LEGACY

The Stellar Heritage Series
by Bob Mauldin

Legacy

Spheres of Influence

Far Horizons

When One Door Closes

LEGACY

Stellar Heritage

Book One

BOB MAULDIN

BLADE OF TRUTH

PUBLISHING COMPANY

Published in the United States by
Blade of Truth Publishing Company, Forsyth, Montana

Cover art: Covers by Christian

This is a work of fiction. All characters, places, and events
portrayed in these stories are either products of the author's
imagination or are used fictitiously. Any resemblance to actual
persons, living or dead, events, or locales is coincidental.

Contact the publisher via email at:
chadd@bladeoftruthpublishing.com

ISBN-13: 978-1-64248-006-1

To my awesome beta readers: Dylan, Darlene, & Jennifer. Thank you for your hard work.

To Joshua for walking into my life and changing it completely and for helping fulfill my dream of being an author.

To my Honey; without you this work would never have been started—or finished.

FOREWORD

It is with a heavy heart that we write this...

In November of 2019 Bob Mauldin tragically passed away. Bob was not only a great man, but a phenomenal author as well. The stories in his head that he never put on paper will be sorely missed. However, his legacy will live on in the works he did get down on the page.

When we came into the picture, Bob already had his four book series completed for a number of years. At the time, we didn't have a publishing company so we decided to show him how to self-publish the works on his own. Plans changed as we founded Blade of Truth. Now we had an easier avenue to share Bob's work with the world.

We were barely established as a publishing company when Bob took a chance on us and asked us to publish *Legacy*. It was with much excitement that I was able to come to him after only a couple of months and tell him that people loved his book. We took on the rest of his series and started the editing process. We published his second book, *Spheres of Influence*, in July 2019 with plans to publish the last two books in early 2020.

Then November came and Bob passed away, but not before he could see the success of his books and the support many readers were showing him. He passed after experiencing his dream of being an author come to fruition and we were blessed enough to be a part of that.

The last two books in the *Stellar Heritage* series are published posthumously with permission from his family. This may be the end of a great author, but his legacy will live on in the hearts and minds of his readers.

Joshua & Sarah Chadd
Owners, **Blade of Truth Publishing Company**

INTRODUCTION

I've always been fascinated by the concept of Roswell. More to the point, I've always been fascinated by what would have happened if, instead of the government, it was civilians who'd gotten ahold of something alien and fantastic.

The year 1947 brought with it hope for a newer, happier world after the end of the greatest war the planet had ever seen. It also brought the beginnings of the Cold War, the Iron Curtain, and, in the United States, a rumor, still unverified, of an alleged spaceship crash in the desert outside Roswell, New Mexico.

The year 2001 *should* have begun a bright new millennium, but over three thousand souls were lost in one senseless act of violence on September 11th, and the whole world writhed for years… and *more* people died.

The year 2010 should have been well into the first part of a bright new millennium. Instead, it brought more of the same—food shortages, race riots, sarin gas attacks, and suicide bombings—killing innocents on both sides, all designed to get the world's attention so some group could espouse some great cause, political or otherwise.

With all of this came *more* of the same—anger, hatred and fear, frustration over the inability to effect any changes in the systems causing all this misery around the world, giving way to resignation concerning one's fate. At least one of these conditions applied to the vast majority of the human race, it is sad to say, except for a few favored nations where the standard of living was such that the citizenry, for the most part, knew about the conditions in other parts of their world but felt more than a little divorced from them.

Many of those favored nations would fall by the wayside, devolving in time to the very status they looked down on in those so-called third world countries.

The bright, new, long-awaited millennium finally dawned, bringing with it something alien… something fantastic…

PROLOGUE

Trajo kep Kuria launched the shuttle and moved away from the great factory ship for the last time. The virus had finally gotten to him, even with all the precautions. He should have known. The Spirits of Space would never let him get away with over nine hundred murders, even if it had been for love and even if it was unknowingly.

He remembered the necklace and its silvery setting, entwined with the sigil of Rami's minor house at the bottom. She had placed it around his neck herself on their wedding in the little chapel overlooking the port city of Quillas the night before the *Dalgor Kreth* left on its mission. The gava stone center was almost two inches across and showed the esteem that she and her house were held in by clan sel Garian. Once, he'd been proud of the associations that one piece of jewelry had entitled him to. Now he saw it as evidence against those who would use him so callously and kill so many.

Before leaving the bridge for the last time, he recorded a final message detailing his treachery and naming all those responsible for leading him to his part. He then placed the damning testimony under a security lock with the captain's personal code. He had left the Chalweh—the only personal item he allowed to remain aboard—hidden and revealed its location in his confession, all to show the Matriarch how deeply she'd been infiltrated by Isolationists.

All he had to do was input the codes, and at the specified time Rami had told him, the program would activate several strategically located bombs that would make the ship have to return, setting back the Expansionist agenda by several years at least.

What Rami hadn't told him—and maybe hadn't known herself—was that the explosives were attached to vials of frenda vesh, the death plague. None could survive in the confining space of even so large a place as the huge factory ship. Built in space, and a small village unto itself, the *Dalgor Kreth* was incapable of landing on a planet. She and her crew mined the asteroid belts that made their existence possible, shuttling the finished products to a colony planet's surface. Even though he was a crewmember, he'd never been intended to survive, he now knew, and the ship had never been meant to arrive at her destination.

As per policy, a shuttle was launched each time a ship left otherspace to check for damage, and he had the privilege on this particular occasion of being the lowly soul assigned the boring task of inspecting the unending field of metal that comprised the hull of a factory ship.

From time to time, ships entered normal space in the direct path of a meteor swarm, or even less likely in the middle of the swarm itself, so it was standard practice to make such inspections. Finally, the program he'd inputted activated itself. This time, when the *Dalgor Kreth* dropped out of otherspace, the bombs had gone off. It was the thing that had saved his life, even if it was only for a few more months. He'd been launched at the same time that the small explosive units had ruptured vials of the virus throughout the ship. But before he could finish his chore, the radio had informed him of what was transpiring aboard. During one of his final lucid phases, the captain had transferred control of the ship, and Trajo had felt his wristband tingle for several seconds.

After the voices finally ceased, he flushed the tainted air into space and finished the grisly task of removing all organic material to which the virus might attach itself and survive. Sealed inside a construction pod from his inspection ship while removing the last few corpses, he'd had time to admire the irony of the situation the Spirits of Space had placed him in. He'd finished his morbid tasks and returned to the shuttle, waiting the recommended time and then some before ordering the closing of all ports and restoring the ship's air from uncontaminated spares on board.

In the months that followed, he'd tried to find a home. Someone, possibly the captain, had erased all astrogation data from the computer, and others had evacuated the dead bodies and all of their possessions up until the last few no longer had the mental capacity to carry on. Those few were the ones he'd had to remove himself.

He knew as little about his section of space as anyone would who'd never traveled the airless pathways between the stars. His home star was one of a trinary system, his own sun being the reddest. Ordering the ship's computer to begin compiling data and rebuilding the astrogation library, he also ordered that any such system was to be investigated.

Now he sat in the command seat of a shuttle, leaving the *Dalgor* for the last time. Months had passed as the computer searched out system after system with its long-range scanners. Each time had been a false alarm until the last stop. Sitting in orbit around the reddest star of the latest trinary system, the ship's instruments picked up intelligent signals from a hotter, yellower star than his people would usually colonize.

The irony of that made him laugh. The Spirits had led him to a new race in the stellar neighborhood. The Shiravi knew of only one other, and that one had been rejected as a belligerent, warlike race. From what the computer had translated while he was in otherspace, streaking toward the planet its inhabitants called Earth, these beings might hold the key to the defeat of the Korvil. But the information needed to get back to Shiravi. If only he hadn't contracted the disease himself. Even now he could feel the ice rushing through his veins.

Choosing a landing site wasn't too difficult. A continent in the northern hemisphere reminded him of home. And, since the atmosphere was breathable, he could at least pretend he was home. The stars would be different, of course, but he would feel the wind on his face one last time.

The virus running through his body bloomed again and the toxins flowed through his system, greying his vision and numbing his hands as the shuttle nosed deeper into the waiting arms of the gravity-well fast enough to overtax the heat compensators. Terror welled up in him at the thought of not getting one last breath of fresh air, but that fear also gave birth to the hormones that finally gave back his vision and the use of his hands. Dripping sweat, he brought the shuttle back under control and keyed the onboard computer to land the shuttle in the valley he'd chosen while still aboard the *Dalgor Kreth*.

Maybe, he thought, *dying will give me relief from this burden. Maybe the Spirits will allow me to rest if these beings can advance fast enough to help bring down the Isolationists who willed this turn of events*.

Hands trembling over the controls, he carefully settled the shuttle into the secluded valley and shut the engines down for the last time. A spasm wracked him as the plague began its final assault on his body, and he coughed blood onto the deck. He staggered from the control room of the shuttle and through the empty cargo section to the door, pressing the controls that would give him his last look at a living world.

And maybe, just maybe, he could use those two aliens he'd seen on his scanners in the last few seconds before landing to get back at all those who had used him. If this race had the curiosity and aggressiveness indicated by their space technology, they'd be a good choice. And if the two he'd seen on his scanners had either or both of those traits, they'd be waiting somewhere nearby. Of course, they wouldn't understand what he had planned for them, but if those Kath-e-vel spawned Korvil Raiders could copy the ships they stole, then perhaps these could, too, especially with a full-sized construction ship waiting in orbit. Maybe they could stop the Raiders, and maybe they could eventually deal a death blow to the Isolationist movement that had used and discarded him. He would never know, of course, but he did hope.

"Oh, Rami, did you ever really love me?" he asked himself as he started down the ramp to get the only revenge he had left…

CHAPTER ONE

Katherine Hawke regained consciousness slowly, her eyes fluttering open. For a time, she just lay there, feeling the cold, hard ground beneath her as impossible images replayed in her mind and her eyes finally focused. The first thing she saw, mere inches from her face, was a small alpine-like plant found in the Montana Rockies every spring. It threw a shadow from the full moon shining down on her. After a few moments, she was also able to make out the sage and mountain grasses that were struggling to cling to the steep slope.

Beyond that was… something else—a craft of some kind, shaped vaguely like a space shuttle. This one was still glowing red from its fall to Earth, and Katherine could feel the heat on her face.

It didn't fall; it landed! And I've had enough experience designing loads for shuttles to know that this isn't one, she mused fuzzily.

At this point, she realized that her head and right arm were hanging over the edge of the steep bluff she and her husband, Simon, had climbed, lugging a telescope to do some stargazing. Slowly rolling over until she was on flat ground, she looked at the moon above, realizing from its position that only moments had passed, and hours of memories poured into her head.

Their yearly camping trip was meant to clear out

"cabin fever," as Simon called it, away from man's presence. There were places in Montana where one could pretend that no one else had ever been and that no other people existed. The occasional vapor trail and far-off sound of engines usually came as a bit of a shock somewhere around the third day, except that it had rained for the first three days.

This year, she and Simon had brought their friend Gayle Miller along. Gayle had stayed in camp, not caring to hike up a steep, muddy trail in the dark.

"I'll keep the fire going so you can find your way home," she'd said jokingly. Her idea of fun was to read a book by the light of a Coleman lantern and feed an occasional stick of damp wood to the warming blaze.

Katherine sat up carefully, a wave of dizziness stopping her just short of upright. When the feeling passed, she took stock of her situation. First, she was apparently unhurt except for a small gash on her forehead that had bled more than a little before beginning to clot, courtesy of some small rock kind enough to break her fall. Standing up uncertainly, she looked toward the telescope and Simon. By the light of the fully risen moon, she could see him struggling as she was, only *he* didn't know why.

Or maybe I don't either, she thought acerbically.

A flash of memory surfaced—the sky growing brighter as whatever was at the bottom of the bluff came down, Simon looking up in astonishment as the sky turned red, and then... nothing. She heard a groan as he struggled to sit up. Whatever had made her pass out had worked on him as well. She struggled through the few paces toward him, and her balance and energy returned more with each step. She knelt down beside him and, pretending to wipe leaves and twigs off, checked him over for any injuries.

Pushing her hands away, he said, "Nothing broken. Just bruised and battered. What the hell *was* that?" He slowly got to his feet, and she wrapped her arm around his waist as much for herself as for him.

They were standing several yards back from the edge of the bluff so Simon hadn't yet seen what she had. "Well, it kinda looks like a space shuttle," she said, nestling close to him in the chilly Montana night, her head on his chest. At an even six-foot, Simon's arm draped around her five-foot-two frame comfortingly.

He rested his chin on top of her head for a moment and then jerked it up. "Looks?" he asked incredulously. "Something moving that fast had to have crashed. What makes you think it was a space shuttle?"

"Come over here," she said, pulling with the arm she had around his waist. "You tell me. And I did say 'kinda.'" Her flashlight found the edge of the bluff.

The moon's cold white light tended to suck the color out of most things, but the craft at the base of the bluff was still sending heat waves into the air, and the field behind them was wavering. Small fires had started near the ship but quickly extinguished themselves due to the rain-soaked ground.

Smoke drifted around the slowly cooling ship, blurring its outlines—first here, then there, always tantalizing and not giving a full view of the thing. A shift in the winds blew the smoke clear for a few seconds, and the pair stared down at the huge ship. It stood forty feet above the bluff, which was about sixty feet above the valley below. At sixty feet wide and nearly two hundred feet long, it nearly filled their end of the small valley.

"It had to have landed under its own power," he said, almost to himself. "And we don't have anything that can do that."

Katherine looked up at him. With the moon behind him, his face was hard to see, his eyes hidden in shadow. She felt a quiver go through the arm around her shoulder. "Who do you mean by 'we'?" she asked. "Even the Russians and Chinese don't have the capability to land something like this under power, and practically VTOL, too." Getting no response—pretty much expected under the circumstances—she added, "Remember, I have a doctorate in physics and I had to learn the cargo capacity of a shuttle, along with lift, drag, mass, momentum, and other things like vehicle configuration, and that is no normal shuttle down there." Occasionally, her time at MIT still came in handy.

Tech Sergeant Hoskins jumped when he heard the first ping in his earphones. He looked at the data stream running down the right side of his display and immediately flipped a switch, pressing three numbers on his keypad. It only took seconds for a captain to arrive.

"What do you have, Sergeant?" he asked, clearly irritated at being disturbed. Nothing at the shift briefing had indicated any reason to expect anything out of the ordinary.

The sergeant pointed at the image on his screen. "Sir, my first guess was junk falling back to Earth, or a meteor, but then this curve showed up. I called as soon as I confirmed that there had been no recorded launches." The sergeant pointed at a line of data slowly scrolling down the screen. "It's definitely decelerating."

The officer picked up a red phone on a nearby console and held it to his ear while continuing to read the display over the technician's shoulder. "Sir, Captain Martin in Operations," he said by way of introduction after a short wait. "We've picked up an incoming bogey as of three minutes ago. Preliminary data is that it is not, repeat, *not* a missile. The object appears to be under power and decelerating and shows every indication of having originated from outside our atmosphere. We have a tentative landing area somewhere between Wyoming and the Canadian border."

He listened for a few seconds and said, "Sir, yes, sir," then hung up the phone. "Sergeant, you will continue to monitor the bogey until it drops off your screen. And try to get something from our orbital assets, too. Make sure you have all of this on backup. I'm not going to take the fall if General Dalton doesn't get all the information he needs."

"Yes, sir." The sergeant wouldn't have this cushy assignment under Cheyenne Mountain if he wasn't good at it, and all recorders had been running from the first. Still, he knew where the feces would land if anything went wrong and offered a silent prayer.

I am definitely going to have to pick a better place to pee next time, Katherine thought, not taking her eyes off the craft below. *A spaceship.*

Shuttles needed long glide-paths and long landing strips. This thing had come almost straight down at a considerable speed for it to have glowed so brightly. The light had illuminated the whole top of the bluff just before she blacked out, and its ability to decelerate caused her to worry somewhere in the back of her brain. But in the forefront of said brain—trained in analytical thinking and possessing a master's degree in systems analysis and a bachelor's degree in theoretical physics—was the desire to go down and examine the craft immediately. Her eyes took in the smoldering vegetation around the ship or… whatever it was.

Looking up at her husband, she said, "Okay, Simon, give. You've got to know something. Tell me."

As a former DIA agent, he was sure to have some of the answers she wanted. The expression on his face told her a lot but not enough.

"Well, I was briefed twice before we were married and I got promoted to agent supervisor, but I never really expected to see one, even if they did exist. Some of us stayed up nights tossing ideas around. What if the powers-that-be were right? We had to have control of that knowledge or we'd eventually cease to exist as an independent nation. That's what I was trained to believe, but here and now, I'm not so sure. There are groups of special troops stationed all over the country set to act as quick-response teams. Our government has a name for them: ALERT teams. Stands for 'Alien Landing, Emergency Response, Tactical.'"

Ever since the bungled attempt to hide the crash at Roswell in 1947, most governments around the world had instituted programs allowing them to mobilize forces specifically designed to contain situations such as the one Simon and Katherine now found themselves in. Although acting under a variety of names, groups similar to ALERT were stationed all over the world in hopes of getting to a craft first. There had been unsubstantiated reports out of South America, Russia, China, Egypt, and a number of other places in the intervening years, but none had ever hinted at an intact craft.

Katherine glanced back at the vessel below. "Why didn't you tell me about this before?"

Simon immediately responded. "Need to know, Kitty-me-love. Besides, I never expected to actually see one in the first place. And I've been out of the loop since I retired."

She surveyed the scene below her, agreeing in principle. The smoke drifting back and forth on the ever-changing winds added a surreal quality to the overheated craft. Decades of reading science fiction hadn't prepared her for this moment, but it did deaden the pain. Hell, she'd even brought the latest Honor Harrington book along for reading material. Three miserable days of rain had left the ground a soggy mess, and she and Simon had had to slog through more than one small swamp to reach the switchback trail up the ridge. At least the dampness kept the heat of the craft's entry from allowing the brush in the area to do more than smolder a bit before dying out.

The newly risen full moon cast sharply defined shadows, and Katherine's breath caught in her throat as she gazed in wonder at the ship that sat exposed in the silvery light. No earthly craft could have landed in that confined space, except some of the more advanced vertical take-off and landing types, the ones called VTOLs, and this certainly wasn't one of those. It had no props or fans at all. Shaped essentially like a shuttle, it had floated over her head and apparently landed under its own power.

Apparently, she thought, because its passage had knocked both her and her husband out in some unknown fashion, and now it sat at the bottom of the hill.

Katherine tried to fit this new information into her worldview. She was bombarded daily with news programs full of travel warnings—anthrax vaccinations and scenes of almost unimaginable suffering from all over the world. The burning questions posed by the immaculately dressed commentators were about madmen pushing the button, trains derailing, toxic spills, drive-by shootings or some other psycho committing another unspeakable act in their particular slice of heaven, all topped off at the end with an upbeat, heart-warming fluff piece about a kitten that survived a fire. Hell, that was the reason for their yearly retreat in the first place! And now this.

"What was that you said about something called ALERT teams?" she asked. The possibility of government agents dropping out of thin air suddenly unnerved her more than a bit.

"They're teams of specially trained agents whose mission is to get this thing out of sight and into a place where it can be studied."

"Like the Roswell ship?" Kitty asked sarcastically. "We've been getting dribs and drabs out of that for the last fifty years, and they still haven't admitted its existence." Within the circles she used to run in, it was a well-known fact that advancements like the transistor and fiber optics were a direct result of technology from crashed alien spaceships. And that was a wrecked one; here sat an intact vessel.

"How long before one of those teams arrives, and how many will be involved?"

"Why do you want to know?"

"Look," Katherine said patiently, an internal clock starting to tick in her head, "in this day and age, this kind of thing can't be kept secret. Too many countries have the ways and means to track it and grasp the meaning of what we have here." She spoke almost as if to a child. "If the U.S. gets hold of it, everyone is going to want in on it out of pure fear that one entity will gain too large an advantage over everyone else. And I truly wouldn't be surprised if it was one of our allies that did the first button-pushing if we didn't give in to their demands."

Simon shook his head. "I've lived with you way too long, woman. You're beginning to make sense. So, we keep it out of everybody's hands. How?"

"If we can't convince the occupants to leave immediately, I don't know what we'll do. If they don't go, it sure looks like World War III to me." At that moment, a high-pitched whine interrupted the crackling and popping of cooling metal coming from the now-darkened ship. As the pair on the ridge watched, a hatch opened in the near side, hinged at the bottom. When it was fully extended, its edge rested on the ground about twenty-five feet from the hull.

A dim red light shone out of the opening, and for a time, nothing more happened. Kitty asked Simon again, "How long for one of those teams to arrive?"

He thought for a moment. "Assume a unit stationed at Malmstrom," he said, naming an Air Force base in north-western Montana. "Not really expecting an event, they'd be a bit unprepared for an immediate activation. Confirmation, authorization, and execution would take some time. Besides the team itself, there would be at least a half-dozen scientists, helicopters to ferry them here, support craft to provide ground troops or perimeter duty as necessary. You're talking between forty and sixty personnel roused from a dead sleep."

He looked at his watch and then at the moon, which had been below the mountains when this started, and saw that it was almost two-thirty a.m. "I'd say two hours for the first of the group to arrive, maybe a little less. Those would be primarily special ops units to secure the area. The brains will arrive at a more leisurely pace. Most of those guys will be civilians, and they'll have all sorts of equipment to study this thing with. But jets scrambled from the same base could arrive here within half an hour for a preliminary fly-over. They're equipped with infra-red and UV, as well as normal cameras, and they would probably be F-15s or F-16s."

Kitty usually told Simon just what she thought, and this time was no different. "If we let our government have that ship, no nation on Earth will believe the U.S. doesn't have it, and I see World War III coming out of that." Sometimes, when she was at her most insecure, she tended to repeat herself.

Simon had started to give her an appraising look when the light from the interior was blocked by something moving around inside. "Looks like our choices just got a lot more limited," he said.

Gayle reveled in her solitude. It was all that Kitty and Simon had said it would be—deer actually walking into their camp—and with the total absence of civilization's noise and light, the stars spilled across the night sky like jewels from the hand of God. Finally.

The first three days had been a pain, though, with all three of them pretty much confined to their tents. A front had stalled, bringing three days of off-and-on rain. There'd been no campfires, no breakfasts over an open fire, nothing. Everything had been done in the cramped quarters of the two tents—dreary, to say the least, and not what she'd been led to expect. Kitty had apologized several times a day, but she had no control over the weather. At least it hadn't turned cold and snowed, a distinct possibility at this altitude even at this time of year.

Kitty was her best friend, of course, and had been for over thirty years. And Simon was, well, Simon. Him, she'd only known since just before the wedding. It was obvious that he adored Kitty, but even after fifteen years, she knew virtually nothing about his life before their meeting. His early life he talked about easily enough if pressed—trouble with his father, some juvenile scrapes that left him with the choice between military service or jail—but her delicate and not-so-delicate questioning over the years still left a blank spot in the life of her best friend's husband.

It was that very mystery she focused on as she fed the fire, gazing outward into the darkness. He had easily fit into their lives while keeping a part of himself secret, at least from her, which could mean Kitty was also keeping a secret from her. She kept trying to brush the idea off as paranoia, but the memory of one of the times she'd brought the subject up kept coming back. Kitty had brushed it off, saying, "Oh, that. National security stuff, like how we met."

"So, he was a spy?" Gayle had asked.

Kitty shook her head. "I think the term 'field operative' or 'field agent' would be more appropriate. Not everything he did was clandestine. I mean, he just walked into MIT and started asking questions. No spy stuff. Just good detective work."

Gayle had learned to let the matter lie, and Simon *was* likable enough. And he did love Kitty; that was obvious. He doted on her. More to the point, Kitty loved him, too, which was where Gayle usually left off in her musings. She added another log to the fire, propped her feet up, picked up her book and began slowly turning pages by the light of the Coleman lantern.

Her first indication that something was amiss was when the pages took on a reddish tinge that couldn't possibly have come from the lantern. She glanced first at the campfire, thinking it had somehow flared up. When that proved to not be the case, she started looking for a fire somewhere in the area, unlikely as that was with all the recent rain. But the red glow continued to increase, throwing vague shadows across the campsite. After a few moments, she looked up and her mouth fell open.

Roughly triangular-shaped and glowing a bright, cherry red that was already dimming, the thing dropped from the sky and floated over the butte where Simon and Kitty had put up their telescope before it set down at the base of the ridge.

Heart pounding, she picked up her .223 rifle and a flashlight, hesitated for a second, and took Simon's obsolete military 30-06 M-1 rifle instead, opting for the heavier stopping power if needed. Slipping quietly through the darkness with a hunter's deftness, she made her way toward the strange craft between her and her friends, the smell of smoke getting stronger the closer she got.

General Herman C. Dalton worked to keep his hand from shaking as he spoke into the phone.

"Colonel, you are to have your team in the air in no more than twenty minutes. Is that clear?" He listened to the response and the question that followed. "Right now, all we can say is that your destination is somewhere in Midwestern Montana. Your pilots will be updated en route. Two F-16s out of Malmstrom have just been scrambled and will take care of the overflight. Yours is the closest team, and I expect your advance people to be on the ground within ninety minutes. And Colonel, no slip-ups. I want that area completely interdicted. No one in and no one out until we have all the information we can get."

The general then turned to the conservatively suited man sitting in an overstuffed leather chair. "Operation Sidestep is underway, sir," he said as humbly as a certain sergeant had spoken to a particular captain not too many minutes before.

"Good," the man answered. "The Director will be pleased if this goes well."

The general was another of those who knew

what happened when things didn't go well, and he said a silent prayer of his own because the director *wouldn't* be pleased if there was any kind of screwup.

Trajo kep Kuria looked out the hatch at the alien mountainside. He was going to walk out into that unfamiliar environment and feel true wind on his face one last time. The icy breeze on his face burned a bit. Part of that was the virus, of course, but he did come from an older, smaller, hotter planet.

Almost anywhere but the tropics would be cold to him. And here he would die, within the hour probably. Even his mind wouldn't focus, and he wondered what he'd just been thinking about the aliens.

CHAPTER TWO

Simon's pulse slowed towards a semblance of normal, his eyes drawn to the little valley below. Formed during the last retreat of the glaciers that had covered North America thousands of years ago, it had provided a sanctuary for both him and Kitty for nearly fifteen years. Every spring, when cabin fever drove them out of their home in Billings, Montana, it gave them almost everything—a small artesian spring that burbled over and around rocks left behind by the long-gone glaciers, a fair-sized pond complete with brookies, a small stream bleeding off the excess water, wildlife strolling around, and near-complete seclusion provided by an access road only four-wheel-drive vehicles could navigate. And even those had to be on the small side to get past some of the constrictions on the road in. All-in-all, it was an almost perfect place to let the cares of running their small security company wash away one week each year.

Across the small valley, the beacon that was their campfire blazed, tended by Kitty's friend, Gayle Miller. This year they had included Gayle in their escape from cabin fever, but it looked like their trip was going to be anything but free of stress. Simon idly wondered how she was taking the situation.

He turned his eyes back to the thing at the bottom of the steep slope. Deep inside, he felt a sadness slip over him, knowing that this sheltered haven would never be the same again. Simon glanced down at the woman beside him. His height often made him feel protective toward his wife, but she carried twice the mental firepower of anyone he knew. That was how she'd captured him.

Looking for a leak in their cold-fusion program, Simon had been the overt operative on the team sent to MIT to investigate the situation. Even though Doctor Conroy was a brilliant physicist, he made a lousy spy. Kitty, as she preferred to be called by her friends, had been assigned as his research assistant while she worked to get her own impressive string of letters after her name, and she'd kept a log of all the good doctor's connections to the university mainframe. While his personal password would only operate the terminal in his office, everything leaving and returning to Conroy's machine had gone through Kitty's terminal first. Noticing certain oddities, she'd long before quietly begun making backups of all e-traffic in a secure file located elsewhere in the massive amount of data in the university's restricted access section.

When he found out about Simon's presence, Conroy panicked and tried to send just enough data to Kitty's terminal to implicate her, but she'd already planned for such an eventuality. Anything being sent to her terminal from his was automatically re-routed right back to his own station, renamed, and hidden among his own research notes.

Even as he was being led away, hands cuffed behind his back, Conroy didn't seem to comprehend the twists that had led to his arrest by federal marshals. Simon knew, though. He knew that without the foresight and ingenuity of one Katherine Cattin, PhD., with a B.S. in systems analysis among her other accomplishments, uncovering the culprit could have been a lot harder.

A whirlwind romance followed, which was the talk of the Agency for a time; then, as with most things, the tempest blew itself out, until the wedding. After the honeymoon, Simon found a notice among all the other stuff in his inbox transferring him to field-operative handler. Reading between the lines, he knew that he was no longer considered a good risk in the field since he now had someone else to worry about as well. What could happen if he were covert and someone found out about his wife?

Two years he'd foundered on, trying to fit into a world of suits and ties, parties, galas and intrigue on higher levels that held no real interest for him. Finally, he tendered his resignation, moved to Billings, Montana, Katherine's hometown, and set himself up in business as a security consultant. Hawke Security was a well-respected concern in the year 2010 when one camping trip changed the course of life on Earth almost as much as the meteor that had wiped out the dinosaurs.

Now, he stood on a hilltop and looked down on a sight that his fellow agents—former fellow agents, he reminded himself—had only whispered or dreamed about. Once he'd been reassigned to the position of handler for field agents, he'd become privy to some of the more esoteric briefings bestowed on the upper echelons. Those evening bull sessions that revolved around all the "what ifs" now stared him in the face.

The here-and-now snapped back into place when

Kitty prodded. "So, what are we going to do, Simon?"

Kitty, for her part, hadn't been idle while studying the thing. Heat-glow gone now, the moonlight sketched a roughly triangular shape sitting in the narrow strip of land between the pond and the ridge they sat on. The general shape of the craft below would make a casual observer think they were looking at one of the space shuttles. Closer examination, however, showed that not to be the case, even leaving out the impossibility of its apparently powered landing in such a restricted space.

Kitty saw that the dimensions were more than a little off. While it had a round, cigar-shaped main body, flattened on the top and bottom, fat stubby wings and a tall stabilizer, something just looked subtly wrong about the whole design.

"Look," she said quietly, seeing the lights change, too. "And don't even try to tell me it's one of ours. I already know it's not."

Simon's other senses brought him information that he took in, stored, and analyzed almost subconsciously—the wind blowing Kitty's long red hair around while it also scattered the smoke from the several small fires below, as well as the smell of the lodgepole pines competing with the odor of overheated metal and smoke whenever the capricious wind blew from the right direction.

"What the hell is a shuttle—whoever it belongs to—doing landing in the middle of a National Forest?" Kitty asked, pushing against Simon's side until she stood unsupported. Reaching up, she felt around the cut on her head, and her fingers came away bloodied again. She let her arm fall to her side, thumb rubbing over her fingertips, feeling the blood rather than seeing it and knowing there would be a lump in the morning.

Kitty felt the shrug of his shoulders. "I don't know, Kitty," he answered quietly. "One thing I am sure of is that that is way beyond anything I was ever told about. Of course, I've been out of the loop ever since I retired."

Kitty looked up at her husband's face, hidden in moon-shadow. "What do you mean, 'anything you were ever told about?' You never told me about anything like this."

Simon shrugged again. "Like I said before, hon—need to know, and you didn't. Besides, I may be out of the Agency, but I'm still bound by several laws about revealing classified material." He looked again at the shape in the darkness below and shook his head. "Of course, need to know just went out the window." Reddish light spilled out of the open hatch onto the ramp and a small section of ground around it. "It's all moot now, but I sure never expected to see something like this."

"What do you mean?"

"That," he said simply, nodding in the direction of the ship below. "Who do *you* think built it? You said it's not one of ours. What do you base your opinion on?"

Kitty looked back at the craft in their little valley. "You know I worked on some of the low Earth orbit satellite projects after… Conroy," she said hesitantly. "Not as classified as your work," she said sarcastically, "but we did need to know things about the space shuttles, like their dimensions, both interior

25

and exterior. That thing isn't shaped right. Too long, too wide, too… I don't know."

"So, who built it?" Simon prodded.

Kitty shrugged. "No one on Earth has the tech base for it. Who do *you* think built it?" She realized the two of them were just temporizing. All these facts had already been gone over.

Simon stated positively. "This thing *flew* over us."

Kitty was silent for a time, replaying the last few seconds before she'd lost consciousness. A hollow feeling began to form in the pit of her stomach. Hesitantly she asked, "Okay, so who does that leave?"

Simon said, "Aliens."

"Don't you *dare* make fun of my choice of reading material, Simon," Kitty said tartly, already having come to the same conclusions.

"It's not a line, hon," Simon said gently, "And I read the same stuff as you, thank you very much. So. After I got promoted sideways, I attended a number of briefings on what to do in the event of something like this, and some of us, other controllers, talked about it amongst ourselves—the ones who were cleared for it, that is."

Kitty stared into the dark spaces where Simon's eyes hid. "So, we're looking at real live aliens?"

Simon chose not to answer the accusation Kitty had leveled at him.

She stared up at him in the dark. "You're not kidding, are you?"

Simon shook his head. "No, dear, I'm not."

She looked back at the ship in the valley. "What does this mean?"

Simon's gaze followed his wife's. "It *could* mean that the balance of power is about to shift drastically.

It *could* mean that the U.S. is about to get an advantage no one else will be able to match."

Kitty's voice came quietly to Simon's ears. "Or it could mean the end of life as we know it."

Montana nights tended to be on the chilly side, even in late May, and especially above six thousand feet, but Simon's shiver hadn't come from the errant winds. Rather, it came from the profusion of possible futures his mind conjured up, one possibility leading to another in an ever-increasing cascade of maybes until it was all just a blur. Some of those paths led to the best long-term gain for humanity. Others ended badly, with humanity suffering more in the long run, some less dramatically. But a few led to the stars. He held Kitty tightly, his shiver passing to her.

"If that ship doesn't leave soon, you could be right, Kittyn."

CHAPTER THREE

"So, tell me," she said quietly, "what *do* you think is going to happen?"

"Truthfully?" Simon asked. Shaking his head, he said, "We're out of time. That's the future down there, and we're in deep shit—personally, as well as a race. The people who are going to show up soon are good enough to figure out who camped out here sooner or later, so even if we leave, they'll be knocking on our door. And as a race, well, this isn't going to be a Roswell kind of thing. Too many people have too many ways of finding things out for this to be kept under wraps for long."

He ran his hand through his hair. Kitty knew that gesture. Whenever Simon felt trapped or was unsure of his course of action, he fussed with his hair. "No nation on Earth can be allowed to have that much of a technological edge over the others. Balance of power, remember? I think that before we could figure out how to use what's down there, other nations—China surely, Russia possibly, even France and maybe Germany—will try to get their share of the pie. Of course, we'll deny it, but word will leak out. I see a coalition rising up against us to turn it over to the world. I see us refusing, throwing up roadblocks while we try to get some advantage before world opinion forces someone to do something drastic."

Kitty contemplated his words. "So, this is major."

Not a question, a statement of fact.

"Unless that thing takes off," Simon confirmed, "very major."

The two observers noticed another change in the light from the interior of the craft at the same time. It looked like something, or someone, was moving between them and the interior light source. They stood rooted as a figure stepped into the doorway.

Stepped, Kitty thought, legs shaking. *One head, two legs, two arms. Maybe it's a human ship after all, and things aren't as desperate as Simon thinks.*

The figure leaned against the doorframe for a moment and then stepped over the threshold. It seemed to sag, as if it suddenly shouldered an extra burden, and staggered two paces forward before sinking to its knees.

Knees, Kitty was almost giddy with relief. *He's human after all.*

In the dim red light pouring out of the interior, the figure looked like it was trying to stand but only succeeded in kneeling upright before falling off the side of the ramp into the shadows.

"Honey, I think he's hurt. I need to get down there." Simon started to move toward the edge of the bluff.

For the first time in her life Kitty was afraid of the wild darkness of her native Montana. "Not without me, you're not! I'm not staying here alone. Besides, you might need help."

Simon hesitated, deciding. He handed her a flashlight and pulled his mag-light from its nylon holster on his belt. "Okay, but be careful." He took her free hand and slipped over the edge of the hill, beginning the long slide to the bottom.

As she scrambled down the sloping face of the knoll with a small patch of light her only guide, Kitty thought, *This is crazy! We're going to break our necks trying to get to a space shuttle in the middle of the night in the middle of a forest!*

She skittered down the slope just feet behind Simon, using one hand to keep herself more-or-less upright, the other shining her flashlight ahead so she could maneuver around the shrubs, rocks, and occasional small trees that kept appearing in the tiny circle of light.

They reached the bottom and Kitty hissed at a stitch in her side and a new gash in her palm. Simon came over and looked at Kitty's hand. He took a small package off his belt, opened it, and placed it over the cut. Wrapping the ends around her hand to hold the gauze in place, he said, "Pre-loaded with antibiotics and a painkiller. I'll do a better job as soon as I can."

Simon shined his light to the right, revealing a stubby wing set low on the stern of the vessel out of which protruded a landing foot or skid. Pointed up, the beam revealed a heat-seared wall some forty feet high. The two felt the craft's residual heat, though it was quickly dissipating in the night's chill breeze. "This is almost beyond belief," Simon muttered, taking in all the details his eyes could focus on.

"'Almost' isn't a word I would use," Kitty said sarcastically. "Where's the pilot?"

To the left, no flashlight was necessary. A pale red light washed out of the opening, illuminating the ramp and part of the ground in the near vicinity but leaving everything close to the ship in shadow. They had come down with the ramp between them and the fallen pilot. But what about the rest of the crew? A ship this size had to have a crew of at least five or six. Shouldn't they be coming out as well? The two of them had made enough noise coming down the hillside. Loose pebbles still clattered down the slope.

Kitty watched Simon start to move slowly in the direction of the ramp some twenty feet to their left. She started to call out to him to wait but just followed instead. She watched him reach for the old Army .45 caliber pistol he always wore in the woods, fearing something bad was just ahead. Her heartbeat slowed when she realized he was merely checking to see that the leather flap was still fastened down.

Simon stepped gingerly onto the ramp from the side, crossing the fifteen-foot expanse in silence, watching the interior as he made his way across. Kitty followed onto the strangely textured surface and glanced into the interior of the craft as well, seeing nothing but an unbroken expanse of floor. Simon let out a breath that brought her attention back.

She moved up beside him when he motioned her forward, his light never wavering from something in the shadows on the far side of the ramp. Their near-vertical, controlled slide down the face of the hill in a darkness broken only by the wildly swinging beams of their flashlights and a full moon had been bad enough. But this! This was just un-bloody-believable! She'd figured the pilot was a human being, even after what Simon had told her. Of course, she had. After all, who in their right mind would *really* expect a UFO to drop out of the sky right in front of them? It just *had* to be next-gen technology not yet released to the public

He had told her of his military service and how

he'd joined the DIA after leaving the Army so he could keep doing something for his country. The problem had been that he wasn't one of those who easily tolerated the regimentation of military life. That was why the DIA had been perfect for him until they'd gotten married. On some deeper level though, she struggled. She just couldn't believe he hadn't told her about this years before.

Until now. Apparently, you could take a spy out of the business, but you couldn't take the mindset out of the spy. Speared in the twin beams of their flashlights lay indisputable proof.

"Simon! He's red!" Kitty stared in fascination at the… person… crumpled on the ground beside the ramp. "I mean really red. Look at his face!"

The ochre light spilled from the open hatch and mixed with the beams of their own lights, revealing a sight Kitty could hardly tear her eyes from. The pilot, the alien, slowly moved to lie flat on his back. His, because there was no evidence of breasts showing under the form-fitting, bluish garment he wore.

He looked back and forth between the two beings standing over him. There was no hair on his head, no eyelashes, and no eyebrows, and the lack of the latter gave him a permanently startled appearance. The eyes themselves were a slightly lighter shade of red than his skin, the nose had no cartilage to give it form, and the fingers seemed to have at least one extra knuckle each.

How must we look to him? Kitty thought.

He leaned away and coughed something dark onto the ground.

Finally breaking free from the trance he seemed to have entered at the sight of the being on the ground,

Simon said, "We have to do something. Help me get him up."

Simon stepped to the far side of the alien, and as he and Kitty squatted down and reached out toward him, the man—for that was how they both thought of him—said, "K'lat! Muvara chi. Liperin se." As he spoke, the alien struggled to get himself into a seated position.

The two humans looked at each other. There was no way to know what the alien had said, but the intent was obvious: they weren't to touch him.

"Stop!" a voice said from inside the ship. "I cease. Touch not."

Time seemed to stand still for Simon. His thoughts raced. *Two aliens?* The weight of the pistol on his hip comforted a small part of him, and he suddenly realized just how small a part that was. But the voice from inside had said, "*I* cease." He looked first at Kitty, then at the open doorway into the vessel. Images filled his head as scenes played out to their logical, and sometimes illogical, conclusions, and all of them left much to be desired.

Simon took on faith that whoever—whatever— was translating for the alien was capable of working the other way as well. "What can we do to help?"

As the translation rumbled out of speakers somewhere inside the ship, the alien seemed to relax, though his expression remained guarded, if any earthly description could be applied to a face so different.

"Keppa sil," the alien answered. "Chi a sumara do jora, kiya liperin se."

Seconds later the voice sounded from inside the huge ship. "Very little. I would feel a planet's breath once more before I cease."

Simon was acutely aware of the passage of time. He asked, "What happens to your ship when you... cease?"

"It will cease also," the alien answered. "I would see that not happen."

"Me, too, I think," Simon muttered.

Kitty spoke up from beside Simon. "How can that be prevented?"

The alien thought for a moment, or perhaps gathered his strength. The impression both humans got was of less than good health—the short breaths evident by the movements of the nasal skin flaps and the labored rise and fall of the skinny chest.

"I am the last of the crew," came from the internal speakers. "When I cease, the ship will know by this." He held up his wrist, encircled by a silvery metal band covered in colored designs. "To prevent the capture of our technology by... others... we make our ships cease when the last of the crew dies. This can be prevented if one of you agrees to wear this. It will identify you as the captain and allow you aboard. The technology will be yours."

Simon stared at the alien as choices flashed into his mind—possible outcomes, branching alternatives, countermoves—trying to think several steps ahead while still maintaining a degree of adaptability to adjust to the exigencies of the moment.

To Kitty's eyes, Simon seemed frozen, a condition she'd only witnessed on rare occasions. It was a form of meditation that she'd begged him to teach her. He said he could sometimes see the possible futures laid out on a grid, one that changed even as he examined the individual moves that led to certain conclusions. When she asked him how he could change things merely by looking, he would only say, "The observer always affects the observed."

Now, if he was right, time was running out. She deliberately broke his train of thought with a question. "What do we do, Simon?"

Simon jerked as if a small electric current had hit him. He looked down at the alien. "How much time do we have to decide?"

"Keppa sil. Muvara se," the alien said, and the translation boomed from inside the craft.

"Very little. I cease."

She knelt down beside the alien. "Who are you, and why are you dying?" She gazed into the improbably red eyes, a shiver running down her spine.

"I am Trajo kep Kuria," the red man answered through the translator, almost brusquely. "I die because of stupidity. I was tricked into releasing a plague aboard the ship. I thought it was an explosive that would damage the ship and force it to return to Shiravi, my home-world. There were explosives, yes, but they were only small charges to release the virus and it was to have killed me as well. I would see the ones who have done this punished." His hand shot out and grabbed Kitty's wrist. "You are my last hope. Find my world and send this message to the Matriarch—Isolationists have a deeper hold than you realize. Beware."

Before Kitty could do more than start to pull out of the alien's grasp, his hand fell limply to the ground.

"Virus?" Simon questioned, kneeling beside his wife. "What good will it do us to do anything after being exposed to who-knows-what kind of disease?"

"You are safe," the alien said. "This disease is

one that targets only those of Shiravan ancestry. Our systems are too incompatible for you to be affected. Now, you must decide."

A thoughtful tone entered Simon's voice. He turned to look at his wife kneeling beside him, still surprised at her acceptance of the situation. "If I was still with the Agency, I'd probably turn it in. But being married to you for fifteen years has mellowed my outlook a bit. Now, I'm not so sure that turning it over is the best idea. We could try to move it farther back into the mountains, staying below radar level, and hide it until we can figure out what to do with it. We could also turn it over to an international consortium or something. But whatever we do, we have to take the wristband, now."

"You two *would* be right in the middle of something mysterious."

The voice out of the dark made Kitty jump.

"Damn it, Gayle! Don't *do* that!" Simon exclaimed, lowering the pistol and putting the safety back on. Even in the dark, her waist-length blonde hair stood out. "What the hell are you doing out here with a rifle—*my* rifle?"

Before she could reply, Kitty said quietly, "Okay, do it."

Gayle looked over and saw the alien move his fingers over the surface of the wristband in a complicated pattern. "Holy sh… I mean, Jesus Chr… I mean, God damn!"

Gayle's last New Year's resolution had been to quit cursing, but given the situation, Kitty felt her friend had shown remarkable restraint.

The two women had met on the first day of first grade. Kitty had been dropped off and was making her way across the playground through the mass of yelling second through sixth graders, lunchbox in hand, when she heard first laughter—unpleasant laughter—and then screaming. "Let me go, you bastards! I'll kill you, you sons of bitches!"

Kitty started to head away from the ruckus since she'd been raised that a proper young lady didn't use that kind of language or associate with those who did, but a glimpse of the screamer changed her mind. *She's smaller than me!* she thought. Six-year-old Kitty saw the little girl being held against the baseball backstop by two bigger boys while two others reached through from behind the chain-link fence and were busily tying the poor girl to the fence by her long, blonde hair. Kitty, victim of the O'Reilly genes that had given her unruly red hair, was also victim to a sense of outrage that knew no bounds. At the tender young age of six, she knew wrongness when it hit her in the face, and she had to do something.

She made her way around the growing crowd of yelling schoolchildren until she was behind the two boys industriously tying the blonde girl to the fence. She didn't have a plan; she just ran straight at the boys, bowling one over completely and swinging at the other bigger boy's head with her lunchbox. An altogether satisfying sound came from the meeting of the two hard objects, but the boy's head began to bleed from a nasty gash above his eye. Yelling at the two to get away, she kept swinging the box until the two boys ran off.

Kitty began to try to untangle the messy knots in the now-silent girl's hair, completely oblivious of the quiet wall of children staring at her from the other side of the fence. Knowing that some of her actions caused more pain, she was surprised that the girl said nothing, made not a sound. Finally, there was only one knot left.

"I can't untie this one. I can cut it with my scissors or go call a grown-up. What should I do?"

"Just cut it. My mom is gonna be so pissed!"

Kitty found her new school scissors in her pocket and sawed at the mass until it finally fell apart. She wound the section of hair around the scissors and slid them back into her pocket at the same time the teachers arrived.

The ensuing brouhaha got her dad recalled to the school before home room, along with the blonde girl's mother and the parents of the injured boy. Kitty stood beside her dad, looking at the carpet in front of the principal's desk.

"It's abundantly clear, Mr. Cattin, that your daughter was only doing her best to defend the other little girl from a group of bullies that, quite frankly, we've been having trouble with for some time." He did have the nerve to stare at the boy's parents when he said it, "My problem is that she actually injured Danny Batten pretty badly. The cut on his forehead is going to require stitches, and his parents want an apology. I believe I can put this aside if she'll just apologize to him."

Kitty pouted. "I won't 'pologise! I *can't*." The principal caught the stress on the last word and asked why. "'Cause then I would be a liar, and my daddy said I should never lie. I'm not sorry, and I won't 'pologise." She glared at Danny Batten, reducing him to ashes in her mind, and then looked sullenly back down at the floor. "I'd do it again, too," she muttered.

The principal looked as if he hated what he had to say next. "Then I'm afraid I'll have to suspend you for a week, Miss Cattin, just because you won't tell him you're sorry." He tried to say it kindly, hoping she'd change her mind, but it was to no avail. Stubbornness was another Irish trait she'd acquired from her mother.

There were two positive notes that emerged from the incident. One was that Kitty never had to fight again. Her reputation had been made, and it grew with each year she went to school with the same kids. The other was that it started a friendship with Gayle Miller that spanned over three decades. The downside was the anger Danny Batten carried around forever after.

The two girls, later women, were seldom seen separately. For the week of Kitty's suspension, Gayle was over every day, helping Kitty keep up with her homework and filling her in on what was going on with the bullies. It seemed that as a result of one little first-grader tackling two bigger boys, the other kids had decided they could do something to defend themselves against the milk-money thieves, the smokers, and the drug pushers, and were just saying no long before it became a First Lady's battle cry.

A sharp metallic snick marked the passing of the wristband. She stared at it, Simon's light shining off it. Composed of a mostly silvery metal, the band was largely covered with colored spaces that had to be some form of information input. The wristband felt both light and heavy at the same time. Her original thought—that it was merely ornamental—went out the window as she remembered the long red fingers moving across the surface of the two-inch-wide band.

"Guys, can either of you explain what's going on here?" Gayle's voice had risen an octave, signaling her approaching panic. "I saw this thing land over here where you two were playing with your telescope, so I grabbed Simon's bear-stopper and headed over. I don't know what I expected, but it sure wasn't this!" she exclaimed, gesturing with the weapon.

Kitty shook her head, trying to rid herself of the impending sense of doom that washed over her. "It would appear," she said stiffly, "that we've just had a real-life, honest-to-God spaceship handed to us."

"And how long do we get to play with it before the big boys show up?"

Simon stood up from beside the body of the alien. "If we don't get out of here, and soon, we won't get to play with it long at all. This guy just died. At least, I think so. His chest moved up and down just like ours until a few seconds ago." He ran his hand through his hair.

Kitty looked at Gayle and shrugged. She then laid her hand on Simon's arm. "Darlin', we need you to put your old DIA hat on. What would you do if you had a three-person team here and needed to move in a hurry?"

"Divide my forces," Simon answered immediately. "Someone stays here to see if we can get some kind of control of the ship while the other two go break camp. But we're *not* a DIA team."

"But we're all we've got. What do we do first?" Kitty just stood there and looked expectant.

Simon came to a decision. "Gayle, are you in on

this?"

"See if you can get rid of me," she answered.

"Okay, you two go forward and I'll go aft. I'm betting you'll wind up with the control room, and that," he said, pointing one thumb over his shoulder, "should be the engine room. I'll do a quick recon and meet you up front. Then we split up, but not until I'm sure that whoever gets left here is as safe as we can hope for." He glanced at his watch. Miraculously, only twenty minutes had gone by since he first looked at it. That meant *maybe* twenty-five from first contact with an ALERT team.

Simon led the way up the ramp and across the threshold into the interior of the ship. His sense of balance fought for control as the gravity seemed to lessen instantly. He held onto the doorframe for a few seconds, looked at the ceiling, and jumped straight up. Kitty and Gayle looked appropriately amazed.

"They've got some kind of gravity control," he said as his feet reached the level of their heads before stopping and floating back to the floor. "Well, ladies," he said as his feet hit the deck, "shall we go exploring?"

"I'm not sure. Are we going to meet any more of… those?" Gayle asked worriedly.

"I don't think so," Simon answered. "He said he was the last crewman. How about you, hon?"

"You're the expert here, Simon," Kitty temporized, adding sarcastically, "I've never had a need to know, remember? But whatever happens needs to happen soon, according to you. These ALERT teams you talked about. How soon will they show up?"

Simon glanced at his watch, a purely reflexive

gesture. "If F-16s were scrambled out of Malmstrom, we should be getting an overflight within half an hour, figuring NORAD recorded the descent and some of the newer thermal imaging satellites confirmed it. Ground forces? That will depend on where they're based and what kind of transport they have. Choppers at the least for the forward troops, the ones who will secure the area. After that, it's anybody's guess when a supervisor will arrive onsite. Won't be long though."

Kitty shrugged. "What's the worst that can happen if we fail?"

Simon looked at his wife sharply. "When did this become a 'we' thing?"

She looked back just as sharply. "You've been saying 'we' ever since this started. But it actually became 'we' the day we got married. If things go wrong, we can always give it to the government, can't we?" Kitty asked.

"I'd have to say yes. We'd have to negotiate for our freedom, but that shouldn't be too hard if it comes down to that. Look what we have to bargain with."

Kitty said simply, "Then let's do it."

Simon looked at his wife. "Are you sure? We're moving into circles where the air gets pretty thin, hon."

"Simon." The name came out with enough snap to make a drill sergeant proud. "We have to go with our strengths, love," Kitty said into the surprised eyes of her husband. "You're the one with the experience in this kind of thing. We go with your feelings, and the way you keep looking at your watch tells me we're running out of time."

"Okay, we take the ship. Maybe find a more

remote place to keep it hidden until we can arrange a transfer to an international group. By the way, I didn't see anything even remotely resembling food or drinks aboard. This thing must have a mothership in orbit somewhere."

Gayle stood at Kitty's shoulder and whisper in her ear. "You want to explain all of this to me?"

"Simon can fill you in later, and I'll vouch for it, I hope," Kitty said, temporizing. "Then you'll know almost as much as I do. It seems that Simon was a bit deeper into clandestine operations than he ever let on. Honestly, girlfriend, that didn't cause this situation, but he wasn't as surprised as I would have thought. Now we're getting a spaceship and the whole world is going to be after our asses."

CHAPTER FOUR

Katherine Hawke had continued her studies after she married Simon, attending classes at Montana State University, Billings. Math was her first love and had been ever since she figured out that no matter what, three plus five always equaled eight. Always. The simplicity of the thought appealed to a child afloat in a life that changed from one day to the next due to the vagaries of being a military brat.

By the time her parents were killed in an automobile accident shortly after she turned twenty-three, she'd exhausted most of the avenues available to her mathematically. What was confusing to most people, she found crisp and clean. All a person had to do was plug in the right values and everything worked out. Why couldn't they see that? Theoretical mathematics led to practical applications, and soon Kitty had a degree in advanced physics to go along with an impressive string of other accomplishments, including systems analysis.

The three stood in the control center of the ship, gazing at the layout. Simon had found that the rear of the vessel was indeed the engine room and that it was uninhabited. The center two-thirds of the ship was one big empty space, and the front of the ship had this cockpit. Chairs for four beings fronted consoles covered with incomprehensible symbols. She knew that someone was going to have to take charge, and she *did* have the captain's wristband.

It was the last course of study Kitty had focused on. "We need someone to figure out if we can get this thing off the ground, and somebody's got to go break camp." Kitty could tell that Simon was conflicted. He always had trouble when it came to his idea of defending her. He needed to allocate his resources effectively, and his defensiveness was getting in the way.

"Simon, why don't you and Gayle go break camp and let me work on the controls? That way, you can fill her in on what we know so far and give her a little background on just how it is that you aren't surprised by all of this."

It had been easier than she'd thought to get him to do as she wanted. The concept bothered her on some levels and pleased her on others as she watched two flashlight beams bobble away into the darkness. She'd finally had to resort to stubbornness and pointing out that time was running out to get Simon to leave her there to study the controls. She sat down in what she thought of as the pilot's chair. It was the only one with weirdly shaped joystick-like controls on the arms.

Katherine Hawke wondered at her own actions even as she began to study the controls in front of her. She'd always been a law-abiding citizen until then, and this would push her over a line that couldn't be uncrossed. Of course, she had the support of Simon and Gayle, who were of the same mind. She shook herself, both mentally and physically, and went to work.

She let herself feel the ship around her and was immediately aware of the fact that her feet dangled at least six inches off the floor. Built for beings who probably averaged a bit taller than normal for Earthmen, the chair cut off the circulation to her lower legs if she let them dangle long. That fit with her impression of the alien just outside the cargo bay door being tall, even though he was on the ground. She shivered and looked over her shoulder.

Shaking the worrisome thoughts from her mind, she settled herself as best she could and closed her eyes, imagining herself taller and with a longer reach. *As if*, ran ruefully through her head. She took a deep breath and let her taller, longer-limbed self handle the controls, then opened her eyes and looked closely at the control panel before her. Dark panels set in obvious patterns stared back up at her. Smooth to the touch, there were some symbols that could only be seen from certain angles. "Back-lighting, dammit!" she prayed.

She climbed down out of the chair and began a systematic search of the four stations. Some of the panels were duplicated, and some weren't.

Duplicate controls, she thought. *Probably connected with Flight Operations*.

The seemingly unduplicated controls would most likely route mission-specific information to the particular crewmember for which it was intended. A circular depression in one surface defied all guesses, especially once she noticed an opposed depression in the undersurface of a small shelf protruding over the panel.

She walked back to the center station and studied the control board. A muddy brown button sat apart from the others on that panel and was duplicated nowhere else in the room. She tentatively reached out and touched it. Akin more to the touch-sensitive screens on some computers, it neither moved nor clicked, but the entire panel lit up. Looking right and left, she saw that the other three stations were live as well. The odd depressions still sat dark and useless.

Now the various buttons were indeed back lit and she could make out what had to be lettering on each one, accompanied by a pictogram. Kitty realized that she was copying Simon's tic—looking at her watch. Thirty minutes had passed, and all she'd managed to do was get power to the control boards. At this rate, they'd be old and grey before anything significant was accomplished. She jumped up and slammed herself into the pilot's chair, folding her legs under her. "Damn! Where's a Rosetta stone when you need one? How am I supposed to figure out an alien language in the next ten minutes?"

"Is this a request for information?" a voice reminiscent of the alien translator inquired.

Kitty nearly jumped out of her skin. "Who wants to know?" Her heart pounded in her chest at the unexpected surprise.

"I am the control center for the Shiravan colony ship *Dalgor Kreth*. Do you require assistance?"

"Hell, yes! How do I fly this contraption? And how do you speak English?"

"The main control board is laid out to represent the ship itself. Now that the board is activated, all you have to do is touch the symbols for the engines and then the launch indicator. The vessel will go into prelaunch condition, and all automated systems will be under the control of the shuttle's onboard computer. The controls on the arms of the master seat regulate the acceleration and attitude of the shuttle."

As Kitty watched, two symbols—supposedly the engines—and then one—probably the launch indicator symbol—flashed on the board as the voice spoke.

"The left control handle regulates the power applied to the engines, and the right control determines the attitude of the vessel. All languages were recorded and decoded when I moved into orbit. Once your speech was identified as English, mid-west, I was able to translate for Captain kep Kuria and now am able to speak with you."

"Wonderful," Kitty muttered. Aloud she said, "The left is the gas pedal and the right is the steering wheel." A motion outside the cockpit window caught her attention. Two sets of headlights bounced and swerved across the end of the little valley, seemingly disconnected from anything earthly in the now nearly moonless depression that was the small valley they were in. "That would be Simon and Gayle," she said out loud. "They're not going to be able to get the trucks up the ramp. Can I move the ship so that it faces the other way?"

"That can be done. Another option is to open the ramp on the other side of the ship." Kitty looked closely at the new light that had begun flashing and finally noticed the outline of the ship inscribed in the surface of the control panel. She thought to test the system, and instead of pressing the blinking light, she pressed the light that would correspond to the open door opposite the newly flashing button. Hearing a noise coming from the center section of the ship, she slid out of the chair and hurried to the control room door in time to see the ramp closing off the view of the hillside she'd scrambled down less than half an hour earlier. She returned to the control panel and pressed the other ramp button, rewarded with the sounds of it opening.

"Can't you operate these controls without my assistance?" Kitty asked.

"No. No voluntary controls can be accessed by the control center. All functions must be input by a… human being." Kitty was certain she heard a slight hesitation in the computer's atonal voice.

"You seem to be speaking better than you did when we first arrived," Kitty noted aloud. She continued to study the control panel in front of her and monitor the progress of the two approaching vehicles.

"I have been accessing several hundred English language audio and video transmissions. I have been able to identify and store more than four hundred and fifty thousand words in a variety of languages up to this moment."

Kitty stopped in her tracks as a thought struck her. "Hold it. You said something about automated systems being under the control of the shuttle's onboard computer."

"That is correct."

Kitty's heart began to pound. "Am I in the shuttle you were speaking of?"

"That is correct."

"If I'm on the shuttle, where are you?"

"I am aboard the Shiravan colony ship *Dalgor Kreth*, in orbit around your planet."

Kitty climbed back into the pilot's chair to chew on this new bit of data and saw the two sets of headlights rounding the far end of the little lake. Soon, they'd be on the old Forest Service road leading to the meadow the ship sat in. At that point, it would only be a matter of minutes before the threesome was reunited.

"Is there room aboard this *Dalgor Kreth* for this shuttle?"

"The *Dalgor Kreth* is thirty-eight hundred of your feet long. The landing bay is capable of holding three shuttles and one fuel scoop."

"Oh, God. Simon is gonna shit." Kitty was already making plans of her own. And there was no need to bother Simon just now. She stared down at the wristband she had chosen to wear, one of the few major unilateral decisions she'd made in their marriage. For a moment, possible futures laid themselves out before her. It was too much information too fast, but she *did* know that she was keeping this ship.

Kitty stumbled slightly as she stepped over the threshold of the ship onto the ramp. The change in gravity was unexpected. Her muscles had acclimated a bit even in the short time she'd been aboard. She walked to the bottom of the ramp and watched Simon stop their S-10 pickup at the end. Gayle's Jeep stopped behind it. The two drivers got out and met Kitty at the ramp.

"Well, Miss Systems Analyst, it looks like you're getting a handle on things. It was the other side that was open before, right?" Gayle looked down the side of the ship in the headlights of the two vehicles. "That's too stubby to be a wing, isn't it?" she asked, peering toward the stern of the ship.

"I think you're right." Kitty looked that way, too. "Probably just housing for the landing gear. There's another one up there," she said and motioned toward the nose of the craft.

Simon waved his hand to get their attention. "Sorry to interrupt the discussion on alien spacecraft design, but the clock's ticking, ladies. We need to figure out where we're gonna stash this thing. I've got the topos on the front seat."

Kitty waved back. "We've got to get those two vehicles aboard first. If we back 'em up to the rear wall, they should be okay if I don't have to do any fancy flying."

Simon looked intently at his wife, raised one eyebrow slightly, and nodded. He looked at the ramp, easily capable of taking both vehicles at the same time, and walked back to the truck.

Gayle followed and asked Simon quietly, "Is this a good idea?"

Simon nodded, smiling. "Oh, yeah. We leave no tracks, offload the rigs somewhere else, and then I'll drop this thing in some hollow somewhere and hike out. I'll take some pictures first, of course, so we can prove it when we go public." He sat down, turned the key and drove the little pickup into the cavernous interior of the ship that was nearly fifty feet wide. He turned left, turned the headlights off, and drove to the end of the bay near the door to the engine room, jockeying the truck around and backing it up until it nudged the rear wall. Setting the parking brake, he turned off the engine and grabbed the maps.

Gayle followed more cautiously, and Simon waved her into position.

"Kill it and set the brake!" he yelled from the far side of the Jeep.

Gayle joined him and they turned toward the front of the bay. Dimly lit with a reddish illumination that seemed to come from the ceiling panels themselves, the room was huge. Simon had rarely seen larger rooms in most buildings, except, of course, for public places—opera houses, sports arenas, and the like.

Thirty feet to the ceiling, Simon judged, by nearly fifty wide and almost a hundred long. "This thing hauls some serious cargo." He noticed the scuff marks in the deck plates as they walked toward the cockpit.

Gayle's voice, usually carefree, betrayed her concern. "Where's Kitty?"

"I hope she's in the cockpit, Simon answered. "Damn, but it's strange to be saying something like that."

"Why?" Gayle kept pace with Simon with difficulty. At only five-four, her legs needed to take more steps than his did, but she recognized the unconscious worry on his face and didn't say anything about slowing down. "Kitty said you knew all about this stuff."

"Not about *this*," Simon said, waving his hand vaguely. "About the teams deployed to *intercept* this. That would be the ALERT teams I told you about. This is as new to me as it is to you." They strode about ten feet up the steps leading to the cockpit door. "Kitty! Where are you?"

"In here! And you'd better hurry. We've got company!"

Kitty was bent over one of the panels when

Simon and Gayle entered the control room of the ship. The first thing they noticed was that all the panels were lit, and they walked over to see what she was looking at so intently. Between the bowl-like depressions of the mysterious panel was a cylindrical column of light. It took Simon a few seconds to recognize the little valley they were in, then the surrounding foothills. Then, two moving green dots caught his eye.

"What are those?" he asked, pointing.

"That's company. Computer, how far away? And how soon until they arrive?"

"Accessing measurement translation program. Sixty miles. The craft seem to be suffering from the mountain winds. Estimated time of arrival is four minutes, twenty-eight seconds."

Simon jumped perceptibly when the computer spoke. Kitty noticed and looked into his eyes for a few seconds before turning back to the controls.

Gayle interrupted. "I see five more dots headed this way. It looks like slower and lower, but definitely headed right for us."

Simon was silent for all of three seconds as his mind translated the distance into time. "If the first two are F-15s, they shouldn't be traveling over Mach one in these foothills; updrafts play hell with fast planes at low levels. So, we've got about four minutes left, like the computer says. They can't really get this far into the mountains. It'll be a high flyover with some pretty sophisticated cameras and smart bombs. The other five are probably Blackhawks with enough combat-ready troops to secure the area. Screwed, blued, and tattooed." He shook his head. "If we get the vehicles out of the ship, we might be able to keep from going to jail for trying to steal this thing. If it was just me, that's one thing. But I can't let you two take any of the heat on this. Federal time isn't all it's cracked up to be, trust me."

"Oh, ye of little faith," Kitty said. She climbed into the pilot's seat and asked, "Computer, how long for the engines to rev up or whatever they do?"

"Full engine power is available as soon as the engines are activated. Cargo has been detected in the bay. Stasis field should be activated before take-off."

Simon stared at his wife in astonishment. He opened his mouth to speak, but she reached out and touched a flashing light on the panel in front of her and the emotionless voice responded. "Stasis field activated." She pressed another button, this one not flashing, and sounds came from the cargo bay. Simon stuck his head out the door to see the ramp swinging into place and sealing itself.

"Wait!" Simon yelled. "Lower the door. I've got to get the telescope from the top of the hill!"

Kitty watched the green dots closing on their location, two much faster than the others. She ignored Simon, touched two buttons in succession, and the ship seemed to come to life. A vibration that had not been there a moment before ran through her body. An outline of the shuttle appeared on the forward glass, a form of head's-up display. Kitty touched another button and felt her stomach lurch. A hum came out of the air for several seconds, along with a stronger vibration felt in her butt, finally ending when the computer said, "Preflight operations complete. Anti-gravity field at seventy percent, landing gear retracted. Shuttle is ready for departure. Pilot has control."

Simon stormed into the cabin. "I wanted that telescope," he said fuming.

Kitty said, "Look at the radar. I'll get you another one later. Right now, though, if you'll excuse me, I think you need to sit down." Kitty gripped the two control arms and said softly, "Left is gas; right is steering wheel." Louder she said, "You grab a chair too, Gayle. The ride could get a bit bumpy."

Simon stared in awe as his wife began to operate the alien ship. She spun it a full 360 degrees, looking for her adversaries—dozens of men in combat Kevlar with their weapons trained on the shuttle's front screens and half a dozen Blackhawks trying to keep her boxed in.

"Outer doors sealed. Vessel ready for flight."

Simon started to speak, then changed his mind as Kitty clenched her fists twice, reached out, and gripped the joysticks. She pulled back on the left stick and Simon noted a difference in the vibration coming into the soles of his feet.

He glanced at the device he could only think of as a form or radar, and blanched. "Kitty, this thing says those jets should be back in about a minute. It also says we're about, oh, six hundred feet higher than we were a few seconds ago. What did you *do*?"

"Simon, another way to say systems analyst is to say efficiency engineer. All I've done so far is to guess at what would work best for a tall, two-armed person, plus getting a lot of help from the computer. As for what I've done specifically, I've pulled back on the left-hand control arm, seeing what happens when I send power to the engines while not giving a specific command to the attitude control. Apparently, it rises up in one place if the directional controls are in neutral."

"There goes one of the jets," Gayle commented. "I just saw his exhaust, and the radar thingee shows both of them past us and turning for another pass."

"Kitty, if you've got any ideas, now's the time to pull them out of your hat." Simon glanced at the radar and back out the window. "I don't know whether they've been ordered to shoot first or order us down and try to take us intact."

"Give me a few seconds here, dear. The way you talk about my driving, you should quiet down. And now I get to drive in three dimensions." Kitty centered the left-hand control and said, "Let me know if our altitude starts to drop. I either have to apply constant power to stay at one height or the ship will do it automatically when I center the control. It will give me a few seconds to try this…" She slowly rotated the right-hand joystick, and Simon watched the outline on the front screen slowly rotate at the same speed.

"Any change in altitude?"

"None that I can see," Simon answered. "We seem to be holding at a constant height, according to this, although we've moved several miles away from the mountains."

"Okay," Kitty said. "I think I've got this. Tell me about those planes."

"F-15s, most likely," Simon said. "Capable of Mach two-plus. The plus is classified. Usually carry two or four air-to-air missiles—"

"No," Kitty said, interrupting, "I mean, *where are they?*"

"North and east of us, turning for another pass," Simon replied. "This is where I would order them to fire if I was calling the shots and was so inclined."

"Dual radar lock-ons," said the computer. "Engage covert systems."

Kitty glanced at her panel. "You guys look for a flashing light and push it, quick."

Gayle almost yelled. "I've got it! Pushed it. Now it's on steady." After a short pause, she asked, "What did I just do?"

"You probably activated some kind of stealth or jamming system," Kitty answered.

Simon commented dryly, "If they can see us, they can still shoot at us. They just fall back on seat-of-the-pants flying and good old-fashioned luck to hit their targets."

"Then we'll just have to be gone when they get here." Kitty held the angle of the ship in the forward screen steady at about forty-five degrees from level and pulled back on the power control.

Simon expected a heavy SOB to sit on his chest when Kitty fed power to the engines, so he was off-balance when nothing happened. Off-balance was apparently the catchword of the day. He'd felt off-balance ever since the ship had flown overhead, like something out of one of the original Star Trek shows, only without the bad acting. He said, "I don't think we ..." His voice trailed off.

"Simon, what?" Kitty's voice carried more than just concern in it. A tinge of hysteria added its own modifications to her voice.

"Uh, situation stable at present. No sign of the jets. It appears that we're about two hundred fifty miles up and climbing, and I don't feel a thing. Do you have a destination in mind?"

"Well, yes," Kitty said a bit diffidently. Simon knew Kitty. The nonchalant attitude was just a pose. He could tell how scared she was by the way she hunched her shoulders. "I just needed to be somewhere safe for a few seconds so I could take the time to ask a question. Computer, how do I find the main ship?"

"Astrogation data is available through the left-hand station."

Kitty looked over her shoulder. Gayle was closest. "Gayle, be a friend and press the button that should be flashing on your control panel, okay?" Kitty asked sweetly. "You've just been promoted to Astrogation Data Specialist."

Gayle looked at Simon, who just shook his head and shrugged. Gayle shrugged back and pressed the button indicated.

"Accessing orbital data. Increase distance from the planetary surface to twelve thousand miles. *Dalgor Kreth* will appear as a medium-sized green dot on the forward viewscreen as soon as it clears the edge of the planet. Use the right-hand control arm to orient on the dot and apply power slowly with the left to pull up from behind. When you reach the proper distance, the automated landing sequence can take over if you put the ship on remote-pilot." A light that was centered on the main control panel began flashing.

"Hon," Simon asked softly, "how did you get the computer to talk to you?"

Kitty let go of the power arm and waved her hand nonchalantly. First, she said, "Computer, take us slowly to orbit, then let me know." Then she looked up at Simon, her whole posture screaming for attention. "Once I had the power to the control panels on, all I did was ask myself a question out loud and the computer asked if it was a request for information. After my heart started beating again, I asked, and it answered." She sat silent for a while, listening to the sounds moving the ship farther from Earth. "Then I had to decide whether we're really going to turn over what we've found or find a way to keep it."

Simon interrupted. "*You* had to decide?"

"Yes, dear. After all, I *am* the one flying the ship. And that's another thing. I say we keep it. You'll have to be in charge of most things. Any recruits we manage to find will respond to a mature male quicker than a tiny, red-headed girl."

Simon sat back, apparently thinking about what his wife had just said.

The view outside the cockpit window took on the true colors of space—black highlighted by every color in the rainbow, or to be more precise, in the stellar spectrum. The Earth's atmosphere washed out the color from most of the smaller stars, leaving a neutral white speck. Beyond the upper reaches of the atmosphere, the stars gleamed like jewels strewn upon the velvet darkness of space.

Kitty watched the slowly changing vista for a while and then moved the attitude control a fraction, turning the shuttle so that they were able to view Earth from an ever-increasing height.

"Oh, my God."

Kitty looked over her shoulder to find Gayle standing there, one hand on the back of Kitty's chair.

Gayle was staring at the planet below. "I think I can make out Japan down there," she said, pointing.

"Right," Kitty said. "And there's the northern part of Australia. They're just starting their morning. If we keep on going, we'll see the lights of some of the larger cities of Russia and Europe."

Simon, mouth opening to speak, got interrupted as the computer announced, "We have reached twelve thousand miles above the planet's surface. If you wish to dock, begin reducing power by pushing the power arm forward until the image of the ship is stable in the holographic display."

Kitty did as instructed until the image of the ship was centered in the display and holding position above the Earth. She let out a sigh and dropped both hands into her lap, massaging her forearms, and then looked into the display. No medium-size dot.

"Computer, can you increase the range of our scanners?"

"Navigation station has the controls for that, as well as the homing beacon. Left-side station."

Kitty waved Gayle back to the station. "Let's find the ship first. Gayle, press whatever flashes, and then we'll see what happens."

"Okay," Gayle replied with little enthusiasm. "I just hope I don't open the door or something."

"Certain actions are not possible when the vessel is in flight status."

"That's just reassuring as all get-out," Gayle said sarcastically. Presently, a pulsing green dot appeared in the display. Kitty, now comfortable with the controls, moved the shuttle closer.

Gayle had a confused look on her face. "Kitty, what are covert systems?"

Kitty stared at the holo-display glowing in the forward window and twitched the control arm, adjusting their course while watching the dot that represented their ship move closer to the dot the computer called the *Dalgor Kreth*. "Simon would be better able to answer that, really."

"Not really, Gayle," Simon demurred. "I don't know any more about this stuff than you do. But I have to agree with Kitty. The term 'covert systems' could apply to any number of things technology-wise. It does look like it foxes radar though."

Kitty sat up straight in her chair. "No cuts, bruises or contusions, ladies and gentlemen," she said lightly. Simon looked at her, asking with his eyes. She pointed out the window. "I think we've reached our destination."

Gayle was the first to see it. "Looks like a two-by-four from here," she observed.

"That 'two-by-four' has room to park this shuttle, two others, and something called a fuel scoop," Kitty stated quietly. "We're still a long way off."

Simon peered out at the sight. "I don't have anything to reference it against. How big is the damned thing?"

"The *Dalgor Kreth* is two hundred thirty-six feet high, six hundred and eighteen feet wide, and three thousand eight hundred forty-one feet long," offered the computer.

As they approached, the shuttle seemed to slow down on its own. The size of the larger vessel became more apparent the closer they got. Simon began to comprehend the true size when a door slowly opened low on the side of the gigantic craft.

"It's huge! Something like this had to have been built in orbit. I wonder if they've had any contact with humans before."

"From what Kitty told me, I'd have to guess not," Gayle offered. "Otherwise, the alien would have been able to speak English, don't you think?" Simon remained silent.

The shuttle floated into a large space in the side of the gigantic mothership. Noises and vibrations came from beneath their feet, and then the ship settled onto the floor of the chamber. Several seconds later, the noises they'd come to associate with an active ship began to disappear one by one as the ship shut itself down.

"I guess you never really know what you're hearing until you can't hear it anymore," Kitty said. "So, this is the end of the trip. What do we do now?"

"We should definitely leave the ship—this one, that is. We need to find out if the alien meant that the crew of the shuttle died of the plague or the crew of this bigger ship, too." Simon suited action to words and headed for the exit ramp.

Two buttons were flashing alternately when he arrived at the door.

Gayle looked at them and asked, "What does that mean?"

"How about we leave them alone for a while? Could be that something isn't ready to operate," Kitty surmised, looking over her shoulder at the other door and imagining that she could see that one flashing, too

Simon was about to comment when the panel steadied down. He reached out and pressed the button with the open ramp symbol on it. "My guess is that the atmosphere had to equalize," he said as the door first popped out about four inches, then opened. Simon stepped out onto the ramp and shivered. "Cold out here."

Large enough to hold the shuttle and three others as well, the room was lit by the same dim red light as the inside of the shuttle. Simon walked to the front of the shuttle and looked down the line of vessels. Their vehicles sat at one end of the row.

Kitty's voice brought his attention back. "This one looks like ours, don't you think?" She stood on the deck a bit forward of the ramp, hands on hips, looking from one vessel to another.

Simon peered into the gloom. While the hangar (for that was all he could think of calling it), was definitely brighter than the inside of the shuttle, it didn't do much to help human vision. Kitty's form was little more than a silhouette as she stood at the mid-point of the shuttle about seventy-five feet away. "I think so, dear," he said, pitching his voice to carry without quite yelling. "The next space over has another ship that looks the same from here. Looks like a fourth ship parked way down there, but I'm not positive. I'm gonna take a quick look."

Simon strode down the line of ships until he stood in front of the fourth one. The ship sitting there bore only a slight resemblance to the other shuttles. It was squatter, with no windows at all, and somehow it seemed more… used, more worn. He walked back to where Kitty waited, straining to make out details in the reddish half-light. To his left was the hatch that served as exits for the ships he passed. His steps quickened when his imagination gave him all the gory details of what could happen if someone cycled the airlock while they were out of a ship. At the same time, his mind felt numb as the implications of what they were doing finally struck home.

Simon reached Kitty and slid his arm around her waist. She hugged him back, then quickly pushed away, looked him in the eyes, and said, "We are standing in an alien spaceship, and you go wandering off! Both of you! And left me standing here! What the hell got into you?" The tremor in her voice told him just how tightly she was wound.

Simon was saved from having to respond when Gayle appeared out of the gloom. "I found a door in the wall back that way. Looks like a more complicated system than on the shuttle though." She nodded her head back in the direction she'd just come from.

"Well, then, that would be where we need to be," Simon declared, a feeling of unease settling onto his shoulders. "Ladies, let's go." He put his arm back around Kitty's waist and pulled her close. "Unless you'd rather stay here?" he asked jokingly.

"No, I'm coming, Simon," Kitty said. "Where you go, I go. That's what I promised fifteen years ago. I just didn't imagine this!" Her voice started to quiver, and she took a deep breath, eyes closed. "We're on an alien spaceship, twelve thousand miles above the Earth. It just takes some getting used to." She waved a hand in the direction Gayle had indicated. "But maybe we should get started, so let's go."

Her enthusiasm growing more evident with each step, Kitty walked alongside Simon, disengaging his arm from around her waist and sliding her hand into his. Her head moved from side to side as she looked for some sign of the inhabitants, passengers, or crew of this larger ship. Gayle, right behind her, was doing the same.

"So, what did you see?"

"Just about the strangest thing I've ever seen," Simon proclaimed.

Kitty began to hiccup, followed immediately by hysterical laughter.

Simon noted the manic quality in her laughter. "What's the matter, hon?"

"The matter is that we're on a spaceship God only knows how many miles from home and you just saw the strangest thing in the world; that's what. The first thing that went through my mind was how did your mother get here ahead of us? Okay, so she's not exactly strange, just a little bit eccentric," Kitty temporized, "but my mind isn't exactly working right at the moment. Can you say for sure that yours is?"

"Well, no," Simon agreed sheepishly.

"So, what's so strange, Simon?" Gayle asked lightly, trying to divert the conversation onto another track. "If it's not your mother, what is it?"

"Don't you start, too!" Simon growled. "Just a weird ship. Sorta like these three shuttles, but more... I don't know. Just different. You should see it."

"Okay, dear. Why don't we do that before we leave here? We might not get another chance for a while."

The trio walked around the front of the second shuttle, affording everyone a better view of that quarter, and moved across the open space to stare at the squat, half-melted-looking ship sitting alone at the side of the room. Roughly the size and shape of the shuttle they'd ridden up there in, it had a broader, less aerodynamic bow, and didn't seem to have any viewports or access except through a front opening that resembled a scoop. Its battered appearance gave it the impression of being either very old or heavily armored and even more heavily used.

"You're right, Simon, that's even stranger than your mother." Kitty giggled. "Sorry, darling, I'll get myself under control sooner or later."

"Sooner would be better," he growled under his breath. Aloud he said, "I'd like to get a better look at that one. Why so beat up?"

"We can do that some other time, maybe," Kitty said, clearly uninterested in the strange ship. "I can't help but feel that there's someone here somewhere. How sure can we be that we're alone on this thing?"

CHAPTER FIVE

"If I were running the show," Simon said, "I'd be right on the other side." He indicated the door Gayle had found in the back wall of the landing bay. "And I'd expect someone on the other side of this door except that we've been here for over half an hour now. Maybe that alien was actually telling the truth about the ship being uninhabited."

"That's fine for you to say, but I'm not in as big a hurry as you are," Gayle said, standing beside him. "Kitty, I'm going to borrow one side of your husband for comfort. You can have the other." She moved back a step and looked around Simon at the door. Placing her right hand on his shoulder, she looked at Kitty and reached for her hand.

Simon looked over the door. It wasn't really more complicated; it just had more moving parts. A wheel was centered in the door with twelve cantilevered bars attached, much like watertight hatches in use on Earth. The door opened outward. "I think that if this side was still in vacuum, this door wouldn't open, anyway. The pressure on the other side would keep it shut. Like in a submarine," he said to the girls. "Ready?"

"No," Gayle said flatly.

"Not really," Kitty agreed, "but go ahead. We're out of options, aren't we?"

Simon shrugged, stepped forward, and turned the

wheel firmly. The bars smoothly disengaged from the bulkhead and the wheel stopped with a faint click.

When nothing happened, he pushed on the door and it opened as smoothly as the ones in the shuttle, but this far more massive door absorbed the energy of Simon's push and stopped about half-way open. The sight that greeted them was… anti-climactic. The same red light and deck plates continued into the murky distance, with nothing in sight but the floor. Simon spoke first. "There's nothing. Warmer, though. Let's look around."

"This is going from scary to spooky," Kitty said.

Simon pushed harder on the door. Before he could stop it, the door pivoted all the way around and banged against the metal bulkhead. The resultant clang echoed back twice, indicating a very large open space ahead of them.

"Well, there went our last chance to sneak up on 'em," he quipped, stepping through the hatch. "If any of them still exist, remember."

Kitty and Gayle followed Simon through the door into a red-tinged, nearly formless void. The only point of reality was the deck stretching out of sight until Kitty reached back and grabbed the wall for support. She tilted her head up, eyes following the wall into the gloom, and saw a straight line. Immediately, her depth perception asserted itself and she recognized the ceiling about twenty-five feet above her head. She let out a breath she didn't know she'd been holding.

Simon heard and turned away from his fruitless scan of the area in their immediate vicinity. "What? Are you okay, hon?"

Kitty smiled. Even though his face was in deep

shadow, she knew worry lines were pinching the corners of his eyes in a most unattractive manner. "I'm fine, love. I just discovered the ceiling." She knew it sounded inane, but she didn't care.

Simon and Gayle looked up as well. Kitty saw the gleam in Simon's eye when he looked back at her. "Now I don't feel like I'm under a microscope. Just a bug on a plate. A subtle difference, but an improvement, I think."

"Wanna make a map or something?" Gayle asked. "I have a notebook and pen in the Jeep." She laughed nervously. "Or we could leave a trail of shredded paper. A paper trail. Get it?"

"Not a bad idea," Kitty agreed. "I'll get them and handle making the map. Maybe it'll help me stay focused." She glared meaningfully at Simon and walked purposefully back to the shuttle. She'd complained only moments before about being left alone, and now she was walking off on her own to prove… what?

Not being able to see the far side of the room due to the dim lighting, Simon chose to begin the map from the open shuttle bay door. He arbitrarily turned right and began counting paces aloud while he considered the notion of confronting Kitty about her inconsistent behavior. A team leader needed to be able to depend on the actions and attitudes of his team. And she had specifically asked him to act as a team leader, thinking of her as an asset rather than a wife. It was hard, but he was trying. He realized before opening his mouth that he had almost fallen into the trap of thinking he really was on an assignment. He decided, also, that the two women were holding up remarkably well under the circumstances and that discretion was certainly the better part of valor.

A door appeared out of the gloom. This one had a small, lighted panel next to it. Set into the bottom of the panel was an icon that could be interpreted as an up arrow if one stretched the point, or maybe an 'A' without its crossbar. Touching it opened the door onto a small chamber that would be crowded if a dozen people were in it. A strip of buttons graced the inside wall next to the open door, and the bottom one was lit.

"Elevator, I'll bet. Looks like I've got a new saying for a while—form follows function. Let's see what else we can find. I suggest we finish walking the perimeter of this… room."

"You're in charge of the reconnaissance mission, dear," Kitty said.

Gayle remained uncharacteristically silent.

The first piece of… machinery that manifested out of the gloom startled the explorers at first. While looking the device over, whether accidentally or not, Gayle pushed a button that was set apart from the others. A faint hum emanated from somewhere inside the thing, and it rose up off the floor about four inches.

The noise made Simon jump. When the machine rose in the air, he said, "Okay. Who did what? We need to be careful here. I don't want anybody getting hurt. We're a long way from a doctor."

"Sorry, Simon," Gayle said, her voice not quite carrying the sentiment. "I'll be more careful." She pushed the button again, this time obviously, and the hum died out as the thing settled back to the floor.

The mysterious shapes that presented themselves after that didn't evoke quite as much apprehension as the first. Several different types of machines were noted during the walkaround of the room, and numerous racks affixed to sections of the walls held unidentifiable objects, possibly tools.

Reaching a second corner, Simon announced, "A little over two thousand feet. I figured this thing was big when we docked with it, but two thousand feet?"

"Well, the computer on the shuttle did say it was over thirty-eight hundred feet long," Gayle said, following her two friends along.

Simon began pacing along the next wall until they came to four more doors. "This area should coincide with the hangar bay we arrived in. How many shuttles do these folks need at one time?"

"These doors do look like the one on the other side," Kitty commented. "That one should be an elevator if the little panel is the same, but these are separate." She walked up to the nearer of the three remaining doors and knocked on it to hear the clang. "Why are there three separate doors over here and just one on the other side?" She gripped the wheel in its middle and spun it until it stopped. "For once, I'm opening the door for *you,* Simon. Be my guest, but be careful." She bowed facetiously and swept her hand in the direction of the new room.

Simon shook his head, an unreadable smile on his lips as he turned to the new room. He instantly dubbed the three ships they found 'fighters,' each having its own launch bay. And what beauties these little ships were! Sleek and deadly in appearance, they looked for all the world like Vipers out of the old TV show Battlestar Galactica. Noting the open cockpits, Simon itched to sit in one and see how it felt. But acceding to his desire to find out for sure if anyone else was aboard, he passed on the idea. Reluctantly, he closed the door and began to count paces again while Kitty made a notation on her pad. They passed the door they'd tentatively identified as an elevator and kept walking.

Arriving back at their starting point, they took stock.

"We're in a rectangular room about two thousand, three hundred feet long by about six hundred feet wide, not including the shuttle bays," Kitty read in the dim light. "This end has two bays with seven ships—three shuttles, one weird one, and three fighters. There are two banks of three elevators each at this end of the room and one each at the far end. No other doors that we saw. Correct?"

"That's the way I figure it. The big question is why does such a huge space exist? Twenty-five feet to the ceiling gives us a lot of square footage." Simon looked thoughtful.

"Something like thirty-four-million-plus square feet of space." Kitty looked up from another page of the legal pad she was fast running through.

"Are we ready to take a ride upstairs?" Simon asked.

"Not me," Kitty announced. "At least, not yet. I don't know about you two, but I need to get a bite to eat. And I'm in serious need of a bathroom. Not necessarily in that order, either. Why don't you two go to the Jeep and let me take care of other things for a minute, okay?"

"Hold on and I'll join you," Gayle said. "I don't think we should run around here alone. Simon can fix us something to eat and I'll get the necessaries." Minutes later, she walked back out of their shuttle carrying the porta potty. "Simon will be okay for a few minutes. Let's find a corner. I guess I'm glad this happened on a camping trip, or we'd be in deep… trouble," she finished lamely. Her resolution to quit cussing often caused her to have to stop and think before she said something.

Returning to the Jeep, the two women found that Simon had lunch ready. "Cold cuts, cheese, crackers, and pop," he said. "Comfort food."

The two women took their time, dragging the meal out until Simon got up in frustration and began to pace toward the shuttle cockpit. Gayle looked at Kitty and raised one eyebrow. When Kitty frowned and nodded her head just once, Gayle wiped her hands on her jeans in lieu of the napkins Simon had forgotten and went after him.

"Hey, Simon," she said when she found him. "Let's talk a minute, okay?"

"Sure," he replied, idly running his hands over the arms of the pilot's chair.

"I'm really not up to any more exploring today," Gayle confessed. "And Kitty isn't either. She told me when we went… Anyway, I've had enough shocks for one day. I'd suggest we take a nap or something," Gayle advised, motioning Simon to follow her. "Look at your watch. It's almost midnight," she said over her shoulder, leading Simon back to the Jeep. "I know I've had a long day. And if any aliens show up, it's a safe bet that they'll wake us up. We can close the ramp on the shuttle and get that much extra warning. It makes a racket opening up. The more I think about it, the more sure I am," she said, getting into the front seat and reclining it a bit. "Besides, don't you want to be at your best if that alien was wrong and we finally do meet his friends? You go close the door, Simon. It's lights out for me."

No alarms went off, and no aliens woke them up at blaster-point. But the lighter gravity did make for some interesting dreams. Simon stretched the kinks out of his back and legs, grateful for the sleeping bags and air mattress. "Okay, ladies, rise and shine," Simon called. "If you can't shine, then just rise. I'll be right back."

Visions of alien pilots herding this shuttle around for hours on end made him go back to the cockpit, roll of paper in hand. "Even aliens gotta go sometime, damn it." Rapping on a blank section of bulkhead, he finally found what he was looking for by putting pressure on a section of plating the size of his hand. The door receded about an inch, then slid silently into the wall. The facilities thus revealed were strange, to be sure, but keeping his new mantra in mind, he made them work.

Feeling more than a bit pleased with himself, Simon strolled back to the Jeep. "Guess what I found, ladies. Here's a clue," he teased, aiming the roll of toilet paper at the back of Gayle's head.

Gayle, closer to being awake, got the picture first. "Cool! I don't guess you can imagine how I felt last night. I had dreams of being caught with my pants around my ankles by a bunch of snickering aliens. Where is it? Kitty! Potty call!" Groaning, Gayle crawled out of her sleeping bag and limped around. "My foot's asleep! Shit! Kitty! Let's go! Your man has made himself useful and found a bathroom!" No one said anything about her lapse into profanity.

Returning to the Jeep to find breakfast almost ready, the two women smiled at each other. "I guess we'll keep him around for a while," Kitty said. "He does have his moments."

Breakfast finished, Simon strapped his ever-present pistol on his hip and said, "Let's go, ladies. The elevators await. Kitty, got your pad?" At her nod, he set off down the bay and opened the door. When the ramp stabilized, the three of them went to the still-open bay door. "We're going to have to come up with names to call things around here until we get set straight by whoever's aboard, although at this late date, I'm beginning to believe we really are alone. Someone should have come to see why a shuttle docked and no one got off, if there was anyone left aboard, that is. Shuttles, fighters, launch bays, and the big empty room so far. Okay?"

"Any preference as to which elevator we want to use in the big empty room, boss?" Gayle questioned frivolously.

"Nope. The closest one will do," Simon said, pointedly ignoring Gayle's tone. "They all had the same strip inside the door. I counted them. Apparently, this ship has eighteen levels. I hope we don't have far to go before we locate someone."

With Kitty scribbling furiously, the three stepped into the elevator. "Press the top button, Gayle. That's the obvious place to start. Not that 'obvious' means anything in a situation like this, but it's as good a place as any." Simon didn't really expect to find much on the top level. He hadn't seen anything that related to windows as they neared the immense ship, but his ingrained training made him want to start at the top and work his way down.

Gayle pressed the top button on the strip, and they felt the weight of a swift ascent as the chamber moved up. The door opened to more red light and still no occupants. They stepped out into an empty corridor and stood there uncertainly. Closed doors met their gaze along the corridor. There was a door just a few feet to their left, and the corridor then stretched off to their right, ending in a bulkhead door. "I really expected to find someone here," Kitty said peevishly, "regardless of what that alien said. How could everybody on a ship this big die of a plague? Can it really be that fatal?"

"Anything's possible, Kitty," Gayle said. "There are documented instances of entire tribes dying of smallpox back in the 1800s, from infected blankets issued by the Army, if I recall." She shivered. "It wasn't an easy death, either. It's possible that whatever killed these people was extremely effective. But if that's true, there should be bodies, right?"

Kitty froze. "Thanks for that mental image, girlfriend." She turned left and went to the door in the bulkhead, inspecting it. "No airtight seals here, guys. Just one of those plates like in the shuttle. Well, here goes nothing."

Putting her words into action, Kitty pressed the plate and watched the door slide into the wall. The corridor ahead of her, some twelve feet wide, stretched off into the distance. "Simon, start pacing off distances, please," Kitty said as she began walking. "We'll go as far as this hall will let us and then start looking into rooms, I guess. Does anybody else notice how much we're saying that? 'I guess?' Quite a bit, I guess." She giggled, and that set Gayle off.

"Not this early, please, Kitty," Gayle said with a chuckle.

The corridor they traveled ended at a T-type intersection. "Five hundred feet, Kitty," Simon offered. "You do realize that the length of this section of the ship is in addition to the big empty room downstairs? Down below? Whatever. This section adds to the length of the ship as a whole."

Kitty noted the figure on the map. "That makes it twenty-eight hundred feet long, so far," she said. "We've passed ten cross-corridors. Let's go left," Kitty said.

An hour later, the three were more confused than ever. "This whole floor is mostly what looks like weapons sections with a few sets of living quarters for personnel. Dozens of rooms, and not one of them looks like they've been used recently. No personal possessions, no pictures, no nothing. I really don't get it. Could it be empty? How can someone lose a ship this big?" Simon sat down on a bed he would have killed for the night before. A metal shelf extruded from the wall and was covered with a thin yet amazingly comfortable mattress.

"At least we won't have a problem finding bathrooms again," Kitty quipped. "But the idea of this thing being empty really bothers me. Let's go down to the next level."

As the threesome headed back toward the

elevators, Gayle said. "Remember how the computer said this ship was thirty-eight hundred feet long? I want to know about the missing thousand feet."

"Probably the engine room or section or whatever," Simon said. "About the last place we'd be likely to find survivors, if any, which I'm beginning to believe less likely by the minute."

The second level proved to be simply sleeping rooms, exercise rooms—judging by the odd-looking equipment scattered around the floors—and large rooms with oversized tables and benches that the trio thought were eating areas or gathering places. After a more than cursory but less than complete inspection, they moved to the third level.

This time the elevator doors opened onto a larger corridor than the other two, and Kitty's heartbeat went up the instant she stepped into the corridor. There was a feel to this level that she hadn't sensed on the first two. She watched Simon's hand brush his pistol—an automatic response to an unknown situation. Recognizing the incongruity of his response, she snorted quietly, an action that didn't go unnoticed by Simon.

"So, what's the drill here, boss?" Kitty asked, deliberately deferring to Simon's expertise. She'd listened to more than one story of recon in enemy territory and was unsure whether she was glad he was unarmed or not.

Simon glanced around him. The abnormally wide corridor, compared to the only other two they'd seen so far, stretched out ahead of them like the other two, but where corridors had branched off, leading to blocks of housing and communal areas, this one seemed to have a more... managerial... air to it. It ran straight and direct, with only two cross corridors until it reached a set of double doors that were the first of their kind so far.

The two previous decks had rooms with doors that were marked by different symbols above a series of other figures painted beside the door. Just above that was a plate that, when pressed, opened the door. These doors had their designations fronted directly on them, although the now-familiar, hand-sized plate was still set beside each door.

A more thorough investigation of this particular level turned up rooms dedicated to things the three humans could only guess at. In some rooms, consoles sat dark beneath blank panels or screens; in others, the control panels flickered with electronic life, the displays scrolling along faster than the human eye could comfortably follow. Other rooms gave no clue to their reasons for being that the three could identify.

Standing in front of yet another point of entry, Gayle placed her hand on the now-common panel found beside most doors, expecting another room full of more unidentifiable items. But this door slid into the wall, revealing a sight that caused her to hesitate. Her eyes flickered around the room, taking in as much as she could without passing over the threshold. She finally managed to break away from the scene and turned to find Simon just coming out of a room across the corridor. "Simon, come here," she said excitedly. "This whole level has been work-spaces and labs and stuff. This room looks like a secretary's office. Maybe we're getting close."

Simon glanced into the room and shrugged. "Could

be. Extra chairs along the walls. A desk guarding the only other door in the room. Maybe the captain's outer office."

Kitty turned up at Simon's elbow, having finished looking over the room she'd been assigned. "What have we got?" she asked, peeking around the doorjamb.

"A mystery," Simon replied. "What did you find?"

Kitty shrugged. "Nothing earth-shattering. I got one of the consoles to show me a few star systems. One of 'em might be ours. The sixth planet was ringed, but it showed ten planets instead of nine."

Gayle bowed at the waist and waved Kitty into the room. "Here's our mystery. All the rooms we've seen so far have been dedicated to something specific, like your last room and the star systems. This room looks like it was designed for people to just sit in."

Kitty walked in and stood beside the desk. She stared around the room and then sat in the over-tall chair behind the desk. She ran her hands over the surface, along the sides, and under places she could easily reach. Turning a bemused look on her husband and friend, she said, "This is a receptionist's desk. I don't know how yet, but she has a way to let her boss know who's here. He'd be in there." She thumbed over her shoulder at the door behind her. "This is a waiting room."

Gayle grinned. "Told ya so. I've been in enough of 'em."

The next series of rooms, after figuring out the secretary's door opener, proved to be a suite, and was just as frustrating as all the other rooms had been.

"What do these people have against personal effects?" Kitty complained. "Not one personal item anywhere. No pictures, recordings, clothing, games, toys, nothing. It's as if there was never anyone aboard, but we have the alien's story that there were more crewmembers. And the computer said so, too."

"Which we haven't heard from in a while," Gayle commented. "Computer?"

"Attending." The same voice came from apparently empty air.

Gayle looked around the room she and her friends stood in, sat down on what was obviously a lounger, and said, "I'm not moving until I get some answers." She glared at her friends. "We need to know things, damn it! How many people are needed to operate this vessel?"

The response, while immediate, wasn't one any of them wanted to hear. "It requires one hundred thirty-seven crewmen to operate the engines and navigation systems. Seventy-five are assigned to sensor duty and record and input data to the computer continuously. One hundred are assigned to routine shipboard maintenance. Another seventy-five serve as cooks and other shipboard tasks. Five hundred thirty-one crewmen are assigned to operate the factory section. The total complement of this vessel is nine hundred and eighteen."

Simon sank into a recliner-type chair, stunned at the number. Gayle's mouth had dropped open during the recitation, and Kitty slowly sat down on the lounger opposite Gayle.

Simon asked a question in turn. "What do you mean by factory section?"

"This vessel's purpose is to go to a star system,

preferably with an asteroid belt, manufacture the materials needed by a colony, and deliver those goods to the planet selected for colonization. When the colonists arrive, basic shelter will already exist, and all other necessities will be stockpiled for their use."

"So, your builders were going to colonize our system?" Kitty asked angrily.

"No. Colonization directives dictate that only planets with non-sentient life are suitable for colonization. This vessel went off-course after the plague struck."

Kitty had climbed out of the chair and was roaming the suite, listening to the computer's answers. She opened a door and stared for a few seconds as a smile flowed across her face. She leaned against the doorframe, one foot cocked over the other, arms crossed, and gazed around the room. Images out of Star Trek flashed through her mind as she took in the scene.

Rectangular rather than circular like the *Enterprise*, this bridge had nine different stations, each composed of a pedestal-style control panel in front of a chair. Two faced the front of the room, if the front was defined by the several huge screens showing off-colored pictures of the Earth. The rest all managed to find space along the sides of the room, leaving one other chair set slightly apart and above the others. She stood away from the jamb and walked into the heart and soul of the titanic structure they were in.

Kitty was studying the viewscreens when she heard Simon and Gayle come in. All the screens needed to be color-adjusted, but the center one was very obviously Earth. Florida and the Gulf of Mexico were proof positive.

"We wondered what had happened to you. Whatcha got?" Gayle asked.

"Control room," Kitty declared. "Or more appropriately, the bridge. And not a soul in sight. If anywhere, this is the place I would think to find someone. Ten people to operate the entire ship. That doesn't seem right."

"Maybe," Gayle proffered as she walked through the room examining the consoles, "ten is all it takes to command it in flight. And at that, there would have to be some kind of shifts, wouldn't there? We assume these people sleep, given the fact that they have beds, so we have to assume that they get tired and need to be relieved."

"And of course," Simon said, finally getting a word in edgewise, "there are other people to run other stuff. We've only been on three decks, now. Computer, did this plague you mentioned kill them all?"

"Yes."

"Just as the alien claimed," Simon said. "So, we ask questions about how to run this ship and you answer them?"

"As much as I can. There are very large portions of my database that have been deleted."

"By whom and for what reason?" Gayle asked.

"Unknown."

"And now we die, too?" This from Kitty as she sat down in the single central chair.

"No. The records that continue to exist appear to define the plague as species-specific."

"You keep using words like 'I' and 'my.' Are you self-aware? And what are your functions?" Gayle asked.

"No. My functions are to oversee the operations of the factory levels, calculate courses, and estimate threat levels under hostile conditions."

"Factories? Threat levels?" Ever the master of understatement, Kitty said, "I think we need a lot more information than we have at the moment. Tell us everything you can."

"Yes, Captain. My construction was completed just over a year ago as time is measured on the planet below ..."

CHAPTER SIX

"Sir, we have a preliminary report on Event Alpha," the dark-suited young man said.

"Yes?" John Porter, Director of the Defense Intelligence Agency, took a few seconds to switch gears. He gave a harried look at the folders in the young agent's hands.

"The event in Montana, sir," the agent said, knowing his boss's propensity to focus on one thing at a time.

"Ah, yes." The light came on. "I hope we managed to salvage something from the situation."

"Well, sir, we did find the spot where the unknown landed, but it managed to get away just as forward elements of one of our air cav units arrived on the scene. I have the radar records of both the landing and the departure. I also have radar and visual records of the F-16 that actually got within range. Audio recordings of the conversation between the pilots have been provided as well. And NORAD tracked the vessel back out of atmosphere until it disappeared from their screens. No reason was given for the disappearance."

At a gesture from the director, the agent set the pile of folders and discs on the edge of the antique desk. At a signal, he sat down in the straight-backed chair opposite his boss. "Put it in a nutshell for me, Agent. I have to make a report to the president later today."

The young man started his recitation. "We have evidence of recent use at a local campsite across the lake from the landing site. The place was pretty well cleaned up, but we managed to come away with quite a bit of Intel. Near the edge of the hill, overlooking the site, we found blood. We were able to come up with an exact DNA match—one Katherine Anne Hawke of Billings. Did research work in particle physics at MIT some time back. We also found a telescope on top of the ridge with an inscription on it. 'Merry Christmas, Simon. Love, Kittyn.' We pulled positive prints of both suspects off the telescope. Our forensics teams found a strange background radiation and something very crispy that they're pretty certain wasn't conceived on this planet."

The agent went on. "We didn't have to look far to find Simon Hawke, either. Metaphorically speaking, I mean."

"I don't have the time or temper for metaphors, Agent. Finish this."

"Yes, sir. Simon Andrew Hawke. And an interesting individual he is, sir. It seems that he's a former member of this very agency. Left thirteen years ago after being side-lined for getting married. Seems he wasn't cut out for military life, so he crossed over when he had a difference of opinion with Army higher-ups. Made an effective agent. His most notable case was the Conroy affair about sixteen years back—the physicist smuggling secrets to China. He's been living in Billings, Montana for the past thirteen years, which is just about five hundred miles from the event site. And with his wife's blood on the ridge and the fingerprints of both on-scene, we can pretty much wrap this up as soon as we get our hands on either of the Hawkes." The agent flipped a page on his clipboard. "One other thing. The ALERT team leader ran down the same information and sent someone in to find Hawke. It seems that he and his wife are out of town. Annual spring camping trip or some such, according to some chatty neighbors."

The director's expression was not one that would be found on a happy face. "So, what do I have to tell the president? That this was just the break we needed to put us ahead for good? That no one would ever be able to threaten the U.S. again?" The director looked the agent in the eye. "You get Hawke in here immediately. I want it spread quietly to every police agency in the country that Simon and Katherine Hawke are to be taken alive. I want as much on this guy as we can get. Then we'll know who has what to say."

Kitty went to bed thinking about the implications of what they could actually do, and the next day a long and involved interrogation of the computer was begun by the three humans. One question led to another and one topic to another until what would have been early hours for most from their time zone. Their adrenaline levels were just too high to allow them to stop. Among other things, it turned out that the ship had teleportation technology. This would prove invaluable to the three conspirators, for that was surely what they had become.

Finding this second, larger ship had changed all of Kitty's ideas. No way could this technology be given to *any* governmental or quasi-governmental group, or sooner or later one of the bigger nations would gobble it up whole and begin to wring its secrets from it for their own military gain, bringing about the very future they were trying to avoid. And now, with the discovery of the existence of the larger ship, even Simon recognized the wisdom of not giving it up.

The need for rest finally made itself felt, and the three strolled back to their vehicles in the shuttle where Simon prepared dinner from canned goods, an ice chest, and a Coleman stove. The trip back up to the third level gave them time to talk more about future plans.

"If we're going to keep it, we need to learn as much as we can about it," Simon said. "None of us have the grounding to do more than be button-pushers here. We need to have at least a basic understanding of what type of forces we're dealing with or we're going to get bit in the ass. And sooner rather than later."

"What do you suggest?" Kitty asked. "I'm still thinking of you as the team leader. You've got the expertise in this type of situation."

"There's never *been* a situation like this!" Simon exploded. "Getting the ship, any ship, if we could, was part and parcel of our mission statement, *the* mission statement, that is," Simon said, stressing his self-distancing from the decision. "But development of its technology was supposed to take years. And we were just in acquisitions, so to speak. Hell, look how long it took for fiber optics to get into general use after what supposedly crashed at Roswell got taken apart down at Groom Lake. The predictions were that it would be years before we understood enough about the technology to keep from blowing anything up."

"So, what do we *do*?" Gayle asked. Simon looked at her, his face devoid of expression. "Hey! Don't give me any of that!" she protested loudly at his favorite blank look. "Remember, I *just* found out you're a spy. I guess that's what comes from letting your best friend marry outside their community, huh?"

Kitty grinned at her friend and shook her head slightly. Simon shook his harder and focused on Gayle.

"I'm sorry, Gayle. I was concentrating on your question, to be honest. And don't blame Kitty. I never told her everything. National security and need-to-know clauses in my contract. I resigned for the good of the service after I couldn't hack a desk job. So that means I *was* a spy."

"Kitty said you weren't cut out to sit around all day. That was true?"

"As far as it went," Simon admitted, leaning back in his chair, trying to find a comfortable position. "The thing is, the Agency, the DIA, that is, doesn't approve of married field agents. If you have those kinds of ties—a wife, kids, a life outside the Agency—you're less likely to take advantage of delicate circumstances when they present themselves. So, I got sidelined, made a handler for active agents. Didn't work for me, so I quit. Came to Billings, and you know the rest."

Gayle looked at Simon as if she'd just met him. "Do you miss it? The adventure of all that spy stuff?"

Simon smiled, his eyes focused on something she couldn't see. "I wasn't James Bond, kiddo. Most of what I did was boring—footwork, paperwork, details. I spent a lot of time in libraries. As a matter of fact, that's how I met Kitty. Not *in* a library but because of one. I needed to know a little bit about low-temperature physics for the assignment at MIT where I met Kitty."

Gayle persisted. "You still haven't answered the question. What do we do?"

"We do the same thing any other team does when it finds itself in need of assistance," Simon said. "We follow the manual on this." The looks of confusion on both faces made him laugh outright. "We call in experts." He'd leaned forward to stress his point and then resettled into a different position in the chair.

Kitty looked sharply at her husband. "I thought we wanted to keep this ship out of government hands?"

"We do. I *do*," he said, emphasizing the second syllable. "We find our own experts. Actually, all we have to do is locate one, someone with a background that would let him or her accept all this." He waved his hands vaguely, "And a background that will let them bring together enough like-minded individual scientists as possible to give us a good working knowledge of the ship's systems—if not *why* they work then at least *how* they work. We find our initial contact outside the usual channels and let him or her pick the next candidates."

Gayle was perplexed, and it showed. "Even if we get some scientists to tell us what we can and can't push, we're still going to need a crew. Where are we going to get them, and how are we going to make sure they'll follow orders? Or won't form cliques and try to take over or something? And just what will *we* be doing with this thing?"

"All good questions, Gayle," Simon said easily.

"Who do we know ourselves who would believe us without proof? Let's start out with our closest friends and then decide who we should contact first. As for the rest of your questions, I have only one answer." He looked over at Kitty. "I know how you feel about martial law from some of the things you've said over the years, dear. But I think that the only way to control a group as disparate as the one we're contemplating is going to be through some form of military rule. How are you going to feel about being a part of that?"

Kitty thought for a moment before she replied. "It depends on what we're going to do with the technology. I do get a voice in this."

Simon nodded. "Of course you do. After all, you're the captain, and the ship answers to you because of that wristband. But we have to find out what we've got before we can decide what we can do with it. I believe this ship belongs to the whole planet, not just one country, at least until the original owners show up to claim their property. I want to be very careful about what we tell the world in general, and when, so we don't cause too much disturbance in the economies of the world. Best way to do that is to take the—what did the computer call her?—*Dalgor Kreth* out to the asteroid belt and build her twin just in case her real owners show up. Then we can give her back without any losses. We'll recruit crew the same way we recruit scientists. I'd say that we should build a cadre of people loyal to us personally before we start letting a lot of relative strangers aboard."

Gayle said, "I know just the right bunch! My little brother and some of his friends would love to get in on this. I'm sure of it."

Simon smiled at Gayle's statement. Grant Miller had definitely received the height in the family. Standing six-foot-three, he was about average in the post-high-school football-team crowd he was often found with. They could bring Grant and his buddies aboard, with Gayle being head of security for a time, and then the real business of figuring out this nightmare could begin.

"Good idea, Gayle." Simon slapped the arm of the chair. "I like the way you think. We have to work on our friends and acquaintances and let them do the same to others in their broader circles of friends." Gayle beamed at the compliment, but it didn't last long. "I figure we all need to start taking on the responsibilities of getting this enterprise underway. And you getting Grant and his friends is just a start. Satisfied, Kitty?"

With some misgiving, she nodded slowly. "Okay. But just because we set up on a military structure, I don't want to lose the… the," Kitty searched for a word. "Oh, I don't know how to say it. See, the government knows we've got the ship but not who we are. They're gonna try to make us out to be the bad guys when I think most people might come around to our way of thinking. I want us to be the good guys in this."

Simon nodded. "We'll find our scientist. You two can do it from home. I'll lay a few false trails Earth-side and get in touch with some of my old platoon. I know one who'll be perfect for security officer."

Kitty worriedly asked, "Dear, how are we going to move bunches of people around without getting caught at it sooner or later?"

"We'll use the transporter technology to simply

beam in and out. You heard what the computer said— line of sight and inside most buildings but not underground."

"Simply," Kitty said, mimicking Simon. "You're willing to trust yourself to that kind of technology?"

"Not without some testing," Simon admitted. "I'd say send down something very expendable, like a bag of trash. When we beam it back up, if it still looks like trash, I'll try it myself. We'll still have to get us and the vehicles back to the surface, though, so that means at least one more shuttle trip.

"Oh, yeah. Gayle can pull into her driveway and beam out, no chance of her being touched. I, on the other hand, want to know what they know. The questions they ask and don't ask will tell me a lot. I'll just have to improvise to get out. I'll bet they identified you from the little blood you left behind. My telescope was engraved with both our names, and Gayle is our best friend. There's no way we're just gonna be able to just walk around on the loose, but going to the house is the only option I have to learn anything. And they know I'm an ex-agent. They'll be on their toes for the little tricks I know. I'm almost sorry you're going to miss the dance.

"We're about to be investigated to hell and back, dear, so we better have an airtight transportation system. The shuttles are good, but now that they're known, I'd rather not use 'em for a while. So we'll do a lot of transporting."

"Well, I'm gonna need some things from home. All of us are," Kitty said. "How safe would it be to transport into the house and back out again?"

Simon thought about it a minute. "I'll bet they've got our phones tapped, computers bugged, and audio and video pickups all over our houses by now. Why not just appropriate what you need from a store and leave a voucher saying the U.S. government will take care of the bill? Sign your name and I'll bet they do it," he finished, laughing.

Gayle applauded lightly. "That might just work. You think on your feet pretty well."

Simon shook his head. "If you can't think on your feet in this business, you're dead," he said with a straight face. "I'm not exaggerating. And as far as thinking on my feet is concerned, I'm about out of the ability to do that until I get some rest. I think I'm gonna go find a bed."

Kitty's own face was carefully blank until the door closed behind him. She looked at Gayle and just said, "I've got to sleep on it too, but I do have some reservations."

Simon woke from a restless night. The gravity thing had kept him thinking he was falling every time he closed his eyes for more than a few seconds. And the dreams hadn't made it easy to rest, either. But a trip to the shower reduced his irritability enough that he was able to face the world at last. He found clean clothes laid out on the bed with a piece of the yellow notepad on top, saying, "Meet us on the bridge."

Simon, Kitty, and Gayle sat around a too-tall table in too-tall chairs in a suite of rooms they'd started calling the captain's quarters. Gayle now wore a wristband like Kitty's. The girls had gotten up earlier than Simon and explored more of level three. One room boasted a machine that would custom-fit a band for any wearer. The first order of business was to get one fitted to Simon's arm.

A door led directly from the bridge to the captain's briefing room and quarters, and was the only set of rooms to have a private bedroom and bath, as well as the fact that the amount of space allowed for a lot more people to be coming and going. It boasted the only living room they'd so far seen aboard the ship, as well as a room they called a private office, connected to a smaller room that was connected to the main corridor. "Looks like any standard office I've ever seen," Kitty said as she walked around the suite. "Secretary sits out here at the desk. The big boss sits in there." She nodded toward the inner office as she looked over an instrument panel on the small desk.

The last room in the suite was the one they were in. "Conference room?" Gayle said, guessing. "I'm betting you can get twenty or more people around this table once we get it lowered and have some more chairs brought in."

Simon nodded in agreement. "For mission briefings, daily reports, and that sort of thing, maybe. It's perfect. Three doors that let people in from the secretary's office, the captain's office, or the captain's private quarters." A thought crossed his mind and he smiled. When the two women looked perplexed, he added, "Of course, it would make a hell of a room for poker games, too."

Kitty bristled at Simon's comment. "These people were... are... aliens, Simon. You can't just go assigning things like that to them. There's no telling what they did here."

"You're right, Kitty," Simon said slowly. "But I can make some assumptions about them. I have to.

For instance, they were concerned with their physical wellbeing. Why else would there be obvious exercise rooms aboard? They also colonize other planets to perpetuate their species. They eat, drink, shit, sleep, and all the things we do."

He stood up and began to walk around the table. "They lose things... like this ship. They have enemies or they wouldn't need weapons like those fighters down below or the cannon we found mounted on level one. And they need room to expand or they would never have built this ship. If they just wanted to explore, there'd be no need for a factory ship." He fell silent, but continued to pace—something Kitty had only seen him do when he had a really tough decision to make.

"Okay, we have a bunch of unknowns," Simon said, "and very few knowns." He began ticking off points on his fingers. "Starting with not knowing why the alien chose us, humans, in general, and Kitty to give the captain's wristband to. We don't know why large chunks of the computer's memory have been wiped out—things like all the astrogation data. We know nothing at all about the race that built the ship other than their language in the computer, which could come in handy in the future if and when we run into them. We have no *real* idea why a colony ship would be coming here and no idea who their enemies are."

"You're right, Simon. The knowns are very few," Kitty said and looked at the pad in front of her. "We know the translation program will allow us to relabel all the controls so we can run this ship. And we know we *aren't* going to be able to run it because it takes over nine hundred people, and we don't know that many people. We'd have to put a lot of trust in a lot of people, and I just don't know how we can do that."

"Two more unknowns," Gayle added. "How these aliens react to strange races, and how they react to strange races that have some of their technology. And, I want to know how you're so sure they have enemies in the first place."

"Well," Simon said defensively, "it's just logic. First, until we got the ship, or until we met the alien, we could always believe we were the only intelligent race in the universe. But then we got hit in the face with reality. There *is* another intelligent race out there. And if there's one, there could be a second, third, fourth, or fifth. Even more. Knowing of two— ourselves and whoever built this ship—lets us extrapolate other races. Looking at the ships in the bays on the lower level tells me that if there are races other than our two, then at least one of them is an enemy of the people who built this ship. If you don't have enemies, you don't need weapons.

"Now, as for the technology level. You heard the computer on the bridge," Simon continued. "We have a matter transmitter aboard. That means we can beam down and up just like Star Trek as long as we have these bands and someone stays aboard to operate the controls, which can't be automated. That's a hell of a plus, even if it's restricted to ships of this size due to the size of the equipment. Matter conversion takes place in the factories, and the ship only needs to have the fuel supply replaced every five years. Personally, I need time to think about all this. And we don't have a helluva lot of that at our disposal."

"It's something we all need to think about," Kitty said dryly. "Truth to tell, I already have some ideas to bounce off you two. These guys have exercise rooms, mess halls, kitchens, showers—all the things needed to allow this many people to function, like you just said. It's like a small city, and we've only scratched the surface. We've just seen the top three levels of the living area."

"What *I* want to see is the factory section," Gayle declared.

Simon grinned at her. "Well, I've only got the beginnings of some ideas. Believe it or not, I had this dream last night, and the more I walk through this ship, the more concrete it becomes. Most of 'em get lost after a while, but this one…" He shook his head. "I'm going for a walk. Maybe I can get something to gel."

Kitty and Gayle looked at each other, and Kitty said, "Okay, Simon. You do that and we'll toss a few ideas around in here."

"Let's do our idea tossing while we go through the factory section," Gayle suggested. "That's what this ship is all about, and I want to see it!"

They agreed to meet in two hours in the shuttle bay for lunch, and when Simon arrived, he started in without preamble. "We ran into each other enough times for you to know that I spent a lot of time in the factory section, too. That's an amazing place! Anyway, I was wandering from room to room, trying to get a feel for what should be going on. If this thing was properly crewed, so much would be happening— pulling asteroids into the converter for breakdown into raw materials, moving those raw materials to the various rooms, making parts, and moving them down to the lower level for either assembly or loading onto a shuttle to be transported to a planet's surface. There are computer terminals in each of the rooms to tell the machines what to make and a larger one in what appears to be a control room that has image after image of things that this ship can build—from sheds to skyscrapers, from cars to tanks, from planes to spaceships. All the infrastructure of a colony world."

"Let me guess," Kitty cut in. "I know you, husband-mine. We already have the infrastructure, and you want to build more ships. Where are we going to get the people to crew this one, much less others? And why would we want to build ships in the first place?"

"Because whoever lost this thing is going to want it back sooner or later. I'd like to have the time to duplicate it and some of those fighters to defend what we build before its owners show up. Maybe we can be strong enough to hold them off long enough for us to get a permanent foothold in space."

He busied himself with turning some of the stored food into edible meals for them. As he opened packages and combined things, he continued. "First, we need to learn as much about this thing as we can before we crew it. And for that, we need scientists. I sure don't know any we can trust, so we'll have to come up with a plan. Table that for now. We'll want to get the trucks down since we don't need them up here. That means we learn how to fly the damned shuttle, get Gayle and the Jeep back to a remote location, and get back up here. I'll drive our truck home and get the original confrontation settled."

"Oh no, Simon Hawke. I know your temper and the willingness of the DIA to negotiate. They get you and we're dead in the water.

"Nice try, Kittyn, but you can't have your cake and eat it, too," Simon said. "I know the routines these guys will go through. Do *you* want to be on the end of their questioning? I think not."

"And," Gayle added hastily, cutting Simon off, "we can start looking for scientists to come up here."

"And these," Kitty said, laying a few metal disks on the tailgate of the Jeep, "are locator disks. Found 'em in the same room where the wristband machine is, or whatever you want to call it. Hand one to a person, press the red button on your band, and you and the other person will be transported to the ship if the two are close enough together. Or, it'll work as a single-function device. The person holding it will be transported alone if they press the button on the upper side. At least, that's what the computer told us. We found the transporter room, too. We missed it on our first walkthrough. At least, I don't remember seeing it. It will allow four at a time to beam up or down. So," she said, changing the subject, "who's going to pilot the shuttle?"

"Why don't we all practice at it?" Simon suggested. "Three heads and all that. I think getting back up here will be the same as before. Hopefully. Just get close enough and let the auto-landing program take over. Get the computer to help us relabel the controls and maybe we can figure out the rest for ourselves. That is, if the thing is as user-friendly as you think."

"And try to keep us stealthed. And go back down at dusk, so we have less chance of being seen," Kitty said practically. "If that button works like it did before without anything on the radar, then we might just get away with it. Both vehicles get home, and we can also get to work finding someone to bring in on this."

"Agreed," Simon said after a little thought. "The more the merrier, I think."

Two more days found the trio ready to depart. Day one had gone into relabeling the shuttle controls and learning how to use the transporter. First, a bag of trash the three had accumulated was beamed down to a little-used campsite with a locator disk inside the bag. What looked like a shower of blue sparks surrounded the bag and then it faded from sight. When it was beamed back up, Simon went through it.

"Looks like trash," he announced, unscrewing the cap from a Pepsi bottle and taking an experimental sip. "Tastes like pop to me," he said, causing Kitty to scold him for his foolhardiness.

"Lighten up, hon," Simon admonished his wife. "Someone has to try it out sooner or later." He walked over to one of the hexes on the floor and turned to face the two women. "Now, just do the same thing again, this time with me. Wait about thirty seconds and bring me back."

"I'm not sure I like this, Simon," Kitty said, voice atremble. "What if something goes wrong?"

Simon walked back to Kitty and wrapped his arms around her. "Nobody said there weren't going to be risks, Kittyn. But sooner tested, sooner known. Besides, I'm the logical candidate." He leaned back and tilted her head up with a finger under her chin. "In two minutes, this will all be history and we can get on to other things. So, let's do it, okay?"

Kitty took a deep breath and said, "If anything goes wrong, I'll never forgive you. I understand the need to know, but I don't like to risk losing you to some alien ..." She reached up and pulled his head down for a long kiss. "Two minutes, no more," she said firmly after breaking loose.

With a sideways look at Gayle, Kitty walked over to the console and began to press the combination that would dematerialize her husband. Simon walked back to the hex and stood, waiting.

Kitty's finger paused over the last button.

Gayle asked, "Do you want me to do it?"

"No. He's my husband, and if anyone's going to be responsible, it has to be me. But I don't have to like it." Without looking up, she pushed the final button and Simon disappeared.

The second day was used to learn to handle the shuttle. Since it was a powered vessel, keeping control was only a matter of staying out of any major atmospheric disturbances once they started down. Test flights around the bigger ship were successful, except that landing in the relatively small bay was tricky. Simon cheated by pressing the return button on all three approaches to the ship and let the landing system take over. The stealth button lit up each time it was pressed, so it was assumed that the system was in operation. Only a lack of visitors would confirm that once they got back to the surface.

Deciding where to land was a problem until Gayle remembered something.

"The rifle range! Outside of Acton, Simon. We went there last year to sight in our rifles just before hunting season. There's that wide valley, and the ramp should let us drive right out onto the road. All we'll need to do is open one gate, and bingo, back in Billings."

"And it should be easy to find," Kitty put in. "Just north and west of town. We come in from the east, keep Billings on our left, and we should see that valley fairly easily."

Simon looked at the control panel in front of him. "We don't have a lot of options. Too far away will take too long to get home. And if the stealth works, it won't matter anyway," he concluded. He looked at his watch. "Let's get some rest. It's still a few hours until dark."

Kitty spent the last few minutes before departure in the control room, looking at the planet as it spun below them. This would be a dead-reckoning flight.

I wish I hadn't used the word 'dead,' she thought.

The sky was clear over most of the Pacific Northwest, so she was able to pick out the jewel that was Billings and headed for the shuttle. "Cargo net on?" she asked.

"Check," Gayle answered from the left-side control panel.

"Stealth on?" she asked, looking at the panel.

"Confirmed," came from Simon, seated to her right.

"Bay doors sealed?"

"Confirmed," Simon said, looking strangely at Kitty.

"Okay, depressurizing," she said, pushing the newly relabeled button. "I'm really glad this thing is built as well as it is. Have either of you noticed that there isn't a real airlock on board? Or on the big ship, for that matter. Apparently, these folks never landed anywhere there wasn't air to breathe."

When the door opened, she grasped the twin joysticks and pulled the left one backward, raising the ship off the deck slightly. She then pushed forward fractionally on the right, which moved the shuttle out of the bay and into the bright light of a full sun.

Wish I'd been a Nintendo player, she thought. *This would probably be easier.*

The trip down wasn't without incident. No one had noticed the turbulence on the flight up. They'd been too keyed up probably, but on the trip down, it scared the hell out of all of them. The hull temperature stabilized, so Kitty kept the speed constant until they hit the jet stream. None of them had even considered it, and the violence of the impact knocked Kitty's hands off the joysticks long enough for the ship to break through the lower layer and right itself.

"Ignorance is going to get us killed," Kitty said after she got her voice under control. "The first thing I'm going to do is find a pilot, *then* a scientist."

Thirty minutes after leaving the ship, Kitty set the shuttle down in a little valley just north of Billings. "Cargo net off, Gayle," she ordered. "Radar shroud is still online, so we have a few minutes at least. I'd like to talk to Simon alone for a few. Can you get the Jeep out by yourself?"

Kitty felt him shudder when he put his arms around her. During their entire fifteen-year marriage, they'd never been separated by more than a few hundred miles. Now, it was going to be twelve thousand miles, and all of them straight up. "Don't worry. If anything happens, I'll just press the button and you can beam me up. God, that sounds weird to say! Gayle will beam right out of her truck, and I'll face the DIA waiting at home. It won't be easy though."

"I could try some of the contacts I have at MIT, but that's been a long time."

"Yeah, I know," Simon said, nodding in agreement. "Who's going to believe you when you say, 'Guess what? I've got a spaceship!' Still working without a clue?"

"So far. But you know how Gayle and I get when we start tossing ideas around."

"Indeed, I do, love. I've had to deal with the aftermath of some of the schemes you two have worked out. Just remember that whoever you go after, he or she doesn't know you. Be gentle, okay?"

"Yes, dear." Kitty kissed him lingeringly. "Think that'll hold till you get back?"

"I hope so. And there's no time for more. Gayle just pulled up in front of the shuttle." Simon took her by the arm and guided her to the stairs. All the words he didn't know how to say tangled in his throat, allowing none to get out, so he just hugged her one more time. "I better go. We could have been seen landing. I love you. Now get back into the cockpit before I... just go!"

Simon turned Kitty around and gave her a small shove as Gayle honked her horn.

Leaning out the window, Gayle yelled, "Let's get moving!"

Kitty closed the ramp and watched the taillights move off over the hill. Still feeling a strange pressure deep in her chest, she reached out to press the return button but stopped her finger just before contact and leaned back in her chair.

Why not? she thought. *I never said I wouldn't. Of course, neither of them asked me.* Grinning at that, she gripped the joysticks, pulled the nose up, fed power to the engines, and took the craft back up out of the atmosphere. *I'll still let the autonav land it, but this is fun!*

CHAPTER SEVEN

Kitty's return to the larger ship was somewhat complicated. Owing in large part to her lack of knowledge of celestial mechanics and astronavigation, she couldn't find the damned thing! Understandable, perhaps, in light of the state of human space exploration, but potentially fatal, except for the failsafe homing system built into the shuttle's controls.

She'd never really considered the fact that getting from the ground to a particular point in space in a fully powered vehicle was an entirely different matter than getting from space to a particular point on the ground by seat-of-the-pants flying. Nor had she considered things like orbiting satellites. Simon had quipped, "Expect the unexpected and you... we... might all survive this." This comment had come just before Simon fired up their truck and followed the Jeep up the rutted road to the Forest Service gate.

Five minutes after Kitty left Simon and Gayle, the radar lit up with several blips. She looked over her shoulder at the empty radar operator's display, gripping the joystick controls and working to match orbits with the three blips. But turning that way to see the results hurt her neck, so she finally swiveled her chair around so she could see better. From there, she kept wanting to look over her shoulder out the forward viewscreen but suppressed the urge to do so.

When the three blips were stationary in relation to the icon that represented the shuttle, she pulled back on the left grip, increasing power to the ship's engines.

The power increase threw the ship into a higher orbit, passing near one of the blips as Kitty used the right stick to maneuver around the obstacles. Rising to a higher orbit put the shuttle above most satellite traffic, and the radar screen went dead, hologram fading out of sight in a matter of seconds.

She'd faced back to the front and begun to search for the *Dalgor Kreth* when she realized just how fruitless such a search would be. *Easier to find the proverbial needle in a haystack*, she thought sheepishly.

"Computer, display main ship and this shuttle," she ordered.

She turned the chair back to view the display. The green spot in the center she understood to be this shuttle, so she assumed the pulsing blue dot farther out to be the big ship. "What do the little yellow dots mean?" she asked aloud.

"Artificial satellites placed in predictable orbits for various purposes by the indigenous species of this world," the computer replied.

Kitty studied the various spots of light and ran her hands over the joysticks. She slowly fed more power to the engines and threaded her way through the satellite layer, gradually closing the distance between the green spot and the blue. She glanced over her shoulder out the front of the cockpit and was rewarded with a three-quarters view of the Earth, the terminator swallowing the mid-Pacific before her very eyes. A chill ran through her when she thought about how long she'd dreamed of seeing this very sight. Watching coverage of live missions whenever possible and every documentary that came her way couldn't have prepared her for the emotions welling up inside.

Her hands trembled slightly as she twitched the controls so that more of the planet became visible. Blue, green, and white predominated as she'd always known, but the browns, tans, and greys of deserts and mountains were visible as well. Adding to the palate were the variegated greens of the coastal shallows fading into the deep blue of the open seas. The British Isles and Western Europe were just coming into view, their large, well-lit cities showing as expanding patches of light along coastlines and most of the major rivers.

Her breath caught in her throat and a memory floated, unbidden, into her consciousness. She could no longer place the speaker or the particular mission, but an astronaut had commented on the fact that no national boundary lines could be seen from space, a remark significant enough to resurface at this time. She looked down at the planet slowly turning below her and realized that the only boundaries *were* those imposed by man. A sense of insignificance verging on impotence washed over her until she remembered that she had possession of an artifact capable of giving her species an unexpected technological advantage if only the squabbling factions would give up bickering over a few square miles of land and unite under one banner to work toward a common goal.

For the first time since this whole thing started, alone and without the distractions of her husband and friend, Kitty tried to clinically diagnose her—their—

situation. They were three humans in possession of alien technology of unknown potential. Of course, the government didn't know there were just three of them. That was a plus, but the low numbers were a definite liability, which was why they were going to find a scientist to turn to.

Kitty knew Simon had downplayed the danger he faced, even though he knew the caliber of people he'd be facing in a way she hoped she and Gayle never would. She also knew that some bright young agent would correlate the disappearance of an ex-agent living in the vicinity of this incident and start asking questions.

A thought occurred to her. "Computer, are we cloaked from electronic surveillance?"

"Yes, Captain. But we are not cloaked from the lesser technologies. Specifically, from devices that manually magnify light."

"Damn," Kitty muttered. "Some amateur astronomer is eventually going to see us and report an anomalous body in orbit. The shit will really hit the fan then." One thing she did know was that most astronomical discoveries were made by amateurs.

What would she do if she were leading the opposition? Knowing they could just beam out was small consolation. First, if they got arrested and used their wristbands to escape, it would confirm that they had the ship. Second, it would demonstrate the level of technology available, and it was just too early for that.

People like the ones they were looking for tended to focus their attention on particular parts of the sky. Once the bigger ship was reported, every eye on Earth would be staring straight at them.

"Can you evade incoming missiles?"

"Considering the level of technology exhibited by your race so far, there is nothing that can approach us without being destroyed."

Kitty relaxed slightly. "Anything that gets too close, you will destroy unless your sensors report humans aboard. It's remotely possible that NASA or somebody else could send a manned vehicle up to get a closer look. You will inform me of either situation before you take action."

"Yes, Captain."

Kitty thought long and hard about the repercussions. At present, only the U.S. and Russia could mount manned missions to inspect the ship, but a number of other countries could send up unmanned missiles with fairly sophisticated gadgetry aboard. Anything beyond that would require the cooperation of the whole world, setting the stage for a one-world government, and there were still too many madmen and patriots alike unwilling to give up any of their hard-won ground for that to happen anytime soon. What they—the madmen and patriots—needed was a common enemy, and she smiled uneasily at the idea of becoming that enemy.

Kitty brought the shuttle into traffic-control range of the bigger ship and let the automated process take over the docking procedure. She had too much on her mind to attempt the maneuver under manual control. The shuttle banked into its final approach and Earth slid out of view to the rear.

She turned her thoughts back to the task at hand. First and foremost, she planned to talk to the computer at length. That, in association with a far more thorough inspection, should help her answer any questions, or at least know where to look for answers when the conscript came aboard. She no longer wondered whether or not there would be a recruit; she just wondered when.

Simon turned onto his street two blocks before he normally would. Even late at night he spotted the grey sedan parked a block from the house.

"I'll bet there are at least ten agents in the area," he said to himself. "I hope Gayle doesn't have any problems."

Simon backed the truck into the driveway, intending to unload the gear into the garage and take the clothing into the house. Watching from the corners of his eyes, he saw one of the cars pull up to the curb as he opened the tailgate and began to pull their camping gear out of the back of the truck.

He pretended not to see the two men until they were almost on him. He looked up and then looked closer—a classic doubletake—and said, "Johnny! You're about the last guy I'd expect to see these days." He dropped the tent he'd been lifting out of the back onto the tailgate and shook the man's hand. "What brings you here after all these years?"

John San Martino gripped his ex-partner's hand firmly, sighed, and said, "Let's not play games, Simon. We were partners, for Christ's sake. You saved my life on more than one occasion. I got assigned to a case and your name keeps coming up in all the wrong places. We need to talk."

"Is this a back room thing, or can we talk while I

unload the truck? Then we can go in the house and have a beer like civilized adults."

"We can talk here as long as you play straight with me, Simon," San Martino said, leaning nonchalantly against the side of the pickup.

Simon looked at his ex-partner from hooded eyes as he pulled a long grey case out of the back of the truck. He handed it to San Martino. "30-06. Never leave home without one. My pistol is on the passenger seat." The tone was pure banter, but the gaze was speculative. He lifted the tent back onto his shoulder, turned around, opened the garage door, and walked to the back wall. He set the tent on a shelf and came back to the truck. "So, what do you want to know, Johnny?"

"You're going to make me go through the whole routine, aren't you?"

"Yep," Simon replied, hauling an ice chest out of the truck and setting it aside with a grunt. "If you're official, we need to be on the up-and-up all the way across the board, don't we? I know your boss—who is that these days?—wouldn't like any of the particulars to be overlooked." He hooked two folding chairs with one arm and snagged a folding table with his free hand. Carrying them inside, he said over his shoulder, "Let's stipulate that you've read me my rights and I understand them. Come on, John, get specific."

"We found your telescope, Simon. Has your prints and name all over it. Were you *expecting* a landing? Do you have some kind of connection to these landings we've been set to watch for?"

Simon walked back to the truck, thinking. "Oh, come on, John. I'm an amateur astronomer, and you know it. I saw whatever it was come down and I got the hell out of there. I had vacation time coming, and I really needed it this year. You remember Kitty? Katherine? We're having some troubles right now, and I needed to get as much distance from her and money troubles as possible. Then that thing put an end to that."

"So, why did we find her blood at the scene if she was nowhere around? And who was the third person? Woman or small child? And there are the tire tracks in but not out. Those same tracks go across the clearing and into thin air. Not to mention three indentations in the soft soil that said something heavy sat there, and there were some small fires caused by whatever it was when it left. And let's not forget the supposed remains of something definitely not from this world. You see, we've got quite a bit, along with the tires on your truck, which is now under a national security seal."

Sleeping bags and a mattress were tossed into a corner, pillows tossed at the porch, and Simon pulled out the last item—an oversized canvas suitcase. He closed the tailgate and picked up the suitcase.

"Okay, John," Simon said, sighing hard. He wiped his hands on his pants and picked up the ice chest. "Come inside and I'll tell you everything. All I need to do is empty the ice and put the perishables away. Forgot all about the 'scope at the time. When you guys are finished with it, I'd like it back. It's a gift from Kitty. You know how wives are about stuff like that."

"So why didn't you report it, Simon? That's the question on everybody's mind."

"Everybody's?" Simon repeated. He picked up

two crates of food and moved them to the back porch, along with the chest. "Or the director's? You seem to forget, I'm a civilian now. Yes, I still have classified information, like the existence of ALERT teams, and I knew troops would be on the ground within the hour, most likely. But you should also notice that I just got home. When have I had time to report anything?"

Simon opened the back door and sidled into the house with the big suitcase. San Martino followed him, carrying the rifle. Simon dumped the suitcase in the middle of the floor, laid his pistol-belt on top, and stepped out the back door, grabbing the ice chest while ignoring the remaining agent. He quickly put perishable items in the refrigerator and pulled out two beers. Stepping into the living room, he handed one to San Martino.

"Sit down, John, and tell me why this is going to be the last beer we share. Oh, and the third set of prints belong to a girlfriend of Kitty's. Gayle Miller is her name."

San Martino set the beer down unopened, an action not unnoticed by Simon. "Because you're dead center in the middle of something a lot bigger than any of us, Simon. And your wife is in it up to her ears, too, along with her girlfriend. That's one sharp woman you've got there." He looked around the living room and shook his head. "This is as far as you could get in thirteen years, Simon? A four-bedroom house in Billings, Montana of all places? Home of the Freemen, the Unabomber, and now Simon Hawke."

Simon looked at the place he'd called home for thirteen years. It looked fine to him, and he felt sorry for the agents who never knew where they were going to be from one day to the next. Of course, he was in the same boat now but in a distinctly different way.

Their home was a mixture of the two of them, and Simon and Kitty had managed to make dust-ruffled furniture co-exist with a mounted eight-point whitetail rack and gilt-framed oil paintings of mountain scenes. A blue Persian rug tastefully set off the light oak furniture that was sitting on burnished hardwood floors.

"Actually, I'm rather happy here, John. I run my own business, come home to my own bed every night, and only have my wife to answer to. Why would I jeopardize that?"

"I don't know, Simon," San Martino admitted. "But our profilers say it's extremely likely that you're mixed up in this. And remember, you helped train me. I know you. That's why I was assigned to the case. And I don't like getting the old Hawke smoothness in full force. You almost had me there."

Simon just grinned. It wasn't fun to give his old friend the runaround, but it would keep the waters muddy long enough to cover some of their tracks. He cracked his beer and took a pull.

"You know we're going to have to interrogate Miller, too. We have to cross-check all the information," San Martino said tiredly. "You know how the game is played, Simon. So far Miller and you and your wife are the only ones we can connect to the… incident. We need to know how you got separated, how you got away in the first place, where you've been, and who you've talked to. We're going after all of it, Simon. We want that ship."

"Sorry, John," Simon said. "Can't help you with

the ship part. I don't seem to have it on me." The sound of a car door slamming brought the two men to their feet. Simon looked out the window to see Gayle walking up the sidewalk. He let out a silent groan.

Simon started for the door, but San Martino raised a hand. "Allow me, please." He opened the door just before Gayle could knock. "Come in, Miss Miller. Simon is waiting for you. My name is John."

The blonde walked over to Simon, a perplexed and somewhat apprehensive look on her face. She took a deep breath and turned to face the stranger. "Mind introducing me, Simon?" she asked brightly.

Simon was secretly surprised by the composure she showed, walking into the situation almost blind and knowing there was going to be trouble. That was obvious from her stance. He'd sparred with her a couple of times and knew how much trouble she had pulling her punches, even sparring. But pissed off? Hell, he'd been out of his league when she was just warming up. Her blackbelt wasn't for show, and she practiced regularly.

He was going to have to keep his attention on San Martino and just hope Gayle could hold her share of the line if push came to shove. He noted that she wore a long-sleeved shirt, a common-enough event in Montana in the springtime that even his own long sleeves didn't get remarked upon. And of course, the two pieces of identical jewelry wouldn't be noticed… at least not until they were hauled out in handcuffs.

"Gayle Miller, my ex-partner John San Martino of the DIA. It seems that John wants some answers to some very touchy questions."

At Simon's introduction, Gayle stepped forward, a thousand-watt smile lighting up her face. "If you were Simon's partner, I'm glad to meet you. We could use a friend in all this mess." She held out her hand to the agent.

"John isn't the friendly face you think he is, Gayle," Simon warned. "As a matter of fact, he's here to arrest us. Isn't that right, John?"

Gayle jerked her hand back, her expression going blank. She looked at Simon, who had sat back down on the couch, the picture of a genial host. Gayle slowly sat down on the other end, almost as if she expected the couch to bite her. Simon noted that her foot was ready to strike in the direction of San Martino's knee. He wasn't sure she had the reach though. If he could get the agent a little closer ...

Gayle dropped her hands into her lap. "Don't you need a warrant or something before you can arrest us? And don't you need to prove that we've done something?"

"Miss Miller," San Martino said patiently, "we've got all three of you linked to a place and time where an... anomalous object... appears to have landed." He held up his hand to forestall interruptions and began ticking points off on his fingers. "We've got the telescope with both Simon and Katherine's prints on it found at the scene. We have blood samples taken from the scene that match Mrs. Hawke's DNA. We have shoeprints that likely as not match your boots and tire tracks that probably match your Jeep. And there's always the Homeland Security Act that lets us do pretty much what we please."

"How do you know all that?" Gayle interrupted.

Simon held up his hand. "They're very good at their jobs, Gayle. I should know; I used to be one of them. As a matter of fact, I trained John. No good deed goes unpunished, right?" He turned back to San Martino. "Go on, John. I'm sure you've got more."

"We've got NORAD and several satellites verifying that something entered Earth's atmosphere and landed in a small valley about five hundred miles from here. We've got tire tracks leading into the area but not out. We've got those same tracks leading us around the edge of the clearing and into a small meadow, finally vanishing as if by magic. And we've got a mass of... something... burnt to a crisp. DNA analysis just doesn't have a place to put what we've got."

"This is all circumstantial, you know," Gayle said, finally finding her voice. "There's no way it's going to stand up in court."

Simon patted her arm. "There isn't going to be a trial, kiddo. We're about to be disappeared until they have all they can get out of us. Even then, we might not get back to our normal lives."

"Well, you're not about to disappear me," Gayle stated positively. "I've got plans."

"Miss Miller, we really don't care what you have planned. We're going to ask questions and you're going to answer them."

Gayle put her best indignant look on her face. "You threaten to haul me away to some governmental limbo and you want my help? Please, allow me to cordially invite you to go piss up a rope."

"I'm truly sorry you feel that way, Miss Miller, because the accommodations aren't going to be like Club Med." San Martino didn't sound as if he much cared either way.

Simon crossed his legs and leaned back on the couch, seemingly totally unconcerned. Gayle merely seemed ready for whatever action she needed to take.

"I'm really surprised that you didn't see the need to bring more than four men to take us in, John. You know I never work without a fallback position."

"'What I haven't forgotten," the agent retorted, "is your ability to make the best of any situation. That's why this mission wasn't restricted to just four men. Those are just the front team. You were meant to see them, Simon. You must be getting soft." He crossed his own legs and finally reached for the beer he'd set aside earlier. He twisted the cap off, dropped it deliberately on the floor, and took a healthy swig. "I brought a full tactical assault team. The rest of them moved into position as soon as you came into the house."

"Simon," Gayle asked worriedly, "what does an assault team consist of?"

"In this case, knowing John, a full platoon of forty men, armed for a small invasion, armored against anything except a nuclear explosion, and with orders to shoot to kill if any of us step out of the house. How'd I do, John?"

"Pretty good, Simon, except that they are required to shoot to stun. We want the information, see? I can give away things if I think I might get something in return."

"A full platoon, John? Did you bring air-mobile support as well?" Simon asked tersely. "I guess I should be impressed that you think you need that much firepower to bring us in."

"Simon, Simon, you know how it is. The women are pressure. We really don't believe they know that much. Now, your blonde friend did surprise us a bit. Three different blackbelts in three different disciplines. All deadly. But that we can counter. It's you we have to neutralize. You forget that I watched you kill two men with your bare hands in less than ten seconds. I'm not going to make the mistake of underestimating you. But even you can't talk your way past forty men who have no ties to you whatsoever."

Gayle looked at Simon with a measure of respect she hadn't shown before. "You *let* me win, you son-of-a-bitch!" she hissed, referring to their sparring matches.

"Not once," Simon said defensively. "We were fighting by the rules, and you beat me by those rules. If you want a no-holds-barred match sometime, I'll try to go easy on you."

Gayle huffed up and started to say something, but San Martino stood up impatiently. "Enough of this domesticity. We have transport waiting to take you to a secure location. Miss Miller, if you ever find yourself in a position to take Simon up on that free-for-all, I suggest that you don't."

"No way to talk you out of this, John?" Simon asked lightly.

"I have my orders, Simon."

Simon's face clouded up. "Ya know, as soon as I remembered I'd left the telescope behind—easy enough to do in all the excitement—I knew somebody would be here sooner or later. I wasn't expecting *you,* but I guess I should have. Playing on my loyalties and all that."

Simon let his body posture relax, leaning back into the couch and projecting less aggressiveness than he had seconds before. "You know, you were one of the ones who used to get together and discuss just what we'd do if something like this should ever really happen. As I remember it, you were one of the advocates for blowing the thing to kingdom come, Johnny. What happened to change all that?"

"I decided to live in the real world, Simon. My agenda is whatever my bosses tell me it is. And at the moment, that's acquiring all the advantages possible for the U.S. in a rapidly deteriorating world situation."

"Well, I have an agenda of my own, old friend, and I can't be letting you interfere with it," Simon informed the agent, sadness in his voice. "It was always a given that we could count on each other. It's too bad you've gone and let the powers-that-be brainwash you so thoroughly. I could have used a friend on this one. As it is, you've just forced me into that fallback position I mentioned earlier."

"One word from me and this house will be assaulted from all four sides," San Martino said regretfully. "You're not getting out of this one, Simon. Face it, you're weaponless and surrounded, and no one knows you're here."

"Let me guess, John. That word would be 'indigo.' At the agent's look of confusion, Simon laughed out loud. "You come here thinking you know me, friend. Well, I'll let you in on a secret. I've grown in the thirteen years I've been gone. The love of a good woman will do that to you. You, on the other hand, haven't. Just remembering your activation word should show you I know more about you than you do about me."

"What I know, Simon, is that *I've* got the upper hand here. You have no chance to get away."

Simon smiled. "I know you're wired, John. Are you set up for video, too?"

"Why?" A suspicious look crossed San Martino's face.

"You just said that I had no chance to get away. I'm about to prove you wrong. I also intend to take Gayle with me. I just hope that this is on video so your boss can see what he's up against."

San Martino was livid. Not in his wildest imaginings had he expected the interview to go this way. "Okay, partner, I'm calling your bluff. If you think you can get both of you past forty armed men, especially after warning us, go ahead and try." He spoke into his lapel. "Condition Red. Take down anyone leaving the house."

Simon looked over at Gayle. "Let's go."

Gayle just nodded, stood up, and pressed the return button on her wristband. While San Martino's eyes were on her, Simon hit his own at the same time.

San Martino's eyes went wide as Gayle vanished in a cloud of blue sparks.

"Sorry it has to end this way Johnny, but sometimes people do change." He snaked his foot out and caught the pistol-belt, transferring it to his hand as San Martino's pistol appeared. Blue sparks started to flow past his eyes and San Martino's face evaporated, replaced by the reddish light of the transporter bay.

Kitty stared thoughtfully into the open hatch. The computer had told her where to find the access hatch to the main data storage area, and she'd wound up here. It was located in the factory section, or the computer room as Kitty called it, and was merely an empty room with a door in one wall and this hatch.

Closing the hatch, she used the single door to enter the room, and what she was staring at reminded her not of a computer but rather a bowl of Jell-O, more than anything else.

The entire mass, some four cubic feet, appeared to be back-lit by a light that came out a glowing, iridescent green after it passed through the... "proto-organic gel," as the computer had called it. Lights flashed on and off within the mass, the product of something called "whisker-lasers," which was the computer's way of writing information to, and reading from, the memory core.

Baffled by the advanced technology, she asked the computer how someone would go about removing data from the memory core.

"Data deletions can be ordered from any of a number of consoles throughout the ship, but it would be most convenient for someone to do it from either the bridge or the environmental control center," the computer responded.

"But how do you recognize a valid order?" Kitty probed. "Or could anyone have given the order to delete astronomical data and all data on the original builders?"

"It would require the deletion request and passwords from two ship's officers."

"So, let's trace the passwords. Can you do that?" Kitty asked.

"No. All passwords have been deleted."

"So that leaves?"

"No way to determine who deleted the information."

"Wonderful," Kitty muttered as she listened to the pneumatic hiss of some device sealing the access cover back into place over the computer core. She stood up and massaged a kink out of her back. "First thing we have the new guy do is find us a computer specialist with imagination and vision. This is lightyears ahead of anything we've got. Somebody has *got* to want to study this!"

She began walking down the corridor away from the computer room, looking into each room she came to. Sensors turned the lights on as she entered a room and turned them off again as she left. Along with the lights, the sensors activated a console located near the door of each room and a variety of different machines. Pressing buttons on the consoles produced few results.

Probably needs certain keys pressed certain ways to activate 'em, she thought. *Or maybe, there has to be raw material in the room for the machines to make something.*

All rooms provided virtually the same results, with only a few buttons lighting up or doing anything at all.

It was the picture window that gave it away. Kitty's heart beat faster as she slowly walked across the room and put her hands on the glass, looking down into a huge funnel-shaped hole leading into the bowels of the ship. She then looked up at the rim some two hundred feet above. This had to be the matter converter that shredded asteroidal material into basic components for the various factories and assembly areas. That placed her roughly in the center of the huge ship.

She turned around, forcing her attention back to the job at hand. All the consoles in this new room were considerably more advanced and probably more complicated than the others. And there were no machines, just the various workstations, six in all, scattered around the room. Near the window, a separate console sat fully powered and operational. Even the usual flat-screen-like panel always located on the right side of all consoles looked bigger and somehow more imposing.

Guessing that this was the main control room for the factory section, she looked back out the window and remembered one of the training flights they'd made before taking Simon and Gayle down. She had circled the ship while learning the controls, and she'd looked at just about every inch of the exterior. This funnel was the matter converter. Centered in the upper side, the converter penetrated almost halfway into the ship and was capable of taking asteroidal material in chunks of up to almost two hundred and fifty feet in width. Larger rocks were sliced up by lasers mounted in the tractor beam towers that circled the rim.

The oversized flat-screen on the main desk was displaying the image of a device that was slowly rotating through all its angles in the upper left corner of the screen. On the right side, a column of figures scrolled from top to bottom. Beneath the small image, an expanded view of the device took up the rest of the screen.

Beneath the display was a confusing array of buttons, and one was flashing. Taking a deep breath, she pressed the glowing spot on the panel and the image changed. First, it was a full-screen view of a different object. Then the image shrank into the upper left corner and the screen displayed the same information it had for the previous image. The next images were of a spaceship, one with a distinctly more warlike look than this one or the three little ones in their bays.

An alarm interrupted her. She shut the panel down and headed for the Transport Control room. The panel identified the alarm as Gayle's transport request, so she got to watch her friend sparkle into existence. Simon's wristband was flashing as well, so she quickly reset the panel and beamed him in, too. Having been in a seated position when the beam-up occurred, he naturally landed flat on his butt, muttering curses at alien technology.

CHAPTER EIGHT

Unexplored territory, Simon thought, standing in front of a perfectly normal door on factory level sixteen. After his return to the ship, he'd begun to do a more systematic search, and he was facing the last barrier to their exploration.

He spun the now-familiar door lock. This door, though, opened in such a way that if the room were decompressed, he wouldn't be able to open the door against the exterior pressure. Once all the bars were fully retracted, he pulled on the door, noting the strength necessary to get it moving.

Engine room, he decided as he entered the oversized room. Several of the shuttle test flights around the giant ship had passed by the stern of the vessel. Three huge black nozzles marred the otherwise smooth rear of the ship.

He'd figured then that they were engine exhaust ports, and now he was pretty sure he was looking at the other end of those holes. Before him were three cylinders, each hundreds of feet long and easily sixty feet high. But it wasn't the engines that took most of his attention. That was accomplished by a huge, ill-defined yet solid-looking sphere floating equidistant between the floor and the ceiling.

Besides a low railing completely encircling a dark-colored area directly beneath the sphere, the only other structures in the room were dozens of tubes and the supposed engines. Attached to the sphere's surface by no obvious means, two tubes ran from the sphere to each engine while others disappeared into the walls for purposes unknown.

In exasperation, he wrote, "Let whoever the girls pick out decide what kind of scientists we need and who to choose."

Simon stifled a yawn and looked at his watch. Shaking his head at the amount of time he'd spent going even this far, he headed back to the captain's quarters to dine on some of the oh-so-appealing MREs he'd offloaded from Gayle's Jeep.

"Grabbing a little rack time wouldn't hurt, either," he mused aloud later, cleaning up the residue of his meal. And putting how to dispose of the trash at the top of the list would probably be a wise move. He jotted that final note on his pad and left the large room in search of his bed.

Somewhere between lying down and starting to worry about something else, a fitful slumber finally overtook him. He walked through a murky darkness, alone except for shadowy, unidentifiable… things… at the edge of his vision—things that never seemed to get any nearer, staying just out of reach.

Simon dreamed, and knew that he dreamed, of darkness and light. Oh, yes! The light. For just as the darkness brought visions of fear, hysteria, and loss, so did the light bring visions of splendor, glory, and hope.

When he woke up, it was to a feeling of disorientation. Normally not one to remember his dreams other than vaguely, this one stood out due to its complexity, but that wasn't what left him uneasy. The darkness was complete, and as he lay there, a slight noise, more of a low-level vibration in the air itself, intruded upon his consciousness. He reached out to turn on his bedside lamp and banged his hand on a metal surface. "Damn!" he muttered.

The feeling of falling or floating had been very real just before he'd awakened. He sat up on the side of the bed, letting his feet swing a bit until he realized they should be touching the floor. That was when the events of the last few days snapped into focus.

"Lights," he said into the darkness, and a red glow pervaded the room. "I've got to do something about the lighting. This can't go on. It's too depressing. Like being at battle stations at all times."

He padded into the bathroom, noticing the extra height on the fixtures there, and made a mental note to see about having something done about that, too. After throwing water on his face, he went back to the bedroom and got dressed, then worked his way through another MRE packet and went to the bridge.

"Computer," he said as he entered.

"Attending."

"The lights on this ship are not... adequate... for humans. What can be done to change them?"

"The lighting can be adjusted to any wavelength required. Please define the parameters."

Simon thought for a few seconds and said, "How about something more appropriate to the planet below. "Say high noon halfway between the equator and either pole." The room immediately brightened to a harsh glare. "We're on the right track," Simon commented, quickly shading his eyes from the light. "Less intensity, please." The glare seemed to dissipate somewhat, and after a few more adjustments, he was satisfied with the level. "Let's set that as the standard all over the ship, please."

"New configuration locked."

Simon smiled as he walked off the bridge, thinking about how pleased Kitty would be at the change. That happy thought led directly to the realization that he was feeling better without ever having suspected that he'd felt less than well.

It must have been all that red lighting, he thought.

He stopped in the corridor and looked at the legal pad that seemed to have become his constant companion. He noted the rumpled and dirtied edges, the dog-eared corners, and wondered if there wasn't a better way to keep track of his to-do list. His eyes focused on a single word, underlined twice, at the bottom of the page—fighters. Much easier to read now in the brighter light, the word brought direction to his otherwise aimless wandering.

He stepped into the elevator and punched the button for the lowest level. The floor fell away and he fell with it, enjoying the sensation and thinking it probably had something to do with the lower gravity. He was feeling the weight returning when it dawned on him that the numbers on the control panel were in English. The lowest button had the number eighteen on it. He then noticed that the three was highlighted in red.

Because it's the command deck? he asked himself. It was as good a guess as any.

Simon walked out into the cavernous space and immediately noticed the difference. Where the lighting had once been dimmer and more indirect, he could now see the light strips running the length of the room. Their intensity also allowed him to see the circular openings, all irised closed, in regular rows between the light strips. He noted his observation and moved on to the fighter bays.

The sleek little ship sat in its stall, looking as if it had been built the day before, but the image was ruined by scorch marks around the engine nacelles. Though it was grey over most of its surface, there were markings on the erect fin at the rear of the ship.

"Probably ID numbers," Simon guessed.

Walking all the way around the ship, he added to his guesses. The legs the ship sat on had no tires, only ski-shaped feet or skids, making him think of Earth-manufactured vertical-take-off-and-landing aircraft, but the small wing surface argued higher speeds than the skids suggested.

He shook his head at the discrepancy and looked for a way to get to the cockpit, but no ladders or other machinery were present in the room, and no handholds were apparent on the body of the craft. Experimenting in the lighter gravity, he flexed his knees and jumped for the edge of the cockpit some twelve feet off the floor. His fingers missed the edge by a matter of inches, so on the next attempt he crouched deeper and pushed off harder. This attempt netted him a handhold and left his body dangling down the side of the ship. He lifted himself up by the strength of his arms alone until he was able to get first one elbow and then the other over the edge and wriggle into the single seat.

Moving a helmet designed for a head slightly different from his own, he set it on the fighter body just outside where the canopy would seal and looked over the controls. A joystick-style system sat in the obvious place for a bipedal creature, and an abbreviated instrument panel, dark and lifeless, was arrayed just below the seal and wrapped around the front of the compartment. A pair of pedals were just out of comfortable reach in the recesses under the control panel.

Form follows function, Simon subvocalized for the hundredth time—at least for people of the same general type of body structure. His hands found a series of pockets on either side of the cockpit, and he idly stuck his hands into each one, finding nothing until he slid his fingers into a small pocket on the bottom right side. He felt a sizable lump in the little pouch and managed to jam two fingers into the narrow pocket. Pulling up slowly, he worked the item out of its hiding place to find that he was holding a smooth, dark-green stone in a heavy silvery setting, dangling on a long chain of what looked like the same kind of metal.

He looked at the necklace for a while, wondering at the significance of the design completely encircling the oval green stone, if any, and wondering why it was here when the rest of the ship was so nearly sterile. He held it up to the light and studied it for a minute, watching it dangle. Shrugging, he slipped it into his pocket and returned to his examination of the cockpit.

The seat was a bit too large for him, a condition he was used to from the chairs, benches, beds and other sitting places aboard the rest of the vessel. But it was less so, it seemed, than those places. He noticed as well that he had to lean forward only a bit to reach some of the hand controls.

Maybe their pilots are required to be smaller than their average, he mused.

Simon closed his eyes and let his hand find the

main joystick-style control, wrapping his fingers around it. Contoured to fit a hand different from his own, it felt awkward, but it went along with the feeling that the ship was designed for a being somewhat taller than himself. He opened his eyes and, after another look around, climbed out of the cockpit and perched on the edge. He put the helmet back in the seat, suppressing an urge to put it on, and eyed the drop to the floor.

It's called a deck, he told himself, and let his body slide free of the little ship.

In the lighter gravity, it seemed that he floated to the deck, flexing his knees to take the shock of landing. His hand touched the deck to steady himself, and then he rose to his full height. He walked around the back of the craft again and looked at the twin orifices he found there. Not truly holes that led someplace deeper within the vessel, these were capped with a translucent material set about three feet inside the holes. The edges of the metal at the most aft portion were discolored by, he imagined, the titanic and unknown forces that propelled the fighter through space. The same discoloration showed on three smaller and similarly capped orifices located at the front of the ship.

Attitude controls? he speculated.

Knowing that he wasn't going to take this thing out for a spin anytime soon, he reluctantly closed the hatch and headed back to the command deck.

The two women noticed when the lighting changed.

"I'll bet this is Simon's doing. Good for him," Kitty said.

She and Gayle had been discussing how they were going to find a suitable candidate to recruit, and they returned to their conversation.

"We can't just beam back down and start making phone calls, Kitty said. "Simon mentioned something about a way to hack into public communications on Earth. Let's go see what we can find."

The two women wound up in what Kitty called the master control room for the factory section. Bringing power up to the main board activated a dozen or more auxiliary terminals around the room. "Computer?" Kitty asked, hopefully.

"Attending, Captain."

"I want to know about that device that will let us access and use Earth-side communications without detection."

"Simon Hawke has already researched that data, and I have found and reconfigured a device that will perform as requested."

On the main screen was a flat-looking device, slowly rotating through all its axes. "Placed on top of any power transformer in close proximity to telephone lines, it will provide total access to all communications without the possibility of discovery, barring a physical inspection of the transformer itself. It merely needs to be placed on top of the transformer and access will be instantaneous."

Kitty asked, "Do we have enough material to build three of these? Backups would be nice. And make sure that any tampering registers here before the device fries itself."

"Instructions have been downloaded to manufacturing, room thirteen-dash-seven. The process requires initiation by a person. Will two backups suffice?"

"For now," Kitty hedged.

She Gayle made their way down to 13-7, finding the systems live, schematics already inputted, and a single light flashing on the activation panel.

"I guess we just push the button," Gayle said. "That's all we had to do on the shuttle."

Kitty nodded and, with only a hint of hesitation, pressed the button. "Okay, computer. What happens now?"

"In about an hour, you will find all three devices waiting at the far end of the assembly machine."

"Thank you, computer," Kitty said, feeling a bit self-conscious about thanking a machine. But the damned thing seemed so… normal. "Come on, Gayle. Let's go get a bite and start figuring out where to put our little packages on Earth. They need to be obscure places, ones that aren't too likely to need repair often."

Choosing three spots was the work of minutes after a light lunch, with Simon showing up for once. The operations panel in the transport room was live as they entered the room. Simon took the three devices—dinner-plate-sized with several short antennae on top—and placed them on individual transport hexes. "So, what's the plan after we get these things in place?" Simon asked casually.

"First, we go shopping," Kitty said. "I think we can convert power to Earth-side stuff like computers and start looking for our first victim." She looked at her own clothes and then pointedly at both Simon and Gayle. "We can't just appear somewhere, so we're going to have to appropriate things for a while. Once something gets scanned into the computer, we can send the originals back. Hell, most things can come from the homes of recruits—new clothes, state-of-the-art computers, and food! I'm sick to death of MREs. If we spread our perishable purchases out over the whole world, no one will be hurt. Plus, with anything appropriated, we'll send it back as soon as we can get it scanned. It's a victimless crime, except for the food part."

Simon went quiet and stared at the deck for a time. Finally, he said, "Well, that sounds like a plan to me. Would you like do the honors?" He bowed toward the transporter panel waiting for coordinates for the three devices.

Kitty shook herself and walked over to the panel. She had to stretch her short frame to reach some of the buttons on her cheat sheet, but each device winked out of existence.

CHAPTER NINE

It took two days to find all they needed to make life more comfortable. With the big computer's help, they found one of the kitchen areas—mess halls as Simon called them—and began filling the shelves of the refrigerator/freezer with food. It turned out later that both cold sections were inside a modified stasis chamber. The temperature was allowed to reach a certain level, and the stasis turned on automatically until the door opened.

The computers were beginning to pay off as well. Hooked into the Internet, it took Kitty and Gayle just an afternoon to find their first recruit, though a battle still raged about how to approach him.

"We don't have to convince him," Gayle said, taking a sip from her coffee as the two women sat at the table. She pawed through the printouts and found the downloaded picture of the dark-haired astrophysicist. "All we have to do is get him aboard, and the ship itself will convince him for us."

"True," Kitty agreed, "but anything less than him going along of his own free will is going to cause him to resent us." She stood up and walked around the mess hall. "We need to get his interest and make him *want* to come aboard, not kidnap him."

"Leave that to me," Gayle said. "Of course, you realize you're taking all the fun out of it if I can't just throw a rope around him," she kidded.

"This is who we've come up with," Kitty told Simon. "First of all, we asked ourselves who would be most likely to believe us in the first place. The answer was obvious… after we hit on it—a SETI scientist. They spend all their spare time sitting at some radio-telescope looking for little green men."

"And right now," Gayle added, punctuating her comments with a fork, "this guy is our best bet. Because of the limited range of the telescopes anyone can get, there are only a few people in the world who ever get access to the big dish. We got this picture off an astronomy website he runs. Dr. Stephen Walker, PhD, thirty-eight years old, single, degrees in astrophysics and mechanical engineering, and right now he's down in Arecibo looking for signals from space."

The three began exploring ideas about how to confront their choice until Gayle finally said, "My mother once said there were two ways to get a man's attention. And since I can't cook, let's send me to Arecibo and see what I can do. He'll have trouble resisting these!" She grinned as she wiggled her chest at her companions.

"If I was single, I'd agree with you." Simon grinned back and looked at Kitty, whose face was carefully neutral. "Looks like we have a new personnel officer. Now for *my* news. I've been working with the transporter, so now we can beam Gayle right into Arecibo. It only works in line-of-sight mode, but from our altitude, we can beam to and from just about anywhere in this whole section of the northern hemisphere, and that includes Puerto

Rico. With the sensors this thing has, we should be able to drop her within a few feet of whatever location we choose." He turned to Gayle. "Ready to go to Puerto Rico?"

"You bet! But first, I need a change of clothes, especially for the tropics. And maybe someday, I'll get a chance to do some sightseeing!"

The three conspirators went to the transporter room and Simon showed off the console. "The sensors on this ship are so refined that I can almost read over the shoulder of someone on the surface."

"The colors and the general lighting, are... correct now. What did you do?" Kitty asked as she looked over Simon's shoulder at the console's screens.

"Just talked to the computer," Simon said. "I got it to adjust everything for human eyes. You should see the viewscreens on the bridge!" He consulted a piece of paper on the edge of the console. "Cheat sheet," he admitted. "Don't want to drop her anywhere but home, now do we?"

"I'd hope not!" Gayle put in. Simon motioned for her to go stand on one of the transport hexes and went back to the console. "Uh, Simon? Is there a chance that I can be... you know... beamed *into* something? Like a bed or a wall or something?"

"No," he replied, standing back from the console. "As a matter of fact, you should come see this. Kitty, too. You'll both need to know how to do it." Kitty stood beside Simon, eager to see the finer details. "First, the physics of this machine is that the pads," he said, pointing at the four hexes, "must be set up close to a field generator of some kind, I guess you can call it. Anyway, the sensors on board this thing will determine if there's enough free space in, say, a room, or your garage, Gayle, to allow a transport to the indicated destination." He scrolled a cross-hairs-type indicator across an expanded aerial view of a neighborhood. "I've already got Billings in the computer as a main reference point." He set the crosshairs on an intersection and turned to Gayle. "North is at the top of the screen. This is the intersection of Juniper and Ash. Which house is yours?"

Gayle indicated a spot. "Two houses up from the second corner."

Simon moved the crosshairs and put his finger on a button. "Increasing magnification." Hearing Gayle's breath hiss at the speed of the magnification process, Simon smiled. He'd had the same reaction the first time he zoomed in on his own house. Touching two other buttons, he said, "This thing uses some kind of pulsed energy beam to target the house. They—we—use it as a carrier wave to piggyback sensors on and read the destination. One of 'em is a sonic-type sensor to tell if there's enough room for the package—you or me—to be delivered, so to speak."

Kitty immediately caught the implication. "So, if there's no room, the machine won't transport her?"

"Exactly," Simon confirmed. "Kind of a fail-safe. These people were... are masters of user-friendly technology, it seems. Everything is set up so that it takes more than just one mistake for someone to get hurt. You should see the things I call constructions pods—self-contained miniature spaceships with grappling arms used to build things in space from components built here." Simon shook his head. "There's just so much stuff! Right now, though, we need to get Gayle on her way."

"Right," Gayle agreed. "If I'm going manhunting, I need different clothes, and that's just for starters." She walked back to the transport hex, turned to face Simon and Kitty and said, "I'll buzz you tomorrow morning. Don't go far."

Simon pressed the sequence he'd written down on the small paper attached to the side of the console and Gayle disappeared in a shower of sparks. No sooner had she disappeared than Kitty spun around and punched Simon in the arm.

"That if-I-was-single comment was some crack, Simon!"

He grimaced as he rubbed his arm. "Well, yours got my attention first. And they still have it. Besides, I'm right, aren't I?"

Kitty said deprecatingly, "Well, yeah. Our Dr. Walker is in for a bit of a shock."

They looked at the map and Simon said, "We need to drop her just outside of town in a secluded spot. Won't do to have her spotted beaming in." He scrolled the screen to show Puerto Rico. "This looks good. No nearby buildings, and only about a mile from town. Among other things, the computer has infrared scanners so we can make sure there are no people around and drop her right before sunset. She can get a room and look up our guy."

The pair walked out of the transporter room and down the hall towards the captain's quarters. Halfway there, Simon remembered a discovery he'd made the previous day. "Hon, would you like to see something? I think you'll enjoy it, if you aren't too tired. You've had a busy day."

Kitty heard the excitement in Simon's voice and

asked, "Can you give me your impression of this little surprise in ten words or fewer?"

Simon's head tilted to one side a bit. After a few seconds he said, raising a finger for each word, "So cool it's almost frigid. In a word, spectacular. Nine. How's that?"

Kitty bowed slightly and waved her hand in a sweeping move, palm up. Simon, not to be outdone, held his arm out for her to take and led her to the nearest elevator. Exiting on level one, uppermost in the ship and devoted mainly to sensor arrays and weapons pods, Simon led his wife down a maze of corridors until he came to a small airtight door. Opening it, he exposed the first set of stairs Kitty had seen aboard the ship.

Curious, she climbed them, stretching her legs on the slightly oversized risers, and emerged into a spacious, hemispherical dome near the bow of the ship. Awestruck, she raised her head and stared at the sight outside. The dome was turned away from Earth at the moment, so she felt as if she'd stepped into the airless void of space. The velvet blackness was pierced by a myriad of tiny colored lights. Her breathing came in small gasps at first. Knowing that the ship was in orbit only helped a little.

A feeling of insignificance threatened to wash over her when she thought about the plans they were making. She melted into the comfort of Simon's embrace, knowing the feeling of protection was illusory but grateful for it nonetheless. Simon put his arm around her shoulders, pulled her close, and copied her stare into infinity for a time she never would be able to accurately define.

Simon tensed slightly, breaking her mood. She

looked up into his grinning face. "What? Am I going to have to set a limit on how many times you can surprise me on any given day?"

His grin got even bigger, telling her that he did indeed have something else in mind. "I found something earlier today," he said, confirming her suspicions. Most men were so transparent, although she had to admit that Simon did pull off more than his share of surprises. "It may be the only personal artifact on board this thing, and I immediately thought of you."

He reached into his pocket and slowly pulled the necklace he'd found in the fighter into the light. Bringing out the chain first, thereby stretching out the moment, he finally let the pendant slide from his pocket and begin to sway back and forth. At the sight of the dark green stone glowing brightly in the starlit dome, he froze. "It didn't do that before," he commented wonderingly.

Kitty gasped and her hand reached involuntarily for the stone, glowing green in the darkness. She cupped the pendant in both hands, feeling the weight of the stone and its intricately carved setting. As she held it, the glow increased visibly. "It's so beautiful!" she exclaimed. She turned the piece over, examining the back. "What makes it glow?"

"I have no idea," Simon admitted. "It didn't do that when I found it in a small pocket in one of the fighters," he said, slipping the chain over her head and settling it onto her neck, the pendant lying between her breasts. "I just thought this would be the best place for it."

"Words can't express how I feel," Kitty said, pulling closer to Simon's side. "Ecstatic and scared.

Humble and cocky. A lot more scared than anything else, I think."

"I know what you mean, dear. I've had just as much time as you to get over my feelings of insignificance, but I don't think I ever truly will." He turned her to him. "As a matter of fact, I thought that this might be a good place to ..."

"Simon!" Kitty's voice expressed her total shock at his suggestion.

"Why not?" he asked innocently. "I locked the door coming in, and can you think of a better place to initiate our new... home?" He pulled her to him and began to caress her back.

An indeterminate time later, with clothes scattered everywhere and naked to the universe, Simon's last conscious thoughts were of the novelty of making love under a rising Earth and how the stone glowed so much brighter against Kitty's bare skin.

Gayle beamed into the transporter room the next afternoon dressed for a hike and carrying a small backpack. "I've got an idea about how to snare our pigeon. Don't ask. If it works, I'll tell you all about it."

Kitty grinned. "Knowing you, I don't need to ask; I can guess. Poor guy won't know what hit him. Just be gentle, okay?"

The sensors on the ship were easily able to discern a clearing and nearby trail, as well as the fact that there were no humans within two hundred yards of the spot. Gayle beamed into a small clearing on a hillside overlooking Arecibo. The first things she noticed were the heat and the humidity. Fifteen seconds in the new environment and her shirt was already plastered to her skin, making her think about pulling a bra out of her backpack.

The air had an almost physical quality to it, heavily laden with the smells of tropical flowers mingling with the odor of decomposing vegetation. It was a smell she felt she could tolerate but never entirely get used to. She took a deep breath, reaffirmed her opinion, and listened intently for sounds indicating that anybody was nearby.

I guess I could just say that I had to pee if someone sees me coming out of here, she thought.

She stepped out of the clearing onto the trail, oriented herself on the lights of the small town at the bottom of the hill, and headed down to locate her quarry.

She walked quickly along the path in the growing dusk, slapping at mosquitoes the size of small planes until she passed between two ramshackle buildings and found herself on the main street of the little town just as the sun finally set. Looking around, she saw a sign painted on the wall of a building not too far down the street. Remembering her one semester of high-school Spanish with something less than fondness, she translated it as Hotel Arecibo.

Walking in the front door, she was relieved to see a counter off to one side that had the universal look of a check-in desk. Opposite the desk was an open door leading to a dining room. As she reached the counter, a young woman, most likely in her early twenties, stepped out of a doorway behind the desk.

"Yes, senorita? May I help you?"

A few minutes' haggling got Gayle a small

bungalow behind the main building for a surprisingly cheap rate, considering the fact that it was one of the few with air conditioning, as well as hot water. The desk clerk told her dinner would be served in an hour and would only cost a little more. She paid in advance and, almost as an afterthought, asked, "Are there any other hotels in town?"

"No, senorita," the girl replied. "This is the only hotel. There are not enough touristas to make it a profitable thing to do here. Although I just rented a cabana to two American men."

"Did they say anything about staying long?" Gayle asked, interest aroused.

"No, senorita, and I don't think they will," the girl said with a smile. "Their room has no air conditioning."

Gayle walked down a crushed-shell path to her bungalow. She passed a dozen or so cottages in various states of repair. Clustered at the far end were several outbuildings that were most likely used for storage of maintenance equipment, sorely in need of repair. She found her room, stepped inside, and turned on the air conditioner. She let the air blow over her for a moment before stripping off her sweat-soaked shirt and pants.

Not up to stateside standards, she thought, giving the room a once-over, *but air-conditioning and hot water make all the difference in the world. Or out of it.*

She let the air conditioner lower the temperature and suck some of the humidity out of the room before she stepped into the shower. Changing into a pair of khaki shorts and a light blouse, and this time wearing a bra, she strolled back to the foyer and into the dining room.

The desk clerk was on duty as hostess and told her to pick any empty seat. She looked around at the six tables. Each table was set with four places and had two or three people already seated, except for the one in the far corner of the room. Seated at that table was the man she'd come to find. And all by himself.

She looked around the room, trying to identify the two Americans who were undoubtedly agents of one alphabet agency or another, but none seemed any more unusual for this time and place than any other. If anything, she was the one who was out of place.

If this gets any easier, she thought, heading toward her prey. Stopping behind an empty chair, she put on her sunniest smile.

"Hi! Mind if I join you?"

Dr. Walker looked up from a scatter of papers covered in graphs and cryptic figures. "Uh, sure, Miss ...?"

"Miller. Gayle Miller. What are you working on?" She slid a chair out and sat down, pointedly looking at the papers on the table.

He made a vague gesture at the papers and then swept them into a pile when he realized she actually meant to sit with him. "These? Just some frequency tables and astronomical charts. I work at the observatory. You know, just outside town. I'm Stephen. Stephen Walker. Hi."

It turned out to be homestyle dining with their only choice being what to drink. Both chose a local beer that Stephen said was palatable. As the meal progressed, Gayle showered him with questions about space and the big telescope even allowing that she believed in aliens, too.

"Too?" Steve asked, eyebrows reaching for his hairline while the last bite of his dessert hung on his fork.

"Yes, too, Stephen. You do prefer Stephen, don't you? I think it sounds so debonair." Gayle leaned forward, exposing more than a fair amount of cleavage. "You wouldn't be listening for signals from space if you didn't believe, now would you?" she said, pressing. "I've always believed that there has to be someone else out there. And it would be so cool to make first contact."

"Well, yes, I guess I do believe, Miss Miller," Stephen admitted a bit sheepishly. "And while I can't say that I *expect* to find proof of alien life, I do *hope* to find it. It's just that the distances are so vast that at the speed of light, it would take forever for any signal to arrive. Remember, we've only had video signals going out for about sixty years. We've had radio a lot longer, of course. Those signals are just now beginning to arrive at some stars. Assuming that one of those stars has a planet with intelligent life on it, and assuming further that they are capable of receiving and decoding our signals and want to respond, it would take the same length of time to get word back to us. So, I only have hope of finding *evidence* of somebody else out there, not actually talking to them." He pushed his plate away and took a long pull on his beer. "Tell me, what brings you to Arecibo?"

"Oh, I had a little shore leave coming, and I've always been interested in the big telescope. I thought I'd come out here and see it."

"Shore leave?" Stephen asked. "Are you in the military?"

"No," Gayle said with a laugh. "I'm the personnel director for the Morning Star. It's a cruise ship docked at San Juan." Getting into her role, she made up stories about her life and continued to show interest in Stephen's work. Questions starting with, "How do you ..." and, "What about ..." finally made him break down and invite her to his room to show her some of the intricacies of radio-astronomy.

'Bout damn time, she thought. *I was beginning to think I'd lost my touch.*

Neither she nor Stephen noticed the two men who got up and followed them out moments after their departure.

The next morning Gayle carefully extricated herself from between the sheets and a sleeping Stephen Walker. Deciding a shower was in order, she sauntered into the bathroom, grinning. Putting the next phase of her plan into motion, she set the alarm on her watch and turned the shower on. Climbing under the water, she tunelessly hummed anything that came to mind, making sure the good doctor was awake. She stepped out and began drying her hair as she walked back into the bedroom to find him looking her way.

"So, I *didn't* imagine last night," he said.

"No," she replied, grinning, "you didn't." She watched as a blush spread from his face down below the sheet he held in his hands. As she was about to sit down beside him, her watch began to beep, and she regretted having set it for such a short time. *Oh, well*, she thought. *The hook's been set. I'll reel him in later.* Aloud, she exclaimed, "Damn! I'm gonna be late," as she slipped her blouse on.

"Late? I thought you were on vacation," he said.

"Yes and no. I'll explain tonight if I can see you again," she said, stepping into her panties.

As she gathered up her shorts and shoes, he just said, "Uh, sure."

"At seven for dinner, okay? Okay."

Shorts and shoes in hand, she stood in the middle of the room, said, "Bye!" and pressed the button on her wristband. The last thing she saw was the sheet falling to his lap as a look of astonishment spread across his face.

Simon and Kitty were in the transporter room when Gayle beamed back in.

"That's just about the coolest thing ever!" she exclaimed. "So, what are you guys doing?"

"Well, I *was* going to go down for breakfast, but right now I think Simon should go. Care to explain why you're half dressed?" Kitty didn't seem to know whether to be mad or crack up laughing.

Simon said, "That must have been one hell of a plan! I'm not going anywhere till you fill us in."

Gayle looked at her shorts and shoes and said, "Oops!" Putting the rest of her clothes on, she filled them in, finishing with, "And I've got a date for dinner tonight. We'll see then how well I set the hook."

Gayle walked into the dining room at seven p.m., black short-sleeved shirt and trousers showing off her figure and managing to look vaguely military at the same time. The effect was heightened by her long blonde hair being pulled back into a ponytail. Dr. Walker was already seated at the corner table without his papers, so she walked over.

Stephen saw her in time to stand up. He looked hastily around the room, but seeing only the familiar faces of his fellow guests, he relaxed a bit.

"I'm alone, if that's what you're worried about, Stephen," she said, stopping opposite him. "Buy a girl a beer?"

He waved his hand at the chair across from him. "I'd almost convinced myself that it had been some kind of weird dream or something. Otherwise, I'd have to be going crazy." He sat back down in his chair, hands on the table and fingers spread as if he needed some physical connection to the world around him.

Gayle slid into the opposite chair and started to open her mouth, but Stephen held up a hand. "There are other explanations, though." He stared into Gayle's eyes. "One could be that I wasn't dreaming, and you actually possess the technology I saw." He stared a few seconds longer, then said, "That assumption is bolstered by the fact that those two gentlemen over there," he nodded to two men across the room, "came to see me today and grilled me quite intensely about our evening and why you didn't leave my room this morning. If I work that assumption, then I have a truckload of questions. Let's leave the obvious 'how' for later and go straight for the big ones. Why? And why me?"

Grinning sheepishly, Gayle glanced in the direction of the table Stephen had indicated. Impishly, she waved in their direction. "Can you guys hear well enough?" she jibed. "Going straight for the throat," she said, turning back to Stephen. "I expected that. I'll explain the 'how' later. As much as I know." She leaned closer and began to whisper. "I'll bet this drives them crazy. Anyway, we need you, or more specifically, someone with a certain set of qualifications. That's the 'why.' You were the first one we found who fit our criteria—those being a belief in extra-terrestrial life, a working knowledge of both astrophysics and mechanical engineering, and a spirit of adventure. Besides, I needed some way to get you to listen seriously to what I came here to tell you."

"What I came here to tell you," he mimicked. "Let me guess. You beamed down from the Enterprise for a little R&R." Sarcasm dripped from his words as he waved two fingers at the waitress.

"I'd consider it a personal favor if you'd keep your voice down." She looked quickly across the room. "Just let me talk until dinner arrives. After dinner, I'll finish up and answer all your questions, okay?"

He nodded.

"First off, I lied… some. But then, you've already figured that out. The ship I'm on isn't the Morning Star. It doesn't have a name. Yet. I *am* the personnel officer, and temporarily, the recruiting officer. And to answer your next question—no, I don't plan to recruit any other personnel that way. So far, we have a crew of three, and we need over nine hundred more. You're the first person we've contacted."

She began to tell the story from the time she'd seen the shuttle land. Dinner arrived and they ate in silence, leaving without dessert. Walking down the main street, they came to a bench and sat down. Two shadows quit moving as soon as they did.

She finished up, adding, "The rest you know, except that I spent all day on board just dreading this conversation because I had no idea how you'd react."

He looked through her for a moment, and then spoke. "Do you really expect me to believe any of this?"

"No, but I do expect you to keep an open mind. Especially after this morning." Even in the dark she could see his face turn red. "Not *that*. I mean the other thing. I can prove what I say, every word of it. And if I do prove it, it validates everything you believe in, doesn't it?"

He looked at her thoughtfully. "Okay, just how do you plan to prove it? I assume you have a plan."

Gayle stood up. "Of course I have a plan. Follow me," she said, getting up and heading between two buildings.

They passed between the two houses and stood only a dozen feet from the jungle.

Dr. Walker turned to Gayle. "Well, how do you plan to prove you're not… prove such an outlandish story?" His voice betrayed his discomfiture at his predicament.

"Prove I'm not insane?" She reached into her pocket, pulling out a small round disk and holding it out to him. "This is a locator beacon. At present, it's slaved to my transporter activator," she said, lifting her left arm and displaying her wristband. "If you hold it while I activate mine, we both beam up and you get to visit a real, live spaceship built by the very aliens you've been looking for. The decision is yours."

Feigning indifference, she leaned up against the side of one of the houses, determined to out-wait him.

Dr. Walker paced a short distance. The lights from the buildings illuminated only a very small portion of ground. He turned the disk over and over in his hand. At last he stood before Gayle.

"Okay. Let's get this over with. If you're nuts, you're outta here. If not, well ..."

Gayle stood up and quit examining her fingernails in the near dark. She looked around for the two men from the restaurant. Not seeing them, she said, "I do like a risktaker!" She eyed him speculatively. "Where's the disk, Stephen?" He held it up and she nodded, reaching for her wristband. "Watch that first step," she said lightly.

As the walls of the transporter room phased in, Gayle watched the doctor. He looked at Gayle.

"Uh ..."

She shrugged. "Told ya so." She winked at Kitty, who'd been standing by to activate the beam when Gayle signaled. Gayle introduced the two and added, as she walked toward the door, "Okay, Stephen. The hard part's over. Let's go." She stopped next to the transport console and waited for him to make up his mind.

A confused look on his face, he walked stiffly over to her. "Look, suppose I don't want to go through with this or decide to back out. I mean, is it too late?"

Gayle laid a hand on his arm. "Stephen you're not a prisoner. I said 'visit,' and that's exactly what I meant. Let's go meet the rest of the crew."

Gayle pulled gently on his sleeve, but he ignored her, focusing on the transport console itself. He looked a question at Kitty, who nodded her head and stepped back so he could take a closer look at it.

"You said you found an alien ship," he said to Gayle. "How is it that everything is in English?"

"We've had some small successes dealing with the computer that runs this thing. You should have seen the lighting before Simon got the computer to change it to Earth normal," Gayle said. "Ask Kitty how dismal it was."

A bird might look at a snake the way Stephen looked at Kitty.

Holding out her hand, she said, "Katherine Hawke, Dr. Walker. Please call me Kitty. It's a pleasure to meet you. And the light really was pretty bad. So dim that you couldn't see from one side of a room to the other in some of the larger spaces. But Simon will tell you more about that." She looked at Gayle. "I believe he's in the ready room."

Simon stood and put out his hand as Gayle entered the room, leading Dr. Walker. "Welcome aboard, Doctor. How are you holding up?"

Walker gave a small shrug. "Better, I think," he said, taking Simon's hand. "This is a bit much to accept, you must admit. And I'm not saying that I do accept it. I've seen some pretty good special effects in my time. I still need proof, Mr. Hawke."

Gayle interrupted the proceedings. "Simon, Stephen, I have to go talk to Kitty for a bit. Will you excuse me, please?"

Her request was only peripherally heard as Stephen nodded his head without taking his eyes from Simon's. Gayle waved a hand at Simon and left the two men to talk. They released their grip and sat at Simon's gesture.

"Good. I must admit that we engineered all this just to talk to you, but neither Kitty nor I were aware of Gayle's tactics. What we want is for you to join our little band of merry men. All of what I have in mind can be explained during a tour of the ship, as soon as you're up to it, of course. Coffee?"

Simon got up and poured Stephen a cup from a thermos sitting on a side table. He had beamed down and brought coffee back for their visitor as soon as he knew for certain that he'd arrive. "Something normal to help him keep his head on straight while he adapts to the idea," he'd said by way of explanation, and it seemed to be paying off.

During the tour that followed, Simon explained why Dr. Walker had been recruited, what some of their plans were for the future, and a bit about their timetable. One idea that Simon had conceived of was a way to marry their benefactor's solar cell technology to automobiles and even homes or, on a grander scale, cities. "We need to do something to get a cash flow started," he said.

Showing a flair for the dramatic, he saved the final pitch and a visit to the bridge for last. With a full Earth showing on the viewscreen, Simon asked, "So, interested in signing on? This isn't going to be a picnic, but when will we get another chance at this kind of technology? I see a lot of hard work ahead, but with perseverance we should be able to get this crate to work for us just as well as she did for her original owners."

Simon looked at Gayle, who had returned from her talk with Kitty. "Some of this, we just got from the computer. With a full crew, this ship is capable of turning out a basic-design space dock in about six to eight months. That dock will be able to turn out spaceships, depending on the size, at the rate of about two a year."

Simon turned back to Dr. Walker. "We'd like you to set up planet-side operations for the solar cell project and then turn it over to someone of your choosing. Until then, you'd be wearing a bunch of hats, just like the rest of us. I'll expect you to be my liaison between the scientists you approach and me, so getting yourself away from Earth-side operations as quickly as possible will be a prime consideration. Then you'd be free to be on that first trip if you want. And another thing—your expertise in astrophysics guarantees you a position aboard just about anything we build."

Dr. Walker looked at the planet below. "Of course, I'm interested, Simon. But the devil's in the details."

Nodding his head, Simon answered, "Of course. Getting paid is just one of those details. And I can't cover that at present. Which is one reason I want to get the solar cell project I have in mind up and running, soon, along with a newer, improved battery. We should be able to realize revenue from that at a fantastic rate. We're talking free fuel here. And once we add anti-gravity, we have George Jetson's car. Tell me that won't make millions… billions! You'll have full access to all engineering specs to develop it, and you'll probably come up with a lot of other ideas, too. Then there's the planet-side setup, which is more money we don't have. And officers and crew to pay. I would hope for precious metals from the asteroid mining, but I'm not betting on it. No one knows what's out there. And after we start turning out ships and crewing them, we'll need even more money. A space-based population is going to require a space-based economy, so I guess one of the specialists we're gonna need is an economist."

Kitty and Gayle walked in, and Simon looked at the three of them. "Here's what I propose," he said, growing excited, "crew this ship, go to the asteroid belt, and build a space dock. If we can build another ship like this one, then we can set this ship adrift heading back toward home. We should be able to make an educated guess as to which way to send it. And by 'we,' I mean a whole crew, including the scientists we want Stephen to talk to. Maybe the aliens will find it before they find us and give us some breathing room before we have to start dealing with an alien race."

He turned to Stephen. "Incidentally, you'll need a wristband like ours to pull the disappearing act for your people."

Gayle looked worried. "Suppose the previous owners don't like the fact that we've duplicated their technology? Suppose they don't like the competition?"

The talk went on for a long time, fueled by imagination and their surroundings.

The plan was finally modified to producing smaller, more heavily armed ships to begin with and the duplicate later. At this, Simon winced. More people.

Consultations with the computer showed just how many—five hundred plus for each ship built that followed the lines of the one they were on, minus the factory section. Those would be the battleships.

Smaller ships, smaller crews.

"Something I saw when I was wandering around in the factory section was a list of ship types. A type I didn't see was a carrier for fighters, which leads me to wonder if they never thought of that, or if fighter tactics won't work against their enemies.

"One way or another, they were talking about a lot of people—not percentagewise when looking at Earth's population levels, but still, someone was going to notice, especially when they planned to siphon off the best and brightest."

"Can I put in my two-cent's worth here?" Stephen interjected. "It's a change of subject, but we seem to be doing that a lot. I think I can do more good up here after getting the first few groups of scientists settled in. I know a mechanical engineer who would be perfect to run any production facilities, after getting the patents on solar cells and batteries, of course. All these things take time. And that's what we're talking here—time to create, patent, develop, market, and produce. And it's all going to take money. Do you... do we... plan to crew this ship on a hope and a prayer?"

Kitty and Gayle both started to talk at the same time. They stopped and looked at each other, knowing each had the same idea, and Gayle jumped in.

"That's exactly how we're going to do it, Stephen! Look at where we are! There are enough starry-eyed... excuse the pun... people down there to crew a thousand ships, given the chance. And for free! To live and work in space, and not on a space *station*, but on a space*ship*. Yeah, some will get bored and quit, but there will be more just standing in line."

Kitty chimed in. "But how long can we keep that big a people-drain a secret? Someone's gonna notice, and then the shit's gonna hit the fan. Especially the scientists, for God's sake! Our government thinks of people like that as national resources. Remember, I was part of that program for several years. What happens when a bunch of 'em start to disappear? We need to play this as close to the chest as possible, but I don't think we're going to be a secret for very long. I mean, they know about the shuttle already. I hate to be a wet blanket, but we need to keep the possibilities in mind."

Simon managed to break in. "Good ideas, everyone. And we *are* probably already compromised. This ship is going to be the only real refuge we're going to have for a long time to come. Stephen, it sounds like you're going to fit in real well. I think you're going to be a major asset, and I'm delighted to have you aboard. And I agree that you should handle your situation as you see fit. I don't have the expertise to tell you how to do it. Gayle, we'll work on the logistics of recruiting nonscientific personnel. See what you can come up with, and we'll brainstorm it. And Kitty, good points. Like I said, we're already compromised, especially after my visit from San Martino. And those were probably his people in Puerto Rico, too.

"I'd hoped for a little more time," he said, "but we'll have to make our plans and keep one step ahead of the law. We're going to have to provide safe havens for our recruits as well, and that will include their families, eventually."

He stood up and started to pace, thinking out loud more than anything else. "Now, we'll soon have a lot of people beaming up and down. Security is going to be a problem. We need security personnel before those scientists move in. And I think we'd better restrict access to the computer—need-to-know type of thing. Speaking of which, we should get a computer person up here soonest. Kitty got a chance to look at the computer. The main unit is located in a small room at the back of deck three. She managed to get a panel off and look inside. It looks like some kind of green Jell-O or something. When I asked about it, I was told that it's a proto-organic gel, whatever that is. It seems that the computer is alive and stores things at a cellular level with super-fine lasers."

The meeting seemed to have come to a conclusion for the time being, and Stephen took advantage of the lull to ask about getting specs on the technology he needed. He wound up with a trip to the factory control room and a shiny new wristband. As he prepared to beam back to Arecibo, he commented, "I've only got three more days on my stay there. I can start contacting people and dropping a few hints. But I'm going to have a problem with my new shadows."

Simon gave him a shopping list of professions to include, and added, "You're the expert here. Add anyone you think will be helpful." Standing at the transport console, he watched as Stephen vanished.

Back in the mess hall, Simon turned to other concerns. "First, Kitty, I think we should move the wristband machine into the meeting room." They had decided to use a room near the captain's quarters for the initial meetings with newcomers. "That will free up a room right off the bridge just for orientation.

And under way, it can be used as a breakroom or something. Next, Gayle, your job is to schedule your security personnel. We're going to have to start keeping the transporter room manned at all times, soon."

Kitty looked up from the pad she was busily scribbling on. "Also, proper tables and chairs for the mess halls and... ready room. Let's call it that to prevent confusion, okay? And you have a job, too, Simon—deciding on a chain of command. You spent five years in the Army and have a better understanding of that than we do. And how about uniforms?"

Simon went for the easy one first. "How about what Gayle's wearing? Black shirt and pants. Call it space black. Lots of pockets for regular onboard activities and fewer for dress wear, if we ever get to that point. We'll decide on rank insignia later."

Both Kitty and Gayle nodded agreement while Kitty scribbled.

Kitty said, "Tables need to be about three inches lower, and how about individual chairs instead of benches? We'll bring up a couple of chairs and duplicate them in the factories as soon as we have people to work them."

Gayle raised her hand. "I'll take a stab at learning how to run one of the factories. That way I can use some of the people I have in mind for security to get them made. Some of my little brother's friends from high school still keep in touch with him. Big guys. Not tall, just husky. Used to be football players. And intimidating as hell when they want to be."

Kitty threw another comment in. "Nametags on

the uniforms so we know who's who. Also, who's going to handle shift scheduling? Once people start coming aboard, we're going to have to allocate time everywhere so people get some practice at their jobs before we even leave orbit, especially the shuttle pilots since they're the ones who'll be bringing material to the ship for construction."

A week went by before Stephen beamed up again. His time had been spent getting back to the States, contacting colleagues, and starting on the plans for the solar cells and batteries. And being thoroughly worked over by agents of the United States government, who refused to identify themselves further.

The first thing he noticed when he beamed in was a new face in the transporter room. "Who are you?" he questioned.

"Ensign Marshall, sir," was the reply. "Security and transporter tech."

Making his way to the mess hall, he found Gayle having coffee. "I have twelve people meeting me at a hunting lodge in the Appalachians outside of Washington, DC tomorrow. One of them is a half owner. I think most of them will at least listen with an open mind. I've worked with almost all of them at one time or another on various projects."

Gayle told him she'd gotten his name onto a list of speakers at a sci-fi convention in Denver two days after that. "Sorry to fill up your schedule, but it looked like too good an opportunity to pass up."

He winced. "Astronomers don't usually work at this pace, but I can handle it awhile longer. I just wanted to give a progress report and pick up some of those locator disks you used on me for tomorrow. I'll fly in today and get some rest before my guests arrive. I see you managed to get some security set up."

She shrugged. "Wasn't too hard. I picked the three I thought would come over easiest, and they convinced three of their friends. They also got a cousin of one of 'em to come on board, too. You probably met him in the transporter room. They're already running around in their uniforms, calling everyone 'sir' and 'ma'am' and 'captain' and 'commander.'"

Kitty walked into the mess hall during this last. "Welcome back, Stephen. We were beginning to worry about you. It's a good thing those security boys are here now and past the denial stage. Did any of us go through that? And, congratulations, by the way. You are now Commander Walker, senior officer in charge of Operations. That makes you Third Officer, temporarily. And, incidentally, third in line for command. Of this ship or any that we build."

Stephen sat back, stunned. "Command? Me? I assumed you guys were kidding before."

Kitty looked at him sympathetically. "I know how you feel. Denial finally kicked in for me a few days ago. I'm still trying to work through it."

Gayle excused herself. "I'm going to get another batch of those locator disks for you. Be right back."

Simon strode into the mess hall and went to the coffeepot. "I'm glad somebody keeps this thing filled." As he sat down, he smiled. "Well, how's our newest commander? I assume Kitty has already spilled the beans. At least I get to do this."

He slid a small case across the table to Stephen,

who opened it and saw a pair of eight-pointed stars. Looking around at the others, he saw that Simon was wearing the same and that Kitty had what appeared to be comets on her lapels.

"One on each lapel of the shirt you draw from Supply on deck eight. One of our security people has a knack for finding things. I think he'll make a fine Supply Officer. And two are pilots, so they'll learn shuttle operations."

Quite a bit had changed in a week. The mess hall now had eight tables for four, with chairs at each. The conference room had a long table and chairs for sixteen. Security protocols restricted bridge functions and computer access. Stephen now had a room on deck four, rank (high, apparently), and a job. And seven new faces roamed the decks.

"Just what does an Operations Officer do?" Stephen asked with the look of a man who'd received one shock too many.

"Coordination, mainly," Simon said, "between shipboard functions, shuttle crews, factory output, construction crews, etc. You won't be alone. Each department will have a supervisor who'll report to you. All you have to do is keep track of it all and give orders."

Stephen winced. "That's *all* I have to do? This, I'm going to have to digest. And I need to get back so I can take a plane ride. I don't want to arouse suspicion by not having a back-trail. Now I'm acting like I've got something to hide." He raised his hands in the air dramatically, and then let them fall to his sides, his smile a bit lopsided. "Well, I guess I do, at that."

He proceeded to fill Simon in on his visit home. "They were waiting for me at the airport. The next eighteen hours were the worst of my entire life. I made sure to call each of my contacts from a different phone and at different times. I'm sure they all think I've gone over the top. As for the rest of the week, I turned those plans over to a friend of mine and let him have his way with 'em. He promised a working model within a year, and that's including retooling a plant—a couple of plants, actually."

Simon and Kitty accompanied Stephen to the transporter room. "What do you mean by a couple of plants, and where's the money coming from?" Simon asked pointedly.

"Investors," Stephen responded, "all looking to get a piece of the pie when we go public. And I have Adam Gardner overlooking the whole thing. He's a good friend of mine with an uncanny ability to get things done."

The tech on duty reported, "Commander Miller requests that you wait for her, ma'am. She has a package for Commander Walker."

Kitty replied, "Thank you, Ensign." Turning to Simon, she sighed. "I don't know if I'll ever get totally used to this, being the captain and all. It seems too strange."

Gayle arrived in time to hear the last of Kitty's lament. She handed a package to Stephen. "Here are the locator disks. I'll put your insignia in your room." She turned to Kitty and put one hand on her friend's shoulder. "And you'll get used to it, Kitty. I have. Just think about all the men you'll have at your beck and call!"

Kitty stuttered, "I d-don't need men at my beck and call!"

Simon laughed. "One of the perks of command, dear. Let's send Stephen on his way. And us, too. You realize that this will be the first time we've been down together since we got this old girl? Been thinking about a name for her, too. How does *Galileo* sound?"

They all agreed that it was an appropriate name, so it passed unanimously. Kitty nodded at Stephen's armband. "Contact us when you're ready. We'll be waiting anxiously."

Gayle put a hand on his shoulder. "We'll put on a good show for your friends, Stephen." She leaned forward and kissed him on the cheek. "That's for luck." He turned beet-red as she turned to the young man at the console. "Activate transporter, Ensign."

Two days later, an ensign knocked on the Hawkes' door. After she read the hardcopy, Kitty said, "We have an hour to get dressed and meet our guests. I know my part; just don't fumble yours. I'll call Gayle." She shook her finger in Simon's face.

She had spent much of her free time the past two days learning about military protocol from him. His five years of service was about to pay off in a most unexpected way, indeed. And she'd switched ranks with him after a long discussion. She felt a male captain would go over better in the beginning, and he had the ability and knowledge to pull it off.

Those two days hadn't been without incident, either. An Agent Daniels, FBI, seemed to like to pop up when least expected. Just that morning he'd knocked on their front door. Kitty and Simon had only beamed in moments before, and that only after a scan of the house showed no occupants. Persistent, he wanted to know where they'd been and insisted on seeing Simon as well.

Sticking her head into their office, she told Simon about their visitor.

"Don't worry about answering questions about where we've been since we got back," Simon said. "He shouldn't know any more than San Martino. Let's see what else he has."

What he had was footprints, none distinct enough to ascribe to any one individual due either to the weather or contamination by other feet, but they were of a size with both Simon's and Kitty's at the scene of an… event that was yet to be explained. "Yes, Agent, those could be my footprints. I do camp in the area from time to time. But, we don't know what you mean by an 'event' any more now than we did then. And I've already been over this with Agent San Martino. Care to enlighten us?" Simon asked.

Demurring, Agent Daniels left, but not without a parting shot. "It's my job to know when something doesn't smell right, and I can say without hesitation that something stinks here. You aren't leaving the house by any means I can see, yet you're very seldom here. Your truck is here, but where are the Hawkes? See what I mean? We will talk again, I promise you."

Any response would have been made to a very angry back as it made its way to the grey sedan parked at the curb.

As the hour expired, 'Commander' Hawke walked self-consciously into the transporter room and went to the tech on duty.

"I didn't introduce myself when we came aboard. Too much of a hurry. I'm Commander Hawke," she said and shook hands.

"I'm Bill Hodges, ma'am. I guess that's Ensign Hodges, now. But you're really the captain, right?"

Kitty smiled. "We're all making adjustments, Ensign. We'll be having some visitors shortly who'll probably appreciate a male captain for now. Watch for Commander Walker's signal."

Not knowing quite what to expect, but trusting Stephen's judgment, she told the ensign to begin transport as soon as the signal arrived, which resulted in four very bewildered men staring at her. "Welcome aboard the *Galileo*, gentlemen. Would you please step forward so Ensign Hodges can bring the next group up?" Motioning with her hands to one side of the room, she drew them away from the transport pads. "Again, please, Ensign." Three men and a woman were next to experience the effect while the first four stared goggle-eyed.

"Son of a bitch!" escaped from someone's lips before he managed to control himself.

"Again, welcome aboard the *Galileo*. Would you please step forward so Ensign Hodges can bring the next of your group aboard?" She motioned toward the first four, and the current group moved slowly off the pads. "Once more, Ensign," she ordered. As three figures emerged from the sparks, she recognized Stephen. "I believe that will do, Ensign, thank you."

The ensign put the console on standby and moved away from the gaggle of visitors.

Kitty turned around to confront her guests. It was amazing what one could do under the guise of military protocol! Still, the mere thought of ordering people around like she'd just done gave her fits. To think that she had that kind of power and responsibility only made her throw up once a day... usually.

"Ladies and gentlemen, once again, please let me welcome you aboard the *Galileo*. I am Commander Hawke, and if you'll follow me, I'll take you to the captain." She turned and walked to the door, which whisked open in front of her. Remembering how unnerving that had been the first few times, she stepped into the corridor and turned back. "Ladies and gentlemen, please. The captain is waiting."

One man took a hesitant step forward, then another. The moment gone, the rest followed into the corridor, Stephen bringing up the rear. Keeping her tone light, Kitty led the way down the corridor, apologizing as she led the group to the ready room.

"Sorry about the long walk. The mechanics of transporter technology seem to require that the transporter pads remain in close proximity to the generators and an entirely separate computer that handles our beam technology. Some of the things you'll find here will seem subtly wrong, like the people who designed all this just think differently than we do. For example, we haven't found any evidence of art or esthetic values aboard. Just utilitarian rooms and furnishings."

As she finished, she led her charges into the ready room and pulled the newest toy Simon had found out of her belt. Holding the commlink to her mouth, she said, "Commander Miller?"

"Miller, here."

"Commander Miller, please inform the captain that his guests have arrived in the ready room. And bring a couple of pots of coffee from the mess hall."

"Right away, Commander. I'll have Ensign Hodges bring the coffee," came in a voice from the small instrument Kitty held. The group of scientists looked at each other nervously.

The woman spoke first. "I'm Dr. Joanna Barnes, Computer Sciences. This is all kind of hard to believe, Commander. Sit anywhere?" she asked.

Kitty nodded, understanding. "I know what you mean. I've been here for weeks now, and I still find myself running head on into denial around every other corner." She waved her hand at the table. "Anywhere there's a notepad, Dr. Barnes."

Everyone took a seat, Kitty at what would be the captain's right and Stephen at what would be the captain's left. Simon walked into the room just as the last person was getting settled. Kitty and Stephen got to their feet while the rest froze. Striding to the head of the table, Simon ordered, "Be seated, Commanders." Reaching his chair, he said, "Welcome aboard. I am Captain Simon Hawke, commanding officer of *Galileo*. This is my First Officer and wife, Commander Katherine Hawke. You are already acquainted with Commander Walker, and here comes Commander Miller with refreshments." All eyes turned to Gayle as she entered, not for the coffee she brought but for the figure she cut. Where she'd found time to tailor her uniform was anyone's guess, but it did turn heads.

"Good evening, ladies and gentlemen. Sorry to be late." She rolled an ordinary cafeteria cart before her and stopped about midway down one side of the table. She set a pot and a tray filled with cups and a stack of saucers at each end of the table. From the lower level she brought out cream, sugar, and other things people ruined good strong coffee with, duplicate sets going to each end of the table. She then sat down quietly at the lower end of the *Galileo*'s officer chain.

Simon leaned forward and crossed his arms before him on the table. "Thank you for coming, even though none of you really believed it was possible, but the fact that you showed up at all tells me your *desire* to believe. Of course, your natural skepticism won't let you fully trust this even yet. A tour of the ship later will finish that job, I assure you.

"I'm sure Commander Walker told a good story, including our feelings about turning this vessel over to any one government. Well, I can't stress enough how right she is. This vessel won't be another Roswell. Nothing this big can be kept secret from the government. Too much leakage. And if one nation did get it, all the rest would want in. If not, I can see some neighborhood bully saying, 'If I can't have it, you can't either.' Then there's the very real possibility that if things managed to stay quiet, absolutely none of this technology would reach Joe Citizen for a hundred years. It would get shuffled into some agency's black budget and never seen again. On the other hand, if *we* keep control, the technology *will* get to the people. Some of it is already in the works. Talk to Commander Walker sometime. That's his department.

"You folks have the unique opportunity to bring more technology back, whatever you can find that will be of benefit to humanity. You'll have an almost totally free hand in that department. There will be only two restrictions. One, no weapons or propulsion technology goes down. That's firm. Two, I have final approval on just what does go down. That, too, is firm. I can't allow anything too advanced to show up too early. Remember, smallest waves possible. Does anyone have problems with the situation as I've outlined it?"

Several hands went up, and Simon recognized a crucial point when he saw one. He sat up straight in the chair. "I'll bet I can guess what you're thinking. How about, 'How dare you think you know what's best for humanity?' Or, 'What gives you the right?'" All the dissenters' heads nodded in unison. "Well, let me tell you a secret. I don't know that I *do* know what's best, but I believe that I do know what's worst, and turning this vessel over to any one government down there is worst. The balance of power would change so drastically that no other nation could let it go unchallenged. I believe turning it over would eventually spell the end of humanity as we know it. Ironically, keeping its secrets as long as possible and doling them out piecemeal is what will help humanity the most. The process will take years, and thought must be taken at each step.

"More than military disasters are ahead if we do this the wrong way. There would also be economic disasters as entire industries disappeared and new ones were born. What would happen to the displaced people? Too many at one time... see what I mean? What happens to the loggers when lumber is no longer needed? Or to everyone in all the oil-related industries when oil is no longer needed? Multiply that by all the other changes and you have chaos. We cannot be the cause of that. The only path we can follow is the one we're on."

By the time he finished speaking, Simon was on his feet. Sitting back down, he said, "Ladies and gentlemen, I apologize for the harangue but not for the content. I feel very strongly about this, and I'm afraid it shows."

Kitty broke the spell by reaching for the coffeepot. Filling her cup, she passed it to Dr. Barnes, who had seated herself on Kitty's right. "Okay, you've heard the serious explanation. You should have heard him when we first came aboard. 'I found it! It's mine! I'm keeping it!'" she mimicked, falsetto. Laughter ran around the table until Kitty waved her hand. "No, he didn't really say that, but I'm his wife and I know he thought it!"

Simon sputtered. "Well, who wouldn't! But back to business if you please. Second call. Who still has reservations? This time only two hands went up. Simon frowned. "I wish we could change your minds. If they do change, I'm sure you know how to contact Stephen. Now, I am sorry, but the rest of this meeting is classified. Commander Walker, would you escort our two guests back to Earth?"

Gayle stood up to take her turn as Stephen left with his charges. "Now, for those of you who remain, we need you to tease as much information out of this ship and its computer as you can. You were selected because Commander Walker considers you Earth's best and brightest in your individual fields. We're in the position of the man who'd never heard of electrical fields but knew that if he flipped a particular switch, a particular light came on. We want... no, we need to know how, why, who, where, when, and even what, if it applies. Toward that end, Commander Hawke and I would like to take you on a tour that is, quite literally, out of this world!

CHAPTER TEN

Kitty and Gayle led the scientists off in two groups, leaving Simon alone in the ready room.

"There you are," Stephen said, finding him poring over the now-tattered legal pad. "I think those two will be back. Both have commitments they couldn't get out of." He sat down across the table and poured a cup of coffee. "I'm sure you noticed that not one of them said a word?" Simon nodded, his expression saying that he had no idea where Stephen was headed. "I think they're afraid of you."

"What!" Simon sputtered. "Afraid of me! What the hell did I give them to be afraid of?"

Stephen grinned and took a sip of his coffee, stretching the moment out for effect. "Oh, I don't know. Your severely businesslike attitude perhaps, or the way you steamrolled them and took control of the whole conversation, then just dismissed the two who weren't able to commit without even asking for an explanation. What do *you* think?"

Simon smiled ruefully. "Maybe you're right. I just wanted to do a good job of explaining myself and get 'em on board. We do need them, as well as every one of their friends they can convince to join us. We also need their good opinion of us. Maybe I shouldn't have too much to do with the science types?" he said, looking across the table.

"I've been thinking, Stephen. You know about

the time limit we're under before the original owners come looking for their property? We figure we've got about five years unmolested, according to what we got from the computer. That's not knowing anything about where the original owners are located, by the way. After that, all bets are off. When someone comes knocking on our door, we better be ready. How are they going to react to our having their property? Or pirating their technology? Or even being in space and setting ourselves up as competition? These questions have already been asked, but there can't be any answers until we actually meet them. I just want to be prepared for friend or foe."

Stephen sat down with a frown on his face. "What can we do? They have more ships and more experience than we do. Supposedly."

Simon sighed. "I'd say that's a safe bet," he said glumly. He leaned back in his chair. "Here's how I see things. This ship is probably listed as missing by... whoever. Our first contact will most likely be with scout vessels looking for ship and crew. I checked the computer about that class of ship. They're lightly armed but fast. If they find this ship manned by other than their own, I'm betting they'll scoot for home. Also true if they find other ships present. Either way, if we can detect them first, we open up other options. Let 'em go and know we only have a couple more years, at best, or let them know we know they're there and let them know that we let them go. Or try to take them out. Or some other option I haven't thought of yet. The problems come in if they detect us and we don't know about it. They could come back in force and we'd be sunk."

The two men sat in silence until Stephen poured himself a cup of coffee. "Seems to me like we should gear up even further than you first imagined. Look, we've both been going through the computer, what we can of it, that is. And we've both made observations, things such as the need to get the fuel plant built first. That's what, two or three months? All automated. Then, the first space dock will take six more. How long to turn out a ship?"

Simon leaned forward and refilled his own cup. "About six months more for the design I have in mind—about a thousand feet long, with more beam weapons, but lighter, missile launchers and plasma cannons, whatever those are, and crews of about five hundred. It would be a mean bruiser, but there are no shields. We need to figure out if we can make shields and then figure on a third power source just for the shields. When not used for shields, that third source could be added to the engines for greatly increased output, making it almost as fast as a scout and measurably faster than anything else in its class. Or it could be funneled to the weapons, making us the equivalent of a full battleship. At least, that's what I get when I fiddle with the numbers."

Stephen took the notepad and pen and began to doodle. "Okay. Let's say the fuel plant is done. Six months for the first dock and six for the second. And in that second six months, the first dock has produced a ship. Six more months for the third dock, and the first two have put out two more ships. Six months for the fourth, and the other three have put out three more ships. After two years, you'll have six ships. Every year of operation after that, you get eight more ships, unless you begin to vary the sizes."

Now a frown traced its lines on Simon's face. "We're back to people, again—four docks at almost six hundred apiece, six ships at five hundred each, and this one at eight seventy. That's around six thousand, Stephen. This grows by leaps and bounds. How are we going to control this monster?"

Stephen shook his head. "I'm not the one you need to ask. You set up the chain of command here, so do it again on a higher level. Call it Fleet Level."

Simon threw his hands up in the air. "I'm not able to think on that level right now. Let's just take this one step at a time. Get a crew, build a fuel plant, and build a space dock. Until we get near the end of that program, I'm not going to worry about the next step."

Stephen stood up. "I have to get our visitors back soon, so I'm going to make a quick trip to my room. I'll see you before I beam down. Oh, here," he said, placing two locator disks on the table. "Maybe Gayle and Kitty should collect the others, too." He strode to the door, stopped, and looked back at Simon. "And you shouldn't worry about it, but you should be thinking about it. If you don't have any idea about our direction, who does?"

Not waiting for an answer, Stephen strode from the room, leaving Simon staring at a notepad covered with scribbles and one much-circled number.

Simon stood as the first tour group returned. He realized he was frowning and tried to turn it into a smile. What he came away with was something less than a frown.

"Ladies and gentlemen, during your tour,

Commander Walker pointed out that I presented an image that was something less than... amiable. For this I apologize. I'm not used to public speaking, as you've undoubtedly figured out for yourselves. It's just that I," he said and paused, looking for words, "I feel *so* strongly that turning this ship over to any one government or group would be the worst possible course of action for humanity. So, I hope you'll allow me the opportunity to change that first impression at another time."

As soon as Simon finished speaking, the visitors began to seat themselves at the table. One man remained standing, however, and began to speak. "I'm Adam Gardner, Captain, and personally, I've put up with a lot worse to work in less interesting places." He glanced around at his companions. "Besides, Commander Miller has explained how much pressure you folks are under. She also outlined your general plans for the future. I won't presume to speak for the others, but for me, where do I sign?"

The other three were echoing Gardner's sentiments when Kitty led her entourage into the room. Simon repeated his apology to the new arrivals, sat down, and looked around the table.

Spreading his hands in an all-encompassing gesture, he inquired, "Well, folks, what do you think of the *Galileo*?" The dam broke, and not one sensible word came out of the babble that followed.

Kitty got control of the situation by the simple expedient of tossing her notepad out into the center of the table. It landed with a sharp report, halting all conversation instantly.

Gayle took the rest of the pressure off. "Commander Hawke does have a way with words, doesn't she?"

As the laughter died down, Kitty put forth a suggestion. "How about everyone starting a list of questions, comments and suggestions? We can go over them at future meetings. What I'd like to do right now is get each of you outfitted with wristbands like ours." The physical effects and general use of the transporter had been explained as well as possible by Kitty and Gayle during the tours. "One thing to remember—beam-up is not automatic. Make sure you're in a secure location. Since that place is where you'll usually return to, a locked room is always good."

Stephen found his colleagues in the briefing room getting fitted with their wristbands. As the last one was finishing up, he stepped forward. "Folks, we need to get you back to Earth." At the shocked looks he got, he laughed out loud. "Get used to it. Those wristbands make it a fact of life. One thing of note— those bands are connected directly to the computer on board the *Galileo*. If you wind up under too much pressure or get given something to change your basic metabolism or some such, the band will notify the computer and you'll be beamed out of your situation. It's a bio-monitor, pure and simple, and lets us know your location and general situation as well. It won't automatically beam you out just for getting incarcerated or overly, shall we say, excited. Your stress levels have to go pretty high before that happens. Otherwise, you have to request a beam-out by pressing the red spot on the band. If at all possible, try to do that where the results won't be seen."

Stephen and Gayle had started to lead their charges back down to the transporter room when

Kitty spoke up. "There's one more item of some importance to most of you. We've found that our anonymity has been breached already. Who says our government isn't good at its job?" A few nervous titters sounded in the room.

"Anyway," she continued, "so far, it appears that only we four—me, my husband and Commanders Miller and Walker—have been identified. Make an active effort to keep your involvement unknown or you, too, will be receiving late-night callers. If that should happen, and you don't want to escape, tell 'em everything they want to know. Tell them also that the wristbands are attuned to each specific individual. Even if they figured out how to get it off without destroying it, it still wouldn't work, at least not as a transporter. It becomes an automatic listening device and locator beacon at that point, but you don't have to tell 'em that part." With a wicked little grin on her face at the thought, Kitty turned and headed off to find Simon.

She found him in the ready room, slumped in his chair and glaring at his notepad. "Okay, I know something's wrong. Spill it." She sat down beside him and grabbed a coffee cup.

He slid the notepad toward her, picked up the pot and filled her cup. "Stephen has suggested that our best course of action is to expand the plans we've already made to go from one dock to four. In two years, we can have six operational ships. That circled number is how many people we'll need by then. Over five thousand." Simon sat there, tapping a pen on the table. "These numbers scared me for a while. I was only in charge of forty guys—a rifle platoon, for Christ's sake! Not even a jeep."

Kitty leaned over and laid a hand on Simon's arm. "I've never seen you quite this indecisive about anything before, dear. You always seem to know what you want and how to go about getting it. And here you are... dithering. What's the worst that can happen? We could all get dead, of course, but that's going to happen sooner or later anyway. You've always told me that if you act like a boss, then people will look at you as one. Okay, you've set yourself up as one," she said, her voice trembling. "So, start *acting* like a boss. All we've done is up the scale."

Simon spent a long minute thinking over Kitty's comment. "Okay. The only thing I can see to do is take the opportunity and run with it. I guess if we don't pull it off, we can always give the ship to something like the United Nations rather than a single country. But I must say that you surprise me. You're the last person I would figure to push for keeping this thing to ourselves."

"In a perfect world, I wouldn't," she retorted. "But have you looked around lately? The sarin gas attacks, India and Pakistan with nuclear weapons, shit starting in the Middle East, and to top it all off, look at the similarities between Drake and Hitler. Both of them stole the leadership of their respective nations, and both of them immediately started wars. At least Drake has the dignity not to grow a mustache. He looks silly enough as it is."

Simon looked at his wife as if she'd grown a second head. "So, you've got this all figured out, have you?"

"No," she answered, sitting down across from

him. "But I've got some ideas. Hell, you gave me the glue to bind it all together."

"Me? What did I say?" Simon sounded defensive.

"Well, it was more your dream than anything else. Remember it? You said you could never forget it. It happened on one of your first nights aboard and it was about starting an empire."

Simon's features got more animated as he recalled what she was talking about.

"But," Kitty said, going on before he could speak, "I applied that technique you taught me to the situation. I kinda tranced out and looked at the possibilities as my mind laid them out for me as far into the future as I could go. In most of the futures I saw, we were better off keeping the technology away from the powers-that-be down below." She was referring to a meditation technique Simon had taught her, picked up on his travels somewhere in Asia. He'd always been rather vague about just where.

Simon thought for a time, now lost in that realm himself where some of the more probable futures were laid out, almost like chess moves. Cutting the visit short, he said, "I see what you mean. You do realize that this means the government is going to do whatever it takes to get possession of this ship, don't you?"

"Yes," Kitty said, reaching out and taking Simon's big hands in her tiny ones. "It means that since they can't get at us, they're going to go after those we care about. My folks are dead, but you ..." Her voice trailed off.

Simon spoke well of his mother when he spoke of her at all, but only once had he spoken of his father. An innocent question had once led to a half-hour rant that ended with a penitent look and a heartfelt apology. And it had never been repeated. Nor was mention of his father ever made again, by unspoken consent.

Now, though, things were different. "They aren't going to care if you hate your dad. They're going to pick him up, along with your mother and brother. Wanna bet they use the words 'protective custody?' You're going to have to face him sooner or later."

"The later, the better," was all Simon said. Pointedly changing the subject, he said, "That thought about my old platoon was really first rate. For now, though, let's get Gayle and Stephen in here. Send for Ensign Marshall, too. And the two pilots."

Twenty minutes later, the four ship's officers were seated around the conference table. Simon took a breath and said, "It's time to fish or cut bait, people. I've been worried about personnel, but I'm going to go ahead as if that were assured. If it doesn't come to pass, well, we'll cross that bridge when we get to it. This way, we can start training them as fast as we can get 'em.

"Gayle, among other things, you're Communications Officer. That puts you on command staff and in line for command. Our two pilots are going to start hands-on training tomorrow for shuttle/fighter training. Stephen, you need to get ready for the convention in Denver. Let any of us know if you need help with that. Kitty and I will be reachable by wristband at all times once Stephen gets to the convention. We'll use the same routine we used on the scientists, only this time it will be on whoever you can manage to attract. If a system works, go with it."

Gayle jumped in when Simon took a breath. "The convention center is expecting a couple of assistants."

"Fine, just don't take any unnecessary chances," Simon said, agreeing to the unspoken request. "You guys work it out and let me know what you plan to do."

Before Gayle could respond, Ensign Marshall knocked on the door, both pilots behind him. "Ensigns Marshall, Johnson, and Quinn reporting, sir." He stood at a civilian's idea of attention and saluted, mimicked by the two pilots.

Simon self-consciously returned the salute and said, "At ease, Ensigns." He proceeded to fill the three men in on their duties. "All three of you will start flight training. Tomorrow, you start hands-on training... in the bays. No excursions until authorized. Johnson and Quinn, you're both promoted to lieutenant, junior grade. Ensign Marshall, you're promoted to lieutenant and temporary Chief of Security. I want you to get as intimate a knowledge of this ship as possible. As a temporary Security Officer you need to have that knowledge of this vessel. As soon as you can demonstrate that, you'll be posted to commander. We'll get insignia to you when we have them. Wait for me in the briefing room. We can discuss things in more detail shortly."

Gayle spoke up as the three men left the room. "They'll have those insignia before you know it, Simon. John—Lt. Marshall, that is—and I designed insignia for all officer ranks and made up a few sets of each rank up to commander, only one for captain, and none for the admiral ranks. We just did designs for those. We still need to do the enlisted ranks, though. We made them in one of the smaller factories down on deck four. They'll draw them from Supply before going off shift. Trust me. I know those guys. Ensigns wear a small silver pip we call a planet. lieutenants jg wear a silver crescent moon, lieutenants wear a gold crescent moon, lieutenant commanders wear a silver eight-pointed star, commanders a gold eight-pointed star and captains wear a silver comet with a tail. Hope that meets with your approval. And I guess I should pass stuff like that by you first, huh?"

Assuring her that it did indeed meet with his approval and noting that he'd already seen a few, he called for questions. After all three demurred, he closed the meeting. "Good luck, Stephen. I hope you're as successful as you were today. Call if and when you need anything. I guess that's all for now, folks. I've got people waiting in the briefing room. Meeting adjourned."

The mess hall had been rearranged into auditorium-style seating to accommodate the thirty-five young men and women who'd attended Stephen's lecture. Their presence was a direct result of what Stephen called smoke and mirrors.

"Without the smoke or mirrors," Gayle said to Kitty, her nervousness causing her to forget for a moment that Kitty had been there, too.

The presentation easel had read Teleportation in the Twenty-First Century, on the first line, Lecture from 6 p.m. until 7 p.m. on the second, and Guest speaker Dr. Stephen Walker, PhD., M.A., B.A., M.S. on the third. The time had been scheduled between two of the more major events of the convention, and it was hoped that enough people would drift in to make the whole thing worthwhile.

Almost forty people wandered into the room before Stephen took the microphone. "This is really not my forte," he said, "public speaking, that is, but thank you for coming. I'm not here to lecture on the possibilities of teleportation in the twenty-first century but to show you that we actually have it."

The room started to buzz immediately, and Stephen, a teacher as well as everything else, waited for his moment. "Teleportation exists, but the ability to teleport is currently beyond *human* reach. That means this ability comes from an outside source. We, humanity, were lucky enough to get possession of alien technology, and it's in civilian hands. I have with me an officer of a very large and dedicated spaceship. One of the pieces of technology aboard this remarkable find is the teleportation device, and we propose to demonstrate it to you right now."

He gestured to Gayle, a striking figure in her space-black shirt and pants, boots polished to a high gloss, and golden hair in a ponytail that reached her waist as she stepped to the lectern. "Ladies and gentlemen, I'm relatively certain that not one of you believes we can prove teleportation exists in a single hour. I propose a quick and easy way to prove it." She reached into the lectern and pulled out three transporter disks.

"These are tickets to a real, live, working spaceship. It's not the *Enterprise* or the *Millennium Falcon,* but it *is* capable of building those ships. Let me put it another way. What we're doing is recruiting volunteers for a crew. All we ask is that you go along with the gag until you're convinced."

She tossed the disks out into the audience where each one was looked at and passed around for a few seconds. At that point, Gayle stopped all inspections with an announcement. "I'm about to push a button on my wristband. I trust you've noticed that we're all wearing them," she said, raising her own. "I'll press it in ten seconds. At that time, anyone holding a disk will be transported aboard the *Galileo*, as we've named our ship."

"You should have heard the commotion the ones left behind caused," Stephen complained. "I thought we were gonna be raided by convention officials. The only thing that saved us was Gayle and the first three finally beaming back in."

"Well, we had to show 'em enough of the ship to prove it wasn't a setup," Gayle interjected.

"Anyway," Stephen said, "the rest of the group got so into questioning them that they forgot all about us for a while. Finally, some of the braver ones said they wanted to take a ride, too. Eventually we got the entire group up for short tours, gave them an address to come to the next day, and sent them on their way. I'm both pleased and surprised that thirty-five showed up."

The three commanders stood out as they walked to the front of the room in their solid black uniforms, facing the group of young people from behind a long table. Kitty, as senior officer present, called the meeting to order by tapping on her as-yet-unfilled water glass. She was finally getting comfortable telling the story of how they'd come by the ship and what they planned to do with it. To start, she, Gayle, and Stephen answered questions for about twenty minutes, stopping when Simon entered the room.

Stephen had been watching the door and spotted Simon first. He stood up and announced, "Captain on deck!" Kitty stopped in mid-sentence, and she and Gayle jumped to attention.

Simon took his place at the table. "Be seated," he said to the three in black and the few who had hesitantly risen to their feet as he made his way to the front of the room, making a mental note of each person who had stood, however hesitantly.

"Commander," he said to Kitty, "if you would finish your presentation." He'd been listening to the meeting via commlink and timed his arrival accordingly.

When Kitty reached the point where she, Stephen and Gayle had been sent to Denver, she shut up and looked at Simon, who began his part of the presentation.

"I'm Captain Hawke, commanding officer of the *Galileo*. Ladies and gentlemen, I believe we have a unique opportunity here, a real chance to start something new, an ability to make a difference like no other group in history. Until now, mankind has just dreamed about the stars—written about them, wished for them, and wished *on* them. Now, we can actually go there. Those of you sitting here today can eventually be in command of some of the first ships to visit many of those stars. There's a hitch, though."

He hesitated for a moment to let that sink in. "The… people who built this ship are going to want it back, and they're going to come looking for it. My officers and I believe they'll do whatever they have to do to get it back. Now, I'm not saying we won't give their property back to them, but I *am* saying we're going to duplicate it first, along with all the technology it contains. We also need to worry about whether these aliens are going to object to us being the new kids on the galactic block. To that end, I propose that we start a program of building and expansion like nothing seen in the past hundred years. I'm asking you to make a sacrifice equal to that of the patriots of the American Revolution. I'm not talking about an overnight project here. We have five years minimum to build up, gear up, and prepare to either repel invaders or greet visitors. So, I ask you now to give me your time, your bodies, and your hearts, and we can forge a whole new direction for humanity—a direction that has Earth as a beginning and the entire galaxy as a destination. But only if we take the opportunity chance has provided for us.

"Now, if your manner of transport hasn't convinced you of the truth of the situation, then the tour we're about to take you on should do the trick. Afterward, there will be another question-and-answer period, followed by interviews for each of you who choose to sign on. If you have any skills that will qualify you for specific berths, we'll find out about them then. Those without specific skills who wish to join the crew will be given a few simple aptitude tests and assigned positions. As soon as the first ships start rolling out, those of you who've qualified for posts on those ships can be transferred to the new vessels and assist in the training of your new crewmates. If you find yourself in a post you don't like, you can cross-train for another as soon as it's available. So, if there are no questions, we can begin the tours."

As the visitors were anxious to see a working starship, they kept their questions to themselves for the present. Simon had three security officers on hand to make the tour groups a manageable five persons each. He took the first group out the door and onto the bridge while the other groups started out with different primary destinations in mind, emptying the auditorium out almost instantly.

After an hour of tramping around the ship answering questions, Simon was glad to get back to the mess hall. He fielded more questions until Gayle led her group in, turned his five over to her, and strode from the room. He slipped onto the bridge and through his quarters, heaved a sigh of relief, and sank into his chair.

Later, all three found him lost in thought, staring at a view of the Earth. "So this is where you've been hiding." Kitty said. "We were beginning to worry. And where the hell did that speech come from? Do you have any idea what kind of reaction you got from those kids? They're so hyped up, they're ready to leave orbit right now. We got them to calm down some though. They're all going back down to get friends to sign on. I think you may have just solved our personnel problem all by yourself."

Stephen joined the conversation, saying, "And you sent *me* to that convention? And what, exactly, *is* our direction, Simon?"

Simon looked up, sat up straight, and spoke in a subdued voice. "I've been dreaming about that very thing since we first came aboard. The problem is that when a secret is shared by more than one, it isn't a secret anymore. We've recruited some of Gayle's friends, you, about a dozen scientists, and almost three dozen others who'll come aboard as crew and recruiters, as well as any of their friends, almost without any kind of guarantee of their loyalty. Our decision to keep the *Galileo* to ourselves and crew her is going to cause a hell of a reaction when word gets to the right people. I'm sure there's been a lot of scampering around, trying to find out something concrete already. And trust me on this, those guys know their jobs, so it won't be long."

Simon sat quietly for so long that Gayle started to speak, but Kitty held her hand out and shook her head. Finally, he spoke again.

"Once we take this step, it's a certainty that none of our lives will ever be the same, not to mention the lives of a bunch of people we're asking to blindly follow us. We're going to have to achieve an equal-but-separate status, and the technology on board this ship is all we've got. Our lack of numbers is a definite liability, but at the same time, we're going to have to start being careful who we let in. I have some ideas on that for a later meeting."

Once he got started, the rest just flowed out. "For the short-term, our direction is towards independence, although everybody concerned will know just how dependent we really are on Earth, at least for now. We'll outgrow that need rather quickly and become a separate, self-governing branch, a branch that will eventually absorb the parent as they get the technology we have aboard and join us or stay earthbound. It's a dream I started having right after Kitty and I first came aboard. Now it looks like that dream will come true. If I had to give it a name, I'd call it 'The Terran Alliance.'" Simon looked at his three commanders—one his wife and two his friends. "I'm serious, guys. Tell me you don't feel it, too, and I'll walk away from this right now."

Silence reigned on the bridge for a moment that seemed, to Simon at least, an eternity. Gayle was the one to speak for the trio. "No, Simon, we feel it, too. We just didn't have the words for it. You brought it to life and given it a face. I say let's go start an empire!"

Stephen grinned and bowed. "Emperor Simon the First! And his Empress, Kitty!"

Simon exploded. "No! Emperors rule by decree, and I don't see our Alliance ruled that way. As soon as we have enough people, there will have to be elections. And I guarantee that my name will not be on the ballot! All I want is my own ship and a chance to see things that no man has ever seen before. That's another part of my dream, and no way is that going to happen if I'm anything other than a ship's captain. This boy's happy with Captain Hawke. Period. End of discussion."

Kitty addressed the silence that followed Simon's ultimatum. "Whatever you say, dear. I'll go along with you, but that's quite a way into the future yet," she said, as if to a child. She laid a hand on his arm and smiled, taking the sting out of her tone. "Change of subject. I don't think you have to worry about being too imposing to other people anymore. I overheard a couple of those kids actually bragging that they got the captain as a guide. And we got twelve females in this bunch, by the way. Gayle and I won't be alone anymore. Also, Stephen suggested an additional function for the wristbands. I checked with the computer, and it's doable. I did have some trouble getting it to respond to me at first, but we now have a way to let people know we need them without being obvious. It's a mild electric shock, more like a tingle. That way, anyone down below can be told to report aboard before we leave orbit. It can also be used to call specific individuals or identify persons who are requesting a beam-up."

Simon considered what she'd said. "Good ideas. And that's to all of you. Looks like we've got a real good start here. Now all we need are about eight hundred more people."

CHAPTER ELEVEN

Two weeks had produced significant changes. The first batch of recruits had talked to friends, who talked to other friends, and the first group of thirty-five turned into over seven hundred new faces living on, training on, and otherwise finding reason to be aboard the gigantic city/ship.

During the first few days after the convention, Simon, Kitty, and Gayle conducted interviews with all those who accepted wristbands. Gayle's second contribution to the crew—nearly a dozen large, intimidating friends of her brothers—acted as additional security and escorted each interviewee back and forth as they were called up from the lower levels.

A more professional security solution was in the works though. Simon had contacted his old platoon, and almost the entire unit, another thirty-three, joined outright. Six were either dead or off the grid, as some called it. They would absorb Gayle's original force and train them up to Simon's standards.

Since none of the three were professional interviewers, they finally decided to just chat with each and see how it went. Simon specifically focused on education and home life when he sat down with an applicant. He laid out his ideas and listened to how each person reacted to what he had to say, then went into chat mode to draw out their inner thoughts and let the answer to his final two questions count for as much as the whole conversation up to that point.

"So, how do you feel," he would ask casually while refilling a pair of coffee cups on the small table between them, "about leaving home for almost a year at this point in your life?"

The answer was invariably some form of, "Are you kidding? Look around us. How could I possibly pass this up?"

The second question usually caught the interviewees by surprise. "Do you realize that every government on Earth wants this ship and will do anything to get it?"

Only twice did Simon make a note that the applicant wasn't ready for a position aboard the *Galileo*. One other impressed him enough—twenty-two years old, finished high school a year early and moved on to college, majoring in physics while getting respectable grades in creative writing—to ask Kitty to talk to her and give a second opinion.

However, the one thing all four were universally agreed on was finding others to take over the interviewing process.

The scientific staff had been hand-picked by Stephen, and they were soon found poking into various and obscure portions of the ship in search of… whatever. The Science Department had grown to somewhere in excess of one hundred and was making great strides with cataloging the technology, or at the least getting an idea of what could be grouped with what, as far as basic effects were concerned.

Several things had already emerged for certain

from that quarter. First, the massive matter converter, the teleportation system, and a small device found in the mess halls currently called a food processor, were offshoots of the same technology. Second, the computer had a virus that was slowly lobotomizing it.

The propulsion system was giving the scientists fits because they'd finally figured out that the basic fuel was antimatter monopoles. And Doctor Barnes had identified the fact that the computer was infected with what was quite probably the same virus that had killed the crew, being composed, she guessed, of the same material as the aliens themselves.

Each day ended with a debriefing for the four friends, and three weeks after the first scientists had come aboard, Stephen sat down at the ready-room table and started without preamble.

"I have bad news and good news, and it comes in the same statement. The computer is lobotomizing itself, according to Dr. Barnes. Remember her?" Even Kitty had made a comment some time back that the computer was getting harder to work with. "Apparently it's a gradual thing." He put his feet up on the desk, indicating that the matter wasn't about to bring their dream to an abrupt end. "It seems that somehow some of the virus that killed the crew got past the hermetic seal on the computer housing. It goes after higher brain functions first, so we're losing its speech programs and most of its self-willed protocols. We'll still have the autonomous functions, though, like environmental controls and gravity control. Now, before we go any further, I've got to say that I like the idea, in a way. If there are any lingering… things in there, like commands we haven't found, they should be gone by the time we get the upper hand."

Simon nodded. "Joanna Barnes?"

"Right. Anyway, she seems to be on the trail of a way to fight this virus. It looks like information is written to and read from the memory core by means of something she calls whisker lasers. Doctor Barnes thinks that since the original owners used their own proteins, the core was susceptible to the virus and it was only a matter of time before it happened. She and a hand-picked team worked day and night to identify the virus and now are in the process of getting the computer to disinfect itself."

"I really don't want to sound like too much of a dummy," Simon said, "but how will she do that? If the core is infected ...?"

"Apparently," Stephen said, "all she needed to do was clear a portion of the gel manually, then get a set of commands inserted into the cleared core, and the computer would take control of the lasers and target and destroy any traces of the virus remaining in the gel itself."

"And has this process worked?" Simon asked worriedly. "If we don't have a working computer ..."

"As far as we can tell at this time, it's working," Stephen said. "It isn't as simple as I made it sound, of course. Barnes has assembled a team on her own to fight the infection. She has medical doctors, computer techs, laser specialists, and I don't know how many others working on the problem. She seems to think it will only take a few more days before the system is cleaned up. One good thing is that because all the colony infrastructure data was in so many places in the factory section, we seem to have kept all that. We did lose all data on the alien language though. Apparently, no one bothered to copy it out. I guess they thought they had plenty of time. The bright spot is that we can reprogram the computer to our specifications as we go, and by the time we're ready to leave orbit, we should have a full set of instructions for it. If not, we can handle most functions manually."

"Well, then," Simon said, "as uncontaminated space becomes available, start inputting anything you think we need—navigation programs, astronomical data, whatever. If we're going to leave orbit and start building a space dock, we need all the information we can get."

"I've got it under control," Stephen said.

Simon's feet joined Stephen's on the ready-room table as the end-of-day briefing wound down. "The news about the computer is both good and bad as far as I can see," he said. "I don't know how much 'disk' space we have, but keeping unnecessary things off the hard drive is one of the things people try to do with computers. This virus looks like it's going to do that for us, whether we like it or not. The fact that most of the things we call ship's services are going to survive is good. The bad part is that we're losing all language skills, astrogational data, and automatic traffic control. Also bad is that we have no idea what else we've already lost or will still lose before Dr. Barnes gets this thing under control. It's good, however, that Dr. Barnes and her team think we may have that accomplished in the next few days. It's also good that Stephen's people think we can make do with manual control of most of those things until someone can work out new programs to handle autonomous functions."

He waved a sheaf of interviews in the air. "Another good thing is that every one of these kids has more formal education than I ever dreamed I would get," he said. "And Kitty and Gayle say damn near the same thing about each one of their interviewees." He tossed one interview out on the table. "Eager, ambitious, intelligent." Another paper. "Enthusiastic." Another. "Determined and smart."

He laid the balance of the stack on the table carefully. "One thing I don't want to do is fall into the mindset that it takes age to be prepared for service aboard this ship. Everything is new to all of us, and I think that the younger folks we attract, which is going to be a very high percentage, are just as capable, maybe even more so, as any of the four of us at this table tonight. These are the people that the future 'captains of industry' would be drawn from under other circumstances, and I think we can use most of this bunch as the core of our primary command teams. We could put them in charge of various departments or make them second in command to one of Stephen's people until they're competent to run the department themselves."

Kitty raised her hand and asked, "Are you sure that's the best course of action? Shouldn't we have older people in charge?" She let an embarrassed look cross her face. "I don't want to sound like I'm discriminating based on age, but I guess that's what I'm doing, isn't it?"

Simon grinned at her. "Yes, you are, dear. And I was guilty of the same thing for a while until I started reading these interviews. You haven't seen Gayle's or mine, but they all say things like 'conscientious, level-headed, responsible, or trustworthy.' Keep in mind that these… kids have all had a chance to spend time away from the nest, and while a few aren't ready to take on the burden of command, most of them seem to be. And as far as I can see, we got a lot better than we deserve with this first batch." He hesitated for a moment and then said, "Another problem I see is that we need teachers in various disciplines, so a priority on our return will be to recruit as many people capable of teaching astronautics, physics, and anything else we decide on to the rest of the crew. I would imagine that some of the scientists already aboard would fill those slots admirably. They'd get to stay aboard and study the ship while training people at the same time. We get the best of both worlds— older heads laying down the framework and younger, more ambitious people to implement our decisions."

He effectively ended the session by adding, "We really should reward the courage and adventurousness this batch showed in making the trip up here in the first place. Command will be a good way to punish them for that courage, don't you think? Besides, if you look at this thing as a military operation, we have the captain, first officer, security chief, and science officer all in agreement about a course of action. We will, of course, add members to this council as we come to trust them. We'll keep ultimate control among ourselves and can demote or retrain anyone we think isn't making the grade. But since this has turned into a military operation, there can be only one captain, one final authority. Unfortunately, that happens to be me, thanks to you," he said, looking meaningfully at Kitty. "I'll gladly trade positions with any one of you if that's a problem."

The offer to step down was ignored by all present as each one planned their next moves.

All levels teemed with people moving from one place to another as they learned their new jobs or carried out some chore necessary to the comfort and well-being of over nine hundred people crammed into one big container. Some were already moving into quarters and spending more time aboard than on Earth.

The pilots had started making training flights with the shuttles, and there was a waiting list for fighter training. That one was going to take some time because the differences between a shuttle and a fighter were enormous, the main one being that the fighters weren't flown by intuition or by the seat of the pants but by a more direct neural interface. Fighter pilots wore a skintight suit containing a myriad of receptors connected to various ship functions. An accompanying helmet tied the pilot into the sensor suite, accessing the heads-up display and even throttle control.

Half a dozen engineers were aboard getting the factories prepped, and most positions were fully staffed. The bridge crews were shaping up, and Astrometrics, led by Stephen, had identified six different locations that were suitable for space docks.

Construction pods had been located in a ring around the aft end of the factory section, brought online, and had crew training to use them. These were one-man, self-contained miniature spaceships in their own right. They were the workhorses of the construction projects, designed to take a completed equipment assembly out of the main ship and move it into space for installation. Twenty-four of these nimble craft were on hand to perform whatever task was assigned them.

And there was still a trickle of recruits coming in. By this time, most of the more glamorous positions had been assigned, and the occasional recruit would show something less than boundless joy when they found out that the only positions left open were either janitorial, maintenance, or something equally boring and dismal. Sometimes it was only due to the confidence and spirit of the interviewers that the potential recruit agreed to sign on in one of the less sought-after positions.

Stephen had department heads reporting to him on a regular basis, and two scientists working in the engine room had detected a small fluctuation in one of the magnetic containment fields. They had adjusted it and established protocols to monitor both fields while automatically keeping them at optimum.

Some very interesting observations were beginning to come in about their ship. Some of the technology was well in advance of Earth, such as the monopole energy source, warp engines, artificial gravity, and transporter. But other things seemed rather anachronistic beside them. Most internal data transfer was by fiber optics, for example, and most things were powered by electricity produced by generators that wouldn't get a second glance on Earth. The scientists were having a real problem trying to come up with a hypothesis to explain the disparities. Links were built to allow Earth equipment to run on the ship's power.

One report that caught Simon's attention was about the power source. The science-types were all abuzz about finding actual working equipment based on ideas that were still just theories to earthbound humanity. Apparently, the original builders had discovered monopoles, a fairly recent theoretical possibility to Earth scientists. What was most interesting to Simon was that antimatter was involved. It seemed that monopoles could be created artificially and that it took one north monopole and one north antimatter monopole to create power. If they were put in conjunction with each other in a containment field, they generated power. The mechanism was simple, apparently—that is, if you had the technology. North poles tended to repel each other, and matter and antimatter tended to attract each other. If an antimatter north monopole was placed next to a normal-matter north monopole, the dynamics of the situation created power that could be tapped. At rest, they provided enough power to keep all ship systems active. If pushed together by manipulating the magnetic containment fields, they produced enough power to move the ship at normal speeds. If pulled apart by the fields, they produced energy quantum levels higher, thereby allowing warp drive. The scientists were starting to call it a quantum drive. And apparently, that strange ship down on deck eighteen was what went after the necessary material to produce monopoles scooped from a sun's corona, which explained the badly warped armor plating.

But the other news was what made Simon's day.

He'd been worrying about how he was going to feed this crowd. So far, most of them had been beaming down to their homes, keeping the problem at a minimum. Once they left orbit, though, the problem would be how to keep enough food on hand.

"We've been studying the transporter as everyone is calling it," a little man was saying. Simon never could remember his name. "It seems," he began, "that the device has a cousin, so to speak. Have you noticed the alcoves in some of the rooms, primarily the ones we've set up as dining rooms?"

"I have," Simon said hesitantly, not sure where this was going.

"Well, it appears that those alcoves are a kind of matter converter. We think—that is, my colleagues and I think—that if we can get control of those alcoves, we can start programming them to produce whatever we want them to, such as well-done steaks, or soup, or oatmeal ..."

"And how did you arrive at this conclusion?" Simon asked, all ears.

"We simply followed certain trains of thought, Captain," the man said. "First, we have all that organic material between the hulls of the ship. We figured it had to be more than shielding, as some surmised. Then, when we found the conduits that led to the various... terminals, for lack of a better word, we became certain that they had a specific function. From that point, we just followed the wiring, and we got the connection, if you'll excuse the pun. In other words, we can program the computer to give us whatever we want in the way of organic foodstuffs. It just won't do anything like take organics and turn them into metals, plastics, or other materials."

Simon, Kitty, Gayle, and Stephen became a panel that summarily decided which of the volunteers would fill which position. Nine of the ten possible command slots for each shift had been filled. Tactical officer, also known as second officer, was still vacant because there was no vital need to fill it yet, although there were several names under consideration.

The first draft of the command roster put the four friends in four of the top seven positions in first shift, with one other older person filling out one of the top slots. John Marshall, a sergeant from Simon's old platoon, took command of all security with an automatic promotion to full commander, which left only three people new to the group. Second and third shifts would be made up completely of newbies, a move Simon thought would show one and all that there wasn't going to be any discrimination.

Meeting daily, the command team grew from the original four members to nine. The exotic, more than slightly alien surroundings tended to keep most people off balance enough that for most of the time leadership questions were overlooked in the welter of other things to do.

The primary command team began to mesh, bringing problems to the daily briefings for solutions that didn't readily present themselves elsewhere. Simon decreed that each officer on the command team was responsible for their alter egos on the other two shifts, so each person became responsible for training at least two others in the time remaining before the ship left orbit. The most common things being brought to the staff's attention were the newest discoveries about the vessel and frictions between crewmembers as they shook down into a functional whole.

During today's meeting, the chief medical officer waded into the fray with his diagnosis. Not a regular participant at the daily briefings, Dr. Harrison (Sandy) Penn said, "Crewmembers are beginning to experience boredom, pure and simple, even considering where we are."

He suggested exercise equipment as a starter, and it was brought aboard and copied. Card games and board games began to appear around the ship, and the computer began tapping into satellite broadcasts of radio and television for storage and replay. Crew quarters and recreation areas were equipped with receivers so watching television was becoming popular in the off shifts.

"But don't let it become the only form of relaxation," Dr. Penn warned. "And," he added, looking directly at Simon, "you should probably have more interaction with the crew. I haven't been aboard long, but I've already heard two things about you. One is that you're secretly one of the aliens that built this ship, and the other is that you tend to keep yourself apart from the regular crew. The second, in my opinion, tends to reinforce the first. You should get out among the crew more and show them you're as human as they are."

Simon fumed as Kitty, Gayle and Stephen broke out in gales of laughter. Kitty was the first to find her voice. "What must they think of *me*? I'm married to him!"

Glances passed among the newer members of the command team until Shirley Dahlquist, appointed to navigation officer under Stephen and some of his Science team, said diffidently, "The doctor is right, Captain. Your reputation started out pretty good among those of us who got accepted early on, but the newest recruits don't see much of you. The talk in the rec rooms after shift turns to all sorts of things concerning the ship and the command teams, especially you. Having been the first one aboard the ship who recruited the rest of us, you've earned a reputation, whether deservedly or not. Keeping yourself apart from the crew only makes people talk more, and some of the rumors are just..." she said, hesitating for a second. "I was going to say out of this world, but you know what I mean."

Kitty, still chuckling at the thought of Simon as an alien, said, "Hon, you should make yourself more visible. We all should, for that matter, but you most of all." She held up her hand as Simon started to protest. "I hear stuff, too, and Shirley's right. What our people need is the occasional inspirational talk that all good managers know how to give. You've got to tell the troops that they're doing a good job, and they need to hear it from you."

Simon's face turned red as he tried to find a way out of his dilemma. "I'm not a public speaker! I don't have any idea what to say to people or how to say it!"

The silence that greeted Simon's outburst stretched out enough to begin to be uncomfortable. Amy Carpenter, newly appointed to helm officer, first shift, diffidently said, "Captain, I think the biggest thing that has people spooked about you is the fact that you're planning to keep this ship away from the government. That takes a lot of guts, sir, and it makes people wonder what else you're capable of." She looked around the table before continuing. "Captain, I have some public speaking experience. I'll be happy to help you write a speech to give to the crew, if that's what you need. Actually, it's not so hard to do. I thought I could never get up in front of folks and say something, but I found that with practice and a belief in what you have to say, it's actually rather easy."

"Thank you for your offer, Ms. Carpenter," Simon said, discomfited by the statements of his new Helm officer. "I'll think about it and get back to you."

Engineers were busily going over and amending plans for the first dock. While no changes were being made to the operational side, several people voiced the opinion that the oversized ceilings, chairs, tables and various other equipment needed to be reworked from the outset to make it more human-friendly. Control panels were lowered to a more workable level, along with the aforementioned chairs and tables, and the theme carried itself over into things like beds, toilets, door handles, and as many things as could be thought of ahead of time.

Parameters were changed in the computer, keeping the original plans separate for safety's sake. The fuel plant, being fully automated, needed no changes. As soon as the ship arrived at the spot where they were going to build the plant, the *Sundiver*, as the fuel scoop had been named, would be sent on a three-and-a-half-month round trip to pick up its cargo of coronal material needed to begin operations. Controlled by the computer, no other supervision would have been necessary. But with the loss of the computer's higher functions, a team of astrophysicists would program the maneuvers into the *Sundiver's* onboard computer and track it all the way.

A departure date had finally been set for moving the *Galileo* out of Earth orbit and into the asteroid belt. The last of the crew were called back, accounted for, and a final countdown begun. It had taken three months to get to this point, and tensions were running high. Until that moment, no power had actually been routed to the engines, and until that happened, all that had gone before was just an exercise.

There were quarters for forty more people than were actually needed, and they were filled, too. Once the dock, tentatively named Orion, was operational, over five hundred volunteers would remain aboard to begin production of the first ship and would stay aboard for up to one year. That would leave just over four hundred aboard the *Galileo* for the return to Earth orbit. More crew would be recruited, and they could then head out to build dock number two.

Simon walked onto the bridge ten minutes before departure. Looking at the crew bringing the behemoth to life, he smiled slightly at the memory of a couple of unofficial, clumsy attempts to suborn a few of the crew. Simon was the first to admit to the efficiency of alphabet agents, but with only a large point made in the papers nation-wide about the missing civilians and none made of missing scientists, everything else stayed quiet, except, of course, for the late-night radio talk shows.

All stations but tactical were manned, and all stations but his were backed up by an extra crewman for training purposes. He took the command seat when Kitty relinquished it and listened to her report.

"Engine room reports all systems optimum. Computer is green and course is laid in, Captain. All departments report ready and all personnel have received the ten-minute warning. Stephen will monitor things from the engine room. You have the con."

Simon sat down and ran his hands over the controls built into the arms of the chair. He looked around the room at the expectant bridge crew and back to his wife.

"Thank you, Commander, I have the con," he said formally. He looked at Kitty, winked, mouthed the words, "I love you," and, with a slight hesitation, entered the codes that removed the ship from standby.

A low murmur that had gone unnoticed made its presence felt by its cessation as the bridge crew turned to their posts. An almost subliminal hum filled the air, and a barely felt vibration made itself known. Pressing a button on the arm of his chair, he announced, "All hands, this is the Captain. Secure all stations. We break orbit immediately. All our work is about to pay off. From this moment on, the course of human history is going to change as we embark on the grandest project since the pyramids were constructed. Good luck to us all." Leaving the PA live, he said, "Helm, on my command, engines ahead slow."

The crewman reported back, "Engines ahead slow on your command, Captain. Course laid in for position Alpha." Commander Amy Carpenter, Senior Helm Officer, looked over the crewman's shoulder at the console, nodded to Simon, and patted the crewman on the shoulder.

A stronger vibration began to make itself felt as the engines took the power being forced into them. From this point on, all experiences were new to each and every person aboard the enormous vessel. Simon watched several people exchange glances as their bodies registered the almost subliminal pulsations. He wasn't immune to the experience himself and found himself looking at Kitty.

A thin smile crossed her face, and she laid her hand on Simon's shoulder. Her gaze went to the forward viewscreen and the image of an Earth that would never be the same again.

Calling up a screen showing the same information Stephen would be looking at in the engine room, Simon double-checked his own readings, took a deep breath, let it out slowly, and gave the order everyone had been working feverishly toward for over three months. "Helm, ahead slow." Barely noticeable, the image on the viewscreen receded as the ponderous ship began to slip away from Earth.

CHAPTER TWELVE

A seriously agitated agent of an agency only recently admitted to by the U.S. government waited anxiously in his boss's outer office. Rather than appear to be anything other than totally relaxed, he flipped through the documents collected into a manila folder on his lap. For two weeks he'd been following leads on what he'd first thought to be a doomsday cult similar to the Heaven's Gate bunch, looking for possible ties to terrorist groups operating on U.S. soil.

Finding his old partner dead-bang in the middle of the whole thing put an entirely different light on the operation. And the rumors of alien spaceships caused him no end of worry, especially after some of the things he'd already seen. Pure *X-Files* stuff, but the actual facts seemed to him to be even more disturbing than that.

The secretary had been busily typing during his entire wait, and veteran that he was, he still jumped when she spoke.

"Agent San Martino, the director will see you now."

The agent closed the folder and stood up, walking to the door to the inner office. He took a deep breath, opened the door, and walked in. "Thank you for seeing me on such short notice, sir. I believe you'll find that what I have to show you will justify your time."

"Just get on with it, Agent. I have an appointment on the Hill and not much time today." The heavy-set man behind the ornate desk set a small sheaf of papers aside to give his full attention to the agent.

"Sir, I was present when the ALERT team scrambled for that sighting in Montana earlier this year. I have residue that our best forensics experts say can't possibly come from this planet. It was regrettably charred but enough remained. I personally saw the craft make its escape. It was I who found the link between the event and Simon Hawke, who just happens to be an ex-agent and an old partner of mine."

San Martino took a breath. "I faced him one-on-one, and he sparkled out of existence right in front of me. And don't look at me like I'm going nuts because I know what I saw."

Before he could go on, the director held up a hand, stopping him. "Agent San Martino, relax. I'm fully aware of the sparkle effect." At San Martino's look, the director said, "What? Did you think you were my only line into this situation? The White House is even more interested than we are."

The agent looked at his boss and asked, "So, I'm just confirming what you already knew?"

"Yes, but not entirely. You're bringing in new information, like Hawke having been your partner. You'll have some insight into the man."

"I don't think so, sir. Simon Hawke isn't the man I knew fifteen years ago. He has a different look in his eyes. I wouldn't trust my own analysis of him in this situation."

The director looked his agent over. "Well, you're going to have to get a handle on it. We need that technology."

The comment jogged a memory in San Martino. "Sir, if we were to get control of that ship, how long would it be before the rest of the world governments found out?"

"What do you see as a result, Agent?" the Director hedged.

"I mean, like, what would the U.S. do if, say, the Brits or Chinese got the ship?"

"We'd have to pull an emergency preemptive strike on China and hope we were in time. The Brits, I don't know. Why?"

"It's just that I would expect the Chinese to react in the same fashion, sir. It almost seems like the situation as it stands is perfect. The ship is completely crewed by Americans, with the exception of a few scientists. Keeping them quiet is going to be a small problem as they come back home and we get them for debriefing, but we still wind up with the data ahead of anyone else on Earth." A moment of silence passed, and San Martino said, "Then, we impress upon them the consequences of staying with such a traitorous bunch."

"Do you think you can convince enough to make a difference? It seems even to me that the idea of really traveling in space is going to overcome many people's loyalties. Or so say some of my other informants." The director looked at his watch openly, deliberately. "Agent San Martino, you are ordered to get someone on the inside of this group as soon as possible."

San Martino looked the director in the eye. "That's going to be a problem, sir. The ship just broke orbit and headed for the asteroid belt. They're gonna be gone close to a year."

The director looked San Martino in the eye. "Then that's how long you have to figure out how to capture at least one person from that ship. Dismissed."

San Martino closed the door behind him and started down the hall. "Damn you, Simon Hawke. Damn you to hell!"

CHAPTER THIRTEEN

Six days and eighteen shifts. That was what was projected for the enormous ship to reach its destination. Stephen's Science team recommended running systems up to speed slowly, since there was no longer a reliable database to draw information from.

Simon was near collapse when Kitty lowered the boom late on the second day.

"Simon, no one knows any more or less than anyone else about what we're doing. You said so yourself. You have a shift, I've got a shift, and Lt. Commander Grimes has another. And all three of us have assistants. I'm telling you right now that if you don't go get some rest and quit staring over our shoulders, mine included, you're going to have a very lonely trip, Captain Dearest. The rest of the staff are taking their off shifts, and you need to do the same. We're all agreed. We need you to be on top of things when we reach Alpha. Do you want me to get Dr. Penn to make it official?"

Simon opened his mouth to argue.

"No, Simon," Kitty interrupted before he could speak. "You set up the rules. If you don't follow the rules, you can't complain when others don't. So, I'm making it official." She stood at attention and spoke an age-old formula. "Sir, I relieve you."

He deflated and gave in to the inevitable.

Answering in the same way, he smiled, "I stand relieved, Commander Dearest. You have the con." When he thought no one was looking, he kissed her and left the bridge.

As they approached a rendezvous with the point in space the Astrometrics officer called Position Alpha, Kitty thought, *Simon is going to be pissed. But it* is *my shift*. Aloud, she ordered, "Helm, all ahead slow. On my mark, reverse engines and make us dead relative." The bridge was silent for a long minute until she said, "Mark. Report dead relative." Conversation returned to a low murmur as each station worked their minor miracles getting the ship ready to go back into standby.

At last, Helm reported. "Dead relative. Position Alpha acquired, ma'am."

A low cheer sounded on the bridge until she hit the all-ships. "Attention all hands, this is the first officer. It gives me great pleasure to report that we have reached position Alpha. Good job, one and all. Operations Officer, please report to the bridge as soon as possible. First Officer, out."

Kitty looked at the arm of her chair, pressed a combination of buttons that she had rehearsed several times, and the ship settled back into station-keeping mode. The vibrations that had become white noise made themselves known by their absence. Curiosity getting the better of her, she called up a view of Earth. All eyes went to the viewscreen as it came alive.

A small voice quavered, "It's not there!"

Kitty ordered, "Magnification ten, coordinates zero-zero." While the stars behind didn't seem to change size, the image on the main screen focused on the Earth/Moon system and zoomed in at a speed that made a few of the bridge crew mutter in awe. Centered on the screen was a large blue dot accompanied by a smaller white one.

Only the faintest of smiles betrayed Kitty's emotions as she congratulated herself for all the hours she'd spent with Stephen soaking up all she could about the environment she was going to be living and working in. It was difficult keeping up with all these young people eager to see their dreams come true. Her only recourse was to spend as much time as possible with the Science teams, learning as much as she could retain about the ship itself, as well as everything she could get her hands on about the asteroid belt. She felt like a teacher just one jump ahead of her students.

Unfortunately, not all the crew had had time to do more than learn one specific job. Looking over at her Helm officer, she said, "Think about just how far away we are, Commander Hill—over one hundred and forty million miles. Okay, team, secure all stations. It's time for the construction crews to take over."

As she shut her console down, Lt. Commander Donna Hill asked, "Where are all the asteroids, Commander?"

This time Kitty's smile broke through. Of the nine-hundred-plus people aboard, roughly ten percent were scientists of one kind or another. The remaining fraction was composed of the original thirty-five volunteers and all the contacts they'd made over the months it had taken to get the ship fully operational again—friends of theirs, and friends of theirs in ever-increasing circles. While almost all the volunteers knew something about space, having grown up in the 'space age' after all, some stereotypes still remained.

Kitty responded, "There's a lot of space out here, Commander. And as many as there are, most asteroids are pretty small—under a mile, in fact. It's not like the movies. I suggest you do some reading on the subject. You can download some material from the computer after you go off shift."

The young lieutenant commander took the suggestion seriously and replied in a quiet voice, "Yes, ma'am."

Stephen entered the bridge, deflecting Kitty's attention from the embarrassed junior officer. "Everything under control?" At her affirmative response, he winked and said, "Ma'am, I relieve you."

Kitty stood up, waved to the command chair, and replied, "Sir, I stand relieved. The bridge is yours."

The rest of Stephen's Flight Operations staff started arriving and Kitty waved her crew toward the door. "See you at the meeting this evening, Stephen. Break a leg."

Kitty walked into her quarters and found Simon sitting on the edge of their bed, reading over a sheaf of status reports. "Looks like the factories are all ready. And the flight crews are as ready as they can be without actual experience. Marshall, Johnson, and Quinn will be supervising crews for a while. According to Chief Engineer Baylor, the *Sundiver* will be dispatched within the hour. By the time it returns, we'll have the fuel plant finished for sure and a major dent made in the habitat section of Orion. Looks like you and I are out of work for a while. Want to learn to fly one of those fighters?

Kitty gave him an appraising look. "Sounds like fun. But I have something else in mind." He looked up just in time to see one hand unbuttoning her shirt. He never saw the one that turned out the lights.

The completion of the fuel plant was two weeks behind the original estimates. Nine hundred people don't all learn at the same rate, and it had taken time for a group of that size to learn to work as a team—actually a series of teams, or to be more precise, three sets of teams since the plants ran twenty-four hours a day. Simon forgot that in his effort to get the entire project up and running.

There were a great many things he and others hadn't considered, like how what they had could attract all the kinds of people they wanted—starry-eyed dreamers willing to take part in one of the greatest endeavors of all time just for the sake of being there—as well as the kinds they didn't want—those trying to escape from something or those working for interests other than those of most of the crew. Those were the ones who would, out of idealism, nationalism, fanaticism, or something entirely different, try to take the ship and fulfill visions of their own.

They tended to forget that most of these kids had grown up with some of the most sophisticated sci-fi scripts and graphics of all time and were damn near brain-washed from the beginning to think of life aboard a spaceship as regimented. The initial three months of recruitment had weeded out a lot of those who thought of the *Galileo* and Simon's plans for her as just a game or who weren't ready to commit themselves for whatever reason. All the way up until departure, there were those who'd said that it was all a hoax. Those were the very ones who wouldn't sign on and would be susceptible to inquiries from the various agencies detailed to look into the mass disappearances of so many people.

Another problem was the fact that not all of those who'd volunteered to work in the construction pods were able to do so. A significant number of people couldn't adjust to zero-gravity.

One of the original volunteers had an uncle in need of work, and when she approached him, the uncle managed to talk most of his crew, some twenty men in all—high-steel men—into coming along. Of course, this was after a suitably convincing courtesy visit by Gayle and Stephen's "smoke and mirrors." It was from this group that most of the pod jockeys had originally come. Used to working in high places, it was just another job to most of them. A welding torch was a welding torch, after all. It was just the location that had changed. Simon shook his head when he realized these men wouldn't be there if not for the fact that the year 2010 had brought more of what its predecessors had left behind—declining job-markets, inflation spiraling out of control, and the stock market dropping as war finally broke out in the Middle East.

The factories were busy turning out components on a twenty-four-hour basis but were still running below their projected optimums. The shuttles were flying far afield, scooping up small asteroids and dust into a type of force field that extended from each side of the vessel. The unloading process was simplicity itself. They merely stopped above the converter opening, turned off the force fields, and moved off. The tractor beams and lasers mounted around the rim of the huge hole would do the rest.

Several dozen green specks, the business ends of the pod thrusters, flitted around the installation as the finishing touches were being seen to. Completion of the plant was expected that evening, the last details of the fuel plant's docking port and some shielding over critical components being the last items on the checklist. The small satellite stationed nearby had already been activated so that the *Galileo* would have greater control of the docking procedure when the *Sundiver* returned from its trip through the corona of the sun.

Simon and the rest of the command staff decreed a twenty-four-hour day of rest. In an all-ships address, he commended the entire crew for their hard work, and in a private meeting with his senior officers and department heads, he said, "Tell your people to have a good time. Just make sure that the ones who have duty don't get crocked. Let them know their turn will come as soon as we get ourselves situated at Alpha-two."

Over the two months the *Galileo* had been in the belt, the daily and weekly progress report sessions had semi-officially become known as staff meetings. Who exactly started it, Simon never found out and would gladly have strangled the perpetrator. He left the latest meeting more than a little unsettled. His discomfiture was at the deference that he and Kitty seemed to be held in by the members of the crew. Gayle, and to a great degree, Stephen shared in this circumstance as well. His ingrained sense of keeping to the shadows warred with the necessity of keeping visible and visiting the various departments. Informal talks with section heads invariably filled in gaps in written reports.

It was on one of his inspection tours that he found advice from an unexpected direction. "Surround yourself with people who know what they're talking about, Simon. God knows, you can't do it all yourself," Gayle chastised. She took two steps to his one until she managed to get ahead of him and spun around to block him from going any further. She poked him hard in the chest with her finger to get his full attention, then shook it under his nose. "No boss can. Presidents have cabinets, CEOs have boards of advisers. Face it, friend," Gayle said, calling up stories Simon had told her of his Army life, "you're not a platoon sergeant anymore."

The two friends walked into Simon's private office and sat down. The meeting they had just left dealt mostly with the adjustments people were having to make to work in the new environment and the close living conditions. It had been an emotionally draining experience for Simon. He still felt that there were better people for the job than he.

"No, no, no," Gayle said, wagging her finger. Now that she finally felt that she knew the full background of the husband of her lifelong friend, she somehow felt more at ease in his presence. "While I get some of the spotlight, it's you and Kitty who seem to have become the focus of everyone on board. You are, after all, The Captain, and these kids are romantics all the way through. Not to mention a bunch of totally indoctrinated sci-fi nerds." Gayle held up her hand, stopping Simon from protesting. "I mean that in the best possible way, of course." Her grin was matched by the first smile Simon had shown in hours. "These are just the kind of people we need out here right now. Idealists, dreamers, crazy fools willing to risk their lives to live in a sci-fi series. Just like you and me."

"But why me, Gayle?" Simon asked plaintively. "I sit in those meetings week after week and those people look at me like I have all the answers. And I don't! Sure, we decided a male figure-head was better at first, but it could just as easily have been Kitty. You two found Stephen. It took all four of us to get the first group aboard. Stephen got the scientists, and those kids as you call them, brought the vast majority of these people aboard themselves. So why me?"

The answer he got stunned him. As much by content as by its source. "Because every great endeavor needs something or someone to personify it. In this case it's Captain Hawke and Commander Kitty. You're it and that's all there is to it. Besides, you don't have to do it all alone. You've already got your staff in place. Use it, Simon. Let the people who have made it their business to learn about specific aspects of this ship tell you what they know, then you decide what to do with the information. That's the job of a captain, isn't it?"

Simon struggled to find a response to Gayle's argument. With a shrug and wry smile, he finally accepted the inevitable. "What would I do without the women in my life? I never knew you were so insightful."

Having cleared out a couple million cubic miles of space, it was taking longer to get material to *Galileo*, so the factories were shutting down. There were only a few things left to install anyway, so even fewer factory units were needed at the last. Then, for safety reasons, the ship would move some millions of miles away to build the actual dock. If something should go wrong with the fuel plant, no one wanted the *Galileo* or the slowly growing base anywhere near it. Dr. Harmon was sure the blast, if there was one, would be easily detectable on Earth.

Lt. Commander Lucy Grimes, officer in charge of the third shift as much by luck as catching the captain's and Commander Kitty's attention during the initial interviews, squirmed uneasily in the command chair and punched in the sequence that brought the ship to life. She glanced at the first officer, who was watching from one corner of the bridge.

"Don't look at me, Commander," Kitty said. "You have the con. I'm just along for the ride."

The young commander faced forward, keyed up all-ships, and with a quiver in her voice said, "All hands, this is the bridge. Secure all stations. Prepare for acceleration." She shut off the intercom and, giving herself a mental shake, ordered, "Helm, set course for Alpha-two. All ahead slow."

Commander Kitty left the bridge shortly after they got underway, and Lucy spent the next three hours coaxing the giant ship into just the right position. She would normally have two more hours on her shift, but since they'd arrived at their destination and gone back to standby, she called Stephen to the bridge and turned the ship over to him.

Lucy had only moved the ship about ten million miles, but she was sweating by the time she put the ship back on standby.

Only ten million miles! she thought. *That's what? Four hundred times around the Earth? We're going to have to find a whole new way to think about our universe.*

Afterward, she returned to her quarters, showered, changed, and made her way to the junior officer's rec room on deck two, sinking into one of the lounge chairs with an audible sigh. At twenty-two, she was the youngest officer to sit in the command chair by quite a few years, and she felt as if people were looking at her all the time, judging. Eyes closed, she sat without a thought about what was going on around her until she heard someone sit down heavily next to her.

Looking over through one slitted eye, she saw her shift second, Rob Greene, looking at her with a worried frown on his face.

"You're too tense, boss. Why don't you go see 'Chiko? She'll work those knots out and you'll be able to relax." Rob and Michiko Greene were one of the few married couples aboard. Rob was Lucy's Science officer, a few years her senior, while Michiko was second shift Nav officer. 'Chiko, as she liked to be called off shift, was a five-foot-one bundle of Asian dynamite with the ability to massage knots out of a steel bar. They'd both been at the DenverCon and were among the first group Stephen and Gayle had recruited, along with most of the rest of the bridge crews.

"What I'd rather have is a long, long soak in a hot tub, Rob. But, thanks. I just might do that."

As they sat there, the rest of her team began to filter in. They were led by Virginia Wade, who peeled off, grabbed a couple of pots of coffee from the food processor—now regularly producing a variety of beverages thanks to the science types—and poured all around before landing in a chair of her own.

"Thanks, Ginny," Lucy said gratefully. Then she turned back to the group as a whole. "Okay, team, we have business to discuss. This came up at the last staff meeting, and the captain would like all the input he can get. We didn't have much time for it to become a problem with the fuel station, but we're going to be here for six months or so, trapped in an oversized tin can. What can we do to keep from going stir crazy?"

"How about some kind of sports?" This from Helm, David Sipes.

"Sure, Dave," Virginia mocked. "Just tell us, what sport do you know that fits our space—no pun intended—limitations? We want something that requires teams so we can involve as many people as we can, don't we?"

Dave looked hesitant. "Well, I managed to bring a basketball aboard, so we could build a few nets. We've got enough height down on deck eighteen, but that won't give enough people something to do. A lot of folks don't like basketball for some strange reason. How about something that uses the ball with new rules for our particular circumstances?"

"Let's hear what Rob has to say. He's sitting there with a mile-wide grin on his face and not one word coming out of his mouth," commented Mustafa Morgan, third shift weapons officer. "He sure looks like the cat that got into the cream to me."

Lucy set her cup down and slowly turned her chair around to face her shift second. Draping her legs over one arm, she stared pointedly at her second officer. "If you've got something, you'd better spill it. I'd hate to send you back to 'Chiko in little pieces, Rob."

As everyone's attention turned toward him, Rob raised his hands in defeat. "Okay! I give up. It was Dave's comment about height that helped me put some things together. 'Chiko and I spent a lot of time exploring the ship early on. We've got a place to go play, people. And I'm about to give it the old Greene twist. Come with me and don't ask any questions."

No amount of threatening could get him to open up. Lucy sighed and climbed out of her chair. "This better be good, Rob. If it turns out to be a joke, you'll wish you'd kept your mouth shut, I promise you!"

A crooked grin split his face. "Trust me. If this doesn't get your imaginations going, then you're all dead from the neck up! Besides," he said in a mock-hurt voice, "you insisted, so don't blame me if you don't like it." He stood in the doorway and looked back. "Motivate yourselves for ten minutes. We'll either be heroes to the crew, or Captain Hawke and Commander Kitty will have our heads for trophies. You, too, 'Stafa. We've got to stay together on this. United front and all that. A team, remember?" With a mysterious glint in his eye, he headed for the elevator and the rest strung out behind.

Deck eighteen was an open space twenty-six feet high, eight hundred feet wide and twenty-seven hundred feet long, starting at the nose of the ship and running all the way back to the forward engine room bulkhead. Most people thought the oversized deck was for storage of parts waiting to be taken to another location. The five hundred feet beneath deck seventeen shared a bulkhead with the habitat section above, effectively making two rooms out of the space. It was to the smaller section that Rob Greene led his shiftmates.

"This place is almost ten and a half million cubic feet, guys," Robert said. "And I know how to use it. Just follow your Uncle Rob, and you won't regret it. I hope."

They trooped out of the elevator and Rob shepherded them to the center of the huge room. Their voices echoed in the cavernous emptiness.

"Just stand there. I'll be right back." Raising his voice as he headed to a far wall, he explained, "'Chiko and I use this level for jogging. Totally empty. We figure it was used for storage of manufactured parts by the aliens. Anyway, on to part two." At this point, he had reached the wall. The distance was too great for anyone to see what he'd done, but a panel popped open, revealing a control board with glowing status lights.

"Let your imaginations fly, guys. And why don't you fly, too?" With this comment, the gravity cut off like a light bulb and he twisted in the air, braced his feet on the wall, and pushed off straight toward them, gliding along about a foot above the deck. At the last second, he tucked his knees to his chest, wrapped his arms around his lower legs, and did a creditable imitation of a bowling ball picking up a spare. Bodies scattered haphazardly, and he drifted to the opposite wall amid loud and inventive curses. "Think about the possibilities. Zero-G sports! Get creative!" He used his arms and legs to absorb the shock of hitting the wall and spun around, floating about a foot from the wall. Watching his teammates founder around, he laughed, "Been there. Done that!"

Reactions were varied. 'Stafa sat Buddha-style, floating upside-down in relation to the deck, while Velma fruitlessly tried to swim. David reached the ceiling, tried to grab a projection, missed, and drifted off at a new angle.

Virginia groaned, "I think I'm gonna be sick!"

Lucy finally yelled, "Aha! Thank you, Professor Weston!" Those who could looked her way in alarm. Their eyes widened as she turned her back to the wall with the open panel, took off one shoe, and threw it away from her. This gave her a small amount of momentum toward the wall panel. That shoe was followed by the rest of her clothes, one piece at a time.

It was a totally naked Lucy Grimes who finally reached the panel "Uncle Rob" had opened. Studying it for a moment, she pressed a button and slowly slid a lever about halfway from the bottom to the top. As she did, her team, along with her widely scattered clothes, slowly drifted to the floor as weight returned. As everyone was getting to their feet, they were startled by the sound of clapping.

Velma, closest to the elevator, saw who was standing there. "Oh, my God! Captain on deck!"

Everyone, including a very red, very naked, Lucy Grimes, came to attention. Simon and Kitty stood just outside the elevator door, and Simon's back was to the room as he inspected the call panel.

"At ease, people," Kitty ordered, a grin plastered on her face. "Get your clothes on, Commander. Some of you help her get them together. By the way, who is

Professor Weston?"

Lucy began to get her clothes on, aided by her team. "Ma'am, he was my physics professor. One of Newton's laws of motion—I forget which number— is that for every action there is an equal and opposite reaction, or something like that. It just made sense." With shirt and pants on, shoes in hand, she stood there, head down.

Kitty tapped Simon on the arm, and he turned around. "That was quick thinking on your part, Commander," Simon said carefully. "No one else on your team thought of it. I think posting you to commander of third shift was a good idea. Now, how did you people figure this out?"

Rob Greene stepped forward, intentionally trying to deflect attention away from Lucy. "Sir, my wife and I thought the area would be ideal for jogging, to keep in shape. One off-shift, we saw one of the little service robots open the panel and check the settings or something. After it left, we looked at the panel and figured out what it was for. It was a remark by Commander Grimes that made me put it together. She said we needed to figure out something to keep people from going nuts out here. I brought the team down and showed them. I had an idea that we could come up with some kind of Zero-G sport for the crew to get involved in, helping prevent boredom. I was just starting to tell 'em my idea when you showed up. May I ask, sir, how you happened to be here?"

Simon answered, "It's not anything supernatural, Commander Greene. Commander Hawke and I happened to be on the bridge going through some ship schematics when the gravity went off down here. If we'd been looking at something other than the habitat section, we'd never have known anything was going on. We came to see what the problem was and got here just in time to hear Commander Grimes thank her professor. That's all."

Kitty got a thoughtful look on her face. "I think you have something there, Commander Greene. Personally, I like it. Why don't you go brainstorm it and see what you can come up with? Involve the other shifts and departments, too. The more the merrier. Submit your proposals to your shift commanders, and they can pass them on to us." She glanced at Simon before continuing. "We'll offer a prize or something for best idea. We can get more people involved that way, I think." She laid a hand on Simon's arm and started to turn to go but spun back as another thought struck her. "And, Commander, any more discoveries of this magnitude are to be reported immediately. "Understood?"

Rob nodded vigorously as Simon and Kitty disappeared behind an elevator door.

Stephen leaned back in his chair, regarding Simon and Kitty almost gleefully. "This looks to be very interesting. As a matter of fact, I think I'll submit a proposal of my own."

Kitty made a face at him. "I'm coming to know you pretty well, Stephen, but for the life of me, I don't have a clue. What do you have in mind?"

He ran his hands through his hair. "Just putting some things together. One of the engineering teams found a weapons locker yesterday. It contained hand weapons and longer-range, rifle-shaped ones, as well as a few heavier weapons. Those come with a backpack power supply, and I suspect they're some type of portable plasma cannon or particle beam."

Stephen shifted in his chair as two sets of eyes gazed at him unpleasantly. He went on quickly. "The find was on the docket for tomorrow morning's briefing, but I did have time to check out the weapons and put them under a security lock. The pistols and rifles are variable-strength lasers. We tested those, very carefully, I might add. We'll wait awhile before we test the ones with the backpacks." He doodled unconsciously. "The rifles and pistols have internal power sources. If we make a few dozen pistols that can't do anything more than emit a harmless beam of light and add some body sensors, we can have something like the laser tag of a few years back. Throw in some large balloons that will drift in the air currents of a Zero-G environment, and there you have it. There could be teams of four or five, and the winner would be the team that kills all the rest. There could be eliminations, play-offs, trophies for the winners, all that."

Kitty clapped her hands. "I love it! If one of the crew can come up with that, let's give them the credit, though. I think it would be good for morale. Maybe we should have a competition for the best ideas. Eventually, after we get more ships, we can have an all-ships competition. What do you think, Simon?"

He made a gun out of his thumb and forefinger. "I think you and I better be on the same team. I know how good a shot you are. Does that answer your question?"

A week later, game fever had taken full control.

During that same time, long-range scans reported receiving the *Sundiver's* return signal. Stephen, as ops officer, ordered a recon flight to oversee the docking from a safe distance, of course. The flight was scheduled to leave in a week, and, as the shuttles were all involved with factory supply, it would be the fighters making their first extended trip away from the *Galileo*. Simon was spending a part of each shift training for the flight. He had put himself under the same regimen as the rest of the hopefuls and would have to qualify in the top three to get assigned to the mission.

CHAPTER FOURTEEN

After the incident with the gravity control, Simon sat down with his inner circle and had a talk. The two months building the fuel depot had been the shakedown cruise for the fledgling spacemen, and at first it had seemed like things had gotten done more by accident than on purpose. As time went by and nothing blew up in their faces, the various members of the crew began to mesh as teams worked toward a common goal. The newness of their situation, combined with having to learn new skills and coming to grips with the fact that this was no science-fiction show, took almost all the time and energy anyone had to spare.

Television and movies pirated from Earth satellites and beamed to the huge construction vessel helped fill the few empty spaces, but now that the ship had reached its final destination, more people were going to have a lot more spare time on their hands.

"That's what I want to avoid," Simon opined as he took his seat at the table. "Spare time is not a good thing when so many people live so closely together. We need to find something that will redirect the excess energy that comes with hand-to-hand combat into something more suitable to spare time."

Kitty nodded her agreement. "I've got an idea that this thing with Zero-G will figure in very prominently. But whatever it turns out to be in the end, a diversion of some kind is going to be needed."

Stephen picked up a pen and aimlessly scratched it over the pad in front of him. "I think we need to go a step farther than that, Simon," he said hesitantly. When Simon faced his way, Stephen continued. "I think these engineering updates should be released to the crew in general. At least part of 'em," he said before Simon could voice a protest. "Maybe not the technical details, but the fact of their existence. I think we need the imaginations of everyone on board to come up with the innovations we need to make this a going concern for humans."

Stephen leaned forward, body language conveying his intense interest in the subject. "For example, just last week one of the groups I'm overseeing came up with a way to manipulate the capture fields. I know, we can do that already. The shuttles, and to a lesser degree, the fighters, can pick up asteroids and drop them off at the converter, and it grabs them and pulls them into itself. What this bunch did was to find a way to use them *inside* the lower deck. Now a shuttle can enter the main hold and load or unload anywhere without the necessity of maneuvering on its own. We can have a field operator pick it up and move it to whatever position we want."

"That's a good use of resources, Stephen," Simon said, "but I don't see how that applies to allowing the junior staff and the rest of the crew in on what gets found or discovered."

Stephen shook his head. "You don't have the whole story, yet. Two days later, these guys are playing around with the effects of their research, moving this and that from here to there, and one of the crew down on eighteen for whatever reason stopped to watch. It was her comment that got the guys off on another tangent. She asked why it wasn't possible to turn the field sideways and use it for see-through doors over the exterior hatches. Forty-eight hours later, there are several generators down on eighteen, and they've shut off a section of the deck." He went into lecture mode. "The procedure we follow right now is to move equipment ready to be incorporated into the dock down to eighteen, close off the deck, and pump the air out. Then we can open the hatches and the construction pods come in and haul all the stuff out. We reseal the hatches, pump the air back in, and start all over."

Simon waved his hand dismissively. "I know all that. Where is this going?"

"It's going to man's basic nature to do things the easy way, Simon," Stephen said. "We—and I say we because by this time I was as involved as anyone else—can make that field selectively permeable. We can get it to pass metal, but not air molecules. Glass, or what passes for glass, but not anything else. Or just program it not to pass just two items, like, say, air or a body, which is really several different items, and we can push all that equipment out the side of the ship and the pods can pick it up there without depressurizing the hold at all."

"That's a lot of time and effort saved," Kitty said appreciatively. "I wonder why the original builders never thought of it."

"We may never know, Kitty," Stephen admitted. "But the point is that we can use the input of everybody to find new uses for some of the things we see around us. Restrict the information to too small a group and we're bound to miss a lot."

"Agreed," Simon said after listening to Kitty and Stephen for a bit. "Let's start easy, though. We already have morning staff meetings to lay out the day's general orders."

He'd finally embraced the full concept of making the *Galileo* a quasi-military organization, knowing Kitty's reservations about any military in general, and had adopted as much of the military lexicon as would fit their situation. Where necessary, he innovated.

"We also have weekly staff meetings to discuss progress and problems. Let's set up a site on the computer where people can go to see what we've discovered so far and how we use it, allowing them to make suggestions for other uses—a bulletin board that gets looked at on a regular basis. Stephen, it's your job to oversee setting up the site. You can conscript anyone you need to help with data input. That will help ease the boredom problem a little.

"Ladies and gentlemen," Simon said to the various department heads, standing up to signal the end of the meeting, "let each of your people know about this. I want everyone looking for new ways to enhance our capabilities."

The chain of command that had developed almost of its own accord surprised Simon when he mapped it out one night. Effectively, there were two distinct and separate crews aboard the great ship. One was the operations crew, responsible for the daily operation of the ship in flight mode. The other was the construction crew, responsible for getting the factory section running and the completed parts funneled out to the construction site where the pod jockeys assembled them into a functioning fuel plant, space dock, or whatever.

The factory section had a foreman/chief engineer heading up the construction project. The job of directing the huge spaceborne factory complex was normally directed from an office Simon had found on one of his trips around the ship, but Flight Control operated from the bridge communications console and Daniel Baylor, Chief Engineer and production foreman of the construction process, could often be found there. He had developed into Simon's alternate, taking control of the ship when it was in construction mode, even so far as having the ship moved when a particular section of the belt was mined out. On those rare occasions, he called Simon, Kitty, or Lucy Grimes and their on-duty bridge crew to settle the ship into a new location.

Staff meetings became increasingly more complex as time went on, to Simon's consternation. Whenever possible, all three shift commanders from the operations crew were present, often with their seconds. Also present would be the heads of Engineering, Computer, Life Sciences, Astrogation, and Flight Control, along with their seconds. Navigation and her second would be along when the need for moving the ship was to be considered. If everyone attended, they would constitute a fair-sized group, so normally the only time a second would show up would be to replace a busy senior officer, keeping the meetings to a manageable size.

This particular meeting coincided with the

completion of the fuel station and would deal in part with the movement of the *Galileo* to its new location for the pièce de résistance—the six-month construction of the space dock Orion—so everyone and their seconds planned to attend. Kitty had scheduled the meeting to be held in a mess hall on deck three, allowing everyone some breathing space. A few of the attendees had had little prior experience with Simon, so Kitty wanted the extra space to allow those who felt less comfortable a slight remove to indulge themselves.

Simon waited until the last arrival was seated and stood up. "I want to thank all of you for being here, and I'd like to get right to business. It has been brought to my attention that we need to have more people in on some aspects of the decision-making processes. We have two distinct and separate divisions aboard this ship—those whose job it is to run the ship, and those whose job it is to build the new dock. We also have the distinctions of more-or-less military versus civilian, male versus female, younger versus older, religious versus nonreligious, and any other differences that come to mind. These divisions are not being enumerated to cause any problems, but rather to highlight the fact that we have a lot of diversity here, and we need to take advantage of it. Different people think in different ways and see the world from slightly different perspectives. That's why I am so insistent on everybody sharing information."

Simon looked out at the sea of faces before him. "In six more months, we'll be done here, and some of us will go home. I hope most of you will choose to stay on, filling the roles of teachers for the next wave of volunteers. I believe there will be a problem for those who do leave us, and that's going to be with our government."

Simon looked down at Kitty, who found herself suddenly very interested in the notes on her pad. Finding no help from that quarter, he forged on, hoping he wasn't stepping on too many toes.

"So far, it seems that most people have the idea that we're coming out here to build something and go home. Nothing could be further from the truth. We're here to establish a permanent deep-space presence, and not the haphazard type of thing going on in Earth-orbit."

Several looks of confusion and a couple of downright anger greeted his statement.

"I said haphazard, and I meant it. Look at what we have back there. Several governments are putting people into space, trying to gain an advantage over the others. It's only recently that we've seen any cooperation between nations to get the International Space Station up and running, and actually damned little of that And what will this bold endeavor allow? A paltry half-dozen scientists at a time to go up at incredible expense to perform experiments that won't have any effect on the planet for years. Letting those in power know what we're building out here will put a halt to those projects eventually, and the funds currently being funneled to them can be redirected to other programs as we eventually take over the extraplanetary component of humanity for the foreseeable future."

The confused looks had faded, and the angry looks had morphed into confusion.

"Once we reveal ourselves to the world at large,

that is. The government already has some knowledge of us. This group is going to be our think tank. You are the best of the people we've recruited so far. There will be other recruits, to be sure, and some will be brighter and smarter, but your advantage is that you're the first. You won't be the last, and you'll have to work to keep that advantage, but that's what's going to make this such a great opportunity for everyone."

Simon looked at Kitty again and saw that she had boldly written the word, "Yes!" on her pad. Heartened, he went on.

"I've asked you here today because, as individuals, you each see situations differently. The discoveries we make aboard this ship will impact all of us immediately and directly, and sooner or later, every member of the human race. It's going to be your input that will help determine which directions we take at different points in time. Stephen, would you repeat the example you gave me?"

Stephen stood up and related the story of the crewman and the shields, finishing up with a plea. "It's going to take the combined minds of everyone on board to figure out the applications to which a lot of our discoveries and innovations can be put. It's therefore necessary for everyone to become familiar with these concepts."

Simon had started to get back up when a raised hand in the back of the room caught his attention, and he recognized Navigation's second, nodding for him to speak.

"Sir, Lt. Commander Jeremy Hoke. Some of us spend a lot of time discussing the... political ramifications of our situation. Will that be something we discuss here?"

Simon nodded, smiling. "Yes, Commander, it is. Along with anything else that affects us—crew morale, discipline, disciplinary actions, personal problems, personnel problems. You name it; we can discuss it, and hopefully come to a decision that will be acceptable to everyone."

He hesitated for a second, and his expression went carefully blank before continuing. "But don't let it go to your heads. This is not a democracy! It can't be. Only one person makes the final decisions, at least for the indeterminate future. My vision is for a new segment of the human race, for a while anyway. There's no doubt that we need the Earth for recruits, for vacations, for retirement—if things get that far— for raw materials we can't get out here, and any number of other things. Plus, that's where most of us have families, not to mention that Earth is genetically coded into us. I don't think we'll ever escape a need for Earth. And the people in power back there are going to have to come to the realization that they need us and what we'll shortly be able to provide.

"We'll be hounded," he predicted, "coerced, pressured, intimidated, and bullied to give up what we've found and gained. And all so one regime can expand its sphere of influence over another. It's my opinion that we need to see to it that the balance of power on Earth be kept as it is and not tipped one way or the other by the ownership of this vessel and its knowledge. It's to that end that I've decided it will stay out of earthbound hands and stay in ours. The cost of doing anything else is just too high."

Simon noticed a young brunette raise her hand. *Damn! So many of them are so young*! he thought.

When did that happen? I didn't get married until I was older than these kids. Aloud, he said, "Yes, Commander?"

"Miranda Lee, sir, Flight Control," the woman responded. She had an odd look on her face, and it took Simon a minute to see both reluctance and determination warring there. Determination won. "Sir, I've spent more time listening to these discussions than getting into them, but it seems to me that I'm involved. How can we possibly stand against Earth?"

"Good question, Commander," Simon said. "The answer is really simple if you take two things into consideration. One is that we have the right to say no, and the other is that we have the power to enforce it. Aside from the fact that we can build ships and docks, we can come and go as we wish, undetectable by radar and at speeds they can't match. And if you haven't already figured it out, that last one means that we're now essentially UFOs."

A nervous titter ran around the room for a second before Lucy Grimes' second spoke up. "What about our families and friends, sir? We've already seen how governments react to threats, and this one is going to scare the sh—I mean, well…"

Kitty took pity on Simon and fielded this new question. "Commander Greene, isn't it?" At his nod, she went on. "This is a time in the history of the human race like no other. The Greeks, Hannibal, Napoleon, Hitler, Genghis Khan, Pol Pot and others whose names I'll never remember all wanted to control the world, or at least that portion of it that they knew existed at the time. And look what happened to them. The big question is *why* it happened to them, and the answer is fear, which we have going against us, I admit, but those people didn't have this ship. And they didn't have our motivation. Theirs was and always will be to dominate everything around them. We want to give all of this to the world as soon as possible, making it a better place for every nation—which, by the way, will be measured in years rather than the decades we figure it would take if we turned her over. To directly answer your concerns about friends and family, I'd say that they're going to take some heat, yes, as the government tries to get a handle on us. It's just a fact of life that we'll have to deal with until we can make them understand."

Kitty had come to her feet and caught herself before she started to pace. "But—and this is the part that you'll have to take my word for—they won't take heat for long because they aren't part of this. Our system, the one we left behind and will someday return to, is basically sound. Internments of Japanese and Germans in World War II and other transgressions have happened and will again, quite probably in this case as well, but the outcry of the common people will put a stop to it. Especially when we go public and start releasing some of the technology. One of the conditions of sharing that technology will be that anyone being held in connection with us be released. With the abilities this ship gives us, we'll be able to make sure that everyone on the planet knows what's happening, and one thing I can say for sure is that wrongdoing just can't stand up to the light."

Lucy walked into the rec room. Two weeks had

passed since her embarrassing encounter on deck eighteen. The funny thing was that not one word had come back to her about it—nothing from the captain or Commander Kitty, nothing from her bridge team, and no rumors or snide comments from the rest of the crew. The dread with which she'd started meeting each day began to fade as time went by, and now she walked confidently.

Rumor had it that David Sipes was in the running for his soccer idea, as well as Rob Greene, who'd been in close consultation with Commander Walker for days. His was the one she secretly hoped would win, even not knowing what it was, because it would bring prestige to the shift. Of course, several other ideas were on the table, too, so anything was still possible, but one could always hope.

She looked around and found that third shift had commandeered one corner of the room and were holding a chair for her. She sank gratefully into it and groaned.

"I think I spent too many hours in that damned fighter. And whoever had it out before me doesn't know how to change socks!"

Glancing at the other team members, Rob walked around behind her and began to knead her shoulders. "You need to take a break, boss. And, speaking for all of us, we have a surprise for you. Come on."

Lucy shuddered. "I think I'll pass. Your last surprise is still too painful to think about."

The team laughed good-naturedly. "No, boss. This one is from all of us. Do a favor and play along, okay?" Ginny begged.

"Oh, all right. But it better be good!"

Ginny grabbed one hand and Mustafa the other, and they pulled her groaning, protesting body to its feet. They led her to a door she didn't remember being there a few days before.

Marcus Randall, security officer of the team, whipped out a cloth and blindfolded her.

"Hey! What's this?" she cried as she was propelled through the door that had been opened after her eyes were covered.

"A surprise, boss. A couple of the guys down in fabrication and reproduction owed me big time," bragged David, "so I called 'em on it. Okay, take a look."

Lucy removed the blindfold and gasped.

"Yep," Velma confirmed, "the only hot tub on the ship at the moment, and it's all yours, for the next hour, at least. After that, there's a waiting list, I hear. But you have the privilege of being first, so we'll just leave you alone."

Marcus was the last to leave, and he pointed to the door. "The door unlocks about five minutes after the warning light and buzzer comes on, so don't let any grass grow under your feet when your time's up."

Lucy's ability to move returned about the time her body started to rid itself of the effects of the surprise just handed her. A slow grin spread over her face and her hands began to pull off her shirt almost of their own volition. For the next hour, all thoughts not connected with pure animal relaxation banished themselves from her mind.

All except one. All her life she could remember a sense of knowing that her future was preordained. Now the heat and water acted like drugs, focusing her mind on a thought—that the place she found herself in sure added another dimension to her universe. A small smile at her own wit was soon followed by a light frown as her mind free-associated the possible futures that lay ahead, and she shivered at the fear she finally recognized at her core.

CHAPTER FIFTEEN

Simon fired up the systems on the sleek little fighter and held it in neutral, calling Flight Control. "Control, this is Fighter One. Status green. Prepared for launch." Sensors told him that the air was being removed from the bay and that when the doors opened, a gentle pressure on the control yoke would move him out into space. He was aware that, if necessary, the doors could be opened almost instantly, wasting the air and allowing the fighter to exit the bay much faster. As the door finished sliding out of the way, he caressed the accelerator, watching the bay slide past him. After clearing the bay, he angled the little ship slightly so the drive field wouldn't cause any damage to the hull. Moments later, he was in a loose formation with the other two fighters. Lucy Grimes flew one. The other was under the control of a man Simon had met only a few times before. Dieter Rausch was an ensign from one of Chief Baylor's manufacturing crews. Apparently, he was a natural pilot. He'd out-scored Simon in every way despite all of Simon's practice. Lucy had finished a close third.

The three pilots would be in their cockpits for the next twelve hours, flying to the site of the fuel plant and back, plus the time onsite observing the docking. They flew just above the plane in which the asteroids orbited. Fighters, being smaller craft, had correspondingly shorter scan ranges, so it took a while to come into range of the fuel plant's transponder. They spent the first five hours in straight-line flight until Ensign Rausch, who was leading at the time, reported receiving a signal from the fuel plant. Stephen had had Engineering reconfigure the transponders of all vessels and installations to operate on a frequency that was unlikely to be discovered by unwelcome visitors making anything less than a full scan of the system. They continued to fly sunward until the *Sundiver's* signal was picked up.

Simon and his companions cautiously flew into visual range of the automated shuttle. Engineering had replaced almost the entire surface of the squat, ugly vessel in preparation for its first trip into Earth's primary, but one would never know that from the sight that greeted the three pilots. The effects of its trip had left it looking much as it had when he'd first seen it in *Galileo's* launch bay—armor plating warped, projections melted, and a section of plating missing. His sensors detected a wobble in the drive field, and a small antenna projecting from the hole left by the missing plate was the source of the signal they homed in on. They followed the stubby vessel until it finally mated with the plant, and Simon turned his ship toward the *Galileo*.

"Okay, folks, mission accomplished. Let's go home," he said.

Lucy was leading the flight as the fuel plant disappeared behind them. Simon signaled to her, "Commander Grimes, report."

Seconds later, Lucy answered, "Yes, sir?"

Laughing into his headset, Simon accelerated past her. "Tag, you're it!" Watching his instruments, he saw both of the other ships traveling together. First, one sped up, followed almost immediately by the other.

"Hey! Wait a minute! How can we tag each other in spaceships?"

Dieter answered first. "You don't need to tag, Commander. All you have to do is pass one of us."

The three fighters slid into their bays, and technicians began to go over the ships as the pilots went their separate ways. Simon found Stephen and reported on the success of the *Sundiver's* mission, Dieter went back to his department, and Lucy was off to shower, change, and head to the rec room.

On a ship the size of the *Galileo*, as in any enclosed environment starved for any information or diversion, news traveled fast. By the time Lucy arrived in the rec room, almost every junior officer not actively on shift, and a few that were, had crowded in to welcome her back. Most she didn't know, but by now she realized that any excuse to party was a good excuse. Virginia sidled through the crowd and pressed a beer into her hand.

"Where'd this come from?" Lucy whispered incredulously. "We're going to get so busted."

"Not even. Special dispensation from Commander Kitty," Virginia retorted. "There are three parties going on right now, and one of them is for the captain. Commander Kitty gave the word to unlock the food processors' restricted levels enough to allow beer for tonight, so we're having the first kegger in space in your honor." Virginia stepped up on a chair, pulled a protesting Lucy up on another, and addressed the room. "Ladies and gentlemen—if there are any present—our guest of honor, Lt. Commander Lucy Grimes! Queen of the asteroid racers!"

Cheers shook the walls, glasses were lifted (and spilled), and Lucy's mouth dropped open. "What... how?" she spluttered incredulously.

Rob and Michiko appeared out of the crowd.

"Let me guess, Lucy. You forgot that the *Galileo* has much better sensors than those puny fighters," 'Chiko said. "We kept track of your entire trip, especially your return flight. Word got out and everyone on board started betting on the winner. I don't think anyone was more interested than Commander Kitty. Actually, I think 'pissed' is much more accurate. I sure wouldn't like to be in the captain's shoes right now."

Lucy paled in horror as she stepped down off the chair.

Rob grinned. "Lighten up, boss. Rumor has it that Commander Kitty is only upset with the captain for starting it. For once, the first officer gets to pin back the ears of the captain, not that we lowly junior officers will ever hear what she has to say. All you did was follow the captain's lead. The fact that it turned into an all-out race isn't exactly your fault. The fact that you won, now, that's a matter for celebration. You're an official hero to all the folks in this room!"

The *Galileo* had been on-station for just over a month now, and the habitat section of Earth's first deep-space station was nearing completion. Another week would see that finished, followed by two more for power generation, and then the pressure of so many people living so closely together could be alleviated by moving a large number aboard the new facility. At that point, work on the actual dock assembly would begin. The factories that weren't involved in the habitat section were turning out some of the larger assemblies that would go into the dock proper. By far and away the largest of those was a duplicate of the smelter. It was half finished already and floating in position trailing the habitat, as were several dozen other modules that were scheduled to be installed at different times during the construction project, not to mention three new stripped-down shuttles and twenty-four new construction pods. The shuttles were for feeding the smelter, and the pods were to handle the actual construction of new ships after the *Galileo* returned to Earth. Projections said four more months after the habitat section was done and they could head back to Earth.

Simon was going over reports with Stephen in the ready room. "Dr. Penn says injuries are up. Nothing major so far, but he says it's only a matter of time. These games are the main problem, of course. Stopping them would start a mutiny, so what can we do?"

Stephen tossed his pen onto the table. "You said it yourself—mutiny if we try to stop it. So, I have a suggestion." Simon looked up from his reports expectantly. "Do the only thing you can, Simon." Stephen took off his shirt with a vicious grin, revealing a series of laser sensors. "You can show your support for the sport if not for Walker's Wildsiders. Exhibition games start in about an hour."

Simon shook his head in resignation. He had to show support. After his little screwup with racing back to the ship like a teenager with a new hot rod, Kitty would never let him hear the end of it if he didn't. Plus, one of the teams in the first exhibition was Kitty's Kommandos.

He slapped the table with one hand. "Of course I'll show support, Stephen. And, privately, I hope the Kommandos wipe the deck with your butts." Turning the conversation back to the construction of the base, he asked, "So, when do we need to fire up the fuel plant?"

"All the material is in place," Stephen said. "We can send the signal any time. That way we can send a ship out to tow the finished fuel cell and send the *Sundiver* back for installation as soon as power generation is completed."

The game forgotten for the moment, the two men lost themselves a bit longer with deciding how to handle some of the minutia that constantly threatened to take all the fun out of having a spaceship.

Simon changed from his uniform to something less conspicuous, feeling that he needed to appear at the games in an informal capacity. Deck eighteen, forward, had been transformed into an arena. Cables had been strung from floor to ceiling in a random pattern, some of which had four-foot plastic (or something like plastic) balls suspended from them at different levels. About three dozen other balls lay around the arena. One end of the room near the gravity control panel had been walled off by some clear material put out by one of the factories. Cables were strung in an orderly pattern for spectators to anchor themselves once the gravity was turned off.

The rules were simple—kill your opponent by hitting the proper sensors. Some sensors caused an arm or leg to be immobilized. The sensors would light up with a reddish glow, and if it was for an arm or leg, one of the three referees would disallow that limb's use. There were five players to a team, no substitutions after the game started, and no quarter until one team was dead.

The gravity was still on when Simon found a place among the nearly two hundred fifty spectators in the gallery, some of whom were in laser-tag garb. He saw Lt. Commander Grimes and her team off to one side, wearing what looked like bathrobes, for crying out loud. They were in one of the later exhibitions, he supposed. As he waited for the first match, Kitty slipped into the space beside him.

"We're in the fifth match," she explained.

He looked her up and down in surprise. Her flat-black outfit could have been painted on, and sensors were strapped to various parts of her anatomy. Kitty chuckled merrily. "Gayle is something of a seamstress, you know. And she had a field day with this new fabric." She pirouetted beside him. "See something you like, big fella?"

Simon was saved from answering by three men in traditional referee's stripes walking out onto the arena floor. One blew two short blasts on a whistle, consulted a clipboard, and announced, "We need the first two teams in the arena immediately. That will be the Neutron Stars and the Astronuts."

Ten men and women walked into the arena, each armed with a laser pistol that had been redesigned specifically for the human hand and powered down for the games. One team was dressed in standard black ship uniforms with multi-colored stars sewn on, and the other team sported gaudy rainbow-patterned outfits. Starting positions had been predetermined, and the Neutron Stars in their rainbow outfits took position at the far end of the arena. The referees spread out. One asked if both teams were ready and then signaled to the gravity control operator, who cut the power.

Both teams held their positions while the referees moved from one loose ball to another, giving each a random kick or shove until all were in motion. At the next whistle, both teams exploded into action.

Each team had different tactics. The Astronuts operated more or less solo, each having picked out an opponent, while the Neutron Stars worked as two teams of two, with the fifth player flying solo as backup for whichever twosome needed support.

The Neutron Stars handily beat the Astronuts, the Moon Men trounced the Starwalkers, Walker's Wildsiders squeaked out a victory over the Novas, and then it was time for the match between the Martian Maniacs and the Queens of Outer Space.

The Maniacs were already in the arena when the five bathrobe-clad women entered. The team captain of the Maniacs asked the Queens if they intended to fight in their robes, and Lucy looked him up and down.

"Oh, no," she drawled, a sound of superiority riding the accent. "We're just waiting for our attendant."

At this announcement, another young lady walked up to the Queens, who began to hand her their robes. The catcalls and applause were deafening. The disrobing had revealed five nearly nude women dressed in sensors, mini-thongs, pistol belts slung low, and nothing else—very distracting for the all-male Maniacs, whose team captain lodged an immediate protest to the boos and jeers of the crowd.

The referees put their heads together for a moment, and one referee spoke for the group, "In the matter of the protest by the Maniacs over the manner of dress exhibited by the Queens, considering the fact that no mention is made of uniforms or clothing in the rules of combat, we find that the Queens may wear anything, or nothing, as long as all sensors are worn and no sensors are blocked. Let the combat begin."

Gesturing to the panel operator, the referees set the loose balls in motion, and at the whistle, the contest began.

Lucy's teammates were Velma and Virginia from her bridge crew, and Ensigns Toni Putnam and Miranda Lee, both training for bridge positions. The five bare-breasted women started out using the same tactics the Neutron Stars had used to such good effect. Within a matter of minutes, Velma had been shot in one arm and Toni in a leg.

Shifting tactics on the fly, Lucy yelled, "Cue ball!"

Immediately Velma grabbed the nearest ball, wrapped her legs around it, and with her pistol in her good hand, got a push from Virginia. She sped off toward one corner of the Maniacs' territory like a cue ball's bank shot, firing wildly.

The other four advanced to the centerline of the arena, and at Lucy's shout of, "Cables!" pushed off the stationary balls. Firing cautiously, they flew toward different anchored cables in enemy territory. Using the cables to change trajectory, they each kept firing at anything that looked male.

Distracted by Velma's ricochet tactic, and not being able to disable or kill her because of the ball she'd wrapped herself around, the five Maniacs were all "killed" within five minutes of the starting whistle. The final action took less than two minutes from the time Lucy yelled "cue ball." At the referee's command, gravity was restored, and the teams sorted themselves out.

Holstering their guns, the Queens of Outer Space strutted from the arena, beaming from ear to ear as they slipped back into their robes. It took longer for the crowd to stop cheering than it had for the Queens to beat up on the Maniacs. So far, they were the only team to win their match without having a team member killed.

Simon turned to Kitty, only to find her gone. As he looked around, he finally saw her entering the arena for her match. Her team's opponents were the Rocketeers, dressed in black and silver. At the signal, the Kommandos began to advance. Two pairs and a solo looked like it might become a standard tactic. Kitty's team varied it only slightly as their pairs were on the flanks while the solo worked the center.

The Rocketeers tried a tactic no one else had yet. Each grabbed one of the loose balls, and the team moved together as a group. The balls made a formidable wall through which none of the Kommandos' shots could penetrate. To their advantage, the Rocketeers were able to fire around the sides and between the gaps at their opponents. They concentrated their fire first on 'Chiko Greene, Kitty's solo. Then, at the Rocketeers' team leader's direction, they fired at each remaining member of Kitty's team. They lost two of their own in the doing but eliminated the Kommandos rather handily, much to Kitty's chagrin.

Four months turned into just over three. Orion's new shuttles were pressed into service alongside *Galileo's* three, and with six shuttles supplying the converter, the factories went into overdrive. Between that and the instant attraction and near total devotion to what was now being called Z-Tag, almost everyone was too tired or too caught up in something to be bored.

Even the scientists had kept busy. Much had come of poking into the dark recesses of the computer core, some of it disturbing, such as not understanding even the basic mathematical principles behind which most systems operated. As the staff sat in the ready room going over reports, they all realized they'd dodged a major bullet in that there had been no deaths. They'd had quite a few injuries—half a dozen broken bones associated with construction, multiple cuts, scrapes, sprains, abrasions, and more broken bones from Z-Tag. All in all, they'd walked away clean, primarily due to the amazingly trouble-free technology aboard the ship.

Chief Baylor would remain with the dock for about six months, long enough to turn out one new ship that was now being called a battlecruiser. He and almost five hundred others had volunteered to stay and handle operations. Since the dock was technically capable of independent motion, Chief Baylor would be promoted to captain.

The modifications to the original dock plans had been instituted, but a last-minute clamor for an arena for Z-Tag had gone up. Extending the lowest level of the dock—now being called a base but soon to be formally named—had been, if not easy, at least straightforward. Adding extra height and grav lines to the lowest level had accomplished the task.

The three fighters would remain behind and assist the shuttles with their duties since they also had capture fields, albeit not as strong as the shuttles. New fighters, designed to human dimensions and specifications, had been built to replace them. Engineering estimated that anywhere from two weeks to a month could be cut from the production schedule by their addition.

In the final days before the *Galileo* headed back to Earth, a large portion of the organic material stored in the holds was transferred to the base for the food processors, personnel received their new assignments for the base as well as the *Galileo*, new chains of command were worked out, and base's new computer core was activated.

The activation of the new core touched on one of the darker discoveries. The computer itself was semi-organic in nature, composed of about four cubic feet of proto-organic gel, just like the *Galileo's*. Information was transferred to and from the gel by way of micro-thin lasers that would write and read to and from different sections of the core. As the information in the *Galileo's* computer was being transferred to the new one, it was discovered that one section was being consistently skipped. It could neither be copied over to the new core nor could it be read. The Science staff hypothesized that it was probably a personal diary or a formal report under some kind of lock.

It started simply enough. Simon needed to know the date. It wasn't until he glanced at the calendar and figured out the present date and Orion's commissioning date that an icy feeling of disaster barely averted washed over him. Simply remembering was enough to get him off the hook, especially way out there, but ever the romantic, Simon had been obsessing for the last several hours about what he could do to make the occasion special for Kitty.

He wandered the corridors of the *Galileo* aimlessly until he found himself on the bridge. The number of people at duty stations surprised him for a moment until he reminded himself that the commissioning ceremony was just a week away. Communications was one of the stations that was constantly manned since it was used as flight control for the entire construction process. Now, with construction winding down, everyone who could find the time—and that was most of the people aboard— were lined up to get a chance to fly one of the fighters. That meant increased traffic and increased personnel on comm duty.

Gayle looked up when he entered the room, then returned her attention to the pilot she was coaching. "Relax, Ensign," she said into the microphone. "You just need to realign your frame of reference. Your computer still thinks it's aboard the *Galileo*. Didn't your instructor warn you to realign as soon as you left the ship? Lower righthand quadrant of your control panel. Small green knob. Turn it clockwise until it lights up." She cocked her head for a second. "Very good, Ensign. Now complete your flight and remember to realign when you re-enter the flight deck. I'll personally check your flight logs later. Control out."

Gayle took her headset off, shook out her hair, spoke quietly to one of her control team members, and came over to join Simon. "What's up, boss? You look… strange."

"Do you know the date?"

"The date?" Caught flat-footed, Gayle stalled for time. "No, I don't. Should I? It's pretty easy to lose track out here."

Simon nodded. "That's just my point. We're going to commission the base next week, so I had to look up the date because I want to make up a plaque or something to give to Daniel during the ceremony."

"Okay, so far, but what's the big deal?"

"Today is February 7th. One more week will make it the 14th, our sixteenth anniversary," Simon confided. "You know we always do something special. But look where we are. What other man has given his wife an anniversary in the asteroid belt?"

"Hold it, Simon, let me think. You know by now that most women just want to have special occasions remembered, and Kitty is really no exception to that, but out here ..." Her voice trailed off as thoughts raced through her head. "How about you say something during the ceremony? Maybe at the end? Just to her? And afterward the two of you can have one of the most romantic dinners on record. I have just the place. You know the observation deck. Run everyone out and it will just be the two of you for a quiet dinner. Consider all the details taken care of." At his look of disbelief, she added, "Duty roster for one shift and a romantic dinner. I've got a week to figure it out. You better take me up on it, friend. It's likely to be your last real peaceful moment for a while."

Simon sat in silence for a few moments. "I can do that. All I have to do is come up with something to say." Already beginning to formulate a way to add what he wanted to say to Kitty into what he'd prepared to say to Daniel and the ship's company, Simon wandered back to his quarters.

Gayle, for her part, returned to her console, put her headset back on and smiled. *Too bad you can't collect on bets you make with yourself,* she thought.

Kitty had come to her not five hours earlier with the same dilemma and received an almost identical solution. It was an incredibly easy thing to do since she'd been anticipating the situation for over a month after her own need to know a date. Hell, she'd had the dinner planned for most of the last month anyway, but it was just so much simpler when one's victims cooperated.

With the exception of skeleton crews on both the *Galileo* and the now-completed space dock, everyone was present on deck eighteen. Simon and his staff stood facing Chief Baylor and his staff. Stepping forward, Simon addressed the ship's company.

"Ladies and gentlemen, crewmates and friends,

the day we've worked so hard for has arrived. The better part of a year has been spent one hundred and forty million miles away from Earth to build the first true space station in humanity's history. The friends and comrades we leave here today will start writing the next chapter while the rest of us go back to Earth to repeat the process—recruit volunteers and build another base.

"We stand here today as the salvation of mankind from her own follies and from outside aggression. It's all too clear that it's possible for mankind to destroy itself or be destroyed by some natural cataclysm or, as we now know, from alien interference.

"But right now, I have something of a happier nature to do. I have the pleasure to formally announce the completion of our first space base, and I have the honor of naming it Orion. I also have the pleasure of introducing its new commanding officer. Commander Baylor, step forward."

Daniel Baylor, Commander, Terran Alliance, (even if only in the minds of those present), hadn't been told the full story. Simon and Kitty loved to spring surprises wherever they could; it tended to liven things up. Daniel knew he'd be in charge of the new base for a while, but that was all, until now. He'd held several positions, as had most of the crew, and had actually held two different ranks simultaneously—commander and chief of operations, equivalent to a captain—for the construction projects.

As he stepped forward, Kitty and Gayle came out. They smiled at his confused look and met him halfway between the two groups of officers. Reaching up to his lapels, Kitty calmly removed the two golden stars of a full commander and placed them in her pocket. Turning to Gayle, she opened the case Gayle held in both hands, and, one at a time, replaced the two gold stars with the silver comets of a captain. Taking one step back, she saluted.

"Congratulations, Captain Baylor."

The cheers were deafening, even in that large space, and continued until he returned the salute. Kitty and Gayle returned to Simon's group, and the newly promoted Captain Baylor went to stand in front of his staff.

Simon spoke again. "Captain Baylor. It is now my duty to relinquish command of Orion. As the only officer present with the rank to assume command, do you accept?" At Daniel's nod of stunned acceptance, Simon smiled. In a voice that didn't carry past the two command staffs, he said, "Acceptance is usually verbal, Dan, but I'll take what I can get." Raising his voice to carry to the entire company, Simon continued. "Captain Baylor, as commanding officer of the *Galileo*, I wish to present you with this plaque." Stephen handed him a cloth-covered object, and as Simon took it, Stephen removed the cloth. Revealed for all to see was a highly polished brass plaque, three feet long by two feet high, with three lines of raised letters:

ORION BASE
COMMISSIONED FEBRUARY 14, 2012
CAPTAIN DANIEL BAYLOR, COMMANDING

Handing it over, Simon saluted and said, "Hang it in your reception area, Captain." Then, dropping the salute, he shook hands with the new captain.

Turning to the assembled crew, Simon announced, "Ladies and gentlemen! Captain Daniel Baylor!"

When the second round of applause and cheers died down, he addressed the crowd again. "I have an announcement to make at this time. Actually, what I have to say isn't so much to you as it is to one particular individual."

The crowd was suddenly aquiver, anticipating something major. Simon turned to his staff lined up behind him, looked straight at Kitty, and said, "Honey, I want you to know that I haven't forgotten our anniversary." Silence reigned over the operations deck at this announcement, and he let it continue for a short time. Turning back to look out over the assembled crew he said, "Since men first started promising women things to get them to marry us, women have been promised everything imaginable, including the stars." A titter of laughter ran through the crowd.

He turned back to Kitty and said, "I really don't remember exactly what I promised you way back then, hon, but I know it was to love and cherish, help and protect—all the standard things men say to women at times like that. We mean them, but sometimes we just can't deliver. I'd like to think that I've delivered on all the promises I made all those years ago."

As Kitty started to speak, Simon raised his hand. "Let me finish. Today, I am the first man in history to have the opportunity to fulfill one particular promise." Emotion held back his next words. "Kittyn, so far, I've only managed to give you an asteroid belt. In just a few more years, at most, I *will* give you the stars... with the help of all of these good people around us."

The applause and cheers went on for so long that Simon finally held up both hands to quell the noise. "Okay, people! You've all got your assignments. I want to break orbit in twenty-four hours. Dismissed!"

The director eyed Agent San Martino as he sat in the chair in front of his desk. Although it was more or less designed to be uncomfortable, San Martino seemed relaxed.

"Well, what have you got for me?"

San Martino shrugged slightly. "We know the ship hasn't come back to Earth yet, and we have a loose net of agents monitoring the families of all the missing people we can identify. We know about every scientist that has gone missing, and interrogations have all been unsatisfactory. Seems like every family repeats various versions of the same story about them taking a vacation to get away from the stress of work.

"As for the civilians, we've got over six hundred possibles identified. We have the school records for the general area and have been canvassing most of the businesses in the area. We've checked missing persons with every police agency from Cheyenne, Wyoming to Great Falls, Montana. We've leaked stories to the press, hoping someone will come forward with information. And we're paying special attention to the relatives of the Hawkes'.

"Also," he continued quickly, "we've managed to find a few of the people who, for whatever reason, turned down the offer or were turned down. We're having a little better luck getting information from that latter bunch, though even that's sketchy. The timeline we've worked out is that they should be gone about a year, and the rumor is that whatever they're building out there, at least some of them will stay behind to operate it."

The director stopped him with a gesture. "I'm going to see the president in a few minutes. These plans for the return of the ship are all well and good, but can you give me anything in the way of good news?"

"I hope so, sir. Among the missing is an agent from this very agency. We're not sure, but his disappearance coincides with the last few people reported missing. We're desperately hoping that he got aboard but didn't have time to report in."

"And that's it? You haven't come up with anything better than a desperate hope?"

San Martino shrugged again. "We've discovered and are watching what appear to be several teams in the area. It's getting to be a real pain in the ass to keep from actually running into one of them. And from what information we can get, they all appear to be working for different countries or different agencies." This last came out with some asperity.

"If and when the time comes, terminate those teams with extreme prejudice, except our own, of course. I leave it to you to deal with those delicately, Agent."

Taking the tone of voice as dismissal, San Martino stood up and simply said, "Yes, sir," on his way out the door.

Almost two thousand miles away, Agent Daniels of the Billings division of the FBI was working leads of his own. When the disappearances occurred, he'd begun the original investigation and was quickly relegated to the shadows as the DIA took all control of the situation. But one thing they couldn't do was stop him from investigating the disappearances in his own assigned area. He'd been called to Washington once and read the riot act. His response was, "If that's all you had to say, you could have done it by phone." He hadn't really expected to get out the door, much less being allowed to return to Montana.

He immediately started looking into his own old files and soon hit upon what he thought was the main cob up someone's butt. About eight months earlier, a lot of people had disappeared. Now the higher-ups were sticking their noses back into the phenomenon.

Knowing from experience what might happen, he ordered three large moving vans and a crew to strip the Hawkes' house bare after a full set of pictures had been taken. He felt bad about doing this, but he needed to make a point, get a reaction. He left a phone with his number attached and exited the house, locking the door behind him. Several days went by with no repercussions, so he settled back to wait.

CHAPTER SIXTEEN

Simon and Kitty stood in the reception area of Orion, the last members of *Galileo's* crew to leave the new station.

Simon shook Dan's hand and said, "Time for us to go, Captain. We'll be back in a month or so. Keep in touch and good luck." Realizing that the new captain already had a mountain of work ahead of him, the two *Galileo* officers beamed back to the ship that was waiting to take them back to Earth and another load of recruits.

Running at half speed, the *Galileo* took a leisurely orbit back to Earth. Full speed for the colossal engines that powered the factory ship was possible inside a solar system, but the scientists and engineers had decided it wasn't worth the time savings to push things too close to the limit until her full capabilities were better understood.

Eight hours into their homeward flight, with all systems optimal and all screens clear, Kitty sat in the command chair, musing abstractedly about the romantic dinner she and Simon had shared the night before. Dinner in the dome of the *Galileo* was something that could only be described as out of this world. A precious whole chicken had been sacrificed so the cooks could prepare dinner for the anniversary pair.

Her attention was diverted as the comm reported

an incoming message carrying the urgent prefix Simon had devised for intra-ship messages. Communications had twice checked in with Orion to test the higher-powered communication system they'd installed, and the last thing she'd expected was a message from the new dock at that particular time.

"Let's hear it, Ensign," Kitty ordered, letting the thoughts of how she was going to repay Gayle for her duplicity in last night's dinner slip from her mind.

The next sounds that came through the speaker froze everyone in their tracks.

"Mayday, mayday, mayday! This is Orion Base. We are under atta—" The signal cut off in mid-word, leaving only interstellar hissing in the background.

For five interminable seconds, Kitty sat there, stunned into immobility. Then she began issuing orders.

"Helm, get this ship turned around, now. Navigation, plot a course back to Orion Base at best speed." Hitting all-ships, she announced, "This is the first officer. All hands prepare for immediate maneuvering. Captain to the bridge, on the double." Turning back to her bridge crew, she ordered, "Comm, I want full scans of the entire area. Everything is to be recorded completely. I want every sensor we've got on full. Do I make myself clear?" That last was rhetorical, and she really didn't expect to get an answer. "And re-establish contact with Orion."

By the time Simon burst onto the bridge, the feel of the ship itself had changed. What had once been a subtle vibration had become a heavy pulse felt deep in the bones of everyone aboard as the engines labored to slow the giant ship down and turn it around. Kitty filled him in on the little they knew and her subsequent actions.

Communications interrupted. "Ma'am, still trying to re-establish communications with Orion. No luck so far."

Kitty only replied, "Keep trying until you do." She looked up at Simon as he stood beside her. "Do you want to take over?"

He laid a hand on her shoulder. "No need for that; you're doing fine. But I do want all weapons systems manned and free as soon as possible."

Hitting all-ships, Kitty called her weapons officer to the bridge. They'd been too complacent, she now saw. But who would have guessed that anything like this could happen so soon? And just who or what the hell could be attacking Orion? There should have been several years yet before they had to worry about the owners showing up.

Lt. Commander Thomas Breen, second shift weapons officer, showed up seconds after the announcement. It appeared that he'd been on the way without being called.

"Get to your post, Thomas. Orion has been attacked and we're going back to help. Make your weapons live and free." Turning to her Nav officer, she said, "I want a best estimate on a return to Orion."

Simon taught me well, she thought. *Even I can't hear the quiver in my voice.*

Navigation responded almost immediately. "Been working on it, boss. We're already turned around and pushing her close to red line to get back what we lost. At max acceleration, we're four hours out." Frustration tinged her next words. "For all the good it's going to do us."

Simon stood there for another twenty minutes until Kitty again gave him the choice of taking over or getting off the bridge. "You're not doing any good staring over everyone's shoulders. Either take the con or let us do our jobs, Simon."

He grinned ruefully and patted her on the shoulder. "You're beginning to get the hang of this, aren't you? I'll be in the ready room. Let me know when the situation changes." He leaned over to kiss her cheek and whispered, "You could send some fighters out ahead if you think it best." With that, he walked off the bridge.

Twenty minutes dragged by interminably, the numbers on her watch moving at half-speed. Kitty ordered two fighters to scout ahead, keeping the third one out but closer to the ship. The only sounds were the muted voices of the bridge crew taking reports and issuing orders to the various departments. The very air pulsed in sync to the throbbing coming up through the deck plates.

Another twenty minutes passed, the outer black pressing in on her as her tension grew. Among the steady radio traffic between the two fighters and the *Galileo*, her comm officer found other sounds just now being reported by the fighters.

"Ma'am, I'm picking up faint signals from what seems to be a shuttle. Both fighters agree and both have authenticated another fighter answering their hail. We're also picking up what appear to be two high-power drive traces on an outbound vector."

"Any chance of catching them?" she asked hopefully.

Silence reigned while Helm and Navigation bent their heads over their respective stations, sending data back and forth. Finally, Nav said, "Sorry, ma'am. Even the fighters can't get close to them under their theoretical maximum."

"Keep those traces under observation and record them for analysis. Communications, what do you have for me?"

Comm replied, "Ma'am, I'm picking up faint traces of what appear to be shuttle transmissions aimed at the station. I'm trying to enhance the signal. Signal clearing. Transferring to bridge audio."

The signal cut in mid-message, "—*ion* Base, this is Shuttle Two. Please respond. Please respond." Panic oozed out of the speakers as the bridge crew listened helplessly. "I have a damaged fighter in my capture field. Pilot needs assistance. I'm headed for dock. Open the bay. I repeat, open the bay. This is Shuttle Two. I am two minutes from dock. Open the bay. I have a damaged fighter in my capture field. Respond. Respond."

As the shuttle pilot's transmission ended, another voice came in stronger, one the entire bridge crew knew well. Ensign Miranda Lee had elected to stay with Orion and had opted for Flight Operations. She'd come to love that sleek little craft and had been out helping the shuttles supply the base with material for the smelter when the mayday came in.

"Shuttle Two, this is Fighter Three. I have a visual on the docking bays. Bay two is clear. Repeat, Bay two is clear. You are clear to dock. Base cannot respond. Their antenna array is shot to hell. I have the *Galileo* and three fighters on my long-range sensors. She's on a return vector and appears to be about three hours out. I'll fly cover until she returns. I see two outbound drive traces. No telling if there's anything else waiting for us."

The *Galileo* established communications with the fighter, as well as with the shuttles now inbound to base. The two new fighters arrived on the scene and began to fly cover and search and rescue. No trace of the third fighter was found. Kitty called Simon and filled him in on the situation as it appeared at that time—Orion apparently functional but damaged to an as yet unknown extent, cut off from communications, all shuttles inbound, one fighter damaged, one missing.

Three hours later, the *Galileo* sat dead relative to Orion. Kitty turned the bridge over to Lucy Grimes and met Simon in the transporter room, and they beamed over to the base.

The two materialized in the middle of a scene of furious activity. Kitty grabbed the arm of a passing ensign and asked for Captain Baylor.

"The last I heard, he was in the infirmary," the distracted junior officer said.

They found the captain sitting on the edge of a table, his arm in a sling, giving orders. Simon, eyeing a row of sheet-covered bodies, was beyond speech.

Kitty, ever sympathetic to the feelings of those around her, put a hand on Daniel's arm and asked, "What can we do?"

Looking up from someplace far away, he answered in a voice devoid of all emotion, "You can get those bastards."

Kitty looked down at the bodies on the deck. "You know we can't do that right now, Daniel. There's no way the *Galileo* can match the speed those two vessels were making. But I promise you we'll get them. The only question is when."

Walking over to the row of bodies on the floor, Kitty knelt and uncovered the face of each of the seven. At the last one, she fell to her knees and gazed down for a long time.

"This will not go unpunished, Toni. Not one day will go by that I won't look for a way to pay them back," she whispered.

She knelt there for so long that Simon began to worry. As he was about to go over to her, she finally slipped the sheet back over Toni Putnam's face and stood up.

"Simon, if there's anything that can be done, I'm going to do it. I helped her pack, for God's sake!"

It was a Kitty that Simon had never seen before. Steel tinged her voice as she added things up, tears streaming down her face. "Seven dead. One missing. One fighter destroyed and one missing. Damage to the base. What do you need from us, Daniel?"

Daniel corrected her. "That's three missing, Kitty. Two of my construction pods haven't checked in. I need pilots out in shuttles looking for them and the other fighter."

Looking him in the eye, she said, "I'll take care of it. You and Simon get started figuring out how we're going to get back on our feet here. I'm going to contact Stephen."

An hour later, six shuttles and all fighters were searching in ever-widening spirals for the missing. It was not an easy task since it had to be conducted in three dimensions. Space had never looked so vast to Kitty as it did from the deck of a rescue mission. The pilots were all from the *Galileo* as Daniel's people had enough to do. Just getting airtight seals into place and putting in a new antenna array was a strain on already frayed nerves.

After several hours of fruitless searching, one shuttle stumbled on a curious item—a piece of debris that had no business being where it was, much less existing. An engine pod of a design that didn't exactly match anything in their databanks was floating in the middle of a slowly expanding cloud of plasma.

Simon and Kitty, joined by Stephen, were sitting in Captain Baylor's office. Simon began speaking first.

"Dan, I'm sorry to have to start on this, but we need to. I know you need time to mourn, but we need to get to work to prevent this from ever happening again. Gayle will take care of matters as far as seeing that our dead are cared for until we can get them home." He shook his head. "Daniel, I thought we had a few years at least. We all did. I think we still do have years if we're talking about the people who built the *Galileo*. What information we have shows that the drive fields of the two ships that ambushed you are not typical of the types of drives we're using. We speculated early on that the original owners had enemies. Because of the weapons, that is. Well, apparently, we were right. I don't know if we were attacked because they thought we were the original owners or if they just don't like the new guys. But it doesn't really matter, does it?

"What we need to do right now is to start analyzing all the data we have and see where it takes us. I need to know just what *you* have on scans that might shed some light on this. I already have everything from the *Galileo's* data banks, which is precious little. We were too far away to get good scans."

Daniel reached over and picked up a commlink. "I'll have everything sent down immediately." He spoke at length and put the link back on the table. "We were running the shuttles and fighters as much as possible, so we have a lot of data to go through. Flight ops should have recorded all of it. We'd been bringing two weeks' worth of material into the station area and parking it all around so we wouldn't have to fight just to stay ahead of the factories. Then the bastards just popped up out of nowhere, or so it seemed at the time. Now we know that there were three of them and where they'd been hiding. How they got there is anybody's guess. We weren't looking for trouble. We were just waiting around for the smelter to go online full time. The construction pods could move 'em around as easily as a shuttle in the area of the base—easier, in fact, because they're smaller and more maneuverable. Communications was running as well. And we do have hard data on what happened. They hit us and they ran. Distress calls from two of my pods were cut off mid-word. We didn't have time to get a fix on that, but the missing pods were scheduled to start bringing in smaller rocks from the rear of the base."

Simon's next comment was deeply impassioned. "More than anything else, I want to know why they ran. They had enough time to turn this base into toothpicks. Why didn't they? I'm glad they didn't, of course, but what stopped them? What did they want, and what stopped them from finishing what they started?"

Finishing what they started was an apt comment. Aside from two destroyed fighters and two destroyed or missing construction pods, the only real damage to the base were three well-placed shots, one that took out the antenna array and two that hit the base proper. Of the seven known dead, two had been outside the base at the time of the attack—a crewman repairing an antenna housing and Toni Putnam, the other fighter pilot. And there were still the two pod jockeys to account for.

Hours of poring over data was giving everyone headaches. They were reduced to going over and over the same things without making any progress. Stephen had been called in to get a fresh viewpoint but to no avail. Charts and diagrams covered all available surfaces. When they broke for dinner, they were still going in circles.

As they pounded on the same points one more time, Simon said, "I don't understand. It looks like they had a perfect operation planned. They came in from your rear, made a pass, and took out one section of the base. There were two of them at that time, and apparently one missed, if he fired at all. They knew when to strike and what to hit. They waited till we were out of range, came in, took out the antenna array so no signal could get out, and then the records show them hightailing it out of here. What happened?"

Kitty jumped up. "I have an idea, and I think I may know an answer to that question. I'll be right back." She took off so fast that Simon didn't have time to ask what it was she knew.

He looked at Stephen and shrugged. "Any idea is better than none. Let's see what she has."

Five minutes later, Kitty was back, accompanied

by an unruly stack of papers. She sat down between Simon and Stephen and pointed to a section amid the chaos.

"We've got the scans of the intruders, but nobody thought to add the ones of the legitimate traffic. Look here. See. This is where they made their first pass, and this is their second." She set one scan above the other so all traffic was visible. "Here is pass number one. Notice that the fighter is hidden from their position by these asteroids." Another chart. "Here is where the Mayday went out. Watch the fighters." She kept moving back and forth between the two sets of data. "The bogies rendezvoused back at what I call position one. Here comes Quinn's fighter. See. He got close and something upset his containment field. It blew, and now we have the engine pod of their third ship to study. Here are Toni and Miranda heading back to base to see what the shouting is about. Okay. The other two bad guys panic. Maybe. Want to bet they weren't expecting us to have left fighters behind? So they make another pass, maybe hoping Quinn was the only one. They'd already gotten the antenna array, so they make a second pass. Toni fires two missiles without her targeting computer, misses, and gets hit herself. Then Miranda fires and hits one of their ships. I *know* one of those ships was hit. Here are the scans from the *Galileo*. See the drive traces? The lead one is strong and steady. The other one is fluctuating. It's having trouble keeping up. They panicked. They ran."

Kitty leaned back in her chair, breathing hard. "Those ships are bigger than a fighter by a long shot. They could have stayed and taken out Miranda *and* the base, and caught us by surprise, but they ran.

Now that they know that we know they're out here, I don't think they'll be back unless they have an overwhelming superiority. And they don't, or they would already have done it. They're just sitting out there somewhere, watching us and waiting for us to screw up. Or they're waiting for backup. That's the way I read it. And I'm right, damn it!" She stood up, glared at the three men sitting there, turned on her heel, and left.

The two staffs were gathered in one of the mess halls on Orion since they needed the extra room they couldn't get in Daniel's office. They began to discuss options.

Gayle was of the opinion that since they weren't a real military outfit, many of their people were going to want out now that the situation had turned sour— too many people, in fact, for them to continue operating both the *Galileo* and Orion.

Daniel looked at Gayle and spoke deliberately. "I don't know about you, but I've already spoken to my people. There were only two or three who wanted to go home. And when they found out what a minority they were, they changed their minds. It wasn't cowardice; it was simply that they were thinking the same way you were."

He glared around the room. "We're not talking fear here, we're talking anger. My people are royally pissed. You people realize what we're forging here, don't you? I think only Simon and Kitty truly see what's happening. My people don't *want* to go home; they want revenge! And if it's in my power to help them get it, then I'm here for the duration!"

A plan worked itself out of the confusion.

First, the *Sundiver* was going to have to be reconditioned and sent back for another load of coronal material. Since she was unpowered for the entire voyage except for the initial boost in-system and docking at the end, it was considered an acceptable risk.

Second, they would delay the building of the first battlecruiser. Instead, they'd start building a fleet of fighters using plans from the computer—slightly larger fighters than the ones originally provided by the Builders, as the previous owners were now being called. It would still be a one-person vessel but capable of carrying four missiles instead of two and having a more powerful beam capacity. Engineering estimates gave them almost one hundred fighters of the new class in the three months it would take the *Sundiver* to get back. There was enough material, Stephen's people estimated, to power several dozen of the new fighters almost immediately.

Third, the *Galileo* would remain on-station for two additional weeks, adding her production capacity to the newly commissioned Orion.

Fourth, they would send the *Galileo* back to Earth, recruit more people and return. Simon's original idea of building a carrier-type vessel was hauled out, dusted off, and approved, but when it would go into production was another matter.

Fifth, they would maintain full scans at all times, reporting any anomaly immediately. So many things needed doing all at the same time.

CHAPTER SEVENTEEN

Simon pushed as many distractions aside as he could so he could concentrate on the report of the recovered enemy engine pod.

"It's like an older version of what we're using," Stephen said. "My people don't have any answers, but it looks like what we have is several upgrades better than what they have. They've got to use a lot more power to achieve the same effect, and that doesn't include our own improvements. If they think we're the Builders, they won't be expecting some of our upgrades, and if they *are* the Builders ..." He just couldn't think of an appropriate end to the sentence.

The tentative conclusion arrived at after much analysis of available data and even more guesswork was that the three alien vessels probably crewed around forty beings apiece. This assumption was based on the apparent engine output and relative speed of the vessels as they appeared on the scan records. While it was theoretically possible for ships the apparent size of the ones that attacked Orion to have power cores big enough to give them warp drive, space limitations should prevent that unless they gave up something in weapons space—another bit of evidence for the smaller ship theory. It was therefore suspected that there was a mothership hiding somewhere farther out in the solar system.

Realizing that the mood aboard the two vessels

was near the flash point, some way was needed to divert the attention of officers and crew alike. To this end, the gaze of the staff fell on Ensign Miranda Lee. She was the only survivor of the little fighter wing, and there was computer verification that she had actually damaged one of the vessels. This meant she had most likely been instrumental in driving the intruders away, thereby possibly saving the lives of all aboard Orion who'd survived the initial attacks. The combined staffs decided to honor her.

A ceremony was called for. It would take the undirected anger that was beginning to manifest itself in unhealthy ways and redirect them. Ensign Lee probably wouldn't like the idea of a ceremony in her honor, but she would perform her duty. And if that didn't work, she'd just have it forced on her. She had to surrender her anonymity for the greater good—at least, that was what she'd be told. Simon suggested a medal, and the idea passed by acclamation. Stephen wanted to call it the Stellar Cross. Kitty and Gayle wanted to design it.

Three days later, repairs were finished on the *Sundiver*, and she began her second voyage to the sun without ceremony. Repairs to Orion were almost done, and her antenna array had been replaced.

There was now a maze of small asteroids around the base itself that required a rather circuitous course to get in or out. Six shuttles were bringing material to the two smelters, and parts and assemblies were beginning to stack up. The new fighters were going to be assembled in record time, it seemed. In honor of the pilot lost in the explosion that had given them the enemy engine pack, the new fighters would be called Quinn-class. A new class of missile was being constructed as well. Once more, technology was being changed to fit new circumstances.

There was enough material on hand to give power sources to twenty of the new fighters, with enough material left over to convert into antimatter for warheads and propulsion systems.

The new warheads were a marvel. Equipped with proximity devices, as well as contact fuses, they would wreck enormous damage, if not total annihilation, on whatever they hit. The missile itself was normal enough by all the standards of construction supplied by the Builders—a small fusion drive pushing chemical explosives very fast. The differences were that the warhead was now a small amount of antimatter riding in a containment field powered by an externally mounted field generator. Mounted ahead of the containment field it generated, the generator and field died if the missile impacted anything, releasing the antimatter at a fraction of the speed of light, followed instantly by the explosion of the drive generator. Hopefully, this would take place deeper within an enemy vessel, multiplying the damage exponentially.

With twenty improved ships carrying a total of eighty much more destructive missiles and improved beam weapons, the original owners would be hard pressed to recognize their own equipment, or combat it. And rudimentary shields were being tested in hopes of mounting them on the new fighters, as well as the *Galileo* and any ships Orion turned out.

Kitty stepped up onto the dais, and the milling crews began to sort themselves into their various subgroups. When it looked like everyone not on duty was present and in their appointed places, she called them to attention. They stood in the larger section of the *Galileo's* lower hold beneath the factories. It had become Engineering's project area when not needed for one of the ongoing construction projects associated with Orion. Weeks of work had gone into the project that emerged after the attack on Orion. Changes were made and assessed against other changes, dead ends were reached and circumvented, and obstacle after obstacle was surmounted in a prodigious effort to bring this latest project to fruition.

Before the assembled group sat a thing of deadly grace. Sleek, flat-black, and about a third again as large as the original version, this new vessel, the Quinn-class, was already being called a Mamba because of the snake's deadly reputation. Simon stood to one side and looked the vessel over for a moment.

Turning to the assemblage, Kitty ordered, "At ease. Ladies and gentlemen, we are here for several reasons today. One is to commemorate the lives of our dead. We will miss them, but their efforts have not been in vain. We will build on their efforts and carry on.

"Another reason is to present our latest innovation, the Mamba, and give recognition to those who've brought this new fighter into being. From department heads down to factory operators, engineers, pilots, pod jockeys, and all the support personnel who made it possible for those directly connected to this project to get the job done in an amazingly short time, you are all responsible for what has been accomplished here. You all deserve recognition, and after this ceremony, you'll be released from duty for twenty-four hours except for skeleton staffs who must remain on duty. Sorry. It can't be helped, but you'll get your twenty-four hours after those shifts." This last was said with a small grin.

"And still another reason is to give special recognition to one of our company who has, through her dedication to duty and her selflessness, brought that recognition upon herself. Ensign Miranda Lee, front and center."

As Kitty spoke, Simon walked up beside her. While the new Mamba was no surprise to any of the crew, it had been rumored that something else was to be announced at this ceremony. The unveiling was expected by one and all, of course, so almost everyone found some excuse to be on deck eighteen for the event.

Kitty stepped to one side and Simon took over the microphone. He looked out at the expectant faces, letting the suspense build until the ashen-faced ensign had finished walking stiffly up to him.

"Ensign Lee, reporting as ordered, sir." Her salute was crisp and sharp, though her eyes said scared.

Motioning for Kitty and Daniel to join him, Simon pronounced, "Ensign Lee, you have shown a greater-than-expected devotion to duty. It's an unfortunate fact of life in any military organization that dedication of that kind is never rewarded, but instead the individual is punished."

The silence that had grown when Miranda was

called forward was broken by a buzz of low conversation as the crew listened in confusion to Simon's pronouncement. Hadn't she saved damned near everybody's lives? Hadn't Kitty herself just said so? Simon's smile took some of the sting out of his words, and the unfortunate ensign's emotions flew across her face in a steady progression from confusion to consternation to total befuddlement.

"The punishment you'll be subjected to is more responsibility, Ensign," Simon said, causing her face to return to confusion. It also caused the noise to die down in anticipation of... something.

Simon reached out and removed the small silver pips from her lapels one at a time, pocketing them. He then turned to Kitty, who stepped forward and opened a small case so Miranda could see the silver stars of a lieutenant commander resting on a black velvet background.

As he pinned the insignia of her new rank on her, he said, "With more responsibility comes increased rank. It is my great pleasure to promote you to lieutenant commander." Finishing the second star, he stepped back a pace and saluted her. "Congratulations, Commander."

The assembled crew cheered until Simon held up a hand.

"Folks, we're not yet through with Commander Lee. Captain Baylor, if you please."

Relinquishing his position to Daniel, Simon winked at the new commander. In a voice that reached only to her and Kitty, he whispered, "Chin up, Commander. It only gets worse!"

Daniel took his place in front of Miranda. "Ladies and gentlemen, there are times that require special attention. As a commanding officer, it's my responsibility to recognize your performance and act appropriately. This is one of those times, and it is my happy duty. Commander Miranda Lee, for acts of bravery above and beyond the call of duty, specifically in defense of Orion Base and your fellows against overwhelming odds and with no regard for your own safety, I am proud to bestow upon you this medal."

Turning to Kitty, he opened a second case that had been slipped to her while all eyes were on Daniel. Inside, on a layer of black velvet, lay a golden cross. Symmetrical in all dimensions, it was about two inches high and highlighted in silver. Attached to it was a golden ribbon lined with silver. Picking it up, he turned back to the dumb-founded Miranda.

Holding the ribbon apart with both hands, he reached out, and in a move that had its beginnings somewhere in mankind's misty past, Miranda bowed her head so he could slip the ribbon around her neck.

"Commander Lee," Daniel intoned, "I have the honor of bestowing upon you the first Stellar Cross of the Terran Alliance. Know that from this day forward, you and all future holders of this medal embody all that is precious and unquenchable about our spirit. Know also that when you wear this medal, you are entitled to be saluted by all ranks at all times. Woe be to those who neglect this duty!"

Stepping back a pace, Daniel stood flanked by Simon on one side and Kitty on the other. He came to attention, as did Simon and Kitty. The three of them saluted Miranda as one, and Daniel added, "Congratulations, Commander." Turning to the assembled crew, he announced, "Ladies and gentlemen, Commander Miranda Lee, first recipient of the Stellar Cross of the Terran Alliance."

It took two more days for Engineering to okay the new fighter for trials. When it was finally ready, Simon and Daniel made it a point to be on hand for its maiden flight. Simon had to admire the efforts of the engineering staff. The new version of the Mamba still resembled that of the original, but at almost eighty-five feet in length, it was a full third larger. A correspondingly larger engine pack gave it greater speed and maneuverability. The pilot was protected by what the engineers called an acceleration drain or grav-drain that bled off some of the g-forces associated with higher speeds and turns.

A new device straight out of R&D had also been added to the craft. Several of the scientists had become obsessed with the capture fields used by the shuttles, and they'd already devised shields that would allow certain things to pass through, allowing easier access to the dock. Now, they were experimenting with an actual force field capable of protecting an entire ship, be it fighter, shuttle, or a larger ship. And the flat-black finish, along with its sleek aerodynamic styling, gave it a look of menace just sitting in the bay.

Lt. Commander Lee entered the bay wearing a black, short-waisted jacket over a grey, form-fitting suit and strode directly to humanity's first true deviation from Builder technology. Helmet in hand, she walked around the vicious-looking craft, thoughtful admiration evident in her gaze, one hand occasionally caressing the skin of the ship as she made her visual inspection. She rounded the nose of the experimental ship and saw the two captains waiting for her.

She walked up to the two men, saluted, and said, "Good morning, Captains," bringing her hand back down without waiting for either officer to salute back.

Simon chose not to comment on the casual nature with which she approached military protocol. He'd tried to teach them that courtesies such as proper saluting helped define a regimented society, like juniors showing respect to seniors and seniors returning it. But he'd finally come to the realization that most of the civilian recruits would never understand. They did try though.

Besides, he thought, *it's not as if my five years instilled that much discipline in me, either*.

Daniel, equally oblivious to the niceties of military courtesy, returned her salute as casually and asked, "Well, Commander, what do you think?" He pointedly did not mention the purple bruise under her left eye.

Lt. Commander Lee looked over her shoulder at the ship. "She looks hungry, sir."

Surprise flickered across Simon's face as he looked at the ship once again. "That she does, Commander. That she does. Well, she's all yours. Take her out for her trials. You get all the time you need, and the only tests you can't perform today are the aerodynamics. You have four missiles aboard with dummy warheads and bogies to match out there somewhere. We'll observe from the bridge. Good luck."

The captains headed off the flight deck, discussing the upcoming trials in low voices. As soon as they were in the elevator, Simon asked, "What about that shiner?"

Daniel answered with a twinkle in his eye. "What I heard was that there was a disagreement about who would be flying the trials today. Looks to me like it got solved."

Simon shrugged. "Can you delay her departure for about ten minutes? I've arranged a small surprise for her. I told her there were four simulated bogies out there. In that, I wasn't lying. What I need you to do is hold up her departure for a bit so I can get set up to ambush her. I have her old fighter and one of your stripped-down shuttles prepped and ready for launch out of one of the *Galileo's* bays."

Daniel nodded in agreement. "I see. The Mamba outperforms both craft, but not knowing what's coming should give us a better idea of the craft's capabilities and her ability to handle surprises."

Simon just grinned. "Once she's used her missiles, we'll jump her. It's one thing to know what to expect, and it's another entirely not to have any idea what's going on. I think it'll be a good test of both the craft and Commander Lee. I'm beaming over to the *Galileo* now, so if you can handle that delay for me, I'd appreciate it." Shaking hands, Simon beamed out, leaving Daniel to go on to the bridge.

Commander Lee's departure was delayed for almost fifteen minutes by an unusually strict systems check. Engineering wanted nothing to happen to their prize pilot. Another ship could be built, but not another Miranda Lee. Her mystique was already starting to spread. At last, she climbed into the cockpit, put her helmet on, and became one with her ship.

Engineering had taken the original fighter designs and beefed them up, not stopping with the weapons systems and engines. Joanna Barnes and her team had installed a miniature version of the *Galileo's* own computer, which accounted for a small portion of the increased size. The proto-organic nature of the gel forming the computer meant that it had to be fed, so a section of the ship had organic material stored between the inner and outer hulls to feed the living computer.

The main difference was that the computer in this fighter must be constantly fed, unlike the *Galileo*, which stored years' worth of food between its inner and outer hulls. While the power core gave the little craft virtually unlimited flight time, its computer needed to have its stores replenished on a regular basis—at least weekly if not on standby.

Built into the helmet were hundreds of sensors that connected a pilot directly into the computer. Information came to the pilot in three dimensions on a heads-up display on the inside of the visor, giving the pilot a real-time 3D image of all space within scan range. The effect was as if she were flying in the center of a bubble.

The downside of the system was that the pilot and computer tended to bond, learning each other's ways and quirks. The analogy used by Dr. Barnes was that for another pilot, it would be like riding someone else's horse. It would work, but not well and not for a while.

Miranda and several volunteers had spent two totally frustrating days in the cockpit, running simulations programmed by the war gamers among the crew to get the bugs worked out. While she hadn't aced everything thrown at her, she came away with an appreciation for this new generation of vessel. A lot of the scenarios had been pretty absurd, and some just weren't possible to escape with the limitations imposed on her by the computer and the programmers.

Miranda ran through her preflight checklist, checking each item off her HUD with a thought. She accessed her intra-ship link and said, "Flight Control, this is Mamba One. Communications check." When she received confirmation, she reported, "All systems green. Request permission for power-up."

Flight Control's voice was close in her ears. "Systems green, aye. Permission to power-up granted. Launch bay clear and locked, outer doors opening. You are cleared for launch. Good luck and good hunting, Mamba One."

Miranda watched the bay doors split down the middle and retract into the space between Orion's double-walled hull. She fed minimal power to the engines, mindful of the exhaust that still baffled the scientific team, not that it mattered to her as long as the deadly little ship moved when and where she wanted it to.

Not truly exhausts in the technical sense, the apertures that emitted whatever type of energy that pushed the *Galileo* and her children through space still stumped the eggheads on Stephen's research teams. This energy tended to blacken the metal around the points where they exited the ship, and the back walls of the launch bays exhibited scorch marks consistent with the expulsion of energies producing high heat levels. Oddly enough, or not-so-oddly actually, the metal of those walls was more than twice as thick as even the exterior hull.

Miranda slid the Mamba out of its bay, able to tell even this early that she had something more than an ordinary ship. The static tests performed for two days inside the bay had given her no real indication of what the ship was capable of, but the simple act of moving it away from the larger ship told her that here was something as far beyond the original as a Ferrari was beyond a Model T.

Her heart began to pound and her mouth went dry. She took a sip of water and willed herself to relax. Letting her senses acclimate themselves to the HUD built into her helmet, she moved off to her predetermined starting point above and ahead of Orion.

A course had been laid out through a portion of the asteroid belt that hadn't been cleared out completely so the Mamba's handling characteristics could be evaluated. Miranda put the agile craft through a series of maneuvers assigned by Engineering, weaving her craft through the asteroids in the same manner that had gotten Captain Hawke a much-rumored scolding from Commander Kitty back when the first fuel plant was being finished. Speed, agility, and maneuverability in all respects exceeded every parameter Engineering had established or imagined.

Special telemetry devices had been installed in her craft so Engineering could keep up with her systems in real-time. Those devices constantly transmitted data on all the ship's systems to prepositioned relay satellites, so when she suddenly diverged from the program by diving straight into the densest part of the belt she'd seen so far, a howl in her headset brought a smile to her face. Already, her instinctive feel for this deadly ship told her that she had a tiger in the tank. Her smile turned into a teeth-bearing grin when she opened the throttle the rest of the way, and the howl rose to a shriek as Engineering ordered her to slow down.

She spun the little craft around, trusting in her HUD to keep her aware of anything larger than a small pebble, and the newly installed shields would take care of those. Another thing that added to the size of the new fighter was the installation of shields based on capture-field technology. It had been discovered by R&D that the fields used to snare asteroids for the smelter could not only be tuned to specific shapes, but with the right application of power and field generation, they became shields that would deflect anything that got in their way. Missiles would detonate at a short distance, their energy dissipated—theoretically—and anything else that smashed itself against the screens provided a quite unexpected fireworks display.

Twisting and turning through the obstacle course she'd run through once before, this time in the other direction and at a much higher speed, she wondered at the silence that had replaced the spontaneous screams of moments before. That was one of the perks of flying a fighter—no one could hear her screams of pure joy. Flipping the ship end-for-end and applying full power, she stopped herself quickly enough to strain the capacity of the augmented grav-sump, adrenaline flooding her system as she felt herself greying out.

Setting all of her controls to idle, Miranda slid her helmet's HUD up and looked out into the emptiness of space. Opening her commlink, she said, "*Galileo* Control, this is Mamba One, reporting completion of performance trials. Request permission for phase two."

Knowing she had overstepped her prerogatives, her heart beat with more than just the adrenaline of moments before. Expecting a reprimand, or more likely, a recall, she was thrown off balance by a voice apparently straining for control. "Roger, Mamba One. You are cleared for phase two."

Miranda's surprise vanished as she thought about the next phase of the trials, and a tiny, little-girl-like grin twisted her lips as she surveyed her new hunting territory. "This time, I get to play with the *guns!*"

Knowing what was coming, she enabled her combat computer and pulled her HUD back into place, putting her trust in the computer's programming. Keeping a close eye on scan for the bogies she knew would be there, she held her ship to a little over half the speed she now knew it to be capable of. Just ahead and slightly to the left of her course, she saw a small cluster of asteroids. Knowing something was coming, she figured it would be a good place to watch and instantly saw the drive trace as it flared into being. Locking her computer onto that trace, she twitched her craft lightly, increased her speed a fraction, and when she'd achieved target lock and optimum range, she fired.

One missile fired, and with one sustained burst from her twin pulse lasers, one bogey was down. Seconds later, she picked up twin engine signatures.

Acquiring both in her targeting computer, she locked them in, armed and fired two missiles, and fired on one with her lasers. Looping back around, she went after the other to confirm the kill. Then she turned back onto her original vector, looking for number four.

Presently, her long-range sensors registered the drive trace of a ship cutting obliquely across her path. Her ship acquired target lock and veered off to one side in a preprogrammed maneuver, lining up to launch a missile. Engineering had said that the programs would allow a pilot more time to assess a situation in the early stages of an attack, and Miranda tended to agree as she noted the sensors reporting an increase in power output from the target, followed almost immediately by a course change. She looked at the icon on her HUD that represented her autopilot, blinked twice, and went manual.

Maneuvering her ship into position behind the target, she armed her remaining missile and slowly increased her speed. Wondering if Engineering had anything else in mind, she kept a sharp lookout. Closing to within five hundred miles, she ordered her computer to fire, feeling the now-familiar lurch as the missile left the tube. With her lasers armed, she followed the missile in, staying a little behind and to one side. There were barely two hundred miles between her and the missile when it connected with the engine pack of the bogey and exploded in an exceedingly bright flare—bright enough to grey out her HUD for a long second. She added the effect to her mission recorder.

"Well, I know my missile was a dummy, so I'll bet those geeks put a piece of antimatter in that bogey to throw me a curve. Okay, guys, that was your last trick." She opened her commlink. "*Galileo* Control, this is Mamba One. Four up, four down. Mission accomplished. Request instructions."

"Mamba One, this is *Galileo* Control. Roger mission accomplished. You are cleared to return to base."

Heading back to base at a leisurely half speed, Miranda felt very pleased with herself and her craft. "What a sweet thing you are. We're going to kick some alien a—" Three separate alarms erased her self-satisfied feeling instantly.

How the hell did something get that close? she thought wildly.

Something had moved into her rear aspect while she'd been congratulating herself on that fourth target! Sensors reported something trying to get a target lock on her, setting off another alarm. The third alarm reported a missile launch from another direction entirely, and she twitched her control, rolling the ship to port and down, and increasing her speed to evade her pursuer, who was continuing to gain. *There's two of 'em!* she thought, an edge of panic feeding her nerves. She let the pursuer get to within his apparent target window and then dazzled him with a full burn on all boosters.

"That ought to fry the front of his ship off." Finding the distance growing between her and her pursuer, she found the bogey on an intercept course. "Must be the one that fired on me."

As she was taking this in, the bogey on her tail cut loose with laser fire that would have sizzled past her cockpit had there been air to sizzle. Twitching her ship again, this time to starboard, she found a small cluster of asteroids on her screen, and against all training, dove her ship into their midst. Emergency deceleration and a hard turn to port and down brought bogey number two onto her screen. Acquiring target lock, she powered out of the cluster and opened up with both lasers. Scoring several hits on the bogey, identical in design to the older style shuttles the *Galileo* carried, she saw a flare of light from its engine pack as it skewed sideways. Not finding bogey number one on her screens at all, she quickly reversed course and ducked back into her hideout. As she started to pull her ship into the cluster, she began calling home.

"Mamba One to base. Mamba One to base. Reporting bogeys. Real bogies! One down, one active. This is not a joke, people. I have just taken out one bogey and one has dropped off my screens." As she uttered these words, her vessel lit up with several laser shots, and all her systems went dead.

Sitting in the darkened cockpit of her crippled fighter, Miranda began cursing her own stupidity. With her sensors dead, she could only sit there and wait for the bogey to come back and finish the job. She didn't even know if her message had gotten out. After several minutes of nothing, she finally cracked.

"Damn you! Come back here and end this charade! But winning one battle won't win you a war, you bastard!"

Drifting in the silence of space, without even the whisper of her life support system for company, Miranda lifted her visor and waited. She finally noticed a small, red, blinking light among the darkened instruments of her control panel—one small light to hold on to in that great darkness. She stared at it for a time, then reached out and touched it. Instantly the light went out, and several seconds later, all of her systems came back online.

With the return of her systems came her radio and an incoming message. "Congratulations, Mamba One. You found the reset button. Consider yourself fortunate that this is only an exercise and you *have* a reset button. You are cleared to return to base. Report for debriefing as soon as you've settled your craft."

Recognizing the voice, she muttered, "I don't know how Commander Kitty does it." As she located the base on her screens and began her approach, she muttered, "I could kill that man."

Lieutenant Commander Miranda Lee, first recipient of the Stellar Cross of the Terran Alliance, was thoroughly pissed at herself. *Too damned cocky*, she thought. Well, she'd just had that kicked out of her. She eased the nose of her ship through the force field and into the docking bay. Mad as she was, she realized that the engineers and science teams were doing a good job. This new force field, for example. The Builders had possessed the technology, but for some reason, they'd never adapted it to this use. Now it wasn't necessary to pump the air out of a bay so a ship could enter or leave. The selective field made life so much easier.

Likewise, the interior capture fields. Adapted from the shuttles, they caught an entering ship and the docking crews could move it to wherever they chose. She shut her systems down as she felt the field take hold and began to get ready for the ass-chewing she foresaw in her future. As she stepped down the ladder provided by the deck crew, an ensign was waiting.

Saluting, he said, "Ma'am, Captain Baylor's compliments, and would you report to his office in one hour?"

The hour Captain Baylor had granted let Miranda shower and change before reporting. *Might as well look my best for the funeral*, she thought gloomily. At the appointed time, she knocked on the captain's door and was ushered in and asked to sit down before she could go through the formula of reporting. She found herself sitting opposite the highest-ranking members of the combined crews.

I have to quit this. I'm not going to be able to survive the attention, much less any combat! she thought.

Captains Baylor and Hawke, and Commanders Hawke, Walker, and Frost were all present. Frost was the new Chief of Engineering for Orion, and probably the one who'd screamed the loudest when she red-lined her ship.

The debriefing went much better than she'd expected. The only low point was when Chief Frost chewed her for exceeding her red lines. She defended herself by stating the obvious—that it was absolutely necessary to know exactly what her vessel was capable of—and she bordered on insubordination by saying that she would do the same thing again under the same circumstances.

Having been questioned extensively by most of the officers present, Miranda was feeling very wrung out, but she was beginning to think she'd walk away from this debriefing clean until Simon spoke. He went over, in great detail, everything she'd done during her encounter with the fighter and shuttle, continually asking, "Why?" It turned out that the pilot of the shuttle was Commander Kitty, who apparently had been annoyed but not all that surprised when her craft was disabled so handily. As they discussed her maneuvers, Simon made a point of stating that there was no wrong move for her to have made, as up until this point, there was no such thing as space combat tactics.

"In this field, we're quite literally flying by the seat of our pants," he cautioned. "So, all in all, you are to be commended for your performance today and for the way you handled yourself throughout the entire exercise."

Simon ended on that note, and everyone stood up to leave. As they did, Kitty maneuvered herself beside Miranda. Placing her hand on Miranda's shoulder, she slowed down to let the men go on ahead. In an offhand tone she commented, "Apparently you weren't aware that there was a cockpit voice recorder on your vessel today." Miranda looked at Commander Kitty questioningly. They reached a juncture in the corridor, and as Kitty prepared to go to quarters, she looked both ways before confiding, "There are times when I could happily kill that man myself." Turning on her heel, she left a stricken Miranda standing alone in the hall.

CHAPTER EIGHTEEN

Simon was furious to the point of a total meltdown. Two reasons were that his wife and First Officer refused to allow him to get her out of harm's way. But the second reason was the one responsible for most of his anger—she was right.

It had started the day before, on an upbeat note, oddly enough. Simon and Daniel had been on the *Galileo's* project deck when the last Mamba, number twenty, was brought in for its systems check shortly after the power core had been initialized. The crew and technicians present let out a ragged cheer, acknowledging the promised celebration as the interruption in Orion's basic mission ended. Thirty days of nonstop production had produced those twenty ships, their eighty antimatter missiles, and more than enough pilot-hopefuls to fly them.

Kitty and Miranda had started a training program using one of the original fighters to familiarize trainees with their future craft, as well as the more unpleasant task of identifying those who weren't going to be able to interface with the upgraded neural net well enough to serve in a flight capacity. Getting a long-range patrol up and prowling the fringes of Orion's sensor range became a priority issue, and permanent if sketchy air cover would become the rule before the *Galileo* left.

Now that Orion had some protection, the *Galileo*

could go back to Earth and pick up more volunteers. Simon had made a list of the people he wanted on that trip, and Gayle and Stephen were on the list because they made a good recruiting team. Several of the first thirty-five from the DenverCon were on it because of their contacts And he wanted Kitty as acting captain.

Simon had broached the subject several days before the *Galileo* was scheduled to depart. The confrontation in the Hawkes' quarters began when Kitty told Simon no.

Kitty sat there calmly and waited for Simon to run down. When he finally paused to take a breath, Kitty jumped in with both feet. "My turn." Simon opened his mouth, but Kitty spoke first. "Shut up for a minute," she said, breaking one of their rules never to use those two words with each other. "This isn't as much captain and first officer as it is husband and wife, and you know it. You want me away from here so I'll be safe. But that leaves *you* here and in danger."

She laughed at the startled look on his face. "I'm perfectly capable of figuring out the same things you are, dear. Now, one of us has to go back and supervise replacing the recruits. That should be you since some of the decisions have to be made on the spot. And I," she said, fists on hips, "don't want to leave here with my job half done."

Kitty finally decided to put Simon out of his misery. "Besides, Captain Dear," she said, a half-nasty smile on her face, "you aren't cleared to fly one of the new ships yet, so you can't teach anyone else how to fly one. You signed the order that gave me and Miranda the power to license a pilot, and neither of us will certify you in the time we have left, so I stay and you go. And Miranda and I have things under control. You need to realize that I can handle my end here, and that you're the one most qualified to handle things back on Earth. Besides, we can keep in touch by radio." Her decision had been hard to put into words, and her voice cracked at the end.

It took some doing, but Simon finally bowed to the inevitable, and two days later the *Galileo* finally left for Earth. The night before departure was a strange experience for most of the crew. They were about to watch their comrades leave again, and the last time had produced some very unpleasant results. For Simon and Kitty, it was a problem because they'd never been separated by over twelve thousand miles for an extended time in their sixteen years of marriage.

The strain was beginning to get to everyone, and it was almost with a sense of relief that the *Galileo* made her way out of the maze now surrounding Orion and disappeared into the deep black.

With the *Galileo's* second departure, a new sense of purpose began to infect Orion and her personnel. Plans had changed again, but the fluidity of plans around the two large craft had become a hallmark. Now the theory was that if three of the old-style fighters could run off their attackers, then surely twenty of the newer, meaner version could keep them safe until the *Galileo* could get back, especially with the maze in place.

Consequently, Daniel kept patrols out at all times. He had Engineering, already overworked, design a series of sensor buoys that would warn them long before any craft could sneak up on them again. These would be placed by some of the farther-ranging patrols, first in near-Orion space and later farther out on the edges of the solar system by ships going out on their trials or on patrols.

Kitty Hawke, now Wing Commander, and her executive officer, Lt. Commander Miranda Lee, shared an office built into one corner of the flight deck. With the extra personnel left behind by the *Galileo*, lured either by the mystique of the new Mambas or a sense of outraged duty, they'd been able to man all twenty fighters.

Orion returned to its original purpose of building full-sized, long-range ships. Two weeks after the *Galileo's* departure, the keel of the first vessel was nearing completion. With the additional assistance of the Mambas not on patrol, Orion's Engineering department estimated the completion of the first ship sometime in November of 2011.

Kitty chafed under the knowledge that Simon had gone back to Earth and left her with all the potential problems that were inherent in that situation, even though she'd fought for it personally. Privy to all the staff meetings up until the *Galileo* had left, she was as aware as anyone else of the possibility that the government—U.S. that is—would most likely be all over them as soon as it became aware of their return. The days that passed with no report of trouble were a balm at the end of each weary day. The first week was a no-brainer because it would take that long for the huge ship to get back to Earth. Each day after that gave her more hope that they'd misjudged the situation.

Her reason for staying with Orion was still a

valid one, and from the moment the *Galileo* disappeared into the inner system, she and Miranda had had their hands full training the new pilots in the fine art of fighter control. That they were making up rules and tactics as they went along was obvious, but it was a start.

Kitty's days began early. She got up, showered, had a hurried breakfast in the mess hall nearest her quarters, and hurried to her office on the lower deck. By the time she arrived, the morning Flight Operations shift was on duty, crawling over the off-shift fighters like so many ants over their queens. By the time Miranda arrived, Kitty had the day's training and patrol rosters posted, had made coffee, and was going over the reports from the previous day, as well as the late shift's reports on flight readiness for the assembled fighters waiting on the main deck.

The calm ended the evening she stopped by the radio shack—called that for some esoteric military reason she never bothered to ask about—and read the evening report filed by the *Galileo's* Comm officer. Surprisingly, she read, it was reporters who'd first begun to harass the returnees, the government a close second. Transport Control was busy pulling people out of jails until the authorities gave up on that and just started asking questions. Her emotions, already low after having to wash out two gifted pilot-hopefuls earlier in the day, she couldn't take the stress any longer.

Tears rolled down her face as she made her way back to the room she shared with Miranda. Expecting Miranda to be gone, as was her usual habit, Kitty didn't wipe the tears away as she entered her apartment. Her thoughts were only for the bed she wanted to cry herself to sleep on.

Miranda looked up from the report she was reading and said, "You know, I used to read novels. Now I feel lucky to make it through one of these reports before bedtime." It took that long to register the tears flowing freely down her boss's face. She set the paper aside and moved to Kitty's side, using an arm around her shoulders to guide the weeping woman to a chair. Seeing the crumpled-up piece of paper so obviously from Communications and knowing that the *Galileo* had only been back at Earth for two days, Miranda guessed at the worst possible scenario. "Kitty! Simon… is he okay?"

Kitty nodded wordlessly as tears and sobs emanated from the despondent woman. "Yes, at least so far. It's just that everything is getting so complicated, Randy," she managed to choke out. "I trust Simon to handle things there just like he expects me to do the same here, but I'm just not… I don't have the experience he does with things like this!" Kitty waved her hand in the air, trying to indicate the whole of her life at present but only succeeding in making Miranda look at the paper she had clutched in it.

Not knowing exactly what Kitty was referring to, Miranda focused on the paper and managed to extricate it almost intact from Kitty's grasp. Reading it twice to make sure she missed nothing, Miranda said, "Kitty, dear, we knew this kind of thing was going to happen. Remember, Simon told us the government would do all it could to take the *Galileo* away from us. And truthfully, I wouldn't mind giving her to them after we dismount all the weapons and wipe the computer. Now that we've got all of her information duplicated on Orion…"

"It's not just that, Randy," Kitty wailed. "I had to wash out Rita and Larry today. They each did fine in the old trainer, but neither one of them could tolerate the helmet." "The helmet" was a euphemism for the neural net built into the suit and helmet of a pilot that essentially made that pilot one with her ship.

Connected to the net via connections wired into the helmets, almost twenty percent of the applicants reported a buzzing throughout their entire bodies— never enough to impair their senses, but enough and then some to distract them from the concentration needed to fly one of the new ships. The condition disappeared the instant the pilot removed her helmet, leaving the two women guessing that the problem lay with the person and not the new system. "And I don't like not being able to talk to Simon when I need to."

Miranda listened to Kitty talk well past the time the two of them usually went to dinner. Taking the opportunity to call the mess hall while Kitty took a restroom break, Miranda ordered a couple of plates delivered to their room before the stewards went off duty. Finally, the commander of the new fighter detachment, worn out from worry and stress, went to bed. Miranda tucked a light blanket around her boss's shoulders and turned out the light.

Looking back from the door, she said, "You've got tomorrow off. We've only got two more pilots to certify, and I can handle that. Get some rest and call Simon. I know you won't be able to talk to him, but you can message and reply as often as you want until you can get this talked out."

Simon's mission to Earth wasn't faring as well as operations aboard Orion, primarily due to the people equation. The return of almost five hundred people to the Denver/Billings area after a nearly year-long absence had been a recurring topic of discussion at the weekly staff meetings. So vocal were the arguments that Simon had had to step in a number of times to separate potential combatants.

Preferring to lead from the best position available, Simon tended to listen to both sides of an argument, let the two sides get all of their information on the table, and then try to sift through the partisan posturing to hopefully arrive at a solution that would work for all involved.

From the snippets of conversations heard and overheard in daily shipboard life over almost a year's time, Simon surmised that a goodly number of the crew accepted for the construction of Orion had told no one they were leaving for any number of reasons. Most or all of them would be listed as missing persons, and any one or two would arouse considerable attention when they showed up. But almost five hundred…

Surprisingly, just under half had stayed in the asteroid belt to begin construction of the first ship. Their continued absence would be commented on in light of the return of so many others. And there was the very real problem of telling eight families about the death of a loved one, having to convince them that it was no hoax. And it irked Simon that one of the missing only had a name. No one could ever remember him—Derek Carter—ever talking about his background, so he had no one to contact.

Simon still felt a bit uncomfortable with his

position at the head of the table. His five years in the Army had brought him to the illustrious rank of sergeant and placed him as second in command of a platoon of forty men. A long visit to the observation deck, awash in Earth-light, and a lot of soul searching helped him let go of the fear of failure and embrace the vision that had slowly grown more vivid since finding the *Galileo*.

He sat up straight in his chair and leaned his forearms on the table, his actions bringing the current growing argument to a halt.

"This isn't a prison." His expression told the assembled group that this was Law. "We don't have the right to keep anyone from beaming back down if they want to. Everyone aboard this ship is here of his or her own free will, risking their lives gratis for a dream.

"I happen to know that there are several dozen who've made it clear that they want off and won't be coming back. I've spoken with most of them, and they know there will be no protection for them when the authorities find out who they are and where they've been. In keeping with the consensus reached here in prior meetings, I've asked these volunteers to cooperate completely with any officials who decide to question them.

"Now we get to the great majority of the people aboard the *Galileo* as of this moment. That so many have chosen to stay is something I find… amazing." Simon shook his head, smiling slightly. "That so many have chosen to give up so much to do this also amazes me, especially after what happened." His voice trailed off for a moment, echoes of the attack on Orion rebounding around the room. "But," he said forcefully, jarring a few to closer attention, "we can't hold anyone back who needs to take some time off. We're going to be here for at least a couple of weeks, and if we don't let these people off, there will be a mutiny. We need to keep the good will of our unpaid crewmembers, ladies and gentlemen. And they are supposed to be recruiters as well, so they have to have the freedom to go back down and take their chances just like everybody else. We'll just make sure to bail them out as necessary. To that end, you will go back to your departments and tell your people that we'll begin a beam-down schedule right after breakfast tomorrow morning."

Simon raised a hand. "Beam-down will be by reverse order of rank, lowest ranks first. See if you can get some to postpone their beam-downs to keep ship's services running until we can get replacements, and then they'll have their chance to visit home if they want to. I'm pretty sure a lot of them have families to reassure.

"I've listened to all of your arguments, and I've decided it's going to be impossible to keep our return a secret, so now is the time to start grabbing some airtime with interviews. Beaming out in front of a live camera will go a long way toward helping our recruiters prove their stories."

He sat back up and let a speculative look take residence for a minute. "We need to re-crew fast, and some attention will help. Getting new people found, convinced, aboard, and partially trained is going to take some time, and our people are the ones who'll do the finding of those recruits for us, so we can't sequester them aboard. That would be denying ourselves the use of a basic resource."

Simon's face hardened slightly before he spoke again. "I'd like to see about setting up some sort of underground network before the shit hits the fan, though. Everyone please submit a written plan based on your knowledge of Denver and your friends and acquaintances to address the problem of recruiting covertly if the need arises. I've had Engineering make up a few radios to keep in touch with whoever we decide to do business with because sure as God made little green apples, we're going to be the targets of everyone on the planet who thinks they should be in charge of what we have.

"Those who choose to leave our service will give up their wristbands and will be encouraged to cooperate with the authorities, telling everything they know. As soon as they're identified, they'll be hauled in and debriefed, but since we're still in the unfortunate position of merely duplicating what we have without truly understanding the underlying physics, there isn't much chance that they'll give away more than we want them to. The other side of the coin is that once humans know something is possible, they'll worry at it until they find the way— or at least *a* way. I've decided that we will *eventually* give all the technology aboard this ship to Earth, but the two things we won't give up in the foreseeable future are weapons technology and our power technology."

He glared around the table. "There are some things we need to keep to ourselves to ensure our own survival, and make no mistake, that's something we must do to keep the world from destroying itself fighting to get control of this ship. The problem is that if we keep it, we become the enemy in the eyes of every government on Earth. Another unfortunate characteristic of human nature is to be afraid of someone who has more power than you do, and we represent more power than any group in history. That's going to engender a lot of fear in high places. Our job is to prove to the general public that we aren't the monsters some will try to make us out to be. Exposure is our best friend, but I do want to wait until we have the beginnings of a second crew aboard before we start making our existence general knowledge."

Simon placed his hands on the table, drained of all energy after his speech. He looked at Griswold when the commander asked, "Sir, I can see writing off assistance to the ones who opt out, but what about those of us who just visit home and get arrested or something?"

Simon looked at him blankly. Hadn't they gone over this a dozen times? "Just press the red recall button twice for emergency beam-up, Commander. The wristband you wear," he said, holding his up for all to see, "is essentially a bio-monitor, as well as a communicator. We've set the parameters of all wristbands so that if you find yourselves in positions of great stress, the computer will automatically beam you out. If you're slipped a drug, your vitals will change, and the computer will beam you out. If you start to drown, the computer will know and beam you out. Of course, there's always the old standby of pressing the emergency recall button. So, if it's not an emergency, signal for regular recall, please."

Silence greeted his final statement until he waved a hand. "Ladies and gentlemen, you've now got a lot more to think about, so I'll leave you to implement the departure of those who wish to quit us and the leaves of those who only wish to visit home and family. Make sure the first group understands what they face and that the second keeps a low profile until they can each get a few new recruits lined up. And check for volunteers to stay aboard for a few extra days." His voice trailed off and he sat quietly for a few seconds until he seemed to reach a decision.

He stood up, bringing all at the table to their feet, a response he still felt less than comfortable with. The senior Engineering officer said, "Tenn-hut!" and everyone stiffened to various positions of attention until Simon left the room. As the door closed, he heard, "At ease," and shook his head in continuing bemusement at the turn his life had taken.

The first thing reported to the *Galileo* by those who made the initial trip was the intense interest expressed by a multitude of hard-faced men and women most generally described as dressed in cheap suits and wearing dark glasses. The questions asked by this group ranged from where people had gone to when they were expected to return. No aspect of the lives of those departed or those known to have been associated with them was overlooked. Relatives, teachers, friends, acquaintances, even clerks at known hangouts had been harassed for the first several months after the *Galileo* departed. Apparently, the government had spared no expense in searching out possible crewmembers and keeping a soft surveillance going.

Pointed questions concerning secret technology,

thinly veiled hints at treason, and horrible consequences from the benevolent, freedom-loving government that spawned these dour-faced, humorless people had managed to get some results from a variety of sources. By the time the *Galileo* returned, more than a little bit was known about the situation in places Simon and company would have preferred to have been kept in ignorance for a while longer.

The initial furor had died down during their long absence, but that didn't mean eyes weren't watching from the sidelines. Officials, primarily police and hospitals, were on alert to report the presence of any of hundreds of names that showed back up in Denver and other cities, while Simon's and Kitty's house, unknown to them, was under constant surveillance.

Two days was all it took for word of the reappearances of hundreds of missing people to filter out to the press. Reporters who had covered the mass disappearances the previous year paid heed and dug addresses out of their archives. Thus armed, they went in search of the returnees, as often as not finding the object of their search.

Before the first responses to Simon's lefthanded request to speak personally with the mysterious agents swarming all over the area came back, the news shows started airing interviews with returning crewmembers.

The first one was the most dramatic, of course. Any time a totally new experience impacts someone's life, it tends to stand out. And in an unusual twist to last year's bizarre disappearance of almost eight hundred people from Denver and surrounding areas, a Denver news anchor said to a rapt audience, "It has been reported that some of those missing people are starting to show up in areas they were seen in just before their disappearances. Our Jennifer Martinson was able to track down one of these missing people, and the results are guaranteed to amaze you. Please keep in mind that this is untouched footage taken earlier today."

The screen blanked out for a second and returned to what looked like an impromptu interview with a shoulder-mounted recorder trying to keep the reporter and her subject in the same shot.

"I'm Jennifer Martinson," the woman said, holding her microphone so the logo of the local CBS affiliate was visible. She stood in front of an anonymous brick wall, leaving the viewer to wonder if that was by happenstance. "I'm talking with John Grant, reported missing almost one year ago. John has turned up with many of the almost eight hundred people reported missing from the local area last year." She looked at the black-clad person standing beside her and asked directly into the microphone, "Can you tell us where you've been for the past year, Mr. Grant? And are you associated with all the other people who've turned up recently?" She moved the microphone towards the young man.

Hesitantly leaning forward to speak into the proffered microphone, John Grant said, "I've been working in outer space for the last nine months. And all of those people were there, too."

The expression on the reporter's face, trained to remain impassive regardless of what was said to her, slipped a fraction before she was able to regain her composure. "Can you tell us exactly where in outer space you've been working? To the best of my knowledge, NASA hasn't been sending up hundreds of workers for any special purpose. And what are the requirements to get a job like that?"

"Well, the requirements, for me, for all of us, was being in the right place at the right time," the crewman said. More than a touch of pride entered his voice. "And for the last nine months, I've been working in the asteroid belt helping to build humanity's first real deep-space facility."

"Really, Mr. Grant?" Condescension evident in her voice, the reporter asked, "And how did you get all the way out to the asteroid belt?"

Looking more uncomfortable with each question, John Grant answered, "We've got a spaceship, ma'am. Our captain and his wife found it. They were the ones who got us to come aboard and go build the space station."

The reporter looked at the camera, her expression revealing that she now felt she had a total nutcase on her hands. "Okay, Mr. Grant. And what does this captain of yours and his wife want to do with a space station in the asteroid belt?"

"They're going to use it to build more ships."

"What kind of ships, Mr. Grant? And why?"

"The first big one is going to be a battlecruiser," Grant said proudly. "And we're going to need 'em to protect us from the aliens who are going to come and try to take back their ship."

The reporter smiled at the camera. It wasn't a nice expression, more like a pit bull realizing it was going to be able to take a kitten apart without any repercussions. "Really, Mr. Grant! Aliens?" She stepped closer to the man, pushing her microphone ahead of her like a sword. The camera followed, giving the viewer a look at the face of John Grant as he found himself backed quite literally into a corner. "What do these aliens look like? And where are the rest of the eight hundred, Mr. Grant?"

Unused to attention from the pretty young reporter and the camera filming his every word, the young crewman began to get flustered, and when his heartbeat hit 150, he disappeared in a shower of blue sparks. Jennifer Martinson looked from the empty spot in the corner to the camera once, then again, and asked, "Did you get that?"

Simon sat at his desk, facing Stephen over a series of reports. "Another emergency beam-up. Reporters, again," Simon commented, smiling. "The government has already gotten tired of all the 'escaped from custody' reports. Now they're just questioning anyone they catch on the spot. So far, it seems as if someone with a real cool head is covering this."

Stephen looked at Simon speculatively. "I know what you said during the meetings, but you really did expect this, didn't you?"

"Of course I did, Stephen," Simon said patiently to his friend. "What did I ever say to make you think I didn't believe this would happen? After all, I *was* part of that mentality for almost fifteen years. You just wait until this time tomorrow. Fully half of all emergency recalls will be back due to escapes from police or government agents. What about your people? Are you having any trouble with them?" Simon was referring to the scientists aboard, most of whom had come aboard at Stephen's request and had stayed for at least the first round trip to the asteroid belt.

"Yeah," Stephen admitted, a sour look on his face. "But at least most of them are reaching a few of their friends before they either go back to their lives or stay for another tour, so to speak. Are you sure you want to let some of them be interrogated?"

"Of course. And that's exactly what it's called—a tour of duty. It was the plan all along, Stephen, to let the authorities know what we have. I *want* them to know." Simon gestured broadly, indicating not only the ship but more. "The technical knowledge alone will help humanity get a leg out into the universe. If we can understand what we have, so much the better. But right now, I'm happy just being able to reproduce it. Since we still don't understand how to make antimatter or how to even begin to formulate the math to understand the physics behind our force fields, there's no harm in letting some of our people be questioned, as long as the people who do the asking do it nicely. None of our people will be subject to pain or jail. And they don't know *what* we have right now. They're gonna have to get a spy aboard."

"I still don't see why you want the authorities to know what we have," Stephen said. "I would think you'd want to keep it a secret."

"Different people down there are going to want different things, Stephen. Imagine what the United States would ask for: maybe the antigrav, maybe something else. But what about one of the flood-ravaged, third world countries? Would they want antigrav or a way to make safe medicines and food?

What will people like the Saudis do when the world no longer depends on the oil they produce? Maybe we should approach them to find out if they'd like to get in on the ground floor of a unique power storage device, coupled with a reliable, long-lasting electric motor. What would they pay us to be the sole producers of these motors and power systems to the world's automobile makers? Maybe we shouldn't have given that one to your friend, Victor.

"I'm going to sell, trade, or lease what we have here for the rights to come and go as we please, and we'll recruit the same way. Some of your people should tell their interrogators that they should be dealing with me rather than going after the small fry."

Stephen had one of the hardest jobs of all. The scientists of the United States are watched, just like the scientists of other countries. They were the points around which ideas coalesced and new breakthroughs occurred—national treasures to be kept under close surveillance. Keeping surreptitious track of these individuals had been a task of certain agencies since before the Cold War. To have so many disappear at once—some one hundred and twenty scientists stretching out over almost every discipline—had caused quite a stir, to say the least. Some of the more out-there conspiracy theorists clung to the belief that the disappearances in Denver and those of dozens of scientists clustered mostly along the east coast were related.

The efforts of the scientific community, along with the return of so many of their peers, brought a steady stream of scientists aboard over the next two weeks. Some stayed, drawn to one ongoing project or another, seeing the possibilities for research on things they could otherwise only dream of. Others only stayed long enough to find out that the ship was real, having been approached surreptitiously by one agency or another. They were ordered to observe as much as possible and report everything they saw, paying special attention to aspects of the technology that might be reproducible on Earth.

Within days of the *Galileo's* arrival back at Earth, dozens of scientists had had to use the recall function on their wristbands to escape durance vile from government agents, most certainly, but in some cases it wasn't exactly certain which specific governments were being represented. And the new hires were reporting advance visits from solemn-faced men warning of dire consequences if their edicts weren't met.

Simon quietly congratulated himself. He'd learned many years before that if anyone wanted a project or idea to leak out, the best way was to try to be mysterious about it. Truth be known, visibility was what he wanted, and as much as possible. The fact of their existence had been spread all over television, radio, and even the tabloids, for crying out loud. Now, that didn't mean much to Joe Average, even when the headlines read, "Earth has Spaceships!" Conspiracy theorists had had a field day right after the first disappearances, especially those who managed to get airtime on some of the late-night talk shows. Every possible answer for the disappearances was forwarded, including the right one, which got little mention after the anonymous caller got off the tollfree line.

Eventually, the calls died out almost completely.

Those who knew for sure kept a low profile during the first set of absences, and those who only suspected could never turn up so much as one body. So, no one outside the government had enough proof to do more than speculate… until now.

CHAPTER NINETEEN

The efforts of the group Simon had come to think of as Lucy's people brought new faces up at the rate of a dozen a day, and not surprisingly, there was a lower incidence of interference with them from government agents as it was almost impossible to pick out who was being approached to join up. The science-fiction crowd was more open to the possibility that the *Galileo* really existed and were easier to convince to go for a ride.

The rumors and stories told by people who'd been approached but declined to join the original mission, coupled with the return of people known to have disappeared almost a year ago, had the *Galileo* fully crewed two weeks after arrival in spite of governmental interference. And, of course, it didn't hurt that CBS kept replaying the John Grant interview. Nor did it hurt when the other major affiliates began airing similar interviews to the point that they became commonplace in less time than it took to get the ship re-crewed.

There were a few problems that needed to be attended to, but most of them could be handled by delegation of authority. However, two problems stood out, and Simon, Gayle, and Stephen held council in the ready room. Simon, being Simon, took the easy one first.

There were more applicants than they had room for. "Take applications," he said. "By that I mean to get their names and numbers and tell them we'll get in touch when we have an opening. Meanwhile, we'll only take those who can be vouched for by someone already aboard."

Simon had been following the news as it was beamed from pirated satellite intercepts directly to the *Galileo* and Orion. Election campaigns were just heating up. How that would affect their actions was unclear. President Drake was running for re-election based on his record of having stomped so hard on terrorist groups around the world, doing his best to maximize the fact that the Republican agendas had effectively gutted the stock market and brought the country to the brink of depression.

The Democrats were working to keep Michael Drake in the Oval Office so his more moderate policies would help to reduce the violence directed at Americans and American interests around the world. The eternal hatred of the have-nots for the haves would ameliorate any positive effects that ploy would have, though, Simon feared.

Stephen had been investigated during his absence by the FBI and other agencies, as well. Most of the missing scientists who'd gone joyriding on the *Galileo* suffered the same fate, even to the point of having their relatives checked for suspicious activities. The flurry of investigations over the mass disappearances of almost eight hundred people from the Denver area had produced few real connections between most of the missing persons beyond a curious affinity for science fiction. An east coast reporter working on the disappearance of so many scientists at about the same time noted the same curious fact, though it was buried among many other observations and never really got the attention it deserved.

Gayle's disappearance, along with a few others with whom she had a passing connection, had caused a minor stir in Billings local news stories for about two weeks. Simon and Kitty had been mentioned as well in a separate article, as was the disappearance of half a dozen young men thought by some to have gone off to a religious retreat.

Gayle visited her parents with Simon on her second day back. They had called to make sure her folks were home and then told them the story. To prove it, they beamed into the living room of her parent's house.

The first thing they heard was her mother's scream and the second was her father's profanity. Half an hour later, after her mother had recovered from her faint, Simon and Gayle showed them a video of all the things they'd done over the last year, courtesy of Kitty who'd had the foresight to record events as they unfolded.

Simon and Kitty weren't quite so lucky. Since Kitty's parents had died in an automobile accident when she was twenty-two, they'd been living in the house she'd acquired from her mother's estate. Using part of her inheritance to set up an account that would pay all the property taxes automatically, they figured they had all their bases covered. What they hadn't figured on was the tenacity of Agent Daniels.

Gayle's father was the one to break the news to Simon. "There was an FBI agent here asking about you shortly after Gayle left. And he stopped by several times after that, too. He seemed to think you were involved, but we told him you couldn't have done something like that. He was intimating that you had killed her without actually using those words. I think now that it was just to get us rattled so we'd tell whatever we knew, but what could we think, you know?"

"That's not a problem, Mr. Miller," Simon said positively. "I've dealt with this guy before, and so has Kitty, if he's the same one. I was planning to go over to the house and pick up a few things I know Kitty would like to have when we get back. I think I'll call him from there and get something started that's going to set this whole world on its collective ear, if I haven't already done so," he amended sheepishly.

Simon beamed into his house to find it totally empty. The only thing left was a telephone on the floor with a note from the overzealous agent. "If you want to get your property back, contact me." At the bottom was a local number.

Waiting for the connection to be made let Simon get his emotions back under control. Somewhat. At the sound of the agent's voice, Simon growled, "Okay, thief, you've got my attention, but you may decide it was a bad idea on your part. Get over here and tell me what you want." Beaming back to the ship, he picked up a transporter disk and called Lucy for backup. The two beamed back into the house and waited for the soon-to-arrive Agent Daniels.

"I'll give him some credit, Commander," Simon said as a grey sedan pulled up in front of the house.

"It only took him about fifteen minutes to get here. And now we're going to put an end to his interference."

The agent walked through the open door without so much as a knock. "Well, Mr. Hawke, I'm glad to see you've come to your senses. You want to tell me what's going on?"

Simon just grinned. Tigers would run from his expression. "Sure, Agent, I'd be happy to. You see, you guys were right. We *were* out there when the ship landed. Oh, yes," he said at the startled expression, "it was a ship. And we managed to get away with it just before the stormtroopers showed up. Here's just one of the smaller things we found aboard our pretty new ship." He reached into his pocket and pulled out a transporter disk.

Simon hadn't informed Lucy about his plan to virtually kidnap the agent. She watched him toss it to the agent, and a small noise escaped her.

"Don't worry, Commander," Simon said softly. "He'll find out sooner or later, anyway. If we make a clean breast of things, we might get some leniency. Right, Agent? Besides, you must be up on all the stuff going on with our people coming back after all this time, right? You were expecting me, weren't you? How else would you have been here in just fifteen minutes?" Simon winked an eyelid at Lucy as the agent's eyes rose from the disk in his hand.

"So? What is it?" he asked, pointedly refusing to answer any of the questions Simon put to him. "And how does the girl rate the title of commander?"

Simon spoke from across the room. "Just as to-the-point as ever, aren't you, Agent? Only this time, you managed to see to it that we didn't get to keep our stuff. Petty of you. Real petty. And this 'girl' rates the title of commander because she does a commander's job. Just like I do a captain's job."

The agent, face reddening, answered the accusation. "Petty? No. You can have your stuff back. I just wanted to get your attention."

Simon had been pacing around his empty living room. "Well, you managed to get it, friend. Now let's see if you don't regret it."

He'd stopped pacing right in front of Lucy. Standing with his hands behind his back, Simon watched the agent examine the disk in his hands. Pressing the spot that activated his beam-out along with the slaved disk Daniels held, he transported back to the ship.

Immediately upon his arrival, he called out, "Security, arrest that man." Pointing at the agent standing there in total shock, he watched as the two security personnel first disarmed him and then stepped back. "Okay, Lieutenants, I accept responsibility for this man. Hold on to his weapon until he's cleared to beam back down."

Simon turned back to the speechless agent and watched as he suffered another shock. The standard, person-tall shower of blue sparks formed over one of the hexagonal spaces, and Lucy materialized in the middle. The sparks died as she stepped off the spot. Bringing the agent back to reality after he witnessed his first beam-in, Simon said, "That's why you and your people aren't going to get what you want this time, Agent. Come with us and you'll see just what it is we found."

A quick tour of the ship ended up in the ready room. Simon seated himself and then waved to the other chairs. "Sit anywhere, Agent. Let me present my First Officer, Commander Lucy Grimes, my Science Officer, Commander Stephen Walker, Ph. D., and my Communications Officer, Commander Gayle Miller." As he slowly dropped into a vacant chair, Lucy sat also, followed by Gayle and Stephen, who had attached themselves along the way.

Keeping in mind the fully crewed nature of the ship and the impending departure that had everyone running around like a stirred-up anthill, Simon asked, "Okay, tell me. Are you going to release my stuff now? And put it back?"

Gasping like a fish out of water, the stunned agent asked, "Is that all you can think about? Look around you!"

The four looked at the agent instead. "What do you think we've been looking at for the last year, Agent... Daniels, is it?" This from Gayle as she turned her full attention on him, devastating when she was so close. "And how about you try to guess what we've been *doing* for the last year." Leaning across the table, she picked up a remote control. Pointing it at a screen to one side of the room, she started the video Kitty had begun making right after the *Galileo* reached the asteroid belt.

Instantly, a view of the stars showed clearly in the small screen. Time-lapse editing showed Orion begin to take shape from the things shuttled from the bigger ship. More scenes played—shuttles and fighters bringing in material for the smelter, people playing Z-tag, two construction pods sliding an assembly into place while another welded a seam.

Leaning toward the agent as the screen went dark, Gayle, cleavage exposed for effect, asked the faltering agent. "Quick, Agent. What are you going to do, now? Arrest us? All eight hundred of us? What about the ones out in the asteroid belt? How are you going to get at them? Do you have any answers to any of these questions?"

Forcing his eyes to travel up to Gayle's face, the agent stammered, "I… don't know. I suspected something, of course. But, this… I need to pass this on to my superiors."

Stephen decided to have a little fun of his own. "So, tell me, Agent. Just what are you going to do when you find out that your bosses know all about us, and that they've been keeping you in the dark all this time? Just what can you say that won't get you shipped off to… someplace very remote and cold?"

"Well, I…" Getting some of his composure back, Agent Daniels asserted, "I'm just going to have to confiscate that video."

As he started to get to his feet, Lucy raised a hand. "Don't get up, Agent. I'll get it for you." Pulling the disc from the machine, she slipped it into a plastic case. Smiling wickedly, she said, "I don't think you're going to confiscate anything off this ship that we don't want you to have, Agent, so let me save you the trouble and make you a gift of this one. We have *so* many copies."

Handing it to him, she said, "Some of the equipment on this ship—we call her the *Galileo* by the way—is very much from Earth. Nowhere did we find any evidence of videoing for personal use, although they do have a way to store videos in the ship's main computer. We haven't had any reports from our scientific staff to that effect, anyway."

Half an hour later, Agent Daniels, dismissed by

Simon and his other officers, made the trip back to the transporter with only Gayle as an escort. Armed with the disc and his pistol, unloaded, he was about to be transported back to Earth.

"Tell me, Agent, just where is the superior you'll be reporting to?" Gayle asked, all innocence.

Standing on one of the hexes, he said, "Washington, DC."

She signaled the transporter tech to step aside and handled the beam-down herself. "Well, I hope you don't have any problems getting that disc to him. You do realize that time is of the essence, don't you? Good luck, Agent. We'll see you in anywhere from six months to a year." She looked over the control board settings and, nodding to herself, reached out to activate the system.

As Gayle was about to energize the beam, the agent spoke hurriedly. "And tell Mr. Hawke I'll have his house restored to normal right away."

Gayle looked at the reeling agent. "That's *Captain* Hawke, and don't forget it!" Reaching out again, she energized the beam and Agent Daniels sparkled out of their lives.

Stephen had his share of difficulties, too. It had been hoped that a solar cell project would generate some revenue that could be used to resupply the ship with luxury items or used to perhaps pay for the time of someone whose expertise was needed and couldn't afford to be gone long without recompense. Stephen had recommended an engineer for the project and recruited him, turning over a considerable amount of information from the *Galileo's* data banks early on so he could begin production of these advanced cells.

After getting no answer to a phone call, he beamed into the house of the engineer and sat down to wait. An hour and two beers later, Victor McCord unlocked his door, turned on the light, and, to his credit, didn't flinch. His eyes took in the two empties sitting on the table beside Stephen, and he brought another two from the kitchen, opening one for himself and handing the other to his friend.

"Okay, spill it," Victor said without preamble. "And if it's not the best damn story I've ever heard, that's the last beer you'll ever get from me."

For the next half an hour, Stephen talked, the beer mostly forgotten except to wet his throat. He finished and sat back, arms crossed.

Victor brought another beer. "Well, you do spin a great yarn, friend. Now, how do you convince me?"

A crooked grin on his face, Stephen asked, "Do you really want to be convinced?" At his friend's slow nod, Stephen handed him one of the videos Kitty had made.

An hour and two more beers later, Victor argued, "This is good, I'll admit. But I've seen better special effects at the movies. Got anything else?"

"As a matter of fact, I do. How would you like to see where I got the data on those cells you're so busy turning out?" At the engineer's bemused nod, Stephen tossed him a disk. Climbing out of the armchair he'd appropriated when he beamed in, he warned, "This will be easier if you're standing, Vic." Looking down at the disk in his hand with confusion on his face, Victor stood up. Stephen advised, "Remember, buddy, you asked for it!" and activated his wristband.

Victor was convinced. Finally. They sat in the mess hall, drinking coffee he'd seen materialize out of bright blue sparkles. They talked about the problems associated with the solar cell project—very few, actually. The patents had gone through, and he'd drawn some interest from the private sector. But the big surprise was the defense contractor who wanted exclusive rights. Remembering Stephen's request, he'd demurred and gone ahead with the project privately. Some speculative money had come in. He'd taken an option to lease on a building that would be the manufacturing facility, and some of his friends were retooling existing equipment to fabricate the new cells. The batteries would be farmed out to another company, built to the specifications Stephen stipulated.

The *Galileo's* return had coincided with the next phase of Victor's job—the actual production of the new cells and their storage batteries—and after a tour of the ship and a good long look at the fighter in the bay, Victor was ready to go back.

"That fighter is the old model," Stephen said. "The newer, faster versions, twenty of them, are still out there."

Victor shrugged. "I'm an engineer. I can guess what the new one's look like. And I'm going to see one, sooner or later. Right now, though, I have to finish getting this project up and running. One more year, and you'll have a very insistent volunteer."

Taking Victor back to the transporter room, Stephen said, "I'll go back down with you. One of the most amazing sights in the world is to see someone beam out. And you know there are no hidden gadgets. It's your own house, after all."

As they stood there, Transport Control beamed in a young crew woman. Victor, agog, said, "I'm going to find out how that works! Really, Stephen, there's no need to go down with me now. I've seen what a beam-in is like, and I'll assume a beam-out to be much the same."

Agreeing that it was, Stephen shook his friend's hand. "We'll be back in about a year. I'll be in touch as soon as we make orbit. Good luck, Vic. And be ready to take a ride next time." Gesturing to the on-duty tech, he watched Victor beam out.

CHAPTER TWENTY

Lucy decided she hated being in command, but actually, it was okay in a way. When she was just in charge of the third shift, it was cool. Most of the time all she had to do was sit there and maybe order a course correction, but that was before she'd found out what Simon's definition of rank and command structure really meant.

She'd never completely understood her own idea that everybody on the first two shifts would be senior to her in rank. Simon, on the other hand, felt somewhat differently—a misunderstanding, really. He hadn't realized Lucy didn't fully comprehend her position, not understanding its importance in Simon's worldview.

She'd thought she was just in charge of the third-stringers, sort of, but Simon had explained the facts of life to her when the *Galileo* headed for Earth, leaving Kitty on Orion. Now Wing Commander Hawke, Kitty was going to oversee the formation and training of the defense network around Orion, which left a gap in the command structure of the *Galileo* for the voyage home.

Commander Walker was in charge of the Research and Development division and Commander Miller was senior Communications Officer, also overseeing factory operations when the *Galileo* was in construction mode. With the captain being the captain—*Duh!* Lucy thought, working her way through the logic—that was all four of the Firsters.

"With Wing Commander Hawke on Orion, and since Commander Walker isn't a line officer and Commander Miller is... working in other areas, that moves you to First Officer," Simon had told her when he'd called her to his office the day before the *Galileo* left for Earth. "And you've been in actual command of this ship eight hours a day, seven days a week for quite some time. Let me ask you a question, Lucy. Who better to run second shift and be First Officer than someone who has experience running third?"

"But..." Lucy said, searching desperately for an answer. The reality of what the captain was asking her finally struck home. "I can't run second shift! I mean, sir, everyone on the second shift bridge team outranks me."

"Not anymore, Commander," Simon said. Smiling, he slid a small case across the desk to her.

Hand shaking slightly, she picked up the black velvet case, guessing what was inside. She opened the lid to reveal the gold eight-pointed stars of a full commander.

Her mind churning, she looked from the stars in her hand to the man behind the desk several times before she could formulate a response. To her horror, she heard herself ask, "Do I get my bridge team, sir? I'm not sure I can do this without them. I mean it's not all my doing that our shift runs so well. I depend on them a lot, sir."

Simon smiled, "I appreciate your loyalty, Commander, but the fact is that to do so would effectively demote those already on second shift for no apparent reason other than favoritism, and that's not going to become a practice aboard any ship I have control over. Do I make myself clear?" He ended on a firm note that sounded stern even to himself. When the new commander silently nodded, fear evident on her face, he relented.

"This is going to give you a broader range of experience, Commander. Learning to work with others is a part of life. Besides, your new team is expecting you on the bridge at fifteen hundred hours tomorrow." He smiled at the nervous Lucy. "Relax, Lucy. I'm going to give you the same advice an old sergeant gave me way back when—if you act like you know what you're doing, most people will believe it. Confidence breeds confidence, Commander, and you need to project it. Now, this bridge team is pretty much intact. They did lose their Helm officer to Orion, though, so you can bring yours over. That way you'll have at least one familiar face on the shift until you get used to the new ones."

The thought of David Sipes sitting at Helm did calm her some, she had to admit, but getting used to the new position and faces was going to be a bitch.

She'd thought the move to second shift was going to be a problem, but whatever she'd expected never materialized. The bridge team was polite to her, calling her "ma'am," and following instructions without hesitation. She did get a few sideways looks that she thought could have been her imagination, but she was never certain. The few times she met her old team in the rec room was the only point at which she got to let her hair down. They razzed her unmercifully about her promotion, but she knew it was all in fun. Nevertheless, it had been a hectic week, absorbing the new situation. Rob Greene was feeling the same since he'd been promoted to Lucy's old position.

Now they'd arrived at Earth, and Lucy's trip home to see about getting some of her friends to join up had been interrupted by a strange incident. Ensign Lisle Gower had been in a TGI Friday's dressed in civilian clothes when she was approached by an anonymous man and woman asking for her by name. The two had given her a letter and asked her to deliver it to Captain Hawke.

"They acted okay, but kinda stiff, you know?" Gower said. "It did do some good, though. All my friends got to see a couple of MIBs give me a letter with the presidential seal on it, and then they all followed me outside and watched me beam up. I was gonna let one come with me to tell the others what had happened, but this seemed more important, so I told them I'd be back and just beamed out in the middle of the parking lot. You said we should be more obvious about it—beaming out, that is. Did I do right?"

The implications were clear, Lucy realized, tapping the envelope Gower had handed her on the arm of the command chair. The girl had indeed done right. Captain Hawke wanted as many people as possible to know about their existence, feeling the exposure would help ease the problems dealing with a government that wanted their ship, but they'd expected a greater respite before the government began sending this kind of message to the captain.

"Of course, Ensign," she said, sending her back

down to her friends.

"Well, the only thing to do is to pass the buck," she mused and continued tapping the envelope on the arm of the command chair while she waited for the captain to arrive.

When Simon appeared on the bridge, Lucy handed the envelope to him. "This has to be related to that FBI agent. God, but he's quick. Didn't Commander Miller drop him back in Washington? In order for him to get that," she said, gesturing to the letter, "get back to Colorado, and get it to one of our people, well, *someone* greased his wheels."

Simon tore the end of the envelope open and shook the single-folded piece of paper out. Reading it, he looked up at Lucy. "Get Commanders Miller and Walker to the ready room. And be there yourself as soon as you can, Commander. Looks like things have just heated up down below."

Lucy stared at him as he left the bridge. If a man could skip without actually doing so, then the captain had just done a credible impression.

Gayle and Stephen walked into the ready room and found Simon and Lucy already there. The letter lay on the table before them. Seating himself, Stephen reached out and grabbed the piece of paper, bringing it over so he and Gayle could read it.

"Is this for real? And who would we send? It can't be you."

Gayle added, "Hell no, it can't. And where would we meet these people? And on such short notice. And I'm not sure I like this phrase," she said, pointing at the paper. "What does 'in the best interests of all concerned' mean, anyway?"

Simon lifted his hands in surrender. "Don't look

at me. I'm sure I don't know, but there's a way to find out. Stephen, why don't you set up a meeting at the earliest moment? I don't want to delay departure any longer than I have to with all these new people on board."

Taking the business card that was stapled to the letter, Stephen said, "I guess the lodge would do again. I still have the key I never returned before we took off last time. I'll beam down and give this Special Assistant to the Office of the President a call. I'll let you know what happens as soon as I can."

"Brandon Galway," the no-nonsense voice said, grating out of the speaker. "Who's this?"

"I'm Commander Stephen Walker of the *Galileo*, Mr. Galway, and I'm under the impression that we're supposed to talk."

Setting up the meeting was the work of minutes. When Stephen asked how long it would take Galway and crew to get to the Appalachians, he was told that they had a helicopter at their disposal and that he should just name the place.

"Okay, Mr. Galway," Stephen said, "about five miles past Rawley Springs you'll see a cutoff into Washington National Forest. Take that for about five miles and you'll come out at a hunting lodge. There should be enough room to land a chopper."

Given an arrival time of an hour and a half, Stephen responded, "Very well, Mr. Galway. Just make sure you four are the only ones there. And unarmed. We have ways to monitor things like that, you know."

When Simon heard about the arrangements, he

could only say, "Good work. I want all four of you to have a sidearm. The new lasers could give you an advantage or even things up if your gun ban gets disobeyed. Full uniforms as well."

The roster for the away team had broken down to Lucy, Stephen, Gayle, and Commander John Marshall, their Security Chief. All four went to their quarters to change into clean uniforms and draw weapons from the armory.

Keeping track of the air traffic in the area via the *Galileo's* sensors, the four members of the team were informed that a helicopter seemed to be heading straight for the lodge and would arrive in about fifteen minutes. Lucy, as First Officer, was in charge of the mission, and in addition to the weapon on her hip she was wearing a headset identical to those her other team members wore. That way, everyone could keep track of what the sensor crews were reporting, as well as keep in touch with each other if they should get separated. Their headsets were connected to the new commlink that had been built from some of the plans found in the computer. Despite its small size, it was able to reach the *Galileo* some twelve thousand miles above.

Ten minutes before the chopper was estimated to arrive at the lodge, the team beamed down to the parking lot outside the two-story ranch-style log structure. Stephen pulled the key from his pocket and opened the front door. Looking around to see that everything was in order, he waved the others in and, pushing the door closed, set about making coffee in the oversized pot on the divider between the living room and kitchen.

A few minutes later, they heard the rising sound

of the whirlybird as it cleared a ridge half a mile away. Almost immediately, the sound began to drop as the craft settled in the precise middle of the parking lot. Lucy, getting updates from above, gave the okay. Even though she was years younger than the others, she had the responsibility of command. Taking time for a deep breath, she remembered the captain's advice about appearances.

"Seems like there are five people in that thing, folks. Commander Walker, would you be kind enough to greet them and ask them in for coffee?"

Stephen watched from a window as four men stepped out of the helicopter and, bending over, ran several dozen feet away from the whirling blades. A silhouetted figure stayed at the controls of the idling machine. They conferred in a tight group for a few seconds and then headed for the lodge. Stephen watched them walk up the stone steps and across the wide wooden porch. He nodded to Marshall to open the door as the lead man reached for the doorknob.

Hesitating only fractionally, the four U.S. representatives entered to a scene they hadn't expected. There were four people in the room, all in identical uniforms, and a good-looking blonde was pouring coffee into obviously expensive cups on equally expensive saucers. Stopping just inside the door, a short, stocky man looked each of the *Galileo* crew over.

"Looks like you have a lucrative business going here. I'm Brandon Galway, Special Assistant to the Office the President. This is Colonel Michael Babcock, USAF, Steven Mitchell from NASA, and… a member of the security services."

Lucy stepped forward, hand extended. "Pleased

to meet you, Mr. Galway. I'm Commander Lucy Grimes, First Officer of the *Galileo*. With me are Commander Walker, Science Officer, Commander Miller, Communications Officer, and Commander Marshall, our Chief Security Officer." As she named each one, they nodded their heads in turn.

Lucy looked the four men over. Galway could have been a linebacker in a former life. He had the kind of build any coach would love to see in a defensive formation. The Air Force officer was in uniform and the NASA guy looked the part of a rocket scientist, complete with pocket protector and pens. The unnamed man at the back of the group Lucy faced would never get a second look on the street. Plain in dress and appearance, he would blend into virtually any crowd. Here, he stood out like a sore thumb since Galway had made such a production of not naming him.

He was the first to speak, baiting her, she realized. "Kinda young to be second in command of a spaceship, aren't you, young lady?" he taunted.

Keeping her temper under control wasn't the easiest thing to do. Too many times in her short life she'd had to defend herself against those who would give her the same kind of grief. "Who are you? And what experience do you have with spaceship crews that you can make that determination, sir?" she threw back.

Glowering in anger, the little man started to make a rejoinder when Galway, the obvious leader of their group, silenced him with a wave of his hand.

"Now that we have the amenities out of the way, can we get down to business?" Sitting down at the head of the table that separated the two groups, Lucy waved for the visitors to be seated as well, preempting the right to set the tone of the meeting. She picked up a coffeepot, filled her cup, and set it down as close to Galway as she comfortably could. "Your fourth still hasn't identified himself, and until he does, he can wait outside. I was raised to observe the amenities."

Galway shifted uncomfortably in his chair and said, "He's a member of a group even I don't know the name of. Let's just call him Mr. Smith."

"Well, that's very original." Her sarcasm wasn't lost on Galway or Smith. "So, tell me, Mr. Galway, what's so important that you'd call a meeting like this at such short notice? We're due to leave orbit as soon as this meeting is over, so you'll forgive me if I don't have time to spar with you. Tell me what you want, and we can discuss the details without any beating around the bush, if you please." The captain had briefed her on how to handle these people. She was to make them state their position and wasn't to let them draw her into any confessions or giving too much away.

"First, I want to express my displeasure at the fact that you people are wearing weapons. That's a violation of the agreement we made prior to coming here," Galway huffed.

This brought an immediate response from Stephen. "Mr. Galway, I asked *your* group to come unarmed. You never asked the same of us, though we would have come armed in any case. We're the ones at a numerical disadvantage. Now, please state your reasons for asking us here. We can leave any time, you know."

Taking a deep breath, Galway looked at his little

security man and spoke. "We're here to demand that you turn the vessel you found over to your government. It's the patriotic thing to do, and the law is very specific on this point. It's called the right of eminent domain. Confiscation is allowed under the laws of the United States. Besides, you have no idea what you have and no idea how to use it. Also, having private citizens in possession of such a thing is a threat to our national security. We have no recourse but to insist on this course of action." Sitting back in the chair he occupied, he smugly folded his arms across his chest and waited.

Lucy grinned. "The Captain said you'd take that tack. Well, here are some facts for you. Even though he didn't explicitly mention eminent domain, I will tell you that, if I'm correct, it only applies to things actually *in* the United States. Our ship was found in what amounts to no-man's-land some twelve thousand miles above the Earth. Let's add to that the fact that we *do* know what we have and how to use it. As evidence of that, let me play a video for you, a new one. Commanders Miller and Walker will narrate."

Motioning for Commander Marshall to put the disc in the player, Lucy sat back. Over the next hour, Gayle and Stephen explained what was showing on the screen. It would have taken far less time if they hadn't been repeatedly interrupted by one or other of the four men.

"Gentlemen," Lucy began after the disc ended, "this second video shows you that we *do* know how to use *our* ship." Everyone noticed the stress she put on the pronoun. "And turning this vessel over to any government on Earth would be stupidity of the worst sort."

Outpacing the objections that naturally followed that comment, she went on. "Do you know what would happen if we do as you demand? How would Russia or China react to the United States having the kind of technology that our ship represents? You, my anonymous friend, how do *you* think they'd react? Or all the other countries of the world, in fact? We say that the best thing is for the 'status' to remain 'quo,' so to speak. That will keep this country and all the others on this mudball from taking each other out in some kind of nuclear frenzy. We consider that to be patriotism of the highest caliber. And as we have both possession and a tactical advantage, I think we'll keep control."

Deftly fielding the questions of the four men from the government, Lucy and her team finally hammered home to them that there was no joke, no special effects, and no attempt to defraud, defame, coerce, or intimidate.

"Remember, you came to us, gentlemen," Stephen interjected. "Right now, one hundred and forty million miles away, we have four-hundred-plus people trying to carve out a piece of the universe for the human race. We don't intend to keep that away from the rest of Earth. On the contrary, we intend to give it to the people of Earth, eventually. Please note, I said 'to the *people* of Earth,' gentlemen, not to one country or group. But until we get a few problems solved, the most notable of which is that we've already been fired on by unknown aliens—and fired back successfully, mind you—we must keep as much distance between us and you as possible. We're still figuring out how to do that since we have to keep returning here for more personnel and to bring back those who get tired, want out, or need to be buried. Yes, buried. As I said, we were attacked, and there have been casualties. We have seven confirmed dead and three missing. This isn't a picnic we're returning to."

Gayle found a chance to make her voice heard. Knowing that her physical attributes made most men underestimate her, she tended to let it go on most of the time, but in this instance, she decided to demonstrate that she wasn't there just for show.

"We're now fighting for our lives out there, Mr. Galway." Turning her not inconsiderable attention toward the leader of the opposing group, she continued. "We are few, and space is vast. I realize that's an understatement, but there it is. We have a chance to move the human race forward a quantum step, and giving the ship to you wouldn't accomplish that. As a friend of mine said, 'They'll study it into some black budget, and no one will ever benefit from it.' That's a paraphrase, but you know what he means. So, we keep the ship, and we're going to carve out a foothold in space for the human race whether you like it or not!"

Not a word came from the four men, and a cloud seemed to hang over them as they sat there. Lucy tipped her head to one side, listening to a report from the *Galileo*. She looked at her visitors. "Gentlemen, are any of you expecting company? Four men in a sedan heading toward this cabin at a high rate of speed, perhaps? If you are and can contact them, I'd suggest you wave them off. If not, we're out of here, and our next meeting won't be under such pleasant circumstances."

Commander Marshall rose and went to stand at one of the windows, looking out onto the parking lot with pistol in hand. At this, Galway's security man looked at Galway, who nodded at him. He got up and left through the front door.

Galway temporized. "Look, we had to take our best shot at things. Truth is, I feel a little like you do. I want to keep things as they are, having a vested interest in the status quo. But I also have to answer to a higher authority. Balancing those two can be pretty tricky sometimes. I imagine that if you don't know that yet, Commander Grimes, you will before too much longer. Those guys in the car had orders to infiltrate if they didn't get a signal from… him. Now that we know how hard it is to sneak up on you, I'm sure it won't happen again."

Lucy glanced at her watch. "Mr. Galway, this thing in my ear is a terrible nuisance sometimes. It just informed me that we're running out of time. So, here's what we want: A base on each of three continents—North America, Europe, and Asia—free passage for our personnel when they return from their tours of duty, and no restrictions on recruitment. These are things we expect you to work out with all of Earth's governments while we're gone. In return, we'll start giving out some of the technology on board to begin improving the lives of all Earth's citizens. There are, of course, two restrictions on that. We will not trade propulsion or weapons technology."

Lucy closed her eyes for a moment, thinking back to some of the conversations she'd listened to and, lately, been involved in. "The real kicker to the whole situation as we see it is this—if we give something to you, Mr. Galway, you can be sure that someone in every country on Earth will be given the same data. There will be no exclusivity."

Stephen picked up where Lucy left off. "I want you to keep in mind, too, what a Pandora's Box this kind of deal can be. Let me give you an example. Today, in this country, there's a company forming to build improved solar cells and storage batteries. That's all well and good. But how about when we offer you a device that will cancel weight? Not mass, my friend, just weight. Marry that to an automobile equipped with the new battery and solar cells, and whole industries would vanish overnight—gasoline companies all the way down to distributors because those batteries will run an electric motor at seventy-five miles an hour for a week. Add to that all businesses that support internal combustion engines and all businesses that have anything to do with tires, Mr. Galway. And those are just a few off the top of my head. So. One small... gift and how many millions of people will be unemployed around the world? What about the countries that produce the oil the world will no longer need? I say take what I've said here back to your boss and tell him to be very careful about what you demand and what you—"

Lucy's wrist jerked and she looked down at her arm. Blue sparkles formed before her eyes as she looked back up to see two men barreling into the room, guns drawn.

"Keep the same phone number, Galway!"

"I will not tolerate this!" Lucy shouted, rampaging through the bridge. "I want to know how two men can get past our sensor net and get that close to us!

Those two fucking Neanderthals weren't kidding. Weapons out and looking for someone to shoot."

Stephen, silently in agreement with her, was busy picking through the data to come up with just that answer. "It seems, Commander, that the lodge is in an area that blocked some of our sensor sweeps. Somehow, and don't ask me how, those two got into the area before we beamed in and worked their way into the lodge. If the others in the car hadn't shown up, we wouldn't even have been on the lookout. Imagine the potential damage from that. We got lucky, and that's all there is to it."

Simon chose that moment to walk onto the bridge after waiting for the few minutes it took for Lucy to regain a portion of control. "Luck is about all we have going for us, people," he said, looking to bring the atmosphere on the bridge back to something approaching professional. "And that's been from day one. All we can do is make the best of any break we can get and try to minimize any damage." He turned to Lucy. "Debrief in my office, if you please, Commander."

Lucy stood at attention as Simon circled her like a... hawk, not blinking. She couldn't get the image of a bird of prey out of her mind, searching for just the right moment to strike.

"In front of junior officers, Commander?" he asked inches away from her ear, his voice almost a whisper. He walked all the way around her again, coming to a stop in front of her. Raising his voice to conversational level, he continued speaking. "Losing your temper is not out of line, but I will *not* tolerate outbreaks like that in front of the crew. *That* was out of line." He turned his back on her and walked to his desk, the set of his shoulders telling her he wasn't through.

He sat down, deliberately staring at her the whole time. "When your subordinates see you lose control, their confidence in you can be severely impacted, which in turn can cause problems at crucial moments, problems like hesitation to obey orders instantly. And instant obedience is required out here or else people can die. Easily. These people, like you, Commander, are volunteers. They don't have to obey; they obey because they want to, because they trust you, and because they trust that I made the right choice putting you in command." Simon had gone into lecture mode, his voice smooth and firm, his eyes compelling her to look at him and daring her to look away. The Law was about to be delivered from on high. "These people only follow what I say because… hell, I don't know why they do, but they do. And they're only going to as long as the people I pick to lead them in my place don't let me down."

He took a deep breath, obviously choosing his words with care. "Outbursts like the one I just witnessed are marginally acceptable in a staff meeting but not in front of the crew. If that's not acceptable to you, I'll see to it that you're dropped off the next time we get back to Earth. Otherwise, you'll make it your personal mission to see to it that each and every officer on this ship learns what happens when that rule is broken the first time. And remember that while 'first time' implies a second time, second time means *last* time."

Simon leaned back in his chair and looked up at

her. A chime sounded, saving her from further chewing. He smiled, taking her by surprise. It carried all the way to his eyes, which had remained hard up until then.

"All I have to do is remember some ass-chewing I got and give it to someone else when they screw up, and I sound like a damn genius, don't I?" He shook his head sadly and glanced at his watch. "Right now, we have a ship to get under way. And as it's my shift, I want you to get some rest. We'll let your actions decide your fate. You show up for your next watch and I'll consider this matter resolved. You don't show up and I'll still consider it resolved." He looked at her for another minute while she stared a hole in the bulkhead over his shoulder. After another eternity, he said, "Dismissed."

Lucy closed the door behind her with a sense of doom averted. He hadn't canned her. She'd known she was wrong as the words were coming out of her mouth, but she hadn't been able to stop. She blamed it on post-adrenaline letdown, but for whatever reason, he hadn't canned her.

And why wouldn't everyone follow him? she thought. *Yeah, it's going to take some time and work, but I see the vision Simon sees. And it's obvious that Commander Kitty sees it, too.*

Six days later, the *Galileo* slid back into place beside Orion, ostensibly to drop off extra supplies for the food processors and to add and transfer crew, but also to show those on the space dock that they hadn't been forgotten. Just over a month had passed since their departure, but to Simon it had felt like a year.

"I'm going to be too old for this before we get the third dock built, Dan," he griped. Putting his feet up on Daniel's desk, he sipped gratefully at the scotch sitting in front of him. "And I'm going to have to do something about whoever's been smuggling booze, even if it does hit the spot right now." He knew better than to ask who among his crew was bringing the stuff aboard for Daniel, and he let the matter drop. "So, how are things going out here?"

"First, who said it was smuggled?" Glancing at some printouts on his desk, Daniel shrugged. "And as well as can be expected. We haven't had any more visitors. We now have a sensor net that covers an area extending from halfway to Mars out to about the same distance from Jupiter. That's lateral. Front to back, I'd say somewhat less." Front to back referred to the areas ahead of Orion and behind her in the asteroid belt.

"As for the ship itself, we're about a quarter done. The construction is primarily from the inside out, as you know. As each section is finished, it's pressure tested, and the next one out is started. Installing the hull plating itself effectively finished that portion of the ship, and work started on braces so we had something to build on, so-to-speak. Now we can pick up the pace. All the time that the beam extruders were turning out the keel beam, spars, struts, main braces, and so on, others were turning out deck plates and hull plates. And the other factories were busy stockpiling wire, cable, fiber optics, switches, control modules, seats, tables, nuts and bolts, and everything else. Now it's just a great big jigsaw puzzle.

"Everything has been reconfigured to our own

physical parameters, of course. That translates to more decks and more storage space and will make things a little less claustrophobic for everyone who works on her."

Simon took another sip of the scotch, eyeing the amber liquid speculatively. "We'll be able to mount heavier lasers and more torpedoes, too?"

"Oh, yes," Daniel affirmed. "And even the newest thing out of R&D. I'm just glad they got the specs to us in time to allow for the interior modifications."

Simon looked from his inspection of the drink in his hand to Daniel. "I've read all the reports that come across my desk. Did I miss something? The only thing I know is something about reconfiguring the capture fields into selectively permeable barriers." He secretly patted himself on the back. A year ago, that phrase would never have entered his conversation.

"Right," Daniel said, slipping into teacher mode, finding it an aid in helping someone reach the answer by themselves. "Now take those same barriers and add a little more power to them. Remember, we've got power to spare out of an antimatter core. Push 'em out past the hull of the ship and you've got what?"

Simon unconsciously set his drink down, forgotten, as the imagery Daniel's words evoked cascaded through his mind. "Force fields!" he exclaimed. "Meteor shields, antimissile defenses." His voice trailed off, and he looked up at Daniel.

"Exactly," Daniel said. "And if we'd had that technology when those ..." His voice cracked and Simon knew what was going through his mind.

"I wish we'd them back then, too, Dan, but we

didn't," Simon said, feeling the same pain Daniel did. "At least we have them now, though. Retrofit Orion and…" His anger over the deaths of people who'd trusted him he filed in a safe place. Someday he'd be able to pull it out and deal with it, but now was not the time.

Instead, he fell back on the age-old tactic of changing the subject. "Did I see a white hull as we came in?"

Daniel sat up, relief showing on his face, and nodded. "One of the engineers found a way to add coloring to the hull plates as they come out of the factory. Takes a little more time to set up, but once in place and functioning, it doesn't slow anything down. And it makes the ship look less like the *Galileo* and more like a ship from some other race. Also, white reflects light, and the ship won't require as much energy to cool it. We're carrying the idea inside the ship, too. Humans are color-oriented critters, Simon, so we're using light colors in the work areas and corridors, and restful pastels in the gyms, mess halls, etc. We're still debating what to do with the personal quarters. Have you thought of a name for her, yet?

Simon looked his friend in the eye and smiled. "Yes, I have. And for the next five after that, too. I intend to name them after six of the premier science-fiction authors of my time. They will be named the *Arthur C. Clarke*, *Larry Niven*, *Isaac Asimov*, *Anne McCaffrey*, and *Andre Norton*. And the one you're building right now, the flagship of our battle fleet, will be named the *Robert A. Heinlein*. I'm sure they'll be referred to by the surnames only, and that's all right with me since I won't mind being captain of a ship named the *Heinlein*. And I just hope he won't be turning over in his grave at the thought that a fighting ship is named after him, but he really shouldn't since he spent a good part of his life in the navy."

Daniel looked at Simon questioningly. "I was never a sci-fi reader before this, but I've read some of the stuff the guys brought with them." He shook his head, eyes casting to and fro, as if in search of an answer. "Still, I don't get your choice of names."

Simon leaned forward, eager to find another topic to get them back to the present. "It's not so much the particular authors, really, although they're the ones I read the most avidly when I found a new title on the shelves. It's just that science-fiction authors are responsible in very large part for the fact that we have such an easy time getting volunteers. And sci-fi writers have been in the business of asking 'what if'… for the last hundred years or so. Surely you've heard of Jules Verne?"

"Well, yeah!" Daniel exclaimed. "The submarine show. Now that was a piece of engineering. Cheesy monsters, though."

Simon laughed out loud. "Well, Danny-me-lad, that book was written in the late 1800s, so that was science fiction in its day. But look at the subs we've got today. And sci-fi authors predicted force fields a long time ago."

He turned serious as quickly as he had laughed. "I wonder why the Builders never took their technology to that level?"

Daniel shook his head. "I don't think we'll ever know, Simon. Too much cultural difference, I'll bet."

Simon finished up his courtesy call on Orion's skipper and returned to his quarters on the *Galileo*, somewhat miffed that Kitty was still out on one of the continuous patrols. If not her sensors, then her radio should have informed her long ago of the *Galileo's* arrival. He'd only been back for a couple of hours and already he was hearing gossip about the commandant of the fighter wing—how she spent as many hours up and out as possible, and how she was turning the fighter wings into an elite group of... what?... loyal to her and her vision of what a fighter pilot should be. Could this really be the even-tempered woman he'd married? And to make a pistol a part of the uniform? A vision of her tear-streaked face kneeling over the shrouded body of Toni Putnam crossed his mind, and he shivered involuntarily.

Kitty sauntered into their quarters and dropped her pistol belt in a corner. After draping her flight jacket over a chair, she draped herself over Simon.

"Long time, no see, lover." Pulling him to his feet, she tugged on his sleeve until she got him moving in the direction of the shower. "Help me scrub the stink off, okay? Then I've got plans for the rest of the night. Randy's got the watch, and we're clear until I say otherwise."

After a much-needed shower and a desperately needed reunion with her husband, Kitty was relaxed enough to broach a subject she'd been thinking about for the entire month of Simon's absence.

"Simon, how far have you thought this out?" Long hours in a Mamba had given Kitty's philosophical nature time to worry over the future. "Right now, you see the possibilities of getting open recognition. What about when—not if—some government gets pissed off at not getting what they want fast enough? We've already seen our own government trying to arrest our people. It's thanks to the wristbands and your foresight that they were able to get their jobs done without anything worse happening, but that can't go on. Someone will get hurt no matter what we do. We all hoped we'd have at least a little more time before publicly revealing ourselves, but that didn't happen. So, we make the best of our situation." Looking over her shoulder at Simon as she briskly dried her now shoulder-length hair, she saw the amazement on his face. "What?"

He grinned, propped himself up on an elbow, and sighed. "You seem to have… embraced our situation rather completely for an avowed pacifist. Come back to bed and tell me about it."

And cradled in her husband's arms, she did.

"We've been out here for almost a year now. And while I'm out there," she said, waving in the general direction of the bulkhead, "I have time to think. I figure there's a point at which there's no going back, and I think we've already passed that point. We're going to need a fallback position for when we're cut off, officially, from Earth."

Simon marveled at how their thought processes coincided. "I mentioned that to the staff when we were on our way to Earth," he said. "We've got the beginnings of just that in place—a couple of people we can trust to help steer volunteers our way without having to worry too much about whether or not they're agents of some kind."

"Hell, Simon, it's the second most common topic for discussion in any group, and most of the groups are composed of college-age people. You know how they like to chew on something once they get their teeth into it. And," Kitty went on in a lively tone, "we need to instill some traditions in our fledgling republic. We'll probably have to quote the Declaration of Independence at Earth eventually, so getting people motivated early is a good idea. The Mamba pilots are a highly visible group, so use them to motivate our own people and attract newcomers."

They talked for hours in the limbo Kitty had created for them. And after their reunion idyll ended by common consent, Simon and Kitty dressed for their evening appearance.

"We can't miss dinner," Kitty proclaimed. "It's traditional on the first day back."

Simon nodded in agreement. "Fine with me, but I gotta say something about that fledgling republic comment of yours. When what we've started building here can grow on its own, then it can be a republic. By that time our group will have grown and split into many segments—a civilian population, service industries, police, courts, military, everything any civilization needs to survive. Diversity. Right now, we're only a military branch. We have to build and recruit the rest. But let's get to dinner, since it's now traditional," Simon said, changing the subject. "We can throw this out on the table for our own bull session later."

For the most part, mealtimes had settled down to the ends of shifts, so there were three meals served every day by the people assigned to the kitchens. For reasons known only to themselves, most folks didn't seem to take too well to the food processors. It made no difference that the egg they were eating had come from a processor; when people wanted an omelet, they wanted it prepared by the hands of a fellow human being. Therefore, a kitchen had been constructed, and cooks plied their arcane skills within.

Time was measured in the age-old twenty-four-hours-in-a-day manner, and dinner was being served to those who had the evening shift free, which included most department heads. Because of this, Simon wasn't too surprised to see Daniel in the mess hall, along with Stephen, Gayle, Lucy, and Miranda Lee.

"Waiting for us to come out of seclusion?" Simon asked, smiling. "So, what's up?"

"What's up is that everyone wants to know what happens next, Simon." Daniel looked up from the depths of his coffee cup. The number one ongoing discussion centered around just that question. Simon, having determined to keep overall control of the *Galileo* in his own hands, was in effect being called upon to put up or shut up. Closing both eyes and drawing on the strength of his wife sitting next to him, he jumped straight into the deep end.

"The immediate next step is to start the next dock and let Orion get on about its own mission," he began. Opening his eyes, he glanced around the table. "The next step after that is harder. I originally wanted to stay out of view longer than this, but our government—while not exactly composed of the brightest bulbs on the sign—isn't stupid and figured out enough that we couldn't stay hidden if we wanted to. Here's what happened on Earth."

After relating his part, Simon let Stephen, Gayle, and Lucy tell their tales.

"So, we go completely public when we get back with two lines of attack. One is overt. How do we go about openly recruiting? And the other is covert. How do we set up clandestine lines of communications if worst comes to worst? Call me paranoid, but from now on we need to consider the possibility of tech spies, sabotage, and worse. Prepare a proposal or proposals for me to review. There's no rush on this since we have to get number two built before we spend any more time on Earth.

"Next on the table is the question of command. In the next eighteen months or so, we're going to need three base commanders and ten more ship captains, not to mention crews. Stephen has indicated that he wants to opt out of command and stay more in the science branch. I agree that we can get more use from his abilities if we follow his suggestion, so I'm left looking at five of my next nine captains and base commanders.

"Daniel, you may not like this, but you're going to be the only captain among the base commanders. I'm looking at a chain of command that will leave one person in overall charge of all the bases—that being you or your replacement—to coordinate the building of ships. Standardization will be the watchword. I want any ship able to be serviced at any station, refueled and rearmed as necessary. We need one man to handle that, and you're elected. The others will have the rank of base commander. We have Orion, and we're going to build Gemini." Noting the look on Miranda's face, Simon gave her his attention. "Speak up, Commander. This amounts to a staff meeting, and if you weren't supposed to speak up, you wouldn't be here."

Stephen leaned across the table and stuck his hand out. "Welcome to the team, Miranda. I got conscripted the same way. My advice is, take a deep breath and just say what's on your mind. He doesn't bite."

The rest laughed as Simon reddened and Miranda swallowed a lump in her throat.

Miranda began by saying that she wanted to opt out like Stephen had and started citing reasons why she wasn't a good choice for captain. Simon let her ramble for a bit and then cut her off.

"Miranda—and in these meetings, we're all on first-name basis—I've got something more in mind for you than being just a ship's captain. But right now, I need people I can trust in those control seats, so I want you to take the position anyway. And here's the carrot I've got to dangle in front of you. At some indeterminate time in the future, we're going to have fighter squadrons… and fighter carriers. Do you want to be in command of the fighter squadrons? Before you give any kind of answer, let me point out that most of the jobs on both the *Galileo* and Orion are being handled by people your age or younger. And here's another thought for you—you're just as qualified as anyone else to do a job no one has ever done before. But I need you to have some command experience. It's not something that needs to be answered right now, but do think about it and we'll talk about it later."

Next, Simon turned to Daniel. "I guess now's the time to tell you that I'm stealing not only your assistant but about half your crew. The crew, I'm replacing with fresh faces. Your assistant, I'm not. I figure that if he's good enough to be your straw boss, then he can handle a dock on his own. We may run out of qualified people to captain the docks. I'm open to ideas," he said, looking around. "Submit them any time, people."

Tossing a folder on the table, Simon said, "This is what we've come up with for crew transfers. You get half of my volunteers, and I get half of your trained personnel. We can juggle specifics later, but I want to get under way within forty-eight hours."

CHAPTER TWENTY-ONE

Simon, Kitty, Lucy, Gayle, and Stephen, along with the newest member of the inner circle, Adam, sat at the ready-room table. Kitty still held the rank of wing commander, and she'd taken charge of all of Gemini's fighters, beginning her version of training almost immediately for every pilot aboard. Miranda Lee had been left in charge of the fighter detachment aboard Orion, and Kitty was more than a little upset at not getting her position as first officer back. Simon had to explain that it wouldn't be fair to Lucy to remove her from the position just because Kitty was back.

Adam was Simon's candidate for base commander of Gemini once it was completed. An accomplished mining engineer, he'd come highly recommended, and to his credit, he was an avid sci-fi fan.

"It always helps, Adam," Simon said, referring to Adam's sci-fi propensity. "Most of our volunteers are hardcore fans. I swear, if we allowed costumes, you'd see Klingons walking these decks side-by-side with Ferengi."

He laughed and poured Pepsi over the glass of ice the steward had set on the table in front of him. "Sooner or later, though, you're gonna hit the wall, as we call it. You're gonna wake up some morning and say, 'That was the most realistic dream I've ever had!'

Then you'll step out of your cabin door, find out it ain't no dream, and wind up in sick bay until we can get your head screwed back on. I want you to remember what I just said. I just love to say 'I told ya so.'"

The *Galileo* stopped at Earth long enough to drop off some last-minute returnees and headed on out to the asteroid belt across the solar system from Orion. Position Beta was one hundred eighty degrees around the belt from Orion, and that put the sun in the way of any direct communication at most times of the year, so a relay satellite had been constructed prior to departure. Dropped off along the way, it provided a link to their compatriots so far away and allowed direct news from the underground forming on Earth. Slow though it was, it was the only way to keep in contact at those distances.

First things being first, a new *Sundiver* was built and sent on its way, courtesy of the original shuttles the *Galileo* had brought along. Next, three more shuttles and a dozen fighters were constructed, powered by cores also brought from Orion. Then, and only then, the *Galileo* went to work building the fuel plant. The shuttles received power cores and joined the three already in operation. The fighters were immediately pressed into service, flying patrols and doing double duty as shuttle alternates. By the time the *Sundiver* got back to the fuel plant, the *Galileo* would have moved on to its new location and the construction of Gemini would be well under way.

A goodly number of personnel aboard the *Galileo* were now veterans, and the training of new volunteers continued apace with the construction of the new dock. Within weeks, the habitat section was finished and the overcrowding ceased, although the new section would depend on the *Galileo* for power until the power plant processed the *Sundiver's* first haul.

Start to finish, this second dock took eight months, power plant included. The old hands from Orion made the whole process go much smoother than before. At least this time someone knew what they were doing from the start. The only circumstance of real note during that time was that Orion finished its first ship and immediately began the second.

Simon had originally intended to take that first ship for his flagship but changed his mind somewhere along the way. He prepared a message to Daniel, congratulating him on a job well done, and outlined his ideas. With treachery and deceit the top topics at more than one of the staff meetings, Simon had come away with some new security precautions whirling through his head. Since the commissioning would have to wait for the *Galileo* to return to Earth and pick up a new set of volunteers, Simon decided to wait on even activating the new ship's computer core. He wanted to make some changes to the basic programming and figured to take the third ship to come off the docks or reassign whoever originally got command to another and take her himself. He confided some of his suspicions and intentions in a letter to Daniel, dropped the message at Communications, and went to bed.

Simon waited on the sidelines as the available personnel of both the *Galileo* and soon-to-be-commissioned Gemini milled around deck eighteen, waiting for the activation ceremony to begin. It was known, of course, that Adam Gardner was going to be promoted to base commander. It was his firm hand and eagle eye that had kept things moving, and it was his presence, somehow always at just the right time, that kept the construction crews energized. It was gratifying that there had been an overabundance of volunteers for this second base.

Simon studied the faces of the people standing below the dais, shaking his head. He knew just how important ceremonies like this one could be, but he was still learning how to be an effective public speaker.

Just goes to show you, he thought, *even the upper echelons have to learn new jobs*.

The cooperation necessary to accomplish the prodigious task that was now almost behind them had formed a bond among these faces looking up at him. Now, he needed to cement that bond with *him*.

The babble began to die down as he stepped up to the microphone, and soon the last voice went silent. Simon said nothing for a moment. He let his eyes pass over every face he could, recognizing some but not as many as he would have liked. Leaning toward the microphone, he said, "Thank you."

He let the moment linger for several seconds, then said, "Thank you one and all for believing in the dream that we few not only can but *do* give our allegiance to advancing the human race so far in so short a time. We're still learning about the technology we're using. Every day something new comes across my desk, and I wonder what's ahead on this totally surreal journey. Only time will tell where all of this will lead, but that's the way it is with… pioneers—they lead the way and others expand on their work. This station, Gemini Base, will stand alongside Orion and two future bases as mankind's most outstanding accomplishment for many years to come."

Simon swept his gaze over the entire audience, including everyone in his next words. "None of this would be possible if not for the vision, dedication and endurance of you, the builders of this new facility. Now, the time has come for all your work to be put to the ultimate test. Very soon, we'll be activating Gemini's computer and leaving behind a crew to begin the process of turning out some of the first ships capable of taking humanity to the stars. That being said, I now call upon Commander Gardner to step forward."

Adam stood stiffly as Simon replaced his old insignia with the new golden stars surrounded by an oak wreath, denoting his new rank, and shook hands all round with his staff. Stephen then stepped forward and handed Gemini's commissioning plaque to Adam.

"It gives me great pleasure to present you with this plaque, Commander. We all wish you the best of luck in the coming months." He snapped a salute to the new officer, and Adam returned it clumsily as he transferred the heavy plaque from one hand to the other.

Stephen smiled at him as he stepped back amongst Simon's staff. "I think the audience is waiting for you to say something, Commander," he prompted.

Turning to the assembled crews, Adam looked

everyone over for a few seconds and then said, "You folks all know me. I'm not a fan of long, flowery speeches that say I couldn't have done any of this alone. Take it from me, this plaque belongs more to you than to me.

"Now, I'm sure you've all been waiting for this announcement—assignments will be posted tomorrow. Some of you will be staying here with me, and the rest of you will be going back to Earth to recruit more volunteers, but your names are at the top of the list for the next ship built. Until those lists are posted, people, I want you to enjoy your parties, for tomorrow we toil. Company dismissed!"

Immediately after, continuing a tradition started only eight months earlier when Orion was commissioned, parties broke out all over both bases.

Adam Gardner, newest commander in the fleet, poured drinks all round. "If you can call two docks and two ships a fleet," he grumbled good-naturedly, and his audience chuckled. Gemini's conference room was comfortably crowded with five of the *Galileo's* crew and six of his own staff. "Okay, Simon. I know. 'Take the long view.' I'm trying to do that. I think my problem is the same as most of the people at this table." At Simon's raised eyebrow, an affectation he'd raised to an art form, Adam went on. "I keep stumbling over reality. I really *am* living in a science-fiction story!" Laughter rippled around the table. Adam raised his glass and said by way of a toast, "To Gemini. May this base age gracefully and bear many young!"

Simon woke up with a headache. "Why did we get warp-drive and not a cure for hangovers?"

Kitty threw a towel at him and grinned evilly. "The cure is to eat first and drink slowly, not-so-bright hubby of mine. Remind me, why did I let you marry me?" Easily dodging his lunge, she stepped to the door. "You shower and I'll go tell Lucy to get the *Galileo* ready to get under way. Courtesy call on Commander Gardner in one hour. Meet me in the transporter room, okay? Okay. Love you! Bye!"

Good-naturedly grumbling something about uppity women, Simon headed to the shower and an hour later met Kitty and Lucy at the elevator.

"Good morning, Commanders. What's our status?"

This last was directed at Lucy, who promptly answered, "Sir, course for Earth is laid in. Everything and everyone needing to be transferred have been. All factories report deactivated and locked down. Drive is online, all stations manned, all instruments green."

Simon looked his first officer up and down. "Very good, Commander. Now, how about you fill me in on these uniform changes."

While they waited for the elevator, Lucy began to explain. "Sir, this is the result of one of your suggestions to work on ideas for overt recruitment. The uniform was too bland. If we're going to recruit openly, we need to look like a class act. Commanders Miller and Hawke think so, too."

Simon stared at Kitty with no visible expression on his face. Over the past several days, Simon had seen more and more uniforms with odd patches on the shoulders. He'd expected to be informed of the changes at one of the morning briefings, but so far, none had been forthcoming. Now, on the day the *Galileo* was ready to leave for Earth, he could see that every crewmember of both the *Galileo* and Gemini were wearing shoulder patches on their uniforms. No one would admit to actually starting the practice, but Simon was sure Gayle had had a hand in it somewhere.

"It actually started when we last arrived at Earth. Everyone's left shoulder has a round patch about two inches across," Lucy explained. "It has a stylized Earth with an accelerating ship above it and the words Terran Alliance stitched into the design. On the right shoulder, you'll see three different patches, depending on their duty station. All of them are the same shape. One reads *Galileo* and has an image of a crescent moon taken from a drawing by Galileo himself. The second reads Gemini and has a pair of twins holding hands. The third says Orion and has the constellation on it. We'll soon have to start making ones for each ship as it gets commissioned."

Some of the right-side patches carried another above emblem them—a partial arch that read "Mamba Pilot."

Finishing up as they arrived at the transporter room, Lucy blurted out, "And I think we need to have baseball caps as part of the uniform, too."

Seeing the patches on the transporter tech, Simon gave in to the inevitable.

Gayle and Stephen were in their respective departments handling last-minute business before departure, so only Simon, Kitty and Lucy beamed into Gemini's reception area. Adam's executive officer was there to greet them.

"The commander's compliments, if you please. He'll be with you momentarily."

Acknowledging the young lieutenant commander, Simon eyed the reception area. His eyes came to rest on the plaque Stephen had handed to Adam the day before. It read:

GEMINI BASE
COMMISSIONED: NOVEMBER 17, 2010
COMMANDER ADAM GARDNER,
COMMANDING

As he read the lines, his chest filled with the pride of accomplishment, but then a chill ran down his spine as his vision greyed out for an indeterminate time. He got a glimpse down the long, cold tunnel of history to a caveman stumbling through unfamiliar territory. Forcing the vision down, he got himself back under control and turned from the plaque as Adam entered the room.

"We'll be back soon, Adam. Or someone else will. We're heading for the *Heinlein's* commissioning by way of Earth to pick up more recruits, so the new ship could be the next vessel you see. She'll come this way on her trials. You know, the more ships get built, the less we're going to need the *Galileo* as a taxi service. We *may* move her into Earth orbit and leave her there as a waystation until we're able to replace her. We also need to keep in mind the fact that by the time we get that first one crewed, we're going to have to get a crew for the second ship, and your first won't be far behind that! Possibly in the same month."

Lucy offered her goodbyes as first officer, and

then Kitty spoke for herself and delivered Gayle and Stephen's apologies.

Laughing, Adam waved the apologies aside. "It's not a problem. Everyone knows what a slave driver Simon can be. By the way, boss, did you wake up with a headache like mine?"

Pain flickered over Simon's face. "Not like yours, I'll bet. Mine was bad enough to be a phenomenon in its own right!"

"I'll bet you guys are glad you didn't have to drive the spaceship home last night, huh?" Kitty quipped.

Adam's exec appeared outraged at the familiarity, and Adam observed, "Colorado College of Mines turns 'em out serious, apparently. But don't worry. I'll have him trained right by the time you get him back."

One final round of handshakes and the *Galileo* slid into the depths of space, having brought her second child to term.

Rising up out of the plane of the ecliptic, the *Galileo* made her way back to Earth. As soon as she was clear of the sun's interference, Simon sent word to Daniel that the *Galileo* would dock with Orion in about a month with new recruits and any replacements and supplies they might need, so he should start his wish list. Meanwhile, the crew selected for the first ship was frantically training for their trials right after the commissioning ceremony. Only the officers hadn't been named yet.

Kitty glared across the suite at Simon as he paced back and forth—a habit newly acquired, she noted, and one that needed to be broken before it totally destroyed her peace and tranquility. Launching a large pillow at his feet and one more at his head, she growled.

While fending off the attack to his head, he stumbled over the pillow at his feet. Simon turned an astonished gaze onto his assailant.

"If you don't sit down, the road is going to get a lot rougher! What's bothering you? You're not a pacer!"

Giving the pillow at his feet a half-hearted kick, Simon sat down on the edge of their bed. "It's the next phase, Kittyn. It's as obvious as the nose on my face. I know what I need to do, but I'm having trouble convincing myself."

Kitty crawled up on the bed and sat cross-legged behind him, starting a slow massage on his shoulders. "It must be a doozy. You don't call me Kittyn often anymore. All I'll say is what my grandma used to tell me—if there's right and wrong, choose right. But sometimes the right choice can be painful. Do what you think is right, and I'll support you. We all will. Now relax, or I'll go sleep in one of the empties. We've got three more nights before we reach Earth. Wanna spend 'em alone?"

Knowing that he wouldn't be able to see the *Galileo* didn't stop Simon from looking up into the clear night sky. Standing in his backyard at one a.m., he wondered why he felt so heavy. Stephen assured him that the people who knew about that stuff had long ago recalibrated the *Galileo's* artificial gravity to ninety-nine-plus percent of Earth's gravity. Plodding back inside, he promised himself to test that one someday.

The interior of the Hawke home was back to normal, including the pictures on the walls. "Son of a bitch took pictures, I'll just bet," Simon groused as he looked at the note taped to the television asking him to contact the number below. Copying the number and leaving the note where he found it, Simon vowed, "I'm going to teach a class in contact, Agent Daniels, and you're going to be my star pupil."

Looking around the living room one more time, Simon picked up the small suitcase at his feet, nodded at Kitty, and pressed the button on his arm that took them back to the *Galileo*.

Stephen dropped in on Victor McCord and Lucy beamed into an empty alley four blocks from the White House. Locating a phone, she dialed a number and counted the rings. On the fourth, a disgruntled voice rumbled in her ear.

"At six in the morning, this better be good."

Biting back her laughter, Lucy said, "This is Commander Grimes, Galway. Is that good enough for you?"

"Marginally, Grimes, marginally," the grumpy voice responded. "I have this line transferred to my home when I'm not in the office. You could have picked a decent hour to call." He felt the hair rise on the back of his neck at her next words.

"I'm *still* pissed about our last meeting, Galway." The tone of her voice brought him wide awake in an instant. "There's something you need to start figuring into your equations, friend. You never, ever, upset a girl with a spaceship. She might drop a rock on your house. One big enough to make a crater the size of

Delaware." Letting her voice settle back to normal, Lucy commented, "Just be glad Mr. and Mrs. Grimes raised their little girl better than that. Now, did you pass on our requests?"

Getting an affirmative response, Lucy finished the conversation. "Six days from now. Four people, no weapons. Pack an overnight bag, Galway." She hung up the phone, looked up and down the street, and beamed out of the phone booth.

Over the course of the next six days, Rob and 'Chiko, the husband/wife duo from the first batch of volunteers, began sending other volunteers aboard. Their efforts were aided by crewmembers who would beam into a meeting that had been organized by still other crewmembers who'd managed to gather a few friends together. They'd then take a few volunteers up for a quick look around. Usually, after they returned, most of the rest would be anxious for a visit.

Ted and Alice Brandt were twenty-six and twenty-four, respectively. The Brandts had two children—a boy, eight, and a girl, seven. Jim Collier, twenty-four, and his wife Barbara, twenty-five, were the proud parents of a six-year-old boy. Rob and 'Chiko had considered these two couples to be excellent candidates for a clandestine recruiting network. Friends since high school, the three men had attended each other's weddings and continued their friendships on into adulthood. The wives had known each other almost as long, and now that relationship was about to be tested.

The three couples had often gone to see the first showings of many science-fiction movies that had come out over the last dozen years or so, but the credulity of their friends was going to be hard to get through in a hurry without help. For that reason, Robert and 'Chiko had asked Gayle to come along.

"We really believe in these guys, Commander, and we think that if you'd beam in during our presentation, it would at least convince them we aren't nuts."

The sextet met on short notice at the Brandt house, it being easier for the Colliers to find a short-notice sitter for one than the Brandts for two. Robert and 'Chiko arrived last, bringing the traditional bottle of wine that the last arrivals were required to bring, a juvenile holdover from their boisterous college days.

Robert stood on the Brandt's front porch and looked at his wife. "One last chance to back out?"

'Chiko shook her head, not trusting herself to speak. She'd last seen her friends almost a full year ago and had left with virtually no word of goodbye.

"Got the disc?" Robert asked.

"In my purse," 'Chiko managed to say.

"Yeah," he sighed.

He held up the bottle, showing Alice the label when she opened the door. "We're last."

"That'll get you in the door," Alice conceded, inspecting the label. "But it's gonna take a damned good story to get to stay."

She turned away from the door, leaving it open, and Robert and 'Chiko followed her in, closing the door behind them. Robert followed his wife down the short hall and into the Brandt's family room. He stopped just inside the room, hand on 'Chiko's shoulder, and felt Alice's cool reception magnified four times over. Tim Brandt sat on the couch with Jim Collier and his wife Barbara.

Alice, standing at the end of the couch, was the one to break the silence. "Do you two have any idea how many times we've had to answer questions from the police?" She stamped her foot in frustration, a personal quirk 'Chiko had always found amusing up until now.

"And reporters looking for stories," Jim put in caustically, "not to mention private investigators hired by the families of other missing people, not to mention, *again*, psychics, channelers, and even a weekly tabloid guy from frigging England!"

"Aw, give the Brit a break, Jim," Barbara said, sarcasm dripping from her words. "The guy was over here doing a story on cattle mutilations and heard about almost a thousand people gone missing from Denver. Of course he tried to see what he could get."

"Guys," Robert began, "we know this is gonna sound too hard to believe, so we'll just say that, yeah, we were part of those thousand people. Actually, it was only around eight hundred. And until you see our evidence, all I can say is that it was the most frightening and enlightening time of my life."

'Chiko nodded her head in agreement and pulled the disc out of her purse. "We want you to watch this video. I know we have a rule against that and baby movies, but this isn't any ordinary home movie. You just watch. No narration, no nothing. We'll even leave the room."

"Just watch the video and ask questions later. This ain't Amway, guys. We need a favor, and the video will tell you why." Robert set the disc on top of the player and steered 'Chiko out into the kitchen. "We'll be on the patio for a bit, guys. Trust us. Just watch the video."

Robert stopped at the refrigerator on the way out the back door and 'Chiko scolded, "We shouldn't be doing that." It had long been a friendly tradition among the three couples that anyone wanting a drink could go get their own.

"Relax," Robert said, "we *are* still friends. Besides," he opened the door and pulled out two cold Cokes, "that video is going to take about twenty minutes." He handed one can to his wife, opened the patio door, and motioned her out.

The recruiters Simon had counted on had fallen through, so he'd put out word that he needed to find others who could be trusted. Robert and 'Chiko offered to try a few of their friends and were about to find out the results. Knowing the length of the disc helped. Rob and 'Chiko walked in just as it was ending. Picking up the remote, he sat down. 'Chiko set a tray of beers down on the coffee table and sat as well.

"Pretty good special effects," Jim commented. "But the camera work is kinda cheesy."

"Reminds me of a low-budget movie that came out not too long back but no discernible plot," added Barbara. "You said you needed a favor. You need backing to get better camera work?"

"This could turn out to be a good deal if there's a plot to go with all the special effects," came from Ted, ever the entrepreneur. "Could be money in a low-budget sci-fi flick."

Alice was the one to put the brakes on things. "I don't think this is some kind of deal to get investment money, guys. They would just ask. Look at their faces. And remember, we've known these guys for years. I know, for example, that they don't have the kind of camera or computer equipment to do some of the things we just saw." Turning to her guests, she confronted them. "One of the things about being friends for years is that you get to be blunt sometimes. So, point blank, this isn't a pitch for money, is it? What's in it for you? And us, by the way, since you came to us with whatever this is."

For the next hour, Rob and 'Chiko talked. They used the video to point to various parts of their story until Jim finally stopped them.

"All right. Enough is enough. I like the thought of having a spaceship, too, and I've seen some of the stuff that's been on the news. But are we supposed to buy the idea that you guys really have one?"

'Chiko spoke up. "Well, *we* don't have it. We're just crewmembers on it. Senior crew, but still just crew. We don't get to make the big decisions. But since we *are* senior crew, I think it won't be long before we're making some of the big decisions."

Out of deference to his friend, Jim had waited this long before digging in his heels. "Flights of fancy are one thing, Rob, but this is really going too far, I think. Are you telling us flat out that you are both... what? Some kind of officers on a super spaceship?" Standing up, fists propped on his hips, Jim challenged Rob. "I say put up or shut up. I'm sorry, guys," Jim said, looking over his shoulder for support. He turned back to Robert and 'Chiko. "This is just too much. Rob, please either admit this is all a joke or prove it, okay?"

Rob stood up and walked over to his friend.

"Here's part of the story we didn't tell you." Holding his wristband up for all to see, he continued. "'Chiko has one, too. They're part of the *Galileo's* transporter technology. Everyone you saw on that video has one, too. Now, I realize that doesn't prove anything, but this will." Turning to 'Chiko, he said, "You know, I could get used to the expressions on people's faces."

Turning back to Jim, Rob held up the armband on his left wrist. "Put your finger on the red button and press it, buddy. When you do, you'll get all the proof you want. And if it isn't enough, I'll bring more proof when I come back."

Jim gave Rob a calculating look. "Come back, huh? You know, I almost hate to do this. It was a good story, Rob, but… uh?" Standing alone in the center of the room with his finger pointing at empty air, Jim gulped. Quite literally. His friend had disappeared in a cloud of blue sparks, and something in his throat just would not go down. He looked down at the carpet, expecting, what? As he looked to his friends for some kind of support, his finger still poised in midair, something pulled his attention back toward the center of the room. The same blue sparks were fountaining out of thin air. Stunned at the sight before him, Jim backpedaled and fell onto the couch.

The sparks were becoming more solid by the second. Right out of Star Trek, for Christ's sake! There stood Rob where he hadn't been a few seconds before and where he'd stood but seconds before that! And with a blonde. And, oh, what a blonde! Golden hair down past her ass. His eyes went first to 'Chiko, then to his wife. 'Chiko seemed to be expecting the woman, and Barbara's eyes were sparkling.

"Okay, Jim," Robert said exultantly, "proof

enough for ya? If not, have I got a tour for you! Everyone, this is Commander Miller, Communications Officer of the Terran Alliance Ship *Galileo*."

Finishing the introductions as he brought out another chair, Rob said, "And this is Jim Collier. He's a true disbeliever. Or, at least from Missouri."

Gayle looked Jim over. Turning to the other two women, she asked, "All right. Who does he belong to?" When Barbara raised her hand, Gayle walked over to her and shook hands. "Hi. I'm Gayle, and I really am the Communication Officer on a spaceship. I know. Sounds simplistic and stupid when you say it out loud, but it's true. May I borrow your husband for a bit? I promise to return him in the same shape he's in now, which isn't too great. He hasn't said a word since I got here."

Bowled over by Gayle's flamboyant attitude, Barbara looked to 'Chiko for support. "Oh, let her have him for a bit. I promise she won't hurt him. If you want, Rob and I will take you three on a tour, too. Wanna see a spaceship?" she asked with a wicked grin.

Getting a slow nod from Barbara after getting 'Chiko's okay, Gayle said, "Oh, goody. I just love a good skeptic. Here, Jim, stand up and take this." Handing him one of the handy-dandy locator disks, she pulled him to his feet. She said, "Watch that first step, my friend. It's about twelve thousand miles high."

Pressing the button on her wristband, she wished for something more flamboyant, like having to say, "Beam me up," but would settle for the blue sparkle effect.

"Come on, stop staring," she chided as the metal walls of the transport room shimmered into view. "Nobody else can come aboard while you hold things up by standing on the transport pads." Turning to the transport tech, she said, "Ensign, this is Jim Collier. When his wife comes aboard with either Commander Greene, let me know immediately." Turning back to her stunned companion, Gayle asked cheerily, "So, what do you want to see first?"

Two hours later, all four visitors were together in the mess hall on deck three.

"So sue me! I'm sorry! I've been convinced, and I want in. I still think that if we stayed on the *Galileo*, the kid wouldn't be that much trouble. But I'm outvoted, so I give up" Jim said, raising his hands.

Ted laughed along with the two women. "Well, we do have promises for when our kids are old enough. I got Rob to agree to talk to the captain for us. When the kids turn fifteen, they can join with parental consent if, and only if, the parents join for two years, too."

Since each couple had finally agreed to act as clandestine recruiters, both were given a small radio. Made to look like kitchen appliances by paranoid engineers, there was little chance of them being spotted and even less of them being overheard since Earth still hadn't discovered the wavelengths they were on.

Beaming back to Earth with the two couples, Rob and 'Chiko were jubilant.

"Now we can stay in touch. I was afraid we'd wind up choosing different roads. I don't like it when friends drift apart. Good ones are hard enough to come by as it is," 'Chiko said.

The usual round of hugs and handshakes ensued, complicated by the fact that there were three couples involved.

Robert shook his head. "You guys are going to have to get used to this, so we'll just say goodnight, and we'll be in touch soon." He was still amazed that he could see out of the beam well enough to recognize the envious expressions on the faces of their friends as it took effect.

Stephen had no trouble, on the other hand, getting his friend Victor McCord to come aboard. "Oh, I've been waiting for you, pal!" Victor crowed. "I've had things wound up for months, and waiting for you to come back was the hardest thing I've ever had to do. And that includes my final exams and getting married and divorced!"

CHAPTER TWENTY-TWO

Six days to the minute after Lucy hung up the phone on Galway, she called him back. Sounding considerably more alert this time, he commented, "Now why did I expect to hear from you at this exact moment?"

Lucy responded, "Of course you should have expected me. I said 'six days from now,' didn't I? Are the other members of your team ready to go? Good. It shouldn't take you long to drive to a little place in Delaware called Bethany Beach. There are two rooms reserved for you in your name." She named one of the better known motel chains and added, "Once you've had a chance to unpack, you'll be contacted." Looking up and down the street, she beamed out of a phone booth far away from the one she'd used the previous week.

Later that evening, Lucy called Galway's room. "Satisfied with your rooms, Mr. Galway?"

A slight hesitation came from the president's representative. "To tell the truth, Commander, I was expecting the rooms to be paid for, but when they weren't, I went back over what you said. And your words were 'there are two rooms *reserved* for you.' You tend to say what you mean, don't you?"

Lucy shot back, "Well, Mr. Galway, my grandpa

always said that I never learned how to gild a lily. I think that just means that all I know how to do is be direct."

Galway chuckled. "Now there's a phrase I wouldn't expect out of someone twice your age, Commander. But to answer your question, yes, they're acceptable."

Lucy couldn't resist another shot. "I thought they might be. After all, what do four men together need besides an internet connection and the Playboy channel? The reason this place was chosen was because of the meeting rooms. They're totally secluded from the outside world. A lot of companies come here for their retreats. Not even sunshine can get in if it isn't wanted. If you'll go down to the first floor, you'll find that the Compton Room has been reserved for your party. See you in fifteen."

Galway and his group arrived about five minutes early to find the door locked. They milled around uncertainly for a few seconds until the youngish manager came up to them.

"Are you the Galway party?" he inquired. Brandon nodded, and the manager unlocked the door. "Enjoy your meeting."

The four men filed uncertainly into the empty room, pulling the door closed behind them. The little man walked over to the door and checked it.

"I'm not the least bit happy about this, Galway," he complained.

"And what are you worried about, Anderson?"

Galway all but snarled as the agent put the phone back on its cradle after checking for a dial tone.

Looking around the generic box of a room like a million others from Boston to Bavaria, they found a long conference table with eight chairs around it. The big difference was a small metal box sitting on the table. Without the tools that none of them were carrying, nothing could be determined about the box since it appeared to have no seams at all. The only conclusion the four men could come to was that it was obviously not solid unless it was a very light metal or composite.

Having been reassured by a hidden sensor disk on the wall that their opponents were unarmed, Lucy and her team beamed into the room precisely on the mark. The meeting proceeded in an unremarkable fashion. Galway let them know that the U.S. government was ready to cede a small parcel of land to be used embassy-fashion. The location was still to be determined, of course.

"Everything's negotiable," Galway said.

Lucy just smiled. "No, everything is not negotiable. What about the other two bases?"

"We're working on that. The other heads of state involved—and actually that includes all the nations of Earth—are having trouble believing you exist."

Stephen couldn't help getting a shot in. "Maybe that's because you've promoted the 'they don't exist' policy a bit too long and aggressively, Mr. Galway. See what your policies have brought you to?"

The colonel had to speak at this point. "That's not a fair representation, sir. It isn't *our* policy. We just do as we're told."

Stephen countered. "That's what the Nazi's said

at Nuremberg, Colonel."

Lucy stepped into the fray before the two men came to blows. "Children, please! Well, Mr. Galway, you'll have to solve that little dilemma, now won't you? Just remember this: we will not put up with any more delays." Changing tack fast enough to give most people whiplash, Lucy asked Galway in a frank voice, "Let's get the record set straight, here, Mr. Galway. Just what is it that you think we have? A spaceship, yes. But what else do you know?"

Galway glanced at his team, and the little man spoke. "We know you have an alien spacecraft that belongs to the United States, Commander." The man almost spat her title out.

Lucy leaned back in her chair. "Any particulars on that spacecraft? And it actually belongs to its builders. We're just sort of caretakers."

Galway stepped in, keeping the unnamed man quiet. "Analyzing the video footage, we've come up with what is probably in the vicinity of two thousand feet long. What its functions and capabilities are, we don't know. And that scares people. We're assuming it has an interstellar drive. We're assuming, too, that its data banks will have information about this part of the galaxy and its own neighborhood that we can use to our advantage. We also know that you're using it to build what you call space docks and ships, and that you need large numbers of people. The rest is speculation."

Lucy looked at Galway like a bug on a plate. "Okay, I'm going to give away information that's going to save you a lot of time and effort. The ship you assume to be two thousand feet long is closer to thirty-eight hundred feet long, eight hundred wide, and over two hundred high. The first five hundred feet are living spaces on sixteen decks, workspaces on one, and storage on the eighteenth. The last five hundred are engines and power core. The portion in between is factories and a fusion smelter. It's a construction ship, Mr. Galway. The computer aboard has the specs for every piece of equipment needed to start, maintain, and eventually expand a colony world. That *also* includes ships, sir. Many kinds, from little scout craft to ships big enough to turn our planet into ashes. We're still trying to figure out just how it wound up here.

"Our plans. We're going to build four—count 'em, four—space docks in the asteroid belt," she said waggling four fingers in the air. "We've already finished two, and one of those has turned out a ship. We're going out to commission and crew that vessel now, return for more volunteers, and go back to get the third dock started. And here's a secret for you. The second and third ships are already under construction. Once we have all four docks built, we'll be turning out four ships every six months, each and every one with interstellar drives and weapons suitable for space combat. Energy beams, force fields, antimatter bombs, and more."

Lucy looked at the little man at the back of the group, recognizing him from their previous encounter outside Washington, DC. "I see a look of pure fear on your face, little Mr. Anonymous. Don't worry. We won't be using these weapons on you. They're for the folks who'll be coming to look for the ship they lost. Assuming, of course, that we can ascribe our motivations to an alien race and that they show up angry. We believe it will take almost three years to duplicate that ship ourselves, and we don't think they can let that kind of expense go without at least looking for it. If we want to keep it or duplicate it, we'd better be prepared to fight for it. And without other ships, we can't. Also, what will happen when they do get here and we have no defenses against them? Will they come as friends or oppressors? Who was it who said, 'The best defense is a good offense?'" She shook her head. "It really doesn't matter. We have things well in hand and intend to keep them that way.

"And there are others out there besides the Builders. The ship had weapons aboard and in the data banks. That means there's someone they've had to fight. We've been attacked ourselves. Most of our folks don't believe it was the Builders, so that leaves their adversaries. Those could be our friends, given a chance. Or not. Again, we're going to alien motivation. Could be that all space-going folks are going to resent the new kid on the block. So, we'll be as prepared as we can get. We figured five years before the Builders could even show up the first time. That's down to four now and maybe a little less."

Lucy leaned back in her chair and waited. She could tell Galway didn't enjoy his position, and being put there by a mere girl was even worse. "So, tell me, Mr. Galway, what does Earth want? Does she want to feed her starving millions? Does she want to clean up her biosphere? Or do you want to be able to turn lead into gold, Mr. Galway? Tell me what you want."

A bit nonplussed by her direct approach, Galway stalled. "Most negotiations tend to have a lot more give and take in them, Commander Grimes, and your directness is a little disconcerting. You've already made it clear that you'll share no weapons or propulsion technology. How about some kind of shield technology? Something we can use to protect ourselves from attack?"

Lucy nodded, a grimace on her face. "Barely possible, I believe. That can be done. I do want you to remember what you were told in the beginning. We're giving these items to the people of Earth, not to any one particular nation or group of nations. We'll make our shield technology available to the people of Earth if that's what you want. We'll give it to a representative of each nation and tell them not only why they're getting what they're get but also who requested it. I have a hard time believing, Mr. Galway, that all the countries of the world got together and asked for shield technology. You wouldn't be putting yourself up to speak for the entire planet, now would you?"

The anonymous little man fumed, "You can't give that information out to everyone. It's not that we were going to… it's just that we need to be able—"

"Silence, you little prick!" she thundered. "If you can't add something constructive, just be invisible." Getting her temper under control, she turned her back on the infuriating man.

Colonel Babcock stepped in and put an end to the exchange. "I'd be very surprised, Commander, to find out that anyone outside of the G-8 officially knows about your existence, which, as I understand it, goes against the spirit of what you're trying to accomplish."

"You got it right, Colonel," Lucy avowed, watching the little man glare daggers at the colonel. "Maybe you should be in charge of these meetings for your team." Lucy looked at all four of the men facing her. "You need to keep in mind that we are citizens of Earth, too. We have families here, and we want to come back, eventually. Some of us won't stay in space forever but will come home to live and work and raise families of our own. We need to be able to come and go without harassment by the alphabet agencies. Believe me, I know how hard that is for a government to allow. But you don't have any choice, which makes you madder than hell and also makes you doubly dangerous. And that means we have to be doubly cautious. See our dilemma? But you can relax. I don't believe we would give you shield technology, anyway. Sometimes the counter to a threat is as bad as the threat itself. Now I want to get something straight, Colonel. Is it true that only eight governments know of our existence?"

Getting a hesitant nod from the colonel, Lucy went on in a stricter tone. "We're not too far away from breaking orbit, Colonel, so there's no way to remedy the situation now. We're going to be out seven or eight months building the next dock. By the way, Mr. Galway, by the time we finish that dock, there will be two more ships finished and ready for commissioning.

"We'd like to be able to set up Earth-side bases when we get back. We expect that in that time you'll have officially revealed our presence to the rest of the world. And we'll know if you don't. If you haven't, we'll do it for you. How about something visual? Flybys over Moscow, Washington, New York, Beijing, London, Paris, and Tokyo maybe? I guarantee you, it would be something the major news services wouldn't be able to keep from reporting, especially after the flurry of stories last time we came back and this time as well. We're more than willing to coordinate with you ahead of time so you don't get caught with your pants down."

Gayle had to get her two cents' worth in. "Think about this—if we get to set up shop down here, you'll be able to keep track of some of our comings and goings, maybe even slip a ringer or ten in on us. At present, you don't even have that much, as far as we know."

The others nodded at that as if they'd talked it over before coming to the meeting.

The anonymous little man spoke up. "How about putting an observer aboard?"

Lucy hesitated for a few seconds, glanced at her team members and then back at the group in front of her. "It's an interesting idea. Not a subject that has come up in discussion for some reason," she said a bit acerbically. "I *will* say this—it won't be you."

Turning to Gayle, she asked, "Commander, would you take the suggestion to the captain? I think it merits immediate attention since we're so close to leaving."

Gayle nodded and stood up. She glanced at the four men and said, "Gentlemen, if you will excuse me." Touching her wristband, she disappeared in front of them.

"I've seen that a few times now and would really like a chance to look into it," said Mitchell, the NASA man.

"Maybe you can someday, once the politicians settle down and the military decide we're no threat to them," Lucy mused. "The problem with that technology is that it's line-of-sight and very energy-intensive. Only the *Galileo* has it and will probably be the only one for quite a while. The equipment is very bulky, and only battleships or larger can provide the space for it."

Gayle's return moments later put an end to the impromptu question-and-answer period. Looking at Lucy, she said, "Captain is agreeable to the idea of an observer. And he put special emphasis on the word 'an.'" Turning to the men, she added, "Gentlemen, the captain has a suggestion for who that observer might be, if you're interested. He'd be agreeable to having an FBI agent on board the *Galileo*, and he chooses that particular agency because he personally knows an agent who already has some small experience with this case. If you're amenable to the idea, please contact Agent Daniels out of Billings, Montana. And if he's agreeable, he should be at Captain Hawke's house in six hours. Acceptable, gentlemen?"

Declining to answer right away without conferring with their superiors, Galway and his team started to make leaving noises.

Lucy helped the process along by telling Galway, "I'll let the captain know what you've said here. If Daniels is in place, he goes. You'll get a report from him in about seven or eight months. Now, if you'll excuse us, we have departure preparations to finish up." Standing up, Lucy leaned across the table with her hand out. "Mr. Galway, it hasn't necessarily been fun doing business with you, but it has been instructive."

Galway shook her hand and answered, "Commander, you are a breath of fresh air. That's not to say that I'm in favor of doing business this way on a regular basis, understand, but you do get to the core of a problem quickly."

As they were preparing to leave, Mitchell asked, "What's in the box?"

Lucy looked at the box, smiled, and pushed a button on her wristband. When all eyes were on the box, she said sweetly, "Strictly a diversion, Mister Mitchell," as two sensor clusters hidden on the wall disappeared unnoticed along with the team.

Simon and Kitty beamed into their living room about an hour before Daniels was due to arrive. Kitty wandered aimlessly around the house, chafing under Simon's instructions not to go outside and to stay away from the windows.

"If he shows up at all," Kitty commented as time ran out on the deadline. "I have to wonder if he'll have the nerve." She sat down on the couch and started tapping her foot in annoyance.

Simon looked up from the book on his lap. "I'm willing to bet he won't have any choice, hon. Someone is going to make it an order. You're starting to think like an officer. You just need more practice."

Kitty sniffed at him. "I do well enough, thank you. No one has said anything about my leadership qualities, and I get my job done, so there."

Simon slid over beside her, put his arm around her shoulders, and said, "Of course you do. If not, I'd have someone else doing it. But you do need to start thinking with a little more paranoia. It helps to guess what the other guy is gonna do. And if you're wrong, no problem. It's the 'if you're right' part that will save your delicious little ass, my dear. And everyone will be in awe of your superior tactical ability, whether you have any or not."

This time the doorbell rang, and Simon answered it as Kitty left the room. "I didn't know whether to hope you'd show or not," he said. "In any case, come in. You know your way around, of course." Walking across his living room and standing at the far end of the couch, Simon turned to his visitor. "I must admit, you did an excellent job of putting things back where they belong. But you shouldn't have done it in the first place."

Agent Daniels sat down nonchalantly on the far end of the couch from Simon. "And that's why I'm here, right?" Daniels asked as he kicked the overnight bag sitting beside him.

Simon nodded. "That's right, Agent Daniels. I'm a man who pays his debts, even *small* ones. You should have spent more time studying me, and then you wouldn't be so surprised to be here." Raising his voice to be heard beyond the living room, Simon called out, "Hon, our visitor is here. When you're ready, we are, too."

Kitty walked back into the room, a small overnighter in hand. "All done and ready to go, husband-mine." A measurable frostiness entered her voice. "Good afternoon, Agent Daniels. I really would never have imagined that I would invite you into my home for any reason. I can't say that I'm happy to see you, but I trust my husband's judgment."

Exasperation in his voice, Agent Daniels interrupted. "I need some information here, if you please. I have a real problem with this."

Kitty turned her full attention to the agent sitting on her couch. "Just exactly what is it that you have a problem with, Agent? Isn't it your job to find out what's going on?"

The agent was beginning to show signs of agitation. "Whatever my job is, it doesn't usually entail getting on a spaceship with people I'm investigating at the instruction of superiors from the White House."

Simon looked at the agent. "What were you told?"

"Told? I was told to pack a bag, be here at a specific time, and expect an extended trip." This last came at the same time the agent's overnight bag received another swift kick. "I was told nothing else."

Simon looked at him for a long time. "I'll fill you in on all the details later, and you can crosscheck them with your bosses when you get back. But suffice it to say, Agent Daniels, that at the moment it seems you get to be the determining factor in whether your government and the peoples of Earth consider us friend or foe. I'm the one who asked for you to be here, and that was just because I'm an ass.

"I believe another question you might ask is how long you'll be with us. Well, there are two answers to that, and you get to choose the answer you like best. The short answer is a couple of weeks. We're going to be making a trip out to one of the space docks to take the crew out for the ship we've just finished, then we'll return to Earth, pick up more crew, and go out and build another dock. That's out in the asteroid belt, Agent. That'll be dock number three, by the way. If you want off after the two weeks, fine, but I think you'll get more out of an extended stay, don't you? On our return for more crew, you'll be able to leave the ship and return, of course.

"The only restrictions are that there are areas that

are off-limits to you—weapons bays, engine room, fighters, shuttle bays, transporter room. Don't try to get in. Trust me, we'll know. Also, no weapons. Otherwise, you'll be free to go where you want, talk to whomever you want, and draw whatever conclusions you want. Oh, and the extended voyage will be seven or eight months."

Simon reached down and picked up a locator disk. "Remember this? Be sure to have your bag in hand when we beam up."

The agent stood up, took the proffered disk, and slid it into his shirt pocket. Simon glanced over at Kitty. Seeing that she had her finger on her wristband, he did the same.

"Bag, Agent, before it gets left behind."

Tearing his eyes away from Kitty long enough to pick up his bag, Agent Daniels was still able to see her vanish in a very pretty pyrotechnic display. At the same time, the world he was used to began to fade, replaced by another one entirely.

Agent Daniels' second visit to the *Galileo* was considerably different from his first. This time, it was with eyes wide open and of his own free will. Kind of. His superiors had given him little choice, and by now, his own natural stubbornness was making him do something that good sense screamed at him to run from.

Walking out of the transporter room and down the corridor, the three stopped outside a door. "This is my ready room," Simon told the staring agent. "You can leave your bag here for now. We'll send it for later or take it to your billet." Leaving that room behind, Simon led the agent to the briefing room. "I'm going to have to come up with something other than Agent Daniels. We could be around each other for quite a while," he said amusedly. "Who'd a thunk it?"

Walking over to the device sitting on the corner table, Simon ordered, "Put your left wrist in there. You'll get a wristband like the ones the rest of us wear."

Looking dubiously at the dark opening in the side, the agent balked. "Just for my peace of mind, what can I expect sensation-wise? I don't want to get surprised, jerk my arm, and mess up something."

Laughing, Kitty told him, "You won't feel a thing, I swear. Unless she doesn't like you."

The agent looked around. "She who? And what will she do if she doesn't like me?"

Waving his arm grandly, Simon said, "Why, the ship of course. The *Galileo*. That box is full of sensors. When a wristband is fitted, the ship gets a bit of a skin sample and knows you from then on. And if she doesn't like you, she'll keep the hand."

Looking into Simon's eyes, the agent smiled. "I'm calling your bluff. It's a locating device and probably a communicator. You want to keep track of me, so I'll wear one." Confidently sliding his arm into the device, he waited.

Simon manipulated the controls on the side of the machine. "Security level five, Agent. That means you aren't allowed near Engineering, the engine room, weapons bays, shuttles or fighters without supervision. Understand?"

Daniels watched Simon and pulled his arm out when Simon nodded. He looked the wristband over critically and shook his wrist to settle it in place. "Understood, Captain," he said.

The unlikely trio walked onto a bridge that was all brisk efficiency. They made their way over to Lucy Grimes, who was keeping track of the goings-on from the distance of the captain's chair. Simon glanced around the bridge and spoke so only the four of them could hear, "Someday, Commander, I want to know how much you bribe the transport techs to let you know when we come aboard."

Mock penitence in her voice, Lucy quietly replied, "Why, Captain! How can you think such a thing? It's my job to know when you're aboard and where you are. Just in case, you know. Costs nothing except the extra processor rations I give as a bonus to whoever's on duty. And look at all the goodwill I spread among the crew."

Simon stepped back into captain mode. Raising his voice a bit, he said, "Status, Commander?"

Lucy immediately replied, "Sir, course for Orion Base is laid in, all new volunteers are accounted for, and all departments report locked down and ready for boost."

Simon deferred to Lucy. "Very well, Commander. It's your shift, so she's your vessel. Take us out of here. Request permission for my party to observe departure."

Lucy responded, looking pointedly at Daniels, "Permission granted, Captain." She turned to her primary responsibility. "All hands, this is the First Officer. Prepare to leave orbit. Engine room all ahead one third."

Simon gestured his companions over to one side of the room. Keeping his voice low, he said, "Kitty, if you want to leave, you can." Getting a grateful kiss on the cheek, Simon added, "I'll stay with Agent Daniels for a bit and get him settled. See you in our quarters shortly."

Simon had been watching the agent watch the viewscreen on the forward bulkhead. He'd also noted that the agent appeared to be trying to follow some of the bridge chatter.

"That's not a real view, you know. It won't appear to change very fast for a while. And I'm afraid you won't understand much of what you hear right away. Spend time in some of the introduction classes for new crewmembers and see if it makes any sense in a few days."

The two men stood silently for a time, long enough for the Earth to slowly slide off the forward screen. Tossing a small wave in Lucy's direction, he led his charge out into the corridor.

"Always ask permission to enter the bridge. I can't imagine you not getting permission, but you never know. Things could get a little hectic."

Leading the agent back to his ready room, Simon sank into a chair, waving his visitor to do the same. Picking up a commlink, Simon called Gayle. "I need a billet assignment for one Observer Daniels."

The answer, when it came, dripped acid. "We don't have any trash bins on this ship, so I've had to billet him with people. Is that okay with you, sir?"

Stifling a smile, Simon admonished, "Now, now, Commander. He's our guest. I need that room assignment, and I need you to set up a level five services account for him, if you will be so kind." A level five account was basically a subsistence account with unlimited credit for food, clothing, gyms, rec rooms, etc, and no access to restricted areas.

Gayle's voice finally came back. "Deck six, room C-26. I have him rooming with one veteran and one recruit."

Simon thanked her and put the commlink away. Leading the agent to the elevators, he explained the facts of life.

"There are a few specific do's and don'ts that you'll pick up. But there's one general rule that's broad enough that you only need to hear it once. You're locked into a big tin can with almost nine hundred people. Do whatever it takes to make the time you have to spend locked up with us as pleasant for you and for us as possible."

Making their way down to deck six, Simon quickly located room C-26, knocked once on the door, and then opened it. Finding no one present, he motioned Agent Daniels in. Pointing to the empty bunk, he indicated that the agent should place his bag there. "I prefer you have at least one old hand around for the first few days. After that, make your own bed and lie in it. Okay, follow me and I'll give you a quick tour of this level."

Stopping first to key Daniels' thumbprint to the door code, he then showed him the mess hall, showers, library, theater, gym, and other common areas. He also mentioned the hot tub on deck three. "We didn't have one on board when we got the ship. This is a new thing for us, and it seems to be in great demand. Your room is now keyed to you, so I'm going to leave you to your own devices for the next few days. Visit any deck any time. All officers are instructed to answer fully and completely about anything except, weapons and propulsion. Now, if you'll excuse me, I need to go."

During the trip to Orion, Agent Daniels found out a lot about the *Galileo* and the people who ran her. There were essentially three groups of people aboard, the first being the oldest group, with 'oldest' meaning longest aboard. This included Simon, Kitty, Gayle, and Stephen, of course. It also included some dozen scientists and quite a few of the first people recruited from the DenverCon. These were the people in charge. Most of the second generation of people had come aboard after the completion of Orion. A lot of the middle-management positions were being held by those people. And then there was the newest batch, who'd been aboard for only a few days.

Agent Daniels was good at his job, well able to tell the difference between fact and fantasy for the most part. Who could have predicted this, though? And he was soon amassing a pretty fair-sized mental file of the various things people were saying. On his first evening and night aboard the *Galileo*, the agent ate dinner in the crew's mess on deck six and spent most of the evening talking to the newest volunteers and one or two of the people who'd been around since Orion was built.

The next morning, he awoke to an all-too-familiar sound. Reveille. The lights came up to something just short of eye-searing, and he heard one of his roommates say, "Okay, guys on your feet. We've got a long day ahead of us."

Daniels groused, "I'm not one of your volunteers. I'm just an observer. I'm staying in bed."

And the same cheerful voice replied, "Well, if that's what you wanna do, but you're gonna *observe* real quick that if you don't get up right now and take a shower with the rest of us, no one's gonna want to be anywhere near you. You'll also *observe* that if you don't get up, you're gonna miss breakfast."

Staggering to his feet, he found that the body belonging to the cheerful voice was already dressed and bent over slipping his sandals on.

The overly cheerful voice went on. "I'm Crewman First Class Charley McNalley, and this is Crewman Arthur Stein. I already know who you are. Cap'n hauled me up to officer country last night. Tole me who ya are, what ya are, and what I'm supposed to do wit ya. What I'm supposed to do is see to it that you get settled in and see just about every part of the ship and everything we do here. Now I cain't make you git up and do anything, but to my way of thinkin', if you don't observe it, you sure as hell cain't report it. Unless you plan to make it all up. And if you do that, then there was no need to come aboard in the first place.

"The cap'n put you with me 'cause I know what I'm doin'," McNalley went on as he grabbed a towel and soap from a drawer. "Let's go. We get cleaned up, straighten the room, and then go to chow."

The two first-timers followed their guide to the showers. On the way, he continued, "I helped build Orion, I helped build Gemini, and I'm gonna help build the next one that goes up. And probly the one after that, too, cause I'm the best pod jockey on the ship."

At this point the agent stopped him. "Uh, new here, remember? What's a pod jockey?"

McNalley smiled. "That's just the kinda question all the fish ask. A pod is a construction pod. I drive a construction pod. Factories'll turn out sumthin', slip it out past the force field, and I grab it with my pod and go put it where they tell me." He took a few quiet steps. "I'd be doin' more than that, but I don't read so good, so they don't give me more to do."

Agent Daniels, looking for dissent or anything that would show a chink in the armor these people were showing, asked, "Well, wouldn't you *like* to do more?"

McNalley stopped in the corridor. "Well, yeah. I'd kinda like to fly those Mambas. But then, ever'body wants to fly 'em."

Daniels rushed to stop him before he could move on. "Okay, we just hit my stupid spot again. What's a Mamba?"

Having one described didn't quite fill the bill. Late on his fourth day, Daniels went to a class on the Mambas being held down on deck eighteen. There were a lot of classes being held all over the ship. Anyone who knew what they were doing was conscripted to teach the fish something about their new environment. This one was being conducted by Mrs. Hawke.

I guess that's Captain Hawke from now on, he thought.

These were introduction classes for all the new volunteers, some few of whom would stay on the *Galileo*. Some would go to the new ship, according to McNalley, but most would find themselves on Orion since that was where most of the crew for the new ship was being pulled from.

He found himself standing at the back of a group of forty or so hopeful Mamba pilots. Not having had a chance to visit deck eighteen before now, he was simply stunned at the sheer openness of the place. It

410

was over two thousand feet long, eight hundred feet wide, and twenty-six feet high, and this was only a part of the whole. Its primary purpose was to hold finished parts or components until they could be moved to a project and installed. Right now, because the ship was under way, the entire area was nearly empty, leaving one with an eerie feeling. Right now, all that was there was one Mamba and forty or so people seated in chairs around the craft.

Daniels' first view of a Mamba wasn't the impressive sight he'd been led to believe it was going to be from the enthusiastic words he'd overheard in the various common rooms around the ship until he got close enough to judge the size of the vessel by the people standing next to it. Then he was impressed. Oh yes, indeed, he was. This Mamba looked like it was capable of anything just sitting there. Not really prone to flights of fancy, he still couldn't shake the image of a shark gliding up out of the murky depths to wreak havoc on its prey, and a wholly unreasonable fear shivered up and down his spine.

Sitting near the back of the group, he listened eagerly to a recitation of events from Captain Hawke. *She tells a pretty good story*, he told himself as she spoke a little about the construction of Orion and then went on to tell about the attack on the station, the loss of life, and the heroic actions that saved the station. Then she went on to tell how the Mamba had been created to counter the new threat. She talked of their future plan, which was to build a carrier taskforce that would carry these powerful little ships to their destinations and keep them armed and flying against any opponents. And she talked about the possibility of conflict with alien races, a possibility that was all too believable, considering where he was sitting. And the more he looked at that Mamba, the more he wanted to get his hands on one. With ten years behind him as an Air Force pilot, how could he not?

Daniels stood at the end of the line and patiently waited his turn to take a look into the cockpit of the craft. On a couple of occasions, he saw Captain Hawke looking directly at him. He was finally nearing the front of the line when the captain appeared in front of him. Pulling her commlink out, Kitty arranged to have Daniels' tingler turned off.

"So you want to see a Mamba? Well, come on. For now, it's safe to do so." Ushering him up a ladder on one side of the craft, she ducked under and ran lightly up the ladder on the other side. "Well, what do you think?" she asked.

"It's not nearly as complicated as I'd have imagined," Daniels replied. "I flew F-15s for years, and there's a lot more instrumentation on them than I see here."

Kitty went into instructor mode. "Most of this craft is automated, Agent. The computer is advanced enough that some of the techniques now being developed for fighter pilots on Earth are old hat to this technology. Specifically, after a Mamba gets used to its pilot, it can tell what's needed, which is due to its being able to monitor a pilot's brainwaves. After an initial shakedown, the computer can associate certain thoughts with certain actions. The only actions that are not under computer control are the weapons. Those require physical actions to engage. But if you wind up with a bogey on your tail, for example, just knowing where it is gives the computer something to work with and it will help to escape, evade, or retaliate as necessary."

Continuing, Kitty allowed Daniels to actually sit down in the cockpit. "As you can see, the pilot requirements are such that you need to be a fairly small person. "You'd fit nicely, Agent. This vessel is capable of atmospheric flight. Due to the size of the vanes—we don't call them wings—the speed has to be rather high, on the order of about half of Mach one or she loses maneuverability. Anything less than that and we need to add her antigravs to the equation. She can hover on her antigravity generators for a short while, but that's for emergencies only, or for landings and takeoffs. She carries twin high-intensity, rapid-fire pulse lasers, four high-yield antimatter missiles capable of taking a sizable bite out of most anything they hit, and she has an ECM setup that works on levels most scientists have only just begun to think about. It amounts to full cloaking ability."

Kitty stopped for a moment to let the information sink in. She sat on the lip of the cockpit watching Daniels examine the controls.

"Her biggest advantages are her speed and maneuverability in space," she continued. "On rare occasions, these ships can get right up to low-warp speeds. Their biggest disadvantage is their range, which depends on the pilot's stamina. She can't negate all the gravitic stress due to her size, but her grav sump manages to offset most of the problem. Also, there isn't room enough for supplies beyond a few snacks and a water reservoir."

Ushering the agent back down the ladder, Kitty joined him on the deck. "See, Agent Daniels, I can give some of our weaknesses away. Call it a show of good faith." Motioning him away from the side of the ship, Kitty tapped her wristband. "Also, Agent, I apologize for that incident earlier. I really thought you would have tested the limits of your leash, so to speak, and until the last second, I thought you would stop. Please test it now so we can make sure it's back on."

The agent stepped toward the ship slowly until at about thirty feet he stopped. "I feel a mild tingle. Not painful but not enjoyable either. Thank you."

"Don't mention it, Agent." Kitty turned back to her introduction group. "Are there any questions before we end this session?"

CHAPTER TWENTY-THREE

Simon floated into Orion's construction information center, which was even now gestating its second child. Every construction project had a Shack. This was one for the books though. Orion was over two thousand feet long, sitting atop the metal ribcage of some long-dead titan. Extend the main spine past both ends by nine hundred feet each, add twelve oval "ribs" and a bottom spine binding the whole together, and it added up to the space station. But this titan had just recently come into being.

The Shack, which Simon had just entered, was a clear blister on top of the main I-beam. Capable of sliding along tracks along the beam or any of the ribs, it could be at the location of a construction problem almost immediately so the supervisor could make on-the-spot suggestions without having to take the time to get into a pod and go to the trouble spot. Due to its mobile nature, the Shack wasn't equipped with artificial gravity, so most people tended to stay away unless they were pod jockeys or others who were now used to Zero-G.

Finding Daniel busy with several of the new up-and-coming engineers trained on the *Galileo* and Orion, Simon stared out of the transparent wall facing the inside of the ribcage. The pounding heart that always accompanied his visits to the Shack was brought on by the dream being born before his eyes, and the pounding this time was because the dream was about to become a reality.

The vision before his eyes was of a partially constructed hull—Orion's second child. Construction pods moved about the slowly growing shape that would be the third ship in the Alliance Fleet, sparks of light revealing the locations of pods welding or cutting on different segments of the interior while alien atomic torches illuminated the uncompleted portions in stark, intermittent relief.

When Daniel finally left the two engineers overseeing the installation of a new field generator in the starboard forequarter back to their task, he floated over to Simon. "Today's the big day, Simon! Don't you want some kind of ceremony?"

Simon stared avidly out the window. The star field skewed before his eyes as the Shack moved around on the ribcage for a closer inspection of the work area. "There'll be time for a ceremony later, Dan. Usually the grand opening comes a bit after the actual event."

Two pod jockeys maneuvered a sizable piece of equipment toward a hole of questionable size.

"Is that the new generator?"

"Yeah," Daniel said sourly enough that Simon looked at him sharply. "Don't get me wrong, Simon. I'm all for those generators. We just had to do some quick reengineering to get them and their associated field emitters in place. Fortunately, we only had to tear out part of one section. There are eight of those per ship that size."

"So that's why torpedo loads dropped so drastically. I think I'd trade the firepower for the shield any time, though," Simon said, moving toward the far end of the Shack and away from the two engineers.

"I'd think so," Dan said matter-of-factly. "I've still got the hard copy with your signature on it authorizing the installation. But, that's not why you stopped by, is it?"

Simon positioned himself so that he could see the two engineers supervising the installation of the generator. The slowly moving Shack rotated enough to expose the real reason for Simon's visit. He nodded in the direction of the white-hulled warship sitting just outside the dock. "Tomorrow that ship is going to be named the *TAS Robert A. Heinlein*. She'll have to come back to be retrofitted with the shield generators, but for now, she'd the first symbol of what we're capable of. I like the thought of having things like the shields that the Builders never figured out. Could be a critical advantage when we finally meet up with 'em." Simon looked out at the ship as it rotated through his field of view. Daniel could see him come to a decision and reach into a pocket, handing him a computer disc.

It was still easier to have human computers interface with the organic ones of the *Galileo*-class computers when it came to straight input of information.

"Daniel, at this exact moment, only two people know what I have planned for that ship out there. Joanna Barnes helped me write the code on this disc. Actually, it was my idea, and she did all the work. In a few seconds there will be three, and as soon as this one is commissioned, there will be four, and I want this information to stop right there. What I have here is the start-up information for the computer out there—all the access codes, operational information, everything, plus a few extra lines of code. That ship will be able to access any other ship's computer and shut it down, either in part or in total, at the captain's discretion."

Simon slid the disc under an elastic band to keep it in place. "This one is a little different," he said, waving a second disc in the air. "It will be used by all other ships for their startups, and their commands are that they will accept over-rides from that one," he said, pointing at the first disc. "The shutdown codes are buried so deeply in the operational codes that I don't think anybody not specifically looking for them will ever figure out they're there." He laid a hand on the first disc and said, "Call me paranoid, Daniel, but I don't want someone to get hold of one of our ships and give it to the wrong person.

"And, yes, I know it's a calculated risk," Simon went on. "But if only four people know about it, I believe the risk is minimized. Besides, whoever has command of that ship is someone I'd trust completely anyway. So, here's the standard disc," Simon said, stressing the point. "Put it away, and let's get her lit up. After we get her online, I'll keep track of the original. I have a copy of the second disc for Gemini and two more for the new stations as they're finished."

Daniel looked worried and ran a hand through his hair. "I don't know that we need to be that paranoid, Simon, but I do agree that we should err on the side of caution." He slid the first disc into the transmitter, set up the upload, and turned to Simon. "Do you want the honors?"

Simon waved the request aside. "No, Dan, she's your baby. You get the privilege of waking her up."

Daniel pressed the send key and sat back to watch the results. About a minute later, the computer spit the disc out, and a screen flashed the message: *Function complete.*

Simon stared out the porthole at their first ship as it slowly came alive. He was pleased to see the portside running light come on and begin a slow, steady, red pulsation. Neither of the two men could repress their emotions as they saw lights begin to appear in irregular patterns across the surface of the twelve-hundred-foot-long ship.

Simon asked, "How long before we can go over for an inspection tour?"

Daniel's reply was slow and deliberate. "Well, we've had heaters running over there for two weeks now. There are components that don't take well to the cold of space once they get installed. So, I'd say, at a guess, mind you, that we should be able to go... oh, I don't know... how about now?"

Simon gave a chagrined look. "Am I that obvious? Okay, let's go."

Daniel opened the airlock door to the Shack, gave instructions to his assistants, and led Simon off to the main habitat. "I thought we'd take a shuttle over. Soon enough we're going to have to get used to not having the *Galileo's* transport technology. Actually, we've already done that out here, which suits me just fine. You should start getting used to it yourself. I don't know how you people can stand having your molecules scrambled anyway. I'm always afraid I'll go in as Daniel and come out Danielle or something."

Nodding, Simon asked, "How about meeting me in the shuttle bay in half an hour? I need to pick up a few interested parties."

Twenty minutes later, Simon arrived with Kitty, Gayle, Stephen and Lucy, to find Daniel waiting with a handful of his engineers. The shuttle door was open, so Kitty walked directly aboard and found a seat near the front of the passenger compartment.

The rest of the group followed, and Simon noticed that the shuttle had been modified to accept more passengers. This one was more in line with what a shuttle should be. Besides, there were others to ferry large components. Next, he noticed the pilot. To his shock, it was Commander Lee. "I figured you'd have a fit before you'd fly one of these again," he commented.

Miranda's laugh was infectious. "I wouldn't miss this for the world, Captain. Even if it means flying one of these crates. Besides, we want only the best when we have such a high-powered group, don't we?" Her logic was impossible to refute, and her wicked grin said as much.

"Very well, Commander," Simon responded, bowing to the inevitable, "we're in your capable hands."

Commander Lee brought the shuttle online, made sure all of her passengers were belted in, and contacted Orion's Launch Control. "Flight Control, this is Shuttle One... make that Alliance One, requesting clearance to depart. Destination, ship number one. Shuttle will be under manual control. Advise me of any outside traffic."

Receiving permission from Flight Control to depart, Miranda slowly raised her ship off the deck, sliding deftly through the force field and out into space. Checking her screens to be sure there was no other traffic between her and her destination, Miranda slowly applied power.

As they neared the ship, Simon, seated forward with Daniel, said, "Commander Lee, transmit this signal to the new vessel: Open docking bay one, priority override alpha-star-alpha. Then give us a full flyby. I'd like to get an overall view of her exterior."

Miranda acknowledged her orders and momentarily reported, "Sir, instruments show docking bay one open and ready for us to access." She began a slow flyby of the gleaming white vessel sitting alone in the depth of space.

Simon noted the steady pulse of the red portside light, blinking to match the green one to starboard, as well as the occasional interior light that illuminated various portholes built into the vessel. The original designs showed none of those, but it had been determined that since humans are visually-based creatures, it would be necessary to have some kind of window onto the universe to prevent the claustrophobia that grounded a small but respectable number of people hoping for a position on one of the bases or ships.

Simon pointed out to Daniel some of the various features as the shuttle slowly cruised the length and breadth of the new vessel. "I see four torpedo tubes in each octant. Is that correct?" Simon asked.

Daniel nodded and pointed to the forward upper octant. "Each segment is internally independent of the others by virtue of self-sealing section bulkheads, keeping damage to one section from interfering with the operations of the other sections of the ship. You'll notice, though, that the eight separate sections that comprise the forward and stern missile bays are constructed so that the eight forward torpedo rooms are all supplied from one central storage bay. The stern is built the same way so you actually only have two areas that are storing explosive materials. Not including the engine room, of course."

The shuttle glided past a replica of the habitat section of the *Galileo*. The original plans had called for it, and since the one on the *Galileo* was so popular with most of the crew, it was allowed to be left in the design. More important was the addition of the extra power cores in the engine room.

Early on in their studies of the basic plans loaded into the computer's memory, the engineers had discovered a bottleneck in the basic design of the ship's power allocation system. Power taps connected directly to a matter-antimatter core that sent power first to the engines and then to other parts of the ship, depending on the priority of ship situations. Weapons, mostly gamma-burst lasers, drew their power at a higher priority in battle, thereby leaving less power for the engines. The decision was one of fight or flight.

And now, with the addition of the new shield technology, there was going to be the addition of another power-intensive system adapted from Builder technology but apparently totally unknown to them. The solution was evident. It took very little extra space overall to add two more power cores into the engine room. All the controls were already in place for one core and powered one system. The *Heinlein,* as the first ship was to be called, would need to return for a refit of the shield generators, but the data on the systems arrived in time to allow for the installation and activation of the second and third power cores.

Miranda maneuvered the shuttle through the force field and into the docking bay, coming to rest in the geometric center of the space available. She checked her instruments and announced, "Air and gravity optimal. No lumps, bumps, or contusions."

Daniel stood up and made his way back to the hatch. "Well, I told everybody to dress warmly. Commander, let us out."

Daniel turned to face the small crowd staring avidly around the landing bay. "You will notice that we managed to get force screens installed on the landing bay doors, and we're even now working on the plans for how we're going to retrofit her for her shields." He led them out of the bay, lecturing as he went. "Each segment is triple-compartmented. Doesn't mean much normally, but if she should get holed, two major bulkheads seal completely. Like this one here. There's an elevator on each side of the bulkhead and another pair at the other bulkhead. That way, you don't lose an entire ship to one missile."

While Simon had never been aboard this vessel before, he felt right at home walking down corridors that fairly glowed as the pearlescent material used to coat the interior walls reflected the indirect lighting. After all, he'd been involved, albeit in a minor way, in designing her.

Simon commented, "This feels comfortable," a sentiment heartily echoed by all.

The bridge wasn't much of a surprise to the visitors. It was located in the center of the ship, which was considered by some to be the most secure spot, but Simon still felt a bit uneasy. True, there was a lot more mass between the bridge and any possible strike, but Simon was imagining those torpedo magazines fore and aft, as well as the power cores, and that didn't even take into account the large number of high-intensity lasers, plasma cannons, and other weapons between the bridge and outer skin of the ship. Efficient screens were going to be a must, that was for sure. How did the Builders ever send one of these things into battle without screens? It wouldn't take that much to get through the armor plating and blow either torpedo magazine. Were they fatalists? Idealists? Or had they simply never connected the dots? Are their enemies equally armed? Better? Worse?

He shook his head. The debates raged, as to whether the Builders were a young and vibrant race or one in decline. Hell, it was humans who'd adapted the capture fields used to bring asteroidal material to the main smelter for so many uses, all the way to sci-fi's impenetrable force fields.

"The bridge is pretty standard," Daniel said, breaking Simon out of his reverie. "We took the *Galileo's* bridge and adjusted it for the smaller area. "I've been here before. Take a look. Some of you will be working here soon enough."

The tour that followed was totally unexpected. There was color everywhere. Once the engineers figured out how to color the metals, they started to go crazy.

"We found a Lt. Kimura to ride hard on them to keep 'em from going overboard. I'd like to think we put her to good use," Daniel said.

An hour later, they came away with a new sense of what they had wrought.

"Individually targetable, high-intensity lasers," Daniel said proudly. "Thirty of them. At least three, and sometimes more, can be brought to bear on almost any target most of the time. And of course, you must keep in mind that we have more room, so we made the lasers larger, and they have their own dedicated power source."

Simon broke in. "I'm hearing 'almost' and 'most.' What conditions would have to exist for fewer than three? Any blast powerful enough to get us there will have effectively gutted a good portion of the ship already."

Daniel took a serious turn. "If you get to that point, there's no need to know. About the only things that can take this ship out are," he held up a hand and started ticking off points, "superior tonnage or generator power, superior numbers that will overpower even a very sophisticated computer's fire control system, or coming out of warp inside a star. Once this girl gets her shields, I'm not sure even those things could stop her. Except maybe the star."

The missile bays were another marvel. Each of the eight rooms were capable of firing four missiles at a time, making for forward and rear salvos of sixteen missiles at one time, or near-continuous synchronized fire as long as the missiles lasted. Each missile was tipped with one of the new antimatter warheads and was capable of taking down screens, as well as taking out ships. The difficulty lay in the number of missiles required to get through a ship's screens. Tests showed that screens powered by the largest generators could be penetrated. It just took more missiles. Once the screens were down, no mere metal would stop even one of these new breed of killers. And the real nice thing about them was that the other side didn't know they existed. At least, there was nothing like them in any of the computer's data banks. And no shields either.

The boat bays were last on the list, a marvel of compact engineering and efficiency. Each ship in the *Heinlein's* class carried ten Mambas, which launched straight from their bays. The force fields were attuned to the specific energies emitted by the engines and allowed them to escape into space. Upon any given ship's return, capture fields would pull it inside stern first where a crew would be waiting to service or repair as needed.

At last Daniel turned to them. "And here we are, ladies and gentlemen, back at the start of our little tour. If you'll look to your left, you'll see the shuttle that will take you back to Orion." Dropping the tour guide act, Daniel smiled. "We're proud of her. Take good care of her, will ya? Anybody hurts my baby, you'll have to face me." He shook his finger at the lot of them. "All kidding aside, folks, I have things I need to look after. So, let's all get back to Orion, shall we?"

Miranda wasted no time returning the shuttle to Orion. As the passengers exited the craft, Simon handed Daniel another disc. "This one has the crew roster. I'd like to schedule a commissioning ceremony for two days from now. You can release the roster immediately so people can get used to it and get packed and transferred. I was going to take more from you, but, as you'll see, I changed that. Orion will only be supplying a third of the crew. That will minimize your downtime as you train the new people."

Daniel made an exaggerated bow to Simon. "Thank you, kind sir. I'll remember you in my will."

Simon laughed. "Typical straw boss, Daniel. Also, I intend to call a meeting of the senior staff tomorrow evening to announce the officer roster."

Back in their quarters, Kitty put Simon on the spot. "Why won't you tell us who's going to be on the officer's roster? Don't you think we have as much right to know as the rest of the crew?"

Simon gestured at the stack of papers on his desk. "That's everything on anyone who might conceivably fill an officer's position, and I haven't made my final decisions yet. You know I work best under pressure," he said, trying to inject a little levity. "I've only got a little over twenty-four hours to make my decisions. I'll call a staff meeting sometime tomorrow afternoon or evening. If you knew how difficult this is for me, you wouldn't push. The last time we really talked about this, you said you'd support whatever my decision was. Part of that decision is that I won't rush it, and I'll announce the entire officer complement tomorrow evening." Simon began pacing up and down the length of the room. "I'm sorry if I sound testy, honey, but I feel that this is a command decision, and you're trying to use our personal relationship to get more information than I'm ready to give."

Kitty began to back down. "Well, I guess you're right, but it's safe to tell me, you know. I'm your wife, and I won't tell anyone."

Simon said, "That's not the point. The point is that I can't treat you any differently than any of my other officers as far as ship matters are concerned.

You've noticed that I've tried to be scrupulously nonpartisan when it comes to you and duties aboard ship."

Kitty replied a bit testily, "Yes, I've noticed. And speaking of duties, why is it that I'm not first officer anymore?"

Simon responded tiredly. They'd done this one before. "That's a matter of protocol. No officer that serves in a given capacity and gets demoted for any reason stays on the same ship or in the same unit. Promoted up is one thing; demoted gets you a transfer. And we don't have anywhere to transfer Lucy right now. The only two options are to leave her where she is or promote her to captain."

A look of sudden comprehension crossed her face. "So that's it! You're going to make Lucy captain of the new ship and give me back first officer since I've already had experience at the job."

Simon looked her in the eye and said, flat-voiced, "I'm not going to be drawn into this conversation." He picked her up by her upper arms and soundly kissed her, setting her down before she could strike.

Walking to his desk and sitting down, he picked up a folder and began to go over some of the personnel transfers. Looking over at Kitty as she sat on the side of the bed, he said, "Think about the fact that I not only have to decide who'll be officers aboard the *Heinlein*, but I have to decide on promotions for the *Galileo* as well. I'm just glad that once each of these vessels gets a captain, promoting and demoting becomes someone else's problem."

Kitty walked up behind him and began kneading his shoulders. "Poor dear. You're just too tense. You need some relaxin'. A little rest might give you a different outlook." She leaned over and whispered in his ear. "You know, all work and no play is beginning to make Simon a *very* dull boy." As she leaned forward, she noticed that one of the files on the desk had her name on it. "You're not seriously considering me for a place on the *Heinlein* are you?"

Simon glanced down at the desk, reached out and picked up his wife's folder, along with the one under it. Spreading the two folders apart so she could see the other name, he said, "About as much as I'm considering me, dear. Just think, if I claim her, Lucy becomes captain. Chain of command. Now, will you drop it, please?"

Kitty didn't answer. She just dug her thumbs in a little harder until he laid the folder down and let her have her way with the muscles of his shoulders and back. He never saw the dark look she gave him as she worked the knots out.

The next morning, Simon walked into the transporter room and said, "Ensign, if you don't want to walk home, you'll send me to these coordinates and forget I was even here today."

The technician saw the look in Simon's eyes, stammered "Y-yes, Sir," and beamed Simon off the ship.

He found his new surroundings quite comfortable indeed. After all, he'd helped to design them. He was standing in the captain's quarters aboard the *Heinlein*. Functional furniture filled the living room portion of the suite. The dining alcove would seat six in a pinch, and the bedroom was out of sight behind an unobtrusive door in one corner of the room. "It'll do for a hideout," Simon said aloud. "Shouldn't be anyone here until after I name the captain." He sighed, stretched, and sat down. Propping his feet up on the coffee table, he let his eyes slowly close as his dilemma enveloped him.

Strange noises disturbed his reverie until he realized that it was probably just some of the crew coming and going. A ship that had just come from the dock would still need a lot of attention. He poured himself a double scotch and let himself drift back into a light daze as his mind gnawed at the bones of his quandary.

Taking stock of his surroundings for the first time in what seemed like hours, Simon glanced at his watch. Realizing how short his time was, he quickly beamed back aboard Galileo and called Lucy. "Commander, if you'd be so kind as to call the people on the list I gave you this morning and ask them to meet me in the mess hall on deck three, I'd appreciate it. Tell them thirty minutes from now."

Looking to kill close to half an hour without running into anyone he'd be seeing at the upcoming meeting, Simon walked into the mess hall on deck six, not realizing what a stir it would cause to have the captain stop in for coffee. Not wanting to distress anyone, he grabbed a cup of coffee and headed out the door but stopped quickly when he heard a voice calling his name. Looking more closely, he saw a raised hand belonging to Agent Daniels. He walked over to the table and slid into an empty seat.

Recognizing another face, he said, "Crewman McNalley. Everything under control?"

The crewman answered, "Cain't says I complain, Cap'n. But I kinda sat still long enough. It's time for this Georgia boy to git back to work."

Simon nodded at McNalley. "I know the feeling,

Crewman. I like my time off, too, but I get nervous without something to do. I *can* tell you it won't be a whole lot longer. Only a couple more weeks, I think, until we'll be starting on number three."

He turned to the new face at the table. Glancing at the young man's nametag, he asked, "How are you settling in, Crewman Pike? I'm Captain Hawke."

The new volunteer set the glass he'd been holding down on the table to shake hands. "I've got to say how amazed I am at where I am and what's going on."

Simon grinned. "Those seem to be pretty common sentiments for all the new volunteers. I just hope we can *keep* you amazed. A sense of wonder needs to be watered to grow. Speaking of which, after almost a week of orientation, have you found anything that strikes your fancy?"

Pulling a piece of paper from his pocket, Crewman Pike pointed to two job categories he'd circled. "I was studying astrophysics back before I joined, so it looks like either Navigation or Helm would be most suited to what I've been training for."

Simon had to leave the new man with more than that. "Those are both good choices, Crewman, but I want you to remember that a little over a year ago, no one on this ship had any idea what to do on any post. Whatever you choose, you won't have to stay there forever if you don't like it or don't have an aptitude for it. What I'm saying is for you to keep your options open. We hold classes all the time for different positions."

Simon turned to Agent Daniels. "So, Agent, what terrible and subversive plots have you turned up this week? I hear you've been poking into every corner you can find. I also hear you had a run-in with your security parameters. What happened?"

The agent reddened. "Actually, I never saw that Mamba coming, Captain. I was talking to some of the pilots over on Orion when a ship came in for service. I watched it enter the bay and went back to my conversation. The next thing I knew, my wristband started to go off. The technicians had picked it up in a capture field and moved it over by me where they could work on it, so I left."

Laughing, Simon said, "Pretty much what I'd already been told. Just wanted to hear your side. Anything you need?"

Taking a sip from his cup, Daniels finally said, "Well, it *is* a pretty big ship. That commlink you mentioned when I first came aboard would be a big help tracking people down." Simon pulled his own out of his pocket, called Supply, and left instructions for a commlink to be made available to the agent. "Pick it up any time, Agent. Now, if you gentlemen will excuse me, I have to be somewhere in a few minutes."

Simon stepped out of the elevator on deck three to find the entire corridor empty. Puzzled, he stopped at the closed door to the mess hall, took a deep breath, squared his shoulders, and walked into the room.

No sooner had he set foot in the room than Kitty, who'd been standing beside the door, grabbed his arm and hissed, "Simon! Where the hell have you been? We've turned the ship upside down looking for you."

In a voice just as quiet as hers, blue eyes spearing into her heart, Simon answered, "If that question is coming from my wife, I'll answer it in our quarters later. If it's coming from one of my officers, either withdraw it or ask it louder. That way, I can give one answer to the whole room."

Kitty had started to reply when Stephen coughed. She looked over at him as he made a small sit-down gesture with one hand. She stood frozen until Simon quietly added, "Honey, I need you to sit down so I can get on with this. I've been telling you it's not easy." Kitty heard something in his voice she'd never heard before and felt a chill run up her spine—anguish. Reaching out and laying a hand on his forearm for a second, she turned and found her chair between Gayle and Stephen.

Simon stood at his place at the head of the table, watching all the eager faces and not-so-eager faces looking at him. Some of the looks he was getting were tinged with worry.

So many of them are so young! he thought.

When he finally spoke, it was in a voice that was so low it was almost inaudible at first. "I apologize to each and every one of you for taking so long to reach these decisions. That everyone in this room is going to be affected by what I'm about to announce goes without saying, but I have to say it anyway."

He pulled a piece of paper out of his shirt pocket, re-buttoned the flap, and slowly unfolded the paper. "That said, some of you won't be happy, and that can't be helped at this time, but please be assured that no one is being slighted. We'll soon have enough ships for each of you to show your true mettle, ladies and gentlemen."

He looked down at the paper he held, feeling the tension grow in the room. "We'll have a seven-officer cadre—captain, first officer, weapons/security officer, science/tactics officer, communications officer,

433

navigation officer and helm officer. And, of course, three shifts as usual. I'm going to leave it up to the captain to name the other positions. That will be the order of ascension as well. Now, for the position of Helm Officer, Donna Hall to be promoted to full commander. Navigation Officer, Michiko Greene to be promoted to full commander. Communications Officer, Commander Gayle Miller. Science/Tactics Officer, Robert Greene to be promoted to full commander. Please note, ladies and gentlemen, that the Greenes will be promoted at the same time so that neither can pull rank on the other." A small titter of amusement answered back. "Weapons/Security, John Marshall. First Officer, Marsha Kane to be promoted to full commander."

Simon stood at the front of the room and looked at the faces staring avidly at him. "This has been one of the hardest decisions I've ever had to make. When all was said and done, I only had two viable candidates for this first ship, which, by the way, is going to be named the *Robert A. Heinlein*. I found both candidates to be identical in their qualifications for the job, and it actually came down to basing my choice on rank. Of the two possible candidates for captain of the *Heinlein*, my choice is ..." Simon paused to take a deep breath and then continued, "Commander Katherine Hawke. Congratulations, Captain."

The silence after Simon's revelation lasted only a heartbeat as Kitty's and Lucy's faces both fell. Then Rob Greene said, "Yes! Captain Kitty!" He stood up and began to applaud, and the rest of the room followed suit—Lucy not quite as quickly as the others but applauding just as heartily.

The applause dribbled to a ragged stop, and Simon let the silence stretch as long as he could. "Those of you not chosen today for this first posting, please keep in mind that we will have two more vessels within six months, and your names are first in line for any future available positions. Then, three more six ships months after that, and then eight vessels a year from then on, more if we build smaller ships and less if we build larger. Ladies and gentlemen, I believe you all have duties to perform or preparations to make. Everybody not chosen for this ship will be eligible for the second." He stood up. "Lucy and Kitty, if you'll meet me in my ready room in five minutes, we can open the mess hall back up."

Kitty and Lucy sat opposite Simon. He'd thought hard about what he was about to say. He picked and chose each word with care as if skirting a verbal minefield. He addressed Lucy first.

"I saw the looks of shock on both your faces— Kitty's because I named her captain and yours because I didn't name you. That's what I want to discuss first. Although nothing was said, Lucy, I know that you expected to be named captain, and under most conditions you would have been. I didn't choose Kitty because she's my wife. She and I had this discussion last night, although she didn't really know it. I think I've been scrupulously honest about not showing her any favoritism—so scrupulous, in fact, that I think she's had a rougher time of it than the rest of you. The simple fact of the matter is that you're both equally qualified for the position, but Kitty outranked you. Now, I'm going to make life just a little easier for you. In front of a witness, I'm telling you categorically that the next ship completed is yours. And we're talking less than six months, Lucy, so I want you to start training your successor. Also, I'm going to let you choose the name of your ship. Talk to me later and I'll give you your choices."

Lucy said, "Commander Marshall was waiting for me outside the mess hall after the meeting. He explained to me a little about military protocol, so I do understand why you made the choice you did. I'll be perfectly happy with ship number two, and I have a successor in mind already. And I don't think our relationship will suffer."

Simon gave a small sigh of relief. "I'm glad to hear that, Lucy. I think you're going to make a great captain. I'd hate to lose you over something like this. Now, if you'll excuse us, I have some things I need to go over with Kitty."

Lucy stood up, reached over the desk that separated them, and held out her hand. "Truth, Captain. I'm not upset. I'll be happy to take the second ship. Congrats, Captain Kitty," she said as she leaned over and kissed Kitty on the cheek.

When Lucy left the room, the temperature dropped some twenty degrees, and Simon tried to hold off the eruption he saw coming. "Look, honey, what I said in the mess hall and here to Lucy was the absolute truth. But not the whole truth." At this, Kitty's mouth snapped shut. "You are about to become the fourth person to be privy to the following bit of information. The third is Daniel, and he just found out yesterday. The other is Dr. Barnes because I needed her help in writing the code that was used to activate the *Heinlein*. This is a secret we may take to our graves, but then again, maybe not. The big secret is that the ship out there, the *Heinlein*, has an ability that none of the other ships will have. Because of that, only someone I trust implicitly will ever command her. I spent many hours locked up with our computer and Dr. Barnes working this out."

Simon stopped for a breath, and Kitty wailed, "But you're splitting us up!" Simon winced at the volume. "What can possibly be so special about that ship that it requires splitting us up?"

Simon explained about the changes to the operating codes, not only for the *Heinlein*, but for all the others as well, and how her ship would be able to access and shut down any or all portions of another ship's systems. "Life support, weapons, power generation, it doesn't matter. You issue the right command codes, and the ship will go dead. The protocols are hidden behind so many layers of encryption that no one will find them without knowing what they're looking for. And the acceptance protocols on the rest of the fleet will be equally well hidden. Also, any attempt to remove the acceptance protocols or block or circumvent them will result in a total system shutdown for the ship involved."

While he spoke, he watched expressions run across her face. More and more they began to look like what he privately called her Toni Putnam face. Kitty shook her head. "That's a pretty big secret, all right. It's also too much power for one person to have, Simon. But I'll take the ship."

Surprised by her almost instant change of mind, he stumbled. "N-no. That's too much power for one person to have *that I don't trust*. At this point in time, there's only one person I trust as much as me, and that's you. Just between you and me, we started this together, and we'll go as far as we can before someone takes over for us."

Simon began drumming his fingers on the desktop. "Here's something I haven't told anyone yet. Once we get enough ships built and crewed, I envision teams of three ships traveling together, especially when we start to seriously explore other stars. At first, some will go out as singles, but once we have enough, there's no reason to risk our people and ships traveling alone. Two ships like the *Heinlein* and… how about a carrier? We've come an amazing distance by being both daring and foolhardy. I think it's time to throw a pinch of caution into the mix and not send ships out alone.

"Now," he said, pointedly changing the subject. "I believe I heard something about there being a celebration throughout the *Galileo* and Orion. And I know for a fact that you're about to have several very hectic days ahead of you. Let's take tonight and tomorrow night and just relax."

Simon and Kitty boycotted most of the festivities, although nature did finally force them out of their room and down the corridor to the mess hall. As they approached, they could hear a commotion, so Simon wasn't surprised to see a crowd present when they walked in, but Kitty was.

They stopped just inside the doorway and the noise in the room died in a spreading wave, with them at the epicenter. Then one pair of hands started clapping. Presently, everyone in the room was on their feet, facing them and applauding. Kitty looked around the room to see what the cause of the uproar was.

Simon put his arm around her waist, leaned down just slightly, and said, "Honey, the applause is for you." He saw a flush come across her face as he felt her stiffen up and start to take a step backwards. "You can't run from this, dear. Trust me, you're in for the duration. For some reason, all these people seem to like you. You may hate me for this, but for now, you're stuck with it." Keeping his arm around her waist, Simon gently herded his wife in the direction of the captain's table.

Kitty saw the tables and looked up at Simon. "You planned this."

Simon laughed and said, "No I didn't, but I'm not in the least surprised."

Leading her to what would normally have been his place, Simon seated Kitty at the head of the table and sat down on her right. As word spread that Kitty had emerged from seclusion, more and more people began to come by to offer their congratulations. Shortly, the three tables were full. By common consent, *Galileo's* personnel sat to Simon's right and Kitty's new staff sat to her left, including quiet, competent Marsha Kane, whose uncharacteristically dazed expression was further enhanced by the glasses she wore.

Talk inevitably turned to the new ship and plans for her disposition. Simon deflected the majority of the questions for a time by saying, "This next week to ten days, she'll be standing to her trials." He turned to Kitty. "That means, m'dear, that for the first week or so your crew will be engineer and tech heavy.

Some of your regular crew will stay here for that time while you put her through her paces. You'll have the extra tech support for things like repairs, adjustments, calibrations, and such."

A short time later, Kitty turned to Simon and asked him in a quiet voice, "You think you could take me over there and give me a personal tour? I hate to admit this, but I wasn't paying as much attention on the tour as I maybe should have been. I really only went because you did."

Simon patted her on the arm. "Kittyn, it's been planned for a while. I've just been waiting for you to ask."

After the delay that decorum required, Simon and Kitty got up and made their way to the door. Kitty said, "We'll be back before the party's over. Won't be staying long, but we'll be back."

Daniel, seated nearby, turned around in his chair and looked over his shoulder at Kitty. "What do you mean 'party over'? I have it on good authority that tomorrow is going to be all party except for the commissioning ceremony. So I wouldn't worry about missing your fair share of partying."

Everyone within hearing laughed, and Kitty smiled down at Daniel.

Simon stopped in his tracks and turned to Daniel. "And on whose authority do you have it that tomorrow is going to be all parties?" he asked with a chuckle.

Daniel peered up at Simon and said sonorously, "Why, my authority, of course," and then very carefully passed out into the tray of snacks on the table.

Simon took Kitty's arm and steered her through

the milling crowd. True to his word, he led her to the transporter room where they beamed over to the *Heinlein's* modest reception area directly off the boat bays. Simon led her to the bridge, sat her down in the captain's chair, and began to talk. "Unlike the *Galileo*, this is a fighting ship. The slimmer and trimmer she is, the more maneuverable she is, so weight and space considerations mean a lot. This bridge is the equal of the *Galileo's,* only a bit smaller."

Kitty looked slowly around the room, hands unconsciously caressing the arms of the command chair. "And," he continued, "there are repeater circuits that transfer all the information on these consoles directly to your cabin so you can be informed at all times about what's happening."

As the tour continued, Kitty showed more and more distress. She asked all the right questions, but Simon could recognize the signs—fingers rubbing any convenient piece of fabric between them, eyes shifting right and left continuously, as if looking for a way out, face flushed. It was when they entered a laser cannon servicing bay that she finally cracked.

"Simon, these… these things," she said, waving her hand in the direction of the laser assembly, "are the perfect example of why I think you screwed up by making me captain. The only thing I've ever killed in my life is time. I can't kill anything directly. I have to put out no-pest strips and roach motels. And you want to put me in command of a warship?"

Simon leaned back against a convenient bulkhead. "You see, there's the beauty of the idea. Think about it for a minute. Who better than a pacifist in command of a warship? What it means to me is that if you *do* pull the trigger, you had a *damn*

441

good reason. And excuse me while I point out a flaw in your logic. I remember when you found Toni Putnam's body on the floor of Orion's sickbay. I think if you could have gotten your hands on whoever killed her, you'd have killed them without hesitation. And I've noticed a difference in you since then. You're still as loving and caring as ever, and just as quick to find fault with me. But I think you, like some of the rest of us, lost some of your innocence that day. As evidence, your pistol. That's not a Z-Tag toy, love."

With many scenarios chasing themselves around the inside of her head, Kitty decided to head back. Simon, having accomplished his mission of getting his wife to at least question her core beliefs, agreed.

The most noticeable difference upon their return was the absence of Daniel.

"Some of his people took him back to Orion shortly after you left, sir," Robert Greene said as they sat down. The party was in full swing, and there didn't appear to be an end in sight.

Kitty glanced around the table and said, "For once, I think I'll have a beer."

An hour later, after she'd wrapped herself around a couple more beers herself and something to eat, Kitty began to think she could do this after all. Turning to Marsha on her left, she said, slowly and deliberately, knowing the alcohol was affecting her, "Number One, the commissioning ceremony is for two p.m. tomorrow, which is going to allow most of us to sleep off what we're doing to ourselves right now. I think we should have a staff meeting immediately afterwards. We should probably use the ready room here. Time enough to get used to our own once we get moved in."

Marsha turned to her new commanding officer and replied, "Yes, ma'am. I'll inform the staff." Turning her head to the left, she announced, "Officers of the *Heinlein*. Listen up! There will be a staff meeting immediately after the commissioning ceremony tomorrow. Attendance is mandatory in the *Galileo's* ready room." Turning back to Kitty, she mumbled, "Ma'am, mission accomplished," and gently placing her head on her arms, she started snoring.

Kitty looked down at the unconscious woman beside her and asked, "Will someone please help my first officer to her room?"

Rob Greene stood up. "'Chiko and I were planning to leave soon anyway. We'll see that she gets home safely."

Several stumbles and a stagger later, interspersed with more than a few apologies, the trio made their way to the door and out of sight.

Kitty awoke on commissioning day clear-headed and curiously focused. She slipped into and out of the shower in near-record time, and when Simon finally woke up and found her at his desk, a box on the floor beside her was slowly filling up with files.

Simon walked up behind her, bent down, kissed her on the neck, and nibbled one ear. Playfully breathing in her ear, he asked, "Whatcha doin'?"

She replied, "Taking anything even remotely pertinent to the *Heinlein's* operation with me."

Seeing that she had just about finished anyway, he reached out and slid two more files over in front of her. "That should pretty much do it."

Still looking down at the desk, Kitty reached behind her to pat him on the thigh and encountered bare skin. Sliding her hand up a few inches, she asked, "What would have happened if I'd had company?"

Simon kissed her on top of the head and said, "Then they would have seen just how much I love you and how happy I am to see you this morning."

She moved her hand higher and could only respond, "Oh!"

CHAPTER TWENTY-FOUR

As usual, the only place for a crowd this size was deck eighteen. What had come to be known as the projects deck was crowded with people, almost fifteen hundred of them.

And that's not counting the skeleton crews for Orion and Galileo watching via whisker lasers, or the start-up crew already aboard the Heinlein, Simon thought.

He stood in the shadow of a Mamba, looking out over the crowd. The ship and its twin on the other side of the podium tended to focus the audience's attention on the speaker. As he waited for Daniel to introduce him, he couldn't stop his mind from wandering over the events that had led up to this moment. Part of his mind listened to Daniel and another part kept asking what, if anything, he could have done differently. Holding the pages of his speech in his hand, he tapped them against his leg while he fought the butterflies waging war in his stomach.

He had to table his self-examination when he heard Daniel begin to wind down. A quick introduction later, he was staring out at a field of faces. Silence ruled the deck as Simon placed his papers on the podium, grabbed each one, and glanced back down one more time. Finally, he could dither no more.

"Ladies and gentlemen, I wouldn't be standing here today if not for your effort, your dedication, your sacrifices." He stopped for a moment to judge the crowd and heard a murmur in response to his accolade. "I also wouldn't be standing here today if you didn't share my vision of what we can do for the human race." Picking up the microphone, he stepped to one side of the podium. "We are doing more than standing on the edge of a new era." He took a step forward.

"We, those of us living and working aboard five distinct and separate vessels, have actually crossed the line. Just one step, but we *have* crossed. Very few times in history has anyone or any group of people had the opportunity to realize how big an impact they were making on the future. This, my friends, is one of those times. What we do here alters the very destiny of the human race. And we are privileged to know that ahead of time. This place, Orion Base, is a place of firsts." He held up one finger. "This dock is the first deep-space outpost built by humans. And as important as that is," Simon began to put spaces between his words, and as he did, the exterior doors slowly began to open, leaving the entire crew of both vessels exposed to the depths of space save only for force fields. "As important as that is," he repeated, "it pales in comparison to what you've accomplished in the last six months."

The doors finished rolling back and there, illuminated by light that had traveled almost twice as far as most humans had experienced, was a sparkling white ship. Anyone familiar with the *Galileo's* original plans would have trouble believing that the one had been derived from the other. With the annealing process that allowed the engineers to imprint color directly into the hull, deck and wall plates, the ship already seemed to have a life of her own. Her length of over twelve hundred feet, offset by her narrow beam, made her seem smaller than she actually was. Yet the finished product housed twenty fewer crew than originally planned, leaving the crew complement at three hundred eighty. Engines almost the size of the *Galileo's* allowed her to move at speeds undreamed of by the Builders, and she would soon carry shields and armament unmatched by anything in the data banks. On her lower deck were an even dozen Mambas, housed in individual bays that would let any one launch independently of the others.

Simon turned away from his audience to gaze through the insubstantial barrier out to the vessel waiting just beyond his reach. Finally realizing that he was keeping almost fifteen hundred people waiting, he turned away from the vision and back to his audience. He let his gaze drift from left to right over the entire group and then looked down at the podium. He realized unhappily that he recognized even fewer faces than ever.

Replacing the microphone, he gripped the podium with both hands. "I'm going to cut this short. I'm only going to say that where we stand right now and what that ship out there represents is a crossroads in human history. At a normal crossroads, you have four choices, one of which is to go back where you came from. Unfortunately, things aren't that simple here. From where we stand, there are an infinite number of roads we can take. One course is to go back, stick our heads in the sand, and hope the universe goes away. Another is to turn what we've accomplished and the *Galileo* over to the governments of Earth. On the first road, we give up any chance at the universe in our lifetimes, our children's lifetimes, even our grandchildren's lifetimes. As for other roads, well, I'm can't tell you where they lead because we don't know yet, but I can tell you this—I don't like the first two roads, and I won't walk either of them.

"The only things more to say are thank you for walking this road with me this far, and I pray that our association continues for many years to come.

"And now, the real reason we're here today. We have conceived, and you have built, the first ship in the Terran Alliance Fleet. I don't think anybody knows how badly I wish this first ship didn't have to be a warship. But even though she is capable of an immense amount of destruction," he hesitated a regretful second, "I envision her, her sisters, and all the ships to follow to be a constructive force, securing mankind's place in space. And defending, if necessary, our right to be out here.

"From the time the first human gazed up at the stars in wonder to this very day, mankind has dreamed of being where we stand. But it wasn't until the late 19th century that people started to speculate in print. And mostly, it was twentieth-century writers who got us all hooked on the possibilities. Those writers, from Jules Verne on, have fueled our imaginations. We grew up with his stories and those of H.G. Wells in the late 19th century. Most of us, though, grew up reading stories by the premier authors of our times. And the first six ships to come out of our docks are going to honor the spirits of those visionary people without whom most of us wouldn't be here today.

"The second through sixth ships will carry the names *Isaac Asimov, Arthur C. Clarke*, *Larry Niven*, *Anne McCaffrey*, and *Andre Norton*." Simon turned to gaze out upon the ship glowing in the sunlight. "And this one," he continued, "is to be named after the grandmaster of modern science fiction." If any eye on that deck had been looking anywhere but at the ship, it might have seen a small flash of light at the end of Simon's last comment. He hesitated for a few seconds and then continued. "It is my great pleasure to christen the first ship in the fleet of the Terran Alliance. By the power vested in me by the people who share my dream and my vision, I hereby christen her the *TAS Robert A. Heinlein*."

Quite literally on cue, as the last syllable left Simon's mouth, a small glittering cloud appeared at the bow of the newly christened ship. For a few seconds, a small portion of the *Heinlein* was obscured from view and Simon heard mutters of surprise from behind him. He turned back again with a smile on his face and said, "Of all the engineering feats that have been accomplished out here in the last year, you have just witnessed one of the most difficult. Do you realize how hard it is to christen a spaceship with a bottle of champagne?" Laughter broke out on the deck. Simon let it run for a few seconds and then held up his hand. As the sound died, he went on.

"Special congratulations go to Engineering for not only designing the delivery system to get the bottle from here to the *Heinlein* but keeping it liquid until it could smash on the hull and give you all those pretty little sparkles out there. Good old human ingenuity strikes again.

"Now. Those of you who are assigned to the *Heinlein* already know who you are. At this time, I'd like to introduce you to your command staff. For the position of Helm Officer, Donna Hall. Front and center, Lt. Commander." Having rehearsed before the ceremony, Donna Hall walked up onto the dais. Daniels, in the background until this point, came forward to stand beside Simon.

When Donna reached the two captains, she stood to attention. "Lt. Commander Hall, for your dedication to your job and your superior performance of same, you are hereby posted to the Terran Alliance Ship *Heinlein*," Simon said. "With the position come greater responsibilities and duties. Therefore, I have the pleasure of promoting you to full commander. Congratulations, and may you acquit yourself with honor."

During his speech, Simon had removed her insignia and replaced them with the golden stars of her new rank. He stepped back, saluted her, accepted her salute in return, and watched as she pivoted and left the stage.

Naming and promoting as necessary, the two captains continued until only three were left. "Robert and Michiko Greene, front and center." The two officers stepped up on the dais together. Simon and Daniel, each taking one officer, quickly stripped off the old rank and installed the new insignia, finishing at the same time. The four exchanged salutes and then the stage was Simon's again.

Simon again faced the audience. "Wing Commander Katherine Hawke, front and center." At the sound of Kitty's name, the crew who were not in the know began to cheer. Walking as if to her own execution, Kitty slowly ascended the dais, her eyes locked on Simon's. She came to a halt directly in front of him in the same position of attention the others before her had used. Simon finally signaled for the cheering to stop. In the silence, he stared deeply into his wife's eyes, and then said, "I had two choices today. One was to play the part of a happy husband and stand down there while you got promoted, applauding with the rest. The other was to stand up here and pin your comets on you myself." He reached out and slowly removed the golden stars from her lapels. Turning to her newly appointed first officer, Marsha Kane, who had appeared at his side, he picked up the first comet from the small black box she held. After he finished with the second one, he stepped back a half pace and stuck his hand out.

With a slightly perplexed look, Kitty reached out and shook his hand.

"Congratulations, Captain," he said. Then, with no warning, he tightened his grip, pulled her to him, put his left arm around her, and kissed her soundly on the lips in front of the entire assemblage. Whistles and catcalls greeted the sight. Stepping back, he said quietly, "Damn, Kittyn, I hope that doesn't become part of the tradition of promotion." Grasping her by the shoulders, he turned Kitty around to face the crowd. "Ladies and gentlemen, I am proud to present to you the Captain of the *TAS Robert A. Heinlein*, Captain Katherine Hawke."

As the applause started to die down, a voice rose up out of the front row. "Three cheers for Captain Kitty!" At each hurrah, Simon could feel the deck vibrate from the power of nearly fifteen hundred voices yelling in unison. As the third cheer echoed into silence, Simon reached into the podium and said, "Captain, there's one more thing for you to take with you. Apparently, this is going to become part of the tradition as well. He pulled out a brass plaque and handed it to her.

All this fuss for a piece of metal, she thought, and then looked down at the words embossed there:

T.A.S. ROBERT A. HEINLEIN
COMMISSIONED FEBRUARY 10, 2013
CAPTAIN KATHERINE HAWKE,
COMMANDING

Staring at the plaque in her hands, with her name on it, she realized just how thoroughly she'd been roped in by the ceremony. Ceremonies weren't just for the crowds. It bound a person to the event and to the people watching it. The problem with ceremony was that it branded an individual as well, sometimes for the good and sometimes otherwise as in the case of an execution. The ceremony surrounding an event of that nature wasn't for the guest of honor at all.

"Show 'em the plaque, hon," Simon quietly urged, breaking her train of thought. "That's why they all came."

To Kitty's credit, her thoughts never reached her face as she raised the plaque over her head and let the applause—undeserved though she felt it to be—wash over her. She recognized the psychology behind Simon's strategy for what it was but still couldn't get the lump in her throat to go away—not that she would change anything, and not that she could.

Simon, you will pay for this. Worse than the time

you did *forget our anniversary. I promise you that*, she thought.

"The sooner we get these trials done, the happier I'll be. I want to see us get base number three started. We're going to try something different this time," Stephen said to Simon. "I know the *Heinlein* is going to complete her trials with flying colors. Call it an engineer's intuition mixed with knowing how user friendly this technology is. I'm thinking ahead to three things we need to do with one ship in a very short period of time. It's the end of March. We'll have two more ships needing crews by mid- to late April. Meantime, we'll be building... what are we going to name the next base?"

Simon looked up from the collection of papers, files and reports on his desk. "What? Oh, I don't know. I picked two constellations. Let's continue that and you pick the next name."

Stephen added the stack of papers he was holding to the growing pile on the desk and sat down in one of the chairs across the sea of folders that threatened to spill off onto the floor. "We're going to have to get you a secretary before long, maybe two," he said, glaring at the mess. "That office out there is a pretty good indication the previous captain knew how to delegate. You shouldn't have to read anything but synopses and ask for the relevant report if you see something interesting. That would take a lot of pressure off you."

Stephen could see that the conversation wasn't going anywhere near the direction Simon's thoughts were. "Look, Simon. You can't beat yourself up over assigning Kitty to the *Heinlein*. She was the best person for the job as far as I'm concerned. Of course, I'm not married to her," he quipped. "She'll do a good enough job on you when she finds out how much you really dumped on her."

Simon roused himself enough to look up at Stephen. "You're probably right," he said with a lopsided grin. "So, what did you mean by trying something different?"

Stephen said, "Look. What good is the *Galileo* once the habitat section and factory sections are completed? They can finish building the Shack themselves and then start on their first ship. So, we get the fuel plant built, set up the habitat, factory section, and docking bays. We help produce the station shuttles and a half dozen Mambas, and the new dock—let's call her Libra—can finish completing itself. We make a beeline for Earth, pick up crew for two ships, and get back in, I'd say seven or eight weeks. With the Mambas as protection as well as cover, there shouldn't be any trouble while we're gone. Especially if the *Heinlein* stays in the vicinity until we get back. Think about it."

Simon leaned back in his chair, stroked his chin, and put on his pondering face. Stephen tossed a folder at him, and papers flew everywhere. Both men laughed. "See what you made me do?" Stephen complained. "Let's go get a beer."

Simon demurred. "I've got these reports to go over. The Engineering staff seems to think a wobble they found in the magnetic containment fields can be permanently cured with the right filters coupled into the system. They've tried to solve the problem with software filters, but sooner or later they begin to drift again. According to them, the faster a ship moves, the more stress on the containment fields. This time they're looking at a hardware change, and I'm not sure I want to mess with the original design specs on something as critical as this. They tend to get too technical for me, so if you'd look into it and let me know what you think, I'd appreciate it. And I've got something personal to look into."

After seeing Stephen out one door, Simon went directly to the bridge to check on the *Heinlein's* progress. Transmissions came in on a regular basis from the techs and engineers on board, but the *Heinlein's* captain only saw fit to send a personal report once a day. Simon wasn't sure if the point was to make him worry, but he did. And to tell the truth, he even looked forward to the distant tone of voice and terse reports in the daily dispatch from Kitty. He just wished she would let go of her grudge over her promotion.

Six days of trials, and the engineers were putting the *Heinlein* through some pretty stiff paces. They'd spent days going over the parameters she needed to meet, and so far, everything was well within tolerances. Quite a few of the parameters had been drastically exceeded, to tell the truth. Tomorrow was to be the last major trial—an extended boost up to warp speed, then beyond. Simon had told her to head for Alpha Centauri. When she asked why, he only said it was the nearest star and she wouldn't be going all the way there on this trip anyway. It just gave her navigator something to program into the computer.

Every trial so far had come off without a hitch,

even the weapons tests. Here she sat, farther from Earth than any human had ever been except her own crew, of course. Almost eight hundred and ninety million miles from home, shooting at asteroids in Saturn's rings, of all places.

The lasers were even more powerful than expected due to having their own power core to draw from. The poor asteroids never stood a chance. The missiles only needed some fine tuning to their targeting mechanisms. The missile technology, like almost everything else the Builders produced, had been perfected to the point of not really needing anything added to increase its effectiveness. The targeting systems worked perfectly, of course, and it was just the human adaptations that needed to be gone over. Most of the problems lay in the different measuring systems inherent in the computer and the new programs installed by humans. Glitches that surely wouldn't exist for the Builders kept cropping up and needing to be adjusted.

The engineers had turned out several shield generators that would simulate an enemy ship, assuming, of course, that the enemy ship had shield generators. Bets were being taken that there would be no shields to contend with. Generator and power supply were turned loose, and the ship took them out, telling the techs much about what the ship might have to face in a combat situation. Now all that remained were the final engine tests, and then she could go home.

Calling her staff together, Kitty asked them a question. "Are we ready to go for the engine tests?" The usual hemming and hawing began, but she'd suffered through enough of that in the previous week that she'd learned how to stop it before it got into deep technical explanations she'd never understand. Hell, she was sure most of the technical team didn't understand half of what they said themselves.

"Let's cut to the chase, people. Either we know for sure, or we're speculating. Are we sure enough to risk all our lives?" Taking the silence as a commitment to continue, she said as much. "In the absence of a strong verbal dissent, we'll begin the final tests tomorrow shortly after breakfast. I think I'd rather try this on a full stomach and an empty bladder," she joked.

Kitty woke up the next morning in her quarters aboard the *Heinlein* with a feeling of disorientation. She couldn't shake the feeling of something forgotten or missing. The feeling was so intense that even going over her previous days' calendar didn't dispel it. She finally realized that she was waiting for the other shoe to drop. As she showered, dressed, and otherwise prepared for her day, the feeling seemed to become more internal than external, leaving her with a curiously pleasant tingle.

Oh, no, she thought, as she brushed her hair into her usual shipboard ponytail. *I hope I'm not getting addicted to life-defining moments!*

She had checked her repeater screens immediately upon arising to make sure the course she'd given to third shift was being followed, so she decided she had time for a quick breakfast.

Finding the room considerably more crowded than expected, she asked, "Aren't some of you supposed to be getting some rest?"

A voice belonging to a lieutenant commander she barely recognized spoke up. "Yes, ma'am, but I don't think any of us want to miss what's coming up. If everything works like it should, some of us will just be a little tired and go to bed early at the end of our next shifts." He shrugged and added philosophically, "And if something goes wrong, it won't matter."

Kitty sat down at the table next to the philosophical young man and pressed him. "And it doesn't hurt that the technology has been tried, true, and tested for hundreds of years before we got it. It's not new, merely new to us. Now, isn't that right?"

"No, ma'am, it doesn't hurt at all, even if we've added a few twists of our own." This came from a redheaded ensign sitting next to the young lieutenant commander. "We spend a lot of time after shift talking about where we are and what we're doing, speculating on the future. Anyway, ma'am, one of the things that keeps coming up is just that fact—the age of the technology."

Kitty looked at the new speaker more closely and recognized her. She glanced at the nametag on the woman's uniform, and said, "Oh, yes. You would be Ensign Ross from… that would be one of the forward missile bays. We met during one of my first inspections."

The redhead smiled and said, "Yes, ma'am and no, ma'am." At Kitty's confused look, the woman went on. "Ensign Ross and forward missile bay are both correct, ma'am, but I've never had the pleasure of meeting you. That was my twin sister. She's on first shift, and I'm on second. And she didn't quit talking about your visit for days, ma'am."

Kitty looked in the direction the ensign pointed, and her mouth dropped open. Her head swiveled classically between the two, coming to rest, finally, on the one she'd been speaking to. "You mean to tell me that I have a pair of redheaded identical twins on my ship? On a ship named after Robert Heinlein? This is just too hilarious."

The ensign stuttered, "Y-yes, ma'am. Is that a problem?"

Kitty immediately tried to assuage the panic she heard in the woman's voice. "No, it's not a problem. As long as I'm aware of the situation," she said, hedging. "I think I just found the ship's good luck charms. Totally identical, are you?"

"Yes, ma'am. Except that I wear my hair different since we can't wear different outfits."

"And what are your names?" Kitty asked.

"Ma'am, I'm Diana Ross, and my sister is Demeter. And before you say anything, ma'am, our father was a professor of Greek history—with a sense of humor, I might add."

Kitty laughed aloud. "I know what you mean about a sense of humor. My last name wasn't always Hawke. My father's name was Brian Cattin. Try growing up being called Kitty Cattin." The laughter, though muted, was genuine, and Kitty could tell that there was no malice in it.

Kitty finished her meal, made her goodbyes, and went to the bridge where she found John Marshall, her Weapons/Tactics Officer, sitting as shift commander as third shift neared its end. Standing beside the chair, she asked, "Status, Commander?"

He began to detail the status of the ship. Everything from the monopoles, containment fields, power conduits, and field generators to the warp engines themselves had all been triple checked. Simulations showed that she would be able to leave ships like the *Galileo* behind in the blink of an eye, if all went well. And, of course, there was the innovation that that technician in the engine room had come up with—cross-connecting the three power cores so additional power could be routed to any one of the three main systems. She was anxious to see how it would affect the engine trials after how well it had worked on the lasers.

John slid out of the seat and she slid in. She'd actually taken over the shift about ten minutes ahead of time as was her usual habit. And one of the rules she'd instituted was that shift change should occur one station at a time unless there was an emergency. Normally, full shift change, with each station reporting status to new operators, could take as much as ten minutes. Today wasn't normal, and the change was effected in less than five, which still gave Kitty time to talk to the engineers and techs in the engine room and those scattered throughout the ship.

As the last status light on her board turned green, Kitty ordered Helm to move out at normal speed. This would be the first time humans had traveled in excess of the speed of light. All the data said that, in an emergency, the warp engines could be run up from a stop, but the figures also showed that they worked best if the ship was approaching light speed. Consequently, they'd use their in-space drive to cruise up to the lower warp limit and then boost past it.

Since these were speed trials, the instructions were different than anything she'd issued up to this point. Those instructions were to channel as much power to the in-space drives as possible without redlining the drive and see how fast they could attain their maximum velocity. Engineers, techs, and scientists began to monitor their instruments. Kitty cut the intercom into the circuit so all could hear what was going on.

She gave the order to boost, and in less time than anyone thought possible, the ringed wonder of Sol system was a slowly receding dot in the rear scanners. Long before the orbit of Uranus was reached, the *Heinlein* was at the warp threshold, cruising just under the speed of light. This was the point where people could age differently if they stayed at speed too long. Time passed normally for them, but their friends outside the ship would seem to age much faster. The curious thing was that once they went into warp drive, that law of nature no longer seemed to hold, according to the figures they had. Einstein would need several lifetimes to refigure his equations.

Kitty ordered the massive engines cut into the system at their lowest warp settings. She had once asked one of the engine room technicians why there weren't two separate engines for normal space and for warp space, and she'd been told that the whole thing was a matter of the energies produced by the power core. Once the monopoles were placed in conjunction with each other, they found a happy medium where they emitted a tiny amount of energy, an amount that could operate all the third-tier systems without problems for dozens of years. But to move a vessel the size of the *Galileo*, for example, in normal space, more energy was required. In that case, the containment field was constricted a bit, forcing the monopoles closer together, producing enough energy, once routed to the engines, to move the enormous ship around the solar system.

To move at warp speeds, it was necessary to try to separate the two poles. This, for some reason, produced energy quantum levels higher than pressing them together. That energy, when channeled into those same engines, would move the ship up to and through the warp barrier. Slowly, they would be raised up to their max. Over the next twelve hours, they dropped in and out of warp half a dozen times, bringing the ship to a virtual standstill and running her back up to warp speeds, looking for their fastest time.

Their last test was to see how the warp engines would hold up under a sustained near-maximum boost. Kitty had long ago surrendered her chair to the second shift. Marsha Kane had control when the time for the last test came, but Kitty would be on the bridge for the beginning of it. Marsha looked her way and asked, "Course, ma'am?"

Kitty smiled and said, "Set course for Alpha Centauri."

Marsha's eyebrow went up just slightly. She turned to the Nav officer and ordered, "Navigator, set course for Alpha Centauri."

When the navigator called out, "Ma'am, course laid in, sent to Helm, and locked," Marsha got a last nod from Kitty. After checking engine status one more time, she announced the impending test to all hands. Turning back to her crew, she ordered, "Helm, move us out. Normal speed, increasing to maximum in-space. Report when maximum speed is achieved." Shortly, she called the engine room. "Prepare for warp."

As the ship approached its maximum in-space speed, a new panel lit up on Helm's console, who reported, "Ma'am, ship ready for warp."

Commander Kane ordered, "Very well, Helm. Bring us to low warp," and the now-familiar twisting sensation that some said they didn't feel ran through her body as the ship passed through the invisible barrier.

The ship passed that barrier as effortlessly as it had during the short trials, and Marsha said, "Very well. Run us up slowly to maximum warp. Report when we've reached that point."

Kitty could feel the vibration slowly building as Marsha and the rest of the crew pushed the *Heinlein* to her limit. Once they reached high warp, Kitty spoke to Marsha. "Very good, Commander. We are now to run at this speed for twelve hours. Since no one can keep up the kind of concentration we need for that long, shifts will change every two hours for the duration of this test, especially the shift commander. I don't want anyone zoned out. I will be on-call at all times. Just whistle, Marsha. I'm going to my cabin for now."

The engine tests were largely anticlimactic. A huge success, of course, but overshadowed by the weapons tests with all their pretty explosions. The physics of this type of space flight said that when coming out of warp, the ship retained the velocity it had upon entering, so great care had to be taken in plotting courses. Kitty was on the bridge when the *Heinlein* emerged from warp, and she immediately ordered full deceleration and full scan, leaving the area directly astern for last.

A chill ran up her spine as a thought crossed her mind, and she muttered, "More of that life-defining crap. Could I be an adrenaline junkie?"

Finding what they'd expected to find—nothing—they turned their sensors in the direction of the solar system and were surprised, but not unduly, in retrospect, to find that they were receiving a message they'd already received and responded to days before. Kitty, feeling unusually good about how the tests had gone, decided it was time to be a little bit playful. "Gayle, send this reply to the message we just received—Captain Hawke, just how many times do you think it is necessary to tell me to be careful? Sign that Captain Hawke, the *Heinlein*, date it and send it. Rob, can you tell me exactly where we are?"

Robert Greene looked up from his console. "I'm sorry, ma'am, but all I can tell you right now is that we are partway between our starting point and our destination." Before Kitty could explode, he continued, "All kidding aside, ma'am, I can't tell exactly where we are, but I can tell you that if we continued at our highest acceleration, we would reach Alpha Centauri in about two weeks, which makes our maximum speed somewhere in the vicinity of double that of a ship the size and configuration of the *Galileo*."

"That's good enough for me." She keyed the intercom to address the crew. "This is the captain. It's my pleasure to report that we've just completed the last phase of testing. And, I might add, we aced it. Now we can go home. I want to express my appreciation to everybody for a job well done. The time for the return to Orion won't be as long as what we've had to go through up to this point since now we can head straight in. So, ladies and gentlemen, let's get to it. Thank you."

An outside observer would have seen the

Heinlein slowly accelerate to her maximum in-space speed. As she reached her limit, that observer would have seen her apparently blink out of existence while the occupants of the ship went about their duties blissfully unaware of the impact they were making on human history.

Kitty had finished her report, and one of the recommendations she'd made was to keep the computers well acquainted with the various pieces of space debris in whatever area they chose to come out of warp, if possible. She could already see the dangers inherent in traveling to new places and wondered out loud how many ships and people would be lost in exploring their newly expanded neighborhood.

"There's something about two objects not being able to occupy the same space. What happens if we come out of warp inside a moon or something else we can't possibly know about beforehand?" she asked Daniel.

He looked at her and tried to allay her fears. "The people we have rooting around in the remains of the database have been tasked to look for that particular problem. Believe it or not, some of us have already thought about it. So far, what has turned up is a lot of nothing. Since we managed to save some of the data, we have records of many dropouts, without their stellar locations, of course, and never has anything shown up to cause the engineers or astronomers to worry. That isn't to say that it can't happen or won't, just that it seems highly unlikely. Some of the theoreticians think that physics won't let a vessel come out of warp inside another object. That remains to be proven, of course. And how we prove it, I surely don't know. I'm just a lowly engineer, myself."

Kitty leaned back in her chair and an introspective mood seemed to come over her.

"Okay, what's on your mind, Kitty?" Daniel asked. "I've come to know that look."

"I seem to have become more philosophical lately, Dan. What I want to know is what we're going to do with all the ships we're building? I mean, I know we're defending our right to keep the technology now that we have it, and quite likely defending our planet as well, but we don't really *see* an enemy. All we have concrete evidence of is three other ships—one destroyed and the two survivors hightailing it out of the county, so to speak. Sometimes I have to wonder if we're really going in the right direction. It seems to me that we're building stuff we don't really have a lot of use for."

Daniel gave her a penetrating look. "I agree, in a way. But when you think about those ships, you have to ask yourself whose policies they were following. If it was one individual, that's one thing. But if they were operating under the orders of a government, that's entirely a horse of another color. The question I need to put to you is do we dare take any chances? I'd much rather err on the side of caution. And personally, I want to get my hands on whoever was in command when they hit us, hang him by whatever passes for thumbs, and then spend all day carving him into little pieces. Bloodthirsty? Well, I'm not going to defend my position by saying that the human race has been bloodthirsty since it began, but I still want to see the son of a bitch suffer."

Changing the subject, Kitty began to describe her ideas for a large, permanent base. As an engineer, the prospect should distract him from the emotions she could see just beneath the surface. "The asteroid Vesta," she said. "I've been through the database and think I've found a way to turn it into something we can use. It won't be long before we have several thousand people out here, and some of them will become permanent residents while others will need a place to vacation from the ships and bases. It'll take a few years to get it ready for occupation, but here's what I have in mind."

Itemizing the equipment she'd found in the computer, she began. "First, we'd need a power generator and broadcaster. A simple program would coordinate several dozen specialized machines to hollow out the asteroid, and some of the material could be used to seal the interior against air loss. Smoothing off the surface would let us lay out artificial gravity grids like the ones built into the deck plates of the ships, or we could lay the cables on the inside surface before the sealer goes on. Then the inside of Vesta would have gravity. The material culled from the surface and excavated from the interior would follow the asteroid until the *Galileo* arrived to scoop it up and use it to build structures for the interior. Everything except the *Galileo's* part could be done without supervision from humans if we built a computer and programmed it to do the job for us. Once the entrance was sealed, we could introduce air, heat, light and plants to begin oxygen production. I could do an initial survey on the way to Gamma since we'll pass Vesta on the way."

Daniel stared at Kitty, his mouth dropping farther open with each sentence.

"What?" Kitty demanded. "I've looked into this. It'll work, dammit."

"I'm not doubting you, Kitty. I just think we should have thought of this already. When you meet the *Galileo* at Point Gamma, you should be able to skim some of her time and get your machines without causing too much of a slowdown in construction. From what I see here," Daniel said as he called up specs on his own screens, "the factories you'll need aren't the same ones used in dock construction, for the most part. If Simon gives you any trouble on this, have him get in touch with me. This needs to be done, and I'll back it if he doesn't."

Thanking Daniel for his time and support, Kitty left. She desperately wanted to talk to Simon, but he had taken the *Galileo* back to Earth to pick up more volunteers for the next ship. His instructions to her had been to take the *Heinlein* out to Point Gamma where the next dock, Libra, was to be built. Of course, this would be after she'd spent some time there getting her crew sorted out and doing some patrolling to train the recruits.

Included in these instructions was a suggestion that she slowly begin scanning the asteroid belt on the way in hopes of finding any unwanted visitors like the ones who'd attacked Orion. Many people believed there was too high a possibility that spies had been left behind, and after a careful analysis of the records, she'd come to believe the theory was plausible. Still, she wished Simon had waited a little longer before getting Lucy's ship crewed. She agreed time was not to be wasted, but...

Kitty made her way down to Orion's docking bay where her gig and pilot waited. *This is such a waste*, she thought. *I can fly myself around as well as anyone else can. Why does Simon put so much stock in appearances? And why do these people follow so readily?* Resigning herself to the inevitable, she boarded the trim little vessel and waited while the pilot went through her checklist and was pushed out of the bay by the presser beams.

Her gig was nothing more than an oversized Mamba without weapons, capable of carrying a pilot and four passengers. Not warp-capable, it was used to ferry personnel from space to ground or ship to ship. Early on, Kitty had seen the necessity for having two standard shuttles, so a little judicious reengineering had dropped the Mamba complement from twelve to ten so they could tuck the shuttles into the recesses of the *Heinlein's* docking bay.

Two days went by while the tech crew left the ship and the regular crew boarded. Finding room assignments, workstations, and common areas had been a small problem at the beginning of the first voyage, so Kitty had maps made and distributed to the new arrivals. Finally, the *Heinlein* powered up and began to make her way through the maze that had grown around the station. Knowing Simon wouldn't rendezvous with her for almost a month, Kitty took her time, cruising along just above the asteroid belt with her sensors on full, searching for whatever she might find. Knowing she had a one-in-four chance of finding anything since she was only passing one fourth of the belt on her way to Gamma, she felt it would be good practice for the crew. And that percentage held only if an intruder chose to use the asteroid belt as a hiding place. *She* would, she mused, but maybe that didn't figure in the ideas of someone who came from a totally alien culture that had been in space for hundreds of years.

Along with the drills, the regular flights by the Mambas tended to keep most people occupied. Daily reports from the *Galileo* and Orion didn't take up much of her time, nor did her responses since she was still pretty upset with Simon, so she had plenty of free time on her hands. Running performance drills kept all hands occupied, if a little irritated, until she started plugging herself into various personnel slots and taking part herself. It was such a success with the crew that she mandated the procedure for all the command staff.

CHAPTER TWENTY-FIVE

Almost six weeks went by before the huge construction vessel came to rest relative to the *Heinlein* at Gamma. Shuttles and Mambas began to emerge from her dark hull almost immediately. The larger ship had spent two weeks in Earth orbit, picking and choosing from an overabundance of volunteers and letting some of those who'd been gone for almost a year have some leave time.

The third reappearance of so many missing persons added a new dimension to the pressure various government officials were beginning to feel from their constituents. The ramifications of such a monumental discovery were finally beginning to find their ways into the mass media as well. Late-night radio talk shows and supermarket tabloids only added fuel to rumors that were flying through the intelligence agencies of the world like wildfire. Simon smiled at the thought of what those groups were going to do when so many more people disappeared again.

Overcrowding was the name of the game for the week that it took the *Galileo* to get back to Gemini Base. Finally, nearly a third of the volunteers were offloaded at the base. Simon kept his word, investing Lucy as captain, and she immediately named her vessel the *Anne McCaffrey*. The *Galileo* remained in the area while the crew rosters of the base and ships sorted themselves out. It was necessary for dozens of veteran crewmembers of both Gemini and the *Galileo* to be moved to the new ship where they would function as instructors for the newbies who'd been assigned. This left the remainder of the new volunteers to be doled out into the more innocuous positions aboard the three vessels.

Simon, missing his wife more as time passed, ordered the *Galileo* to move out and rendezvous with the *Heinlein* and Kitty.

Kitty beamed over from the *Heinlein*, briefcase in hand, to spend some well-deserved time alone with her husband.

I wonder how much longer this is going to go on, she thought. *I remember something about hunter packs—two ships and a carrier. If Simon will just hurry up and take command of a ship, we can form the first pack and spend more time together. This captain business is really putting a cramp in my love life.*

She walked into the captain's quarters, let her uniform drop to the deck, and headed for the shower. *If he isn't here by the time I get good and wet, then I don't know Simon*, she told herself.

As if on cue, she heard the outer door open just as she was getting the temperature up to blister-the-skin-off-your-body. Turning around, she was just in time to get passionately hugged by the man she hadn't seen in so long.

When the afterglow had faded away into one of those

memories that last forever, Kitty let her satisfied smile turn into an achingly pleasant, joint-popping stretch. She sat up, leaned over and kissed Simon, an unspoken promise implicit in the way her tongue flicked between his teeth and back out again. Turning her back to her husband, she stirred through the pile of clothes beside the bed until she felt the weight of her briefcase.

Aware of the sight she presented, Kitty leaned over and picked up the briefcase. Sitting back up, she felt Simon's hands sliding around her sides to caress her breasts, so she set the case aside, turned in his arms, and kissed him again. Then, pulling away, she gently grabbed his wrists and moved his hands down to his thighs. "Take a break, dear. We just had dessert, and now we need to talk business."

She pulled the briefcase into her lap and hauled out a sheaf of papers. "Before I left Orion, I sat down with Daniel and told him about an idea I had. He thinks it's something we need to implement as soon as we can." She handed the papers to Simon and launched into a description of Project Vesta.

Simon, quickly flipping through the report, did his best to keep up with the details of material allocation and production, transport of same to Vesta, and oversight of the project in its early phases.

Kitty ended with, "And we only have to have someone stop by every month or so to check that things are on track," before leaning back to let the idea sink in. Encouraged by Daniel's enthusiasm, she'd spoken firmly and was pleased with the occasional question, gratified by his acceptance.

"A base like that is just what we need," Simon said. "It can serve as a symbol, as well as an R & R spot. As ideas go, this even tops Z-tag, as far as I'm concerned. But if something can serve two purposes, and one of them just happens to be a PR bonanza, then why not take advantage of it?

"The reasons you gave in the first place are enough, of course, but look at it from the position of those on Earth. A place no government can reach and a permanent base in deep space where you can walk around in shirtsleeves and have room to… what? Play ball? Run races? Anything you can dream up. It would certainly stir up more interest. But this is only one idea off the top of my head, and look where it led. This was your project. Why not watch over it until the time comes to start making it habitable?"

Simon leaned away from Kitty for a second, reaching into the pocket of his own jacket. Pulling out an envelope, he handed it to her, saying, "I've got a surprise for you, too. Read this, Kittyn."

She pulled a single sheet of paper out of the envelope, barely noticing the presidential seal on the corner as she set it aside. She shook the paper open, read it once and then again, more slowly. And then a third time. "Have you confirmed this?" she asked incredulously. "You're going to meet with the vice-president? We're going to get the bases?" Kitty's imagination went into overdrive. "What do we have to give them initially? I assume there has to be some kind of good-faith gesture. And it should come from us. I also think it should be a public meeting. Camp David is where they go to do things quietly. As much media attention as possible is what we need to have."

"Whoa! Slow down, honey. Right now, the only thing on the table is the idea of a meeting. And, yes, with the vice-president, and possibly with senior officials from some of the other countries we could get bases in, too—maybe an Asian representative and someone from somewhere in Europe. According to Galway, through Lucy, we get the bases and then discuss technology trades. And as I understand it, those were the conditions. As for media attention, that's going to be a given, but none of it will happen until we get Libra finished and go back for more volunteers."

Kitty stared at Simon so long he finally had to ask, "What? That's what we wanted. Bases and at least tacit acceptance by the governments of the world. So why the face?"

"Why? Because something doesn't smell right, husband-mine." She rolled out of the bed and began to pace the room. Coming to a stop beside the bed, she looked down at Simon. "I know I didn't marry a total idiot. Since when did any government give away anything without some guarantees first? And they specifically requested our commanding officer? Tell me this isn't a setup, Simon. Make me believe it, *if you can*. Listen, we've been married for what? Over sixteen years, now. You aren't going down there alone and definitely not without backup. Do you understand? If I have to get every single soul off-planet in on that, I can. Don't doubt it for a second."

Simon finally got a chance to get a word in edgewise. "Lighten up! Nothing's been decided, yet." He sat up and pulled Kitty down beside him. "That piece of paper is just an invitation to meet to discuss the details of a meeting, and I haven't answered it yet. The only answer that went back was that I'd think about it. Give me some credit, okay? If it happens, backup is a given. And I won't go alone. Also, what can happen in front of live cameras? And they *will* be live. We'll be able to monitor that from several directions. At the first sign of trouble, the whole team beams out. And that can be done from any of four wristbands or from the *Galileo*, not to mention any other security precautions we can come up with between now and then. But remember, they'll have to be invisible precautions. We can't afford to insult any of the people we want to get something from any more than they can afford to insult us."

Kitty stirred her piled-up clothes with a bare foot and then turned to face Simon. "You'll take care, or else. And here's a guarantee for you—when you go down, I'll be leading the backup detail. Five Mambas flying overhead would give anyone pause, not to mention the PR it would generate on worldwide television, since you like to have things serve dual purposes."

Interpreting the expression on Simon's face as a prelude to denying her the right to fly, Kitty plowed on. "And don't you dare try to tell me no, dammit! If you do, I'll quit and get off the next time this boat gets back to Earth. I'm not one to deliver ultimatums, and you know it. But I mean this! For once, there will be no discussion. If it's safe enough for you, it's safe enough for me."

Changing the subject, which left Simon no option but to accept her final statement, Kitty threw another thing at him. "And you should know, dear, that we certainly do have company out here." She handed him another printout from her briefcase. This one had come about on the way to Gamma just before they'd reached Vesta. "There seems to be an abnormal amount of material in this area trailing

Vesta," she commented. "And while we were scanning, Gayle found a heat source somewhere close. We didn't let on that we'd seen anything, either. I wanted to, believe me! But with Lucy on the way here, I figure we could drop off any mining equipment at Vesta, get the project underway, and then go deal with the problem together. If we work it right, we can trap whoever it is between us and leave no witnesses."

Simon slowly shook his head. "Sometimes I wonder if I did the right thing by making women my first two captains. And here I am considering Gayle for the third." He saw Kitty start to cloud up and hurried on. "I'm not putting you down, hon. You just seem more aggressive than I would have figured a year ago. Hell, it was just weeks ago that you said you shouldn't be in command because you didn't have the killer instinct. I'm not saying that's bad. And I'm certainly not saying I wouldn't do the same thing in your place. You know, if you hadn't suggested it, I probably would have ordered it myself. I've wondered if they could be possible allies hiding out until they've evaluated us. But if there were, I'd think they would have been more open. Or should have been. Who can say how aliens think? At any rate, if they're hiding, they're up to no good, so go get 'em.

"Hey! Let's go get something to eat," Simon said, changing the subject himself this time. "You can meet Victor McCord. He's a friend of Stephen's, and he's going to be our new Base Commander when Libra goes online. He brought his new wife Casey and their two kids with him." At Kitty's shocked look, he went on, "They're seventeen and eighteen. Both are finished with high school, and both are eager to get into the Mambas, of course. And that's all your fault for making those videos. Stephen had to show them to Victor to convince him, and he made copies. He showed 'em to his wife, and when she wanted in and he said no, she showed them to the kids and they triple-teamed him. He brought a list of people with skills, too."

When Kitty inquired as to the skills Victor mentioned, Simon rattled off a list that included theoretical physics, molecular biology, and games theory, among others. Kitty jumped on the last one. "That might be a good place to look for strategists and tacticians."

"I know," Simon replied, "and Stephen said the same thing. Once we get back to Earth, we can look some more of these people up and see if we can recruit them."

By the time Lucy arrived with the *McCaffrey*, most of the equipment needed for Kitty's Project Vesta was already set up. The power broadcaster only needed an internal power source of its own, and the computer that was needed to run the initial interior excavation was being programmed. Kitty called Lucy and invited her to attend a captains' call aboard the *Galileo*.

As the three captains settled into chairs in Simon's ready room, Kitty congratulated Lucy on her command. "And I like your choice of a name, too," she said. After a quick discussion of the *McCaffrey's* trials and Kitty's mention of the redheaded twins, they got down to business.

Kitty called up a display on the wall monitor.

"This is where Gayle found a heat source. I want to go investigate and, if necessary, destroy whoever or whatever is out there. I want you along for the ride, Lucy. What I want is as much advantage as possible. We have no idea what kind of tactics these people will use or what kind of weapons they have." She went on in a much more subdued voice, "I really don't want to be the aggressor here, but I see no alternative. Whoever is out there is watching and evaluating us, learning our weaknesses and possibly making plans to take us out.

"I don't think any report has been sent, or at least no transmissions on any wavelength we can monitor, and no ships have left the system since Orion was attacked. The need to prevent any more reports from leaving this system is urgent. And if we sneak up, so to speak, on this spot, I'll bet anything you want to name that we flush something out. I said we should destroy it if necessary, but let's let the bogey make the first move. Powering up weapons and firing is one response. Powering down and waiting to be boarded is another."

Lucy stared at the display, hoping it would give up secrets she hadn't yet divined. "And how do we sneak up on something like that? It would surely be watching each move we make very carefully, so carefully, in fact, that it decided you were no threat and didn't budge when you passed within less than half a million miles of it. If someone is out there, he—or she—is very good at what they do."

"I've been thinking that we may need to start considering something like submarine warfare during World War II," Simon interjected. "Right now, that captain is just lying there, using passive sensors and gathering data on our progress. By now, they've seen new types of missiles, at the least, and probably the new and improved beam weapons.

"Oh, yeah. Let me tell you both. Some of the guys down in R & D think that real, honest-to-Pete tractor beams are possible. Capture field seams were a walk in the park in comparison and operate within a few hundred yards of a field generator, but this would be something we could use to reach out and touch something from two to five thousand miles away. They say to give them a year or two. I hope we have the time.

"That's another reason I want to see Project Vesta started, Kitty. That much room would give those guys a lot of workspace. And, so far, the free hand they've had has been very profitable. I think that would be a very useful trade technology once it's perfected." The mention of Project Vesta meant that Lucy needed to be brought up to speed on it, so Kitty took the time to fill her in.

"And that's how we'll sneak up on our pigeon. After we set up the equipment and get the power and computer online, one of us heads back to Orion following almost exactly the same course we were on to get here. The other one heads for Earth on a slightly diverging course." She walked over to the display and marked out courses with a finger. "When we reach here and here," she said and looked at the two captains following her finger, "we launch all Mambas and change course directly for the hotspot."

"Whatever's there will have to respond, one way or another. I'm guessing that some of their first moves will be preprogrammed. They could possibly have some passive systems deployed like mines or buoys. But in any event, the ship itself will either have to power up and move or stand down. Splitting each ship's Mambas into two groups will give us four groups of five. If they come in from four different directions and we come in from two others, we'll have them effectively boxed. And if you aren't willing to fire on them, I am." Kitty sat back down and let the ghost of Toni Putnam watch as she planned the revenge that was so long overdue.

Lucy looked at Simon and Kitty. "Okay, look. You two are the bosses. None of us would be here without you, and I, personally, am delighted to live out a dream that no sane person could possibly have expected even two years ago. But I won't fire without a reason that's better than just because they're there. If that's what you're asking me to do, even after what happened to Orion, I quit right here and now. If they fire first, no problem. All bets are off, and I'll do whatever it takes to prevent them from hurting any more of our people. I'll follow that plan all the way up to ordering my people to fire, but I won't give that order without good reason."

"If I believed you were the sort of person to act that way, you wouldn't be sitting here making that ultimatum," Simon asserted. "So, why don't you two work out more specific plans between you and let your crews get some rest. Overworked people don't perform well in a crisis, and you'll need all the cool heads you've got if Gayle's sensor readings are accurate. Now, if we don't have anything else to discuss, let's go get dinner. I'm starved."

Five days of R & R saw both the *Heinlein* and the *McCaffrey* ready to move out to implement Project Vesta. Carried in their small, overstuffed cargo holds were the machines to begin the excavation, and what would not fit inside was carried along in the capture fields of the two warships. That particular method of transport kept both ships moving at minimum speeds, and as had been discussed, the only messages to pass between the ships were about Project Vesta itself. Simon figured that if the *Galileo's* computer could decode Earth languages, then this bogey could, too, so no reference to Project Intercept was to go out over the radio.

All the two ships had to do was stop the tumble of the asteroid. No one really had any idea how to do that until a junior engineer suggested the use of the capture fields. They'd place one ship on either side of the asteroid and slowly increase the strength of their fields—very slowly since the enormous mass of Vesta could wreck both ships if they engaged too quickly. The idea was to have the fields act as brakes on the spin and tumble.

The machinery they'd carried along was parked nearby, and the ships took up their positions. Several attempts were made before any effect showed. Two days of nitpicking, mind-numbing work with the two capture fields finally brought the large rock into a stable position relative to the two ships.

Then the crews detailed to the initiation of the project began to move their equipment into position. Shuttles moved an active power core and transmitter near the end of the asteroid where they planned the main airlock to go. The simple computer, programmed with all the information possible, began to route beamed power to the excavating machines that would go first and do most of the work carving out the various rooms and open spaces. Engineering predicted at least a year to get that done.

Then antigrav grid-wires could be laid in place and covered over. Once air and heat were introduced, humans could enter and begin the process of making the interior a more livable environment. After the wires were in place, another series of machines would be brought in to heat-treat the walls closest to the outer surface of the asteroid, effectively putting an airtight seal in place. Another six months to look forward to.

Implementation of Project Intercept began none too soon for Kitty. As the *Heinlein* headed back towards Orion, the *McCaffrey* headed Earthward. At prearranged points, and at exactly the same time, both ships launched their entire complement of Mambas. Flying in four wings of five, they sped toward their appointed positions. The two warships began their runs toward the faint trace of heat, which was beginning to increase even as they watched.

They were launching six different attacks on one location in space. If there was only one object there, it would be, hopefully, overwhelmed. If it was armed with anything not in their databases, there could possibly be major losses on the Terran side, not so much for the *McCaffrey* but for the *Heinlein* and the Mambas as they had no screens to absorb or deflect anything that might be thrown at them.

The two warships had powered up all three sets

of monopoles. Shields were at maximum for the *McCaffrey,* but they were able to fire their beams at full strength without any loss of maneuverability. The *Heinlein*, still without the new screen technology, would use the cross-connecting capability built into the three power core systems to add to her laser strength or speed as the situation required. The Mambas had only their speed to protect them, and they'd be first on scene.

As Kitty sat in her command chair, she had Michiko feeding constant updates to her battle plot as the distances closed. The heat source became a blazing beacon on their viewscreens as something powered up. Real-time reports began to come in from the first Mambas on the scene.

"Tiger One to base. I have contact with a vessel approximately ten thousand miles distance. Looks to be slightly bigger than the *Heinlein*. Outriders are moving in our direction. I count six. All scans show weapons are hot and targeting systems are trying to lock on."

Tiger and Cheetah Flights originated from the *Heinlein,* and Viper and Cobra Flights flew from the *McCaffrey*. Tiger and Cheetah came in from ahead and to the right, while Viper and Cobra came from behind and to the left. Kitty was above while Lucy arrowed in from below. Twenty Mambas fanned out to prevent an escape. The Mambas of Tiger and Cheetah faced six marginally larger craft. Viper and Cobra went in unopposed. All ships had been ordered to hold fire unless the stranger fired first.

Some had expressed the opinion that the proposed action of the Terrans was *designed* to provoke an armed response, and Kitty couldn't refute it. Sitting at the head of the table during the briefing just before they'd left Vesta behind, she agreed that it certainly appeared that way.

"What other option do you propose, Rob? Should we go in with shields down and Mambas docked? Maybe let them get off a kill shot before we can protect ourselves?" Kitty gave the floor to her Science officer, Robert Greene.

"Captain, that's an unfair assessment of the situation. We just don't have enough data to go on. The possibility of a peaceful settlement has to be explored. We could even be looking at future allies who are evaluating us prior to contact."

Lucy, sitting at the other end of the table, joined the fray. "I don't approve of jumping in and shooting first, either, Commander Greene. But I do think we should go in prepared for trouble. If that provokes the problem, then they probably weren't potential allies to begin with. And if they *are* potential allies, they won't let our aggressive posture force them into a fight. We have a decided advantage in the weapons department, as far as we can tell, but we're also certainly at a disadvantage in the experience department."

"I agree with Captain Hawke," Gayle said. "We go in weapons hot and ready to kick ass. If we don't have to, fine. If we do have to fight, let's do the job right. And remember one thing, people. This is not a debate. These are orders being issued. If you have a problem with them and can't perform your jobs, step down now. Otherwise, you better do it first and question later. The other Captain Hawke agrees as well. The middle of an operation is no time to have qualms about it."

Kitty took the meeting back and brought it to a close. "Ladies and gentlemen, so far, you've all done a superb job, and now we're about to show our teeth because we have to. One thing I know. If you pull a gun on someone, you'd better be prepared to use it. If you're bluffing and get called on it, you're dead, and no amount of questioning by the survivors will bring you back. We bite, folks. And if these people are possible friends, they won't do anything to cause us to draw blood. The only other option is that they aren't friends. And, as far as I'm concerned, that leaves them dead." Her voice was totally without emotion. The image of Toni Putnam was all too vivid in her mind. "If you have reservations, speak up now. Anyone not at their duty stations after operations commence will be taken back to Earth at the first opportunity. Otherwise, dismissed."

No one demurred.

Tiger and Cheetah Flights stopped dead in space relative to the ship powering up some five thousand miles ahead of them. As the ten pilots watched their screens, they saw the six larger craft sweep in toward them. The *Heinlein's* sensors brought the same data to Kitty's battle plot. Fractional seconds after Cheetah One reported missile launches from the craft they faced, Kitty saw the same and ordered all ships to hold their fire except Tiger and Cheetah.

"Take 'em out, and make it decisive, people."

No sooner had the words left her mouth than she saw the ten Mambas scatter as a flight of missiles slipped past them. Cheetah One, in nominal command of the lead units, ordered all ten ships to fire, and seconds later all six opponents vanished from the *Heinlein's* battle plot.

Kitty's Tactical Officer reported. "Ma'am, we have multiple launches from the bogey. She is powered up and her drives appear to be at full. She seems to be going to ram Tiger and Cheetah Flights. I think she was hoping her outriders would at least make a dent she could squeeze through."

"Evaluate motives later, Commander. Right now, we just need facts," Kitty said. "Send to the *McCaffrey*: Bogey is attempting to break out. Her screening elements have been destroyed. Move to intercept. Fire at your discretion. Send to Tiger and Cheetah: Flush your tubes and back off. Helm, intercept course from above and behind. Full speed. Weapons Officer, prepare to fire full spread."

Kitty watched as pinpoints of light erupted from the formation of Mambas in the way of the alien vessel, and then they darted away. The slight haze around the dot of light in her battle plot seemed to diminish as the pinpoints arrowed in like moths to a flame.

"Ma'am, multiple hits registered on the bogey. She appears to have absorbed all of our missiles," Gayle said, whose screens copied those of the Weapons/Tactical Officer.

Kitty heard with part of her mind as she watched the icon that represented her ship closing on the bogey. Acknowledging the report with a wave of her hand, she ordered, "Weapons Officer, fire on my order." A heartbeat passed as though it were an eternity. "Fire! Prepare another spread." When her battle plot showed all forward tubes full, she ordered, "Fire!" and sixteen more missiles tracked in on the glowing dot on her screens.

Simultaneously, missiles from the *McCaffrey* appeared on her display, followed seconds later by sixteen more. Both Gayle and Tac Officer Marshall reported hits at the same instant, and as she watched, Kitty saw the haze disappear from around the dot on her screen just before the *McCaffrey's* second wave melded with it. For a bare second the screen blanked, and when it cleared, the arena held only Terran ships.

A larger slice of eternity passed as Kitty gazed at her screens. Finally, somewhere in the back of her mind, she felt a tension melt away that she hadn't really known was there. And, at the same time, she heard a voice.

"Thank you, Captain Kitty."

Had anyone been standing close enough to hear, they might have been surprised to overhear Kitty murmur quietly, "You can rest now, Toni. And I'll do my best to see that what you lost was worth the cost.

"Gayle, pass the word to all Mambas. I want a full search for survivors, if any, and look for any wreckage. We need some kind of tentative identification on the bogey. Also, when you have time, go back over your sensor logs. See if you can identify any transmissions we might need to be concerned about."

It appeared to be a fact of life that when that many antimatter missiles impacted a ship, nothing was left to recover. One enterprising pilot had gone back in search of one of the missiles that had been fired by the bogeys, and after an unsuccessful hunt, was joined by the rest of her flight. With a little help from the *Heinlein's* battle plot, the now-inert missiles were found. Two were carefully brought "home" in capture fields and the rest destroyed.

Finally, there was nothing left to do but call her pilots home. "Gayle, send to all Mambas: Well done. Return to base."

Kitty ordered a full copy of all sensor data to be transmitted to the *McCaffrey* for Lucy to take back to the *Galileo* so a more in-depth analysis could be made. She sent the two foreign missiles along as well, glad to have them out of her hands. Although it was still technically her shift, she called her first officer, Marsha Kane, to the bridge to take over.

Her mind in turmoil, Kitty wandered the decks of the *Heinlein* until she at last found herself on the flight deck. As she stood in the shadows and watched the technicians service and rearm the Mambas, she saw a technician initial a service log and hang it on the access hatch to one of the Mambas. Recognizing him as her Chief of Flight Services, Kitty announced her presence.

"Good day, Chief."

Anson Hargrove turned around and literally tipped his hat. A son of the Deep South, this was no affectation. Anson, a bit older than Simon and Kitty, had been raised to a different standard than a lot of the younger generation. And he was only on the *Heinlein* due to that upbringing.

Chief Hargrove was a devoted family man. The fact that he'd never had a family of his own at almost fifty didn't keep him from lavishing that affection on his relatives. And when his sister asked him to keep track of her daughter after her husband died in an oilfield disaster, he immediately said yes. This had led him to Colorado State University, where his niece was going to school, and then ultimately led him to a science-fiction convention to keep track of a young country girl traveling in fast company.

Anson had seen people appear in beams of light as he sat in the back of the room his niece had gone to, along with about thirty or so others. Thinking it a great magic trick, he wasn't too concerned until several of the audience accepted the offer to visit the spaceship these people said they came from. Four of the guests took small black disks that were handed out, and seconds later they disappeared in a cloud of blue sparks. Shills, Anson thought, until moments later when they returned in the same manner, expounding on the wonders they'd seen in just five minutes.

Among those early disappearances was his niece. As more sparked out of the room four at a time, he began to worry that none were returning. Even the original four took the opportunity to revisit the spaceship. Worried as much about his niece as what his sister would do to him if anything happened to her, he stood up, walked to the front of the room with some others, and when he was handed a small disk, waited to see what would happen.

And was amazed to see the room vanish, replaced with a small steel room occupied by more of the magicians in uniforms. He immediately asked after his niece and soon found her among a group heading for a meeting room. Catching her eye, he shrugged. Knowing how her uncle felt, the girl just smiled, waved, and kept on into the room.

Finding a seat in the back, Anson listened with growing amazement—a condition he was to be subject to for some time to come. After it sank in that he truly was on a spaceship and that his niece wasn't going to go back, Anson decided to sign on, too. Soon, he'd been evaluated and assigned a job on the factory level.

His aptitude with machines brought him to the attention of a delightfully curvaceous blonde called Commander Miller, and he soon found himself shouldering more and more responsibility. His niece flourished as well.

During the several months it took for the *Galileo* to get underway the first time, Anson took advantage of the fact that he could go back to Earth occasionally and let his sister know that all was well. He didn't tell her about the spaceship part. Margie would never understand. And he'd asked his niece to keep their secret. Now that Marsha Kane was first officer of the first commissioned Terran Alliance warship, he couldn't bring himself to do anything that, in his mind, might jeopardize that position.

Too much family pride, he thought.

Still, he'd told Margie about Marsha's new attitude and how she could be found looking up some obscure bit of data about her new job. "Classified," was all he would tell Margie, "but they let me keep an eye on her." All in all, Anson was very proud of his niece, the first officer.

Chief Hargrove was jolted out of his reverie when Captain Hawke laid her hand on his arm and asked, "Chief, are you okay?"

"Y-yes, ma'am," he replied. "Just daydreaming, ma'am. I'll try to see that it doesn't happen again."

Kitty smiled, and in the manner that had captured the hearts and minds of her crew, said, "Think nothing of it, Chief. Daydreaming is what got us here. As long as you're not doing it at a critical moment, it's no problem. I actually encourage it, come to think of it. Daydreaming can bring us some of our best ideas."

"Well, ma'am, I don't think any ideas will be coming out of this bit of daydreaming, but I'll keep it in mind. Now, what can I do for you, ma'am?"

"Well, Chief," Kitty said with a conspiratorial air, "I really need some quiet time after all the fuss. I was wondering if I might borrow one of your babies for a while. Do you mind? I *am* qualified."

The look Anson gave the tiny captain would have been described by anyone else as a glare, but Kitty had a feeling it wasn't directed at her and was just a way to hold the world at a distance.

"Well, ma'am, I'll be proud to have you fly one of my babies," he said, doffing his hat. "I just finished checking this girl out myself, and she's ready to fly."

Kitty looked up at her big chief technician and said, "I know, Chief. When I saw it was you signing off on the maintenance log, I knew which one I wanted."

Anson turned a deep shade of crimson at the compliment from his captain, and having heard his accent before, Kitty wasn't the least bit surprised to hear him utter a phrase she'd only heard in old movies.

"Shucks, ma'am, I was only doin' m'job."

Chief Hargrove watched as Kitty climbed into the Mamba. He personally checked her seals, put on her helmet, gave her a thumbs-up, and exited the launch bay. Kitty's onboard systems were powering up and showed one red light until the launch-bay door was sealed. No sooner did that door seal than the red light turned green. She instantly began to nudge the fighter out through the force field and into the eternal night. For a time, she maintained a discreet distance from the *Heinlein's* starboard stern quarter until she'd reacquired a feel for the craft. Then, she began to edge away and pick up speed.

Almost instantly a voice came over her radio. "Single Mamba, return to bay. Place yourself on report and confine yourself to quarters until I arrive."

Kitty recognized Marsha's voice and shuddered slightly. "Commander Kane, this is the captain. I'm the pilot of the Mamba," she sent over the commander's private frequency. "I realize now that I should have informed you or Flight Control of my intentions, but I didn't know myself until moments ago just how badly I needed to get out. I need to be alone, Marsha, and I'd appreciate it if you'd let me get this out of my system without interference."

All that came back was, "Acknowledged, Captain. Kane, out."

Marsha told her navigator to keep a special eye on the solo ship traveling ahead of the *Heinlein*.

Kitty shook her head. *Damn*, she thought, *how is it that I can be the captain and still get in trouble?* Needing to do something to set the images in her mind aside for a while, Kitty fed power to her engines. Pushing all other thoughts out, she dove her ship down into the plane of asteroids. She increased her speed, leveled out, and glued her eyes to her HUD. Taking her craft through near-miss after near-miss with asteroids as she went along, she never noticed that the *Heinlein* had picked up speed and was keeping station above and behind her.

All she wanted was for the images in her mind to go away—images of so many people/creatures/beings with thoughts, loves, and aspirations, family and friends they'd never meet again, obligations they'd never discharge. It didn't help that the people she was responsible for had lived because of her decisions. All she could see was the death she'd caused.

Kitty jerked her ship around the last in a long series of tumbling rocks, aimed slightly up out of the belt, then reached over and flipped the master switch that cut all power except for life support. As her ship slowly drifted up out of the plane of asteroids, she screamed. She screamed until it seemed as though her lungs would burst, and the sound in the confined cockpit threatened to deafen her. She railed and ranted at a universe gone mad, and she beat on her instrument panels until her hands were bloody. And she screamed again. And blamed.

She blamed her parents for bringing her into the world and for dying and leaving her. She blamed fate for putting her on a hilltop two years ago. She blamed an invisible alien government, most probably lightyears distant. She blamed a faceless alien commander. She blamed herself. But most of all, she blamed Simon.

No normal person could long maintain those emotions at that intensity, and Kitty soon found herself drained. It was with a sense of great detachment that she noticed the blood running down her hands and into her lap, and she idly wondered how it had gotten there. Sitting in the cockpit of her Mamba, Kitty's mind drifted into that curious state that is neither wakefulness nor sleep. Sharing the universe with only the hard, unblinking, accusatory light of the stars, she sat quietly, waiting for… she knew not what, nor cared.

Her journey through limbo continued for an indeterminate time until she heard a voice call, "Captain."

Too weary to care, she didn't answer. Somewhere in the back of her mind drifted the thought that she had turned the radio off, along with the rest of the systems.

"Captain, I need to speak to you." The voice had an urgency to it that was hard to ignore, but she tried. "I'm not going away until you talk to me, Captain."

Kitty slowly raised her head and asked, "Who's that? I thought I was alone. I want to be alone. I'm the captain. I order you to go away."

The voice disobeyed. "I *can't* go away, Captain. As long as you blame yourself for my death, I'll be with you. You can kill all the aliens in the universe, and it won't be enough to get me to leave. The only way to do that is for you to realize that you weren't responsible."

Kitty wailed. "I *am* responsible! I'm responsible for all of you! I'm responsible for your lives and your deaths. I'm responsible for the deaths of hundreds more on that ship, and I want to die with you!'

"Captain, we're only responsible for the *choices* we make. I chose to join, and those on that ship chose their own paths. You chose to save those under your command today. Do you think they'd have let you and yours live if you hadn't fired? Remember the gun. If you aren't ready to shoot, don't point it at someone…"

CHAPTER TWENTY-SIX

Marsha and the rest of the bridge crew watched in horror as Kitty's Mamba dove into the asteroid belt and sped up. The relative scarcity of material wouldn't normally have been a problem except for two things—the lack of screens on a ship the size of a Mamba and the speed at which it was traveling. She ordered her Helm officer to speed up and stay with the Mamba.

"Above and behind her, if you please. I don't want her knowing we're following."

Any ship under power has a blind spot... directly behind it in a cone-shaped, expanding pattern produced by the immense energies being created and expelled. Sensors couldn't read through that much distortion. So, unless Kitty flipped her ship, she'd never know the *Heinlein* was there.

Two hours passed as Marsha followed the little Mamba, and a collective sigh was heard throughout the bridge as it finally arced up out of the asteroid field.

Gayle, still sitting at her communications console and monitoring the data, was the first to announce, "Ma'am, her ship is no longer under power."

Marsha had noticed this at almost the same instant. She also noticed that there was no deviation in the flight path, and as far as the sensor data could show, the craft wasn't tumbling, which were pretty fair indications that the ship hadn't collided with anything and that for some reason the pilot had intentionally shut down her systems. Concern for her captain was overridden by their last conversation, and Marsha merely kept watch. She ordered the *Heinlein* to change her course and shadow Kitty's ship from the same blind spot. Then, she waited.

One hour turned into two, two finally turned into four, and Marsha could wait no longer. She ordered two Mambas out to intercept with their capture fields and bring the drifting ship in. This decision hadn't come easily. The last hour had been spent making calls to the little fighter and getting no response. Gayle had even traded on their long-time friendship by calling and making increasingly more personal requests for Kitty to answer. When all attempts to talk had failed, Marsha finally took the bit in her teeth.

The two rescue ships rendezvoused with Kitty's craft, and a voice came over the radio. "We have visual on the captain's ship. She looks like she's asleep or unconscious. No response to our hails, no indication that she's even aware we're here."

Marsha ordered the two ships to bring Kitty back, and not needing two sensor stations active at that moment, she said, "Commander Miller, you have the bridge. Order a medical team to the flight deck. Commander Marshall, keep me informed of any changes. I'll be on the flight deck." With that, she left the bridge.

Flight Control had things well in hand. Kitty's ship had just been docked, and the two rescue ships were even then being moved back into their bays. As she strode down the deck to the bay that housed

Kitty's Mamba, she saw a familiar figure stepping through the hatch with Kitty's body in his arms.

With the medical team and curious onlookers around, Marsha could only ask, "How is she, uh, Chief. Is she alive?"

Anger and grief softened the voice of Chief Hargrove as he replied, "Yes, ma'am, she's alive. But look at her hands. Who could have done that to her hands?"

Taking in the steady rise and fall of Kitty's chest and the slight smile on her face—two things at such odds with the blood-soaked uniform and mangled hands—Marsha dismissed the medical team back to the sick bay with orders to have it ready for their momentary arrival.

"Let's not move her any more than absolutely necessary until we can get her on a table and the doctor can have a look at her."

Her secret reason for issues those orders was the expression on her uncle's face. She'd grown up around him and knew that he would sooner give up an arm than the delicate package he carried. During their infrequent conversations, she'd heard him echo the sentiments of everyone she knew, herself included, concerning the high regard in which Kitty was held.

I need to make an announcement at the earliest possible moment, she thought. *Rumors are going to start flying almost immediately.*

The long walk to Medical solidified a resolve she'd had since she'd first come aboard the *Heinlein*, and that was the need for more than one sick bay. There should be one off the flight deck as well, and as she looked at Kitty, she knew just who she'd talk to about that once things settled down.

They arrived at the sick bay to find Doctor Penn anxiously awaiting their arrival. "I knew this would happen sooner or later," he said. At the sharp look he got from Marsha, he added, "I don't mean to the captain specifically. I mean to anybody in general. That they'd get hurt far enough away from sick bay that they'd need to be transported here." These comments were made as he began his examination of Kitty. "Commander, will you clear the room, please? Ensign Dorsey, you will stay to assist me."

To Marsha he said, "Elevators, turns, twists. This ship isn't designed to easily cart injured people from one point to another. We either need to widen the corridors or we need to have auxiliary sick bays in other parts of the ship."

Marsha shooed everyone from the room, saving Chief Hargrove for last. The expression on his face said that he wasn't about to leave, but Marsha looked both ways to make sure they were alone and then promised in a quiet voice, "Uncle Anse, as soon as we know anything, I'll let you know, okay? Let's not disrupt things any more than they already are. Go on back to the flight deck. Please?"

At his silent nod, she turned back to the doctor. "I want you to know that I feel the same way about extra sick bays. After this is over, you and I will go to Simon and insist on some changes in future ships. Oh, by the way, I'm staying, too. If I can help in any way, let me know."

The doctor just nodded and kept up a running commentary for the recorder that hummed at his side.

Doctor Penn first examined Kitty's hands, determined that they were no longer bleeding, and then went on with the rest of his examination. After a complete exam, he told Marsha that the only physical damage was to Kitty's hands. He began to delicately clean the wounds and, where necessary, he either stitched up the cuts or taped them.

As he wrapped both hands in gauze, he told Marsha, "She'll need a pair of hands when she wakes up. I trust you to take care of that. All my medics are male, and I'm sure she'll be more comfortable with a female for certain things. Beyond that, I can find no reason for her to be unconscious. She's sustained no head trauma, and there's not enough blood loss to be significant, so no indications of anything that might bring her to this state. The only possible reason I can come up with at this time is exhaustion—either mental or physical, or possibly both. You do realize that you're in command from this moment on, don't you? And as far as I'm concerned, you will be for the foreseeable future."

A flustered Marsha replied, "I'll certainly take care of seeing to her needs, doctor. I have someone in mind, as a matter of fact. I'd like to see that she's moved to her quarters, if you'd have your people assist me. And as far as being in command is concerned, I want you to return her to duty as soon as possible, without causing her any trouble, of course."

Doctor Penn called two of his medics in and gave instructions for Kitty's transport to her quarters. "First, I'd like to see if we can get her to wake up enough to recognize her surroundings," he said. "It would help if she knew what we were doing to her and would seriously reduce the stress she'd experience if she woke up without any forewarning." He leaned over her and spoke softly but with authority. "Captain? Captain? I need you to wake up,

Captain."

The voice that came to Kitty's ears this time was male, carrying an undertone of concern.

"As far as I can tell, all she needs is rest, Commander," the voice said quietly. "I suggest that we rendezvous with the *Galileo* as soon as possible, and I'd like to talk to her to gauge her mental state as far as I'm able as soon as she wakes up."

Another voice, Marsha, Kitty thought hazily, spoke.

"Very well, doctor. She's in your care. I don't need to tell you what the feeling is on this ship right now. I'll make sure she gets rest, and you call me the instant she'd awake enough to talk."

As Marsha's voice started to recede, Kitty clawed her way to awareness for a moment. "Marsha?" When she felt her first officer touch her arm, Kitty grabbed at it and jerked her hand back involuntarily as unexpected pain exploded from her bandaged hands. "I spoke to her, Marsha. She said I wasn't responsible."

Trying to say all the things one says at a sickbed, Marsha groped for the right words. "That's good, Captain. Don't talk anymore. You need to get your strength back."

"She said I could let it go, Marsha. That I shouldn't blame myself," Kitty murmured as she started to drift off. "She said to remember the gun…"

"Yes, Captain. Now get some—who said those things, Captain?" Marsha asked.

Kitty made one final stab at consciousness. "Toni did, Marsha. Toni told me."

Marsha headed toward her cabin, wondering how she was going to word this message to Simon.

Simon was blissfully unaware of the battle that had taken place outside the *Galileo's* sensor range, having judged the odds that the *Heinlein's* sensors had actually picked up their bogey to be very low. In one respect he was right; the odds *were* low, but not outside the realm of possibility. But as soon as the *McCaffrey's* message came in, he got his nose rubbed in reality.

The report that made its way to Simon as he sat discussing some of Libra's construction details with her future commander gave no details of the battle other than that there were no injuries or damage. It merely stated that the *McCaffrey* was going to rendezvous with the *Galileo* and bring material recovered from enemy wreckage.

The *McCaffrey* parked alongside the larger ship and Lucy beamed aboard, bringing with her all the sensor data from her ship, as well as Kitty's. She immediately called Simon and Stephen to pass along everything she had. Stephen, in turn, woke up several members of the Science staff—it being the night shift—and asked them to make themselves available to start analyzing the new data. The two retrieved missiles were parked a safe distance away.

Lucy handed the sensor data to Stephen, who passed it on to an aide to take to the Science staff. She made a point of noting how many hits it had taken to bring down the enemy ship when their projections hadn't led them to consider it would take even half that many. The conclusions that finally came down from all this data weeks later (and this from people who'd been in space and using this technology for less than two years) was that the ship they'd dealt with hadn't been a craft of the Builders. In the final analysis, they based this decision on the two missiles they'd recovered, along with the earlier bit of wreckage.

Rather than monopole-powered energy sources, these missiles consumed themselves to provide their propulsion in some manner that baffled the scientists. The warheads, if that was what they could be called, seemed to be some form of energy-absorption device. Enough of them striking a target would absorb all the energy from it, effectively disintegrating the craft. This would be harder to do to the *McCaffrey* since her shields had been stiffened by having their own monopoles to power them. Any other missile striking the ship would begin to absorb the energy that bound matter together.

Simon, busy with the minutiae of the *Galileo's* daily routines while keeping his finger on the pulse of Libra's construction and Lucy's report of the battle, was just beginning to realize that the *Heinlein's* daily report was overdue. Once the realization hit, he wrapped up his meeting with Lucy and made his way to the communications console on the bridge, where he upset the ensign on duty by committing the faux pas of showing up unannounced.

Keeping his message terse, all he said was, "*Heinlein*, your daily report is overdue. Please contact the *Galileo* at your earliest opportunity." Not knowing the *Heinlein's* location or situation, Simon gave the comm officer instructions to call him as soon as a reply came in.

With nothing to do while he waited for a response, Simon wandered the ship, making a general nuisance of himself. Only his commlink going off saved him from Victor physically ejecting him from the manufacturing section of the ship.

Although he hadn't been officially confirmed or promoted to the rank, it was general knowledge that Victor was going to be commander of Libra Base, and since the system had worked so well for Gemini and Orion, it had become policy to have the commander and the people who were actually going to crew the base working together to construct it. It tended to slow things down a bit in the beginning, since each base was being constructed by nearly as many newbies as veterans of at least one other trip, but in the long run, the crew of the base knew it intimately from the very first rivet, and they were well able to work together from the first day of ship production.

While this system sometimes caused problems due to the dual chain of command, it normally didn't interfere with the daily workings of the ship when she was in construction mode. In this particular case, Victor was saved from having to exercise a prerogative he wasn't sure he had.

When Simon finally acknowledged receipt of a message from the *Heinlein*, he left for his ready room, unaware of the confrontation that had been averted by his departure.

Simon poured a cup of coffee and sat back in his chair, prepared to enjoy the sound of his wife's voice. He pressed a button on his console, and to his surprise and disappointment, it was Marsha Kane's voice that filled the air. He sat bolt upright, coffee forgotten, at the first sentence.

"*TAS Heinlein*, mission report. Commander

Marsha Kane, commanding per Doctor Harrison Penn's orders. Captain Hawke is under mild sedation in her quarters after an incident. The *Heinlein* is on course to rendezvous with the *Galileo*. Approximate ETA is seven hours from the transmission of this message. The captain is not, I repeat, *not* injured due to battle, and the *Heinlein* sustained no damage. Injuries to the captain are minor, and she'd resting comfortably. Further report to be made in person." Simon was sure he heard a tremor in Marsha's voice. "This is the *TAS Heinlein*, out."

Simon replayed the transmission from the *Heinlein* several more times, trying to glean any more information he could from it. He finally called Stephen, giving no reason other than, "I need a friend." When Stephen showed up moments later, Simon waved him to a chair. "I just got the *Heinlein's* daily report. I think you should hear it." With no further comment, he played the message.

Stephen just sat for several seconds after Marsha's voice faded out. "Simon, I don't know what to say. It sounds like there isn't anything to worry about. You know as well as I do that accidents are going to happen. Marsha wouldn't tell you Kitty was okay if she wasn't."

"It's what she *didn't* say that worries me, Stephen. No mention of what kind of accident, what kind of injuries, nothing. And her word was 'incident,' not accident. And under mild sedation? Something happened out there after the *McCaffrey* left the area. Lucy said Kitty was going to patrol the area, and that's what our first ships are supposed to do. So what could they have run into that would injure one person out of an entire crew, and the captain at that?"

Simon was on his feet, pacing. A flash of Kitty chiding him for just that habit flashed through his mind, and he forced himself to sit back down. "I don't know what to say any more than you do, Stephen. I've listened to that message half a dozen times now, and I can't get any more out of it than the first time. Maybe I just want misery to have company. You and Gayle were with us when we got this business started, and I thought you should know as soon as possible. Gayle already knows since she's out there with Kitty. About six more hours and we'll have all the facts. Or I'll have someone's ass."

Stephen walked over to the wall console and dialed up two cups of coffee. "I thought I'd strangle Marsha for not giving more information, but on second thought, I guess not," he said over his shoulder. "I heard the top-secret stamp at the first of the message, but I'll bet it's all over the *Galileo* and the *McCaffrey* by now."

The hours seemed to drag by, relieved only by regular reports from the *Heinlein* updating their ETA. Sensor data finally showed the ship approaching about two hours before her actual arrival, and Simon haunted the Astrometrics lab, watching Stephen try to tweak any additional data from the sensors.

When the *Heinlein* finally parked on the opposite side of the *Galileo* from the *McCaffrey*, Marsha beamed aboard after a brief message telling Simon she'd come directly to his ready room. Entering alone, she said, "I know you're worried. I would be, too, in your place. Let me tell the story and then you can ask questions." After a detailed summary of events, she finished with, "And Doctor Penn won't let her be beamed over. He insists on having her brought over by shuttle. He's still concerned about her mental state and says that no one knows what the effects are of beaming a fragile mentality."

Simon jumped on one word. "Fragile? Who decided Kitty is mentally fragile? She's about the most stable person I know. Hell, she's the one who's kept me from going ballistic more than once in my life. And look at how everyone out here sees her. She's a rock, damn it."

Marsha looked at Simon pleadingly. "Simon, she's a rock who's talking to dead people. How stable is that? She was out there alone for hours. By her own choice, too. Then when we get her back, she'd tried to beat the control panel of her Mamba to pieces with her bare hands. Simon, please let Dr. Penn talk to her. Maybe she was just dreaming about Toni. But what about her wounds? I've talked to the doctor, and I've seen her hands. Let him do his job, okay?"

Simon finally conceded that the doctor was qualified to make the decisions he had (although it was like pulling teeth to get that admission), and headed for the flight deck.

Arriving as the medics were bringing the litter off the shuttle, Simon bulled his way through them to Kitty's side. His eyes were drawn first to the bandaged hands lying outside the covering draped over her. Seeing her closed eyes and slack expression, he asked the doctor, "What's wrong with her that she needs to be sedated?"

"Well, Captain," Doctor Penn began, "the

problem is that she seems to have taken a holiday." At Simon's puzzled look, he went on. "What I mean is that she's suffered a level of mental distress from which her subconscious needed to escape. Now, I'm not a psychiatrist, but I've seen this before. Since her subconscious can't escape, she has, well, stepped out for a while. I can't say for how long, but she's handling it. From what I can tell from the little she's said since we brought her aboard, it seems that she's had a problem rationalizing the deaths she caused by ordering the attack on that ship. The conversation she believes she had with Toni Putnam while she was out in her Mamba is a manifestation of that conflict. It also appears to have been the catalyst that brought on this fugue. And, oddly enough, I think it's the key to her recovery. She thinks Toni blamed her for getting killed. She also thinks Toni came to her in her ship and forgave her. She needs time to work these things into a new gestalt she can live with. Give her time and encouragement, and she'll recover.

"In the meantime, no stress. Keep things light. Help her feel useful but put no strain on her. That's my diagnosis and regimen of treatment. I know it's not much, but the mind is a tricky thing. You'll have to trust me on this or go back to Earth and get a second opinion."

Simon literally hovered as the med-techs carried Kitty to their quarters. It was quite a little procession that made its way from the flight deck of the *Galileo* up to deck three and the captain's quarters—two med-techs with a stretcher between them, Simon on one side and the doctor on the other. Marsha and Gayle led the way, with Stephen guarding the rear. Simon felt a great weight leave his shoulders as he crossed the threshold into his quarters, the door cutting off the noise of the crowd that had formed in the corridor.

As each person sorted themselves out, Simon wandered the suite, at loose ends. The doctor, med-techs, and Kitty were in the bedroom. Marsha, Gayle and Stephen sat or paced through the living room until a knock came at the door. Startled, Simon just looked at it, and Gayle finally got up and opened it to admit Lucy Grimes.

"Simon, I'm so sorry. I wish I'd known. I mean, I'd never have left her out there if I'd had any idea…"

Simon held up a hand. "Lucy, thank you for everything you've done. You may think you've done nothing, but I think just being here now is a help. It helps me, that's for sure. And Kitty isn't in a coma or anything. She's just sedated. She knows you're here, I'll bet. And how could you, or anyone, have known what was going to happen? Don't beat yourself up over it. Second-guessing doesn't help, and I don't need another basket-case out here. Unless it's me, that is." A lop-sided grin played across his face. "The doctor said she's on holiday. Maybe I should join her and leave you in charge of this menagerie. Maybe then you could pay the penance you think you owe." At the look on her face, he laughed. "Oh? Don't think you screwed up that bad, do you? Well, relax. I don't either. And neither does anyone here, so grab a drink and sit down for a while."

Doctor Penn came out of the bedroom, preceded by the med-techs. The two men left with their stretcher and the doctor turned to Simon. "She's resting comfortably now. She's awake, Captain, and wants to see you. She's not made of glass, but I still don't want her stressed. Answer all questions truthfully. And only two visitors at a time—if one is you, Captain—for the next couple of days. I'll stop in and check on her twice daily, and you can call me if necessary. After that, well, we'll just have to see. Now, can anyone get me some quarters, or do I need to go back to the *Heinlein*?"

Simon called his supply officer to make arrangements for Doctor Penn's stay and then dismissed the doctor from his thoughts as he went into the bedroom to see his wife. Sitting down on the edge of the bed, he reached out and brushed a stray lock of hair from her cheek. "You gave me quite a scare, Kittyn. The doctor says you'll be okay. Can I get you anything?" He leaned over and kissed her on the forehead.

As he started to raise up, Kitty put both arms around his neck and pulled him down into a kiss that spoke volumes on its own. "I know how I'd feel if I lost you, Simon," she said sleepily, "so I think I know how you feel right now. I'm sorry. Sorry I caused all this fuss. Sorry I worried you. And sorry that I worried everyone else, too." Tears ran down her cheeks and Simon wiped them away.

"The doctor said no stress, dear, so let's table this for now except for one thing from me—nothing that happened was your fault. Some people react differently to combat, and you got your first taste with no warning. You thought you were ready but few people are really ready for something like that without a lot of training." He looked down, and in a voice filled with shame, he said, "I used you. I thought all we needed to do was show our presence and readiness to fight. Still, the responsibility is mine, and if you disagree, we can discuss it later when the doctor says you can, and not before. Right now, though, there are some people who want to visit for a few minutes. They want to say encouraging things and offer moral support. Think you're up to it?"

Kitty glanced at the door and nodded slowly. "If you stay here with me. I need that, right now."

Simon nodded and went to the door. Opening it, he beckoned for Gayle to come in. As she sat down in the place recently vacated by Simon, she first reached out to place a hand on Kitty's shoulder and then leaned down to kiss Kitty on the cheek. With her face close to Kitty's ear, she whispered, "If you ever scare me like that again, I'll show you what real stress is all about, you hear me?" Raising back up, she said loud enough for Simon to hear, "If you need anything, just ask. As long as Simon keeps the *Heinlein* in the area, I'll be available. "I was so scared, Kitty. We all were. We're just happy to have you safe."

These sentiments more or less set the tone for Marsha, Lucy and Stephen as well.

Kitty muttered a few inanities to each of her visitors, trying to apologize for the situation. To a person, each refused to let her take any blame. "As a matter of fact," Lucy said, "I think someone should recommend you for the Solar Cross. You planned the action and it went off without a hitch." At Kitty's look of horror, she could only ask, "What's wrong? What did I say?"

Kitty couldn't get the words to come out in sequence. "Murderer. No. Can't."

Tears ran down her cheeks and Simon stepped between the two women. To the stricken Lucy, he quietly explained the situation and Kitty's state of mind as he ushered her out of the room. Turning back to Kitty, he sat and offered his support and love.

After a few minutes, Simon told her, "I'll be right back. Let me run this bunch off and we can have some time to ourselves." Sliding her bandaged hands out of his with ease, he winked. "I'm not leaving, dear. Just getting rid of the well-wishers. I'll leave the door open a crack so you'll know I'm still here."

Simon walked into the living room of his suite to find all the visitors still there. Gayle was in the process of telling her version to Lucy while literally wringing her hands. Stephen, seated beside her, could no longer take it and reached out and took one of her hands in both of his, holding it as she finished. This gesture didn't go unnoticed by Simon or anyone else, but no one saw fit to comment on it, and Simon went back to the matter at hand, which was running everyone out of his quarters. That mission finally accomplished, he went back to the bedroom to find Kitty snoring on the bed. Smiling at a memory that rose in his mind, he drew up a chair, brought a glass of scotch, a glass of Kitty's favorite herbal tea, and a few papers into the room, and sat down to keep vigil over his wife.

Three days brought considerable improvement in Kitty. A continuous stream of visitors had come and gone during normal business hours on this first day of visiting allowed by Dr. Penn. Her aide, Lt. Commander Kimura, assigned against Kitty's wishes, came to her with a strange look on her face.

"Ma'am, your last visitor of the day is here, but I strongly advise that you turn him away. It's Agent

Daniels."

Simon and the doctor had conspired to keep her physical and mental stress to a minimum, using newly promoted Lt. Commander Kimura to screen her visitors and monitor her condition.

"I'll be the judge of that, Commander," Kitty said kindly. "Let him in. I need a diversion from all the well-wishers. And be polite. There isn't any reason to be rude."

"Please be seated, Agent," Kitty said as the agent walked into the living room, waving to a chair that had been placed on the other side of a small table. "Coffee?" At his nod, she called Rukia and ordered two cups, and perversely, a pot. "Well, Agent, how have you been? Keeping busy looking for plots and subverting our people?"

"Keeping busy interviewing anyone who'll talk to me, Captain. Making friends and influencing people. No subversions or mutinies planned, if you're interested," he answered lightly. The coffee arrived and Kitty waved Commander Kimura away.

"I think I'd like some privacy, if you please, Commander. If you really must flutter about, do it on the other side of the door." She watched the woman leave, wounded pride showing in every step. "You can bet Simon will know about my little indiscretion before the hour is up, Agent. Sometimes I feel like a prisoner and take my pleasures where I can find them. Now, what can I do for you? You will forgive me if I don't shake hands?'

"Captain, considering our history, I wouldn't take offense if your hands *weren't* bandaged. How are you doing, by the way?"

She lifted her hands up out of her lap, looking at

them for a moment and then setting them back down. "Physically, as well as can be expected. The doctor says the bandages can come off tomorrow and the stitches can come out in another week. Mentally, well, most of the people around me are treating me like I'm about to explode. Look at the commander, for example. Believe it or not, getting her to leave the room surprised me. I thought I'd have to fight her over it. *I* don't think I'm going to explode, but who am I to judge?"

Agent Daniels poured coffee into the two cups, helped Kitty hold one in her bandaged hands, and took a sip from his. "Well, Captain, I'm glad you worded yourself the way you did because it touches on one of the two reasons I'm here. Let me tell you what the first reason is. I'm the government stoolie, and they're going to want to know everything that happened out there. I'm betting they'll say that their need to know is based on what could happen to Earth because of your actions. So, when you feel up to it, I'd like to request an interview. Not today. It's way too soon, by my estimation, but I wanted to get my bid in." He took another sip from his cup and went on. "It's been my experience that one should always go to the horse's mouth for information, which is why I'd like to talk to Marsha Kane and Lucy Grimes if and when they become available for interviews."

A look Kitty interpreted as discomfort passed over the agent's face. "The second reason I'm here indirectly concerns the rumors running around the ship that say you're a ticking timebomb ready to explode. I don't see a timebomb ready to explode, Captain, but I do see a woman who could very easily have another nervous breakdown. And for what little it's worth, I'm here to offer my support."

Daniels took a deep breath, closed his eyes and seemed to come to some inner decision. "In 1970, I went to Vietnam. I enlisted for my country, you know? They trained me to shoot a rifle and sent me to a place where all the people who didn't look like me either wanted me dead or didn't care one way or the other.

"I was in-country less than two weeks when I went out on my first patrol, and we got into a firefight. I was so scared I pissed myself. I'm not ashamed to admit it now. When it was all over, I'd squeezed the trigger so hard that either it or my finger should have broken. It took my squad leader to pull my finger off that trigger, and I'd never fired a shot. The safety was still on. We lost three people in that firefight, and even today I wonder if any of those three might have lived if I'd done my job right. I'd never have known what I was shooting at, but maybe, just maybe, some of those guys would still be alive. So, what I'm saying is that I know what you're going through. What it boils down to, Captain, is that in a war you do things you wouldn't normally do. Now, I don't know you personally, but because I had to investigate you," here he shrugged his shoulders and gave a deprecating wave of his hands, "I do know a bit about you. And what I know is that you're not some indiscriminate killer. I saw enough of those in 'Nam. Those are the kind of people who will get you killed, not save your life.

"These aren't normal times, Captain. I don't remember who it was that said this, but extraordinary times call for extraordinary measures. And I'll add my own bit to that truism: It also calls for extraordinary *people.* I'm the last person on the face of the planet—hey, I made a joke there—to curry favor with anybody, but I see you, and I see Simon, and I see the hundreds upon hundreds of other people here as extraordinary people. The scuttlebutt I have says you did what needed to be done. That's nothing to be ashamed of or to beat yourself up over. It's just a fact of life. And if the stories I've been hearing from the people I've been talking to have any validity at all, sooner or later there will be a lot more of this. I, for one, will feel a lot better knowing that you and Simon and Marsha Kane and Lucy Grimes and all the others, down to the last pod jockey, are out here.

Daniels stood up and made ready to leave. "Just for your information, Captain, that's the report I intend to give the next time I get back to Earth. I'll probably get off then, too. My superiors will see that report and think I've been compromised. I don't know how much good it will do you and your people, but there you have it. Beyond that, all I want to say is that I wish you the best of luck and a speedy recovery."

Lt. Commander Kimura came back in as the agent opened the door and left. "Ma'am, I guess you know I heard everything that was said in here. The captain, your husband, ordered me to tell him everything that went on while he was gone. You know he only has the best of intentions, and I know it, too, or I would never have agreed to do it, but I think I've just run into something I should keep to myself."

Kitty nodded. "I think so, too, Commander. Simon will know he was here, so we won't keep it secret, but let's not burden him with the full conversation, shall we? All Agent Daniels did was drop in to ask for an interview at a future date and wish me a speedy recovery." At her aide's nod of agreement, Kitty stood up and said, "Well, then. I think we should plan dinner, don't you? Something to distract Simon from our last visitor. Let's call the mess hall and see if we can get someone to put together his favorites—meatloaf and banana pudding. Now would be a good time to surprise him."

A week later, Kitty walked out of the sick bay with her stitches out. She'd already been feeding herself and performing other small tasks, but she felt a line had been crossed. Getting dressed was still a bit of a problem, so Commander Kimura remained as Kitty's aide.

Simon had joined her during the stitch removal and listened to Dr. Penn's admonitions about how she should treat herself for the next week. He then broached the subject he'd been wanting to talk about for a while.

"Doc, look, Kitty's been telling me everything you've been telling her, so I know your opinion of her mental state. Since my own assessment that there's nothing wrong with her mind coincides with yours, what I want is for you to release her back to active duty if you think it appropriate. Before you make a decision, I'd like to say that for the next few months, I want to keep her near me as an adviser." He gently took her hand and pulled her closer. "I want her back in command of her ship eventually, but we've got this meeting with the vice-president coming up, as well as negotiations for bases on Earth and some kind of official status for our people so they don't get harassed or jailed for whatever they know about what's going on out here. These will be executive-level discussions and decisions. What do you think?"

Dr. Penn looked thoughtfully at Kitty. "I think that decision is up to her. As you said, I feel that she's ready to take up her duties. If she thinks she's ready, fine. Otherwise, let her progress at her own pace. I consider her discharged with only once-a-week visits. In about a month, we should be finished completely, which should make you happy, no?" This last he'd said to Kitty.

She looked from one man to the other and took a deep breath. "I have some definite ideas about the meeting and negotiations, so I want in. And if you want to talk, doctor, I'm more than happy to oblige you for as long as you feel it necessary. Does that make the two of you happy?"

Simon nodded and the doctor said, "That brings up my last topic for discussion today. If the *Galileo* follows her current plan, she'll finish Libra, go to Earth, pick up crew for ship number three, take them out to the commissioning, and then go back to Earth for more. Rumor has it that Libra will be finished sometime in July 2013, and two more ships will be ready by August or September. Sometime before then, I'd like to get off. What I have in mind is to disembark at your next visit to Earth and work on getting replacements for myself and crew-doctors for some of the other ships and bases. Psychiatrists and psychologists, too. Believe me, as the population grows, so will the problems. I'd try to be prepared if I were you."

Simon, having heard rumors himself about

people beginning to get tired of tin-can living, was anxious to get these agreements in place and functioning—not just for the Alliance, but for its members. His people needed to be able to come and go with the freedom anyone else would enjoy.

"You bet, doctor. Just remember that there won't be any agreements in place when you get back, which means no protection for you until we can get it negotiated. You'll be running some pretty big risks, especially since you're a doctor. As long as you're informed, I don't have any problem with you leaving. I've said from day one that no one is a prisoner here. Besides, you'll keep your wristband, and if any ship is in orbit, you'll have assistance as quickly as we can. We do appreciate your help in getting replacements, too. Maybe one day you'll want to come back to us. There will always be a place for you. You know that." Shaking the doctor's hand, Simon headed for the door with Kitty at his side.

The two made their way to the observation bubble situated above deck one. As they sat there watching the construction pods add one hull section after another to the habitat section of Libra, Simon finally reached down and took Kitty's hands in his. He held them up so he could see the angry red welts of the healing wounds and gently kissed each hand.

"Honey, I'm sorry."

Kitty looked up when she heard the emotion in his voice and was stunned to see tears running down his face. She pulled her hands free of his, grabbed his head, pulled him to her, and kissed him. "Just what is it you think you have to apologize to me for, you big idiot?"

"For putting you in command of the *Heinlein* in the first place, even though I knew I needed somebody there I could trust. I could have put somebody else in charge. I'm sorry for putting you in a position where a gentle nature like yours winds up going through the trauma I put you through. I'm sorry for thinking there was no chance you'd ever run into a bogey out there that we'd have to take out. I'm sorry that it all came down on your shoulders. I'm sorry you got hurt. I'm sorry that..." He faltered and couldn't say anything more, tears running down his face as Kitty pulled his head to her shoulder.

"Listen, you," she scolded, "I'm as much to blame as you are. I didn't have to accept a commission and go out there. I didn't have to go looking for Toni's killers or give the commands when we found them. I *chose* to do all those things. I can't say that if I'd known where the first choice would lead I would've agreed to any of it, but I did and here we sit today. Now, I'm going to tell you something else. I'm going to repeat a saying so old I should be beaten for dredging it up, but it's true. What doesn't kill you, makes you stronger. And, honey, it didn't kill me. And I *do* believe I'm stronger. Doctor Penn gets to make the final decision on that, but I do believe it's true. I've had some long talks with myself and some longer talks with Doctor Penn.

"People think that I think the long talks I had out there were with a ghost, but I know it was just my subconscious. But the things "she" said to me in that cockpit were things you'd said for real, especially the one about if you're going to pull a gun on somebody; you'd better be ready to use it. Well, I was out there in a damn warship loaded with guns, and I pointed 'em at someone. They called my bluff and I had to use 'em or lose all my people. I've come to terms with that. I think I came to terms with it in the Mamba that day. I'm not saying I'm ready to go back out there… yet, but you don't have to treat me like I'm gonna fall apart. So, let's get on with doing the things we need to do.

"At some point, you were talking about a meeting with the Vice-President of the United States. Tell me about it, dear. Who brought the message? And how do we know it's genuine? If we've got plans to make, let's start making them."

CHAPTER TWENTY-SEVEN

A few reporters worthy of the name—those who did more than just read the predigested pap handed out in press releases—began to stretch long-unused muscles and started investigations of their own. The mysterious mass disappearances of two years running, combined with the reappearances of some of those same people, made for stories with all the ingredients necessary to wring out a week's worth of ratings, or even more.

Those same reporters dug deeper into the files concerning the disappearances and came up with almost nothing. Although it was a sure bet that not all the missing had been reported, the group of persons reported missing around that time numbered in the hundreds. Some estimates said almost eight hundred people had vanished the first time, and those numbers were about the same for the second round.

Relatives had been questioned, friends tracked down and questioned, and habits looked at with greater scrutiny as the numbers of missing increased. Three sets of disappearances had occurred at this point, and each time, some eight months later, most would reappear making wild claims and performing amazing tricks on camera. The only difference was that the numbers of missing were spreading out from Wyoming, Colorado, and Montana.

Most of the missing were young, in their early-to-mid-twenties, but a few were older. Males outnumbered females by a fair margin, and most religious affiliations were represented, including a few who were referred to as practicing atheists. Race didn't seem to be a big factor either, and as the numbers were crunched and the data analyzed, percentages fell within a range that kept investigators stumped, as did the entire case, even when viewed from a distance.

The only thing that even remotely linked most of the missing persons was an interest in science fiction. Tie that into the magic tricks and anecdotes, and the bare bones of a story began to emerge. There was also the fact that the larger, younger group represented a fairly high percentage of college students, a specific that raised eyebrows each time but faded away like so many other speculations. Questions had been raised, but three months later, in the press of other matters of global or political significance, the lack of further evidence effectively excised the phenomenon from the daily memory of the public at large.

Now, in a variety of places all around the United States, a fair percentage of those missing persons had turned up, purportedly claiming to have been voluntarily taken aboard a spaceship and made a part of the crew. And each time they returned they were looking for recruits—volunteers they called them—to join up. When all the numbers were added up, some reporters were looking at an excess of two thousand.

People appearing and disappearing just like on Star Trek had already been seen on television a number of times. And tied into all of that was the rumor that the recent disappearances, so painstakingly coordinated as to happen in over two hundred locations around the country simultaneously, were a response to the arrival of the returnees.

Editors being editors, they had to look at the bottom line first, last, and always. But they also tried to run their papers on common sense, and the tabloids should have been handling the material these editors were receiving. No reputable company was going to advertise in a paper that ran spaceship stories as sensational as these were looking to be.

But editors, some of them, had principles as well and did run the stories, causing a particular late-night talk show host to say, "You heard it here first, several months ago. Just now reaching the mainstream media is the fact that hundreds of our people are in space building ships and bases right now!"

The president's press secretary issued hot denials of government involvement, pointing the finger at overzealous agents of the super-secret DIA as possibly being responsible for the recent reported mass roundups of citizens all across the country.

It took the persistence of one young reporter to actually get a recent returnee to talk to her on camera. Add to that the I-just-don't-give-a-damn attitude of a retiring senior editor who felt the story needed to be told, and the genie was taken fully out of the bottle.

"This is Monica Webb, Channel Eight News," the reporter said into the camera. She stood in an anonymous room beside a young man dressed in all black, with strange insignia sparkling from his collar and unfamiliar patches on his shoulders. "Can you tell me your name, sir?" she asked, turning the microphone toward him.

"John Winston," the twenty-ish man said simply.

"The same John Winston who just up and disappeared from home, college, and friends almost two years ago?"

Yes, ma'am."

"Are you in any way connected with the disappearances of almost eight hundred other people at about the same time?"

"Yes, ma'am."

Getting a little tired of the short answers, the reporter tried a different tactic in hopes of getting more out of this opportunity. "Please, Mr. Winston, explain your relationship to so many people."

"Well, Miss…?"

"Webb."

"Miss Webb, we're all volunteers, I guess you'd call us. We got an opportunity to do something no human has ever done before, and that is to build a factory in outer space."

"In outer space, you say." The reporter looked at the camera, her what-do-I-do-now look classic to behold even though she'd watched the earlier reports avidly. "Building a factory. If that's the case, Mr. Winston, how is it that the government from the local level all the way up has been looking for you and all the others for years now? If you were doing what you say, wouldn't they have known about your whereabouts, and if nothing else, covered it up to keep it secret?"

The young man smiled. "Who said they don't know what I was doing, Miss Webb? I think they're probably more anxious to find me than you were, to tell the truth."

"Are you telling me the government *isn't* involved in what you're doing? That this is a private venture?" The young woman's voice reflected her obvious surprise at his answer.

"Yes, ma'am, entirely," the young man affirmed, seeming more comfortable in front of the camera as the seconds passed. "More or less, that is," he added by way of qualification. "You see, in order to do all that we have to do—build the factories and then the ships they're being constructed to build—we need to have some form of regimentation just so we know who has to be where when and who's in charge once we arrive. So, we're actually pretty militaristic when you get right down to it. We have rank and all of that stuff."

"So what you're wearing is a uniform then." The words came out as a simple statement. "And all your people wear something more or less identical to what you have on right now?" She paused for a second, and Winston nodded. "Can you tell me the significance of your uniform and the symbols on it?"

"Certainly," the man said. "The shirt, pants, shoes, and hat are black. The piping around the collar and shirtsleeves tells people your department. I wear blue because I'm with the engineers." He fingered the collar so the small metal insignia showed better. "I'm a lieutenant, so I wear a golden crescent moon." He then turned one shoulder to the camera, showing a circular patch. "This shows that I'm a member of the *Galileo's* crew," he said and turned the other shoulder forward, "and this is the emblem of the Terran Alliance."

The camera zoomed in on another round patch, which showed a ship leaving what was obviously a representation of the planet Earth.

"Would you explain for our viewers just what the *Galileo* is, please?"

"Well," the young man said sheepishly, "this is the part people are going to have a hard time believing, but the *Galileo* is a spaceship, built by an unknown race for the sole purpose of establishing colonies around this part of the galaxy."

"When you say 'unknown race,' do you mean aliens? As in little green men?"

The lieutenant smiled. "Well, we actually think they're rather tall and red, but yeah, that's pretty much the idea."

"How is it that you get to be aboard an alien ship, Lt. Winston?" The reporter looked like she'd swallowed a bitter pill, clearly expecting something other than the revelation she'd gotten or at least hoping for something different.

"Well, you see, it was found by the captain. Exactly how, I'm not sure. Like he met one of the aliens or something," the lieutenant said, obviously more taken with the pretty young reporter than he was willing to admit. All things considered, she was a rather attractive woman, and he dragged his attention back to the camera with difficulty.

The reporter, perhaps sensing an opportunity slipping away, asked, "And why are you back at this particular time, Lt. Winston?"

The young lieutenant felt his own moment approaching. He'd been briefed a bit on what to say if this happened, along with everyone else in his department on the way back to Earth. Of course there was going to be some attention, and this was his chance to do something.

"We're back here on another recruiting mission. We're supposed to talk to our friends and see if we can get anyone to join up."

"But you already have, by our estimates, nearly two thousand people, Lieutenant."

Winston grinned to himself, letting her lead him right where he wanted to go.

"How many more do you need?"

"Miss Webb, remember when I said we built a factory out in space?"

The reporter nodded silently, a slightly dazed look on her face.

"Well, we've actually started construction on the third factory and left almost five hundred people out there to run it. Spaceships don't build themselves, you know, and they don't run themselves either. After finishing the second base, we came to Earth and picked up enough to crew the first ship out of the first factory. Now, we need to get more volunteers to build another factory to build more ships. The captain says we'll have four factories in all."

The reporter looked at the camera. "Four factories! At five hundred each, that means putting two thousand more people in space!"

"That's just for the factories, ma'am. Then you figure in the crew of the *Galileo*, which is just over nine hundred, and the first ship at almost five hundred, as well as the second ship, and the figure is closer to four thousand right now. Then you add two ships per year per base and you come up with about two thousand people each year that we need to recruit after the last base is finished. There are more people born each minute than that."

Monica thought of a question that might crack

the veneer of confidence this young man exuded. He'd been well briefed and obviously believed what he was saying, but she was betting he hadn't figured on the political ramifications.

"How do you think the American government is going to react to a bunch of its citizens acquiring technology of this level and not turning it over to them? If they don't already know, they will when this interview airs."

"Of course they aren't going to like it. They already don't," the young lieutenant said, causing the reporter's mouth to drop open. "They say they should have it because they know better how to deal with alien technology than we do. But it's going to take them a long time to realize that in this era of global communication, if they did get control of it, the whole world would lose because of it."

Before he could take a breath and continue, the reporter asked, "Are you saying you people would blow the ship up or something?"

"No, ma'am," Winston said decisively. "The problem is that no government on this planet could let any other have that much of a technological advantage. The balance of power can't be allowed to shift so strongly in favor of any country, or the whole world would go up in flames. The only solution is to keep it out of the hands of any government on Earth that would use the technology primarily for political or military advantage."

"And what makes you think the government or the viewers are going to believe you're telling us the truth?"

Throughout the interview, John Winston had been standing in a position most soldiers would refer to as "at ease," feet about shoulder width apart and hands behind the small of his back. Aside from underscoring the idea that the Terran Alliance was a militaristic concept, it was a position ideal for keeping Winston's hands still, hiding his nervousness.

"Well, Miss Webb, I came down here tonight to try to get some of my friends to join up. You found me, so you must have found my folks. If you're any good at your job, you'd probably know by now that we're not real big on family closeness, which is why I'm here and not at home.

"I've already told my friends all that I've told you, and more. And I got pretty much the same response from them that I'm getting from you. I was about to give them a demonstration of what the technology we found can do to prove to them that I'm no liar, and since they're all right there watching us," he said, nodding at a place in the parking lot just out of camera range, "I can show them, you, your viewers, and all the governments of the world at the same time. You'll have to believe that I'm telling the truth because I can do things like this."

With his hands behind his back, the young lieutenant pressed the button on his wristband. Several seconds later, just before the reporter could ask what he meant, he disappeared in a shower of blue sparks.

The woman stared at the vacant space for a few seconds, shook her head, and turned to the camera, microphone before her face like a shield. "This is Monica Webb for Channel Eight," she said, a dazed expression on her face. "Back to you, Mark."

CHAPTER TWENTY-EIGHT

Four months into the construction of Libra Base, it appeared that the U.S. government had decided on a course of action. Not bothering with subtlety, a series of late-night raids began, resulting in the arrests of hundreds of family members of those identified as being part of the Terran Alliance.

The problem with a pirated television signal is that it can't be interrogated. The pirates did manage to get the whole thing recorded, however, so no one missed any of it. The reporter was from a small station in Fargo, North Dakota, and she was breaking a story. Simon and Kitty had to rerun the recording to get all of the account.

The windblown reporter was standing in front of a chain-link fence, complete with manned sentry post and red-and-white-striped barrier blocking the road and some buildings seen well off in the distance.

"This is Sarah Parker reporting live from somewhere north of Devil's Lake, North Dakota. There are many lonely miles to travel to get to this place on dirt roads that haven't seen a road grader in almost twenty years, or so I've been told by local inhabitants. But the road we traveled today looked like it had been graded in the last few weeks. There are no towns nearby, making this a perfect place to … do what? "I'm standing in front of what was an Air Force refueling base until budget cuts closed it down almost fifteen years ago. But today, it appears to be a growing concern."

The camera panned across a barren plain, marred only by the secluded base. Close up, the freshly painted gatehouse had shiny new fencing stretching off to the left and right. There was a control tower and landing strips with associated buildings farther in, and smoke poured out of several chimneys in a cluster of buildings even farther away. The cameraman zoomed in on the plume of dust raised by a rapidly approaching vehicle, the reporter now almost off camera.

"I've received reliable information that this," she said and turned to look over her shoulder as the wind whistled through her microphone, "is the destination for literally hundreds, possibly thousands, of American citizens who have the misfortune to be related to people the government has decided are threats to its existence. Although I hadn't yet been born, I'm reminded of the roundup of American citizens almost seventy years ago because they had the misfortune to be of Japanese ancestry. And German. But there's been no attack here, if you don't count September 11th, of course, and there's also been no mention of anything like that coming from the White House."

A plane—large, green, and windowless—glided through the camera' s field of view, passing the obvious control tower as it got closer to the ground. The approaching vehicle, an unmarked Humvee, stopped and a figure stepped out of the passenger side. Clad in camouflage clothing and a black beret, the man stepped around the barrier and approached the reporter.

The officer said, "This is U.S. Government property. A secure facility. I'm going to have to ask you to leave."

Not much taller than the woman, he seemed to loom over her. The reporter spoke into the microphone, not the least bit frightened by the overbearing way he'd stepped into her personal space.

"Be happy to, uh, Colonel," she said pointedly looking at the eagles on his collar, "if you'd be so kind as to tell me just where this U.S. Government property is. I was under the assumption, as I'm sure all my viewers are," she said, waving at the camera, "that the U.S. Government property starts on the other side of that fence, leaving us outside your 'secure facility.'"

The officer loomed even further, as though acting out a lesson learned in some arcane military class on intimidation. "If you and your pal aren't out of here by the time my MP's arrive, I'm going to have you arrested, young lady."

"You *really* don't want to do that, Colonel," the woman said coolly, not flinching when the officer stepped into her space. She smiled thinly, "I can threaten, too. You don't want to say the wrong thing in front of a camera. The results could just plain haunt you for the rest of your life."

She maneuvered herself so the guard shack was a backdrop to her confrontation with the officer. "Now that we've gotten the amenities out of the way, sir, can you tell me what you did wrong to be put in charge of security at a secret illegal detention facility in the middle of nowhere?"

As loaded questions went, this one was about a six-and-a-half. The colonel turned red at the slight to his military expertise and then realized what the content of the last half of her question had implied. Before he could formulate a response, the pretty young reporter asked, "Why are hundreds, thousands, of innocent American citizens being rounded up in the middle of the night and transported here and other places around the country in planes just like those?

"My sources tell me that for the last two months, this base has been the focus of a lot of military attention—upgrading the security, refurbishing the buildings, getting the power and water back on. The curious thing is that none of the soldiers who pass through on their way here ever come into town. Not to visit, not to drink, not to buy their girls a souvenir, and not even to get away from Army food. I can understand the concept of a secure facility, Colonel, but no passes at all?"

Two more Humvees pulled up, disgorging eight armed soldiers. With their black-and-white MP armbands visible, the armed team fanned out to circle the confrontation.

A nasty grin crossed the colonel's face. "Okay, lady, you've just gotten yourselves arrested. I'll take your boyfriend's disc," he said, waving an MP forward, "and you two are going to wind up at the bottom of the deepest, darkest pit I can find."

A phone began ringing in the guard shack.

The reporter looked startled, as if realizing for the first time just how vulnerable she and her friend were. Then a grin that failed to reach her eyes flickered across her face. Never taking her eyes from the colonel's, she asked, "Disc? What disc?" And then louder. "Dwayne, if you brought the camcorder, I'm gonna see you canned."

"No, boss!" a voice from off-camera interrupted as the camera's viewpoint bounced slightly. "You said you wanted a live feed; you got a live feed."

"So I did, Dwayne, and I'd say it's a good thing you listened." She smiled at the officer again—not an expression of happiness but of pure feral glee. The prey was within her grasp, but she could still lose it all if she didn't spring her trap soon.

"It would appear that you don't know anything about electronics in the new age, Colonel." The soldiers had them almost surrounded now. "There isn't any disc, at least not here. That camera feeds directly to the antenna on top of the van, and that is pointed by computer at a satellite in geosynchronous orbit, beaming our little tête-à-tête into millions of homes even as we speak." She paused to let the information sink in, fighting desperately to keep from shaking or letting her voice break. "Now, exactly which deep, dark pit were you referring to?"

The colonel held his arms out to his sides, bringing the MP's to a halt. "Lady, all I can tell you is that this is a secure facility, and I'm not at liberty to discuss what happens inside that fence."

Dwayne's camera caught the guard inside the shack as he gingerly laid the phone down and walked toward the colonel.

Seeing the look on the approaching guard's face, the reporter knew her time was dwindling fast. Before the guard could interfere, she asked the one question all of this had been leading up to, virtually confirming the rumors a stunned public had been hearing about late-night governmental abductions from all over the country.

"For four days now, military units have been

pulling people out of their homes and taking them somewhere without a trace. All of the reports from Pensacola, Florida to Ottumwa, Iowa, to Portland, Oregon, have one thing in common, colonel—not one unit designation to be found. Odd, don't you think?"

The cameraman, brave beyond belief, deliberately zoomed in on the numbers painted on the Humvcc's bumpers. Where unit designations were usually found was only what appeared to be fresh coats of camouflage paint. He panned back to the colonel and reporter, lens passing slowly over a couple of the soldiers surrounding them before settling into place.

"What have the people you're holding done, Colonel?" the reporter asked. "When relatives and friends report these incidents to the police, they're told, 'We got word from Washington. It's out of our jurisdiction.' Senators and congressmen are being inundated with requests to help find these missing people, Colonel. The information I have says that some of them are being detained here. Why? And who ordered it? And what do so many disparate people have in common?"

The reporter looked at the camera, finally turning her back totally on the colonel. "Ladies and gentlemen, normally the profiles of people detained in raids of this type should match up enough for some kind of correlation to be made. Here we have, reportedly, Democrats grabbed up with Republicans, Catholics with Protestants, young and old, black and white. You name it, we have an opposite here. The occupations range from housewife to police officer, from grocery clerk to political official."

She turned back to her victim. "What have these

people done, Colonel?"

The guard, a sergeant according to the three stripes on his sleeve, finally got the colonel's attention, pointing emphatically to the phone. Flustered, and happy to get away from the little spitfire roasting him alive, he turned away, stepped into the guard shack, and picked up the phone.

Face considerably paler than before he'd stepped into the shack, the colonel walked woodenly back to the reporter. All the while, the camera followed his movements, even recording the silent, "Yes, sir's," he'd repeatedly uttered during the call.

"Miss, I'm afraid you've been misinformed about the purpose of this base. Unfortunately, due to national security restrictions, I'm unable to answer any more of your questions. Even though I'm unable to remove you from public lands, I *am* able to leave you with no further answers." Stiffly the officer turned to head back to his jeep and an apparent trip back to his command facility somewhere inside the fence.

"One last question, Colonel!" the reporter yelled. "It has nothing to do with any alleged detainees, I promise."

The officer, apparently against his better judgment, turned back to the reporter. "What?"

"I've interviewed many soldiers in my time, Colonel," the woman said. "One thing I've been struck by was the fact that every one of them was more than proud of his unit and branch of service. I notice that your uniform has no unit patch on it. It also doesn't have a designation over one breast pocket proclaiming your branch of service, or a patch with your name on it over the other pocket. Do you have an explanation as to why a senior officer would neglect those bits of military regalia?"

"Can someone tell me just what that ass was thinking when he went out to confront that... that reporter?" The last word was spit out with particular venom, and the question was assumed to be rhetorical, so neither agent answered.

The man in the expensively tailored suit delivered his edict from behind a massive oaken desk, his back to the two agents standing there as he looked out over the Washington, DC landscape. "I want him replaced within twenty-four hours, is that clear?"

"Yes, sir," said one of the two agents who'd watched the telecast with the director. "Twenty-four hours. Anyone particular to replace him with?"

"Anyone who can keep his mouth shut!" the suit proclaimed. "And you will begin the release of the detainees immediately."

"Sir!" one agent protested. "We just got them separated and haven't even started on the interrogations."

"I don't give a damn. This has attracted the attention of the White House. The only thing we can do is release the detainees, apologize, and make restitution. As quietly as possible."

"Sir, that will be admitting blame."

"Of course it will, stupid," the man behind the desk growled. "Someone has to be the scapegoat, and who better than some over-zealous idiot of a colonel who will never be heard from again?" He took a second to get himself back under control. "If we release most of the people we've already rounded up, then the few we keep won't be nearly as obvious, will they? The Hawkes' families are separated by thousands of miles. Their absences, along with a few families of some of their top people, will fade into the back pages of the newspapers without the others to bolster them. But the Hawkes, Simon and Katherine, will know that their people are still unaccounted for. And I want you to get that reporter, too. We need to find out who her sources are."

Lucy caught the third or fourth replay of the telecast and immediately had the feeling of butterflies dancing in her stomach—doing the polka in combat boots, to be more precise. She called Robert aside after the piece finished running. "Got any ideas, Rob?"

"About that?" He poked his thumb at the television screen. "Not really. You know how the country's been ever since September 11th." He shook his head slowly, a frown on his face. "Probably more of the same. I'd swear we're headed back to the bad old days of McCarthyism." Lucy crossed her arms on her chest and looked troubled. "What? Tell Uncle Rob what's bothering you, Luce."

"I can't say for sure, but I have to wonder if someone isn't trying to get at us all the way out here." Lucy shook her head as well and sighed like the weight of the world was on her shoulders. "Can you get in touch with your friends, Brandt and Collier, was it? I'd say send them a list of our personnel and let them see if there's any correlation between our people and the ones being picked up."

James Collier, Senior, slapped his hand on the table. For the last hour he'd been listening to a cock-and-bull story from Dave Brandt—whose tall tales were never to be believed—and his own son concerning spaceships, missing people, more spaceships and more missing people. The fact that the third Musketeer, Robert Grimes, was somehow involved only made Senior more determined than ever not to give any credence to the tale that was surely designed to separate him from an as-yet unspecified amount of cash.

But the bite never came. That's what had thrown him for the longest time. The list of hundreds of names, purportedly from Robert, lay on top of a stack of news clippings from papers all around the country.

"And they all match up, Dad," his son was saying. "Every one of those families arrested in the last four days has a connection to one of the names on this list." He tapped the white paper with his fingertip. "But this is the big news. Have you seen the morning paper yet?"

The elder Collier, still groggy from his rude awakening, hadn't made it much past his second cup of coffee and was just beginning to reach a level that would let him think effectively. "Not yet, I haven't. You two just dragged me out of bed, you know? So, what's the paper got to add to this sorry little story of yours, boys?"

By way of an answer, Dave pushed the newspaper across the table, scattering the piles of clippings. The elder man spun the paper around to better read the headline and froze. *MORE LATE-NIGHT ARRESTS IN DENVER AND SURROUNDING AREAS,* the top two lines screamed in bold print. The story beneath it laid out the details, complete with eyewitness accounts from neighbors and friends, and pictures of the abductees. One face in particular leapt out at the older man.

He picked the paper up and began to scan the three columns of print. There wasn't much substance, mostly filler on the missing persons and speculation as to who the abductors were, but two things, no, three, were clear—one, that the stories the boys were telling him were true, at least in part; two, that the government was somehow involved with all these unmarked cars and people who refused to identify themselves; and three, that John Wilder, one of the two abducted city councilmen and James Senior's long-time friend from their days as peace activists, was among the abducted.

"Two city councilmen and two police officers have been abducted, and there's been nothing but stonewalling from the police, even in the face of having to watch two of their own hauled away. Investigations are ongoing," was one quote. "We're doing all we can, considering the amount of information we have to go on," was another.

Senior read through the rest of the article and set the paper down. "So what do you want from me, boys? I'm still not saying I believe in all this spaceship crap, but something sure as hell is going on."

Jim Junior spoke first. "Robert gave us that list, Dad, and he says the names on it are their people. The clippings show that somebody is rounding up the families of the people on the list. We think you should help the people get away who haven't been picked up yet. Maybe to Canada or something," he finished lamely.

Robert and Michiko had wrought better than they knew. They'd known, of course, that the elder Collier had been a peace activist during the Viet Nam War, but they, along with his own son, hadn't known the older man's complete past. The fact was that he was the perfect man for such a situation. He'd helped set up and operate more than one underground network, funneling people out of the country so they wouldn't have to fight in a war they had no belief in. Now he was going to do it again, this time on his belief in the integrity of a mere boy (hadn't he been about that age when he'd gone to his first sit-in and spent the night in jail for it?) who just happened to be one of the two best friends his son had ever had. Dave had joined the two in high school, but Jim and Robert had been friends ever since grade school.

That expertise, so hard-won in the sixties, would be called on again to save more people from the depredations of a rampaging government. "I need to make some calls, boys, but I'm sure I can get something set up. After all these years, there are going to be some holes in the old network, but I'll bet we can get those filled pretty quickly." Changing the subject, he asked, "Are you two *sure* Robert is on the level about all this?" He glanced at the television, now detailing the highlights of a local collegiate sporting event as if nothing were wrong with the world as it spun in its orbit.

"Dad, we've been on the ship. Robert and 'Chiko took the four of us on a tour. We met the captain and some of the officers, as well as a few of the crew. There're hundreds, thousands, of them out there now. You saw the video. Watch it again and tell me you don't believe me."

Dave felt he had to make his contribution to the conversation. "Mr. Collier, there's more than that. There's nine hundred on the big ship alone. They have two bases, and they're building a third with a fourth in mind, and two ships have already been constructed. I'd guess we've got well over two thousand people actually in space. Then there's a few like us who recruit on the sly, so to speak."

The last words that came from the TV before the announcers signed off was their standard hook. "Stay tuned to this station for breaking news on the mysterious abductions as we get it!"

Fifteen minutes later, James the Elder was on the phone to one of his friends, ever mindful of the new technology capable of recording his call. "Echelon is up and running, Sam. So all I'm going to say is that we need to get some of the old crowd together at my place for a talk. This is like the most serious shit to come down since Nam, man." His attention was diverted by a banner running across the top of the muted TV screen. Grabbing the remote, he said, "Turn your set up! We may have more going on. I'm going to try to set my old VCR." He put the phone down and fiddled with the machine under the TV for a moment, missing a fraction of the story.

"This reporter has received reliable information that this," she said and turned to look over her shoulder as the wind howled through her microphone, "is the destination for literally thousands of American citizens who have the misfortune to be related to people the government has decided are threats to its existence."

The aging hippie picked the phone back up and

asked, "Are you listening to this? As soon as it's over, get over here and bring everybody still able to get around without a walker, will ya? I've got more calls to make."

The message time for something to get to Earth from the asteroid belt was on the order of thirteen minutes one way. Then there was the time spent waiting until an unsuspecting recipient realized his friend from outer space had left a message on the interplanetary answering machine. Robert didn't expect an immediate reply and wasn't disappointed. It was almost ten hours before a runner from Communications arrived with a response. Robert thanked him and closed the door. Calling Michiko over, he slid the miniature disc into the player.

"Got your message. Will try to see what we can find out. We'll need a few days to look into it. We'll call you back as soon as we know something," was the gist of the message.

Rumors ran through the *Galileo* like wildfire. The radio operator Robert had used to send his message to Earth started the guess-what-I-heard game before his shift was up. Within eight hours, the story was larger than life, with the governments of Earth planning to strike against the Alliance and use the hostages for a shield. Work slowed to a standstill while every breath was held, waiting on a response from Earth, and the source was the same as the one that had started the trouble in the first place.

Four days passed while the rhetoric grew hotter and

steamier on both sides of the issue. Someone was always glued to the television receiver, keeping track of the developing situation on Earth. National security versus civil rights was the topic on every show that boasted a discussion format and not a few of those that didn't. Experts bandied words, and while the words were sharp, the underlying tone was still a bit incredulous. "That our own country would treat its own citizens this way was so ..."

Entirely believable. The short shrift the Japanese Americans and German Americans got was brought out first, opening old wounds, and the Blacks and American-Indians jumped on the bandwagon, underlining the predominately white, callous, imperialism the United States had fallen heir to early on in its existence. A government, any government, is a living, breathing entity. It has the same basic instinct that single individuals have—the drive to survive—and it will do whatever it has to do to achieve that goal. It would walk over the lives and dignity of "inferior" races to ensure its growth. It would walk away with the lands of others in an attempt to achieve a manifest destiny it possibly shouldn't have envisioned. It later isolated the possible infection of Japanese and German Americans, appropriating their properties in the process, to ensure its own survival. Why *not* believe this newest revelation?

Ultimately, it was Simon's mystique as The Captain, and Kitty's as the unflappable Captain Kitty—though she would be shocked to know that she *had* a mystique—that averted what could have been the

Terran Alliance's first mutiny.

"We can't get there in time, anyway," he pointed out. "Our people are already under military control."

Kitty stood on a podium next to Simon on the *Galileo's* projects deck while the *Heinlein* rode beside the *Galileo*. Word of the raids had reached the *Heinlein* through the daily message relays, and Marsha rendezvoused with Simon as soon as she heard. She looked out over the crowd of anxious faces.

"What's done is done," Kitty said. "I don't mean to sound callous, but there's nothing we can do right now. According to the messages we're getting from our people on Earth, not all of us have been identified, so not all of our families have been targeted. Both Simon and I have relatives in custody, and so do several of the other officers—mostly those who chose to reveal themselves at various times during our last visits to Earth. I think the best thing is to wait and see what happens. The news has broken now, and you can bet that every effort is being made to find out who those people are and get them released, especially if they haven't done anything. And most especially if most of them are good, upstanding Americans, as they're going to be portrayed by every civil rights group looking for a platform to hang their name on. Those folks will do our job for us, and if they can't, well Simon has already said it. We hold the high ground and have the technological advantage."

"This is Sarah Parker, reporting for Channel Four News. In just a moment you'll see the second U.S.

military cargo plane to land within the last hour here at Denver International Airport. The first was laden with people being returned to their homes by the very agencies that were responsible for their illegal detainment in the first place. Planes just like this one are carrying people home from secret locations all over the U.S., like the one reported on in North Dakota." An Army-green plane bisected the camera shot, confirming the reporter's story. "The previous group declined to speak on camera, but we're hopeful that someone on this flight will be willing to talk with us about their ordeal at the hands of the very government their tax-dollars help to perpetuate."

Obviously trying to fill time, Parker said to the announcer on the other end of the camera, "I do believe that if there hadn't been such a mix of people picked up, there wouldn't have been as much fuss raised. By my best estimates, there were no less than four police officers, two city councilmen, a Baptist and a Lutheran minister, and a state representative caught in the largest sweep since the McCarthy era. We've been told that blame is being laid at the feet of over-zealous agents of an undisclosed government agency, and an internal investigation is underway."

Her expression, studiously neutral until that moment, cracked and a look of disdain passed across her face. "Democrats and Republicans alike are calling for an investigation into this latest abuse of power being laid at the front door of the White House. Spokesman Dan Goodall has stated that President Drake had no knowledge of the operation and was as stunned as the rest of the world by the revelation.

"The exposure of this atrocity has spurred Congress and the House to pass a unanimous resolution in record time. Coauthored by leaders from both parties, the resolution condemns the detention of American citizens without due process in the harshest terms without specifically naming individuals."

"Now that one's a little fireball," Simon said appreciatively as he watched a replay of that particular story. "I'm willing to bet it was her first broadcast a few days ago that got the ball rolling on getting our people out of jail. I think we should thank her personally, don't you, hon?"

Kitty stared at the screen for a few seconds before she said quietly, "That woman stuck her neck pretty far out. Someone's really not going to appreciate his applecart being overturned like that. I hope she's got eyes in the back of her head because she's gonna need 'em. And thank her? Sure. Why don't we give her an interview when we get home?"

It looked like the U.S. was going to have to admit that it had been treating with the Alliance, but no such confirmation was forthcoming. "What about all the videos of people beaming out?" one reporter shouted at the presidential press secretary.

"I told you," Dan Goodall said, "that I won't take any more questions on that subject. We're dealing with special effects, nothing more. I suspect that the people in those videos had some accomplices in the matter."

He didn't directly implicate the reporter, but the crowd knew what he meant. Since the news conference was composed entirely of reporters, his comment wasn't taken too well, and a sullen murmur began to make itself heard.

CHAPTER TWENTY-NINE

The months that followed saw the completion of Libra Base and the investiture of Victor McCord as its Commander. Those final two months also saw a lot of radio traffic between Simon and Kitty and the Brandt's and Collier's on Earth. It seemed that all of the detainees, as the hundreds were being called by the media, had been released as promised by an embarrassed administration. The problem was that neither Simon's parents nor Kitty's relatives—two aging aunts in Montana—along with several dozen others from top-ranking Alliance officers, were answering the calls being placed to them by people in the Brandt/Collier network.

Discarding the idea that all families would coincidentally choose the same time to go on vacation, Simon and Kitty suspected the worst. They wanted to keep the information from general knowledge until after Libra was turned over to Victor, so they called in the affected officers separately.

Simon privately vowed to show the Drake administration the folly of its ways. "I don't like the thought of them using our families this way," Simon declared to Kitty. Never really on the closest terms with his father, Simon still felt the anger boil up whenever he thought of it. Family is, after all, family. "Dirty pool, and I won't stand for it any longer than I have to. When we get back, we warn 'em first, and then we drop a rock in the ocean to prove we can do it. If our people are still not set free, we start dropping progressively bigger rocks. We can use the Parker woman to spread the word as soon as we get home. Just get Collier or Brandt to get in touch with her and set things up."

An orphan Kitty might be, but she did have relatives in Miles City. They'd never been truly close, but as Simon said, they were family. Besides, there was a principle at stake.

The last two months before Libra was able to breathe on its own were the toughest on Simon and Kitty. They tried several times through the radio link with Earth to call their respective families, interspersing their own message traffic with that of the others concerned about their families as well. Surreptitious inquiries revealed that their families were among the few still unaccounted for, of those who chose to admit to families at all.

The two talked together late into the night every night, growing more despondent as each message was returned marked: No response.

Curled into a small ball and sheltered in Simon's arms, Kitty asked quietly, "What are we going to do?"

"This is somebody's way of telling us they know who we are," Simon stated firmly. "They can't speak to us directly, but I'll bet they think they got their message across."

Kitty looked up questioningly. "And the message is?"

"Give up or you families get it, basically," Simon said. "But I'm not going to let that happen."

Kitty pushed herself away from Simon's side and stared at him. "What have you got up your sleeve?"

"Look," Simon said, standing up, "attention was what got the rest of the hostages released, and it'll do it again. I sent a message to Collier asking him to get in touch with that reporter, Sarah Parker. I figured she would love to get an exclusive, but Jim sent word back today that she has dropped out of sight. Nobody at the TV station knew anything about it. Even her cameraman, a guy named Dwayne, was missing. Cameras were still checked out to him, and everyone thought the two had taken off after another story."

"And?" Kitty prompted, after a long silence.

"Collier thinks he was followed after he left the station. Pretty sure of it, in fact. He thinks he lost whoever it was in a shopping center."

"So what are we going to do?" Kitty repeated.

"Nothing," Simon stated flatly. "Nothing is going to happen to our folks until they know that we know they have them."

"Wait a minute!" Kitty protested. "That kind of logic gives me a headache."

"The people being threatened," Simon said simply, "that's you and me, have to *know* there's a threat. Without that knowledge, there's nothing to make us change our course of action. Once they know that we know, they can begin to apply pressure."

"So as long as we don't respond, nothing happens?" Kitty asked, unbelieving.

"That's about the size of it," Simon said. "Our folks get away from the hassle of everyday life for a while and have a story to tell forever. There was another reporter who got another story aired about one of our guys—Grant, I think his name was. I want to use that reporter as a backup in case something has happened to Parker."

"But this is our secret for now?" Kitty asked.

"Right," Simon agreed. "For now."

The week before the *Galileo* was due to leave for Earth, Simon called a council of war. Kitty was present, as were Gayle and Stephen. Also present were Victor McCord, in his capacity as Base Commander, Marsha Kane, de facto Captain of the *Heinlein*, and Captain Lucy Grimes, just arrived from her trials in the newly named *Anne McCaffrey*.

"Isn't it a little harsh to call this a council of war, Simon?" Marsha looked a bit edgy at the thought.

"No, it isn't," Simon responded. "First, if you'll excuse the informality, here are your comets, Captain." He slid a black velvet box across the table. "Congratulations. Also, it's time we told you this. My parents and two of Kitty's aunts haven't been contacted yet either. And you know about several others, including Lucy's folks."

The revelation brought silence while the implications sank in. "It's been two months and you haven't said anything?" Gayle said, livid. "Why would you keep something like this secret? And why tell us now?"

"I haven't heard of anyone else who didn't get word back that their folks are safe. So it's just you and Kitty?" Stephen asked, glancing at Lucy.

"Somebody has figured out that you two are running the show," Victor said pointedly.

"We never made any attempt to hide the fact in the first place, and there are a few others as well,"

Simon said, shrugging his shoulders. "At least not after the first few weeks when we started to get rejects. We accepted a few people who later opted out when they found out how long they'd be gone. Had the same problem with the first group Stephen brought aboard, as I remember."

"The reason we didn't say anything until now was so we could get Libra finished," Kitty said firmly. "Then we go back with all three ships and get our folks out."

Simon spoke into the latest silence. "We don't know for sure yet where they are, but it would be a reasonable guess that they're at that same base the Parker girl exposed. With the number of Mambas available to us, as well as two battle cruisers and the *Galileo* herself, we stage a diversion, drop a shuttle into that base, and find our people. We release them quietly, so as not to embarrass their hosts, and then we sit down and talk about a technology release. It's a game of 'I show you my power, now you show me yours.' And I intend to win that game hands down."

Marsha nodded her head slowly. "So it *is* a council of war. You plan to attack the United States less than thirteen years after September 11th?"

"No," Simon stated flatly. "Just one small part of it. At night, and preferably overcast, if possible."

Lucy sat quietly in the corner of the ready room watching the bantering, questioning and planning go back and forth. As the newest member of this august group, she watched the interplay between the various personalities but held her tongue. She specifically noted the way Kitty stood beside Simon, lending her support both visually and vocally. The two played off of each other almost as if it was rehearsed. Then she realized that it was. This scene had been planned two months before, at least in a general way.

She wondered at her role and realized as well that it didn't really matter. The answers had already been figured out and courses of action plotted. All else was just window-dressing.

Lucy was jerked out of her reverie by Simon's question. She didn't register it at first, so lost was she in trying to figure out what was next. But since it had been addressed to the room in general, her lapse wasn't noticed.

"Why me?" Simon asked, complaining again that he wasn't the best person for the job. "Why should it be me who runs this show? There are any number of people who are better at organizing a group as disparate as this outfit is. There's one example right there! Two years ago, I would never have used the word 'disparate' in a sentence. What qualifies me to sit at the top of the heap, handing out edicts from on high?"

Lucy was amazed to hear the question. She started to answer, but Kitty spoke up first. "Because you're right," she said. "Everyone agrees that the *Galileo* can't be given directly to Earth. Doling out the technology is the only safe way to see that the people benefit before the governments and militaries do this time."

Gayle said, "The crucial test is whether our way costs fewer lives to accomplish."

"Is that lives lost or lives destroyed?" Stephen asked. "The technologies we're able to introduce will put so many industries out of business. Of course, it will also create more, but some of those displaced people won't be able to acclimate to the new reality. No matter what we do, we're bound to hurt somebody."

Lucy surprised the whole room, herself included, when she spoke up. "Are you kidding?" She let the front legs of her chair bang onto the deck and continued on to her feet. "You're the captain, and you," she said, turning to Kitty, "are Captain Kitty." She looked at Stephen and Gayle, including them in her next words. "You four are the Firsters. That's with a capital 'f,' in case you didn't hear it. You found the *Galileo* and figured out how to run her."

She turned her attention back to Simon. "Why you? Because you had a vision. The kind of vision people can get behind. The kind of vision that can transform a world, Simon. And all those people out there? They're behind you one hundred percent. Why? Because you let them come along on the journey. You allowed all of us to be a part of what you're building out here. There are nights," she heard herself saying, "when we don't sleep. We talk instead. And we can see the future, too. Why do you think we're all still here? Especially after what happened with Orion."

Stunned by her own temerity, Lucy sank back into her chair. "There's just something about you two that makes people trust you." She was silent for a few seconds, then scrunched down in her chair and added, "And the people you pick to be in charge. And God help me, I'm one of them now." she muttered quietly.

Simon looked at Kitty after Lucy's outburst and then at the rest of the room. "Who says I'm right? And even if I am, why can't someone else be just as right and sit here instead of me? There's an entire government down there that says I'm wrong and is trying to take it all away from us. And until they got caught at it, they were fucking with our families— still are with Kitty and me and a few others. Do they know more than I—than we—do?"

"We have the strength and power to do whatever we want," Stephen said almost apologetically. "As long as we don't abuse that power, we have the right to choose for ourselves how we deal with this situation. No one down there is any better equipped to deal with this than we are. You've drilled that into all of us from the very first day."

Marsha snorted. "Give me two hours with a history book and I'll give you at least six examples in recorded history of larger, less technological societies absorbing smaller, better equipped ones. Of course, I can name a few where the reverse is true, too. Just proves that history is a crap shoot." She smiled slightly. "Now that I've got everyone's attention, which I didn't want, by the way, I have to say that I agree with Lucy. And to put a word on it, you've become a legend, the four of you. There's a mystique that follows you around, and it makes people listen to you and concern themselves with your ideas and opinions."

Lucy, finding strength from Marsha's support, said, "Look at where you have us, and what we've accomplished because of you. Most of us are sci-fi freaks, and you've given us outer space. I remember you talking about a dream of an independent group, a nation, existing not on the Earth but above it. Others heard it as well. Eventually you quit talking about it.

We thought you quit talking about it because your dream was on track. Hell, after all this time, it has become a vision—if not of yours then for the rest of us. And the women share the vision as much as the men. They see half of the First Four being female. Besides, aren't we calling ourselves the Terran Alliance now, anyway?"

Kitty sat beside Simon in shock. Her contact with his body told her that he was in at least the same condition. The words of the two younger women didn't threaten her sanity as much as shake it for a minute or two. To think that she had a mystique! More to the point, she realized that they were right. Multiple confrontations, associations, and interactions raced through her mind, and she saw how the crew acted differently toward both her and Simon, as well as Gayle and Stephen.

She hadn't had time to go into some of the deeper ramifications before Simon stood up, breaking her train of thought. The expression on his face was one she could only think of as distasteful. His words, when he finally spoke, were quiet enough that some had to strain to hear them.

"All I ever wanted from the first day we came aboard was to be a ship's captain, not 'The Captain.' Remember, I'm a sci-fi freak, too. I want to go where no man has gone before first, damn it! I need to think." He looked around the room, bent down, kissed Kitty on the forehead, and said, "Someplace where nobody is sitting around waiting for an answer."

"Damn, I'm glad I don't have to make *his* decisions," Victor said, concern and relief evident in his voice.

Simon automatically made his way to the observation bubble, that unique blister on the outer skin of the ship. A favorite place for crewmembers to visit, Simon was surprised to find it empty. He walked over to one of the walls and stared out at the stars. The *Galileo's* speed, such as it was sitting next to Libra in the asteroid belt, meant that the perspective didn't change much from minute to minute, and hardly at all even from hour to hour.

Simon looked through the transparent metal of the bubble wall. "What a contradiction in terms," he thought. "Transparent and metal, too." He looked to the left and saw the *Heinlein* and then to the right and got a view of the *McCaffrey* riding shotgun. The bulk of Libra was out of sight beneath the body of the huge factory ship, although a portion of a construction spar was visible below the *McCaffrey*, pod jockeys carefully moving another beam into position. Nobody knew why every ship in the database that was battle-cruiser-size and larger had one of these bubbles built into the plans, but it was one of the things the engineers had decided not to change when they began to redesign the ships for human convenience.

Simon had never been a deeply religious person. His view was that though he felt that the human race was more than just a cosmic accident, no caring God would let some of the things that had happened happen, free will be damned. But standing here, looking out at the vista that drew visitors like a Mamba drew pilot hopefuls, he experienced something more than a vague feeling of something greater. Not a conversion, exactly, but a willingness to believe.

Simon was peripherally aware of others coming into the bubble, much as he was aware of the faint vibration bleeding up through the deck plates into his legs. Most visitors tended not to stay long when they saw the captain, hands clasped behind his back, staring out at the infinite dark and obviously lost in thought.

In actuality, though, Simon wasn't really thinking. All his thoughts on the subject had already been thought and all the arguments made, both pro and con. Now he waited. He waited for his subconscious to reveal the decision. After a time, he no longer saw the stars outside the bubble, nor did he see the other ships, running lights ablaze, parked on either side. His mind began to lay out the possibilities, much as a chess player laid out the game many moves ahead.

Simon's mental state was not one that lent itself to straight-line thinking. It was more closely akin to something Native Americans produced intentionally, and it had been brought on by a combination of factors that would not normally exist simultaneously in his life. Worry over family had been lurking in a deep, dark part of Simon's mind for months, pushed there by the rationalization that the government wouldn't really do anything to hurt them to get his cooperation. This was heaped on top of stress, which was heaped on top of exhaustion, with a bit of hunger thrown in for good measure. Now, though, he opened his mind to all potential outcomes.

He wandered through the possible futures, the patterns forming and reforming, the scenarios playing themselves out, sometimes logically and sometimes not. His mind sifted through the various scenarios, evaluating, discarding, searching for a way through the clutter of possibilities that would lead to the outcome he and a lot of others felt was best for the human race. The feeling of not being alone pulsed up through the floor with the ship's vibration, helping to crystallize his decisions.

The visions ended, and Simon finally stirred from the position he'd held for so long, feeling the ache in his knees and back. Decisions and goals finally accepted, Simon stretched the kinks out of his muscles, and with a determination that hadn't been in his step when he'd walked into the room, he headed off to find something to fill the void in his midsection.

Kitty sat in bed and looked at Simon over the mangled remains of the snack tray he'd brought in at three a.m. She shook her head slowly, red hair swaying almost hypnotically. "No apologies, dear. You had to travel your own road to reach the same destination. I have faith in you, and so does everyone else. You just needed to learn to trust yourself."

Simon pushed a piece of cantaloupe across the plate to Kitty and then speared the last piece of watermelon for himself. "You've known for a long time, haven't you?" he asked. "That you were committed to this vision Lucy and Marsha are babbling about."

"Ever since Orion," she admitted, nodding. She stuck her tongue out as Simon bit into the watermelon, taking the last piece of fruit from the plate. "At least consciously. On the other hand, I think my subconscious may have been a little behind my conscious, you know?" She smiled slightly, unconsciously rubbing the numb spot on her right hand, the final physical reminder of her own recent digression from reality.

"There's just one more question to be answered," Simon noted.

"And that is?"

"My decision. Is it fate, destiny, or just colossal arrogance?"

CHAPTER THIRTY

Those same two months before Libra's completion also saw design changes to the newer ships that moved medical services to various places throughout the ships rather than consolidating them in one place. There would also be wider corridors, and generally speaking, a more user-friendly design.

It was also during this time that Dr. Penn signed off on Kitty's complete recovery, and she began to fly Mambas again. She always had her particular craft either serviced or signed off by the head of Flight Services, who'd been trained by Chief Anson Hargrove.

This was the time, as well, to formulate plans for the meeting between Simon and the vice-president. The Alliance's technological advantages were now evident, and most were available as trade goods. At this point, it was only left for the governments of Earth to formally reveal the existence of the Alliance and supply the bases Simon needed for open recruitment. Negotiations for technology rights could then begin after the rest of the hostages were released. Trying to decide what to say to the man, anticipating possible questions or comments from the opposing side, and wondering who—more importantly than any of the above—was going to be involved in the planning and negotiations, was a nightmare from the word go.

One of Kitty's contributions was to get a complete roster of all personnel actually in space at the moment. She was finding out what they knew, what they'd studied, what their hobbies were, and anything else that might shed some light on who they could go to for this most delicate of proceedings. Up until this point, anyone who wanted to volunteer had only needed to be at a collection point and they were beamed aboard, trained, and moved to a more permanent station. Now, however, finding out who each and every one of those people were and what each one knew had become a priority.

Her thought had been that with as many college-age people aboard the ships and stations as there were, surely some of them had been studying something that would be of some use to them. Sure enough, three political science majors were working aboard Orion and Gemini. Simon sent Marsha Kane in the *Heinlein* to pick them up and trade personnel so neither station would be shorted.

As this project worked its way towards completion, Dr. Penn used the radio and the Collier/Brandt connection to try and find a replacement. He also wanted to see if he could recruit volunteers from the medical community for their basic medical teams, as well as for the slowly expanding Alliance Fleet.

Using Stephen to plan most of the details and getting Victor involved in the production planning, Simon got a blueprint for a planet-side base started. What he was looking for was something eye-catching and futuristic since it would be one of the most televised structures on Earth for a while. At the same time, he needed it to perform the functions of recruiting center, headquarters, living areas, and embassy. Simon agreed that it would be a good idea for the Alliance to build their own structure in order to show their expertise, not to mention the fact that there were some aboard who remembered stories about the fiasco of allowing the Russians to build the American embassy in Moscow. It had been so riddled with surveillance devices that it'd had to be torn down and rebuilt from the ground up. Another consideration was the fact that their materials would be proof against anything on Earth other than a nuclear bomb, and the new shield technology could cover even that eventuality.

Simon had originally favored having the first base constructed in the United States, since that was his home country and that of most of the folks crewing the various ships and bases, and he brought this up at one of the first sessions. But after discussion with his new planning staff, it was deemed best to place the first base somewhere in Europe—most likely Switzerland, if possible, as that country had such a long tradition of strict neutrality.

Another topic that got a lot of attention was the requirement that anyone who wanted to could come to any one of the bases and apply. How the various countries worked that one out was going to be something to see, that was for sure, since so many applicants were going to be from places outside the host countries. Another thing to be put forth was that only four things would prevent anyone from volunteering—a physical inability to perform, having a record, intolerance of others, and not being able to speak English. No one thought this last requirement was troubling since English was the most widely spoken language on the planet for business purposes and had been for years. And the press would have a field day with the fact that race, religion, gender, country of origin, and adherence to a particular governmental system wasn't going to be a consideration.

"So," Simon commented, "we've chosen a location, assuming those on Earth will agree to it, and we've set a platform of who we'll accept as volunteers, which is virtually anybody. We do need to keep in mind that from the very first applicants, any or all of them could be spies or plants looking to steal the technology we don't want to release. I'd still prefer to accept volunteers from outside the official channels—that is, from the friends, family and associates of our current volunteers. These will provide a continuing group of people we can be relatively certain we can trust."

Ken Baker, a former construction coordinator on the *Gemini*, asked, "How will we keep people out of sensitive areas, Captain? They'll have to be placed in positions all over the ships and stations. What's to keep them from sneaking in and, say, photographing some installation or other?"

Kitty decided it was time to let out one of the secrets of the wristbands.

"The wristbands you're all wearing can be programmed to either sound an alarm on the command deck or shock the wearer mildly. The shocks get stronger if an attempt is repeated or if someone keeps getting too close to a proscribed area or thing."

She went on to relate a little about the incident with Agent Daniels' wristband the day he tried to get close to a Mamba. "Of course, that function isn't to be bandied about. We may want to see if someone will try to get into a restricted area. We can set their wristband not to shock them and just alert Command. Easier to catch them in the act, so to speak. And pictures of things aren't going to help much without the specs and the factories to produce them."

Simon took the conversation back up. "What I envision is that after we finish number four, which will be named Taurus, by the way, the *Galileo* will be put into a permanent Earth orbit. That way, she can use her transporter to bring up volunteers for transfer to other ships or bases."

Sylvia Parker—poly-sci major, former pod jockey, and current adviser to the command staff—interrupted. "Captain, why not just build a space station in Earth orbit? They're doing that right now—that ISS, they call it, the International Space Station. It will only house ten or twelve people, at best, and requires constant maintenance and resupply. We can build a bigger, better one and do it faster and cheaper. Not only that, but it would have gravity, and if built big enough, it could have its own transporter. Give it some form of propulsion, and it could move to whichever base needed to upload volunteers or download returnees. And it would have the advantage of leaving the *Galileo* not tied down to a purely static function. That just seems so wasteful."

After several months of meetings while Libra Base was being completed, the subjects began to get rehashed and rethought to the point that it seemed that every eventuality had been explored and planned for. Simon decided that nothing more could be gained at the time from further meetings, so he called a halt to them.

"I'd like you to stay aboard, though. Sooner or later, we'll need to get back into this once I've gotten the first responses from the vice-president and his advisers. He's going to want to get all he can for a little bit of land and freedom for our people, but I won't work with this family thing over my head. I don't want to give away too much at one time; we need to keep something in reserve. So, for now, people, I want to thank you for all your input. Feel free to come see me if anything occurs to you. Beyond that, we'll see about finding you something to do on board to keep you busy. Yes, I'm afraid you'll have to go back to work, but once we get back to Earth and start negotiations, I'm sure we'll reactivate this committee."

And so, Libra approached completion. The third daughter of the immense *Galileo* was about to begin her own journey.

Simon and Kitty found themselves alone in the observation bubble. Most people found reason to be elsewhere when the Captains Hawke showed up, knowing the fondness they had for the bubble and the paucity of time they had to spend enjoying each other's company, which was one reason their visits of late had been rather infrequent. It seemed that everyone was doing a dance to see that no one overstepped the bounds of propriety by monopolizing that popular spot.

This night, though, would be a little different.

Since Libra's *Sundiver* had returned, her powered sections were ablaze. Normal construction techniques saw to it that a power core was fired up as soon as possible, so most off-vessel construction didn't require the *Galileo* to provide power to anything but her own massive onboard factory complex.

Simon and Kitty stared out at the vast, nearly completed base and watched the pod jockeys installing the final beams around the construction cage. The personnel staying behind had already been chosen and moved to the habitat section, lessening the crowding considerably. And first thing tomorrow, the *Galileo* would head back to Earth and the next chapter in human history.

Kitty and Simon sat together on a bench that had been constructed around three-quarters of the inside of the observation dome. Kitty leaned into Simon's side, at ease with the familiar weight of his arm around her shoulders. She gazed out into the darkness and watched the lights of Libra and the few remaining construction pods that were still moving about.

"You know," she said, "this is a real strange position to be in for bringing this up, but you should know about it if you don't already." She felt Simon stiffen a little, so she patted him on the leg and said, "Relax, lover. It's nothing bad. Just odd. I heard something strange a few days ago, and I went down to check it out. You won't believe what I found. You'll have to go see for yourself."

"And who or what are we talking about?" Simon asked, turning away from the infinite vista to look down into the face of the woman who'd never steered him wrong in all the years he'd known her.

"Our good friend, Agent Daniels," was the reply.

"Let me guess—planning a mutiny?"

"No, dear. I said you wouldn't believe it, and that would be all too easy to believe. What he's actually doing... I believe the man has finished all of his interviews because as far as I can tell, he hasn't conducted one single interview since talking to Marsha, Lucy, and me after our battle." Simon started to pull away, but Kitty wouldn't let him. She already had both arms around his waist and just held tighter.

"You... he... when you were still... That man is about to get his ass so kicked!"

Kitty spun on the bench to face her husband and placed a hand on his chest. "Simmer down, darling. First thing he did was come to our quarters three days after I got back and was allowed visitors."

"Well, yeah, I knew he'd been there."

"Of course you knew he was there. Rukia told you about it. That was the job you gave her."

Simon pulled away from her, adding a bit of distance for safety's sake. "You knew about that?"

Kitty bestowed a withering look on her not-so-sly mate. "How long have we been married? Of course I knew about it. I suspected it from the beginning. You've always been protective. And now that we're here, you have to be in three places at once, and you have to get someone else to be there in your place. Well, the mistake you made was an obvious one. You assigned a woman to me. We bond easier than men do, dear, so my suspicions were confirmed very shortly. We told you what you needed to know and no more.

"Anyway, back to Agent Daniels. All he did at that time was to request an interview when I felt up to it. So stay off his case about that. He asked nicely, so when I was able, I gave him his interview.

"But what's been going on is amazing. You know he went down to report to his superiors when we were last at Earth. When he came back up, we made sure he didn't bring any contraband with him. We've allowed him to have a recording device, and he's used it for his interviews. He's also had the use of a video camera, as long as he stayed away from sensitive areas. The thing is, when we had his bags checked, we didn't pay attention to the other things he brought aboard. No one said a damn thing about him bringing reading material. And he did."

Confusion played across Simon's face. "Reading material? Are we dealing with a pervert? Why would you think reading material worth bringing to my attention? Am I going to have to get involved after all?"

"No, dear," Kitty said with a sigh. "The type of reading material he brought aboard—well, he's opened a school. He's teaching some of our people down on the lower decks how to read. We've surrounded ourselves with the cream of the crop up here, so to speak, and haven't had time to get to know the rest of our people very well. Some of those surveys we requested are what got my interest started. We have another ship ready to be crewed now, Libra about ready to be commissioned, and two more ships slated to be finished within weeks of Libra's completion. We're about to almost double our personnel, and we don't know the people we have right now.

"I talked to one of the agent's roommates, a Crewman McNalley. I'm pretty sure that's where

Daniels got the idea. I don't know if you remember McNalley, but he came aboard with Chief Hargrove in that group of construction workers Marsha helped recruit at the beginning. Did you know Hargrove's her uncle? That's not for public consumption, Simon. For some reason, they don't want their relationship to be common knowledge. I think Chief Hargrove doesn't want to appear to be using Marsha to get ahead. Why he'd think that is beyond me. The man's a genius in his own right."

Simon shook his head. "I really don't know McNalley all that well. We met a time or two, I think."

"And there is no real reason you should. He's a quiet man, and the best pod jockey we have. He's a smart man, but he's from a place where book smarts don't go much past the seventh grade, if that far. He's older than the average, too—a bit older than us. Hell, Marsha and Lucy are both twenty-four years old and commanding ships. And he gets embarrassed about how he speaks whenever he's around our younger, college-trained people. They make him feel inferior. Apparently this got to Daniels, and when he went down to report to his bosses, he came back with a copy of Hooked on Phonics and began to teach McNalley. It got around to some of McNalley's friends, and for the last three months, Daniels has almost exclusively been teaching school to those men. Haven't you noticed his absence?"

"As long as the computer's proximity alarms didn't go off, I didn't care what he did. No love lost there, hon," Simon admitted.

Kitty went on. "Well, I went on a rambling inspection tour a few days ago, and I found him holding a class on deck seven in one of the crew rec rooms. With a slate and chalk, for God's sake. Where he got those, I'm not sure, but I think he has an 'in' with some of the manufacturing crew. And he's teaching our people to read, write and speak better. He's even teaching them grammar! I was totally stunned by what I saw. And trust me, it's not something he set up overnight. The crewmen I've spoken to are pretty adamant about that. He had to be cajoled into it, but once he started, it seems to have snowballed. And this has apparently been going on for six months, off and on, and almost full time for the last three months.

Simon gazed out onto the night. "Maybe I misread the man. How was I to know? He hounded us, stole our stuff, and made a general nuisance of himself, so I put him right under our noses where he couldn't hurt us." Simon shook his head. "And he still surprised me."

Kitty slid back beside him. "I think you should have a talk with him. You two are a lot alike, you know, and I mean more than exterior plumbing. He was in the Air Force, too. Did you know he served in Vietnam? And he's a prideful, stubborn man, just like you. Don't look at me like that—you are, and you know it. Anyway, I think he's really a nice person. The fact that he's an FBI agent who got on the wrong side of us is no reason not to make an effort. Go talk to him, dear. Please. For me."

"Well," Simon said sullenly, "will you be satisfied if I say I'll think about it?"

Kitty snuggled back into the crook of her man's arm. "Yes, I'll be satisfied if you say it again without that growl in your voice and make me believe you mean it."

Kitty felt the muscles in Simon's back relax and he said, "Okay. You're right. I'll have a talk with him—a civil talk. Are you happy now?"

"Yes, dear. Let's go to our quarters and leave the dome to someone else."

The commissioning ceremony for Libra was becoming a standard thing for Simon, as well as quite a few of the crew of the *Galileo*, but it definitely wasn't for the crew who'd built it. By this time, many of the permanent crew of the *Galileo* had been aboard for over a year and a half, but Libra personnel had only been out there for a little over six months. For them, the novelty hadn't really worn off yet, and they were soon to make Libra their home, as well as their workplace. With this in mind, Simon went to great pains to sound sincere and make the ceremony as upbeat as possible. The last thing he wanted was for people to get the idea that they weren't doing great things, and that was all too possible when great things became a part of everyday life.

As he stood on the *Galileo's* project deck and stared out at the upturned faces, Kitty's words came back to haunt him. He didn't know most of those faces, and quite a few of them were older than the average, as she'd said. His gaze slid over the crowd, and he wondered for a moment which one was McNalley.

Giving himself a mental shake, he started to speak. He praised the dedication of the individuals who were already moved into quarters on the station they'd built. He praised the ability and perseverance of the pod jockeys, shuttle crews, and factory teams.

And he extolled the virtues of the lives they were all about to embark on. As he spoke of the future he foresaw, Simon told them of the heights to which humans could aspire and painted a picture of those in the audience as the forerunners of that future. He reminded them of the folly, too, of thinking that just because they were first that meant they were better.

"It's like being a gunfighter in the Old West," he said, shaking a finger back and forth. "There's always somebody faster than you out there. What we do today and tomorrow will be ho-hum to those who follow even twenty years from now. Don't let that stop you from striving, though. Those who follow won't be able to outdo us without the groundwork we're laying. They wouldn't have anywhere to start if we hadn't built it for them."

He looked out through the shimmering veil of the force field at the station beyond. "It seems to have become a tradition in even this short amount of time for a Commissioning Day ceremony to be followed by a party. Far be it from me to hold up tradition any more than I have to. Ladies and gentlemen, it gives me great pleasure to officially name our third base Libra Base, and name as the Base Commander, Commander Victor McCord."

Following the program that had become a tradition, Victor walked up onto the dais from one side, and, in a slight departure, Kitty from the other. The two reached Simon together and Simon turned to Kitty, opened the black velvet case she carried, and one at a time, pinned the twin, wreath-encircled gold stars of a Base Commander on Victor's lapels. Turning to the crowd, he announced, "Ladies and gentlemen, Base Commander Victor McCord."

Once the cheering died down, he said, "Commander McCord, it is now my duty to relinquish command of Libra Base. Do you accept command?" At Victor's acknowledgment, he pulled the dedication plaque from its hiding place and handed it to Victor, saying, as he had four times now, "Hang it in your reception area, Commander, and good luck." It read:

LIBRA BASE
COMMISSIONED 6 NOVEMBER 2013
BASE COMMANDER VICTOR McCORD,
COMMANDING

Turning back to the crowd below, he said, "Now, with the exception of the crew that must remain on duty, it's time to party!" Cheers resounded throughout the bay until Simon held up his hand. "One of these days I'll figure out whether those cheers are for the end of the speech or the start of the party. Those of you who have duty in the morning or next shift, hangovers are okay, but make sure you're able to do your jobs. Food processors on all decks have been unlocked to provide beer! Dismissed!"

Simon found Kitty and Stephen waiting at the foot of the dais. "Just like old times, huh?" he asked, thinking about the other two bases they'd commissioned in the past year and a half.

"That's true," Stephen answered, "especially when you consider 'old times' to have been just two years ago. And I heard you mention a party. I came from Communications just before the ceremony, and both the *Heinlein* and the *McCaffrey* are on their way in. Lucy and Marsha wanted to be here, but it didn't work out. Actually, the *McCaffrey* will arrive first by about an hour, according to scan"

The three officers walked toward the lift to deck three.

Kitty gibed, "I'm betting you can hardly wait for the *Heinlein* to dock so you can see Gayle again, huh?"

Stephen stammered, "G-Gayle? Um, well, uh, yeah." He seemed to get flustered every time her name was mentioned. "I, uh, we were, uh ..."

Simon began laughing so hard that he had to hold onto the wall of the lift to stay on his feet.

Kitty slapped him on the shoulder and said, "Don't be such an insensitive clod, you, you, man, you." Turning back to Stephen, she said, "Okay, look. We know that you were just 'uh.' Everybody knows that you were just 'uh.' We've known forever. Actually, Stephen, there's been a pool going for I don't know how long now."

"A pool? What kind of pool?" Alarm was evident in his voice even as the question squeaked past bloodless lips.

Kitty grinned. "Why, when you two are going to get married, of course."

The blood drained from the rest of Stephen's face and his eyes went wide in shock. "Married? Us? I don't know what to say." He staggered back until his shoulders touched the wall of the lift.

Kitty stepped up beside him and put an arm around his waist. "Of course you don't know, dear. The man is always the last to know." With her free arm she elbowed Simon. "Get on the other side and help me hold him up. We'll get him to the Officers' Mess, prop him up in a chair, and leave him there until Gayle can get here to collect him."

Parties proceeded as parties do. And in the Officers' Mess, the table that had been set up for the senior officers held Simon, Kitty, Victor, and Stephen, who, after his third drink was heard talking to himself with only the occasional decipherable word, such as "married?" and "me?"

Trying to ignore the stricken Stephen, Simon turned the talk to other things. "I'll tell you right now, people," he said to the group gathered at the captain's table, "number four, Taurus Base, will take longer to build than any of the first three. She's going to be able to build the really big ships—destroyers, large freighters, and another *Galileo*. We've already got the plans laid out. Victor said it would take the best part of a year, not counting the power plant and the *Sundiver*."

Kitty spoke up. "I thought this was supposed to be a party. How about less shop talk and more beer?"

Simon's commlink beeped, and he turned away from the table for a moment. When he turned back, he said, "The *McCaffrey* just docked. Lucy will be along shortly. And scan has the *Heinlein* about an hour out."

The two of them looked over at Stephen, and Kitty said, "Well, we better cut him off or Gayle will kick both our butts."

Simon, feeling the effects of more than one drink himself, said, "She's not gonna kick my butt, I guarantee you that. I outrank her."

Kitty looked up at Simon and replied, "You'll think 'outrank' if she gets here and finds him too far gone for her to get anything intelligent out of him. Don't forget, she's a martial arts champion."

Lucy Grimes, accompanied by the Greenes, arrived in time to ask, "Are we talking about Commander Miller? If we are, I'm in complete agreement with Captain Kitty. She looked around, raised her arm and her voice, and called, "Orderly. Two pots of coffee for the captain's table, please." Gesturing for the Greenes to join her, she sat down facing Kitty and Simon. Looking at Kitty she asked, "How are you doing these days?"

"Fit as a fiddle," Kitty replied. "I got a clean bill of health a week ago. Would you care for a game of Z-Tag to prove it?"

Lucy held up both hands. "Oh, no. I'll take your word for it. Besides, we don't have the facilities on the *McCaffrey* to keep in practice. To Simon she said, "Our scans showed the *Heinlein* about an hour behind us, so Marsha should be along shortly. And I'm sure Gayle will be with her. Just how is it that Stephen has gotten himself into such a state when he had to know Gayle was getting in?"

Simon looked at the young captain and said, "Someone let the cat out of the bag about the pool."

'Chiko spoke up for the first time. "No wonder he's half tanked! Who blabbed?"

Kitty confessed. "I did. The poor man's been hanging long enough. And if he hadn't found out, things would have stayed the same until hell froze over."

'Chiko looked first at her husband, then at the rest of the group, and said, "Commander Miller won't like this." To Kitty she said, "Captain, this isn't wise."

"Gayle Miller has been my best friend for well

580

over thirty years. I feel relatively certain that I'll come out of this alive and in one piece. Besides, *someone* had to move the process along. She wasn't going to say anything, and *he,*" she said, gesturing at the gibbering subject of their discussion, "certainly had no idea. Besides, this is just the push the two of them need. They're likely to be married by the time we leave Earth next."

"And which dates did you have in the pool, Captain?" Robert Greene innocently asked Kitty.

Kitty pulled herself up to her full height, and in her haughtiest voice, announced, "I never bet a nickel on a date. Please check the pool if you don't believe me. So I get nothing out of them getting married on any specific date." An evil grin passed over her face, and she added, "Except for singing." At this point, she performed a small gyration in her chair, her two fists held together, making small circles in front of her chest as she sang, "Another one bites the dust, another one bites the dust, uh-huh!"

Everyone at the table went into fits of laughter, except, of course, Stephen.

Two pots of coffee and two unassisted trips to the bathroom later, Stephen's world seemed quite a bit more stable, the thought of marriage notwithstanding. So Kitty wasn't too worried when Gayle walked into the room behind Marsha. The two newest arrivals found places to sit at the now crowded captain's table, Gayle in a seat that magically appeared next to Stephen. She wrapped her arms around him and kissed him until some joker called out, "Get a room!"

She leaned back in her chair and licked her lips.

"Hmm. Beer, for sure, and you got a rum and coke from somewhere. Able to navigate on your own, lover?"

Stephen, full of pride of self after two successful trips to the bathroom, replied, "I'll have you know I'm perfectly sober."

Gayle, in true form, couldn't resist. "Of all the things you're perfect at, being sober isn't one of them at the moment."

Stephen's blush was seen to go past his collar, but it didn't stop him from asking, "What do you know about a marriage pool? That seems to be the major topic of discussion this past hour." In a wounded voice, he said, "And they're talking about me like I'm not here."

Gayle got a guarded look on her face. "Well, I *do* know about it. It always seemed like more of a joke to me than anything else."

Seeing a chance to get her on the defensive, Stephen asked, "You think a marriage between us is a joke? Am I that bad a catch?" In a louder voice, he asked, "Is there anyone who wants a slightly used astronomer?"

The same joker who'd spoken earlier said, "Slightly is the wrong word to use, but I'll take ya!"

Gayle looked around quickly, unable to identify the culprit. "Why don't you come with me, Stephen? It seems that we have some things to discuss." She glared at all the innocent faces at the table. "I have an idea who's responsible for this, and I'll get you back, Simon."

Simon choked on his beer as Gayle towed Stephen behind her out of the room. "Why me?" he wailed. "I'm innocent."

Kitty laughed. "That is the absolute last word I would use to describe you, husband-mine, even knowing it was my fault. I'm sure you've done *something* this will even the scales for."

As Stephen was towed out the door, the unknown joker couldn't resist one more shot. "If he isn't perfect, send him back. We'll show him how to get the job done!"

CHAPTER THIRTY-ONE

The morning the *Galileo* was due to depart Libra space, Simon called all of his officers together. "This is the last time we'll be together for a while. I want to thank each of you for your assistance and understanding. I particularly want to thank you, Victor, for sticking it out here."

He rubbed his hands together in anticipation. "There are a couple of things that need to be attended to before we move out, so long as I have some high-powered witnesses present. It's been brought to my attention that we, I, need to get a couple of things straight. So, with no further ado, let's get this done."

Gayle stepped forward, holding the now-familiar black velvet box. "First, I am *officially* creating a new staff position—Wing Commander. The job is going to entail keeping track of Mamba production and the training of pilots, initially. I can have anything tacked on later that I see fit. Captain Hawke, step forward."

Kitty stepped up in front of Simon, and he removed her old insignia and pinned on her new ones, showing them to her first. The usual silver comet was central to the design, encircled by a pair of golden wings. "You are authorized to commandeer whomever you need for your office and staff," he said, grinning. "You can thank me later." He stepped back a pace and saluted her.

He looked at the assembled officers. "Next, to

formalize a promotion I've already made, Marsha has already been promoted to the *Heinlein's* . I'll see to it that you get a proper plaque for your reception room, Marsha. And see me later. We need to talk."

Galileo left Libra Base behind. Ahead of them lay another base to be built—an even more extensive base capable of building big ships. Its location was already known. A sizable cluster of asteroids had been found that would provide the materials to keep it in operation for decades, possibly longer. Taurus Base was going to take close to a year to build, but first came several trips to Earth. One ship was already finished, and two others would be ready soon enough that starting Taurus wasn't wise until they were crewed as well. That would put five ships in space, not counting the *Galileo*, and all the Mambas that went with them.

These ships would be cruising throughout the system, patrolling, cataloging the bits and pieces, getting more definitive data on planets and moons, and training their crews. And watching.

Kitty, who as yet had no staff or specific duties, spent as much time with Simon as possible. Attempting to work out a table of organization for her training squadrons had to be balanced with helping Simon prepare for his meeting. There was only a week left before the *Galileo* moved back into Earth orbit, so she was working hard to keep his mind off the hazards he was going to have to face personally.

She knew that the upcoming negotiations were

going to be not only hectic but draining as well. And knowing Simon as she did, Kitty was sure he planned to handle a large part of the negotiations himself. And she knew that after going after that bogey with Lucy, she wouldn't have a leg to stand on if she tried to get him to stay on board. So she bit her tongue, kept her peace, and spent as much time with him as she could.

The *Galileo*, with her escort alongside, finally slid into orbit around Earth, and Simon heaved a sigh. "Once more into the breech," he misquoted. Who, exactly, he was quoting, he wasn't sure, but it seemed appropriate. The two looked down on Earth from the relative privacy of the observation bubble. "This will be the most important one yet—crewing another ship and meeting with Vice-President Reese. Damn, but life is getting complicated."

He turned to Kitty and asked, "Do you ever wish for the days when we were stuck on Earth? I realize we've only been out here for two years or so, now, but it seems like forever. There are things I miss, and I guess there are for you, too."

Kitty looked up at the man she'd shared almost seventeen years with. "Don't tell me you're getting cold feet, man-o-mine. We're way too deep into this to back out, now."

"I wouldn't call it cold feet, hon. But I do miss things. Would you believe it's the little things, like sunsets, snowstorms, and moonlit walks? Remember that sleighride on our third anniversary or the trip to Old Faithful on our ninth?" He sat there, silent for a while. "We never had many friends, and we brought our best friends with us, so this wasn't too hard to accept at first, but you used to like to shop and go for drives and camping and hunting. Those are things I miss, too. Except for the shopping part. Don't you?" He waved an expansive hand. Hastily he went on, "I'm not saying give this up. Maybe I'm just being infected with vacation fever. It's hitting quite a few of the crew. Or maybe I'm just worried about this meeting. Things are about to get pretty rarefied, and I'm not the most diplomatic person in the world."

Kitty snorted. "First, I agree about your lack of diplomacy. Second, we aren't in the world." She hesitated, choosing her words. "At first, I was going to say we were above the world, but I don't want to sound like I think we're better than anyone down there. We're *outside* the world. That, and this ship, gives us a unique perspective. We have a responsibility to our species to continue. We can't give up now. I'm willing to sacrifice sunsets and shopping trips for all this." She cuddled against Simon and smiled. "And we are together, you know. That makes a big difference to me."

Simon grinned back. "It makes a difference to me, too. Okay. So, how do I handle people who've spent their lives manipulating people?"

Kitty sat up and straightened her uniform. "I do miss colors," she said musingly. "Black never did do much for my figure." Turning back to business and moving away from the bench toward the center of the bubble, she continued, "The best way to handle powerful people is to get them on the defensive, keep them there, and don't ever bluff. I'll bet Robert and 'Chiko are already in Denver, and I'm hoping they come back with enough for us to get things rolling." She stepped up to the semi-reflecting inner surface of the dome and inspected herself. "I guess pulling a jailbreak will be enough to let our Mr. Galway know we're back. Things get sticky from there on in."

Jailbreak it was going to be, and through an odd concatenation of events, it was a member of the very government that had kidnapped his family in the first place who provided the necessary information to accomplish their task.

Simon wasn't pleased to find out that Collier Senior had effectively taken over control of the underground that had been forming while Libra was being built—at least, until he met the garrulous old man.

Old, ha! Simon thought. *He's not that much older than I am.*

Collier Senior, mid-sixties, pot-bellied, grey-haired, and pony-tailed, wore wire-rimmed glasses and had a bald spot big enough to rent space on. He also had the sixty's radical mistrust of all that was governmental, disregarding the fact that that same government allowed him to make the protests he did. Any number of other countries would like to see him someplace that light and heat never reached.

Simon and Kitty waited for the Greenes' report on the situation Earth-side and then followed the couple back to the transporter room. The four beamed into the living room of Collier Senior, and Simon got his first look at the aging hippie. Clad in sweatpants and a tie-dyed t-shirt, the older man pulled himself out of his chair to welcome his visitors.

"Robert! I thought it would take you longer to get back," he said, shaking the younger man's hand.

He then turned his attention to Simon and Kitty. "You must be the ones my boy talks about so damned much. James Collier," he said sticking his hand out.

"Simon Hawke, and this is my wife, Katherine," Simon answered, shaking the proffered hand. "Thanks for seeing us on such short notice."

"Not a problem," the older man said, holding the handshake a bit longer than customary. "Somebody's got to keep the man from getting his fingers into all the pies. You've got a lot of balls, dude."

"Just doing what feels right," Simon demurred. "I seem to say this a lot, but if we gave it to the 'man,'" Simon said, dipping into the slang Collier had used, "only the military would get any use out of the technology for-bloody-ever. The little guys like us would never get anything out of it in our lifetimes."

"Still takes balls, though. Sit down. Something to drink? We have beer, tea, and some kind of pop. I'll be having tea," Collier said, patting his paunch. "Too much beer and this is where you wind up."

"Tea is fine with me," Simon said, looking at Kitty and the other couple questioningly as they all settled on the couch across from their host.

'Chiko stood back up. "Mr. Collier, do you mind if I take care of that for you? I know where everything is." She moved off into the kitchen without waiting for a reply.

"You got a good one there, Robert," Collier said. "Make sure you don't let her get away." He turned to Simon. "I asked that you come down here because I have someone I want you to meet, and I don't think I'm gonna let you folks scramble my atoms around like they do on television."

"I know how you feel," Simon said

conspiratorially. "I haven't let myself get on a commercial airplane for years, now. I don't worry about terrorists as much as I do about the people who inspect and repair the damned things. They fall out of the sky with *amazing* regularity."

"You won't fly, and you're willing to travel like that?" the elder Collier sputtered as he waved his hand in the general direction of where the foursome had materialized. "Dude, you have some serious priority issues!" The smile on his face took the sting out of his words.

"You said you had someone you thought I should meet?" Simon prompted as 'Chiko passed around a tray with small teacups and a rather large pitcher on it.

Their host looked at his watch and said, "Jim left the same time Robert did. He only has to drive a couple of miles one way, but he's taking a rather more devious route back. I'm not taking any chances on the man getting wise to our location. I've got a couple of people watching his back in case the dude isn't playing square with us. Shouldn't be much longer."

"Sounds like you're pretty organized," Simon observed. "Also, if you don't mind me saying it, a bit on the paranoid side, too."

Collier took a sip of the tea and grimaced. "Don't talk to me about paranoid. It's your folks who are still in the hands of the man, dude. Tastes better with sugar," he said after another sip, "but I can't have it anymore. Takes a lot of the sparkle out of life. Pretty organized, yeah," he said in answer to the question. He laughed lightly. "Seems like a real turnaround, though. In the old days, the group used to get people *out* of military service, and now you're using it to recruit *into* a military organization. But I will say," the man said, holding up a hand to forestall any response, "that this particular organization just might be worth it. If you don't let go the way our forefathers did and keep a tight rein on things, you might have something worth fighting for." His eyes shifted to a window behind his guests, and he said, "I believe my son is back. I see lights coming up the drive."

"You never did say how you found this guy," Simon observed.

"That's the bad part," Collier answered. "He found us. Or more to the point, he found Jim and David. Left word with them that he was the one who leaked word to the Parker girl and wanted to talk to you. Personally. If he can do it, so can others. So I'm taking precautions. Jim can't be traced to me here since this place is in my wife's name and she and I never officially did the thing, you know? We just never believed that a piece of paper made that much difference."

Kitty's arguments about the sanctity of marriage and the need for a formal commitment died on her lips as a younger version of Collier entered the room. He looked at the guests, particularly at Robert, and raised one eyebrow. Kitty watched the interplay and saw Robert nod slightly. The unspoken answer to the unspoken question was that the captain was willing to meet, and he could bring in his guest.

In his mid-to-late twenties, Jim Collier showed no trace of the beer belly he was genetically predisposed to. Tall and athletic, Collier the Younger stepped over and offered his hand. "Jim Collier, Captain. I didn't get to meet you when Robert and

'Chiko showed us around your ship. It's a real pleasure. And I wish you'd reconsider taking small children aboard the *Galileo*. Think about it, okay?"

The younger man, possessed of an overabundance of energy, moved away from the introduction and quick appeal without waiting for a response, going to the door he'd entered by. "Captain Simon Hawke," he said formally, waving an unseen figure forward, "I'd like you to meet Agent Jared Bench."

The man who entered the room next did so as a cat might, taking in everything in one sweep of his eyes. Simon stood up when his name was mentioned, so the new man had no trouble discerning who was who in the room. "The infamous Captain Hawke, I presume?" he asked shaking hands perfunctorily.

"Infamous, is it?" Simon asked testily. "Is that how they teach you to think about people who won't do what the ever-wise government tells them to?"

"Actually, we're not even supposed to refer to you as captain. You're just mister to us—those of us who follow the party line that is… Captain."

"And why am I supposed to believe that you're on some side other than the one that follows the party line?" Simon asked.

"Because," the agent answered, "I don't believe our government should round up people like we did a few months back. I don't believe any American should be summarily arrested just because it serves somebody else's purpose. We have laws about things like that, and that's one of the things I thought I was standing up for when I took this job. Enemies, foreign and domestic, the oath says. I didn't see any enemies in the people we rounded up. Just scared citizens." Vindication made his voice ring.

"And you were part of it?" he asked coldly.

"Was then, still am," was the subdued reply. "That's how I know that some of your people are still being held. And where." He looked at the elder Collier, directness in the blue eyes he trained on the older man. "I'm not proud of what happened, if that's what you think. If I was, I wouldn't be here now. But staying 'loyal' put me in a position to be able to pass this along."

Simon looked the other man over appraisingly. "I'm told that you said you were the leak that got most of our people released. How did that work? I'd think that you'd be taking an awful chance with your bosses."

"If they find out, hell yes!" The agent looked around the room. "I took some of the crucial data that came in and passed it along to a reporter I know. It was her call to make that satellite broadcast. Then, three days later, she went missing." He clenched his hands in his lap. "That's when I started going over the data myself. It just took time to sift through it all and come up with known associates of the missing people. Up came the names of David Brandt, James Collier, and four others. Statistically speaking, this group shouldn't know as many of the missing as they appeared to. Your son wasn't the first one I confronted, Mr. Collier," Bench said, "but he was the first one to flinch. It wasn't much of a leap to add David Brandt to the mix, seeing as how they were both friends of Robert and Michiko Greene, two of the missing. You people run a pretty tight ship."

Collier Senior asked, "So what's keeping others from following the same trail that led you to my son?"

The agent reached into an inner pocket of his suitcoat and pulled out a sheaf of papers. "Because these are the original documents. The agents who submitted them have no idea what they had, and I'm the only one to have seen them since they came in." He laid them on a table beside the older Collier. "I have no idea what happened to them. I certainly never saw them. And there's nothing left on the hard drive of the computer I used."

"That's all well and good," Robert said suspiciously, "but why come to us? You contacted us. You want something. What is it?"

"Because I didn't leak the location of the detainees to just any reporter," Bench said. "Sarah Parker is my cousin. Who, by the way is missing, along with her cameraman."

"Let me get this right," Kitty interjected. "Your cousin is the Sarah Parker who broke the story of the detainees? And you got the information, how? So far, all we've had the pleasure of coming in contact with is the DIA and FBI."

"Yes, ma'am, she is," the agent confirmed. "And I believe she's being held where your people are. They want to find out how she got word of such a secret operation. And your existence isn't that much of a secret, anyway. It's not something you can cover up that easily, and you haven't been exactly discreet about what you're doing."

"And you're worried she'll spill her guts?" Robert asked acidly, looking for the hook.

"Sarah? Hell, no!" the agent responded proudly. "She can keep a secret. And that's what's going to keep her locked up until they get what they want out of her. Of course, if they go the sodium pentothal route, I'll be toast before I even have a chance to react."

"What do you want us to do, Agent?" Simon asked directly.

"I tell you where your people are, and you bring Sarah and Dwayne out with 'em." The agent looked around the packed room. "And I'm willing to stay here until you get 'em out safely."

Simon looked around the room, getting shrugs and blank stares, all telling him that the decision was his. "We've already got a plan to get them out, Agent. I don't see a problem adding two more to the roster. All we need is the location and someone to tell them that the cavalry is on the way."

"How are they housed and guarded?" Collier Senior asked.

"They're in the same base they were in before, living in one of the barracks. There are about two hundred personnel on the base. Armed guards patrol at regular intervals. That's what the main detachment is assigned to. The rest of the personnel are support—you know, clerks, cooks, engineers, and such."

Simon looked the agent squarely in the eye. "So far, you've been skirting around treason, Agent Bench. It's time to fish or cut bait. "How many people are in the actual guard detail?" This time his voice left no room to squirm.

"A full MP platoon from the 101st Airborne, sir," the agent responded quickly. "Mostly equipped with riot gear, the officers and senior NCO's are carrying nine millimeters. The ten-to-six shift is the least watched, one guard on each floor of the barracks changed every four hours."

Collier Senior finally waved the agent to a chair

and 'Chiko offered him a cup of tea. He took a sip and grimaced. "Would be better with sugar. So what's your plan?"

"The less you know, the less you can tell," Simon said. "At the moment, we don't believe the government knows we're back. We've asked our people to keep it low-key for a bit this time, so the first clue they're gonna get is about two days from now when we make our presence known, assuming you don't give us away, that is. I'm going to take a chance and trust you. Your job is to get word to the hostages, Agent Bench. Tell them to be ready to go at two a.m. two nights from now. And tell them to try to act normal. Just be ready to cut and run. You, of course, will be nowhere around when we get there. Maybe you can be leading the assault on the diversionary force or something. That way, you won't be compromised, and we'll kinda sorta have someone on the inside."

"Kinda sorta?" Bench mimicked. "Aren't you the person calling the shots here?"

Simon nodded slowly. "I seem to have inherited the position, so to speak, but yes, I'm the one in charge. As for kinda sorta, all it means is that for this one instance, our interests coincide, and we won't hold it over your head later."

The agent looked deep into his teacup, possibly wishing for leaves and the ability to read them. "Okay," he said finally, "but go easy on the guards, will you? They have no idea who they're guarding."

Simon, remembering his years in the Army, smiled at the thought of going easy on *anybody* in the 101st Airborne and said, "That time of night, it will probably be a couple of corporals bored half to death.

I don't think we'll have much trouble there. It's going to be the diversion that will be the problem." He turned to Robert. "We can use all four wings."

"Sir!" Robert said, nodding in the direction of the DIA agent. "Shouldn't we let Agent Bench be about his business?"

Simon turned his head and gazed over his shoulder at the agent. "Ah, yes. We'll try to do this with a minimum of trauma, Agent Bench. We are, after all, mostly Americans ourselves, you know."

The agent turned to leave but turned back at the last second. "Captain, there's one way you can pay me back for this." Simon merely looked at the agent and waited. "When the dust settles, and you have whatever it is you want, I want to join up."

Simon stared at the agent for a moment, thinking. "I believe we can always find a place for a man of conviction and compassion, Agent. Until then, I suggest that you walk carefully. You're going to be on the front lines for a while yet."

CHAPTER THIRTY-TWO

The *Galileo's* new command shuttle was poised over the northern portion of the United States, waiting for a signal from the planet below. A gift from Dan Baylor, Captain of Orion, it had been the first official project completed by the new space dock. Specially modified to carry passengers, as well as perform as a mobile command center, its role would be to carry the twenty specially selected members of the rescue team and coordinate the twenty Mambas making up the rest of the rescue fleet.

The target, a closed-down air refueling base named Burgess Air Force Base, rotated through the darkest portion of the night-shrouded side of the planet—dark to the naked eye, that is. The *Galileo's* sensor suite was more than up to the task of laying bare the features on the surface twelve thousand miles below. Thermal imaging, as well as a form of ultrasound, was all that was needed for Simon to start identifying the location of the people still being held by the U.S. government.

It was his years as a soldier that ultimately provided the clues to pinpoint the precise spot. Three different locations had the requisite number of warm bodies, and two of them needed to be eliminated. Simon stared at the screen for a time, then reached out and touched one of several spots. "This is Communications or the computer center, or both in an outfit this small. This is probably Command," he said, pointing at another spot. "Too many people coming and going for it to be anything else."

Not quite touching the screen, he pulled his finger back. "It's possible that they could have the prisoners in the center of all their comings and goings, but their commander probably has them out of the way so they can't get a clear picture of how many there are or get any other ideas about the size of the operation. Lack of knowledge is what keeps people from forming escape plans, and I'm betting they're as far away from the center of things as possible."

One spot stood out because it was so far from the others. Pressing several buttons caused the spot to enlarge, giving Simon a bird's-eye view of a typical army barracks. Two stories tall, the building was designed to hold a total of forty-one men during wartime—four squads of ten men each, two squads on each floor, and a platoon sergeant. One end of the bottom floor held a small room for the sergeant opposite a supply room. The other end held the latrine.

The squads lived in open bays with six to eight windows per side, and there were only two doors, one at each end of the building. One end opened onto a quadrangle where formations would be held when the base was fully operational, and the other, in this case, opened onto a narrow space, almost an alley, that ran the length of one of the airport service buildings.

Simon's attention was drawn from the static display to the tactical. Mambas from the *Heinlein* and the *McCaffrey* began to exit their launch bays and form up into their respective wings. Three more fighters emerged from the *Galileo* and formed up a bit apart from the other ships. They were to make the first move in the rescue.

Simon was also betting that the commander of this operation was nowhere near the base, so his first move was going to be to cut off all communications with the outside world. The orders had to originate from Washington and be sent to the base in North Dakota. That would be two of the places he'd target.

Another gadget in the *Galileo's* arsenal of electronic devices was an electrical jammer. It effectively stopped any mechanical electron flow in a specific area for a specific amount of time. Encased in a force field, these jammers would be dropped at certain locations and activated at the appropriate time. The effect would be devastating. Care had to be taken that no aircraft were in flight in the target areas at the time of activation, or the consequences could be fatal. Otherwise, the simple cessation of the ability to communicate other than shouting would cripple any attempt to interfere with the rescue. It also rendered all electronic equipment on the base useless. No battery-powered, enhanced night-vision, and no weapons that needed anything electrical or electronic would operate at all. Digital watches, microwaves, and everything else in the vicinity of Burgess Air Force Base were going to suddenly stop for no apparent reason. By the time the operations officer could determine that it wasn't a mechanical glitch and sounded the alarm the old-fashioned way, it was hoped that the entire rescue could be done and over with.

Simon watched the operations clock as it turned over

to two a.m., feeling a moment of despair before a chime sounded in the confined space of the command center. Elation filled him for a second, but despair followed right behind it again.

I left home because I could never please the son-of-a-bitch, he thought. *Now, I'm going to save his worthless hide, and he'll probably ask what took so long.*

Swallowing the bile that rose into his throat, he touched a control and said, "Alpha Flight, this is Control. Commence your runs. Full cloak all the way, and report as soon as you're clear of the target areas."

"Control, this is Alpha Leader. Roger, wilco."

Simon heard the same voice as it changed tactical frequencies. "Bozo, you've got the North Dakota target. Golddigger, you've got DC. I'll be taking Cheyenne Mountain. On my mark, dive. Mark."

Simon smiled slightly as he heard one of the pilots ask petulantly, "So why do you get the mountain, Reaper?"

"Because I'm the flight leader, is why," came the response. "And if that ain't enough for you, Bozo, I'm a better pilot and a better shot. Plus, I can whup yore ass when we get back if you don't like it. Besides, all you've got to do is hit North-fucking-Dakota. Now shut up and fly."

Not waiting for Alpha to complete its task, Simon ordered the four wings of Mambas down after a fifteen-minute wait. He could tell by the banter that the pilots were getting restless, and, truth be known, so was he along with his personal flight crew. Only five minutes remained in Alpha Flight's attack runs.

Following at the same speed, the squadron would be ten minutes out when Alpha dropped their cargoes, then five more minutes to activation, then twenty minutes, hopefully, of noninterference from anything that relied on electrical power to function. That still left purely mechanical systems like rifles and light machine guns, not to mention actual physical assault—not an unlikely occurrence, considering the reputation of the unit they were facing. It was those last twenty minutes that would eat up human lives if the right precautions weren't taken.

Hence the jammers and the eight Mambas attacking the base at the farthest point from the prisoners. The ten back-up Mambas would fly patrols around the area outside the jammed space, forcing any flights away if they should get curious about the loss of communication with the secret base.

Simon, in the command shuttle, followed the first flight in, getting confirmation of all three missions accomplished. Five minutes later, he activated the jammers, making certain that the DC one didn't intersect the airport. Cheyenne Mountain would have gone down at the same time as Washington, DC, but Simon waited for two inbound choppers to set down, putting things in that area back by three minutes. Time enough, it seemed, for someone to notice when the link with Washington was broken but not enough to change the DEFCON before Simon shut them down as well. Then and only then did he black out the system around the base in North Dakota.

At fifty thousand feet, Simon ordered flights one and two from the *Heinlein*, to veer off and begin patrol duties in the outlying areas. "Remember, don't kill anyone. Force them back or down. That is all. Copy?"

"Roger that, Control. Turn 'em back or force 'em down. Squadron Leader, out."

Hearing the distinctive click as the flight leader changed tactical frequencies, he heard, "It's our job to watch the boss's back. No one gets through, got it?" Muttered answers came back since all the pilots had already had it drilled into them that there should be no loss of life to the down-siders. "On my mark, move to your assigned locations. Mark."

The shuttle reached the ten-thousand-foot level and slowed to a complete stop. The whine from the engines rose noticeably and the inertial compensators redlined as they performed far outside their parameters. Designed to steady the vessel during landings and takeoffs, the compensators acted like gyroscopes, holding the ship in a particular attitude just prior to launch. Stopping cold at ten thousand feet was asking for a system failure that, while probably not fatal at this altitude, could have severe ramifications if performed much closer to ground—depending on the level of competence of the pilot, of course. Simon ordered the remaining Mambas down into their attack patterns, holding two ships in reserve to guard the spaces the shuttle couldn't cover once it landed.

He looked over the assault team that was formed up at the rear of the compartment. They'd be the first on the ground, establishing a perimeter while Simon and a select few actually entered the building in search of the prisoners. Equipped with laser pistols, as well as the heavier-gauge laser rifles, there wasn't much that would be able to get through. The jamming field that blanketed the area was tuned to the type of current used by humanity at large and totally ignored the power packs and systems of the Alliance personnel.

The members of the ground assault team had been chosen from among all the members of the *Galileo*, the *Heinlein*, and the *McCaffrey*. A request for volunteers with police or military training netted almost two dozen willing and qualified candidates, enough that it was necessary to leave some behind so there'd be room for the prisoners they were going to rescue.

One thing Simon stressed was that the level of resistance had the potential to be fierce, and since the rifles and pistols carried by the guards were totally mechanical, there would be a definite chance of getting shot or killed. "Remember, a bullet can still kill you," Simon reminded the assault team. "It's not the technology; it's the nerves and training of the men holding the guns that decides a battle, and these men are among the best."

The trip back to Earth had produced the crew now assembled. The time had even allowed them to get to know each other a bit, but it would take an actual mission to find out which could be kept for more missions of this type and which would have to be relegated to more mundane tasks. One surprise had been the discovery that one of the assault-team volunteers had, for reasons he refused to divulge, brought with him a set of body armor and a riot helmet. Duplicating and enhancing them with the materials capable of being turned out by the *Galileo's* factories would be easy later, but in the week that passed between the discovery and now, only four sets had been made, and each of those had been specifically fitted to particular individuals.

Simon signaled the pilot to begin his descent as he listened to the chatter over the tactical channels. The diversionary force was already drawing the attention of a considerable number of personnel on the ground, although there was very little firing being done. Knowing it would take time for the unit commander to be brought up to speed without the luxury of telephonic communication, Simon bet on total confusion and delays in getting orders out.

The shuttle set down on its antigravs, the whine barely heard over the noise coming from the base perimeter several hundred yards away. Screened by the buildings between the commotion and the prisoners, Simon felt that the only time they could have been spotted was when they'd dropped out of the cloud layer and floated directly down into the quadrangle. The two support Mambas kept watch on the empty buildings while the perimeter defense team exited the shuttle and set up around it.

Simon stayed at his console, reading the thermal imaging scans provided by the two backups, and spoke into his headset. "Perimeter defense, you have several heat signatures moving toward you from your two o'clock. I make it six warm bodies. Remember, these buildings are set on concrete pylons. If you need to undercut them, you can take out one whole side and the building will collapse. It should happen slowly enough to allow the enemy to retreat or at least regroup. I'm turning the command post over to Commander Shipley. Take your signals from him."

Simon stood up and made his way to the shuttle door facing the building that supposedly housed the prisoners. As he stared at the door, a helmet-clad figure stepped out and gave Simon a thumbs up. Simon strode down the ramp, glancing both ways and noticing the glowing blue flares of Mamba exhausts as they wove a pattern that kept most of the base personnel glued to the far side of the facility.

A feeling of déjà vu shivered down his spine as Simon walked past the platoon sergeant's room and into the squad bay proper. The first face he saw, of course, was his father's. His mother stood to one side, waiting to see how this particular clash between her husband and only child would develop.

Nodding to his father, he looked at his mother and winked. Continuing, he recognized Kitty's two aunts and then noticed the woman standing slightly apart from the others. "Miss Parker?" he asked quietly.

"Yes," she said cautiously. "Who are you and how do you know me?"

"We're the cavalry," he said, smiling. "And as for how I know you, it was your broadcast that got most of our people freed. We're here to repay the favor." Simon looked around the room and then back to the reporter. "My information was that your cameraman would be here as well. Is he being housed separately for some reason?"

"Dwayne's missing?" Sarah looked shocked and worried. "He was supposed to come over and help me edit some footage, but these *people* decided otherwise. I haven't seen him since the day before I was abducted." She fairly spit the last word out.

"Sorry to cause you extra worry, Miss Parker," Simon said. "I think I know someone I can talk to about it, though."

Steps pounding down the stairs brought three pistols to bear until the rescuers recognized one of their own. With chagrin on his face, the commander said, "Sorry, Captain. Upstairs is clear. Both guards are tied up, and there are no other civilians in the building." He turned to yell up the stairwell. "Adams! Move it! We've got a flight to catch!"

Another set of steps sounded, bringing the last rescuer back to the ground floor. "We've got company on the way," he said matter-of-factly. "Looks like about seven to ten possibles trying to flank us and lock the back door. Perimeter defense is on it."

Simon turned back to the prisoners. Before he could speak, the deeper thrum of a Mamba's laser cut through the night air, causing all of the uninitiated to duck.

All except for him*, of course*, Simon thought, watching his father out of the corner of his eye.

The sound of a building collapsing on itself shook the walls, and a huge cloud of dust seeped into the building through every crack. Simon listened to his headset for a few seconds and then spoke. "I'm afraid there isn't time for explanations right now. Mom, Pop, Aunt Cindy, and Aunt Lynn, and you, too, Miss Parker. We have to get out of here now or we'll have a whole lot of very irate soldiers to deal with. I have transportation right outside. There should be enough room to accommodate everybody else as well." With Adams' arrival the body count had risen to almost thirty, including the various families still being held.

"That would be one of these spaceships the government boys have been saying you have?" his father asked sarcastically.

"As a matter of fact, yes, Pop," Simon said curtly. "Sometimes they do know what they're talking about."

"Bullshit," the elder Hawke said flatly.

Simon looked at his father angrily. "Spaceship or not, I've got a ride waiting. Are you going to sit here and let them come at you again?" he asked, nodding at the sound of increasing gunfire. "Besides, do you want to keep Mom in this situation any longer than necessary?"

The elder Hawke started past Simon and paused to look down at the weapon strapped to his hip. "That's not anything I'm familiar with, son," he said.

Simon put his hand on the older man's back and pushed slightly. "I'll show it to you once we get settled in the shuttle, Pop." Simon looked around the room. "Okay, if we're going to finish this without serious resistance, we need to move now." He touched a control on his belt. "Perimeter team," he said, "begin to regroup at the shuttle. The hostages are coming out now. Detail four to lay down suppressing fire. I'll be bringing out the last ones personally."

The guard at the front door looked inside and gave a thumb's up to Simon. Simon noted the enhanced Kevlar vest the guard wore and turned back to the waiting group. "Ladies first, if you please. There are some very angry men on their way to stop us, so we need to hurry this along."

A two-second pause followed while the women looked at each other. Finally, Sarah looked at the windows glowing from the light of the fires started by the lasers. She said, "What the hell," and headed for the door.

Parker walked out the door and was escorted across the open space, up the shuttle ramp, and out of sight. Kitty's aunts, both in their sixties, stopped beside him. "We told them that neither you nor Katie could possibly be involved in something like this, Simon. Are you two in trouble?" Aunt Cindy asked.

"Yes and no," Simon said. "We're working on that right now. Getting you guys out of here had to be our first priority." He put a hand on their shoulders and turned them toward the door. "Now, if you'll let these nice gentlemen lead you to the shuttle, we'll be able to get out of here shortly, okay?"

The two old ladies moved hesitantly toward the strange men wearing the outlandish kinds of clothes they saw on all of those TV cop shows. Both men smiled and spoke courteously, weapons holstered. When one held out a crooked arm, Cindy took it and allowed herself to be led across to the shuttle. Lynn shrugged and took the other young man's arm, allowing herself to be led off like her sister. The other women took their cue and followed quickly.

Simon turned to face his parents. Leaden of heart, he knew he was going to have to face his father, but he could put it off just a short time longer. "Mom, if you'll go with Commander Adams, I'll come along with Pop in just a few seconds, I promise." He leaned down and kissed her on the forehead, telling her in his own special way that all was indeed well.

She looked deep into his eyes for a few seconds and pronounced, "I don't care what they say you two have done. I believe you. They're trying to make you out to be the new Bonnie and Clyde or something. I say the same thing your father did—bullshit!"

"Mom!" Simon was shocked. Not once in his thirty-something years had he heard his mother utter a profane word, and not for lack of reasons. She just always seemed to find a more genteel way to express herself.

"There are very few times when that word can be considered appropriate," she asserted categorically. "This is one of those times and I stand by it." She turned to the waiting guard. "Commander Adams, if you please." To her husband she said, "I'll see you aboard momentarily, John. Don't dawdle. You two can fight when we're all safe."

Schoolteachers! Simon thought. *Ya love 'em and hate 'em at the same time, and I've got one for a mother!*

A flurry of conventional gunfire shattered John Hawke's reverie, lasers whining in return. He spoke, urgency and self-deprecation warring in his voice. "You got your brains from your mother and your bullheaded stubbornness from me, but even I can tell when it's time to cut and run." The remaining men all followed the women across the open space to the unfamiliar craft.

The elder Hawke, last to leave, turned toward the door and walked steadily to it. His wait for a stunned Simon to catch up gave him the opportunity to examine the machine sitting in the quadrangle.

He'd noticed the two lines of uniformed men outlining a path to the door of the craft when Simon reached him and put a hand on his shoulder, pushing slightly. John Hawke took a first step forward but froze when a Mamba drifted into view. His mouth dropped open at the sight of the little ship.

Little! his mind screamed, *that thing's got to be about a hundred feet long!*

The ship fired twin beams of eye-searingly brilliant magenta light into the ground, throwing up dirt, dust and steam as the pilot skillfully walked the reign of destruction across the path of several camo-clad troops working their way around the flaming debris of a barracks building. The push on his shoulder got a bit more insistent, so he hurried down the steps, taking in as much of the marvel in front of him as possible in the few seconds he had.

Simon got his father settled into the seat next to his mother, noticing wryly that the older man had chosen a clear view of the operations station.

I'll get one of the famous John Hawke lectures for sure, he thought.

He pressed buttons on the console and spoke into his microphone. "Mission accomplished, people. Well done. Now all we have to do is get out of here. Ground teams, return to shuttle. Diversionary Mambas, break off and provide air support for ground team withdrawal."

Almost immediately, men and women began to crowd into the shuttle through both sides. Laser whine sounded in reply to sporadic gunshots. The distinctive sound of a Mamba hovering on its compensators multiplied through the open hatches, blowing dust and debris inside. Simon watched as one man entered the shuttle and took stock of all the faces of the rescue mission. "All present, Captain," he said. He looked around the overcrowded cabin. To the teams, he ordered, "Find something to hold on to, people."

"Button us up, Commander," Simon ordered the pilot. Leaning out slightly, he said, "As soon as you have a green board, lift to five thousand and hold." Pressing a button on the console, he said, "Interdiction team, mission accomplished. Be on alert. We are about to disarm the jammer to communicate with the base. Diversionary team, you will transfer to the command of Interdiction Commander Dahlquist when the shuttle reaches five thousand feet."

"On station at five thousand, Captain." Simon's console confirmed the pilot's verbal report.

Simon chuckled to himself when he heard his mother say quietly, "That's not possible, John. You know how I get whenever I fly."

Unable to speak for several seconds without laughing, Simon just sat there, apparently unaware of the stares of his guests. Finally trusting his control, he said, "Attention all ships. I am about to deactivate the jammer. Prepare for possible aerial incursions." Simon pressed a series of buttons, and a light on his panel turned green. He pressed another, and the sound in his earphone was transferred to the shuttle's internal speakers.

"Mongoose, this is Paladin. Paladin calling Mongoose. Please respond, Mongoose." No response came, and the unknown voice called again. "Mongoose, please respond. We are under attack by… I don't know what we're under attack by, but we can't touch 'em."

Simon pressed another button, cutting the voice and background static out completely. He cocked his head, laid his headset down on the console, and said, "Paladin, this is Alliance Control. Mongoose will not be responding for a short while longer. They're still experiencing the same mysterious electrical failure you just did. I have new orders for you."

"First of all," the voice answered, "there is no Alliance Control in my chain of command, so I don't recognize your authority, and second, what makes you think you can give me orders and enforce them?" The belligerent, bullying voice just plain antagonized something deep inside Simon.

His response, when it came, gave no hint of his inner turmoil. "In response to your first point, as the commander with the greater tactical force, I effectively control this entire exchange. And as for your second point, I am betting that you're the kind of commander who won't throw his men away in a pointless gesture. Third, look at the state of your base."

Silence reigned for seconds while Paladin considered that. "Exactly what pointless gesture would that be?"

"Having any of your men on or near this base in one hour."

"What? Are you going to start bombing us? You got what you came for." Incredulity dripped out of the speakers.

"No, but I could if I wanted to," Simon answered, pressing a button. An explosion was heard distantly as the sound was relayed to the shuttle. "That was just a demolition charge to get rid of the equipment we used to cut your power. What I have in mind for your base is a much grander gesture, Paladin."

"What else can you do? We can hold out until reinforcements arrive."

"When I said one hour, I meant it. You are down to fifty-eight minutes. What's about to happen is that

I am going to drop a very large rock on your base. I brought one back with me from the asteroid belt where we've been living and working for the last two years. I thought it would be a nice gesture to donate it to some of the universities of the world so they could study pristine matter from the formation of our solar system."

Simon stopped for a breath, the unknown voice not bothering to fill the gap. "I've decided to give it to someone else instead. I think it would make a much grander gesture to give it to you. The problem is that it's going to be arriving at something like a couple of thousand miles an hour, and it's not a *little* rock." Simon stopped to let that sink in. "I think the grand gesture, the big show of power, the winner of the pissing contest, is going to be the one who destroys the most of the other guy's stuff. You've got a big goose-egg, and I'm about to turn Burgess AFB into Lake Burgess in fifty-six minutes. Are you getting any of this?"

"I'm getting it, but I'm not getting it. You got your prisoners. Why are you telling me this?"

"Because I'm not a monster, like too many military bean counters," Simon answered firmly. "Besides, if I'm lying, you're back in the base in another thirty minutes and none the wiser. If I'm not lying, you've saved your entire command and yourself into the bargain."

"I don't like this, but I don't see an alternative. I'll start issuing the orders immediately." Almost as an afterthought, Paladin asked, "What about civilians in the area?"

"I've had people running any stragglers off for the past half hour. There will probably be a lot of

UFO stories in the local papers tomorrow."

"I want to thank you," Paladin said. "Not many people would have given us warning."

"Just consider yourself lucky that I was raised with compassion." He glanced at his mother for a moment. "The problem is that I also have an ingrained sense of justice that requires that I respond to this incident with a show of force that will make your bosses think twice before messing with us again. The compassion lets you and your men live while the other will deliver a message to your bosses that we are not to be messed with. Also, you should send a couple of men to the detention barracks to untie two of your guards before you leave, Paladin."

Simon cut the connection and reluctantly turned to face the dumbfounded people sitting in the forward section of the shuttle. "We can't sit here for fifty minutes, folks. As good as this equipment is, it has limitations." He ran one hand through his hair and sighed. "I suggest taking the aunts home. We can drop them at Aunt Cindy's farm and be back here in time to monitor the impact."

He turned to Kitty's aunts. "Aunt Cindy, Aunt Lynn, Katie will be by to explain all of this very soon, and we're sorry to have caused you any trouble. We just never expected this to happen," he said, waving his hand vaguely.

"Won't those nasty men just come back and take us away again, Simon?" Cindy asked worriedly.

"I expect to be speaking with their boss in the next couple of days about that very matter, Aunt Cindy. You should be okay, but if they try it again, we'll just have to make sure that there isn't a third." He turned to the pilots and said, "Check your preprogrammed destinations. Access destination alpha and land near the farmhouse you find there."

He looked at his parents. "That'll be one down. As soon as the asteroid hits, we'll get you two home, then the rest of these good folks. Same thing applies—I'll be putting a stop to this soon, but you should be safe enough until I get to talk to a particular individual."

His father raised a hand to get a chance to speak. Simon expected a harangue but was surprised to get a question instead. "How are you going to ensure that the asteroid doesn't miss its target?"

"It's being guided down by two ships designed to move those kinds of rocks around in space. They'll make sure it's on course, and at almost the last minute, they'll veer off and let it finish its run on its own."

"Pretty intense response, though, son."

Simon bristled. "You were the one who taught me that if someone messed with me once to whip him good, and if he messed with me a second time to make sure it never happened again." He looked the older version of himself in the eyes. "The only difference is that this time the bullies have been elected. The level of response to an individual is one thing, but to a government? It has to be something that will make them stop and think or sit up and take notice. I believe I've got that covered."

Simon glanced at his console and then turned to face it completely. "I'm on it," he said to the pilot. He touched a point on his screen, and the isolated farm below appeared in minute detail—barns, silos, main house, outbuildings and large equipment all instantly transferred to the pilot's console. He touched a point on the new screen and said, "Set down there."

Taking off his headset, he turned back to his guests. "Mom, Pop, Miss Parker, I'll be back in a few minutes. I'll be seeing my aunts to their house."

"Wait!" Sarah Parker almost yelled. "Where were we being held?"

Simon looked surprised, but answered, "Call it eastern-central North Dakota, why?"

"And we're where right now?" she asked, ignoring Simon's question completely.

Something in the frank stare she gave him over the tops of her wire-framed glasses made him say, "Call it central Montana. Again, why?" This time his question carried more persistence.

"I'm from Fargo, Captain. I know how far it is from one place to another around here, and we just went around three hundred miles in…" she looked at her watch, making faint beeping sounds, "…about six minutes. Pretty fancy rescue vehicle."

Simon's smile would have done a wolf proud. "We're pretty proud of her, but you should see her move when we shift into second."

John Hawke watched his son usher Kitty's two aunts toward the back of the shuttle. He leaned forward and spoke to the pilot. "Better than three thousand miles an hour? That's around five times the speed of sound. Kind of hard to believe," he said gruffly. For months he'd been questioned by a series of nameless men about just this kind of technology. All that time he'd denied knowing anything. Of course! And now he sat in a chair covered in exactly what he couldn't say, but it was comfortable enough.

The pilot laughed. "And that's about it inside Earth's atmosphere, sir. We're restricted to something in the vicinity of Mach four or five or so. Maybe a little faster if we were more aerodynamic but not much. We try to keep it down around populated areas. But get us out of the atmosphere and she's a bit faster than a Mamba in the long run. Right up to sub-warp speeds is what we hear out of R&D."

The reporter in Sarah wouldn't let her keep quiet. "I know there were lots more people released than would be represented by the number of people here. Where are the rest of your group?"

"Aboard the *Galileo*, three bases, and at the moment, two ships," the pilot replied, "and… well, maybe the captain should fill you in on the details." He turned back to his console and said, "Mikey! I have one vehicle on a straight-line near approach."

"Been there, done that, Jeff," came softly through the speakers. "Beat up old truck, weaving slightly. Probably a drunk headed home."

"Thanks, Mikey." The pilot turned back to the three people sitting in the front row. "I'm sure the captain won't be much longer. We need to get back to the air base soon."

Knowing he wouldn't get anything out of the pilot if he kept pestering him for details, John Hawke asked a more innocuous question. The truth was that the answer to this one question would tell him more than he could get by asking any ten others. "Are you happy doing what you're doing?" His voice trailed off as he pointedly looked at the pilot's collar insignia.

The pilot's face lit up. "Oh, yeah. And I'm Commander Jeff Archer," he said. "Lieutenant Commander, actually. Full commander wears a gold star." He bubbled with enthusiasm. "Wouldn't you be happy if you could live your fantasy? I mean, flying ships in space, away missions, firefights."

"This was a real firefight, son," John Hawke said huffily, "not one of your war games. Real people are risking their lives here."

"I know, sir," Archer said somberly, his face going slack. "I was on Orion when…"

Something in the pilot's eyes, or maybe his posture, told John that his son had reentered the ship. He sat back easily in his chair.

"Thanks for keeping an old man occupied, Commander."

Simon sat down across from his parents and the Parker girl. "I'm glad Kitty's the one to have to deal with that one," he said, sighing. "Take us back to the base, Jeff." He looked at the three people and said, "It's all true. We have a spaceship, and we won't give it to the government. We plan to release the technology to the whole world so everybody benefits. If that makes us bad guys, then we're bad guys."

The few other civilians just absorbed the information since they knew from personal experience what their children had gotten them into, albeit involuntarily.

Simon sat silent for a few seconds and then looked at his father. "This little scene we're having is your fault, you know." At the look of shock on the elder Hawke's face, Simon laughed bitterly. "Not directly, Pop, but you helped instill the values I live by. I'm here—we're all here—because of one of your heavy-handed lectures."

He stood up and looked down at his father. "I remember two things out of all the stuff you tried to teach me. Actually, believe it or not, I rely on both of 'em a lot. One was, 'When in doubt, don't.' That applies to so many things in life, not just passing a car on the road. The other was not to get even with the wrong person or thing. I remember egging some kid's car and his dad called you and complained. I got my ass chewed. You told me that the car hadn't done anything, so I should have left it alone and fought with the kid. When I said you'd whip me for fighting, you told me that the whipping would have been done and over with. Instead, you grounded me for two months. Well, I'm here tonight because somebody else was the egg-thrower and you were the car."

"I don't understand," Doralene Hawke said.

"Mom, somebody's mad at me and was trying to use you as leverage against me," Simon explained. He looked at his father. "Haven't you explained any of this to her?"

"What am I supposed to explain? What exactly did you confide in me for me to explain? How was I supposed to know the truth?" the elder Hawke shot back.

Simon smile wryly. "Maybe so," was as close to admitting his father was right as he would go. "Wanna see what all the fuss is about?"

CHAPTER THIRTY-THREE

Simon sent his second in command, Commander Robert Shipley, down to contact Galway after dropping off the rest of his passengers.

"I was expecting to hear from Commander Grimes," the gravelly voice replied to Shipley's introduction.

"Captain Grimes has been promoted and is too busy running a ship of her own to do messenger duty. I, on the other hand, had a clear schedule and was happy to take a quick look at DC. Now, the Captain says that you and he need to discuss a meeting with one of your bosses, especially since the scales have just been balanced. He said you should get your team together and line up whatever transportation you want out to the west coast. I'll call you back with details later. Have a nice day, Mr. Galway." Shipley hung up the phone, having spoken for less than two minutes.

Robert and Michiko beamed down and placed calls to their friends, the Colliers and Brandts. Specifically transferred back to the *Galileo* for this trip, Robert and 'Chiko hoped to have someone else meet them as well, making life a lot easier all the way around.

The three couples had been in touch via the radios left behind during their last visit while the

Galileo was en route to Earth. The high number of volunteers needed at one time was almost as large as the force trying desperately to absorb them. It would have to be handled in two trips, if that many people could be found. They were looking at almost another two thousand and were hoping to get a fair fraction of that on this trip—enough, if they were lucky, to crew at least one of the three ships waiting in the belt. And that still left Taurus Base to be staffed.

The two-thousand-person figure seemed a daunting number at first. The only thing that made it even remotely possible was the underground that had sprung up in the Denver area. Once converted, James Collier began to show his son how to set up cells of people where only one person in a cell knew about the next one. Making duplicates of the videos and getting them passed around was of prime importance. The video work was amateurish enough that no one could think it fake for more than a few minutes, and it was added to each cell's equipment. Telephone schedules were arranged so that all could be contacted at need, and converts or interested parties could be brought in. Meetings were held for the newbies on a monthly basis, never in the same place twice, and those who agreed to join were assigned to cells.

The process continued to grow and evolve until meetings began to take on the aspect of church revivals, with people showing up from out of nowhere. Once word began to spread about a particular meeting, the Brandts and Colliers, were hard pressed to keep any sort of order. Not able to give a particular date, all they could say was, "Be ready. The call will come. They're on the way back."

The repetition was getting tiresome.

Until the call came. "Robert! Where the hell are you? Are you going to help us? We've got people ready to take our heads off, thinking it's all a hoax. What took you so long?" Ted Brandt was indignant, to say the least.

"It takes time to build a space station, Ted. We got back as soon as we could. And we had an errand to take care of first. Are you able to get some of your people together tonight? I'll stop by to give you something and show you how to use it. We'll put on a little demonstration, and I guarantee that your people will settle down after that."

"You better be right, pal. We can't hold this together much longer without proof of some kind. The will to believe is only so strong, you know. Especially in something that flies in the face of everything these people have been taught to believe."

"I know. I'll see you in fifteen." With that, Robert hung up the phone, turned to 'Chiko, and explained their dilemma. "I think we should give a demonstration like we got when we joined. Want to beam in and freak out a bunch of people?"

She smiled. "I'd love to! Let's go set it up. The best way is to give Jim a locator disk and show him how to activate it when he has his people in one place. You think?"

Agreeing, Rob grabbed the keys to their car and headed for the door.

Robert handed Jim a disk. Ted had been called, and he and his wife were there as well. Babs and Alice looked on.

ⱼgnize these. They send out a signal
√ where to beam down if we haven't
ᴄfore or if it's too crowded. Set it on the
ᵦ.   ᴜ press here," he said, indicating the small
deprᴇ.   ᴜn in the top of the disk, "and the signal is
sent. These are coded to you, so we'll know it's time
for the show. Trust me, your people will believe. And
if you could have a space about the size of a football
field available, that would be great. I've already
spoken to the captain, and he's decided it's time to
start showing a little of what we have to the people of
Earth rather than just our own volunteers. The reason
for all the open space, believe it or not, is so one of
our fighters can come in and land. It won't be able to
stay long, but it should be long enough to make
believers out of the worst skeptics. How soon can
you get your cell leaders and a few from each cell
together? By the way, how many do you have
enlisted?"

Jim grinned. "You said you needed about two
thousand, right?" At Robert's hesitant nod, Jim
laughed. "Well, buddy, we've got about a quarter of
that right now. And if you pull off what you're saying,
I'll bet we can have several thousand more within a
week. We've got people from all over the country
camped out around here. Word spreads, man, word
spreads. You may need to start recruiting from
somewhere else after this. I think it's going to get
way too hot real soon. As my dad says, every good
undergrounder knows when it's time to go under,
himself."

'Chiko let out a small noise. "*Several* thousand?
We could crew all three ships, plus the new base, and
have people left over for the next ships. Some are

624

going to be resentful about being left behind. Perhaps we should institute a lottery-type situation for the time being."

"Maybe, honey, maybe," Robert mused.

"Well, Mr. Galway, we have you booked into the Quality Inn in Billings, Montana." You can check in any time after two p.m. tomorrow," Commander Shipley said. "Two rooms have been reserved in your name. We'll call you sometime after you check in and let you know where the conference room is."

"Billings, Montana," Galway responded with resignation in his voice. "That's where all this started. Where will you people send us next?"

"I really have no idea, Mr. Galway," Shipley responded. "I'm merely passing along the captain's instructions."

Seeing as how it was Simon and Kitty's home turf, it wasn't too hard to have someone inside the airport that serviced Billings and the surrounding area when Galway's plane landed. A disguised Lucy Grimes reported that it actually was Galway and company, then beamed back aboard the *Galileo*. Meeting Simon in his ready room, she asked if he was going to set the meeting up like the last one.

Simon pursed his lips and said, "No, I don't think so. Things like that tend to work only once. I intend to be a little more above board this time. I did tell Commander Shipley to tell them that there would be a conference room set up, so I expect any of their extra manpower to be expended trying to cover all the possible conference rooms we could be meeting in. Instead, I think I'll have them picked up by a limo and delivered right to my front door."

Lucy was aghast. "To your home?" she finally got out. "Isn't that just asking for trouble?"

Simon smiled. "Sure, but why not live a little? It's time to be a little more open. Daniels has been inside—with and without my permission. You know that story. Why not let Galway in, too? But it'll be on my terms, this time. And this session can be more informal. Maybe they'll feel more at ease and a little less antagonistic."

"Well, you know best, Simon," Lucy said dubiously.

"A statement that is not always true," Simon retorted. "Infallible, I'm not. Anyway, we'll let 'em stew for a little while, and then we'll all beam down to the house, call the limo, and have a tea party. I figure me and Kitty at first with two others just to show we aren't alone. We'll have a few security personnel armed and out of sight to discourage unwanted visitors, and then we'll signal you and John to beam in. Another move to show our strength. We'll also have several people around the neighborhood keeping watch. And, of course, the *Galileo* will have her sensors trained on the area the whole time. That should provide enough deterrent to provide an interesting evening without too many surprises."

On the stroke of seven p.m., the phone in Galway's room rang. The voice on the other end told him to get his party together and go outside where transportation would be waiting. The four men trooped out the front door of the motel to find a limousine at the curb. Galway didn't miss the significance of the all-black uniform and baseball cap of the driver.

"Galway party?" the uniformed driver asked. At Galway's nod, the driver opened the door and gestured the men inside. He then walked around to the driver's side, got in, and pulled away from the motel.

At Galway's query concerning their destination, the driver looked into his rearview mirror and said, "Sir, I've been instructed to deliver you without answering questions of that nature, but I *can* say that we'll arrive at your destination in about seven minutes. Normally, I take a more indirect route and point out some of the sights of our fair city, but I've been given to understand that you wouldn't be interested in something like that."

Looking into his rearview mirror and seeing the curt nod Galway gave him, the driver went back to his job of navigating his oversized vehicle through the streets of Billings.

Pulling up in front of a nondescript house on Billings' near-west end, the driver stopped his vehicle and said, "Well, gentlemen, here we are."

A young man in shipboard uniform stepped up and opened the passenger door. The first to venture out of the vehicle was the man Lucy had dubbed Mr. Anonymous, who wasted a scathing look on the earnest young ensign. When the last of the four had stepped out, the young man closed the door and said, "Gentlemen, if you will go to the front door, you are expected. This vehicle will be here when you're ready to leave." He then stepped back into the shadows provided by a lilac hedge and a westerly sun, all but disappearing from view.

The four men walked up to a shingle-sided house

that would have fit perfectly in any middleclass neighborhood in the country. Light seeped around the edges of the curtain that closed off the big picture window, and they could see shadows moving around inside as they stepped up onto the porch. Galway looked at his three companions and hesitated, then looked back at the door and noticed the small sign taped over the bell saying it was out of order and asking them to knock. He did so.

A handful of heartbeats later the door opened and there stood a petite redhead. She smiled and said, "You must be Mr. Galway. Please come in. I'm Katherine Hawke, but you can call me Kitty."

She held out her hand and smiled. Galway hesitated for a fraction of a second, took her tiny hand in his, and replied, "And you can call me Brandon." At this she positively beamed.

"Please, gentlemen, come in. My husband is changing and will be out momentarily. We get so tired of uniform black that I welcome the chance to come down and relax. She waved a hand down her body to indicate the outfit she had on—a cream blouse, tan slacks, and open-toed sandals, none of which hid her striking figure.

As each of the next two men came in, Kitty greeted them by name, showing that she was up on what was going on. "Lucy described you to us, and I'm happy to meet you Colonel Babcock, Mr. Mitchell." As the fourth man walked into the room, she put out her hand and said, "Good evening, I'm Kitty Hawke."

He shook hers in turn and said nothing. As he started to pull his hand free, she clamped down. Having grown up on a farm, she had a grip most men found disturbing unless she toned it down. This time, she let the little man feel the power in her arm.

"Where I was raised, it's customary to respond to an introduction with an introduction. Now, maybe you don't want to give your real name, and that's entirely your business. But, sir, in my house, you will give *a* name for someone to refer to you by, or you can wait outside. And before you say anything else, I said 'where I was raised.' It just so happens, sir, that this house is where I was raised. Now," she said with a smile on her face, "we'll try this again." Still maintaining her grip, she said, "Good evening, I'm Kitty Hawke. Welcome to my home."

The man reddened visibly and said," Uh, good evening, Mrs. Hawke. I'm John Anderson."

Kitty bestowed one of her glowing smiles on the man, and said, "I'm very pleased to meet you, Mr. Anderson. And I like that name." She waved her hand toward a couch and some chairs to one side of the room and said, "Please, gentlemen, have a seat. What would you like to drink? Ensign Martin will take your orders."

A young man dressed in black uniform pants and a white shirt stepped forward. "Gentlemen, we have coffee, iced tea, various colas, caffeinated and decaf, and domestic beer. What can I get you?"

Simon emerged from the bedroom dressed in a V-neck pullover, blue jeans, and cowboy boots, making quite a contrast to Kitty's outfit. "Make mine beer, if you please." Turning to the four men seated in his living room, he said, "Good evening, gentlemen, I'm Simon Hawke." After another round of introductions, hand shaking, and drink orders—three beers and an iced tea for Anderson—the five men sat down.

"Sugar and lemon, sir?" the ensign inquired.

A nonplussed Anderson said, "Uh, just sugar, please."

Simon and Kitty were sitting in a loveseat arrangement facing the four visitors, and Mr. Anderson noticed the two empty chairs. "Expecting company?"

"Yes, as a matter of fact," Kitty replied. "Captain Grimes and Commander Marshall, our security chief, will be along shortly. Do you mind if they just beam in?" she asked in her straightest face.

The NASA representative, Steven Mitchell said, "I, for one, would like to see this 'beaming' phenomenon at a time when everything around me isn't going to hell in a handbasket." Getting no refusal from the rest of the group, Kitty let it drop, and when no one was looking her way, she pressed a button on her wristband.

Simon said, "I really didn't see a need to have a third or fourth member here, but my wife plans these affairs."

Kitty picked up the thread of the conversation as Ensign Martin returned and began passing out drinks. "Well, I felt that four on four was a much more balanced arrangement. So I invited Lucy and John, whom you folks are familiar with anyway."

The ensign stopped beside Kitty. "Ma'am, you neglected to give me your order."

Kitty answered, "My apologies, Ensign. Make that three more iced teas with sugar and lemon for all, if you would. Captain Grimes and Commander Marshall will be with us shortly."

"Yes, ma'am. Right away," he answered and

disappeared into the kitchen.

Kitty held up her wristband for all to see. "This serves a variety of functions, gentlemen. One, of course, is to identify one of us to another. It can be used as a communicator over short distances or a bio-monitor/locator at longer distances. Our ship is, of course, monitoring us at all times. A few minutes ago, I pressed a button that informed our ship, the *Galileo*, that we were ready for visitors. I expect them to—ah! Here they are now."

All eyes went to a corner of the room as two columns of sparks began to form. After about four seconds, Lucy and John stood there in uniform, got their bearings, and walked out into the room. Kitty waved them to chairs and said, "Sit down. Ensign Martin will be in shortly with your drinks."

As they made their way to the vacant chairs, Galway stood up. He stuck his hand out to John and said, "Nice to see you again, Commander." He then turned his attention to Lucy. "I see and hear that congratulations are in order, Captain. Which ship is yours?"

Lucy looked at him sharply. "I have the honor to command the *McCaffrey*, Mr. Galway." Barely hiding her discomfiture at his knowledge, she shook his proffered hand and nodded her head slightly. "You're pretty good at your job, sir."

Sitting back down, he grinned. "That's why I get the hard jobs, Captain. But sometimes just being good at what you do isn't enough. For example, I'm not getting as far as my bosses think I should as fast as they think I should. You should hear some of the things I have to listen to about you folks. Especially the way you get even."

Simon waved his hand grandly. "Had to level the playing field, so to speak. And send a message. Besides, we did North Dakota a favor. Instead of a useless, closed-down airbase, they've got a brand new recreational area—Lake Burgess." The impact zone had touched upon the Ox River. Unfortunately, it had caused tremors felt as far away as Minot and Grand Forks.

Lucy seated herself, still watching Galway warily. Kitty, not missing the byplay, decided to redirect the conversation—whether for good or ill, she wasn't sure. She only knew the subject definitely needed to be changed for a number of reasons, not the least of which was the tension she felt between Lucy and Galway.

"Captain Grimes, I believe you know this man under a different name, but may I present Mr. John Anderson?"

Lucy cast a startled look at Kitty. "How did you... never mind." She nodded formally in the man's direction and said, "Good evening, Mr. Anderson."

After a few more minutes of amenities, none of which were joined in by Anderson, the real reasons for the meeting emerged.

Simon began, "Gentlemen, you know what it is we want, and you know what we've offered. The last time we were on Earth, we had an invitation delivered to us." He reached into his breast pocket and pulled out a much-folded piece of paper, tossing it onto the coffee table in front of Galway. "I assume you have some idea of what this is about."

Galway picked it up and glanced at it. "I should; I helped draft it. Specifically, since you're not a head of state, meeting with President Drake first is out of the question, or more to the point, would not be à propos. That leaves Vice-President Reese. You and he will discuss bases and technology transfers. Our job is to set up that meeting."

Simon nodded. "That's good. I wouldn't want to do anything to upset the applecart." He waved his hand dismissively. "But what about our request that the general populace be officially informed of our existence?"

Anderson finally chimed in. "That's not a good idea. The average citizen isn't going to be able to handle this kind of revelation."

Lucy leaned forward. "And just who do you think *we* are, Mr. Anderson?" she asked. "Remember, before Simon and Kitty found the *Galileo*, they were average citizens. And what about the rest of us? Are you saying we aren't average? And if you are, sir, I, for one, want to know in which direction you think we aren't average. Above or below?"

Kitty stepped into the fray before Anderson could answer. "I think the answers to those questions are ones we don't need to hear right now, although I do want to hear them later. You, Mr. Anderson, may be called on to answer them, and if I were you, I'd think real hard about those answers and the people you'll be giving them to." Turning to the head of the delegation she said, "Mr. Galway, Brandon, my question is—what will happen to those personnel of ours who, for one reason or another, choose to leave our service and return to their lives here on Earth?"

Galway squirmed in his chair. "Well, they'll have to be quarantined, of course, to make sure they don't bring any dangerous viruses down."

"That," Simon said dangerously, "is a load of

bullshit the size of Delaware. You don't seem to be worried about viruses right now, and you haven't been concerned about that at any meeting you've had with our people up to this point. You want to use that as an excuse to detain and interrogate our people. You'd hold them incommunicado, I expect, until they gave up all the information you could get from them. And then what would you do with them? Hold them in some special facility? You know, we need to start playing straight with each other right now, or we might as well not play at all."

Kitty, looking to defuse a testosterone explosion in her living room, spoke up. "Brandon, you need to be aware of something. There are people here on Earth—a very large number of them, from what I hear—who don't know what happens when they flip a light switch. They don't know where electricity comes from, and they don't care. If the light doesn't come on, they'll change the bulb. If it still doesn't come on, they call an electrician. I worry about what would happen if the lights went out, along with the phones, for more than a short while, I really do." She could see the look of confusion in his face. "What I'm getting at is this—we found something. We figured out how to make it work, but we don't know *why* it works, even after borrowing all those scientists. We stick space debris in one end of a thing we've come to call a smelter, and processed material comes out the other end. This we send to various places we call factories. The finished products are put together the way the plans we found in a computer tell us. And what do we have? Three space factories and two crewed ships. Also, one ready to crew and two more ready soon, with another in the not-too-distant future.

"We've got scientists working on some of those questions, but not enough of them. For every guesstimated answer, we get about a thousand more questions. I think that about sums it up. And we still don't think the government should have the ship. You can't do any more with it than we have and probably a whole lot less. I like Simon's analogy best—the one about the caveman who wakes up in thirteenth century England. He might be able to use some of the things he'd find there, but he wouldn't understand it. We are quite literally cavemen, Brandon. Granted, we have a better grounding in science, and granted that what we see up there we don't ascribe to magic. But we still don't understand it. We still have too large a gulf to bridge. Give us time. We'll get the job done."

Mitchell from NASA was waiting for his chance to weigh in. "What makes you think you're better able to figure things out than people who've studied for space exploration all their lives, Mrs. Hawke? We've been at this since the fifties, you know."

"Earlier than that, if you count Von Braun," John interjected. "Surprised that I would know that? Well, some of us have been studying, too. We are *encouraged* to. And just what are you studying, Mr. Mitchell? Ion drives, ram-scoops, atomic drives? Tell us, please. Hell, you're still using liquid hydrogen and solid propellants. I've got news for you, sir. There's nothing up there that you would understand. The scientists we have aboard right now can't say why most things work. We have atomic physicists, nuclear physicists, quantum physicists, string theorists—you name it. And none of them can say for sure why what we have works."

"And we're getting off topic," Kitty said. "I'll

answer your question with one of my own, Mr. Mitchell. Since the scientists we've enlisted say that some of the technology is so far out there that they have a bare glimmer of what the math would be like, what makes you think you could do any better than we have?"

Not waiting for an answer, she turned back to Galway. "What about our people, Brandon? That's one of the points to be decided with Vice-President Reese. The only reason it was brought up was so you could apprise him of what will be on the table for discussion—bases, technology, and freedom from persecution for our people. Is Mr. Reese a veteran? One way or the other, I'm pretty sure he'll have a vested interest in seeing everybody's freedom preserved, don't you?" she asked sweetly.

Galway sat there uncomfortably for a time. "I'm sure he will, Kitty. I'm sure he will."

Simon took a long pull on his beer and waved the empty at the ensign standing silently in a corner. While he waited for a replacement to arrive, he looked at Galway. "You know what I like most about us finally meeting, Brandon? Can I call you Brandon? Call me Simon. What I like is that we can look each other in the eye and spit if we need to. What I mean is that we can get to the bottom of things in a hurry. So. We have several topics for discussion with your boss. Embassies. Tech transfer. Safety for our people. But you haven't even mentioned the one thing we've wanted from the first, and that's revealing us to the general public. How about that, Brandon? Why haven't we heard anything official on the radio or television about our little group?"

Into his third beer, Simon was beginning to feel

the effects and starting to bait his guests. He knew the answer was going to come from another quarter than the one he'd thrown the ball to. "And if we were to get the embassies *without* public recognition, how would you go about keeping it secret?"

John Anderson had just put his tea on the table when Simon put the question to Galway. He stood up, and in a belligerent tone said, "The general population, Mr. Hawke, isn't ready for the revelation that there are aliens out there. Most of them couldn't handle it. We have it on good authority that the best we could hope for would be mass hysteria and panic. At the worst, full-scale revolt."

Simon had been waiting for an opening of this type, and he landed on it with both feet. "I assume your 'good authority' was someone hired by the government and paid by either you or someone so like you that it would make no difference. That particular attitude comes right out of the Middle Ages and has absolutely no basis in fact. Another way to say what you just did is to say that the human race is too stupid to handle the information.

"Are you also saying that the largest portion of the population shouldn't be informed of the smallest? I seem to recall a tribe of twenty or thirty members from the Amazon basin that was a real nine-day wonder some years back. And they won't have near the impact on history that we will. We're over two thousand strong and about to double in the very near future, with a technology that dwarfs anything you have. And you think the people of Earth shouldn't know about it?"

Simon stood up and walked over to Anderson, intentionally stepping into his space. "You know, I have to wonder just who you really are—not so much who you are personally but who you represent. We've pretty much ruled out CIA. And since we have an FBI agent aboard ship, I'm relatively certain you aren't with them." He looked Anderson up and down disgustedly. "And I don't think the Office of Naval Intelligence would have you, so that leaves the DIA, which, if *you're* any specimen, I'm sorry to say that I was one of for several years." At the slight narrowing of Anderson's eyes, Simon knew he had scored.

"DIA. I should have known. Confirmation is always appreciated. I knew a few of your kind when I was in the business. It's nice to know that some things never change. Now I'm going to have to fumigate my house." He shook his head. "You seem to think we're a threat to you, Mister Anderson. Are we a threat because we won't give you our shiny new toy? Or because we're going to let everybody else play with it, too?"

Anderson tried again. "Your weapons and technology are so far ahead of ours that we have to have a serious threat assessment. We don't know what you can do, or will do. If the videos we've seen are real, and I don't doubt that they are, then we have a real problem. And *you* are the problem."

Simon sighed. "You do realize that you just acknowledged that they are *our* weapons and tech? There are a hell of a lot more of you than us. We can't survive without you, but you can survive without us. These are facts even I can see, and you should be able to see them, too. The problem is that if we have to try to survive alone, you could very likely wind up without any of the technology. And we keep trying to tell you that there are others out there who know we are here, now. Add to that the fact that we don't think they are the ones we got the ship from. They want to keep us out of space for one reason or another. Then, there're the ones we call the Builders. When those guys show up to get their ship back, what are you going to do?"

He walked across the room and sat back down. Ensign Martin had set another beer on the table beside his chair, and Simon picked it up. Looking at his wife and friends, he nodded. Not bothering to drink from the beer, he used it to gesture with. "The point I'm making here is this: we asked you to reveal our presence. We gave you the opportunity to put the best light on it that you could, and you did nothing. Well, we're going to do it for you. What we have is another video. We'll show it to you and let you go tell your bosses. So that they will have some warning. I don't like being blind-sided, and I don't think they do either. We are set up to transmit a signal in forty-eight hours to the entire world, one time-zone at a time. This transmission will explain who we are, what we stand for, where we plan to go, and how we got what we have. We'll start with India and Russia because they are on the other side of the globe and it will be eight AM there. Then each time zone until we get them all. Here, watch this."

Picking up a remote control, he pointed at a TV that had been on but muted throughout the meeting. "This is a copy of the tape we will video we'll air in two days. As soon as you leave here, get it to your bosses. Maybe they can put some kind of positive spin on things before the balloon goes up. Sit back and hold on, folks. The ride is about to get bumpy."

Simon pressed play, and the actors winked out,

replaced by snow. Seconds later, an image formed, and there stood Simon himself, dressed in his uniform, collar insignia in place and nametag above his pocket. A dais stood beside him, but behind him was the blackness of space, relieved only by the stars. Off to one side, a ship could be seen. He stood there for a few seconds without saying a word and then began to speak. "People of the planet Earth."

Simon paused the video. "I know that's melodramatic. I didn't want to use it, but everybody said I should because it would get people's attention. I think most of 'em have seen one science-fiction show too many, but I gave in to it." He pressed resume and the video continued to play.

"My name is Simon Hawke and I have a spaceship—a real, working spaceship that's capable of going from one star to another. We call her the *Galileo*. I know she came from outside the solar system because we, that is, Earthmen, didn't build it, so it *had* to come from elsewhere. It's capable of building other ships and bases. At the time of this transmission, the *Galileo* is in orbit around Earth, along with the ship you see in the background. We've named her the *McCaffrey*. How we came to be in possession of all this is a story for another time. Right now, what you need to know is that we have the ship and several other ships we've built over the past two years.

"The reason for this transmission is to inform you of our existence. The governments of Earth have consistently refused to reveal our presence, saying it would cause too much panic for you to know about us.

"As people just like yourselves, that is, average

citizens, we believe the ship we found and all the technology on it belongs to the human race in common. Not to any one country or group within a country, but to all people everywhere. We therefore have petitioned the governments of Earth to grant us three embassies—one on the North American continent, one in Europe, and one somewhere in Asia. We'd like to place the first in Switzerland as they have a reputation for neutrality unsurpassed in history. These embassies will be open to all citizens of Earth where you can come and request a position aboard one of our stations or ships. We wish to trade some of the ship's technology for these bases and for our people's safety when they're not aboard ship. So far, we've had no success getting any agreements of any kind. The only restrictions we've imposed at this time are on weapons and propulsion technology. All else is available to the people of Earth.

"The ship you see behind me is a warship, one of the only two operating ships we've built so far. We have four more in varying stages of completion, along with dozens of smaller, one-man ships we call Mambas. We regret the necessity of making our first ships warships, but the universe is not a friendly place. This ship was armed when we found it, suggesting enemies, and they turned up. We suffered casualties due to their interference, but we prevailed. We don't know whether their aggression was because our bases looked like their enemy's or if they wouldn't tolerate another space-based race. We wish to build freighters, passenger vessels, courier ships, survey vessels, resupply ships, and yes, unfortunately, other warships. We have three operating bases in the asteroid belt turning out ships for which we desperately need crews. Going to the governments of Earth would only defeat our purpose by allowing the weapons technology to get into the hands of people whose only agenda is to increase their own power.

"There is one other thing we want and that is for the people who join us not to be harassed when they come back to Earth—and come back they will. This is their home. They'll vacation here, visit friends and families, and retire here. We don't want our people arrested, detained, debriefed, interrogated, incarcerated, or anything else simply because they chose to work for us. If they were to break the laws of any country, they should, of course, be subject to those laws, but not just because they're our people who'll be bringing their knowledge back with them.

"This transmission is being made at this time because I, as commanding officer, am supposed to meet with and discuss just exactly these issues with various leaders of Earth within the next forty-eight hours. Since our request for acknowledgement has repeatedly been ignored, we therefore take this unilateral step to inform you of our existence. And while it's possible for this transmission to be faked, the visual display in your skies above some of the major cities in each time zone will most definitely not be fakes. This display will begin ten minutes after the end of this broadcast. We invite all interested parties, especially news agencies and scientists with cameras, to step outside and not only witness but film proof of our existence."

The image on the screen reached out and touched the podium he was standing beside. Almost immediately three Mambas moved across the open space behind him. "Those three ships," the recorded

Simon said as he stepped down off the dais, "are ships we call 'Mambas.'"

The invisible cameraman followed Simon as he walked over to and in front of a Mamba parked on the projects deck of the *Galileo*. "This is a closeup of what you just saw outside the force field. This is a Mamba, named after a very fast, very deadly snake, and it has already earned its name. This is what you're going to see in your skies ten minutes after this transmission ends. There will be three of them, and we invite your military forces to try to stop them. We will cause no damage to any of your craft or any of your property, but we're about to give you an aerial display that will prove that what we say is so.

"Please, after this transmission and display, get in touch with your governments. Let them know how you feel. We're betting that you'll feel the same way we do—that this is one of the most wonderful occurrences in human history and that to relegate what we found to some government would be the blackest folly. No one nation could hope to survive if all the others knew they had this ship. Before they could figure out how to use it, the world would end in a nuclear holocaust, and that's our prime reason for refusing to turn it over to any government. Tell your governments that you want the technology we can provide. Tell them that you want to join us on this, the greatest endeavor in human history, and that you want to be able to come and go at your own discretion. Thank you for your time."

At that point Simon stopped the video and walked over to the TV. Silence reigned in the room as he pulled the video out, placed it in a plastic case, and handed it to Galway. Turning the TV off, he turned to his guests. "Well, gentlemen, how did I come off? I tried not to sound too pretentious. I didn't want to sound like I was begging, and I tried not to sound like I was threatening. What do you think?"

Getting no response, he sat back down. "I think your bosses will be wanting to see that at the earliest possible moment. We have several ships available to perform the aerial acrobatics I explained. I think when it's the Eastern seaboard's turn, we're quite likely to hit both Washington, DC and Boston. What do you think? I'm thinking maybe Chicago and St. Louis. Denver, certainly. I had considered Roswell, but then I thought that would be… just not right. They've suffered enough. So, Albuquerque. And what do you think of San Francisco and Seattle? London will get a show, as well as Paris, Berlin, Beijing, Tokyo, Moscow, Sydney, and Johannesburg. Did I leave anyone out? Oh, well, my logistics people will let me know. And just for general information, we've turned off our shields. We can now be seen by any amateur astronomer, or professional, for that matter, about twelve thousand miles straight up. Visual, infrared, ultraviolet, and radio telescopes will have a problem since we don't transmit on any frequency known to man."

The man from NASA, Mitchell, was the first to say, "I think this should be brought to someone's attention immediately."

Kitty asked, "Just how immediately would you like, Mr. Mitchell? I can arrange for you to be in DC in about five minutes."

"You can do that? How?" he asked incredulously.

Kitty smiled. "Why, quite easily. First, we beam you up to the ship and then beam you back down to

DC. Five minutes and your boss will have that video."

Anderson stirred in his chair. "That would be a most inappropriate thing to do."

"Meaning you don't want one of your people out of your sight, is that right?" Commander Marshall quipped. "How about you go up with him? I'm sure we can arrange a small tour before beaming you back to Earth. I'll go with the two of you and make sure you get home safely. I know you want to see her, and I'm sure you've got your knickers in a twist over the fact that the FBI has had an agent aboard for a while now."

Kitty spoke up. "I like that idea, John. I could escort Mr. Galway and Colonel Babcock on a tour of their own, if they'd like." Kitty smiled at the two men.

Galway demurred. "That's a most generous gesture, Mrs. Hawke, but I'm afraid we'll have to decline. How about rain checks for the future?"

Kitty knew when she had a man hooked. "Why certainly, Mr. Galway. And as long as we're near—if not on—the subject, I have something for you."

Getting to her feet, she walked over to where Ensign Martin stood. Reaching down, she picked up a slightly oversized attaché case and carried it back to the coffee table. The men scurried to remove their drinks so she could open it.

Spreading the case out flat revealed an electronic device with a small screen in the center of one half and a rectangular hole to one side. She picked up a device the size of an ordinary cellphone and slid it into the hole. "Now, Brandon, this is a commlink capable of full two-way communication with the *Galileo*. If you'd be so kind as to place your hand on the screen, this device will tune itself to you." She looked him in the eyes and waited while he made up his mind.

Looking at his companions, he shrugged and did as Kitty asked. The screen lit up to a light green color, and a brighter bar of light swept from his fingertips to the heel of his hand and back again.

As the bar disappeared, Galway yelled, "Ouch! What the hell was that?"

Kitty gave him a coquettish look. "Why, Brandon, that was the DNA sample needed to tune the commlink to you. No one but you can use it now."

"Well, it stung," he said petulantly.

"And if I'd told you it was going to bite, would you have put your hand on it?" she asked.

"Probably not," he growled.

"Well, then," she said lightly, "there you go." She reached out and grabbed his hand. Turning it over, she examined his palm. "Not a drop of blood. We won't even need a Band-Aid. Better than a hospital, don't you think?"

Getting serious, Kitty looked at her watch. "I really hate to end our little tête-à-tête, but we have things to do. Busy changing the world, you know. And you guys have got to get on your way so you can try to stop us, or at least make yourselves look less bad. I really wish we could have met under different circumstances. Of, course," she said, "if we'd never found the ship, we wouldn't be playing in such strange territory and meeting such *in*teresting people."

She led her guests to the door, shook each hand and said, "Have a safe trip. And Brandon, don't try to pry open the commlink. It'll melt, leaving you with nothing.

LEGACY

CHAPTER THIRTY-FOUR

Simon sat in his ready room and listened to Jim Collier and Ted Brandt as they pitched their idea.

"Captain, we know what needs to be done to keep these people's attention," Jim said. "You say you want to start beaming them up today, which is fine. We can get them to show up at a meeting, but we need someone to come down and show them that we aren't kidding. So far, all we have is a very large number of upset people. You guys took too long getting back."

He slid a locator disk across the table to Ted. "You're familiar with one of these, right?" They both nodded. "Good, it'll act as a guide for a beam-in. I do need to know the time, at least approximately, so I can have my people on hand. I'd hate to upset any more folks by not appearing when you tell 'em we will."

Getting the time and location of the meeting, he handed Jim a video like the one Galway had taken back to Washington the day before. "You should see this. We plan to blanket the airwaves with this starting tomorrow morning. It's going out worldwide. If this meeting doesn't come off on time tonight, it could be awhile before the ruckus dies down enough to get enough people together for another demonstration. Tell your people we need about four hundred and sixty volunteers packed and ready to go.

And good luck."

Turning his visitors over to their guide so they could beam back down, Simon called Kitty and Lucy to put the idea of playing demonstrator to them. He found that it wasn't as hard as he'd figured. Apparently boredom was a factor that could figure heavily if properly worked. Leaving the situation in their capable hands, he turned to other matters.

Conferring with Flight Control was something that needed to be done in person. He deemed it essential to have the pilots involved as well. They were, after all, going to be the stars of the show starting in just a few more hours. Meeting with the pilots and Flight Control officers on the projects deck, Simon lined out his idea.

"I want the most visually exciting display you can manage, ladies and gentlemen, without cutting it too close—dogfights, playing tag, acrobatics. Have fun with it. You'll be flying in teams of three, and your lasers will be toned down to the point that they're no worse than Z-tag guns. Take shots at each other, but by no means are you to even look like you're firing on a planetary target or anything that comes from Earth. You may most definitely show your superiority by outrunning or flying rings around anything that tries to fly against you, but you'll leave the area as soon as practical without firing a shot at any craft or ground installation. Your lasers won't be able to down their ships anyway, but you could blind someone, and that could be just as bad. If one of you gets too far out of hand, I'll skin you alive in front of the others." None present doubted Simon's ability to do so. "No injuries to the downsiders or their property. All we want to do is impress the hell out of them. Got it?"

At their loud agreement, Simon nodded. "Then I'll turn you over to your individual flight controllers. Have fun, come home safe, and remember, you'll be monitored seven ways from Sunday, not to mention being filmed by every news service on the planet."

Kitty rather looked forward to the impromptu meetings she'd been asked to participate in. If her previous experience was any guide, they'd be a welcome respite from showing newbies around on orientation tours. It was one such tour she gladly turned over to her aide, Rukia Kimura, when she was called to the comm center.

"Mr. Galway," Kitty said. "I wasn't sure we'd be hearing from you today, but I'm glad you called. Or is this a 'Brandon' call?"

Galway's voice sounded strained. "I was hoping to speak to your husband, Wing Commander. And, unfortunately, I think it should remain formal today. It has to do with the meeting we've been discussing."

"I'm sorry, Captain Hawke isn't available at this time. I believe he's busy orchestrating an airshow. After all, our broadcast is due to go out in just under twenty-four hours. I'll have to do for the moment, unless you have a problem dealing with females."

Galway's voice sounded harried. "You know I don't. But, if I may, Wing Commander, this call is to get a specific time arranged for our two principals to get together. You appreciate the demands Vice-President Reese has on him, I'm sure. Not to say that Captain Hawke isn't very busy, as well, but…"

Kitty let him off the hook. "I do see your point,

Mr. Galway. Do you have the vice-president with you? I can get Simon here in ten minutes so there won't be any more delay on the matter."

Galway answered, "That much speed won't be necessary, ma'am. The other thing I was to tell you was that there's going to be a special press conference starting in about half an hour. President Drake will be making an announcement that I'm sure you'll want to hear. I believe that any time after that press conference, Vice-President Reese will be available to speak to Captain Hawke."

Kitty sighed in relief. Finally! "Thank you, Mr. Galway. I appreciate the heads-up and will pass the information to Simon immediately. Do your best to stay close to the vice-president, and try to be in a secure area so he can speak freely. We'll wait for your call after the telecast."

Simon, Kitty, Lucy, and Stephen all gathered around the ready room table. They'd been joined by Commander Shipley and several other officers to view the broadcast and give their reactions, if necessary. Kitty had set up the screen and recording device as soon as she'd informed Simon of Galway's call so a permanent record of the broadcast could be made.

By the time Simon arrived, the room was full, and coffee was on the table. Simon settled himself into his chair and asked what, specifically, Galway had said. She repeated the conversation as close to word-for-word as she could.

"They're cutting it a little close," he said. "Of course, there's a lot more of them that have to be in the loop than there are up here. Can you imagine the uproar this is going to make in Congress? And the House? First, all of those guys will have to be informed and convinced before this broadcast. I wish I could have heard some of those conversations. So, let's see what's on the agenda for tonight."

As the final minutes wore down before the broadcast, Lucy fidgeted, Stephen doodled, and Simon sat still and raptly watched the last few minutes of a primetime sitcom as eight p.m. Eastern time approached.

About ten seconds into an ad promising less redness if one just used a certain eyedrop, the signal suddenly cut off and was replaced by a face most Americans knew, even if they couldn't put a name to it. No one was left to guess for long as the man holding the microphone said, "Ladies and gentlemen, I'm Wolf Blitzer, NBC News correspondent to the White House. I'm standing here in the press room tonight by special invitation, along with several dozen other correspondents from various agencies around the country and the globe who've been able to get here in time. We've been informed that President Drake will be out shortly to make an announcement. Speculation is rampant as to the content, and the atmosphere is charged. No one, least of all this reporter, has any idea what's going on. We've only been told that the president will be out momentarily to make an announcement of global significance."

The scene cut to a newsroom with a male and female anchor staring out at the country from a set with the usual backdrop—a map of the globe surmounted by half-a-dozen clocks showing the time in various places around the world. The man asked,

"Wolf, do you have any idea what could be of such great importance that President Drake would call a conference on such short notice?"

The camera cut back to Wolf, standing in the press room amid a confusing jumble of people and camera equipment. The presidential seal was prominent on the podium behind him, and several agitated people were standing on the stage to each side of the podium, looking confused. The only islands of serenity in view were the secret service agents standing in various places within the camera's view.

Wolf, microphone in his right hand and left hand to his ear, said, "No, Don, we have no idea. No one here has a clue as to what the president has to say, which is why we're at such loose ends tonight."

A mumbled voice spoke from off camera. Wolf looked over his shoulder and then back at the camera. "Don, it looks like President Drake is about to come out now. Yes, I believe he is, preceded by two secret service men. He's stepping onto the stage, followed by Vice-President Reese." Wolf faced the front and stepped to one side so the camera could get a clear view.

The president walked across the stage with a grace belying the fact that he'd been effectively sandbagged by the ultimatum handed out by Simon just a few hours previously. He stopped at the podium, faced the audience, and in an unusual departure for a man who liked to look like he was speaking off the cuff, pulled a piece of paper from his inside coat pocket and made a show of flattening it out on the podium before he spoke.

"Ladies and gentlemen of the press. I want to

thank you for being here on such short notice tonight. First, let me say that I have an announcement of earth-shattering proportions to make. Second, I must say that I will take no questions on this matter tonight. I leave that to my scientific advisory staff. I do feel that the nature of what I am about to reveal to you, and the gravity of the situation, compels me to stand here tonight and make this announcement. What I am about to say is going to be unbelievable, even coming from a president."

Drake took a deep breath as he glanced down at the paper he'd laid out, and his knuckles visibly whitened as his hands gripped each side of the podium. "Ladies and gentlemen," he said as he looked down. He then raised his head and looked directly at the bank of cameras before him. "It is my duty to inform you that… we… are… not… alone… in… the… universe." Not one sound came from any corner of the room as the shockwave moved outward from the podium. The members of his staff on the stage glanced first at each other and then at the president and vice-president as if they, too, were stunned by this revelation.

The president went on. "There has been controversy since 1947, and even earlier, as to whether or not the human race was alone in the universe. Conspiracy theorists said the government cleaned up the wreck at Roswell and hid it, along with bodies and that proved aliens existed. Others have said there was no wreckage, which proved there is no life out there. When I took office, I was asked by various factions to look into the situation. I asked questions. I assigned people to look into it, and nothing concrete turned up. I didn't follow it any further. The exigencies of my office precluded spending any more time on a matter of such seemingly small significance.

"My personal feelings on the matter aside, I, and a very few members of my staff, have been made privy to the fact that citizens of the United States have come into possession of a spaceship of alien origin. Ladies and gentlemen of the press, living, intelligent beings, born on a planet that circles a sun other than ours, built a spaceship, and for one reason or another that ship wound up here and derelict. Citizens of the United States found the ship and took it for their own. They have decided, unwisely, I feel, to refrain from turning that ship over to this government or any other government on this planet. Their stated reason is that to do so would upset the balance of power and precipitate a nuclear war from which we would never recover. Their stated goal is to use the technology that comes from this vessel to benefit mankind as a whole, not just one country or group. As far as we have been able to ascertain in the slightly over two years they have been in possession of this vessel, they have done nothing that did not follow their stated goals.

"They have recruited and trained some two thousand persons, mostly from the United States, and to the best of our knowledge, have three bases in the asteroid belt. Aside from the original ship, they have built and crewed two other ships. Our sources tell us that one more base is to be built, and then each of these four bases will be turning out a steady stream of ships. It has further been brought to my attention that shortly after completion of the first base, it was attacked by persons or beings," here the president's speech stumbled a bit, "of unknown origin. Most likely, we are led to believe, by a second race that is an enemy to the race that originally built the ship our citizens possess. The attack was fended off at some loss of life to our citizens, but they have carried on their program of expansion.

"Now to the reason for this press conference tonight: The Office of the President, along with a select few others, has known of the existence of this group for almost two years. Once I ascended to this office, I was informed of the existence of this group as well. This knowledge has stayed at the highest levels as we tried to work out policies for dealing with this new and disturbing situation.

"Unfortunately, the decision no longer rests with us. Beginning right now, in the time zone that includes Rangoon, Burma, New Delhi, India, Kathmandu, Nepal and portions of Tibet, China and Russia, a telecast is being made to the peoples of Earth. This telecast is designed to acquaint you with this new group and their goals. According to our sources, after each telecast an aerial demonstration will be performed over the major cities of the area. We ask all countries that you do not, repeat, *do not* interfere with the demonstrations or fire on these vessels. They are friendly and are only demonstrating their existence.

"One of the things that has been requested by this group is a series of embassies on Earth. Three in all—one on the European continent, one in Asia, and one on the North American continent. Another thing they have requested is freedom from prosecution, persecution, arrest, harassment, or interrogation for all of their people based on who they choose to work for. They do agree that they should be subject to the laws of any nation they visit. They ask that they be allowed to recruit volunteers for their space-based labor force and earth-side embassies, station personnel and shipboard personnel. In return, they offer access to the technology of this marvelous vessel to increase the quality of life on Earth. They ask that all peoples of Earth be allowed to apply, regardless of gender, religion or ethnicity, and insist that any technology traded is to be given to all countries simultaneously so that no one country gets an advantage over another.

"Artificial gravity, antigravity, new manufacturing techniques, methods to help us clean up our water and air, methods to help restore the ozone layer, methods to make our homes and automobiles more efficient and cheaper to operate, and methods to feed our hungry are among the items this group, this Terran Alliance, is willing to trade for the concessions they have requested. At the same time, these ships will give the human race the universe. I ask you, do not be alarmed. You will be seeing vessels operated by human beings over the next twenty-four hours in your skies. These vessels will be there to show you their abilities and to show you that they actually exist.

"Negotiations with the leaders of this group will commence immediately, headed by Vice-President Reese and attended by representatives of various nations of Earth. Knowing that I am being listened to as I speak, I extend an invitation to the leader of the group, Captain Simon Hawke, to meet with Vice-President Reese at Camp David so negotiations can begin and an alliance can be forged that can take the human race to the stars.

"It is my understanding that two vessels are currently in orbit around our planet at an altitude of about twelve thousand miles. They have turned off their shielding so they can be seen by professional and amateur astronomers alike to make my revelation easier to believe." He looked down at his paper on the dais. "Two major radio-telescope arrays and more than a dozen optical telescopes from observatories around the northern hemisphere have confirmed the existence of two objects at a height of about twelve thousand miles directly above the North American continent.

"I hasten to point out to all the peoples of Earth that this is not, I repeat, *not* an American endeavor. It is simply a matter of Americans finding the technology. And it is they who insist on making it something that crosses all national borders, all racial barriers, and all religious barriers. They are the ones who insist on bases outside the U.S. and accepting anyone who wants to join. As soon as negotiations can be completed, we hope to see all three embassies up and running, but this is not something that can happen overnight. Ladies and gentlemen, thank you for coming."

The president turned to leave the stage, and pandemonium broke out among the reporters. Microphones were raised, voices were raised, and questions were screamed, but, ramrod straight, President Drake walked out of the room, led by secret service and trailed by Vice-President Reese.

It was a full ten seconds before veteran reporter Wolf Blitzer realized his cameraman was filming an empty stage and stepped in front of the live camera. A look of shock was as apparent on his face as it was on the faces of everyone as he said, "Don, for the first time in my life as a reporter, I am absolutely speechless. I can only say that the president's words, if true, speak for themselves, and only time will tell that tale."

The scene cut back to the newsroom and the male anchor said, "What was that about aerial displays?"

The scene cut back to Wolf. "Oh, yes, Don. President Drake said there would be a broadcast from this group of people in each time zone, followed by an aerial display of some type to prove they were telling the truth. We can only wait and see. What I remember hearing is that the first broadcast and demonstration will take place over India, and actually, should be taking place right now. You should be getting reports from that part of the world any time now.

"This is a situation where we will know very soon whether the statements made here tonight by the president are true or whether he has somehow been hoaxed into giving us misinformation, if that is what it is." With one more look over his shoulder at the stage, Wolf turned back to the camera. "It appears that there will be no more from this quarter tonight, so this is Wolf Blitzer in Washington DC. Back to you, Don."

The camera cut back to the newsroom one more time, the two anchors looking as composed as they could, given the circumstances.

Simon reached down, picked up a remote and shut off the screen. "Ladies and gentlemen," he said, "mission accomplished." The sound of cheering made him wince in the confines of the small room. "We'll air the alternate video before each demonstration. Don't want to embarrass our new partners any more than we already have, do we?"

CHAPTER THIRTY-FIVE

Simon handed a disc to Kitty. "Would you see that this gets to Communications, dear? We don't want the wrong one to air. And see if you can raise Galway. We'll send him a copy for his boss so they aren't uninformed. Seems like good manners since we just got all we asked for, don't you think?"

Kitty agreed that it was, indeed, good manners. "But, what are the changes you've made in the second video? I saw the first one, but I actually didn't have any idea there was a second."

Simon seemed to be enjoying himself. "Well, it wouldn't have worked if President Drake hadn't made a mistake. He used the word 'embassies' several times in his speech. I'd used it during our talks with Galway and company, and it got to his ear and came out of his mouth. What the second video does is leave out any reference to disagreements or coercion in getting recognized and refers to us three times as the Terran Alliance."

Stephen, quick to see the implications, spoke up. "You're looking for status as an independent power, aren't you?" he asked. "Only political entities have embassies, and the President is talking about granting them. That is, of course, if the other nations agree."

Simon grinned. "Oh, they'll agree, all right. The only question is how fast. We've dangled some bait already, showing our ships here. And there's more bait to come in the aerial displays. Of course, some countries will try to shoot our guys down. That's a given. But nothing they have can penetrate our shields, and the Mambas are just way too fast, even in atmosphere. My only concern is that our hotshot boys and girls will do something stupid before they get used to flying in atmosphere. So far, all they've done is play around where there is none. I made sure they know to be careful and remember their limitations, but you know how kids with new toys are, especially when they get to show off."

Kitty looked at her husband closely. "This is one even I didn't see coming, Simon. What do you have planned?"

"It's not so much a plan as a dream, hon. And all of you," he said as he turned to the people gathered in the room, "I hope, will see the wisdom in this. If we're independent, we can write our own rules and grow in our own direction. I hope that direction is one that will lead us to the stars as a responsible, caring group—and group is the key word, here. We need to be unified. If we buy into the philosophies down there, we'll wind up just like them—factionalized and fighting over every little word or punctuation in every little document. We need to keep to the bigger picture and follow the spirit, as much as the letter, of whatever we lay down as our operating guidelines. If we stay independent, we stand a chance of influencing them to join us and reunite the human race."

People began excusing themselves to get back to whatever they'd been called from—some to their duty stations and some to bed or time off.

The first to leave was Commander Pritchert,

head of Flight Ops. "I've got people ready to fly, and I need to be there. We plan to have an oversight craft filming each demonstration as well, so I have that much more to do."

Kitty nodded in approval. "Filming is a good idea. We'll have something to show the holdouts about what advantages we have. And if these hotshots know they're being filmed, it might help hold down some of the wilder stuff. They've been told to play around but to be careful. I've also told 'em that anything I find on one of these flights that I don't like, I'll pull their license so fast it'll make their heads swim."

The next several days produced enough activity to keep everyone busy. The culmination was Simon receiving a call from Galway in which he spoke to the vice-president personally and was invited to come to Camp David in three days for a meeting with representatives of most of the more advanced nations and some of the less advanced, as well. "They'd like to know how all this is going to affect nations in the third world," the vice-president said.

Simon replied that the food-processor technology alone would put an end to hunger in most of the world. Given one of the machines, all a person would have to do was put organic material, any organic material, into a receptacle, press a series of buttons, and food would come out the other end. "It's fully programmable, so whatever you want the machine to produce is kept in memory, so to speak, and when you put enough material in and request the item, it will appear. And it can be programmed to refuse to produce items like liquor and drugs of all kinds. Or it can be used in a hospital and programmed to produce the very drugs other units will be unable to synthesize. This is one item we think should be produced and distributed without charge to hungry people around the world. One machine would feed dozens, even hundreds of people. That should do for starters."

Another thing that happened was that new faces began appearing on the *Galileo* again since Kitty and Lucy beamed down to several meetings and sparked near riots at two of them. Beaming out was the only alternative at one meeting where several women tried to grab them to prove they were holograms. Lucy left behind a sleeve and quite a few skin cells in the fingernails of one disbeliever. Kitty fared only a little better when a half-full drink cup that should have passed through her bounced off, covering her with something sticky and cold.

Jim and Ted were kept busy handing out their contact number to anyone who asked. After several meetings, it looked like the total number required for this trip would be met handily. To prevent a recurrence of the last time, Ted suggested that several of the unlucky ones who wouldn't be going this time be given tours of the ship to prove it was real. That, coupled with the president's revelation and subsequent aerial displays all over the world, not only put an end to any disbelief among the faithful, but it assured a worldwide volunteer base that wouldn't be depleted any time soon.

Simon went into a flurry of activity after his talk with

the vice-president. He called in his new security chief, Commander Larry Staples, a former Navy Seal and one of the original members of the crew, his second in command, Robert Shipley, and a lieutenant commander named Olivia Beauchamp to meet with him and Kitty. Along for the meeting were Lucy Grimes from the *McCaffrey* and Stephen Walker for ideas and opinions.

Simon proposed that he, Staples, Shipley, and Beauchamp be the contact team for this initial meeting. "I *have* to go, of course. Staples is for backup, Shipley so that in the future I won't have to be present, and Beauchamp because she's the only one I've found so far who'll admit to being a law student. She wasn't far from taking her bar exams when she decided to take a vacation with us. Now, her knowledge will come in handy.

"I don't intend for us to get entangled in legal disputes though. It's been my experience that if you lay out what you want and the other guy wants it, too, he'll find a way to take it. I plan to let the vice-president and his staff tell us how what we want can be accomplished. Granted, it's simplistic, but some of the best plans are just that. If it doesn't work, we haven't lost anything, and we can look for legal help among the downsiders.

"It's been requested that we don't beam down since too many of the people present aren't familiar with the concept, even from science fiction. So, Commander Staples will pilot a shuttle down, carrying the four of us. I've been informed that a wing of Apache helicopters will be in the air while we're there, strictly as protection, of course, so I informed Galway that a flight of Mambas would fly as backup. This flight, ladies and gentlemen, will not have their wings clipped like the demonstrators did."

Anyone who'd been watching Kitty while he'd been expounding his plan to speak to the vice-president would have seen her eyes narrow slightly. She listened quietly and patiently while he outlined his plan, and her expression darkened visibly when she heard who he planned to take down with him for his contact team. Security chief, sure. Second in command, understandable. But, Beauchamp just because she'd studied law?

A flight of Mambas for cover? she thought. *I told him I'd be along for the ride. I just hope he forgets until it's too late. Shit. I'll fly even if he* does *find out!*

When Simon finished and hadn't specifically assigned anyone to take charge of the cover flight and their pilots, Kitty volunteered her services as Wing Commander. "I'm not doing anything else, anyway," she said offhandedly. "So, who better than a Mamba Wing Commander, and wife, to oversee pilot selection and work with Flight Control to ensure mission safety."

Simon considered the matter for a few seconds, then said, "Sure, why not? I can't think of anyone better to watch my back." He reached out and patted her on the leg. "And it'll teach you not to volunteer."

Radio and television commentators had plenty to keep them occupied for the next couple of days—speculation about the president's announcement, analysts taking it apart, spin doctors from both sides of the aisle ringing in with their opinions, and astronomers confirming the presence of two objects in orbit that shouldn't be there. Simon's broadcast received a lot of attention, and the demonstration flights were featured items. A lot was made of the fact that on more than one occasion a Mamba pilot had missed, and his laser had done no damage to objects on the ground. One scientist said something about attenuated beam strength inside Earth's atmosphere, and the debate over that went on for hours. There were religious views, pro and con, as well as various and sundry nuts able to get airtime— enough material to keep people arguing for years.

Simon had insisted that the meeting at Camp David be covered by the press and televised live. Galway threw a fit.

"Security details are staggering, as it is, Captain. We'll have dignitaries from all over the globe there and no way to guarantee their safety. Normally, it wouldn't be a problem, as I'm sure you're about to point out, but we're dealing with an entirely different set of circumstances. This topic is too highly charged. If the press shows up, the nuts will follow. There'll be demonstrations and possibly riots. I'm sorry, but no press."

Simon balked. "First and foremost, I'm insulted, Mr. Galway. Camp David is one of the most secure places on the planet. Just who will you be needing to protect those dignitaries from?" Simon let the silence from the other end of the connection go on until it was uncomfortable. "You're certainly not going to say that it would be from us, are you? We'll be the only 'unknown quantity' there, so it must be. Maybe we should just call this whole thing off."

Galway got his voice back, and apparently so did someone in the background. Simon couldn't make out the words, but he did hear another voice. "The president has already made the announcement, Captain, and representatives from dozens of nations have already started to arrive. The meeting should go on as planned. This is turning into a circus." His voice died out.

Simon spoke into the silence, picturing the agent sweating as one of his bosses put words in his mouth. "I'm not saying no more secrets, Galway. What I *am* saying is that this is already public knowledge. People have seen the Mambas. Some will surely see the shuttle and her escort. The press can be on hand for that, at least. You'll do more for a space shuttle launch than you will for the first meeting between an extraplanetary power and the leaders of the nations of Earth?" He paused to let Galway respond.

Getting nothing, Simon added, "What arrangements we make, you can keep at a high level and spin them any way you want as long as they don't make us look bad in the process. But the fact of our existence and our comings and goings, well that's history in the making. And I'll bet from all the crap that's been aired on radio and television for the last couple of days that all the major networks would just love to be there to get footage of the first landing of an alien craft. So, here's the deal: if we aren't seeing live transmissions on most, if not all, of the major networks, our shuttle won't leave the bay. Now, we've already acceded to your request that we not beam down the first time. It's time for you to give a little, too. Or are you afraid of something, Mr. Galway?"

Kitty, in the room at the time of the call, felt her heart skip a beat when Simon made that remark. When the conversation was over, she asked as lightly as she knew how, "What do you think the deal is there?"

Simon waved a hand negligently in the air. "Oh, just more of the usual government secrecy bullshit. I just don't intend to let them get away with it."

Kitty left Simon with all of her alarm bells ringing. She beamed over to the *McCaffrey* after making sure Lucy was in and made her way through overcrowded corridors to Lucy's ready room.

"Just how many people do you have aboard this tub, Lucy?" Kitty asked as she sat down.

"Don't call my bucket a tub, dammit," Lucy shot back. "Simon wants to crew two vessels at once, as you know. We're just taking some of the *Galileo's* overflow. My exec, Mark Brenner, is getting one of the ships, so we took on the people who'll be training for command level and a few others, as well. And you know Gayle is getting one of the others, so Marsha is bringing the *Heinlein* in. Simon is having his meeting tomorrow morning, and we're supposed to get underway right after that. It'll only be for a week, so I don't see any real problems. We could do it a little faster, but we can use that week for training."

"True enough," Kitty agreed. "And that brings us to why I'm here. I have a funny feeling about this meeting."

Lucy concurred. "I've noticed that you've been kind of jumpy the last couple of days, ever since the meeting was finally confirmed. Anything specific?"

"Well, no. I want these bases as much as anyone else does, and I realize how important the meeting is. I'd put my jitters down to a wife being concerned about her husband… until I overheard a call between Simon and Galway."

"What did you hear?" Lucy inquired. She leaned forward, laying her forearms on the desk, fingers laced together.

"I was there when Simon was discussing the final details with Galway. And Galway said no media, which Simon refused to agree to. Galway finally gave in. You know how Simon can be. I'd hate to be there when he finally meets the guy as stubborn as he is. Anyway, I just don't feel right. It's not anything I can put a finger on, you know? So. I'm supposed to be picking the pilots for Simon's cover flight. That's my official reason for being here. Simon thinks I'm going to pick five of your pilots, then go sit in the *Galileo's* Flight Control and monitor the whole thing from there. He seems to have forgotten my promise to fly cover for him, and after that call, I'm *definitely* going to be in a cockpit. He'll think someone else is in charge of it right up until something goes wrong. *If* something goes wrong. And that information stops right here, Lucy," Kitty said, tapping Lucy's desk. "He's going to have enough on his mind."

Lucy said, "I have to credit your feelings, Kitty. I have them, too. But this, I don't know. Of course, I'll keep the secret. Just be careful, okay?"

Kitty stood. "Of course. And I'll keep in the background unless there's trouble. Now, down to Flight Control. See you later."

She called Flight Control and requested that four

particular pilots meet her in Fighter Operations. When she arrived on the flight deck, she saw the last of the four entering a room located at the far end of the corridor. She hurried along past the launch bays holding their craft and entered to find all four pilots in deep discussion about the mysterious summons.

After a few minutes of reminiscing, she got to the point. "I'll put an end to the mystery right now," she said. The four pilots, all veterans from the very first group of volunteers, looked at her expectantly. Shirley Dahlquist, Amy Carpenter, Velma Randall, and David Sipes were people she'd flown with and respected. Now she was to fly with them one more time. "As you know, tomorrow morning Simon is going to take a shuttle down to Camp David. We've been informed that there will be a wing of five Apache helicopters to provide protection for the dignitaries there, and we've informed them that we'll have five Mambas flying cover for us. You'll be four of those pilots, and I'll be the fifth.

"Commander Dahlquist will be in charge of the flight." As Shirley started to protest, Kitty added, "As far as Simon knows, you're in command. All radio traffic will come from you, and I'll be referred to as Lt. Johnson. As long as nothing goes wrong, you'll stay in charge. If the shit hits the fan, I'll take over and assume all responsibility for our actions. Clear?" At Shirley's nod, she went on. "I chose you four because I know you. I know how you fly and how you think. I know you'll follow orders, and I know you'll deviate only if you think it's truly necessary. I hope it won't be.

"Orders for the flight are as follows: Going in, it's okay to show off until we get close to the ground.

You need to know how your ships will react in atmosphere if you weren't among the display pilots, so play with 'em. Once we get down, pick a chopper and play one-on-one with it. You will not fire on any individual, installation, or craft, unless fired on first. Keep in mind that there'll be media there filming our arrival and actions, so be on your best behavior. The contact team can beam out if necessary, but that would leave a shuttle on the ground in unfriendly hands. I'll take the responsibility for destroying it, if necessary. The contact team will have their wristbands slaved together. If one person hits the button, they all go. Their bio-monitors will activate the recall if their stress levels get too high, or we can manually recall them if we decide the situation warrants it. The rest will be an improvisation, just like it will be for the contact team.

"We can 'how about' and 'what if' all day long, but that's it in a nutshell. I'll beam over as soon as Simon boards the shuttle, so we won't have much time to talk until the mission. I'll say 'good flying' now and let you check your ships. I'll have the Chief see that a ship is prepped for me, too, and I'll see you in the morning."

She started for the door and turned. "Oh, yes. Remember, my part in this flight is secret. I can't have Simon catching on until after we get back aboard. That's all."

CHAPTER THIRTY-SIX

The alarm went off as if it were any other day. Kitty woke at the first ring but lay on her side, pretending sleep and interpreting the movements of the bed as Simon moved over to shut the ringer off. She experienced a feeling of separation the moment his body no longer touched the bed, believing the mattress transmitted their heartbeats to each other.

She heard him shuffle across the floor and turned over to watch him walk into the bathroom. Laying there listening for the shower to start, Kitty stretched, feeling disgustingly good after the night they'd just had. She smiled to herself, content, until her feet touched the deck.

Why is it, she thought, *that every time I think my life is going well, something happens to upset it?*

The smile faded from her face and she stood up, knowing that the water would be just right and she had to go in there. She smiled again. Simon had known she was awake when he left the room. She often thought they'd been married too long and knew each other too well.

Maybe that's the problem, she thought. *When he starts to predict me, well, I'm just going to have to put some surprise back into that man's life.*

Keeping her nervousness to herself, she stepped into the shower and wrapped her arms around her man, letting her body adjust to the heat and steam of the shower stall. Nuzzling the back of his neck, she said, "Ready for the big day, lover? And after a night like that?"

Simon turned around in the circle of her arms. Obviously more awake and functional than a few minutes earlier, he replied, "You bet. Nights like that only make me look forward to more nights like that." He grinned down at her and kissed her forehead. "Now, woman, no time for fun and games. We'll have plenty of that once we break orbit." He turned back around, feeling her hands pressing against the flesh of his waist. "Scrub my back?"

Showers finished, they both got dressed and stopped in the mess hall for a light breakfast before heading down to the shuttle waiting on deck eighteen.

"Last night'll have to hold both of us until I get back. Now, get to Flight Control, so I know I'm safe." He looked deep into her eyes, kissed her lightly one more time, and turned her loose, then spun on his heel and headed for the shuttle.

Hours before Simon and Kitty had even thought about getting out of bed, Agent Daniels was in his specially selected hiding place, congratulating himself on picking just the right spot. He watched as the shuttle was moved into position by the bay operators stationed above and counted the service techs as they began their morning preflight checks. He would stay sequestered until all support personnel left, which should be enough time to sneak aboard unless guards had been posted.

He'd taken a tour of one of these workhorses with Kitty's permission and had found the best place to hide his less-than-svelte girth. Now, a low chime over the loudspeakers announced lunch. He carefully stood up, the returning circulation almost making him fall. By his best estimate, all the workers had left the shuttle, so he slipped out of the locker carrying the smallest case that would hold his various "finds" aboard ship.

He started to relax and then remembered the force field over the bay doors. Among the items he had on him was a laser pistol "found" in a locker room while its true owner showered off the day's stink. He also got Crewman McNalley to find a way to undo the wristband he wore without it showing on the bridge. He'd gotten a replica to wear at times when he didn't want it known that he was out of his room. And he got McNalley to make a more advanced Taser into the same casing.

Now he had a decision to make—try for the shuttle or go back to his bunk. He was armed with multiple disks, two guns, and terabytes of additional data hidden on various parts of his uniform.

Now was the time, before someone came back early. He pushed the locker door shut with a faint sound and made directly for the shuttle. To his great relief, no one was aboard and no guards called for him to stop. He slipped into the engine room, slid the door into place, and found his hiding spot. After putting his pack down, he sat on it, completely hidden behind one of the oversized generators.

He was still hidden when he heard the returning flight techs, but no one entered the engine room. Soon, he heard Simon's voice, along with several others. The engines began to power up for their prelaunch test while other systems did the same.

"Yes, Sally," the reporter said into the camera, "we're here at Camp David awaiting an historic moment. This is the first time something will land on Earth that hasn't first been launched from the Earth. At least," he continued with a smile on his face as his entire body radiated a palpable sense of excitement, "officially. Stories about Roswell come to mind, crop circles, and many other things as well. But none of those have ever been substantiated. Today we will be able to see something land. I must admit that I'm having a bit of trouble believing all this, Sally. It just seems a bit too… Star Wars-ish. Officials have been very closemouthed about the situation, except to say that we'll be witnessing the first official meeting between this Terran Alliance and representatives from all over the world. What type of craft will land or even how it will land hasn't been divulged.

"Historically, the only flying craft that come to Camp David are helicopters, and the only thing we have to go on so far are all the films of those small fighter-type craft that buzzed the major cities of the world, putting on the aerial displays that are still causing such a furor in scientific circles. In some cases, those craft came to a complete stop and held position for extended periods of time before moving on.

"Where we're set up, just outside the main gate, we have as good a view as anyone is going to get of the landing, if it occurs." The commentator was obviously displeased with not being closer but was unsure whether the unexpected restriction was justified or not. He went on. "I've had the privilege of being present at two space shuttle landings, and I can tell you that what we have here today is a drastic departure from that type of landing. A shuttle essentially glides into a landing area on runways specially designed for a long, rolling stop. The field we've been told to watch is too short by far for anything but a powered landing. And as a pilot, I can say that, considering the area, the angle of descent will be rather steep.

"Whatever's coming down shortly is going to do so in a manner that very few crafts can manage— helicopters, VTOL's like the Osprey, and such. But a powered space-to-ground craft? Nothing in any arsenal on the planet can do it in the space available, Sally. And we are led to believe from the press release," he said, waving a piece of paper at the camera, "that the craft will take off and go back again without refueling."

Another voice, another channel. "According to what we've been told, the vessel will land shortly after eight a.m. and we'll get our first glimpse of the enigmatic Captain Hawke setting foot on Terran soil."

Simon laughed as he turned away from the screen that had been set up on the projects deck. "So, now I'm 'enigmatic.'" He turned to the assembled crowd and said, "Well, folks. Let's go make a deal." He watched as the rest of the away team filed aboard the small shuttle Daniel Baylor had presented to the *Galileo* so long ago.

It hasn't been that long, has it? he thought. *Has it really been two whole years?*

He took Kitty off to one side. "Listen, Kittyn, I

can see the worry in your face. I've known you too long not to know that you've been troubled by this for days. I just don't know how to reassure you. Nothing I can possibly say would do it. You're a wife and your man is going into danger. I'd worry too if the situation were reversed." He smiled deprecatingly, hands out in a helpless gesture. "But the risk is worth it!"

He looked over his shoulder at the waiting ship, slid his arm up to her shoulders, and drew her to him, letting her head nestle against his chest. "Damn it, I know it sounds vain, Kittyn," he said to the air above her head, "but I remember that this is how the U.S. got her independence from Britain. They felt that the distance was so great and the information time-lag so long that it made no sense to remain so closely affiliated. They believed their distant shore gave them the right to determine their own destiny."

He stroked the back of her neck with his left hand. "And if this works, we'll do it without having to kill one person or have one of ours killed. A bloodless secession."

He raised his left hand to her head and let the reddish-gold hair spill from between his fingers, his eyes devouring the sight. "You know I can't do this without you, don't you?"

Kitty pushed back in his embrace, looking up angrily. "I hate it that you put this on me, Simon. You're not asking me if I believe in your vision; you've got more than enough who believe in that. You're asking me if I believe in *you*. And of course, I believe in you. I have since the day we met. I'd have thought you'd have known that, but… you're just a man." She squeezed him tightly for a moment and stepped back. "It's just that I didn't expect this! And I wish it didn't have to be you!"

Simon kissed her, feeling the rapid beating of her heart in the fingertips that lightly stroked her neck. "That's the best compliment I've ever had," he said.

Chief Hargrove waved to her from the last open bay door. She grabbed the helmet he held out as she swarmed up the boarding ladder, throwing her right leg into the cockpit and feeling the ladder retracting before her weight was fully off her left. She wormed her way into her flight harness and settled the helmet onto her head, absently acknowledging the ready status of the ship as the cockpit closed automatically. She had just enough time to realize that the name on the helmet read Hawke, K, and gave silent thanks to whoever'd had the foresight to bring it over from the *Galileo*.

As she put her helmet on, she became privy to the chatter across the open circuits. "Flight Leader, this is Flight Control. Telemetry shows Mamba Five occupied, prepped and ready for launch."

Kitty heard Shirley reply, "Roger, Flight Control. Confirm Mamba Five occupied. Mamba Five, report your status."

Kitty looked down, gave all of her instruments a final check, and reported, "Flight Leader, Mamba Five. Board green and ready for launch."

Shirley's voice came to her again, "Flight Control, this is Flight Leader. Mamba Flight reports all green, ready for launch. Request information on shuttle status."

Flight Control reported back, "*Galileo* Flight

Control reports clearing last computer glitch. Shuttle is preparing to leave the bay. Mamba Flight, you are clear to launch in sequence."

"Flight Control, this is Flight Leader. Acknowledge clear to launch in sequence. Mamba Flight, this is Flight Leader. Prepare to launch in sequence. Ten-second intervals. Form on me and await further instruction."

Kitty immediately felt the distinctive vibration that told her a Mamba had launched. As soon as she felt the fourth one, she began her own internal countdown, and on the mark, took her ship out of the bay. As soon as she slid into open space, her sensors came alive. She found the blips that represented the rest of her flight, moved herself into position, and reported, "Mamba Five, on station."

Kitty looked down at her screens and saw the five small blips of her flight, the larger one of the *McCaffrey*, and the still larger one of the *Galileo*. As she watched, a small blip separated itself from the largest one, and Simon's shuttle headed down at a sedate pace.

Shirley Dahlquist's voice came across the intercom, "Mamba Flight, this is Flight Leader. Escort formation. Johnson, take point," she said to Kitty. "Carpenter, port. Sipes, starboard. Randall, take the rear and watch out for the shuttle's backwash. Remember to test your controls, people, those who haven't flown in atmosphere before."

Kitty, appreciative of the fact that Shirley had assigned her the point so she could assess the situation, led the flight down, keeping their speed well below the levels Engineering recommended for atmospheric flight. As soon as she felt her ship buck, she reported, "Mamba Five. Atmospheric contact."

Both the shuttle pilot and her flight leader acknowledged, and almost immediately Simon's voice came over an auxiliary circuit. "Galway, this is Hawke. Do you copy?"

Galway's terse reply. "Galway here."

"We've just hit atmosphere. We'll be down shortly. Clear a spot."

Galway came back, "If you can land vertically, there's a well-marked helipad that should be able to take a craft up to about a hundred and fifty feet long."

"We'll use the helipad. Hawke clear."

A minute later the shuttle's pilot came on. "Mamba Flight, this is Chief Staples. Transferring commercial audio feed to your channel three. Thought you might enjoy it. Shuttle clear."

Kitty began testing her ship's controls as the six Alliance vessels dove deeper into the atmosphere. With one part of her mind, she listened to the chatter on her ship circuit, and with another she listened to the television audio. "Mamba Five. Fifty thousand feet," she reported.

Immediately on the heels of her report came another. "Mamba Three. Reporting radar contact."

"Mamba Two. Reporting radar lock-on."

"Mamba Flight, this is Mamba Leader. Do not, repeat, *do not* raise shields at this time. Continue your descent. Take no evasive action. Bogeys approaching from east and west and still below us."

Kitty watched the approaching blips, as well as her descent, and heard Shirley challenge the approaching craft. "United States craft, this is Mamba

Flight Leader. We are on approved approach to Camp David at Vice-President Reese's invitation. Halt your approach and state your intentions."

"Mamba Flight, you say. Is there a Captain Simon Hawke with you?" a disembodied voice asked.

Shirley acknowledged the fact that there was.

"Very well then, Mamba Flight, we are your escort."

Kitty's instruments lit up, and she reported, "Mamba Five. Reporting radar lock-on."

She heard Shirley's calm voice continue. "Escort Leader, three of my flight report radar lock-on. That's not good manners. Disengage your targeting systems."

"Mamba Flight Leader, this is Escort Leader. Regret to inform you that we cannot do that. To quote from my mission briefing, it says, 'armed with weapons of unknown potential, and to be considered potentially hostile.'"

"Well, then, I have a surprise for you, Escort Leader," Shirley shot back. On a separate circuit, she ordered, "Mamba Leader to all ships. On my mark, engage shields for five seconds, then disengage. Three, two, one, mark."

After all six ships had engaged and then disengaged their shields, Kitty heard Shirley's voice again. "Okay, Escort Leader, what do you think of that?" The move had made all six ships disappear from the radar screens of the approaching craft, effectively ruining all targeting data and lock-ons.

"Mamba Flight Leader, I still have my orders."

Shirley was silent for several seconds, then said, "That was the simplest thing in our bag of tricks, Escort Leader. Try this one on for size." Switching to the private channel, she ordered, "Flight Leader to all ships. On my mark, reduce speed to zero and hover. Three, two, one, mark. Reengage your screens and continue your descent. Escort Leader, this is Mamba Flight Leader. Respond."

"How the hell did you do th... This is Escort Leader."

"You're just going to have to track us on visual, I'm afraid." Kitty grinned as she heard the suppressed chuckle in Shirley's voice. "If you try to lock on one more time, I'll have to burn out your radar systems, and I don't want to do something like that to somebody who *my* mission briefing refers to as a potential ally. So, we'll just keep our screens up." Switching back to the private channel, she said, "I know we can't do that, but *he* doesn't."

Kitty grinned at Shirley's audacity and reported, "Twenty thousand feet. Extensive radar sweeps. No lock-on."

She listened to the verbal duel between the flight leaders.

"Mamba Flight Leader, my orders are to fire on your craft if you make any hostile moves."

"Well, you're going to have to make your own interpretation of our moves," Shirley said. "We've been invited to Camp David, and we're going straight there, so the only thing you can call hostile will be a deviation from that course. Besides, you aren't carrying anything that can hurt us."

"Mamba Flight Leader, this is Escort Leader. You don't know *what* we're armed with."

"Escort Leader, I have a strong suspicion what you're armed with, especially considering the fact that we're flying over densely populated parts of the United States. You're not going to detonate a nuclear device at this altitude, and nothing else you have can do anything to harm us. Our vessels and shields are designed to take minor meteor impacts at a fraction of the speed of light, Escort Leader, so I suggest you back off on the threats."

Kitty reported, "Ten thousand feet."

Shirley spoke to the U.S. aircraft one more time. "Escort Leader, this is Mamba Flight Leader. I believe you've just reached the point of can't-do-anything-now. We are picking up commercial audio, and all three major networks have us on visual. It's time to put away the brass knuckles and be good little boys. And it's time for me to go eyeball the landing site. Bye, guys!"

With that, Shirley's Mamba dove for the ground with a speed that astonished even Kitty—from just under ten thousand feet to five hundred feet, in atmosphere, in less than twenty seconds. Kitty watched on her screens as Shirley's Mamba came to an almost instantaneous halt.

A few seconds later, Kitty heard, "Mamba Flight, this is Mamba Leader. The water's fine. Come on in!"

Kitty continued to lead the flight down in silence, depending on Shirley to keep control. When she reported the flight to be at five thousand feet, Shirley's voice came over the speakers. "Mamba Flight, level out at five hundred and say hello to your counterparts. Shuttle, you are clear to land."

As she led the flight down at a less breakneck pace, Kitty's attention was caught by the commercial audio band. "Yes, Dan, as you can see, our longest-range lenses are finally picking up the vessels as they approach. The one in the center appears to be built along the same general lines as a space shuttle but perhaps a bit smaller, and it appears to be coming in under its own power. The other four, which look to be similar to the one that appeared here moments ago and the ones that were involved in all of those aerial displays around the world recently, are also coming in under power. One has to wonder at the need for any wings at all when you see this deadly-looking little craft as it just hovers here in the air above us, facing down the five Apache attack helicopters that are circling it."

As her ship hit the five-hundred-foot mark, Kitty said, "Mamba Five, breaking off," and randomly chose one of the helicopters to pair off against. She found herself almost literally nose-to-nose with an Apache attack helicopter, staring into the hard, cold eyes of its pilot, who smiled very nastily when he realized that the pilot he was facing was a woman. She could see his hands move on the controls through the canopy of his helicopter, and he made his craft dart towards hers—a form of aerial chicken.

"So, you want to play, big boy," she said out loud, letting him see her lips move. "Let's see how you react to this one." She nosed her craft forward and raised it level enough that his rotor tip would impact the nose of her ship if he did nothing, and she saw him immediately slide backwards, down and off to one side a bit. She followed, keeping the same reduced distance between the two of them and, smiling prettily, saluted him. She watched the storm clouds form on his face, and though she wasn't a lipreader, had no trouble recognizing the word "bitch" at the end of the sentence he spat in her direction.

As no one seemed inclined to comment on the give and take between Kitty and her opposite, she settled down to keeping one eye on him and one on the shuttle as it grounded. With one ear she was listening to TV audio, and with the other she was listening to the interplay between Shirley and the shuttle's pilot, so she wasn't looking when the unimaginable happened.

Kitty could never have told who it was who first cried out, "It's a trap!" And then, "Oh, my God! He's been shot!" No one would ever be able to delineate the exact sequence of events that transpired over the next few minutes.

At the first yell, Kitty felt the electric rush of adrenaline flood through her body. At almost the same instant, heavy-caliber weapons fire began to impact her ship, and she heard the pang of ricocheting slugs as they slewed away. She immediately brought her shields up and started to turn her ship to see what was happening on the ground. Yells filled her ears, but from the corner of her eye she saw her opposite number slide his craft into her way, smile, and depress a switch. Instantly, two rockets scorched out of the weapons pods mounted on each side of his craft. They impacted directly on the forward shields, dispersing their energy and knocking her back some fifty yards.

She saw his eyes go wide in amazement at the fact that her vessel hadn't fallen, burning, from the sky. She smiled sweetly, thumbed off the safety, and fired twin beams of coherent light into his weapons pods. They exploded gratifyingly, cutting the chopper in half. As the wreckage started to fall, the encounter was already a part of her past, and she spun around, eyes riveted on the grounded shuttle. She saw smoke pouring out of the open hatch, a body that could only be Simon's sprawled at the foot of the ramp, and three camouflage-clad men racing for the shuttle's open hatch. She instinctively fired her lasers, and two of the men went down, the other gaining the relative safety of the shuttle.

Kitty looked around for something else to destroy. The voices in her helmet said there were still gun emplacements active on the perimeter of the camp. As pain ravaged her soul, she saw the last Apache fall from the sky, and she turned her lasers on the gun emplacements still pouring fire on her and her fellows. She screamed in rage as two guns went up in magnificent gouts of dirt and flames, sending body parts and machined pieces in all directions.

After what seemed like an hour but could only have been seconds, there was complete silence in the compound known as Camp David.

Smoke poured across the compound from five fallen helicopters, numerous ruined gun emplacements, the fires started by these events, and from the open hatch of the stricken shuttle, masking much of the damage and softening the visual effect. Kitty maneuvered her ship toward a landing beside the damaged shuttle.

Shirley interposed her Mamba between Kitty's ship and the ground. "What do you think you're doing, Kitty?"

"I've got to get Simon out of there!" she cried.

Shirley's voice cut to the bone. "It won't do any good, Kitty. Look at the bio-monitors."

For the first time since the attack began, Kitty's eyes were drawn to the lower corner of her instrument panel, and the life drained out of her. The bio-monitors of the four team members had been slaved to a small panel of lights installed in the cockpits of the escort Mambas. Four red lights, one for each person, had been glowing brightly all through the descent to Camp David. Now all four of those lights were noticeable by their absence, and the meaning was all too clear: the entire away team had been killed by whoever had attacked the shuttle during the firefight with the Apaches. "We've got to go, Kitty. Let's move."

The voices of her fellow pilots became white noise in Kitty's ears as she said, "We've got to take care of the shuttle. I'll do it. And I'll take care of Simon, too."

Wind carried the battle smoke across the helipad. She could no longer see Simon's body, but she knew where it lay. Then she remembered that there had been three who'd run for the shuttle, and she'd only gotten two. One was still alive inside. He could be the one… She couldn't finish the thought.

Kitty slid her ship around so that she could see into the shuttle's forward viewport. There stood two men in camouflage clothing, desperately trying to get the shuttle moving. Not caring where the other man had come from, she thumbed the intercom override button. "Attention, Earth forces inside the shuttle." They looked up in confusion at her voice. "This is Wing Commander Katherine Hawke of the *TAS Galileo*. You have two choices—surrender or die. That shuttle only leaves the ground with Alliance personnel at the controls."

Knowing they couldn't shut out her voice because of her override, she demanded that the hijackers surrender. "Don't think I won't fire on an unarmed craft, especially when it's occupied by the murderers of my husband."

Hearing the rising alarm in her fellow Mamba pilots' voices, Flight Control, and the voice of the communications officer aboard the *Galileo*, Kitty snarled and locked them out. Ignoring the slowly increasing small-arms fire, she moved her ship around to the side of the grounded shuttle to get a better shot through the open hatch. This left her looking at the backs of the two men feverishly working at the controls, and she saw exactly when they brought the engines online.

In one last bid to keep from firing on the two men, Kitty called them one more time. "Are either one of you married?" she asked. She could see the startled look on the face of one of the men as he turned to look at her. "Did you kiss your wife goodbye this morning?" As the soldier hesitated, she promised, "If you did, that will be the last memory she has of you if that shuttle lifts so much as an inch."

Kitty was contemplating an antimatter blast, and a massive one. The shuttle's power core was going to explode when its containment-field generator disintegrated under the two missiles she'd just armed inside the hijacked shuttle.

The three explosions together should be pretty spectacular, she thought, *for everybody but me. It'll probably set off my own power core at the same time.*

As this thought went through her mind, she saw the look of triumph flash across the face of the second hijacker as he looked over his shoulder at her. The shuttle shifted slightly, she stroked the trigger, and the world as she knew it ceased to exist. Outside, through the gates, the forgotten camera crews continued to roll.

Life went on around Kitty Hawke. A respectable percentage of the compound had been vaporized by the explosions, and observers, after they picked themselves up from the shockwave, were stunned to see that Kitty's Mamba had survived the explosion. Blown backwards by the shockwave and half buried in the side of a concrete and brick building, her ship was covered by the debris still raining down, severely damaged by its impact with the building. Her Mamba would never fly again, but it had saved its pilot's life. The crash webbing, the shields, and the increased structural integrity of the redesigned Mamba had combined to keep Kitty alive but little more as it lay amid the wreckage of buildings and trees only a few dozen yards from some of the closer, more adventurous camera crews.

Perceptions vary from person to person, and while all of the documentary evidence showed that the events following the destruction of the shuttle lasted only seconds, Kitty would forever swear that Consciousness took her own sweet time leaving. In the meantime, she endured an endless visit from Pain and from Sorrow and from Nightmare.

Mostly, she feared Nightmare, because it brought images of death, blood, destruction, and the image of herself with twin beams of fire shooting from her fingers, destroying her enemies as she stood over the body of her fallen mate. She somehow knew those images that Nightmare kept bringing were all too real.

She welcomed Pain with open arms, knowing that for the few moments she allowed it to overtake her, she wouldn't have to endure Nightmare's images. She welcomed Pain also because she knew, somehow, that soon after would come Oblivion. And she prayed for Oblivion.

The four remaining Mamba pilots, unsure what to do with their superior tactical position, milled around above the devastated presidential retreat until one pilot, a little quicker than the others, dove on Kitty's ship and lifted it in its capture fields. The other three, flying escort, followed straight up out of the atmosphere, leaving cameras filming quiet devastation as crews stared first at the departing spacecraft and then back at the immense hole left by the explosions.

EPILOGUE

The nearly Earth-sized planet swung around its reddish-colored primary a bit closer than did Earth around the star its children named Sol, or more commonly just "the sun."

Too faint to be seen from Earth with the naked eye, the dim red star was an unremarkable notation in a compendium of stars notable only for its relative obscurity except to astronomers. The portion of space the red star occupied was only visible from the southern hemisphere and marginally closer to the galactic center than humanity's star.

A tall, red man put down the file he'd just finished reading for the third time. He leaned back in his chair, frustrated. He knew his father would only have needed one reading to arrive at a decision, but his father was three months dead, killed in the same Isolationist attack that had injured his mother and catapulted him into his father's office.

For three months now he'd filled his new and unexpected position as Minister of Spatial Affairs for the Shiravan Polity, and this was the first time he'd needed to do anything other than initial some report.

Not that he didn't keep track of what his position entailed. Oh, to be sure, he did. Too many young, ambitious men had thought to inherit their fathers' positions and rise through the levels of Shiravan society without having to actually work at their assigned tasks. After all, males were not the norm in polite Shiravan society. Only recently had they been allowed outside their compounds to release the females for more important duties off-planet.

Rentec do' Verlas needed to have only a few of them paraded before him, metaphorically, to learn that the system discouraged idiocy, promoting ranking nobles sideways into dead-end positions while more able-minded people went on to head the departments the Matriarch deemed essential.

So he read those reports before signing off on them, sometimes adding comments of his own to show someone that he wasn't the dilettante some thought him to be. He'd already acquired the reputation of staying until the last secretary and runner had gone home for the night before he left himself. Often, the evidence of his late stays would show up in the form of memos found by various secretaries the next morning. Few suspected that he was working at a frantic pace just to keep the position he'd inherited. Fewer still guessed that it was a matter of honor that drove him.

Let the many think his late stays were an attempt to thwart a repeat of the Isolationist bombing that had killed his father. No matter what others thought or said behind his back, he knew that it was an attempt to catch up in a system where those who didn't learn quickly were either gobbled up or pushed aside by the stronger. And it was a perfect place from which to plan and execute the revenge the do' Verlas family required.

Rentec stared blankly out of his third-story window as the Dukara Mountains slowly swallowed the sun, thinking more about the letter he'd have to write in response to the report than the spectacle he still hadn't gotten used to. He glanced across the landing field at the shuttle from the returned colonist hauler *Kemara Vasit*, the sight crystallizing his resolve. He turned back to his desk and reluctantly picked up his stylus, stared at the offending instrument for a few seconds, then put its tip to the blank paper on his desk.

Minister Foran,

Appended is the report from Colonization Ship Captain Serris do' Kerran. In brief, it details her ship's arrival at Descaret Four. Where the colonization ship Dalgor Kreth *should have built a functional base for her load of colonists, there was nothing to be found and no sign at all that the* Dalgor Kreth *had ever arrived at the Descaret system.*

In view of the fact that there were no groundside facilities for her charges, Captain do' Kerran wisely elected to return to Shiravi rather than abandon the colonists to an unprepared planet with few resources or weapons.

It is my opinion that Captain do' Kerran acted in the best interests of her charges and should be commended for her decision. I also recommend that a search be instituted at once for the missing vessel and crew. While the loss of one-twelfth of our colonization fleet is a severe economic blow, it is as nothing beside the loss of life and knowledge represented by the crew.

Ever your servant,
Rentec do' Verlas.

He folded the report and his recommendation

together, slid them into a security seal, and addressed it. Dropping it into his secretary's outbox, he finally left the darkened office for the small apartment assigned to him in the bachelor dormitories the city of Quillas maintained a few blocks away.

ABOUT THE AUTHOR

Bob lived in Montana for over thirty years, since late '85. He fell in love with the state almost instantly (who wouldn't after spending the previous twenty or more years trapped in Houston, Texas). Out in the Big Sky Country, he found the "elbow room" he didn't even know he was looking for. He lived quietly with his two cats and library of nearly two thousand books—about 95% Sci-Fi. He discovered that he liked to write as well and could often be found doing just that. Bob passed away in November of 2019 and is survived by his younger brother. Before he passed, he finished his writing project of more than a decade, The Stellar Heritage series, and he will live on in the hearts and minds of his readers.

Learn more at:
bladeoftruthpublishing.com/bob-mauldin

MORE FROM THE PUBLISHER

Blade of Truth Publishing Company specializes in science fiction and fantasy stories that change the way you view the world.

To find more great books head over to:

bladeoftruthpublishing.com/books

Bringing truth into the world, one story at a time.

Made in the USA
Columbia, SC
14 December 2023

28540574R00424